The Stories of Stephen Dixon

OTHER WORKS BY STEPHEN DIXON

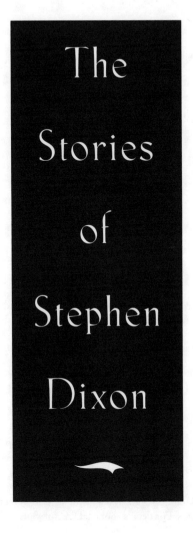

The Stories of Stephen Dixon

Henry Holt and Company

New York

Henry Holt and Company, Inc.
Publishers since 1866
115 West 18th Street
New York, New York 10011

Henry Holt® is a registered
trademark of Henry Holt and Company, Inc.

Published in Canada by Fitzhenry & Whiteside Ltd.,
195 Allstate Parkway, Markham, Ontario L3R 4T8.

Library of Congress Cataloging-in-Publication Data
Dixon, Stephen.
[Short stories. Selections]
The stories of Stephen Dixon.—1st ed.
p.   cm.
I. Title
PS3554.I92A6   1994   93-38509
813'.54—dc20   CIP

ISBN 0-8050-2653-3

Henry Holt books are available for special promotions and
premiums. For details contact: Director, Special Markets.

First Edition—1994

DESIGNED BY KATY RIEGEL

Printed in the United States of America
All first editions are printed on acid-free paper. ∞

1   3   5   7   9   10   8   6   4   2

*Due to limitations of space, acknowledgments
appear at the end of the book.*

To Irving Howe

Contents

Contents   xi

The

Chess

House

"Check."

"Check."

"Just what do *you* mean 'check'?"

"Just what I mean."

He examined the chessboard. There was no doubt he had the other fellow's king in check. The guy must be nuts or something to say "check" right after him. Nobody, absolutely nobody, was near his king.

"So I look like you say," he said, "and I see I got your king."

"You haven't got nothing."

"Then look yourself."

"What are you talking about?" said his opponent. "I see, and I'm seeing right now. *Your* king is a dead duck."

"But where? Just show me where?"

"Right there," the man said, pointing to his white king and then at his queen and one of the knights.

"You're crazy. That don't put me in check."

"Say what you like."

He glanced down. The guy must really be nuts or just pulling his leg, or what? Why can't he say he lost and be done with it? He looked up.

"So check, check, I still say it, right?" the other man said.

"Here, look at my bishop—no, the other one; that's right—and now at my rook. Now don't they got your king in check? No, don't turn away, look."

"Who's turning? I just don't see any bishop of yours. There's none on the board."

"None on the board?" he said, slapping his forehead and then looking up at the ceiling. "You out of your mind? Where are they then, in my mouth?"

"Who knows."

"Don't give me that. Here . . . my finger's pointing right at it."

"Your finger's pointing at nothing."

He sat back in his chair, wondering. So his finger was pointing at nothing, was it? His finger was pointing right at the bishop's cap, right at it, and this crazy man says it wasn't. The kind of people like him who come in the Central Park Chess House shouldn't come. They really shouldn't be allowed, even. Then he held his clenched hand before the other man's face, opened and closed it to show he had nothing concealed inside, and stuck his fist in his coat pocket. He took out a crumpled-up handkerchief, a ballpoint pen, and one subway token. Finally he pulled out the inner linings of his jacket and held them straight out.

"See? Not in my pockets, mouth, and nowheres but on the board." He jokingly opened his mouth wide, showing a missing upper plate.

"I'm not looking," the man said, turning away. "But who knows, you could've hid it somewhere else?"

"Hid it somewhere else?" he said.

"On the floor, your cuff, maybe, but how we're going to play another game without a black bishop beats me."

"I'll tell you how we're going to play—we're not. That's right," he said, when the man looked up surprised, "because that bishop's been staring you straight in the face for the past five minutes—and still is—and you call me a liar? Honestly, I think something's wrong with you."

"That's what I thought you'd get around to," the man said. "But you're the guy they better watch, take it from me."

"Don't worry about me. I'm sane. Me, I got eyes."

"Well, like I always say: some guys just can't take it."

"Can't take too much nonsense, that's what."

"I mean losing. Losing in chess, which is a sportsman's game. If you can't take it here, you can't take anything—no game. When one loses, he should be gracious. He wins, he should be more so."

"My thoughts."

"So you lose, so say so. Me? Do I boast? Do I say anything? I win, so what does it mean to me? A game, nothing else."

"So already you won, you dirty liar? Then fine, say it."

"Lookit, I had enough," his opponent said, pushing back his chair and getting up. "Someone like you could never see when a guy's trying to be fair. But now you've gone too far. Nice I was, but no more so."

"Then good. If you find someone to play with—or cheat with— then play with *him*."

"I'll find. Plenty, I'll find."

"Not with your attitude."

"So you think yours is better?"

"Much!"

"Well, we'll see." His opponent buttoned up his sweater and coat and waved derisively.

The owner of the set bent his head down and flapped his gloved hands at his former opponent. He had first met him this afternoon at the Chess House above Wollman's skating rink, and played with him for more than three hours. He looked up and watched him walk away, stop to stare at another chess game for a few minutes, and finally shuffle into a crowded group of onlookers watching a match between two of the finest chess players in the house. Noticing the man glance at him, he looked down again and began neatly placing the chessmen into a wooden box. He noticed that the intricately carved king had been smudged across the crown where his opponent had handled it. He took out his handkerchief, rubbed some spittle on the king's head until it was clean, and then placed the ivory figure in the left-hand chamber of the chess box. When he looked up again, the man had left the experts' match and was watching a game of checkers or perhaps it was chess. He could hardly identify him through the heavy conglomeration of cigarette and cigar smoke. He held the two black bishops in his hand, then placed them in the box. After slowly putting all the chess pieces in both chambers of the box, he carefully took the ivory figures out again and placed them on the board, hoping that someone in the room would challenge him to a match.

But it was past five, and most of the men began filing out of the Chess House, although he expected that the majority of them— lonely, single, vagrant or retired—had no place to go. After a while, all that remained in the house were a few nonplaying drifters and derelicts who smoked used butts and slept or sat on the benches lining the room, the champions, still locked in their battle, some observers of the match, and his former opponent, who now sat three tables away from him reading a newspaper. He laughed to himself. The poor fool, he thought; he couldn't find anyone to play with, but it serves him right. It'll teach him a lesson he'll never forget. He leaned across his set, held the black bishop in the air and began stroking it, and then placed it in its position in the back row of the board. He arranged all the other chessmen in the middle of their squares, and then looked at his watch.

"Well, it doesn't look you got time or nobody, even to play with, does it?" his former opponent said, standing opposite him, his hands stuffed into his pockets.

"There were plenty to play with if I wanted to."

"Yeah, I saw them flocking to you."

"It just so happens a couple of men asked me if I wanted to play, and I said: 'No dice.' Just wouldn't have been a game."

"Sure, tell me another one."

"Mister, did I ask for you? You play two games with me and right away you own me or something? What about you? *You* get a game? I saw you, you know, looking around, going from one table to another, always trying to horn in. Look, I got a set. I can get plenty of games. It's you. Nobody in their right minds would play you."

"I just don't feel like playing. Didn't ask and wasn't asked—simple as that. They know me here—I'm a *regular*—and they know my look. If I'd've looked like I wanted to play, I'd've been asked. And let me tell you: that set of yours is starting tongues wagging around here—that's right. I mean, just sitting there set up and all—and ivory, no less. You're getting known as the fellow who's always good for a fat laugh."

"Nobody's looking. And ivory's the best you can get. You couldn't get a better one than that if you tried."

"I wouldn't say that."

"Always lots of guys like you wanting to play with a nice ivory set like this."

"Don't look at me, brother. About it being a nice set, well, I seen much nicer." He leaned forward to pick up one of the chessmen, to rub it with his fingertips, but his hand dropped back into his pocket. "It's nice, all right, if you like ivory."

"And who doesn't?"

"I know some."

"Here, touch it and feel if you want, and then tell me who doesn't like ivory." He dangled the black bishop before the man's face. "Touch this one, go on."

"I like the white ones," the man said, pointing to the two rows of white chess pieces orderly lined up on the board before the empty chair.

"Then touch the white ones."

The man touched the white bishop, queen and king, and ran his finger over the jagged crest of the rook. Then, sitting down before the chess set owner could nod his head, he made his first move with the white pawn.

The set owner scrutinized the advanced pawn and his own chess pieces. After briefly fingering his black pawn and tapping it on the board, he picked it up and slammed it down two squares ahead.

The

New

Era

—

I wake up. I had another disturbing dream. In it Winny and I were about to leave the house. The phone rang. She answered it and said into the receiver "Why Frank—grief—how great to hear from you again." As she continued speaking her face changed: became rounder, cheeks rosier, skin clearer, hair longer and blond instead of black. She now looked like the woman I was engaged to ten years ago. I said "Please, we're late." She said to me "Will you cool it a second? I'm talking to someone important." She laughed, traded quips, talked kittenishly on the phone. When the call was over she said "That was Frank Converse." I said "Oh? Seems to be a pretty good friend of yours. In love with him?" "Matter of fact, yes." "Still in love with me?" "Not as much as I am with Frank." "Then that seems to be it then," and I opened the door, said "You know what converse means: reverse." She said "It can also mean a spoken interchange of feelings and thoughts." "Not as a last name it can't," and I left. Her front door opened onto a steep hill of only boulders and stones. I was forced to climb on all fours. That's when I awoke. Winny was already out of bed in her bathrobe and brushing her hair. "Brr morning," she says. The storm windows are covered with crystals that look like palm fronds. I raise myself up. Snowed some more overnight. Just powder, enough to cover prints. "Come on back in bed," I say. "They're not going to open the schools today."

"I have to find out for sure." She goes downstairs. Her son's asleep in the next room. The cat's sleeping on my feet at the end of the bed. The dog's snoring under the bed. The rabbit's in its warren in the toolshed outside and Sammy's fish are in their bathroom tanks and I can hear the macaw jumping from bar to bar in its kitchen cage.

She turns the radio on to the one county station. The announcer talks about the new snow, local car crash, sports scores, growing fuel shortage, meeting today of Persian Gulf states. "Drive carefully," he says, "and if you must go out in this weather, make sure you wear a smile," but nothing about the reopening of schools. Yesterday the high school Winny teaches crafts at and the grade school Sammy's a student at were closed because of icy conditions and a two-inch snow. She comes upstairs, passes the room and in her study dials the phone.

"Number of WRCM," she says. "To learn if the schools will still be closed today. You wouldn't happen to know yourself, by chance? Thanks, dear."

"Does she know?"

"No he doesn't. Only the number."

"Believe me, they can't open today. It's too slippery. That's what the weather report said. Snarling winds, hazardous roads, broken-hip weather, arctic cold. They'll never let the kids be driven on school buses after that accident last year."

She dials. "I heard your news report before but nothing about the schools reopening today. Thanks."

She passes the bedroom to get to the john.

"Closed?"

"Open," she says. She washes. It's my day off from my Christmas selling job in the Little Girls Shop of a department store. The room's cold and the bed's warm. She comes in, nude, and searches her pantyhose drawer to start dressing.

"It'd be nice if you could squeeze in here with me for a minute or more."

"No time. I've no snow tires. If I can't get a ride with Darla, the bus will take me a year."

"You could at least get closer so I can hug you."

"And then mug me?"

"And later kiss and lick and maybe make-a the love with you?"

"Big cock, that's all you ever got on your mind."

"Just a final morning peck then."

"With you one peck can lead anywhere and is never final. I'm late. I'd like to but can't."

She phones Darla, comes back. "She'll call before she leaves to give me five minutes to make the hill."

"Why not call in sick today?"

"Right after I called my assistant principal for a hitch? And they're short of subs as it is and my students are auctioning off their wares today."

She zips up her fly. "Don't forget to call the meter people," she says. The water pipe in the basement froze last night and in my trying to unfreeze it with a butane torch, the water meter burst. We've no water now except for what's left of what we collected from neighbors in pots and jars. I say "Did you get all your vital parts washed okay?"

"What's that mean?"

"Because of the cold water. Don't you always wash your vital parts before going to school?"

"You know I do. But why'd I even tell you if all you can make with it are goosey remarks?"

"I'd nothing else to say and simply felt like saying."

"Why didn't you simply feel like reading from the book you were reading last night before you passed out?"

"I didn't. I fell asleep."

"Fell asleep then."

"Why'd you say pass out?"

"Because you drank so much at dinner and later during the game that I thought that's what did you off."

"I was tired."

"It was a tough day. We were both highly keyed up and exhausted. You're right."

Day before yesterday it stormed and we couldn't drive up till the next day. I live in the city, Winny in the country. She stayed with me over the weekend, Sammy with his dad. Winny and Gil's divorce becomes final this Friday and she's been nervous over it for a week. Gil returned Sammy Sunday night. Before they got there Winny phoned neighbors and asked them to keep Sammy for the night. To get a four-day weekend and drive Winny, I called the store Monday and said I was snowed in upstate and couldn't come that day. The road conditions were treacherous. Winny's snow tires are in her last landlord's barn. Twice we spun around on the road and once across it and were lucky no cars were behind us at the time or in the opposing lane. The car slid again some fifty feet from her house and we had to abandon it in her neighbors' yard. We got back to a freezing house, four-hour blackout, sick cat, few dead fish, no heat till early this morning and the frozen water pipe.

She's dressed. "I had another dream about us last night," I say.

"Same thing? I'm with another man and love him more than you?"

"Yes."

"You worried I'm sniffing around or fancy some other Dan or just want to be alone?"

"No. But I can't explain most of my dreams. I think I make them exist just to torment and bamboozle me. I'll simply have to give up sleeping."

"You do that. And will you help me up the hill with my supplies and walk the dog if you think he has to make? He's good about holding it in if we're out, but if anyone's around he begs to be walked or loses control."

"I don't know why you got him."

"Sammy wanted it. Every ten-and-a-half-year-old should have a dog once. It was a good buy. Nothing, which is unheard of for a purebred chow. And just his face is great protection for us, even if he's scared nitless of strangers and congenitally can't bark."

"You already had the rabbit and cat."

"Even if either barked it wouldn't have helped. Sammy dislikes them. You don't like dogs. The macaw hates us all. I adore all of you though have thought of trading in the rabbit for a couple of egg layers and Sammy's rare tropical fish heap for a pony and goat. Will you walk Bear?"

"I'll ride him. Give me one hug?"

"I've got to get Sammy's breakfast."

"One microbic snug. In the time it just took you to say that and now me this."

We hug. I try to sit her beside me or lay her chest on mine. Nothing doing. She says "Don't be demanding, please?"

"I love you."

"You're my little lovey too."

"I don't know why I said I love you."

"Because you felt like it, *c'est tout?*"

"I said it because I'm insecure about you, though I don't know for what."

"When you do or think just talking to me will help you with the reasons, let me know. Occasionally it's the only way to find out what's bugging you about someone."

"I guess."

She goes downstairs. I dress. She yells up "Sammy? You have to crawl out now if you want to make school on time."

"There's no school," he yells from his room. "My friend Norman said."

"Norman's wrong. I called the radio station. And Darla's picking me up."

"They're wrong. I don't want to go to school. It's too cold."

"Dress hot."

"I can't get out of bed. The floor's frozen stiff. There's ice on the walls."

"Put your shoes on underneath the covers, but hop to it now."

He passes her room. "Don't flush the toilet," I say.

"I won't. I know it's the last flush. But don't ask me to look in the toilet either."

I go downstairs. Winny's eating her breakfast while making Sammy oatmeal, hot chocolate and toast. Coffee's ready. She's let the rabbit in and macaw out of its cage and put food and water out for the dog and cat in three side-by-side bowls. The phone rings. Sammy yells down "It's Darla. Start walking now."

Winny collects our outdoor clothing. "Oats and toast ready," she yells upstairs. "Dick's walking me to the car and will be right back."

"I'm running for the newspaper first," I say, "later with the dog."

"He won't be right back. Lunch money's in your trumpet case. Great day, dear."

We leave. I carry a canister of clay. She says "It's rough enough taking this hill without hauling anything, but forty pounds of clay? Here, let's switch."

"It's okay."

"Men are so strong."

"It's not that."

"Then damnit, let me carry it partway. You can never let anyone do anything for you, especially when you're doing nice things for them."

She takes the clay, gives me her pocketbook and lunch pail. We reach the main road as Darla's car comes. Winny gets in the front seat and I say "See ya, sweetheart." She says "Oh, I'm sorry, Dee. This is my friend Dick." Darla and I shake hands. "Bye," Winny says. I kiss her. It isn't much. Peck I sought for before. They're anxious to get started. I shut the door. The car goes. I wave. They're chatting. I run for the paper, about two miles all told. I mention the headlines to the grocery owner where I buy the paper and she says "Oil shortage in a pig's eye."

"You don't believe it then?"

A customer there says "I've a friend in Jamaica." I say "Jamaica, Queens?" He says "Jamaica the island or sovereign country or whatever the West Indies is or are. He says they get all their oil from us and right now they can get all they want. There ain't no crisis. It's all sludge covering crud."

Sammy's leaving the house when I get back. "Anything wrong?" he says. "Your face. That crease."

"Nothing."

"I'm glad." I rub his hair, pat his trumpet case. Last week he said he was too old for me kissing and hugging him anymore. He goes. I throw open the door and say "Hey, did you walk Bear?"

"Oh God, I forgot. You walk him for me pretty please?"

The macaw lands on my arm. "And Bird. Why didn't one of you put away the rabbit and Bird?"

"You can't expect me to."

"Can't spect me to," Bird says.

I run with the dog. It makes. I'm supposed to say right after it goes: "Good boy, great Bear." I leave him on the locked porch, sit in the living room rocker with the newspaper and coffee mug. The cat jumps on my lap and spills the coffee over the paper. I put the cat out of the house, Bird in its cage and rabbit with its carrot in the shed. I remember I'm to phone the water company. The man who answers says "If your meter burst it means your basement was below freezing and the pipe leading from the ground to the meter froze. It's your responsibility to keep your basement above thirty-two."

"It's okay. I'll pay. But get a repairman over. It's slowly flooding downstairs."

"I'll tell the commercial office."

"Does that mean a repairman will come by today?"

"Look, it's already been a hectic day. Lots of pipe breaks. People don't even know to wrap them with newspapers anymore. Everyone pinning it on the company, of course. Don't make it any worse with your commands for the repairman and me. And I'm sure some other busted pipe calls are now coming in." He hangs up.

The car. Late last night in bed Winny rolled away from me and said "We'll dig the car out together early tomorrow morning, share the shoveling, pushing and getting the snow tires and putting them on before I go to school. I eventually have to learn how to do all those things myself, as I don't want to be a drag or dependent on any man."

I dig the car out, drive up the hill and across the main road and start up the small mountain she lives on. The road's too slippery and steep. I try backing down the hill to park by the main road and the car slides into a snowbank a plow truck made at the side. The wheels spin, my tail's jutting into the road. I try digging the car out. No luck. I run up the rest of the way to the house Winny once rented an attic in and where she said her snow tires were. The housekeeper lets me call a garage. They're all either booked solid for the day or under-staffed or only doing repair work for lack of gas deliveries this week. "Try the state cops for a tow," the last garageman says.

"They'll ticket me. I don't have any snows on, which was what I was after when I got stuck."

"They can pull you in for that one, Tiger, and impound your car."

I run down the hill and try shoveling the car out much harder. Winny's ex-landlady stops her car on the steepest part of the road. "Anything I can do to help?"

"Maybe if you got behind the wheel I might be able to push it out."

"Oh come off it," Giselle says.

She pushes my car from behind while I rev it in first. We finally get it out of the snow with her racing alongside me and I make it up the hill and honk my thanks. She flexes her arm muscles, laughs, points to the mountaintop and makes motions of someone taking a cup off its saucer and bringing it to her mouth.

We have coffee at her house. She tells the housekeeper and me "We're entering a brand-new era, I'm sure you both realize. One of minor and major shortages and mini-crises for the rest of our lives. Everyone's got to start cutting back and changing their priorities and goals or die in their own excesses and wastes. Like we laid off the chauffeur and will redouble the vegetable garden and traded in the less efficient Mustangs and Caddy for two four-wheel-drive Ford Broncos. Takes half the material to make and power to run and does all our trips with ease and most of the more remote logger roads."

We go to the barn. There are two rimless tires there that she says are snows and which to me seem small enough to belong to a Volks. I drive the tires to a service station and ask the owner to put them on.

"You kidding me? Those aren't any good."

A van pulls up at the pumps. "You mean they're not snows?" I say. The sign above the pumps says NO GAS but he starts filling the van's tank. I walk over to him. "Excuse me, but you're saying my tires aren't for snow?"

"Oh they're snows all right, though not much left of your treads and studs."

"Then will you please stop pumping a second and say why you can't put them on?"

"They won't fit your car's what I mean. A Saab or Pinto maybe, but those sizes aren't yours."

It's snowing again. I don't want to take the chance. I park at the station, rest the tires around my shoulders like hula hoops and start up the hill. I put my thumb out. A few feet from the main road a car's coming from the opposite way and I put my thumb hand down. The car stops and the driver says "They look awfully heavy. Give you a lift?"

"It's just another short hill above this one and we're going different ways."

"No trouble. Get in."

"But I don't want you turning from where you're heading and maybe getting stranded on that first curve on Skyview."

"I'll get by."

I get in. Passing the snowbank my car was in I say "That hole's where I got stuck." When we reach Giselle's driveway I say "This'll do fine," but he says he'll take me right to the door.

"Thank you."

"Thank the Lord."

"And thank you too."

"Just thank the Lord," and he reaches past me and opens my door. I get out. On his back window's a sticker saying ABORTION IS MURDER! with a picture of Hitler superimposed on the words. He honks, I suppose his thanks for being able to help.

Nobody's home. I put the snow tires in the barn. The only other matching tires I find look like the front ones for two wheelbarrows. A snow tire that could be for a Volks is strung up on a tree branch behind the barn. I go back to town, buy enough groceries for two days and walk back to Winny's house. The meter repairman hasn't come. There's about three inches of water on the basement floor. The water company man on the phone says if the spigot on the main pipe's turned all the way to the right the flooding should only be a leak and no cause for alarm for at least another day. Sammy calls and says "Think Mom will mind my keeping two gerbils over the holidays?" I call Winny's school and ask the office to have her phone home. Then I think I should have said it wasn't an emergency. I call back. The line's busy. I call again and again. Then Winny calls. She says "First thing, is it Sam?"

"Yes and no."

"Yes and no, goddamnit?"

"Nothing's wrong. I wanted to tell the school it wasn't serious, but their line was always tied up." I go into my day: digging out, getting restuck, more shoveling, Giselle, snow tires, no meter repairman, leaving the car, the hills, abortion, Hitler and Sammy's gerbils.

"I suppose it's okay if they're not the ones that crave hymenoptera," she says, "as for Christmas his uncle's getting him an ant farm."

I say "Do you remember the size number of your snow tires?" She says "Around six hundred dash or something," and I say "Then I think one of your snows is hanging from one of Giselle's trees as a gorilla swing. It has no rim."

"Mine had rims."

"I was wondering how you thought we could put them on with just a jack. All I wanted was to put the tires on so I could pick you up so you wouldn't have to rely on anyone for a ride, but none of it worked."

"You know me, I don't care, though it was sweet of you for trying. By the way, Dick."

"Uh-oh."

"Uh-oh what?"

"Something's wrong. That tone."

"My tone's the same. But I thought I'd tell you as long as your mood seems to be pretty good and you were so concerned about it earlier today."

"Instinct tells me 'ya don't want t'hear, Dickie dearest, ya jest don't want t'hear.'"

"If you don't then I won't go into it. But I can hardly keep it in now, so I'll have to tell you it soon. It pertains to your dream."

"I knew they were saying something I had to fear."

"Nothing to fear. At the most a change in procedure and a little agitation. But I have to get back to class in a minute, so why don't I save it till I get home."

"Spill it now."

"There is someone I've been seeing since you started your Christmas job."

"Frank Converse?"

"No Frank, Converse or any of the other names from your dreams. Just someone."

"Who?"

"I don't think it's important to say."

"Driving up yesterday you said that one of the two fellows next door liked my illustrations. Later I saw the one with the fresher less feathery beard and mentioned I'd heard he'd seen some of my work and he said 'I never saw anything, it must be Otto.' Last night I saw the magazine facedown on your bedside table and it was opened to my illustrations. Now I know you read the story a few times a month ago, so I thought maybe Otto asked you what I did and you told him and he said do you have any of his work around? and you said a magazine with a story he illustrated and he said can I see it? and you gave it to him and he was looking at them and maybe even reading the story in your bed while you were reading that *Depression and the Body* book which I found facedown under my magazine when you two decided to call it a reading quits for the night to make-a the love."

"My good man, you're just too perceptive."

"Today I was thinking my perception would have to travel at a reduced speed like everything else on the road, but I guess I need a governor. He's much younger than you."

"So you're much older than me."

"You never said it mattered."

"It didn't, it doesn't."

"He smells. He doesn't take care of himself. He only listens to jungle music and never speaks to me about anything but copulation and mountain climbing and I can see what he's like by his sty. He might be a scientist but he acts, yaps and dresses like a brutish hood."

"Who can say. And I have to go. I should have told you it this morning, but I didn't want to squelch your one and only paid day off. And it doesn't mean that much, you know. You can stay and for the time being I'll continue to drive in and spend one weekend day every week with you till your job's over and if they don't keep you on for store inventory, though after that I don't know. But I do like him, Dick. It happens. Maybe because we weren't working out."

"We were working out. We would have anyway."

"Maybe we were."

"But you say more than me?"

"I think so. Yes."

I hang up. I pack my clothes and leave the house. The dog whines. I go back to the porch. He bites at his fleas while I try putting on his leash. "Sit," I say. He sits. "Heel," I say and he comes to me and waits for my next command. "Run," and we run along the Tracks behind her house for a mile. The Tracks used to be railway tracks till two years ago when the railroad folded and the towns all around pulled up the rails and ties and turned the road into a bridle path. I give the dog some of the lamb I was going to make stew with tonight, refill the water bowl with milk as he licks my fingers, and say "Good boy, yeah Bear, you're a great love."

The phone rings. It's the water company. Will I be home in the next hour? I unmake Winny's bed and sit and draw it. The repairman comes and replaces the broken meter. Water's flowing throughout the house. I turn off all the faucets, mop the bathroom and basement floors, wrap the basement water pipe with newspapers and twine, insulate the basement windows and door. The cat comes downstairs while I work. It watches. It brushes its body and tail against me and I pick it up by its front paws and walk it up the steps like a rag doll and bore my face into its furry chest. It licks my hair. I pour gravy over its cat food, let the macaw out and clean its cage, let the rabbit into the yard and give it the watercress and celery stick that would have been in tonight's salad and deviled eggs. I leave the house, start down the hill.

"Hey, Dickie old bean, where you going?" Sammy yells from the porch.

"Just a-going. The stage. See ya soon, pardner, and I done plumb come to cherish ya a whole lot," and he says "Okay, see you soon," and blows me a kiss.

The bus to the city comes once every half hour. I wait in front of the frame store for it in the freezing cold. It's snowing big flakes. The bus is an hour late. The frame store owner comes out, locks up and says "With this weather we'll be lucky if she ever shows her face."

Making

a

Break

On the phone she told him he was thirty-three and immature. "Around children you're great. I love your easy, open, understanding ways with them, which you unfortunately don't bring to your adult relationships. You identify better with children I suppose. And like to be around them for all the good reasons we all like to be around them and also because you can act like a silly ass with them without their jumping down your throat like us stodgy adults. Oh, maybe all my interpretations of your behavior and motives might be in or out of order or on or off the mark, but one thing I know is that you've never grown up. Physically, intellectually, you're an imposing man. But emotionally . . . well, you refuse to accept anyone having any value or opinion other than your own, which must put a terrible strain on you. You're also dangerous to be around. Other friends, if they don't like something I do or say, think 'Well that's the way she is,' or at the most say 'Quelle exagération' and be done with their complaint, giving me the same consideration you only give children, and maybe your folks. So how can I continue to see you when I can't be sure you're not going to suddenly flare up and say something vicious to me, one of my friends, or even the local burghers I'm so dependent on, like that nice meatman Mr. Maluggi you accused of cheating me with the weights, but who has a dull thirty-year reputation in my town of unalterable honesty. Maybe most of what I said is contradictory and even sounds stupid and unfair to you but I at least hope my main point got through. You're impossible to be with, Bo."

He put down the receiver after she said goodbye and reread her letter he received this morning, which had prompted his call.

"I feel like a commodity with you, Bo. You want me for something I have absolutely no talent for and are cynical and abusive to me for all the qualities that other people admire. I just don't do it well. Never have and no doubt never will. You'd be better off with another woman or girl who does do it well, which shouldn't be too difficult for you to find. You're attractive and intelligent but just terrible for me, as I can never be sure when you're going to suddenly change from my delightful gentle helpmate into this horrid ogre who for some morbid reason all his own takes pleasure in reducing me to a bawling deranged woman. You're also potentially bad for Tommy, and especially now that she adores you more than she does her New York father, and you make my friends feel uncomfortable and defensive, though there's no reason you should. They're nice people. And they're certainly more tolerant and far-out and less middle-class than you in that they don't always have to broadcast their beliefs or rail out against someone who has a different set of standards and idiosyncrasies, as they don't get as easily threatened as you. I first thought it would be nice having another writer around to walk with and talk to and I feel responsible for urging you to move into this area and rent that big old house, and I don't know what to do about that now. But you changed. Maybe it's the isolation—that quiet house in the country all your own. Or success—the commendable even enviable sale of those commendable even enviable stories—or my own stability: that I live in a community I love around people I love and who love me and that I don't want to be ruining it with your inflexible attitudes and waspish moods. Maybe most of what I've written seems unintelligible and even unfair to you, but I hope my main points get across: I can't afford scandal; Tommy might get hurt; I'm much too fragile a person to continue any kind of relationship with you."

He got in his car, backed out onto the country road, exchanged waves and howdies with his eighty-year-old neighbor Farmer Chapman driving by on his tractor hauling a wagon of manure, and drove the five miles to Bobby's village and pulled up in front of her house. She opened the door as he was about to knock on it.

"Please don't make a scene. There's a neighbor across the street who especially watches everyone's movements and she, being the town's leading loudmouth, I want least of all to see us fight. We'll have a coffee together and then you'll go. And I really didn't think you'd be by. After I wrote you I thought you might drop over. But when you called before I thought that that would do it for you in place of a personal visit."

They went into the kitchen. She put on water for instant coffee, on a tray put cups and saucers, sugar and cream pitchers, silver, biscuits, cookies, napkins, and butter. She said "You familiar with a book with a title of something like *Light Is the Sky Whereunto My Friend Has Flown To* or some such which? I thought you were. Well a week ago our library called and said would I return that book as it was a month overdue. I told them I don't remember borrowing it, but they said because it was borrowed with my card I'd have to pay for its loss. I didn't understand the situation. But to avoid a minor local scandal and because I am on the library's new books purchasing committee and had supposedly fought for the very book I was told I'd lost, I paid for it. Then a couple of days ago the chief librarian called and said they received the book through the mail in a plain manila envelope with no message inside and had I sent it to them that way? I said I hadn't, but she went on about how books if they're mailed should be mailed in Jiffy bags, whatever they are, as books could be marred in manila envelopes, though how fortunately this one wasn't. She also said they'd reimburse me for the money I paid for the book less its month's overdue charges, as they weren't allowed to keep lost book money for a book that later turned up. I forgot about it all till today when the library called again and asked when I was coming in to pick up the lost book money, as they wanted to get the matter off their bookkeeping files and by library law they weren't allowed to send reimbursements by mail. When I went there they made a big point of showing me the manila envelope the book had been mailed in, and I recognized your handwriting and realized the book must have been the one you borrowed with my card when you were my houseguest a while back. You could have at least provided the library with some note of explanation in the envelope. Or have put the book in a Jiffy bag, for you must know better than I what they are. Or else told me you were keeping the book way past its due date, so I could have been prepared for the library's call rather than forced to squirm out of it. Why are you like that, Bo?"

The teakettle was whistling. She poured water in the cups and carried the trays to the living room cocktail table.

"I never know how you take your coffee, as you're always changing from morning to noon. Milk, cream, sugar, nothing?"

"Nothing," and he got up and headed for the door.

"By nothing I meant black. Oh have it your own way. This is just like you. The library incident's just like you. You're childish and mis-sensitive and you never hear a word anyone says."

Tommy was crossing the street with a friend as he got in the car. She ran up to his window and said "Bo, I'm very mad at you, I am. You promised to call to take me horseriding at that ranch on your road, and you never did. If you want to stay my friend you have to keep your promises. Were you sick?"

"No."

"Mommy said you were. I wanted to call, but she said maybe you need to rest more. Can we go riding today?"

"No."

"It's because you and her fought. You're both mad at each other and that's okay. But I hope you don't stay mad as I want to go riding and you're the only one who'll take me. Mommy can't stand horses except to look at and all her friends say they have allergies with them. I like you better than all her friends. It's because you don't act like a baby with allergies or like an old person with me. And you tell scary stories. If I never hear another ghost and Mr. Intermediary story I'm going to also get mad. Will you make one up for me and write me or phone me it soon?"

"The invisibleless ghost," he said, "and Mr. Intermediary met by accident one night on a moonless starlitless road." Tommy and her friend sat on the sidewalk and he cut the motor. "The ghost was returning from a ghost get-together in upstate Canada. Mr. Inter-mediary was walking in the opposite direction and complaining about how dark it was and how he could easily stumble over or into some-thing in his path, what with people being careless about where they throw their moles and moles being careless about where they dig their holes, when they bumped into each other. 'The ghost,' Mr. Inter-mediary said. 'One of those damnable Mr. Intermediaries,' the ghost said. 'And he's got such a nice warm coat on and I'm so cold from my three days up north,' and he snatched the coat off Mr. Intermediary's back. 'That's my coat,' Mr. Intermediary said, snatching back the coat off the ghost's back. 'My coat,' the ghost said. 'My coat. Hoot,' the ghost said. 'Scoot,' Mr. Intermediary said. 'Scoot hoot,' the ghost said. 'I was going to give you a rest from my ghosting tonight. But if I don't get your coat right back on my back, I'm going to scoot you out of your sleep all night with your hoots.' 'Out of my way,' Mr. Intermediary said, and he pushed past the ghost. 'I've a long way to go and lots of holes and moles to look out for without being bothered by you or coming coatless and half-frozen too.' 'The absolute pall,' the ghost said. 'Why you've offended ghosts up and down the Atlantic by shoving past me like that without even being scarcely scared.' And he pressed a belt button. Said 'Darnit, why doesn't this dang belt button work?' And kept pressing the belt button till he took the belt off and chewed and scratched and smacked and thwacked and slammed the belt on its button against the ground till he was suddenly shot into the air, where he circled Mr. Intermediary like a bumblebee as he put the belt back on and said 'I'll show you a trick or two, Mr. Intermediary, sir,' and he dived right down to his head with a ghost grenade in his hand."

"Tommy," Bobby said from the upstairs window. "Oh hello, Bo. Having trouble with your car?"

"He's telling us a story."

"Well after he's through there's something I want you to do for me very soon, dear."

"Call me this week, Bo," Tommy says. "I want us to go riding. And I want you to finish this story or start another one. This one has no ending, does it. They're going to get mad at each other with it getting them nowhere like the last time. And then Mr. Intermediary's going to go home tripping over moles and into holes and the invisibleless ghost will fly the other way to his tree to sleep the whole day away. I'd like to hear a Mr. Intermediary chapter more different and exciting next time, but thanks." Her girlfriend said thanks. They stood up. Tommy said "I wish you were my real father, Bo. You'd make a great one," and kissed the car's door handle on his side and went into the house with her friend.

He drove home, made a pot of coffee, sat down at the kitchen table to start a short story. "Tommy called me at work this morning and told me what she said she would have told me last night if I hadn't passed out in bed: 'You drink too much; you're thirty-three and grow increasingly immature; and though I don't like telling you this over the phone, I definitely want a divorce.'"

He read Bobby's letter and wrote the second sentence. "'The main reason because it's the one I've decided you can never correct is that I never know when you're suddenly going to change from my gentle helpful lovemate into this horrible ogre who for some ugly reason all its own takes pleasure in reducing me to a bawling deranged woman.'"

The phone rang. It was his sister Ray. She wanted him to spend the day with her family at their summer house some twenty miles

from him and be part of a corn and lobster cookout tonight. "But
don't come now less you want to loll around the beach by yourself for
a couple of hours. The kids haven't had their lunch yet, so we won't
be leaving here for another hour."

The third sentence read " 'Maybe most of what I'm saying doesn't
make any sense to you right now or even sound fair, but I hope these
main points get through: my entire well-being can't afford a delay in
the divorce; Bobby might get permanently hurt emotionally if you
don't consent to an immediate divorce; I'm much too fragile a person
to have another thing to do with you till long after the divorce.' "

The story would be called "Negatives" or at least have something
about negatives in the title. It would be called "Something About
Negatives" and the husband for the first part of the story would say
nothing but negatives such as no, nope, none, nah, nay, nil, nix, nor,
naught, nicht, nein, non, niente, neither, nothing, negative, and the
wife he'd model after Bobby and the daughter would be named
Bobby. The last story his agent sold to a magazine was also about a
relationship that ended. It was published this month, and last week
Gerry wrote him from Canada saying she'd been hitching to the
country store for days and the magazine just arrived today and she
read it and loved it but wanted to know if in real life he thought she
was as stupid and sexless as he depicted her in the story.

His sister's house overlooked the Long Island Sound, the point
about a mile away where the Connecticut River began, and on exceptionally clear days, Long Island. He found the key in the showerhouse
where Ray said they always left it, let himself in, made a pot of coffee,
sat in the shade and scribbled out a first draft of the last scene of the
story. It had the wife breaking her vow about not seeing Dom by
breaking down the door of their apartment she'd moved out of and
he'd locked himself in to avoid getting subpoenaed, to get him to sign
the proxy papers that would enable her to fly to Mexico for the
divorce. "I promised to sign them if she came to bed with me one last
time. She said she couldn't come to bed even if she wanted to, as the
front door was broken and somebody might walk in.

" 'If I fix the door so it locks will you come to bed?'

" 'I'll come to bed only if before you fix the door you sign the
papers and let me go downstairs to mail the papers to myself.'

" 'If you go downstairs you probably won't return.'

" 'And once we're out of bed you probably won't sign the papers.
Or if you signed them before we went to bed, then you'll probably
tear them up.'

" 'The only alternative is to choose. If I win the choose then I'll sign the papers, fix the door and we go to bed. If you win the choose then I'll sign the papers, fix the door while you're mailing them and hope that you return so we can go to bed.'

" 'No chooses. You'll simply have to sign the papers, fix the door while I'm mailing them and trust me to return we so can go to bed.'

" 'Maybe you should leave right now, return tomorrow and break down the door again, and listen to the new solution I'll have cooked up by then.'

" 'I'm not going to listen to any of your new solutions.'

" 'Then maybe I should fix the door, you stay here, I'll return tomorrow and break down the door and listen to your new solution.'

" 'There'll be no new solutions.'

" 'Then maybe we should just go to bed, stop halfway through, I'll sign the papers, fix the door while you're mailing them, and when you return we can resume in bed at about the point where we left off.'

" 'Maybe you ought to go to bed alone, get about halfway through, sign the papers, fix the door while I'm mailing them, and when I return we'll go to bed together and start at about the point where you left off.'

" 'Maybe I should sign the papers, fix the door, start in bed without you, get about halfway through and then mail the papers while you go to bed, and while you're waiting for me you get to about half the point where I was, where when I return I'll get in bed with you and we'll resume together at about the point where each of us had separately left off.'

" 'How could I be sure you'd mail them?'

" 'Just as how could I be sure you'd still be here after I mailed them?'

" 'Maybe you ought to sign the papers, fix the door, start in bed without me and get about halfway done, and then we'll mail the papers together, return here, I'll get in bed and start alone and get to about the point where you left off while you're on the floor getting back to where you were before we mailed the papers, and then you'll get in bed with me and we'll resume together about halfway through.'

" 'How could I be sure you wouldn't run away after we mailed the papers?'

" 'Then the only answer is for me to become the good fairy, say the magic words and wave my wand to make you disappear, and then fly out the window like a butterfly to some unknown place way beyond the sky,' and she sprouted wings and golden hair and a silver sari, made several smoky white circles in the air with her wand, tapped the centers of the circles three times each and whispered to me 'Ah-ba-hoo.' " He went for a run.

He was sitting outside trying to remember without rereading what he'd just read, when Ray's family drove up. The poet was referring to all artists when he said something about no prizes or ceremonies for them—"They kill the man"—but the children were on him before he could find the page again: Kirt hugging his neck from behind, Marty and Lou crammed in his lap between the wicker chair arms.

"Take us to the beach, Uncle Bobo," Kirt said. Ray and Dick said Bo couldn't be any more help to them as they hadn't had an hour's peace together for a week. The children got their swimsuits on. Bo found the right page and lines in the recent book of posthumous poems. They made for the sandy beach—Kirt leading the way so he could show Bo the safest route over the jetty rocks, the two girls holding Bo's hands and debating whether he was their favorite uncle.

Kirt laid his towel out on the sand and ran screaming into the water. Bo and the girls lined their towels level with Kirt's and sat down. A woman came up behind them and said "Excuse me, but this here's a private beach and these people in those bungalows up there pay two hundred dollars a week for it."

"I'm sorry," Bo said, "though I think we can stay by the water. All Connecticut shore from half the high-water mark down is for public use I understand."

"That may be true, I never heard it. Just so long as you don't go further up on the dry sand."

They sat on the wet sand. Bo had Lou lie on her back with her limbs spread wide so he could make an outline of her body with his finger. They all packed the inside of the outline with wet sand to make a sculpture of Lou's body. Marty said the sculpture looked like a large drowned doll getting dry. Bo pocked the sculpture's belly for a belly button and asked Lou if her tummy had hurt when he did that. She said she'd rather make a castle.

Kirt appointed himself chief architect, Marty provided the idea of making the castle out of wet sand drippings, Bo dug most of the wells for wet sand and built a wall around the castle to keep the Sound out. They worked on it for two hours. Lou measured herself alongside the castle and said it was longer and taller. The castle looked, when Bo stood up, like the Grand Canyon might look when seen from a low-flying plane.

Marty ran back to the house to get her camera. She told Bo her parents hadn't taken the sailfish out as they said they would but were in bed sleeping. Bo asked a girl sunbathing nearby to take four pictures of them behind the castle. For the first picture Lou stood on Marty's shoulders who stood on Kirt's shoulders who stood on Bo's shoulders who stood. The girl said she thought she missed the castle and most of Bo's legs. For the second picture Bo and the children sat contemplating the castle with somebody else's fist under another person's chin so they'd look like serious city planners. For the third picture they lay on their backs and looked upside down past the castle at the camera. For the fourth they squatted and scratched each other's underarms and were supposed to laugh like monkeys, but Marty told the girl not to snap the picture as it would turn out ugly. Instead, they stood backwards in a semi-circle around the castle and smiled through their legs at the camera. "When the pictures are developed," Marty said, "each of us will get a different one of them."

Bo thanked the girl and ran the quarter-mile length of the beach. Running back he saw the kids running towards him, so he clicked his heels in the air and yelled "Hallelujah" and "Hurray" and the kids yelled "Hallelujah" and "Hurray" and tried clicking their heels in the air but could only do it on the ground. "How do you do that?" Kirt said, trying again. Bo lifted Kirt onto his back, sat Marty on his forearms and Lou facing Marty on Marty's lap, and ran with them like that into the water.

They were sitting on the beach watching a water-skier ski past when two men stopped to look at the castle. "Think they want to buy it?" Kirt said, but the shorter man stepped on the castle, flopped over when his leg sunk up to the knee in the castle, was helped out by a friend and stepped on the castle more daintily till he demolished it. The girls were crying. Kirt yelled "What you have to do that for?" Bo told Kirt to can it and sit down. The man said it was an accident and walked over with his friend. "Why, did it seem like anything else to you?"

"Come on, what are you handing the kid?" Bo said. "And isn't it enough you upset them where you now have to try and provoke us more?"

"Don't give me any of that stuff, you la-dee-da. Because if I upset them by accidentally ruining their castle, you can imagine how you upsetted my bungalow tenants before by running oh so sweetlike on the beach in your bikini," and he imitated an effeminate man bending his wrist and standing in such a way and softening his voice with the last few words. "Because I know what's on your mind, fella. So don't be accusing me of upsetting anyone when you make yourself into such a la-dee-da specimen in front of your kids."

So he thinks I'm queer, Bo thought, or something. Or what does he think? The man was now talking to Kirt, Kirt was arguing with the man. Something about the man having no right. Something about if the public beach starts below the waterline like your father said, then we've the right to publicly bust apart the castle because it's public. Something about the castle not being public but ours because we built it and yours if you only want to look at it. Something about Kirt not knowing what he's talking about. Something about why doesn't the man go away because we were having so much fun before you came. Something about why does a boy have to do an older man's arguing. So the man thinks I'm queer or something, but what do I think of him? I'm thinking I don't want to think of him. He doesn't exist. The silent man not taking his eyes off the ground doesn't exist. The bungalow people standing up to watch the scene from their porches and beach blankets don't exist. Kirt while he continues to argue doesn't exist. So long as the girls continue to cry they don't exist. Neither motorboat saws nor helicopter roars exist. Clouds, sun, sky, sand, surf, salt, birds, wind, me—we exist. I exist on this empty beach on this beautiful day I exist. The castle doesn't exist. Bobby and this whole day don't exist. Yes, the girls exist. I should comfort the girls. "There . . . there, girls . . ."

He told the girls to get their things together. Marty not to forget her camera. Kirt not to say another word. Kirt to help him flatten out the castle and fill in all the wet-sand holes so the man doesn't trip again.

"I didn't trip."

"So nobody on the beach trips. So people don't break ankles or legs or whatever they break when they trip into holes."

They flattened and filled. "Good, you're going," the man said. They walked to the jetty, from on top the jetty looked back. The man yelled to them through cupped hands. "What?" Kirt yelled back. "Don't answer him," Bo said. The man was yelling something about how he's going to sit next to them next time they sit on the public beach. The other man had his back to them.

"I know him and he's an ape as you say," Dick said when Kirt told him the story, "but an ape with a point. He doesn't want us on Sandy Beach and we don't want him at Rocky Cove. The ape understands that. I thought you understood that, Kirt. He's here for business and we for pleasure. And up till now by our not having a thing to do with each other, we've gotten along fine."

"But we always cut our feet at Rocky," Kirt said. "And the sand's not the same for making castles and art."

"Privacy's more important. Next time wear your sneakers to the cove." To Bo he insisted he stay the night. "You're much too silent and reserved. It's that living alone that does it. One full day with us and you'll go home less kindly and talking blue streaks."

At the cookout Marty asked Bo how come he never married.

"Because I haven't found the right girl yet. No, I've found the right girl a number of times, but I was always too young to marry. Oh, I guess I got old enough but just never had enough money to marry. That's not it. I think all the girls I ever wanted to marry ended up not wanting me to or else were happily married themselves. Or it was because I thought marriage would stop me from writing and traveling around cheap a lot and living in a way where I wouldn't have to work at outside jobs that much. No, I suppose I just never believed in the custom of marriage. Or if I believed in it, then that I'd be too unreliable a family provider to marry. Or else, didn't marry because I never wanted to have children of my own enough. Of if I did, then that I'd never make a good enough father. Or if I did, than that I'd never make a good enough husband, which would mean my children would end up losing their good enough father. No, those aren't it either. I don't know. What was the question? Well, some of those answers, none of those answers. Maybe I haven't found the right girl yet."

"I'll marry you," Lou said. "Then you'll be my husband."

"You can't marry your uncle," Marty said.

"I can if he's not married."

Next morning he drove to Bobby's house. At the door she got ready to say something, didn't, shook her head, shut her mouth, let him in, made coffee, stared at him as she set the kitchen table, said nothing. He said "I was over Ray's place for the day—the country one, as the July rentees couldn't make it this weekend so Ray gave them the first week in August if they let Ray have her own house this weekend—and Lou, my youngest niece, she said—actually it was Marty, their oldest girl, who said why didn't I get married? Kirt thought that was a great idea, as all his friends have uncles and aunts who produce cousins and cousins for them, though Lou didn't like the idea of my getting married much. She asked me to hold out for a dozen years till she became eligible. But Ray and Dick, always eager to dispel the most drastically impracticable thoughts from their children's heads and fearful my proneness for aloneness might become irreversible in another year, which would only increase their own worry for me and nurture Lou's incestuous notions, finally convinced

Lou to make it unanimous in that they all wanted to see me married and a father. They voted and even I said aye. We called the folks in New York to make the family unanimity complete, but they were asleep. Now what do you think of all that? Now don't speak up all at one time. Now now's not the time to become tacit and mum. Don't you want to join our family and make it even more unanimous? For no better reason, let's marry so I can edit your manuscripts and you can mark up my proofs. We can return joint submissions to a single file. We can file singles joints to a return submission. We can joint single file and return submissions. We can joint singles to a—say something, any silent thing. Give me a yes, no or maybe. Cat's got your tongue? Then wiggle your eyes, jiggle your nose, twiddle your ears, flutter your thumbs, dilate your lungs. Blink one time for yes and ten times for maybe. Then seventy-six times for no and three times for maybe. Cat's got your eyes? I see, you're shy. Very appealing quality in a woman, being shy. And you've good reason also, with a cat that's got your eyes and tongue and a man who wants a couple of peeps out of you. Just two peeps for yes and three peeps for maybe. What about three short and one long peep for yes quickly followed by five peeps for maybe. Here, take this pen and paper and write what's wrong. Then write six X's for yes and three O's for maybe. Cat got your hand?"

She pointed to his mug. He nodded. She took the mugs and washed them. He said "I meant by my nod that I wanted more coffee." She put away the mugs and sugar and cream pitchers and untouched silver, cookies, biscuits, butter, napkins. She went upstairs and shut her bedroom door.

He wrote on the paper "Dear Bobby, I dropped by but you were out, Love Bo," and was taping the note above the door knocker when Tommy came downstairs. She read it and said "What's that silly note for?" He pinched his neck and said "Ah, ah, throat infection, can't speak but can kiss," and kissed all her right hand knuckles and went to the car. She said "You've had another fight—I heard. I heard also how you can get to go with her again if you don't try to reach her for a month. That's what she told Aunt Peter on the phone last night. She said she was going to tell you the same thing next time you came here or called."

At home he finished the first draft of the story. It now ended with Dom and Bobby going to the beach. "It was our last day together before she flew to her granny's for the summer and Tommy to Mexico for the divorce. We spread our towels out on the sand. A woman came up behind us and said 'Pardon me, sir, but this here's a private beach and our bungalow tenants are paying two hundred a week for its use.' I said I was sorry and hadn't known it was private, but since by state law all waterway shore is public from half the high-water mark down, I hoped she wouldn't mind our sitting on the wet sand. She said 'I suppose that'll be okay,' and we rolled up the towels and sat on the wet sand.

"Bobby suggested making a castle. She designated me chief architect, well digger, moat, wall, tower and tower window maker: she would artistically squeeze wet sand drippings on the towers and walls. We worked on it for a couple of hours. When I stood up and squinted the castle seemed like a real one seen from faraway high ground. Bobby got up to go to the car to get her camera to take pictures of the castle, when a man stood in front of the castle and seemed to be admiring it.

" 'Think he wants to rent it for the summer?' I said, but she wasn't amused. The man was scaring her, she whispered: 'He looks like a people-eating ape.' Short, stocky, hair covering his entire body except for the upper neck to an inch above his heavy brow ridge, arms down to his knees. 'I like the way he looks,' I said. 'Though maybe because it's reassuring seeing a man like myself with hair on his shoulders and back.'

"Suddenly the man was kicking the castle in. 'What the hell's the meaning of that?' I yelled. 'My daughter was about to take pictures of it.'

" 'The meaning's no meaning at all,' he said, coming over. 'I felt like breaking a castle, and since you told my wife this part of the beach's public, I thought that makes this castle public too.'

" 'What I told that woman there—'

" 'Don't touch me,' he said.

" 'Who touched you? I raised my arm past your shoulder to point to that woman there.'

" 'I said don't touch me. I don't like being touched.'

" 'But I didn't. The first time I pointed past you to that woman you spoke about and the second time I was showing you—like this—how I had pointed past you the first time.'

" 'You just touched me. Now I told you not to touch me,' and he swung at me and missed. Bobby screamed. I turned to her to stop her from screaming when the man clipped me in the back. I jumped at him, got him in a headlock and said 'I could get you for assault or something for this so just be a good fellow, relax yourself—that's right—and prepare to walk peacefully away when I let you go.'

"I let him go. He backed off, said 'Go ahead, call a cop. Because

I'd like to tell him how you go around exposing yourself in your tight bikini to all the little girls on the beach. And to this one too, if she really is your daughter.'

"I hit his belly as hard as I could. He dropped backwards into the deep castle moat. I got on my knees and began scooping sand and mud on him while he lay nauseated and dazed. Bobby and I had about completely buried him except for his face and toes when some people came running down from the bungalows. We ran to the jetty rocks, climbed them and got in the car. The man was still in the hole. His friends had only partially uncovered him. His wife was waving a golf club at us and the two men who'd chased us a few feet had their fists raised.

" 'I honked twice at them and drove off. Bobby said she'd never seen me act like that to anyone. I told her I hadn't hit a boy or man since grade school and also since then hadn't raised my voice that loud to anyone except her mother and herself. 'But suddenly on the beach I felt different. I still feel different. Do I look different? Well I'll tell you, from now on I'm going to stay different. From now on the hell with people ordering me about and imposing their stunted views and wanting me to do what pleases them so they can be the masters and fulfill their always unfillable selfish needs. Before I just ignored it. Now I see I can't just ignore it. And if you don't mind, what I'd like doing instead of returning you to your mother's so she can jet you to your granny's while she's off getting the divorce, is spend some more time with you myself.'

" 'I don't mind.'

" 'Say about two months more time with you?'

" 'Mom will mind.'

" 'We'll phone her. You'll plead with her. And if she still won't budge, I'll just have to say I'm kidnapping you from her.'

" 'But before you said you only have enough money to live by yourself for a month. Where you getting it now for our traveling?'

" 'Oh, we'll stop off for a few days someplace and I'll finish the story I've been writing these past weeks and send it to my agent to send it to a good man's magazine. The story's so far about a fairly mild man going through the strain of a divorce he doesn't want, which will mean being separated from his child he dearly loves, and will now wind up with him on the beach with his daughter and meeting a man like that apeman before and suddenly feeling he's been pushed around by too many people like that and by subduing the man he gets up enough courage to kidnap his daughter and sail away let's say on a sloop he steals with her. Then—I'm not finished, because as I said all the story needed till now was an ending—I'll write another story about almost the same people. Though this time from the point of view of the wife who's getting a divorce and sees her daughter kidnapped by her husband she considered crazy long before the kidnapping, and this story I'll try and sell by myself under your name to a woman's magazine. Then we'll collaborate on a child's version of the story, but make it very fanciful with the girl and her mother meeting a real ape from an ape colony on a beach. And somehow the father shows up and does in the killer ape and beats off the ape colony who had kidnapped the mother and child. And because of his newfound courage, he wins back the mommy's love and they all sail off on a raft to live on a remote island and be away for all time from that whole ape culture back there, and this one we'll send to my agent to send to a publishing house as a children's book and sign both our names to it as we'll both be working on the illustrations and texts. Now what do you say?'

"She was ecstatic. We drove home, got my typewriter, manuscripts, clothes, camping gear, at a thrift shop got Bobby a typewriter and some clothes, and that night, after Tommy told me on the phone she was going to have me locked up for life if I so much as drove a single block more with Bobby, we started our drive across country."

Bo had the story photostated, dropped a copy through Bobby's mail slot, banged the door knocker a few times, ran to the car and drove home.

He phoned Bobby an hour later to ask what she thought of the first draft of the story. She picked up the receiver and said before he could say anything "Gah-goo, gee-gee, gig-gen, get-get go."

"When answering the phone," he said, "it's customary to start off with a hello."

Mac

in

Love

—

She said "You're crazy, Mac," and shut the door. I knocked. She said "Leave me be?" I rang the bell. She said "Please don't make a fuss." I kicked the door bottom. She said "Mac, the neighbors. You'll get the police here and me thrown out." I said "Then let me in." She said "Maybe some other day." I said "Just for a minute to explain." She said "There's nothing to explain. The incident's over. It never should've begun. It began and now it's over. So go away. Now don't get me evicted. It's a cheap sunny place. It took me a long time to find. I like this apartment, building and neighborhood and I don't want to leave. You leave. Please leave now? I know you'll feel different in the morning."

I went downstairs and left the building. Coming up the stoop as I was going down it was Jane's closest friend. Ruth said "Hello, Mac, you just up to see Jane?" I said "Yes, and how are you, Ruth? Nice day out. Actually, the whole week's been grand. Some weather we're having. Just look at that sky. No I'm serious: really look at the sky." I pointed. She looked. I said "Blue as can be. And people talk about pollution. But then they also say most pollution can't be seen. The experts say that, I mean, and that what appears to be clean air because the sky looks clean doesn't necessarily have to be clean air but dirty, except it doesn't look dirty because most pollutants, because of something to do with particles and refraction, can't be seen by the average naked eye. Well it's nice having the illusion if we can't have the fact. What I mean is isn't it nice that even if the air's dirty it at least looks clean? Even though it isn't, I'm saying. Or rather they're saying—the experts."

"It's a nice day as you say. And I suppose Jane's in, so I'll be seeing you, Mac. Take care."

"You too, Ruth, and give my regards to Jane. Or rather my love. Here, give her my love," and I wrote on a memo book page "my love," tore the page out and gave it to Ruth and said "Give it to Jane. Tell her I give it to her with my deepest love," and I wrote on another page "deepest love," and gave it to Ruth. "Please tell her I give her these messages with all my love," and on a third page I wrote "all my love," and gave it to Ruth. "Have a good weekend," I said. She said "You too," and climbed the steps and I crossed the street. I looked up at Jane's third-floor apartment. All the shades were raised high. The bedroom and bathroom windows were open a few inches, the living room window was closed. The ceiling light in the bedroom was on, the living room and bathroom ceiling lights were off. Jane opened the living room window all the way and began watering her plants. She turned to look into her apartment. She set the yellow watering can between two plant boxes on the outside window ledge and left the window. She was probably answering the door. "Hi," she would say to Ruth as she let her in. Ruth would say "Hi" or "Hello" and they would briefly hug or kiss one another's cheek or the air beside the cheek but not hug and kiss both. Ruth would take off her coat and put it on the chair next to the door as she always did or at least did when I was there and Jane would pick the coat off the chair and hang it in the closet facing the front door as she almost always did when I was there when Ruth put her coat on the chair. Ruth would mention seeing me and show Jane the pages. Jane would read them, frown, say how these messages were indicative of what she considered my growing craziness regarding her or maybe just my growing craziness. How she was thoroughly tired of my insisting she see me when she doesn't want to. How she was disgusted with my saying how much I care for her when she hasn't any feeling left for me except pity, and maybe not even that. They would go on like that. Ruth would say I had acted kind of strange downstairs. Jane would say "How do you mean strange, outside of these notes?"

"His going on about pollution and refraction and the illusion of the blue sky and such and urging me to look at it though I've seen it a thousand times this week and can very well appreciate a sky without him telling me to and in fact appreciate it a lot less when people urge me to. I didn't know what to make of it all."

"What I make of it is that if he comes around here again I'm going to call the police. I don't know how many times I told him on the phone and in person and once even in a letter to leave me alone. A normally reasonable person would have understood by now. Mac doesn't. He doesn't because he doesn't want to understand. Like a child he's still got to get the thing he's been told countless times he can't have and which will even make him sick. That's one of the things that turned me off to him. Another is that I simply grew out of being fond of him."

"Well I never thought he was right for you from the start. He was just always so eager to please me. There was just something so specially peculiar about his style—and not that he tended to talk too much or was so jittery—that scared or repelled me sometimes."

"I felt the same way in the beginning, but after a couple of dates he didn't seem peculiar at all. He became natural and nice. What I mean is he lost his nervousness or peculiar nature or whatever it is you might call it—that a doctor might call it—and became sweet and calm and generous and we had a pleasant relationship for about a month till something happened in him. He didn't snap. Not that. He simply returned to being peculiar again though in a much worse way than before. Before he was only silly peculiar around people, which we both occasionally found amusing. But lately he became peculiar around people in a way that embarrassed me both for him and myself, and peculiar when we were alone that at times frightened me with the possibilities of where it might lead to. But I'm not making myself clear, am I?"

"You're trying to be tactful, though I understand what you mean. Like that time—"

"Oh let's forget him, because I've had him up to here. Today, yesterday, the night before. Always calling up or dropping by when the last person I want to see is him. Like an hour ago he called to say he was in the neighborhood and I said 'Really, Mac, I'm very busy. I'm busy all the coming weekdays with rehearsals and tapings and in the evenings with acting classes and class exercises and this evening and all day tomorrow with a friend,' though I didn't mention you by name."

"Why not? I wouldn't've minded."

"But it's me. He hasn't any right to any explanations anymore or knowing anything more about my personal life. But he came around anyway and got in the building by ringing a neighbor's bell."

"Didn't the neighbor try and find out who she was letting in?"

"That's what Mac told her as he climbed the stairs. This Mrs. Roy, on the second, she opened her door and yelled for him to leave the delivery carton on her doormat as she didn't want any supermarket roaches in her apartment, but Mac said 'Excuse me, ma'am, but I must've rung your bell by mistake. You should always ask who it is before you tick back. Best way to get burglars in the building,' he said—you know, conning her, as he walks past her apartment apologizing some more for the inconvenience he caused her. She immediately got all flustery with his good manners or I don't know what and said it was a good thing the person she let in by mistake this time was such a nice polite man. Then I hear him coming up to my floor and first thing he says when he gets here is that he wants us to go to bed."

"For what? I don't understand. Came out with it in the hall or in here?"

"Right here. He—but what should I do with these notes?"

"They're your treasures, not mine."

"Dump them, that's what I'll do. Love love love love. But what do you say to some tea. Jasmine or—oh just let me put the water on first. So before—"

"I think you're going to need more water than that for two cups."

"Right. So before, I let him in here. I had to avoid the big scene he swore he'd make in the hall, and immediately he grabs my hand and says 'Jane, I've thought things over and decided the most perfect remedy to all our present difficulties is for us to forthrightly though very calmly go to bed.' I said 'Oh sure, oh thanks, oh anything you say, Mac,' but he still had my hand and when he clutched it even tighter and tried leading me into the bedroom, I told him 'You're crazy, Mac. You're absolutely insane.' I finally had to pull my hand out of his and go to the window and threaten to shout for help unless he left. He said he didn't believe my threat as he didn't think I'd want to cause trouble for myself with the landlord, but as a courtesy to me he'd leave. But once outside the door he knocks and rings and kicks the door to get back in. When I refused he started to cry. Crazy cries. I told him to cry downstairs, cry out of the building, cry anywhere but here, and he said he would. And next thing I know you're ringing my downstairs buzzer and I think it's him and that's why I didn't answer that fast. But when you spoke into the speaker when I turned it on to listen to some sign that it might or might not be him, I let you up. How did he ever give you these notes?"

"On the stoop where we met. Wrote them up one after another in a way that seemed almost logical and clever to me in the sequence and routine he used. But having someone around like him would really scare me, to tell the truth."

"He's essentially harmless, don't worry. He'd never hurt any-one—just bother them to death. But why can't he say as let's say most other men might say 'Well it's over, Jane, and it's been fun, blah-blah'—but not like that, of course. To quietly accept it and dis-appear. Relationships can't be one-sided, I told him. I told him no matter what happened between us in the past, if I no longer have any romantic or affectionate or sexual feelings towards him, then I'm just not going to come around again. He's making me a total wreck."

"Jane?" I yelled from the street.

"There he is again," Jane said.

"Jane? You left your watering can on the window ledge."

"I didn't quite get that."

"Something about my watering can. I left it on the outside ledge."

"What are you going to do?"

"About the watering can?"

"About him. Yelling your name out there. About him still being there."

"Ruth?"

"Now he's yelling your name."

"Ruth? Will you please tell Jane she left her watering can on the window ledge."

"He's going on about something about the watering can again."

"He said you should tell me I left it on the window ledge."

"What I feel like telling you is to tell the police there's a maniac on the street screaming out our names."

"Mrs. Roy?"

"Who's that now?"

"The second-floor tenant I spoke about."

"Mrs. Roy? Will you please tell Ruth, who's a visitor of your neighbor, Miss Room, to please tell Jane she left her watering can on the window ledge."

"Maybe Mrs. Roy will solve your problems by phoning the police."

"No such luck."

"Jane?"

"Good God, Ruth, what should I do?"

"Jane? Will you please tell Ruth to tell Mrs. Roy to tell Ruth to tell you you left your watering can on the window ledge."

"I'm going to call the police."

"Ruth?"

"Do it. Just tell them he's down there. I'll back you up."

"Ruth? Will you please tell Jane to tell Mrs. Roy to tell you to tell Jane she left her watering can on the window ledge."

"Police? My name is Jane Room, Thirty-one East Thirteenth, apartment Three-B. There's a man outside my building by the name of Mac Salm who's constantly shouting out my name in a way to cause embarrassment to me and who's been annoying me for days to get into my apartment....No, I know him. For about a month....I've told him that for a week now, but he still comes around uninvited and causes commotions in my building's hallways and lobby till I'm forced to let him in....No, but I can just as well be protected from his verbal abuse and the mental and emotional harm he's causing me, can't I?"

"Mrs. Roy?"

"Now he's shouting my second-floor neighbor's name....Mrs. Roy....Ernestine. If you had any kind of amplifying device on your phone...Then I'll tell you."

"Mrs. Roy?"

"He repeated her last name."

"Will you please tell Ruth to tell Jane to tell you to tell Ruth to tell Jane she left her watering can on the window ledge."

"He said that Mrs. Roy should tell my friend to tell me to tell Mrs. Roy to tell this same friend to tell me that I left my watering can on the window ledge....Because I was watering my outside plants when the doorbell rang....Not him this time but a friend at the door....I already said he's harmless that way....Well then I said it to my friend here but to you I remember saying I didn't think Mr. Salm would physically harm me....Well I remember....Ruth. I don't see why I have to give her last name to you. If you send someone over and she's still here, which she promised to be, then you can get her full name and address as a witness....Excuse me, but are you going to send an officer over or not?...Yes, this is a complaint.... S-A-L-M. I—thank you."

"He said a patrol car will be right over."

"What was that argument about my last name?" Ruth said.

There she is. At the window looking down towards me. "There you are, Jane. I suppose Mrs. Roy finally told Ruth to tell you to tell Mrs. Roy to tell Ruth to tell you your watering can's on the window ledge."

She took the watering can. "I called the police, Mac." And closed the window, pulled down the shade.

Why don't I leave and not come back as she says? Because I think if I persist in telling her about my love for her she'll once more love me in return. Because she was in love with me once. She once told me that. She said "I was in love with you once but I'm not now." She never once said "I'm in love with you now." Just that she was in love with me once. When was she in love with me? Once when we were on a bus and she curled up in my arms because she was sleepy and cold and it was late and the bus was unheated and we were returning from a dinner party uptown. And another time when we wanted to get to the theater before the movie began and I suggested we run so we ran, she alongside me and running very good for a girl and that smile she gave me then. She was in love with me as we ran, if that's possible. And we held hands during the movie and from time to time looked deeply at one another and gently kissed. She was in love with me then: running, on the movie line when she hugged me, inside. She was in love with me another time when we were in the park. That first springlike Sunday and we fell asleep on the grass just past the shade of a flowering dogwood in flower and just before she fell asleep she was lying on her back with her arms raised and I was leaning halfway over her and we looked at one another without smiling and I was so happy with her that a tear came and instead of wiping it I let it drop on her face because I thought to wipe it was as unimportant an act as to let it fall and then tears came from her and rolled past her ears and neck onto the grass and we kissed each other's eyes. She was in love with me then though she didn't say it. And other times but not now. I hear sirens. "I'm going, Jane. So long, Ruth." But the sirens are for someone else. People passing look at me. They think I'm crazy, drunk or both. I understand that. A man doesn't yell out on the street what I've been yelling without running the risk of people thinking him crazy, drunk, both or something else. But why did she stop loving me? That's what I should yell if I yell out anything else. But she already told me she doesn't quite understand why she stopped loving me. That feeling that allowed her to run along the street smiling lovingly at me went, she said last night when I recalled the incident for her, hoping to reawaken in her the same feeling. That feeling that allowed her to lie or sleep comfortably beside me went, she said before when I half jokingly asked her to come to bed with me. That feeling for wanting to do anything with me went. For wanting to talk to me went. For wanting to even talk to me about why she can't talk to me went. It all went. She doesn't know why it didn't in me but did in her but it did and that is that, she said. All gone, she said. Don't cry, she said. She said she hates to see me cry and might even cry herself if I cry, she said. She said cry somewhere else then, she said. She said she knows how I feel because if this will be of any comfort to me she once loved a man very much who didn't love her anymore but once did and she felt something like what I must be feeling and she knows it's a terrible feeling but she got over it and I will too. She knows. "You're a person with a lot of love to give and I wish what we once had could have continued like it did and blossomed like it didn't but it didn't and love's the one thing in life that can't be forced," she said. "At least from me," she said. She meant for herself. A patrol car was coming down the block. "I won't be bothering you anymore," I yelled to Jane. "I'm sorry for all my ridiculousness about the watering can before and the trouble I've caused you and Ruth and Mrs. Roy and really you've been right all along because like you said when the feeling's gone it's gone and that's that so so long," and I walked to the corner.

Two policemen got out of the patrol car. One asked me to please stand still, lean against the car with my hands on the hood and legs spread wide behind me so I could be searched. He searched me. He said I was clean. He said a person named Jane Room issued a complaint against me. I said I know all about the complaint or at least the reasons for it and she's absolutely right. "I only now know how crazy and wrong I've been. I won't annoy her anymore. I don't know how I can make my feelings any more clear to you on this matter other than to say I'll do anything you want me to do. I'll go to the station house without any bother or leave this block peacefully and never walk on it again if you don't want me to or for as long as you don't want me to. I'll positively not phone or contact her in any way again. I swear."

"All right," one of them said. "No more trouble then."

"No more."

"If there is any, we'll be forced to arrest you. That is, if Miss Room doesn't withdraw her complaint or if she or someone else complains to the police on this matter once more."

"I understand."

"I think he'll be all right, Herb," the other policeman said.

"Okay," Herb said.

"Okay," I said.

They got in the car but didn't drive away. I walked around the corner and along the avenue towards 12th Street. The patrol drove parallel though a little behind me till I crossed 12th and headed for 11th. Then it sped up down the avenue and made a right several blocks away.

As a joke I should walk back to Jane's and yell out her name or something one last time. Something to Jane to thank Mrs. Roy for telling Ruth to tell Jane to tell Mrs. Roy to tell Ruth to tell Jane her watering can's on the window ledge. After all, I could say, the can could have fallen off the ledge and hit someone on the head. I could yell out that in the combined act of our telling Jane about her watering can we possibly saved someone's life or at the least saved someone from getting hurt or at the very least saved Jane from losing or damaging her watering can. I bought her that can at a Japanese gift shop a week ago. But by the time I got through yelling out all this the police would be back, summoned by Jane or maybe Mrs. Roy. Surely Ruth would demand that Jane call the police or Ruth might call them herself over Jane's protests. I would be brought to the station house. I would spend the night in jail. It would be a change. I feel terrible. My stomach and head ache. I still can't accept not being with Jane anymore. I'll have a miserable night unless I'm with her or dead drunk or confined in a cell in a station house and I'll only get deathly sick if I get dead drunk again and Jane will never let me be with her again. "Once I'm turned off to someone I once loved I'm turned off to them for good," she told me today.

I ran along the avenue towards Jane's block. I stood across the street in front of her building. All her lights were on. The bathroom shade was up. The windows in the living room and bedroom were partly open. The sky was no longer light blue but getting dark. "Jane," I yelled. "Will you thank Ruth for telling Mrs. Roy to tell Ruth to tell you to tell Mrs. Roy to tell Ruth to tell you your watering can's on the window ledge." The patrol car was coming down the street. The same two policemen got out. They looked angry. "Ruth? Will you thank Mrs. Roy for telling you to tell Jane—" but the police were on me before I could finish. One got me from behind. He pressed the middle of his club in my mouth in a way where I couldn't push it out or bite his hand. Then I was on the ground on my stomach. Herb had his knee in my back and my arms twisted behind me. I was handcuffed. I was told to stand when I thought I could stand like a peaceful quiet citizen and not before because if I stood before then

I was going to get knocked to the ground but this time by a club. "We're not fooling around," Herb said. "We've got a job to do and you should know that by now."

I said I knew it and was ready to stand the way they wanted me to. "Peacefully and quietly?" Herb said, and I said yes and he took his knee out of my back and helped me up. I yelled "Jane?"

Last
May

———

Two aides come into my father's room with fresh linens and washing utensils and I automatically leave. On my way to the lounge I pass the room where there's a young woman whose mother was brought in the day before my dad and is dying of a more common form of the same disease. The young woman sits beside her mother holding her hand through the bed rails. A glucose-antibiotic solution is being fed to her mother through her other arm. For she was always being fed. Also my father always being fed. But unlike my father, the oxygen tank isn't hooked up and bubbling on top and attached by a hose to rubber plugs inside her nose. Later Marlene will say that so far the doctors think her mother can breathe reasonably well by herself, even though she's been comatose for two days. "I don't want her to get oxygen if she ever needs it. If they insist, I'll pull it out of her nose. For who will know late at night? It'll just be me. I'm sleeping over. I even brought my own pillow from home. I know their nightwatch. I'll just pretend I was dozing through the whole oxymoronic shebang, too wasted to stay awake. I only want her to die."

The second bed in her mother's room's been removed. Is that a sign? Marlene later says that though everyone around here is very skillful and professionally kind, no one seemed that subtle or humorous and that a bed with a patient in it in another building probably did cave in and crash-land as a nurse said. All the other rooms but my father's are for twos and fours. His is the only legitimate single on the floor. "They put him alone at the end of the hall so none of the patients and their guests will have to see him die," my mother said today or the day afterwards, for all this happened a year ago last May. I said something like "What about Marlene's mom near the elevators?" and she said "But they made hers a private," and I said "So? Her door's always open," and she said "Maybe they're too busy or always forget to close it," and I said "And if Marlene leaves the room and no nurses or aides are around?" and she said "Maybe you're right, that poor woman, though why are we still so persistent in wanting to win our arguments today?"

Of course all this is somewhat vague after a year and by nature I'm discursive and regularly forget things in an hour that most people remember for a lifetime, but a lot of it I can still remember pretty clear. My father on his back faceup. That's no task for my memory, for bedsores or not his position hardly changed. The woman also: just a sheet covering them both to their blue hospital gown necks on those warm sunny days. I don't remember if it was just a sheet or if they wore their own or the gowns or pajamas of the hospital or what the weather was like. I know it rained the following Tuesday. And I've newspapers for the three days he was there, or rather the Sunday through Tuesday *New York Times*, as he was admitted on a Saturday and died Monday around noon.

I get the newspapers off a closet shelf. They've actually yellowed in places and begun to crumble at the corners and sides. The President Orders Enemy's Ports Mined. Cavett Stoically Awaiting Word on Show's Future. The temperature date columns in the Weather Reports and Forecast sections say the mean temperature for that Saturday was 63 and Sunday was 62 and Monday was 60, which the columns also say was the normal mean temperature for all three dates. Tuesday, which I didn't save a paper for, was cooler, with what I now read was the *Times*'s predicted and my remembered rain.

But the two of them, their faces pale and gaunt, really bony and gray, eyes closed or thin suffering slits and eyebrows augustly raised, my father bald and her mother with half her hair gone from weeks of radiation treatments, her nose broken and his bulbous but regarding them both from above or in front their noses seemed the same, maybe my father in need of a shave after a day but his thick growth gray to white and virtually indistinguishable from his skin, both with wattles and long slender necks, withered lips, dentures in cardboard cups and mouths oblong holes, they might have looked like elderly brothers born a few years apart and resembling the same parent if they'd been put in a double bed together or in side-by-side twins. And he often dreamed it seemed and a couple of times in his coma laughed out loud and then let out a wide recognizant smile, or else he laughed the last time he was in the hospital a month ago when by the time I got there each afternoon after supper to both see him and relieve my mother he was too tired from the tests and drugs and exercises and mostly slept. I forget. I've notes. Pages of them of what went on then. But they're pressed between the backboard and glass of the sketch I did of him in his bed the night before he died and soon after the funeral framed.

I take the frame out of the dresser, remove the nails, board and notes. The first page reviews my urgent and then aggravated to exasperated calls to his doctor and the drive over and five-minute traffic jam our ambulance got in and this doctor's continental couturier suit and tassel-trimmed patent leather shoes and stylized sprayed hairdo and the first words he said to us outside my father's room, which were "How do you do? We were lucky to get a bed. What can I say? I think I mentioned the last time that each emergency situation is tantamount to another nail being driven into his coffin. I hate to be so blunt or appear insensitive, but for your own sake," meaning my mother's, "I'm not going to let him go home alive."

My mother, who the next day told the doctor she'd given considerable sleepless thought to what he said and decided it was only God's will whether her husband lived or died and he must do everything in his technical power to keep him alive or give up the case to another medical man, had been taking care of my father for a few years. He'd been through various illnesses and numerous operations in that time, for the last year was almost totally bedridden, couldn't stand or even hold a spoon or straw to his mouth or do just about anything for himself. Once a day my mother and I lifted him out of bed by my holding him by his underarms and she the knees, sat him up and sort of balanced him on an inflated rubber tube in the wheelchair and strapped him in with my old college scarf, covered his legs with an afghan she'd also made and tucked in his feet, put his urine bag on his lap so its tube to his bladder wouldn't get caught in the wheels, and pushed him into the living room where for around two hours he napped or watched a television guest show or late afternoon movie or had a digest of the newspapers and family matters and less startling neighborhood events related to him and his professional samples unwrapped and exhibited to him and his dental journal accounts of the latest developments and equipment in his field read to him, all of which he seemed to want to but couldn't show any interest for, and exactly at six was fed his strained food and apple juice and given his pills and capsules crushed or emptied and mixed into spoonfuls of milk while we all watched the local news.

He couldn't speak that last year because of a paralyzing stroke the previous year. Maybe every now and then he emitted a mute "y'ma" or "m'mom" but mostly communicated to us or visiting nurses or visitors of his at home with nods and head shakes and waving his hand no and rattling the bed rails when he wanted to get up and pushing his arm pillow off his lap when he wanted to go to bed and pointing to his genital area when he wanted to defecate or already had and wanted to be cleaned and sticking his finger to his mouth when he was hungry or thirsty and wanted more to eat or drink or had caught some food on his tongue or in his throat and couldn't cough up and wanted it to be picked or slapped out or wanted his dentures put back or removed.

I still live further up the block from their home and have no phone and on that Saturday morning a neighbor in their building rang my vestibule bell and yelled up the stairwell that my mother needed me immediately—"Your father." I ran over to their apartment. My mother said she woke up this morning and found Dad in what looks like a coma. I said "Did you call a doctor?" She said the doctor's answering service said they'll have him call her soon as they can reach him. He was in bed with a wet compress across his brow. I said "Dad, wake up." I shook his face by the jaw. She said don't hurt him. I said I was doing it gently and shook him again. She said he was too weak to be jerked like that: "Just pat his cheek lightly and speak to him close." I said into his ear as I patted him and she rubbed his toes "Dad, get up, it's Bud and Mom and time to have breakfast." She said "He isn't responding, what should we do?" I said "He might be in a diabetic coma," for he was also diabetic and only an artery transplant in his calf a month before his stroke had kept him from losing a foot that had become gangrened because of the diabetes and maybe his life from the amputation because the wound would probably have never healed and become gangrened from his diabetes, and told her to get him orange juice but not too cold. She said she's sure something sweet like orange juice is only good to get a person out of diabetic shock, not coma. "Then maybe he's in diabetic shock for all we know," and she said if he was he'd be groaning and thrashing his arms crazily or just lazily but acting kind of giddy and high. I said "Well maybe the juice will also work for a diabetic coma," and she got a glass of orange juice and as I held up his back and head she put the straw in his mouth and said "Sip, Cy, now you must try and sip," but he stayed a dead weight and couldn't sip in any of it.

The doctor called and said he'd try to get my father a bed at the hospital. I called him a half hour later and he said he was still trying to get a bed. An hour later he said "Your father is two names from the top of the emergency waiting list for a bed." I said "What should we do for him in the time being?" and he said he didn't quite know: "Let me think." I said "Can't you please come over?" and he said at the moment he was up to his ears in emergencies that he could just about cover in his office and on the phone and all his associates were tied up too. I said "Isn't there an emergency doctors home call service?" and he said in this city he didn't think so. I said "*New York* magazine wrote an article and gave the phone number of one which I meant to cut out and then get the back issue of and never did," and he said as much as he wanted to he never had time to read those magazines. "Well shouldn't I at least try and give him orange juice?" and he said "Call an ambulance and go to the Emergency entrance and maybe by then or with just your being there they'll have a bed in a private room. If not, they'll treat him in Emergency and he'll sleep in the men's ward, and if there's no bed there, on a litter in the men's ward hall."

The private room became available as we were admitting him to Emergency, but he had to wait in the hall right outside the room till it was cleaned and the bed was stripped and made and the floor dried. Then an aide came out with a pillowcase of soiled linen and a waste bag and he was wheeled in, put in his bed, immediately given IV and the resident arrived and for the third or fourth time in a year I was asked my father's medical history. I called over my mother because she could recall it all in technical detail and chronological order and also what drugs and dosages he was presently taking and had proven allergic to and the illnesses his brothers and sisters and parents had and died from. Then his regular medical man came and said what he said about not letting my father go home again and that he seemed pretty low and my mother said "Low? You mean his bed?" and he said "No, I mean he's sinking," and I said "Excuse me. I don't want to create any false optimism for you two or me both but he is taking in and eliminating liquids now when he wasn't before," and he said "That's true, though he'll still probably never swallow," and I said "Well I'm not giving up on him, for didn't you say yourself once that the doctors here call him the living miracle man because of his repeated survivals?" and he said "Anyway, he's okay for today so we'll just have to see how he does tomorrow," and shook my hand and patted my mother's back with my father's clipboard and said "Let's keep our fingers crossed," and she whispered to me as he went down the hall thumbing through my father's records "I know I'm going to have a sleepless night mulling over what he said."

My sister Dolly showed up in her waitress dress and hairnet she was required to wear at work and bawled me out for not calling her sooner at the cafe "no matter how much you might have believed I need to hold on to that cheesy job," and went into his room and put her arm around her mum and they both began crying and then it was early evening and my father looked comfortable enough in the pajama coat he'd come from home with and with his breathing light and urine clear and its bag filling up at what seemed a steady level and one of the residents said "It says here 'Dr. Devine.' Is your father a physician?" and I said "Oral surgeon." "Well we'll be fixing up Dr. Devine for the next couple of hours, so why don't you take your mother to the basement for something to eat?"

She said "You and Dolly go and I'll stay with Dad." Dolly said "No, Buddy and you go and I'll stick around and can read. I brought plenty of stuff." I said "Either I stay and you both go or we all go together. For what can we possibly do for him while they're working in there?" Dolly said "But I already had two huge meals at work. Besides, I'll look ridiculous sitting in my greasy uniform with hundreds of waitresses flocking around."

The doctors pulled the curtains around my father's bed and rolled in three small machines. I said to Dolly and Mom "Look, we're wasting time: we're all going together and that's final." My mother said "You have enough money, Bud?" and I said "Lots," but Dolly said "Oh no, it's on me and you can't say it isn't about time. For some reason my tips were good today and really, who the hell needs it anyway—my girls will starve?" My mother said "Maybe we shouldn't talk about money and just go dutch or I'll pay. Yes, I'll pay. No, I don't want to hear any more about it. I said I'll pay."

We went to a fish place in the East Sixties, really our favorite and actually our only restaurant for the past few years and my father's too because of the good food and cheap wine and lively informal atmosphere and clean, Dolly said while we waited at the bar for a table; "compared to every place I've worked in including my own home, spotless." And we really enjoyed ourselves there, pointing out the tables we've already sat at and used to wheel Dad and my sister Sis to and a few more than a few times and who else was with us at those meals and each of us eating lobsters we never dared order before because of their high prices per half pound now even higher and reminiscing about Dad a great deal when he was so verbal and vital and my mother remembering how he used to call me "My little Junsky Boy" after Junior which I wasn't when he wanted to put me in my place and we all drank our wine to that and I remembered he used to call Dolly "Sweet Petunia Child" whenever she emerged from one of her thrice-weekly showers reeking from talc and we drank to that and Dolly remembered the Valentine's Day Mom sent herself a bouquet because Dad thought the holiday a "greeting card and flowers by phone phony flimflam and conspiracy" and we drank to that and never gave her anything on it and we drank to that and became jealous when he saw the card wasn't signed by one of his kids but "an ardent admirer" and bit one of the roses off and ate it and dumped the rest in the trash and we drank again and again to that and I became optimistic over Irish coffee, saying Dad will come out of this crisis as he did all the others when he wasn't given half a chance to pull through and in a month or two he'd be home if maybe in a little worse shape than when he left and with the same and different medication prescribed but more of it and of his daily dose of insulin, but nothing was going to do in the old man and he'd live longer than all three of us and my mother said "Oh, maybe not longer than me but I'm sure you two the way you drink," and Dolly said "I for one know I have a drinking problem though also know it's a problem much justified and easily remedied," and I said "At least he's good for a few more years," and my mother said "Maybe one," and Dolly said that would be her estimate too.

"But if he does come home," my mother said to me, "you will continue to help me out as you've been doing, because I can't do it alone and I'll never send him to a nursing home," and I said "What do you think?" and she said "Does that mean you will?" and Dolly said "Sure, what do you think?" and my mother said "You know it means hanging around the city a while longer," and I said "Oh yeah, I really have a lot of places to go," and Dolly said "If I didn't have a family and job in two different boroughs and a sick father in a third, I'd come in to help out every day too."

When we returned to his room and I saw him with a wood brace taped to his forearm to hold in the IV and the oxygen tube across his pillow and face and the plugs in his nose and his name and today's date and the room number on a card in a card slot a foot above his head on the headboard of the bed and my father flat on his back like a carved limestone knight on a sarcophagus lid my notes say I think I later thought or said and in his white hospital gown on bright hospital linen and the bright center light on instead of the more subdued side lamp and the corridor dark and his face like a store window mannequin's my notes say I uninventively thought but thoughtfully didn't say and also like a face in a casket after it's been prepared for our last respects and the other tube changed and looped over the bed rail from his bladder to the new urine bag below I yelled "Oh no, he's dying, Pop's dying, Dad's doing to die *décidément,*" for it was only then that I knew there was no coming back for him this time and it was only the tubes and tank keeping him alive and in a day or the most two they'd turn off the oxygen and let him in a couple of minutes peacefully or easefully or arduously, horribly, furiously, violently expire just as I'm sure they did with my sister Sis in '66 when they sent me out of her room soon after she squawked in her tracheotimized voice "Why me, B, huh, why me, B, huh, why me?" and who died with her door shut and brudder B right outside and Mudda and Dollop sprinting down the hall and team of nurses and doctors in her single room of the same disease her dada got five years after she died and twenty-five years after they first noticed her café au lait spots but in the end like him sort of succumbed from pneumonia because she was too weak to heave and ho on her own and I fell on my knees that time after they took her tubes out and tidied her bed and led us in just as I did with my dad this time when I perhaps should have been comforting my sister and mother and Dolly said "Come on, Bud, not again," when with our sister she said "Poor S, poor Broth," and both times put her arms around Mom who both times rubbed each of our heads simultaneously while at the same time enjoined her God for her dead, but this time a nurse rushed in and tugged me up by my sleeve and said "Shhh," with her finger over her lips like the much younger nurse or professional model in the Please Be Quiet poster in most of the elevators, lounges and alcoves, "it's very late…past regular visiting hours…you're only permitted up here because Dr. Devine's condition is critical," and I said "Critical?" my notes neither say I thought or said, "He's dead," and she said "Critical…in a coma…comatose…can't see or hear us though believe me he's restful, and there are other considerably sick patients asleep on the floor and we're not allowed to shut his door."

I stayed the night. But the young woman. In her mother's room. Holding her mother's hair. Sitting on the edge of the bed removing a washrag from her mother's head. Sitting on the radiator cover by the window staring at either of our reflections or the sky or skyline or Central Park. Sitting by her mother's bed kneading her fingers through the rails. Parts of her head or arms on the rail's top bar. Body in a plastic bucket chair beside the bed. Leg dangling over the arm of that chair. Moving the padded chair closer and eventually getting into it. Reading. Sleeping. Lids flittering dream signals on the pillow as she sucked her thumb. I first saw her that Saturday night late. My mother said we'd have to hire an overnight private nurse. The on-duty nurse said the private nurses' bureau was closed for the day. Dolly said she'd stay. My mother said "Everybody leaves but me." I insisted I'd stay. My mother said "Justified as it was, Bud, you won't make another big to-do?" I said that scene on my knees was my last: "I'll be useful, only do what I can do and solutely nothing foolish." Dolly took her home and spent the next night with her too. Dolly first phoning her husband from the room to say how unspeakably inconsolable the situation was and forgive him for last night's fight and his walking out and then to her two girls at their grandmèremère's home in a fifth borough about their dear done-for granddad. That, besides Sis, was our family, except for a still interned peripatetic brother in a Ukrainian prison camp for trying to smuggle out doggerel and allegorical pasquinades by Russian writers already interned in the same camp he landed in, which he was then going to translate into several languages and print on his own press in the German West.

So they left. I turned off the overhead, on the night lamp. Got a couple of ales and sandwiches in an all-night deli, placed a towel over the lamp shade to tone down the light. Checked him for feces which if the one overworked aide couldn't come right away I would have for the first time without protest cleaned. Emptied all the ashtrays into the paper bag taped to his bed rail, the bag into a garbage cylinder in the men's room, ashtrays into his night table drawer. Pulled up two chairs to his bed, one for my feet. Moistened his tongue and lips with the glycerin-lemon cotton swabs whenever they seemed dry from the oxygen and his always open mouth.

But that young woman. Shuttling back and forth past her room so many times I once saw her trying to talk with her unconscious mom. I tried to too. Point is I thought I could coax him out of his coma and then out of his crisis and home one day soon. "Dad," I said. "Dad, it's Bud," I said. "Dad," I said, "it's Bud, it's Junsky Boy, it's me. Ah," I said, "you're still probably too weak to speak I suppose. Well if you can't answer me in the usual way, why not try blinking your eyes twice if you can hear me and once if you can't." I said "Maybe two blinks is too tough for you, so only blink once if you can hear me and just keep your eyes closed for a couple of seconds if you can't. Then open your eyes all the way if you can hear me," I said, "and keep them the same way they are now if you can't. Then keep them the same way they are now if you can hear me and want to speak or blink or open your eyes further to me, and the same way they are now if you don't want to do any of those or can't. Then don't do or say or move anything or keep anything the same way if you don't want to or you can't," I said. "Just goodnight. Sleep tight. I won't bother you with another word. Not one. I swear, none."

I did a number of quick sketches of him, seating myself counter-clockwise around the bed and dragging the chair after me, my one detailed drawing done as I stood on the chair above the bed's foot-board. I swabbed, drank, ate, drank, swabbed my own lips and tongue just to get the taste and feel of it and felt the taste was less glycerin than lemon and the swabs could work for an incapacitated person conscious his mouth was dry. I went down the hall to dump the ale cans, wax paper and used swabs in the men's room and stood in the door of the young woman's room. When she turned from my reflection to me I said "Excuse me, Ms., but I'm going—well first off I want to explain that it's not out of any disdain or asininity that I addressed you like that but only because I rarely know what to first address a young woman as anymore. But I'm going to get a few things from the basement vending machines and want to know if you'd like something from there too."

"No thanks."

"Coffee or tea?"

"That might be nice."

"Any special way?"

"What do you mean?"

"Milk, lemon. Meaning milk and sugar or plain milk or black or sugar or black and sugar or nondairy cream or nondairy cream and sugar if it's coffee and milk and sugar or nondairy cream and sugar or just nondairy cream or just sugar or just lemon or sugar and lemon or just hot water with not even tea in it if it's tea. They also have soup. Today's tomato purée."

"Does it have containers of plain milk? Coffee and tea keep me awake. If not, soup's okay. I even have some saltines left in my bag if none come from the machine."

She rummages through her leather bag. "Don't be silly," I say, "I'll pay. One milk or soup literally coming up." I turn to go. "Oh, not lit-erally in any other way but one soup or milk literally coming up" and

I move my hand holding the can with the used swabs inside as if it were climbing and rounding flights of stairs. "I also want to say, and please excuse me if you think I'm sort of meddling and, considering the conditions, talking too much and also for this deluge of excuses, but I think I've some idea what you're going through now, as I'm just about going through the same thing with my father and have as you might have a few times before. So if there's anything I at all can do for you or you want to talk about with someone or just talk about without the other person talking or just to sit silently beside or silently while the other person talks, please, as outmoded or bromidic as this offer and the way I'm proffering it might sound to you, don't hesitate to ask me wherever I am and whatever's the time."

She closes her bag. I go downstairs. In one of the basement corridors I see one of the nurses who worked on one of the floors my father was on in one of the other buildings of this hospital a year or two ago. "Hi," I say. She's in a rush but stops and pulls back the blanket of the bundle she's carrying. "What do you think of our newest baby?" she says. "Just born in Emergency. Hasn't even weeped or peeped or been fed yet or gone goo. But how's your father—Dr. Devine?"

"That's amazing. You remembered."

"But he was so lively and loquacious and refined."

"Not so hot."

"I'm sorry to hear. And I have to run. Taking her to Incubation. Him. They come and they go, I'm afraid. Though that's good, I can also say, and really nothing to be afraid about, though also of course bad."

I dump the garbage. The dairy machine's out of plain milk. The soup's been changed since the last time I was down here a half hour ago to chicken rice. The big decision's between the chocolate drink and many kinds of sodas or the soup. I set the dial and put in the change. Wrapped crackers slide down the same side chute the sugar packets came out of but bounce over the holding lip to the floor.

"No thank you," Marlene says to the glazed doughnut I also brought up. "I'm dieting."

"Save it for later just in case."

"It'll only go to waste with me and I'm prett-near to being old-fogyish with my self-control. Maybe the aide can use it," and she brings it out and returns with some fruit and two petit fours for me and a better vase. She says "Aren't our tulips great? They were left by the last patient but I didn't want them removed." She says "We've one of his best Van Goghs. What have you?" She says "I suppose my brother should be here or say 'You stay the first night and I'll the next.' But what's he got to worry about? He's only just married and twenty-three." She says "That was very nice what you did before. Maybe I shouldn't say that. But that was very nice." She says "We've this cooperative in Queens, my mother and I, and that's hard to give up. I like the country. All my schools since grade school were in small towns. But I like the straight way New Yorkers talk to you. I guess I'll have to live here later on." She says "I've only had my mother. Nobody else. That must be wrong. I know it sounds strange. But I've only had my mother. Nobody else. She was a great person. Now I wish she'd die." She says "She planned it perfectly. Went to the hospital the first time while I was studying for my comprehensives, so I just studied all day here. Then the second time. She waited till I got my degree and two weeks later was back in the hospital. Now she's dying because she knows I've become too dependent on her for my love. She wants me to find someone else before it's too late." She says "Much earlier today I was thinking that arranging the funeral and picking the coffin and lying that I've got the money to pay for it would be the hardest part. But suddenly I've an Uncle Igor. Never saw him in my life and how many a time been told he'd gone down in a drowned ship off the coast of Brava five years after I was born. And here he phones me before and says he'd had a hunch something was wrong with Bunny Jean and he'd just flown in from wherever it is in Wales and is arranging the whole works for us and other than what my mother's union kicks in for the funeral and interment and tombstone and perpetual upkeep of the grave, it won't cost us a dime." She says "For the longest time I wanted to step out on the road and thumb around the globe. But my best friend's sister was picked up and executed by a driver this year. That cured me of hitching again. The bastard was never found. That means he's still around driving cars." She says "I brought my bike along in the ambulance with her, thinking I'd take the two-hour bike trips back and forth each day rather than ride that sorrowful-eyed subway." She says "I'll end up with two big boxes from my mother other than the apartment: my transoceanic radio get-well gift she never opened and a whirlpool bath her ex-lover she said she never loved or made love with gave." She says "Since I was a whittle chile my mother's said she doesn't know if she heard or read this or actually was creative enough to make the statement up, but she feels a kiss is the most direct way to the soul. So excuse me if from time to time I ignore you and bend over her and open her lips." She says "I've this thing about possessions. I just want to own my own tree."

I get a couple more ales and sandwiches and go to his room. He's still the same. I swab. I sink and seat and sway to sleep. Marlene comes in and says "Do you mind my seeing your padre up close before your eyes? He looks like you, in spite of his probably losing so much weight and being so ill. By saying he looks like you it seems as if the son had finally become the father of the man. He's very attractive too. Maybe he looks like you because he did lose so much weight or it could be you who till recently was obese? Is that so? Were either of you very heavy once? Do you think my questions are anything but depressing and out of line? Did he also tipple in his twenties and thirties but give it up after that except for a salubrious shot of scotch every day at work before he left for home? He has a truffle more hair than you and the remnants of a more romantic hairline and broader shoulders, which I bet once made you upset. Endowments like that ought to unalterably be bequeathed to each son. He has beautiful eyes. I can see through the slight partings and the bulge beneath the lids. He also has sensual lips, even if his mouth sags so sadly on the right side, and nice high cheekbones you unhappily don't have and your soulful nose and heavy supraorbital torus and what seems to be an extreme protruding occiput and unneanderthaloid chin and both with your ears unequally elfin as the ears of elves. I called my brother right after you left. He said he'll return my call tomorrow early as he can. He knows I'm alone. He can give a good shit. I hate the son of a bitch. No, that's not even right or especially true, but he's such a weakling. Too sensitive to come to the hospital, he said. Keep the coffin closed, he said. I'm not leaving the limousine at the gravesite, he said. I called him because I couldn't stand not talking to a blood relative any longer and he said I just woke him out of a deep-sea sleep after a great honeymoon lay. I asked him if he'd let me try and make some sense with his lady Dame. He said her mouth was temporarily in debt. I wish I had a man who'd stay with me here or send me home and help take care of my mom for me while I slept. I'm a strong weakling. I don't want to crack. I feel I easily could. So pulling out the plugs and shutting the electricity off wouldn't only be for Jean. Though I'm sure it's what she'd want. On her coma eve she said she was going to tell me the next morning what she wanted done if she became a zombie or the drugs couldn't quench the pain. If I can't speak, write or gesture, she said, then know I've already left you a note in a bureau drawer. I've looked high and low. Did you see the way she tossed around? She's sweating in streamers when the head nurse said that patients in her state aren't supposed to expel from any part. She's not at ease no matter what anyone here says. Medicine is only ten percent medical science and ninety percent intuition and tuition as her orderly said. She's gagging. She's thrashing. She's got the worst comatose blues. I can't stand seeing her this way anymore. Please will you walk me to her room and sit with me for a while with our backs to her bed?"

Want me to hold you?

Do you want to hold me?

I'll hold you if you want.

Even if holding me's not what you want?

I didn't say I didn't want to hold you.

Well do you want to hold me or not?

I wouldn't mind holding you at all.

Then please hold me.

Then you don't mind being held?

I want to be held, I want to hold.

I hold her. She holds me. I kiss the top of her head. She kisses my collarbone through my shirt. You can hear us both sniffling. Her sniffles stifled by my cotton shirt, mine by her hair. Her hair's thick. Her hair's oily and smells dirty. What does she look like? What does it matter? Hair black, skin brown, brows long, size short, body full, waist thin, legs large, feet small, breasts low, rear high, cheeks scarred, neck knobbed, lips gnashed, face plain. Ears, eyes and nose. Bimanal, dentulous, hair from her underarms, chiromanticly complex. Our four arms holding one another till she lets one go and picks up *The Portable James Joyce* on the bed. She opens it, unfolds some sketches and the quartered drawing inside. "They all look like you winking," she says, "but more like you're him. I also draw. Escapescapes, animated finger cartoons. But never my mother now or since she began sphacelating, as I'm sure it'd be in bad taste with mutual risks. She might think it was my supplant for her death mask or maybe accuse me of trying to scare her to death and possibly succeeding and can't you see me arguing back? But what are you reading, or is the book only ballast for your ballpoint pen?" I say "Other Poems—'Ecce Puer' to be exact." She looks at the contents page. I say "Six sixty-three." She looks at her watch. I say "The page." She turns to it, her other arm now on my shoulders, and reads. She says "It's very nice. I read it through thrice. Poignant. Ointment. Kind of childish. Almost

Wildeish. So unJamesian Joyce. Something someone very busy might want to anatomize for one's literature class or memorize for one's father's funeral address. Though I did think the last line should have read 'Forgive thy son' and without the exclamation point, and that there be an h on the O in the penult though where it wouldn't be read as ho." She stands up. "Later," she says and kisses my hand. " 'Ecce Ntric,' " she says from the hall, "will be the title of my work if it'll be an elegy I write."

I go to her room about an hour later. She's asleep in the chair facing the door. Her mother seems to be having bad dreams. She's growling, twitching, squirming, crying but no tears. She then moves her mouth as if she's screaming but no sounds come out. I look for a swab. None around, so I open a new pack that's been in my pocket and swab her mother's lips, and when she sticks her tongue out, her tongue. It seems to quiet her down some. Marlene still sleeps in the chair, thumb in her mouth, face in the pillow, feet under her buttocks, blanket on the floor. I put the blanket on her legs and my hand on her mother's forehead. This quiets her completely. I rub her forehead. Her eyes open but her pupils don't show. I say "Don't worry, Mrs. Hill. Everything's going to be all right with you and with Marlene. I'm a friend." Her mouth opens wide, spit drops out. "Don't speak," I say. Her eyes close. "Though if you do want to speak and you think the easiest way is by blinking, please do, please blink." Her hands shake. "Then don't bother," I say. Sweat pops out on her face and neck. I wipe her dry with my hanky. Her hands tear at the sheets. I hold down her fists. Her legs begin pumping back and forth. I put my hand on her forehead. Her free arm flips up and smacks my side. I swab her lips and try and get at her tongue. More sweat. I look for a towel. Real tears. I slip a pillowcase off a pillow and pat the case on her face, neck and chest. She's growling. Humming. Her hair's soaked. Her expression's total sorrow: the sudden news of the loss of her dearest one; when they have to drag her off the coffin or out of the grave. No swabbing or patting stops the jerking of her arms and legs. "Sleep sleep sleep," I say. She's riding a horse. She's climbing a rope. She's whisking away smoke. Now she's embracing air. I kiss my fingers of one hand and press them to her cheek. "Sorry," I say. She slaps her face and I leave.

I drop by her room around six when the employees' cafeteria opens and call Marlene into the hall and ask if she'd like to have breakfast downstairs. She says she can't leave now as her mother's acting very strange. "She had an unbelievable night. Some of her linens were strewn about. She had to scream 'Demons!' to wake me up. Maybe they were here and are still in the room. I'm waiting for the resident exorcist." I look in. Her fingers are running across her body and over each arm and up and down the bed. I say "I'll bring up some English muffins and a coffee or tea for you," and she says "No thanks." I say "Something else then," and she says "Make it a bagel and container of milk if they have one," and I say "With cream cheese?" and she says "Just with a straw," and I say "I meant the bagel," and she says "I know. Sometimes talking about food. Anyway, I have my mother's glass. But I really should eat. Then when she awakes I can say 'Yes, Mom, I ate.' Actually, she was never a mother like that. Anything. Toasted. Even marmalade. Yes, marmalade. It sounds right for today."

She's not there when I get back. I go to my father's room and find my mother trying to keep all his tubes from coming out or getting coiled while she tries to turn him on his left side so he wouldn't be resting on his deepest bedsores. I say "Sure that's the right thing you're doing?" and she says "Was he in this position all night?" I say "Maybe they think that's the best position for him to get intravenous and oxygen in," and she says "What's the wrong thing?" I hold him, she sticks a pillow and bunched-up blankets between bed and buttock and shoulder as bolsters, he's now on his left side facing the oxygen tank. She swabs, says "Did you notice how clean he was?" tells me all the people who phoned last night, says "The world certainly had a friend in your dad," points to the construction elevator and the first workers of the day soaring through the first ten floors of the thirty-one-story medical center this hospital's putting up, listens to a helicopter overhead and after it passes calls it an unusually low-flying jet plane, says "Maybe he belongs on his back after all," and after we turn him, lights a cigarette and immediately puts it out along with the match. "Look at him. Before I ever get even half so enfeebled I want you to come with a gun or some lethal way where you won't get caught or in trouble, or have I already asked you to promise me that? Well promise me it again. And this was left for you by that abiding angel down the hall whose mother is dying of CA. Where's her family?"

Marlene left me a paperback of Beckett poems with a note paperclipped to the second page of a poem written or completed the year I was born and about saying and being terrified again of begging and loving and not loving and knowing and not knowing and pretending and pretending. The note says "Bunny Jean will hold for the day I'm told. Sorry I couldn't wait, but one of the nieces said I could nap at her flat nearby and I'm literally falling into my feat. But that's nonsense, though as my mother used to say my father used to say about her 20 yrs ere—uh—liberation, ' "That's what happens when you give a gurl education." ' Oh, forget it. Anyying for a yak. Try and have a good day. That's so dumb. You're very kind. I'm my worst when I'm serious. I'm also a compulsive note composer with almost no letup. This poem, probably written about other things, somehow sustained me."

I cab through the park to my apartment on the West Side. A clean-in on my block wakes me sooner than my alarm. Someone has set a stereo system speaker on the sill of the first window of the next brownstone over from mine and people in the street are dancing to its music between radio ads, drinking wine, soda and beer, bi- and tricycling and rollerskating, selling posters and plants and pottery and used everything and stenciled T-shirts promoting this clean-in and the block party next month and playing volleyball with a soccer ball over a net strung across the street from lamppost to parking sign pole, and at the beginning of the block where traffic's been cut off by police barricades, cleaning the street with brooms, brushes and shovels lent by the Sanitation Department.

I call my mother. "Fine," she says. "Even improved I can honestly say. Take your time coming back. Dolly's in-laws and all my sisters are here. You think I should have the phone taken out of his room or are its possible disturbances to Dad outweighed by its immediate benefits?"

"Care to clean in?" the block association president says as I leave my building.

She hands me a street broom. I take it, hold it up to my face as a mustache and give it back. "Can't today."

She sweeps a patch of hosed sidewalk. "Must get every little speck. The enemy is dirt and we shall destroy him. Cleanliness is hell. How's your father?"

"Well—" I say.

"We miss him from last year sitting out front in his wheelchair and how shall I phrase it, observing with skeptical sort of censorious eye our prantics and goings-on."

"He's lived a long time here."

"You mean on earth?"

"The block. Thirty-five years."

"You told me that once. It's still hard to believe."

"Same apartment. And practiced for thirty years of that in what's now the real estate office downstairs. They moved here when I was nine months."

"Nine months? There's a story in that. But he's well. That's great. One day I have to talk to him about the history of this block. The people, the changes. Someone once said there was even a Columbus Avenue el rumbling past. I'll write it up for the block newspaper, or you can if you want. You'll get a byline. And if it's interesting enough, it might even be reprinted in the *Manhattan Block Association News*, which for all I know pays. But why not bring him out now? The committee will see that we're all on our best behavior for him and we can even have a vote now to make him honorary block chairman of the day. Maybe not chairman. He might find that disrespectful. But president. Or just vice."

"Not *well* isn't what I meant. I mean, he's not well. Unwell. He's unwell."

"I'm sorry to hear that. What's wrong? Relapse? Flu?"

"We took him to the hospital yesterday."

"So that was your ambulance. Is he very bad off?"

"Yes."

"How bad? Very very?"

"Very very very."

"Does that mean it's hopeless?"

"It could."

"Not dying?"

"We believe he's dying. The doctors do."

"You mean he's eventually dying. As we all are. But not in the hospital?"

"Yes. It's where I'm going now. I'm sorry. Excuse me."

She backs off, obviously angry I didn't use more tact. Turns her back to me, hands the broom to a Girl Scout and says "Sweep. Clean. The enemy is dirt. We must destroy him," and goes to the wine table and says "Selling well?" and puts down a quarter for the drink and says "Remember: if the president doesn't expect any special privileges, nobody should." But I don't remember our conversation or her movements that well. I had notes. Wrote them down while I walked back to the hospital through the park. Stopped to write them in the park. In the park, when I was walking and running back to the hospital, I stopped to write down the notes about what took place on the block. But for no known reason those notes are not with the rest.

I walk to the hospital through Central Park, part of the way around the reservoir till I get to the East Side at Ninety-sixth. There were many gulls in our drinking water, more than I've seen following a ship or sitting and standing together on a beach. Thousands it seemed. I remember trying to remember the Joyce poem each time I passed a playground. I don't remember the playgrounds. I try and remember the poem now. "A child is torn, a heart is born." No, "A child is born, a heart is torn." No, "A child is sleeping: an old man gone." That's it: "Oh, father forsaken, forgive thy son." Rather—

I pass Marlene's room. Her mother seems peaceful. Marlene's standing behind a shorter man who's crying, his head on her neck, his arms stretched out behind him as though wanting to bring her in close. She sees me, waves, raises her shoulders, the older man she's with turns to see whom she's waving and raising at, I go to my father's room, relieve my mother, am relieved by my mother, my mother and I go downstairs for a late lunch, she rides, I walk, she tells me I must eat, I tell her in her voice she must eat, neither of us eat, she says "What I'd like right now is a stiff lemon and gin, or straight gin," Dolly comes, the in-laws and four sisters were gone by the time I came, an uncle comes, he's a doctor, he looks at his brother's chart, feels his pulse, listens to his heart, pulls up his lids, takes my arm and says "So how are things with you, Buddy?" and walks me out of the room and holds my wrist while he signals Dolly in the room to join us in the hall and says "I got you both out here to say what I couldn't say to your mother because of her already extensive mental suffering, but he's terminal," my uncle's belt beeps, he auscultates his two-way, he holds my mother's hands and says "Whatever happens here with Cy you've nothing to ever feel guilty about, Gay," my uncle goes, I say "Hello?" and "How's by you again?" and "By the way I left your book home by mistake" and "What a day what a day" and "It's always impossible for me to say anything of any merit on the run" to Marlene when I see her briefly in the hall five times, once with her arm around the shoulder of that older man who she whispers "Her ex-nonlover or non-exlover" and indicates by shaking her head while shaking her finger behind his ear that he can't hear, I drink lots of sandwich, eat lots of coffees, dump the paper garbage bag many times and with decreasing easiness tape it back to the bed rail with the same two strips of surgical tape and just about every half hour wash my hands and face, give my father a shave, swab his lips and tongue till my mother says "Don't do it so much or you'll make his membranes sore," cheek his pat, brow his kiss, sit beside my mother, beside Dolly, between them both in the guest lounge watching "Hogan's Heroes" I think and the local news while my father's being washed and changed till I have to get out as one of the guests wants the windows closed because he's got the makings of a cold and all the patients in the lounge are smoking away, get my mother and Dolly and the sickly guest and some patients in the lounge teas and coffees and one buttered bran muffin, in my father's room draw several drawings that I've never drawn anything like before which are a pair of elderly hands squeezing between them the center of something resembling an upended whole human brain.

Marlene and I decide to stay the night. "You going to stay?" "You going to stay?" "I was thinking I might stay." "And I was thinking I should stay." "Good, then let's stay." "Let's stay." My mother and sister will take a cab home and drop off Bunny Jean's friend at any IND subway stop. I walk them to the hospital entrance, the two women climb in the cab and the man shaking and patting my hand as he with the upper part of his coat sleeve rubs away the tears coming out of his nose says "If this is too much of an inconvenience for your family I can always take the crosstown bus."

I go around to Madison for a mixed six-pack of English ales and Irish stouts. We drink a bottle apiece in her mother's room, share a bottle in my father's room, while I'm finishing off another bottle in her mother's room she says "You know it occurred to me before that if your Dr. Devine is the same Dr. Devine who opened an office on Delancey Street in 1923 or 2, then my mother's got a framed photograph of your dad working over her in his dental chair and with a closed couplet by him on the print declaring how this pretty little Rivington Street miss is his first female patient since he left dental school." I say nah, she says yeah. I say "Go on, ya must be kidding me," she says "Ma, will you tell this big lug it's the godshonest truth." We say ha, graze a fist off each other's chin, start to cry, end up hugging one another and kissing the other's hair (me), shirt (she), cheeks (we) and lips, tongues, gums, lungs and after we break she says "That was very nice. Just what I needed. Thank you very much. I'm sure my soul thanks you too," and leaves the room.

Later she comes into the room and sits beside me. We hold hands. I swab his lips, she puts a damp rag on his brow. We hold hands. We kiss, hug. I lick her neck, she scratches my back. I feel her breast, she massages my arm. I put my hand inside her shirt, she says "I don't think I have a bra." I put my other hand between her legs, she says "Wait," and tries the door. I say "There's no lock," she says "Do you have a Don't Disturb sign to put on the door?" I say I don't, she says she does. I say "Don't bother," she says "Don't worry, I'll be back. And it'll give me another chance to check on Bunny Jean." I say "Actually, maybe there'll be less chance they'll come in if we keep the door shut without the sign," she says "They won't see anything even if they do come in." "How do you figure that?" and she says "Maybe we shouldn't even shut the door."

She sits down and picks up my hand and rubs my knuckles across her lips. We kiss, hug. I take the damp rag off my father's brow. She feels his cheek and says he feels warm. I say infection. She says her mother's boiling too. We sit down. We kiss, hug. I put my hand in her shirt, the other hand under her skirt. She scratches my back and massages my arm at the same time. I undo my zipper and belt. She takes off her panties and stuffs them in my shirt pocket and says "Don't let me forget those, for if I'm riding home by bike today my skirt's rather short." She shuts the light, says "I'm very hairy like a man but I don't do anything about it as you won't see," says "One thing else I want to say is I think men are the same throughout the world: they all want to get laid," says to stand, turns my chair to where it faces the window and tells me to sit and sits down on me with her back to my chest and we make love that way, her skirt covering our laps and my arms around her waist and breasts and her hands pressing down on the chair arms to keep us in place, perhaps seeming to someone at the door as if we're admiring the moon if there were a moon or just the ten floors of the medical center frame lit by a single dangling light bulb for each landing at the elevator shaft, and when it's apparently going to be over for me very soon she shoves the back of her head into my mouth and says "Shh shh shh, it's got to be at least some kind of hospital violation and civil offense."

She gets off me, digs out her panties, feels herself and says "You seem to be viscous while every other man tended to be disconnected and leak," and goes to the bathroom across the hall. I zipper up and turn on the light. "Some gal, Dad, am I right? I'm saying, what ya think of her, Pop? Now don't suddenly pretend you've no opinion on a subject when for the first time I'm really going to do what you always wanted me to and that's ask you for some of your good sound straight advice." I search for the pulse in his temple and wrists. Marlene sticks her head past the door and says "I'm pooping out and going to sleep now, Bud, so goodnight." "Goodnight."

We go down for breakfast in the employees' cafeteria right after it opens. On the food line I say "You seem much different this morning—insular, almost aloof and remote. Is what we did bothering you?" She says "No, it's just my mother used to tell me to always be a lady on the outside but a bitch in bed."

When we get upstairs the doctors are in her room and Dolly and my mother in Dad's. "Dad looks a little better today," my mother says.

"What've you two been doing in here?" Dolly says. "The place is a mess." She puts both chairs against the wall and dumps the empty bottles in the trash. "She seems like a very sweet girl, Bud. Married? Engaged? Even if she's got a serious boyfriend—you're a nice intelligent guy who's attractive and ambitious, so what you want you'll get."

I go home, come back around noon. My mother tells me Marlene's mother died a couple hours ago. "She left her name and address and phone number and said for you to call her anytime you want now, as she'll be home and it's all right."

I call. There's a lot of commotion at her house. "Someone wants Marlene," the man who answered the phone says. "Well get her," a woman says, "—she's in Bunny's bedroom." "Can I yell?" "You lost your voice?" "Marlene," the man yells.

Marlene comes to the phone. "I didn't have to pull out the plugs or shut off the electricity or anything. She simply started to shake and cough and I held her up to help try and get the phlegm out and she died in my arms like that. I'm glad we were alone that way and not when I was home or outside her closed door. How's your father? But let me get on the extension." She comes back. "Still there? Hang up, please," she yells. "I'm not that sad. I'm the same way I thought I'd be two hours after it, except awake. Everyone's taking care of my brother. Smelling salts, tranquilizers, a little schnapps, a hitherto retired breast. He's at least allowing people to prolong their legendary heritages while I'm failing to fulfill even their most minimal spiritual and emotive needs. In his own way he's always been far more sensitive than me and I appreciate that in him now, for I see that for everything he doesn't do and is incapable of and in fact exploitative because of this nature, it goes down very deep. You know, you don't have to come to her funeral tomorrow, but will you come?"

"I don't think so."

"It's in your neighborhood."

"I'll try."

"If your father dies within the next few days I won't be able to go to his. As once you're in mourning, the religious-law experts tell me here, I can't go to someone else's funeral for a week or month or even half a year—nobody's quite sure of the length of time for the one surviving sister and unmarried daughter of the deceased mom. I also asked them whether it's against any religious laws to sleep with someone the night before or day of or after the death or funeral and especially with a person not of his or her marriage. Naturally, I said, I was being impersonal and hypothetical with that question and just wanted to satisfy the whopping curiosity that every teacher has when she's a student. The true scholar of the group, a first cousin of Bunny Jean's who till a year ago insisted on sitting me on his knee, said he didn't know but it was an interesting proposition and he was sure the laws were much stricter for the woman than the man and did I mean sleeping in the sense of copulating for the purpose of bearing forth young or solely for pleasure? I said either and he said 'Well it's all written down in those learned books, my darling Marlena, and I'll look it up and report back to you in a week.' I'd love to sleep with you tonight, Bud, and will if you want me to or even if you don't but don't protest. I can sneak out, take a cab to your house. The hell with the expense—the funeral's free. And then slink off just in the nick of to be the first one at the chapel tomorrow morn. Though perhaps some guests will think I was being merciless in leaving behind a brother slipping in and out of semi-unconsciousness all night with only his wife by his side and an unfamiliar uncle from Wales staying over who seems to be growing equally agonized, and because of it cuss me out at the gravesite in my illustrious mother's name."

I say "I'll do my best to be there tomorrow," and hung up and went back to the room, helped Dolly on with her coat and walked her to the elevator.

"We never got to talk you and I," Dolly said and I said "No, we never got to talk much."

"I always think that in trying times like these the family has its best chance of coming together and talking out the things separating and bugging them and so becoming closer by it. But you and I always went in opposite directions as kids. And for the last few days we've been coming and going at different times to different places or the same place at different times, except when we had dinner but got too stewed to speak sensibly then, so we never got to talk to settle anything. Though maybe just saying this to you has settled a lot. At least we spoke, or I spoke. And call me at work if anything goes wrong today and I'll rush over no matter what. I don't like going now, but they're shorthanded where I am and we're pretty short at home and you don't get paid or make tips if you don't come in. Slaves are slaves. And the truth is if there is any money coming out of Dad's will to his children, you know what he thought of me and my life and the baron I married and so he certainly didn't leave me a red cent. You think at least for my little girls he might leave something, but I think he always thought they were too homely and dim-witted and kind of a continu-ing stain on the family and made too much noise. But I loved him—didn't you?—and I love you too."

When I stepped into the hall again I saw my mother waving at me frantically to come back to the room. The elevator was gone. I ran down the hall. She was in the room holding up his arm with the glu-cose and antibiotic needle in it and said "I suddenly looked over before and found it all swollen and wet and blue. The fluid must be going in the wrong vein or pouring out of the one they put it in or just going nowhere once it's in his skin." I was looking at my father. She was saying to get the nurse. I said "I don't think Dad's breathing." She said "What?" I said "Look at him, he's not breathing." I put my arm around her. She threw it off and put her ear to his mouth and hand over his heart. I said "Dad, it's us, what's up, can you hear, you all right?" and felt for his wrist pulse and she said "The doctor, get the doctor," and I ran to the nurses' station and said to the aide behind the desk to get a doctor as my father doesn't seem to be breathing and she said "Who's your father?" and I said "My father, Dr. Devine," and she said "What's the room I mean?" and I said "Come on, he's not breathing, last one down the hall on your left," and she said "The room number—the bed—we don't want to be resuscitating the wrong patient if there is an emergency," and I said "You have to know the room number by now—five-thirteen and there's only one bed," and she said she'll call a doctor and nurse immediately and spoke into the intercom and I ran back to the room and my mother was sitting on the bed beside my father with her arm under his neck and her head resting on his chest and said "Dolly, get Dolly, Bud," and I ran downstairs.

Dolly was getting on the downtown bus across the street on the park side. "Dolly," I yelled. The bus pulled away. I ran alongside it for half a block till it stopped at the light. I saw her in a seat on the other side of the bus and ran around the back and knocked on her closed window and motioned her to pull the stop cord. She raised her eye-brows as if she didn't understand. I pointed to the hospital and ran my finger across my throat as if it were being slashed and motioned for her to pull the stop cord and pointed at the hospital. She was trying to slide the window back but couldn't. She mouthed the words "What? Dad? Something wrong?" I nodded and put my hands around my throat and gagged and pointed to the hospital and for her to pull the stop cord and she pulled the cord as the bus was pulling away. She ran down the aisle and I ran alongside the bus and then the bus was in the middle of the avenue and accelerated to where it was way in front of me but it stopped, she got off, I started trotting back to the hospital till she caught up with me and then we ran together, went up the elevator, ran down the hall, my mother was standing at the foot of the bed next to an aide who held her hand while a nurse was wiping the fluid off my father's arm, and my mother said "He's dead," and the nurse turned to us and said "He's dead, but I have to get the doctors to verify it." The aide said "I'll find them, I know where they are," and left the room and the nurse said to me "Why don't you step out of the room for the time being till the doctors team comes?" and I said "We'll stay here till they ask us to leave," and my mother and sister began bawling and I squeezed in between them and grabbed them each around the shoulder and drew them into me and we all cried like that.

Several doctors and nurses came soon after, asked us to leave, drew the curtains, my mother said "May I stay? I'm his wife," and one of them said "No, really, ma'am, you must leave—please take her outside and wait for us there," and we took her outside, they shut the door, they came out about five minutes later and said "He's dead. Nurse Widner will be out shortly and then you can go in."

Nurse Widner came out carrying a large plastic bag. "He looks much better now," she said. All the tubes were out of him, the urine bag gone, the oxygen tank unhooked and in the corner of the room, the sheets had been smoothed out and the bed lowered to where it was flat and only one pillow was under his head. The three of us stood beside him. I kissed his lips. The nurse said "Maybe you people want to be alone with him awhile. I'll get rid of this," meaning the bag. She left. "Daddy?" Dolly said. She kissed her right fingertips and placed them on his lips. "Goodbye," she said and left the room. My mother kissed his fingers and head and lips and patted his belly and spoke into his ear. We stood there crying with my hand on his shoulder and hers on his knee when the nurse came in and said "Excuse me, but if you're finished, why don't you take your mother to the guest lounge at the end of the hall? Your private physician's been called and he said he'll meet you there quick as he can."

Dolly and I flanked my mother and we all went up the hall. "What can I say?" a visitor said, touching my back. A patient, who was usually plodding up and down the hall and joking or smiling about having to push along with him the rolling stand with his glucose IV on it, looked away when we passed.

"I think we should send a telegram to Russia," my mother said in the lounge.

"You serious?" Dolly said.

"If she wants to," I said.

"I want to. I'm serious. It's only a telegram. Len should know his father died and they should know it too. Maybe it will get him released. Nothing else so far has worked. Say in it—get this down, Bud—say 'Your father, Dr. Cyrus Devine, died this afternoon,' and give the exact time and date and specify what hospital it was and the address here so the Russians can check. Then say 'Request your attendance at funeral at Riverside Chapel in New York City on Wednesday.' We'll just have to hold it up for a day to meet the possibility that Len can come. Also say 'Roundtrip air fare is being sent,' and then wire the money to him at the bank closest to that prison. We've enough around, don't we?"

I said "I've more than a thousand in my bank account."

"You'll get it all back."

"It makes no difference."

"I couldn't even send Len a roundtrip telegram," Dolly said.

"Next send a telegram to the Russian Premier—same address we sent him the others—and say 'Our family most urgently and respectfully requests the immediate prison release of our brother and son, Len Devine, to attend his father's funeral. This is the telegram I sent my brother today,' you'll say and repeat in the Premier's telegram the telegram you send Len. Don't worry about money. Put them both on my phone bill. And don't try to use telegraph language as they might not understand it in English. Then send telegrams to the Soviet Embassy in Washington and the consulate here and say you sent telegrams to the Russian prison and Russian Premier and repeat the entire messages of those two telegrams in each of the telegrams to the embassy and consulate, including the telegram to Len repeat in the repeat of the Premier's telegram. But with these two, judging from my experiences with them, you can use telegraphese for the nonrepeat parts as they seem to understand everything. Then telegram Mr. Boylan at the State Department and say 'My father died today and my mother and sister and I would like Len to attend the funeral. Please do everything possible to help. If the only arrangement to be made with the Russians is for Len to be sent back to the prison right after the funeral, then roundtrip air fare's been sent to him there.' Also say 'I've sent telegrams to the Russian prison and Premier and Soviet consulate in New York and embassy in Washington,' and repeat in his telegram the two telegrams you send the prison and Premier and the one, also in its entirety, to the embassy. Then call Riverside and arrange the funeral. I know this is tough for all of us, Bud, but it has to be done."

I did all that. My father's private physician came. He said "I'm sorry, but I did only think it would take two to three days. They'd like to do a PM on him and I hope you'll consent."

"No," my mother said. "He's been cut up enough."

"Listen to me. Because the doctor's was such a rare disease and the possible hereditary nature of it, this won't only be an autopsy but a complete pathology report as well."

"I think we definitely ought to," I said.

"I'll do whatever these two want," Dolly said.

"It's in your interest to persuade your mother also," the doctor said. "Not only for your brothers and yourself but for the sake of your children and grandchildren or the ones you might have."

"All right," my mother said. "Take what you want but sew him back up."

Dolly said "He's coming," and we went to the alcove while my mother stayed with the doctor and signed the release for the PM. We watched the covered-up body wheeled on a stretcher through the doors to the next hospital building.

We were standing by the elevators when a man got out of the same car the doctor got in and as we were about to get in and said "Devine? The Devine family?" I said yes. The elevator operator said "Going down?" The man said to me "Please let it go," and I signaled the operator to go and the man said "I'm very sorry about Mr. Devine's passing—"

"Dr. Devine," Dolly said.

"Pardon me. Dr. Devine. That would I hope give you even more reason to be sympathetic to what I'm going to ask of you. I represent the hospital's cornea bank and you'd be doing a future cornea transplant patient an indisputably great service with the gift of Dr. Devine's corneas to our bank."

"Go on," my mother said. "Take everything. Take his fingernails if somebody's chewed off all of theirs. Take his nose."

"I understand," he said. "But your husband didn't have cataracts and corneas have to be removed within a few hours of a person's demise. And there's no way else of getting them unless a donor signs a release beforehand."

"Do it," Dolly said. "I like the idea that part of Dad will still be walking around alive."

"If the transplant or plants take," the man said, "it will give from one to two unidentified though always appreciative persons or person with useless corneas or crippling cataracts, partial to total sight."

My mother signed the release. An aide gave me the overnight bag of Dad's things. We left the hospital, took a cab to my folks' place, I went to the savings bank, sent Len the money, went to the funeral home to complete the arrangements.

"Was he a very sociable man?" the funeral official said.

"What does that mean?"

"Will he have many friends and acquaintances and, you know, club and organization members and dental society figures and former patients at the funeral, so we know which chapel to set aside?"

"He had thousands of friends and acquaintances, but most are dead."

He escorted me through the basement to pick out the casket. The first ones he showed in the room right off the elevator were to my taste very gaudy and bizarre. As he showed me through other small narrow rooms with increasingly less gaudy and bizarre caskets, I said "Still too expensive...I don't want dark wood...mahogany's good for pianos...cedar for treasure chests...no brass...no armor...no finish...no nothing...just a plain white pine box without hardware, polish, religious symbols or excessive satin, which I hear is the cheapest and plainest there is." He said "I was going to show you that one. It's in the last room we haven't gotten to yet."

In the office again he asked if the deceased was a veteran. I said "You can still call him by his name or title or my father or Dad or Doc and he was a conscientious objector and went to prison for it, where he first learned dentistry and which kept him out of the war." He said "Way back in what I assume was World War One?" "There were apparently plenty of them then," and he said "Well that's commendable, I guess, considering the present state of affairs in Asia and the low opinion most people now seem to have of that war and the growing respect objectors of many sorts have supposedly received of late. But your father would have been entitled to a two-hundred-fifty-dollar death benefit from the government if he had been a veteran and a chance to be buried free of cost and maintenance in a national cemetery." I said "The cemetery he took care of for all of us long ago, but the benefit would have helped."

Dolly's husband came by that night with their two girls. Dolly said "Sure you should've brought them along? Because the doctor said Mom should be actually getting the first effects of the death about now." Ted said "I told them about Dad and they said they had to be with Grandma and would behave."

Their oldest girl sat on my lap and said she and Sheila and her best friend cried all day when they heard Grandpère died. "I miss him already. I remember he said for him don't say prayers. Daddy took us out of school. He said he won't let us yet because I'm still too young, but I'm going to the funeral and grave too."

A cousin brought over cold cuts and cakes and breads and sodas and beers and made coffee and said "Now I insist you all eat something or I threaten to never leave. Really, I'm only kidding, I would never do anything that bad to you on such a sad day. But take or drink something besides beer, Bud. Food makes you forget and you probably haven't all day."

The Russians never contacted us. The State Department said they'd do everything in their power to help us but didn't think much could be done to join Len Devine with his family at this tragic event. I went to Marlene's mother's funeral the following morning. It was ten blocks from my house. I bought a black tie and dark sunglasses and stopped off at a few bars along the way and got a little high. When I got to the home, intentionally late, hoping to just join the guests in the pews rather than first pay my respects to the family in the sitting room, I found the chapel empty and everybody either in the sitting room or adjoining room with the casket in it or the hall right outside. It was unusual: everyone seemed quite sad. Marlene wore a white dress with a tight belt. Her hair was down, combed out, it shined, waved over her shoulder to her waist, she had eye makeup on, a bra, stockings, clips, I saw, when she leaned over to pick a button off the floor, attached to a brown undergarment to hold the stockings up, her legs looked longer and thinner in raised heels. She saw me, ran over and hugged me and said in my ear "Your being here means more to me than the presence of anyone else." She took my hand and introduced me to her brother. "Bill, Bud. Bud, Bill." Bill said "Nice to meet you, thank you for coming," and "My wife," and pointed to a very young woman on the couch and sat beside her and started crying and she put his head on her thighs and held him.

Two cousins from Chattanooga said they heard how much I took care of Marlene and were eternally grateful. "She's like a sister to us," the man said, "even though she's more accurately my second cousin, and through marriage, my wife's second cousin or second cousin-in-law—I don't know how they put it. Our sons and daughters should only do for us what Marlene did for Bunny Jean," he said to his wife.

"Then I'd say we did our job," she said.

The uncle from Wales shook my hand, stuck a cigar in it, and when I refused it, put it in my jacket breast pocket. I gave it back to

him and said "I really don't smoke anything and don't want to save it
for anyone I know who does appreciate cigars," when he suggested
that, "as I don't want it on me because of the odor unsmoked or
smoked they leave on your clothes." He said "You'll learn what's
good yet," and slipped it into someone else's jacket pocket and said to
me "We both came at precisely the right time, no?"

Marlene said to the cousins "It was the nuttiest thing. Bud's father
and Bunny Jean. Both with the same illness, though of a different ilk.
And both born and bred in the same neighborhood and brought to
the hospital the same day."

"My father was admitted the day after."

"Back to back then, but on the same floor and both in the only two
available single rooms. And in one day flat he became my dearest
friend. If it wasn't for you I don't see how I could have seen it
through." Then she asked how my father was. I said "He died yesterday around noon." She said "That's unbelievable," while her cousins
said "No—that's terrible," and we held one another and the cousins
patted and rubbed our backs and necks and other people said "What's
that? He Marlene's beau?" and a man said "Will everybody but the
immediate family please take seats in the chapel." Marlene said "From
now on I won't be thinking of you or paying any attention your way,
but I will call you at your mother's house and visit you soon."

I sat in the chapel next to the cousins. We were all told to rise.
The immediate family came in, Bunny Jean's suitor holding Marlene's
arm. They sat in the first row in front of the closed casket. Most of us
sat down. A man said "Will the guests please continue to rise." The
officiator came in, stood behind a lectern, spreading out his notes and
opened a book, we all sat. His opening words without reading them
were "Don't be afraid of death. We are all going to die. We share it
with all who have lived and all those who will come after us." The
cousins caught me scribbling this down, so I put my pen and paper
away.

I went to the cemetery in the cousins' car. It was in New Jersey. It
rained. It was a familiar scene. Lots of black umbrellas, people huddled under them around the grave, their heads bowed as the casket
was lowered in, Marlene and her brother shoveling earth on it,
prayers said, two gravediggers standing off to the side and leaning on
their shovels, someone mumbling despondently, the chorus of amen,
the crowd breaking for the long line of waiting limousines and private cars. We got lost coming back and had to go through the Lincoln
Tunnel rather than over the George Washington Bridge. In the car
the cousins and his mother kept on telling me how smart and creative

and kind and sensitive and personable Marlene is and always has been. "What grades that girl got," the mother said. "And you should see the pictures of her as a child. I still have some of them. Professionals used to pay to take her. Even more beautiful than she is now. She's one in a million, Marlene." "One in a century," her son said.

My mother said "That was very good of you to go, though I don't know if it was proper or right." Then we went to the funeral home and stayed till around ten. Quite a few people came. My father's body, only covered by a sheet that was shaped like a casket and hung to the floor, was lying on a layer of ice. It was part of some religious rite that I was unfamiliar with and which my mother had arranged through her sister's temple without Dolly or my knowing of it. All night there we could hear the water dripping into the concealed buckets or basins underneath. Most people who came stayed in the sitting room and talked about the presidential announcement last night: the ordering of mining of all major North Vietnamese ports. I was asked several times what I thought about this news and if I answered I said I didn't really care. "Yes yes, of course, but don't you think it affected the Russians not releasing Len to attend your father's funeral?" and I said "That could be so."

The funeral was the following day. After we returned from the cemetery, many of the guests ate at a buffet table that my mother had prepared the previous day. I called Marlene that night and she said "Not so bad, and you? People are coming in and out of here with pastries all day. I feel like a servant, getting coffee, mixing drinks, emptying ashtrays, running out for liquor and more coffee beans. I'll be paying my respects to your family after my own mourning period's over, which is in four to five days. Anyway, I'll at least be able to catch you on your last mourning day."

She came with candies the last day of our sitting in mourning. Dolly, Ted, my mother and a few friends said she was very cute and certainly the most intelligent and considerate girl I've ever gone out with and I should grab her up fast before some other Romeo does, as she'll no doubt want to get married now that her mother's gone and she's living alone. We sat next to one another and held hands under the buffet table that now only had on it pastries and Marlene's candies and service for coffees and teas. I said "Like to take a walk?" and we walked around the block a couple of times and ended up in my apartment. We sat on the bed and kissed. We lay down on the bed and I felt her breast. She said "You don't seem to want to do it much," and I said "I don't think I do." "Is it still your father then?"

and I said "That has to be it." "I don't really know why it still isn't my mother, unless this traditional mourning period is actually practical and now it's only over for me." She said "You're still the most important person in my life," and told me to call her when I felt better as she wanted to see me very much. I gave her a small magazine that had recently come out and which had some illustrations of mine for a short story and poem. She said she would only begin looking at them and reading the accompanying work on the bus ride home. I said "Take the subway for once—it's quicker," and walked her to the subway, we kissed, she left when the warning signal buzzed that the train was about to pull in downstairs. "The book," I yelled as the train was pulling in and I threw it to her and she picked it up and threw me a kiss and went downstairs. "I'll call soon," I yelled and she yelled, though I couldn't see her, "Please." I waited to see if she missed the train and she did or she didn't but she never came back upstairs.

I didn't call her. All I can say is that I wasn't that attracted to her that last time. I don't know if that's it. But I didn't call her. I wanted to call and say something like "I simply can't see anyone right now— male or female," which wasn't true. "I'm sorry for being so straightforward, which most of the time I'm not, but I don't know when, if when, I'll call again." I don't know why I didn't call her. I either didn't have the courage or didn't want to hurt her or both or it was tied up with my father or her mother or something else. A couple of times I dialed her number but hung up when her phone rang.

Someone rang my downstairs bell about a month later. I went downstairs. There are no tick-back bells in my building. It was past one. It was Marlene. She was a little drunk. She said "I just came from the bar you said you usually go to and I was with friends and looked for you there and in fact had to pressure my friends to go with me there and then decided to leave them when we left the bar and try getting you here." She gave back my magazine. "That meant something to me when I saw them, but nothing now. I only wanted to come by to tell you I think you're the biggest coward I've ever laid eyes on and that if you didn't want to see me you should have said so in the beginning or at the subway station or in your apartment that day. And that if you only found out after that that you didn't want to see me, then you should have called me and said so and I would have known and not hung around for a month waiting for you to call." I told her to come upstairs and she said "What for?" I said "So we don't have to talk in the hallway for everyone to hear," and she said "That's bullshit," and I said "Please come upstairs," and she said "All right," and I took her hand and started up and she pulled it away and followed me the two flights upstairs.

She sat in the chair and I sat on the bed, the only two sitting places in the room. She said "Do you have anything else to say?" and I said "Would you like to spend the night with me here—I would with you," and she said "Of course not," and I said "Just to sleep here and nothing else then," and she said "Don't be ridiculous, do you have anything else to say?" and I said "Nothing," and she said "No explanation why you didn't call?" and I said "No, I've none," and she said "All right, then that's it, then I'm leaving," and she left.

Rose

Up she went and I stayed downstairs, on the street, front of her stoop, waiting for her, minutes went, but she wouldn't come back, so I left, went around the corner, turned back, looked around the corner at her stoop, she wasn't there, crossed the street to look at her fourth-floor window, she wasn't there, all right, she wasn't going to show herself for a while or come running down so quick to say "I'm just confused, Bud, still with lots of stuff to work out, so please forgive me and forget everything I said," I knew that or almost and it was probably better in the end for us both and other rationales and I left, walked, took a bus, went to a movie, couldn't stay, cafeteria, couple of bars, got home and saw an envelope by my door that I thought could be an apology from Louise or some kind of explanation or reversal of what she'd said before about not wanting to see me anymore so I opened it and the note said "It'd be nice if you stayed away for a few months—for at least a year, really, and maybe then we can meet again if we're ready, though I'd get another woman and wouldn't wait around for me if I were you and I hope I'm not being that unkind," and was signed Rose and I thought Rose? I know no Rose and this wasn't Louise's handwriting, and was feeling for my keys while thinking about the irony and coincidence of the note or maybe it was just a message to me from someone else about Louise or even from Louise that for some reason she had someone else write and that name Rose is supposed to mean something that I hadn't figured out yet when I heard my neighbor who lives right next door to me coming upstairs whistling, his special type of whistling, where he employs tongue against palate and almost no lips though plenty of breath control and tunes blown through his front teeth always Dixieland or his version of ragtime and he said "Hi, Buddy," and I said "Hey, how ya doing, Hal?" and he said "Not so hot but I'll survive I guess, you?" and I said "Just fine thanks, and do you know someone named Rose?" and he said "Sure, Rose, my big love," and I said "Well, I found a note of hers in an envelope that I thought was for me but I suppose should've realized could just as well have been placed in front of your door and someone on their way upstairs accidentally kicked it in front of mine or something," and gave it to him and said "I also opened and read it I'm afraid," and he said "That's all right, mistakes are made and every day I'll tell you and maybe by me most of all," and opened it and we said goodnight and he started reading it as he went into his apartment and I went into mine and we closed our doors and I put on a record and opened the refrigerator for some ice water after all that alcoholic drinking and heard a loud noise like a big balloon being busted or a gunshot.

I looked out the kitchen window, didn't know where the noise might have come from, looked out my other window and saw a woman in the next building across the way holding her curtain back and looking at me and raising her shoulders as if she too had heard the noise and wondered and was worried about it and I went out to the stairway landing and heard talking below and said "Hey, every-body okay...anybody in trouble down there?" and a man yelled back up "Did you hear that too?" and I said "Yes, you know where it came from...the street?" and he said "No, I looked, not from the front," and I said "I looked and don't think it came from the back," and he said "I thought it was the floor below mine," and yelled down the stairs "Anything the matter down there, first floor...anyone get hurt or make some shot noise?" and someone yelled back "We're all okay down here...what was it? Sounded like it came from inside the walls," and a woman at the other end of my landing opened her door and said "What's all the commotion? It woke me out of sleep...a car backfiring?" and I said "Could be...could've been just a car back-fire," I said to the people downstairs and the man coming up the stairs said "No, it was a gun, I know a gunshot when I hear one and that was one and I'm sure from this building," and I turned around and looked upstairs and realized Hal was the only one on my floor not on the landing, even all the tenants from the fourth and fifth floors seemed to be looking over their banisters down the stairwell at us so I knocked on Hal's door, no answer and the man from downstairs said "Knock louder, if it's him and he's hurt he might not hear you," and I knocked again and he said "Louder...here, let me," and knocked much louder, no answer and the woman said "Try the doorknob," and he said "You kidding, no one ever not locks their doors anymore," and she said "Just try it, what's there to lose?" and I tried it and the door was unlocked so I opened it a couple inches and said "Hal, it's Buddy, you okay?" and the woman said "Someone could be in there with him," and I said "If so, then somebody he knows, because I saw him unlock his door and his windows are like mine where nobody can climb in," and she said "Still, if you think it's him and a gun wound, I don't want to know about it," and went back into her apartment and closed most of her door but kept looking at us from behind it and I said "Hal, it's me, Bud from next door, I know it's late but your door was unlocked and we heard a noise like a gunshot before and wanted to know if everything's okay," and to the man "Everything could be, you know...it could've been something popping or exploding in his apartment, even a balloon, anything, a small stove accident with something he left in the oven way before and forgot about without first puncturing for steam, for Hal likes to cook, if the noise was from his apartment," and the man said "If it's the stove then even more reason we have to go in," and pushed the door open all the way and Hal was on the couch, chest and face downwards into the cushions, knees on the floor, blood all over his clothes and couch and on the wall with some other stuff and that note on an end table and envelope on the floor.

The police and an ambulance came and they said Hal shot himself and could only have died instantly though they'll know for sure after their ballistics and lab tests and took him away, locked his door, taped a notice on it saying nobody could enter Hal's premises unless authorized by the police, spoke to me about his last moments on the landing, did I see the gun on him at the time, ever see one in his flat, did I know Rose or her last name or anything about her that would help them locate her and I said "I don't other than what Hal said about her being his big love, though that could have been facetious on his part for up till now he almost always seemed to have a humorous or cavalier attitude towards life, which I can only judge from the remarks he made when we passed one another on the stairs or street or I saw him locking or unlocking his door...and my recently hearing from time to time what sounded like the same woman's voice in his apartment late at nights, though sort of strained and muted through our walls, and her heavy clogs when they both left the following day and she'd clunk loudly down the stairs...and a couple times, because they were warm nights and our side-by-side studio windows were open wide, their making love, though I can't be sure it was Rose who I overheard since neither of them, when my record player would go off and I couldn't avoid not listening in, ever mentioned her name," and they said they'd be back tomorrow with more questions and a more thorough search of his place if necessary and left and about an hour later, while I was lying on my bed listening for the third consecutive time to the most mournful modern chamber piece I knew of, though the composer was quoted on the record jacket as saying the quartet was written as an act of religious love and to interpret tonally the mysteries of faith, I heard knocking on my door or Hal's, went to the peephole, saw a woman in front of Hal's door, opened mine and said "Excuse me, you looking for Hal?" and she said "Yes, you know what this notice is about?" and I said "Are you a good friend of his?" and she said "Yes, I've been up here before...you're Billy, Hal's told me about your playing," and I said "Buddy," and she said "Buddy, that's right, I'm Rose...you know if Hal got back and if he didn't, what happened to an envelope I stuck in his door?" and I said "I got it by mistake and read it, I'm sorry," and she said "No, that's good, as long as you still have it and he didn't get it...what it do, fall on the floor?" and I said "I think I've some bad news for you, Rose," and she said "What, he did get back and you gave him the note and he stormed out of here?" and I said "Worse...it's connected with the police notice...maybe you better come in and sit while I tell you, as it's very serious," and she said "Of course serious, but just tell me here, I don't have to go in there," and I said "Okay, I can understand how you feel...well, before, in Hal's apartment, while I was in mine, he shot himself the police say and is dead," and she screamed so loud right after I said he shot himself that she couldn't have heard my saying he's dead, and then seemed too weak to stand almost and the woman tenant on the floor opened her door and said "What now?" and the man from downstairs yelled "Anything the matter up there fourth to fifth floors?" and I yelled back "It's okay...one of Hal's friends, I'll take care of it," and held Rose's arms and she pressed her head into my chest and sobbed and let me hug her and the woman came over and patted Rose's shoulder and said "Poor girl, poor girl," and I said "I think she better sit down," and the woman said "You

want to take her in my place?" and I said "It's okay," and walked
Rose into my apartment and sat down on the bed with her and said
"Can I get you a beer, wine, anything, water?" and she nodded and I
said "Which one?" and she kept nodding and I said "That damn
music," and turned off the record player and got her a glass of water
and wine each and said "This is water and this one's white wine and
you can have both if you want or only choose one," and she took the
water but the glass slipped through her hand, reached for the wine
but I held it to her lips and she drank all of it and I said "Don't worry
about the broken glass, I'll clean it up, just don't step in it, okay?"
and she nodded and I said "I'll get you a towel to dry yourself with,"
and she started crying, so I put the glass down and held her again.

"It was my note, I know it," when I was holding her foot off the
floor to get the broken glass into a dustpan and I said "I wouldn't put
all the blame on yourself, that's unfair," and she said "Well he read it,
right, it was there, opened, right?" and I said "He started reading it
when he went in his apartment and I mine, but maybe he never finished it and was just very depressed about something entirely different at the time and your note was an almost inconsequential
contribution to it, for it wasn't a bad note," and she said "No, it was
cold, too blunt, and short enough to read in the time it took him to
get in his apartment and I knew it would make him sad... that's why I
came back, to either get the note if he hadn't come home yet or to
explain to him face to face what was really in my head, which is that
I've felt very screwed up these past weeks... that note was just a dis-
tillate of about five to six long letters I wrote to him today about how
it wasn't him or my feelings for or against him but me and my wanting to tip my seesaw good and hard for the first time and be absolutely free and uninvolved and doing whatever I want without having
to account or feel responsible for the hurt and disapproving feelings
of any one man, and that—" but the door knocked, I got up, Rose
said "Don't go," I said "But someone's knocking," and she said
"Maybe it's Hal... maybe you lied to get me in here," and I said
"Rose, come on, you know what happened, that police notice," but
she ran to the door, opened it, it was the woman across the floor who
said "I just wanted to check how you were doing before I went to
sleep... good, you're all right," and Rose screamed, pushed past and
ran downstairs sobbing, I started after her and the woman said "Let
her go, maybe it's better," but I ran down both flights, in my
bathrobe, no shoes on or socks, peepholes opening around me, yelled
out her name when I got on the street, but she was halfway down it, a

good runner, and a man bicycling past me on the sidewalk stopped and said "Hey, what's up, she steal something, want me to give her a chase?" and I said "Her boyfriend killed himself tonight in the apartment next to mine and she just found out and I guess went a little crazy," and he said "Tough luck, that's awful, killed himself, God."

Two policemen came by the next night, said the tests and coroner's report definitely confirmed Hal's death as suicide, the body had been picked up by his father and flown across the country for a funeral tomorrow and that an uncle would be by in a few days to clear out Hal's place, and I told them about Rose and how distraught she was last night and if they knew where I could reach her and maybe I could console her in some way if she was alone or had no other good friends or family and they said "We still haven't found a thing of hers, but if we do, why don't you give us a call in the next few days," and gave me their number.

I called the next day and one of the policemen said "We located her phone number on his wallet library card and she was terribly shook up like you said but we know in no way involved criminally in his suicide...it was just another one of those unsuited love affairs that maybe shouldn't've begun and ended up bad as it could have without both of them going and mostly from a misunderstanding and in my opinion these quick changing times...we also told her how you were concerned so much and she said you were very nice that night but to destroy the library card if we could and not give her number to anyone as she wants to work this thing out on her own, but truth is we think someone should see her and told her...a doctor, some minister or psychiatrist which we could help set up for her or even a women's group or clinic, because she's going to need some person to speak to once the initial shock period wears off, that we've found out for singles, but she just hung up on us, and when a lady policeman called back, hung up again, so I'm giving you her number but you won't say where you got it, understand?...since she's in the book and has the last name of Dorsey, you can just say it came from there."

I called Rose for two days and when I finally got her I said "Rose, this is Buddy, the fellow who lives or lived next door to Hal Botenleff," and she hung up and I called again and nobody answered and called the next night and someone picked up the receiver but didn't say anything and I said "Rose, if this is Rose, hold on for a second, this is Buddy again and I want to speak to you if I can...I know what you're going through and it's awful and I want to help you in any way I can," and she said "Then don't call again," but didn't hang up and I said "Rose?" and she said "Yes, the little sweet Rose," and I said "I didn't think you'd still be there after what you said," and she said "Normally I wouldn't have, but I saw I was making the same mistake with you as I did with Hal and every other relatively selfless person I've been insensitive to, so yes, maybe it would be helpful if we talked or if you don't mind, mostly I talked for I don't know anyone sane, smart or concerned enough right now to talk to," and I said "I could come over now if you want," and she said "I'd rather get out of this dump...I've been here for days with the shades down and windows closed thinking and thinking and not learning or understanding a thing more about myself as you just saw and it stinks to high heaven besides, which I can change by opening the windows, but the walls I can't hold back any longer from squeezing me to death no matter how many shades I let up," and I said "Any suggestions where we can meet?" and she said "You do the planning, I can't, though if you already didn't know, I live right around you," and I said "I know, I got your number out of the phone book...you know OJ's?" and she said "I'll be there in ten minutes, can you make it?" and I said "No sweat, I'm on my way," and shaved, dressed, ran to OJ's, she was standing out front, we shook hands, I opened the door and she said "Please, none of that 'holding the door open for the lesser man' stuff...I don't want to be rude again but we got to make this equal in every way tonight excluding the beers and tip, as I didn't bring any change," and I said "Fine with me, though someone had to open the door and I was nearest, and because it was open, I held it for you," and she said "As long as it isn't that 'knock me down lunging for the check and door obsessive machismo' shit," and we went in, sat, had beers, she said "Mind if I have a cheeseburger and fries on you too?" and I said "Not at all, I brought enough, anything special you feel like speaking about?" and she said "Just general things... Hal and me...he was a door man, football freako...no, I just knew him, slept with him, of course, sort of loved him, I don't want to sound mean but do want to say what it is...and then I felt I just wanted to be free of him because he was getting too demanding about wanting to be with me, though I'd told him from the start I only wanted a casual semi-emotional involvement with him, as I wanted to see other men and women, not so much in a sexual way, for getting laid a woman can do any day, but he wanted to marry me, have a child, I already have one and wanted to wait...in other words, he was perfect for me if I'd wanted a permanent mate, I mean we weren't fancy people with unfulfillable goals and most every other thing we both agreed on and liked, so in the end I began telling him I didn't want to be with him all the time or live with him but might one day, but he'd...but I've told you most of this and I really don't want to talk about it anymore, let's just talk about nothing in particular and eat and have fun and one day under better circumstances we'll have beers again and it'll be on me and if we don't, then I'll pay you back some way—by mail," and I said "It's okay, even if we don't meet and you see me walking on the street one day, you can pay me back then if you got," and she said "Deal," and we clinked steins, drank, were silent, ordered more beer and onion rings, I said "Listen, now that you're in a much calmer mood than that night ago and a certain time's elapsed, I want to say again and for the last time that you shouldn't feel it was your fault in any way about Hal...the police certainly don't think so...those things usually start building up years before they actually occur...from childhood even, and with maybe a few previous unsuccessfuls before the real one I've read...he definitely as I said could've been very depressed about many other things at the time which set it off...his work...what he do? because I never got to speak to him much after the previous tenant introduced him as the new one," and she said "High school teacher," and I said "I thought so because of his hours and holidays and sitting at his desk which I could see through our windows, his light going late at night weekdays and especially Sunday nights with I assume him correcting stacks of papers and exams," and she said "Making lesson plans Sunday nights...I teach at the same school but haven't gone back to it yet," and I said "I'm sure they understand," and she said "I'll tell you, even with the economy this bad I couldn't give a damn," and we drank up, ordered more beer, I asked and she told me where she was brought up, her family, older brothers, "I was always such a sweet little girl and superclean daughter and obedient sister and excellent A-plus goody-goody student right through grad school and then devoted housewife and model parent till I could no longer stand doing what everybody was always telling me was worth and good doing and I divorced Jud, though he was another perfect loving mate, and when he asked to have our son for a year I gladly gave Sam to him and it was the best thing I'd ever done for myself outside of having Sam because of the freedom it's given me that I never knew existed till now...but I've done teaching, you can say...proven to myself that I can get a good job and work and support two and even three people as well as any man, something I think I divorced Jud for to find out...but now I'm bored with teaching and outside of the students, there's nobody to talk to there...the men teachers are mostly jerks who can only think of me as a potential lay, and to my department head, no matter how well I do my job and create new courses and love and am loved by my kids, I'm just another incompetent aggressive dumb broad who ought to be fired for not wearing stockings and a bra...and the rest of the women teachers, just like all my old friends, are so blocked with their constant lunch cardplaying and male-dominated views where they think being radicalized is turning in the washboard for the washing machine and getting on top of a man in bed...even the women at my feminist groups are losers to me, radicals for radical sake and some of them so bright as to try out bisexuality for it's this year's fling thing, darling, and so forth... you're not homosexual, are you?...and so I'm right in the center and on the outside of things at the same time, trying to raise my consciousness with women who want to hump me, doing well at work but screaming the tedium jeebies to get out, feeling the time's absolutely right to do something professionally that would better jell with my brains and new outlook and creativity but not knowing what the hell what, and with the one person who understood me best probably dead because of me," and I said "No no, it's not true," and she said "I suppose so, but you know, outside of you right now there isn't anyone I can feel good talking to about all this, now that's a fantastic pity, isn't it? and I don't think most of it's my fault," and I said "It's tough, yes, but I'm sure it will change," and she said "Screw me, let's hear about you," and I said "I was born, raised and public-schooled here and I now compose music," and she said "So that's the piano playing we heard and thought were records—sounded very good," and I said "They were records—are, other composers...when I need a piano I go to a friend's house or former teacher's studio," and she yawned, I said "Tired?" paid up, we left, walked to her building, she stuck out her hand, we shook, she said "Thanks a lot, Bud, you've been very kind in listening to me run on all night," and I said "Maybe if you want we can see each other again to talk some more and maybe have dinner," and she said "Sure, food? anytime...tomorrow?" and I said "It'll have to be dutch," and she said "Well, in that case I guess I'll have to go back to work."

Next night we went out for dinner and three nights later went to a movie and met again the night after that, walked, went for a beer and snack, each time we talked less and less about Hal and their relationship and her guilt and more just about ourselves and what we'd done that day and she seemed to laugh more at what I said and become interested in what I do, done, my plans, and that night I said "Like to go to my apartment and listen to a part of a record some small recording company made of my first quartet along with four other composers—it's a short piece," and she said "I don't much want to go in that building yet and certainly not to the same floor," and invited me to her place, we went, she said "Beer's all I got," and sat on the couch, I on the chair opposite her and I wanted to sit beside her, maybe hold her hand, her body, kiss her, I said "Do you mind if I sit beside you?" and she said "What's on your mind, Tchaikovsky?" and I said "He's good, though not one of my favorites," and she said "I'm sorry, no more composer jokes, they're too easy and so too easily stupid," and I said "No problem, I just wanted to sit closer to you to maybe hold you or I don't know and because it'd be difficult doing it from here," and she said "Sure, I mean to sit, the other stuff we learn about as we go along," and I sat beside her, drank my beer, she her water, put my beer down, and she said "Oh oh, a duet's being composed... excuse me, but I'm a hopeless jokester," and I said "Oh oh's right, mind if I kiss you?" and she said "Nobody's quite ever led up to it like that and then actually asked after the heavy groundwork was laid, or at least not since I was twelve... for you see, a sexual-emotional life wasn't one of the things I was such a superclean Goody Twoshoes at but more an A-minus student, not that I want to encourage you," and I said "I only asked because of the way we met and Hal and that it hasn't been very long," and she said "No, it's all right, I was more in mourning for myself than Hal, but I think that's about over... but I don't want to fuck you, not because of any of that but because I just don't want to," and I said "Okay," and we talked about what a nice place she has and her little knickknacks and then I put my arm around her neck, she gave me her glass of water, I drank from it, she moved closer and put her head on my shoulder, we kissed, I put the glass down, kissed some more, she put her hand in my shirt and felt my stomach and chest, I did the same with her, we started to undress one another and were naked and she said "Let's go to bed... the landlady's nice but a cheapskate with the heat after ten," and we did, made love, I stayed over and next morning we made love, rented bikes, went riding in the park, museum, dinner, slept in her apartment that night, saw each other almost every day after that for a number of months, met what was left of each other's families, her son whom she had for the Christmas vacation, I'd already told her I loved her, then she told me and a month later, while we're cooking supper in my apartment, I said "Rose, I want to marry you," and she said "Yipes, the whole symphony... the chorus, the entire opus and oratorio... you composers... I'm sorry but I don't think so... I don't want to get hitched or another kid or anything so solid and really comfortable like that... that two can live for the price of a breakup or something...isn't it nice the way it is?...loving, plenty of fun and cuddling and no contractual commitments or hang-ups about none...what else can I say?...I got to at least keep the freedom I made for myself, though that doesn't mean never, not that I want to encourage you," and we ate dinner, danced to the radio, did these great ballroom dips and then a double striptease to the music before we went to bed, saw each other the next couple nights and when I said I had a party for us to go to tomorrow night she said "I can't, I've a previous appointment," and I said "With who?" and she said "That's my business, isn't it?" and I said "But don't you think after all this time it's a little bit of my business too?" and she said "A man, all right?" and I said "No, it's not all right, what man, a new man, old man, your father, a distant cousin?" and she said "A man I met who's been subbing at school recently and we were talking theater and he said he'd get tickets to a show and I don't know, I said yes," and I said "Then I'll go to the party myself," and she said "Of course you should, your life shouldn't stop because of me," and we slept together that night and I went to the party the next night and called her the following day and said "Hi, what about a late breakfast out?" and she said "I'm going to have brunch with someone else," and I said "Who?" and she said "Really, you're going a little too far now," and I said "That sub?" and she said "If you have to know, yes," and I said "Just level with me, is he there now?" and she said "You asked, all right...yes he's here and if it'll help to know more, which I'm sure will be your next question, he stayed the night," and I said "In your bed?" and she said "Come on, haven't you had enough?" and I said "Okay, no problem, I'm being dumb, goodbye," and hung up and said "Screw her, I don't give a crap about her," and went out, had breakfast, tried going to an afternoon concert but couldn't even stand on the ticket line and went home and drank wine just to forget her, lots of wine and fell asleep and woke up in the dark to some noise by my door and then something slipping under it, a paper, and I rushed to the door to catch her but she was already downstairs and the note said "It's not that I'm involved with anyone else but that your talk about marriage and now this new jealousy onslaught made me decide again to stay out of any deep involvement with you or anyone for a long time. I'm sorry. I'm just not ready. And nothing much else to say except maybe, if the time's ever better, because we do have so many wonderful things going for us as you've said, then some day in the future perhaps, though I wouldn't want you to hold out for me by any means," and I wrote on the back of her note "I understand and it's okay and believe me I'm not another Hal with this kind of news and that if you think what you're doing is right for you then it's grand with me too, so good luck, long life and everything best in the world to you and I mean that," and drank some more wine, went to sleep and next day reread my note, put it in an envelope, brought it to her building, went upstairs, stuck her keys in the envelope, slipped it under her door and left.

I went home, tried to work, read, drank, fell asleep, someone knocked on my door that night and I went to it and said "Who's there?" and she said "Rose," and I said "What do you want?" and she said "I forgot about Hal, that was so stupid of me, please let me in, I want to talk," and I said "About what?" and she said "Don't be mean, though you have a right to I know, but I don't want to say it through the door," and I said "What's there to say?" and she said "If you're not going to open up, I don't want to but I'll have to leave," and I opened the door and she said "Hello," and I said "Now what is it?" and she said "Oh, molto serioso face," and I said "Sure serious, but no jokes now, what is it?" and she said "I don't want to speak out here," and I said "Why not?" and she said "Because what I have to say is private and might take some time and I don't want to wake your neighbors," and I said "Well I don't want you coming inside," and she said "Why?" and I said "Because we're done, that's why," and she said "I can understand your acting like this and I know you mean it, but that's part of what I want to speak about," and I said "Why, you change your mind about anything?" and she said "I don't know, I don't think so, but I still feel we have to talk to clear up anything that might be unnoticed or out of focus or misunderstood," and I said "Rose, the best thing for you right now is to be outside on your own having your own experiences and testing yourself out on the unknown or something, I'm convinced of that, because I'll tell you, no matter what we say or do here tonight I see the same things hap-pening with us and you over and over again till you do have a lot bet-ter idea what you want or don't want, I know that for sure now or almost... and I'll also tell you, I'm tired of people feeling I'm a bur-den on them because they know I care deeply for them and especially when I thought that deep feeling was being returned or because they feel frustrated or confused because they know I mostly like what I've done and am now doing with my life and because they didn't do what they wanted to before they met me or aren't doing now what they think they can or must do and for some reason think it's because of me or even not because of me but just whatever, all of which might sound senseless or too muddled or high-toned or pedantic or some-thing," and she said "No, it doesn't, and I know it's not you but just me," and I said "Good, but now I'm going to have to say goodnight and shut the door on you rather than with you inside here, okay?" and she said "Not yet, because I think for both our sakes there's still a number of things that have to be talked out first," and I said "Look, don't worry about me, I've been through a similar thing like this a few times and know I'll probably be unhappy again for a while with occasional foothill peaks of cheerfulness and lows of total forlornness but I'll eventually survive, so now please just step backwards a few feet or turn around and walk back out into the hallway but please just get past my door's threshold so I can close it and drink a beer and go back to sleep," and she did and I shut the door, went for a beer while she continued to knock on my door till my next-door neighbor opened up and said "Excuse me, that noise—having trouble?" and she said "Him," and he said "Who?" and she said "Bud, your room-mate, he's being so ridiculous and obstinate he just pisses me off, and I'm also a little afraid for him," and he said "Wait, excuse me again, you got me all turned around, I didn't even know what his name was...I only moved in a couple weeks ago, and afraid for him of what?" and she said "Nothing, let him alone...as he says, he'll sur-vive," and he said "Great, may we all survive, and I didn't mean to butt in just now," and she said "Don't worry, I'm sorry myself...I thought you'd moved in long ago and already met him," and he said "No, long ago I rented the place but because of some litigation between the former tenant's parents and the landlady over the posses-sions and back rent and deposits and stuff, I couldn't get in here," and she said "Yeah? Bud never told me...for I also knew the man who lived there before you," and he said "You mean that Phil or Bill somebody?" and she said "Hal," and he said "Hal, right, I knew it was one syllable...that was an awful story...the landlady told me with all the grisly details," and she said "I'm sure she did...the whole world has to know, but she's crazy," and he said "Were you a good friend of his, or maybe I shouldn't have asked...though the way you said it—forget it," and she said "No no, it's all right...I'm Rose and at the time Hal's best friend you can say, but now I've got to be going," and he said "Wait up, where you going? my name's Jeremy...you shouldn't be walking alone at this hour," and she said "Why, you know the neighborhood?...I've lived here more than a year and never been stopped, and I know how to handle myself... when I go home alone at nights I always put my keys here, between the fingers, key inserts sticking out, and I swear if any man gets rough with me I'd give it to him in the eyes and then kick him in the nuts and blow my little neck whistle," and he said "Whew, man's a killer all right," and she said "I shouldn't be?" and he said "No, Christ, I think it's great and I've been warned, right?" and she said "Not you, but obvious creeps," and he said "Good, and look, I was about to go for the paper anyway, so why can't I walk you to the corner?" and she said "If you're not going to take long," and he said "Only have to put my pants on—want to wait here?" and she said "I'll come in," and he said "I'll put them on in the bathroom, won't be a sec," and the door closed, opened a few minutes later, two of them laughed and talked as they went downstairs, Jeremy returned an hour later and the next day I heard him through our adjacent windows talking on the phone "Hi, Jeremy again.... No, with a G, like in New Jersey.... Then with an N and G like in New Caledonia, listen.... Oh come on.... That's beautiful, beautiful.... All right, divine then, but do I really sound like that much of a phony?... Not half a phony?... Why? because, well, half a phony's better than none at all, no?... Wrong again and I probably do.... No, I really am, Rose, I admit it only to you, but okay for tonight?... Good, say around sixish?... Oops, can't say anything right today, not sixish but a little past six, approximately eleven and a third minutes after six on the nose, better?... Oh, I am a phony, indubitably, unquestionably, and I want to be cured, doctor.... Good, later," and he left the apartment around six, didn't come back that night or if he did it was very late and I was asleep and he had to have left the next morning before I awoke, and I heard him speak to her on the phone many times after that, either through our windows if they were open or faintly through the walls, and she never came to his apartment that I knew of though I did see them on the streets or the patio at OJ's and once leaving a movie theater and always enjoying themselves it seemed, arms around waists, holding hands, once a kiss on the lips while waiting for the light to change, then about three months after he met her I saw him and two friends moving his furniture out of his apartment and I said "Quite a quick turnover for tenants in Three-B," and he said "What can I tell you?" and I said "Where you moving to?" and he said "Near here," and I said "With Rose?" and he said "I didn't want to exactly get into it with you, but yes," and I said "No problem, how is she?" and he said "She's great," and I said "Wonderful, and lots of luck and may everything really go well for you both and I mean that," and he said "Thanks," and we shook hands, I brought down a box of his records and put it into a U-Haul van, saw them a few times in the neighborhood after that, either alone or when they were together, still looking very close, never said hello to them or did anything when he was alone but wave to him from across the street and he waved back and at the post office once I nodded to Rose who was on the next stamp line and though I know she saw me she kept her eyes off me, and then one day I realized I hadn't seen either of them for months and figured they'd moved to another neighborhood or out of the city and maybe got married, while I stayed in the same apartment, rent was never raised, continued to compose, had a couple pieces performed and got a small state grant, taught piano to children at a music school twice a week, almost got married but ten days before the wedding she broke it off, watched tenants come and go in the apartment next door, one I thought a runaway who couldn't pay the rent, then a woman who had to move out when the landlady found she had a dog, now a young couple with a new baby who cries most of the time which seems to bother the other tenants but I kind of like the sound, till about two years after I last remembered seeing Jeremy and Rose, I saw him coming out of OJ's when I was going in and I said "Jeremy, hey, how are you?" and he said "I'm sorry... your face, but your name isn't, and I truthfully don't know where from," and I said "I used to live right next door to you on West Eighty-fourth when you first met Rose," and he said "Rose?...oh Christ, that bitch?...no, maybe that's not fair, though I think it's accurate, but do me a favor, will you?...next time, if we ever bump into each other, don't say her name again," and I said "Okay," and he said "Excuse me, I got to be going," though I was sure just to get away from me and any possible further mention of Rose, and left.

The

Return

—➤

Someone rang my bell. You can't tick back in this building to let the ringer in and there's no intercom. So I went out to the hallway and yelled "Coming" down the stairwell and ran down the two flights of stairs.

Mary, grinning and waving at me through the glass half of the vestibule door. Her hair up, in a sheer shirt. I waved back, opened the door, said "Beeg surprise," and she said "That's my middle names," and I said "Well lookit here, all my gear," and she said "Come on, don't be unfaithful: the lips," and we quickly kissed. She'd brought back my things: clothes, books, records, work materials, probably somewhere in there my two-cup espresso pot and toilet articles. I said "Like to come upstairs a minute before you go?"

"Sure. Let me park first." She left. It took me three trips to haul it all to my apartment. I started putting away the clothes. There was a note on top of the shopping bag of books. It said "It seems so terminal, three weeks and no word from you. I find it kind of sad but nothing either of us can do. I wish the timing had been right for us—you knew better than me last fall and then spring that I had to be off on my own. I hope it doesn't seem too cold my carting back your estate this way. Your keys I used to lock up your place and have thrown under the door. Maybe you've already kicked them clear down your hall into the coat closet like a soccer ball goal. If only we could see each other when we wanted to and have fun without it getting so gripping and glum. But what you expected from me was much more than I could give. It became a pact like I had to live up to—to be like it was. I couldn't—it isn't—you saw and I can't keep you diddling around waiting for me to go through all the living I have to before I'm ready for a more continuous thing with someone like you. So hey. Maybe another day. Okay, boss?"

I ran downstairs, looked for her both ways in front of my building. Ran in the direction her car went to Columbus Avenue and stayed on the corner there looking all four ways for her, gave up after a few minutes and started home.

"Warm day for May," a super I know said.

"I'm only sweating because I was running."

"Me it's because of the weather."

"Newt?" She was coming from the park corner. I walked to her. She waited for a few cars to pass before crossing the sidestreet. I ran to her and she to me. We kissed and hugged, stayed enlaced like that till I said "Movies are better than ever."

"No *versteht.*"

"Your note. I didn't think you were coming back."

"Oh, my note. I wrote it last night. I feel a bit differently today. Though I still think I need a few months' break from you."

"So go. No hard feelings or knocks. But you have to shove off right away?"

"Want to walk in the park first? It looked beautiful when I parked."

"My door's unlocked. And I'm still in my bare feet."

Arm and arm back to my building, hand in hand up the stairs. Socks and shoes on. Socks off, just my sandals on. Just sneakers: wasn't warm enough for only sandals and I could never see myself wearing sandals with socks. Mary drank a glass of milk and retoasted and ate an old buttered toasted roll I'd forgotten about in the stove yesterday. Then we left the building. The landlord, when I apologized, said she wasn't worried I hadn't paid her the gas, electricity and rent. Climbed over the park wall and were on a bench embracing again when a woman I know biked by.

"Hello, Newt."

"Hi," I said.

"Hi, New," her son on the baby seat said.

"Hello, Jim." I hadn't even seen him.

"I got money," he yelled, his mom still pedaling away. The bill blew out of his hand and I stepped on it before it rolled into the lake.

"Hey, Barb—stop," I said. They were gone. "A five. This is our lucky day."

"Do you think I cut myself off from you intentionally and over-dramatize our incompatibilities and then that very cut I made just to get back to the same intensity we had?"

"We might."

"I think I do and if it's true that's sick of me. You're the center of my life. Everything revolves around you."

"I didn't want to ask. But it's all your fellow satellites. Oh well—like to have dinner with me tonight?"

"I'd rather go to a movie and after that a snack. And then we'll be good friends again and I'll go home alone—is that all right for tonight?"

First she had to return some class notes to a classmate for a film course she was taking at the New School. We drove downtown. I said I'd wait outside. She said "Come on in, it won't take long."

The man was waiting for her in the student lounge. He walked over smiling. I walked toward him with her and she dropped my hand and I veered to the side past him into the cafeteria. I wanted to eat an apple. The sign said it cost thirty-five cents. "Thirty-five for an apple?" I said to the cashier, apple in my hand. "This is supposed to be a nonprofit cafeteria."

"If we were selling them from a crate outside it'd maybe cost a quarter. But thirty-five is what it comes to when you take in the upkeep of the place and personnel plus the apple."

I put the apple back and got an orange. Its price wasn't listed.

"Forty cents," he said. "That's a Haifa."

I put it back and got a bag of dry roasted peanuts for fifteen cents.

"That seems fair," I said. "About one and a third peanut per penny."

Mary was still in the middle of the lounge talking to the man. Both laughing, Mary clapping her hands once when she particularly broke up at something either of them had said. The lounge was carpeted and most people sat on the floor, their backs against someone else's back or the wall. I sat on a chair. A man came up to a woman sitting on the chair next to mine and said "Hi, how are you?"

"If you want to know," she said, "I'm doggedly grading exams."

"Maybe I can help you." He sat down next to her. "What's that?" He bent back the test paper to see. "Marx? You're in luck. Marx and Freud are my two specialties."

"Bullshit. They're everybody's here." She gave the paper an A.

"Not getting the best of vibes from you, sis. What's your name?"

"You don't know? I'm supposed to be your sis. But you really want to be of some help to me, take off."

"Sis as in sisterhood. What about a coffee then? Or a beer? They sell it at the caf now."

"What the hell," and she got up and went with him to the cafeteria. Another couple came over. They were very well dressed for this lounge: tie, suit, long pressed dress. He sat, she squatted on the floor. He said "Hiee kwahwahha." She asked how to spell it. He spelled kwahwahha. She wrote it down in her notebook.

"Then that's it?" she said.

"Kwahwahha. What could be after that?"

"Too true." He stood up and she took his seat.

"I'll see you this weekend perhaps?" He gave her what looked like a business card. "This is an excellent place to go Friday and Saturdays around half past nine. I'll be there both nights."

"Not cheap?"

"No, nice. Lots of good African girls go there. Fine music. Topnotch dance. Ethno food that you can't get here."

"Maybe Saturday then. Friday I have to have dinner with the people. If I don't, they write home."

"Good. Then you are being looked after." They shook hands. He left. She opened a book and uncapped a Magic Marker. Mary was still talking and laughing with the man in the middle of the lounge. He took the class notes from her, flipped through to a page, looked serious, sneezed and began jabbing his palm into his index finger. She offered him his hanky. I went back to the cafeteria, got an apple and brought it to the same cashier. "No price rise since the last time?" I said.

"Why make a big deal of it? Money's paper to burn these days. As Marx said—"

"Marx said 'Money's paper to burn these days' or 'is paper to burn'?"

"Man, you're either a hostile type or got a deep-seated gripe. Anyway, as you well know, Marx didn't say it: I did. Though obviously hordes of people said it before me and even Marx might have said it, for it's an ancient cliché: I bet anteceding the Greeks. But what I'm saying Marx said about money that applies to this particular fiscal business of your apple here is—"

"Would you two please continue your political powwow after I've paid?" the customer behind me said. Pointed beard, love beads, long gray sideburns, cultivated curls down his neck and mod clothes: looked like a philosophy prof to me or M.D. analyst. I paid, he paid.

Ry-Krisp and cottage cheese was all he was eating. The cashier saluted me with his paper cup of beer. Three or four dogs wove around the room. I deliberately sat down at the table next to the man and woman who had gone into this cafeteria before for a coffee or beer.

"You're a T.A.?" the man said.

"That's right," she said. "A teaching assistant."

"Don't have to tell me what the initials stand for. What I'm asking is what you do as one."

"Correct papers and proctor exams and such. And in rare emergencies make sudden plane reservations for my professor and subsequent apologies to his wife and take over his class and be appreciated by his students more than he ever could."

"That's all? How'd you get such a cushy breeze—brushing your teeth every morning and your hair a hundred strokes a day?"

"Is that literary crit of my breath and disheveled hairdo?"

"Hold on. I meant it takes nothing out of the extraordinary to get that position, right?"

"If you're a grad student with good grades and proven poverty, you can become a T.A. It's not a glamorous job."

"It is to me."

"Grief. Look at your eyes. Haven't you anything else on that mind?"

"I think it's sort of exciting to think the thoughts I do and to be able to emotionally and physically fulfill them rather than just conceive them. Would you, pardon my tongue, I mean my language, consent to sharing a repast with me later on?"

"I might if we go dutch."

"No other way, sis, no other way."

They drank up and left. "My exam papers," she shouted at the door.

"Leave them."

"You totally crazed?" She came back and also got her sweater off the back of the chair.

From my table I could see Mary still listening to the man in the middle of the lounge. Point 44, his finger jabbed, points 45, 6 or 7. I cut my apple into quarters, cored the quartered core, peeled each piece and sliced them in half, put a couple of seeds in my mouth to see if they could be ground fine enough by the molars for me to swallow, as the entire apple excluding stem and tree supposedly went into those All Natural Swiss or American-cum-Swiss dried breakfast cereals that by the month seemed progressively more popular and expensive and so always out of reach of what I thought I could afford. But the seeds were too bitter to grind further, so I spit them into my hand when there was still something of substance to spit out rather than lose them below my gums, and only ate the mesocarp.

Mary standing beside me: "Where were you? I've been looking all over the place. I imagined you had a change of mind about me or us and beat it home."

"Sorry. Thought you saw me circling around and then come in here. I tried to make myself obvious: waving, doing a junior fan dance. Want something? Coffee or eighth of an apple with beer?"

"We might be late for the movie. Mind if we go?"

We drove uptown to the theater and got stuck in a long traffic tie-up.

"I knew I should have taken First instead of Third," she said, "or Second instead of Lex. What avenue are we on? Look at that guy," motioning to a man waiting for the light to change or just standing there through several greens and reds. He was in a shiny plum jumpsuit and bowler, orange platform shoes with silver heels and soles, by his side a heeling overgrown borzoi. "They're both beautiful."

"I don't know," I said.

"At least he's interesting and his dog's beautiful."

"How do we know it's his dog? They don't look alike and she's unleashed."

"You never especially cared for people with real street flair—not a notable or nadiral flaw of yours, just an impression I re-get. Because how can you not think it's what first and foremostly makes this city what it is?"

"Right now I think, feel, sense and intuit nothing but riding out of this sticky triffic jam."

"Whew, are you ever pissed. You sinking into one of your male menstrual moods?"

"No, I'm going to come out of one."

"That's my man." She grabbed my hand. Let go to slip into gear when the tie-up about ten blocks ahead started to move. "Oy vay ve vamoose on our una and only luf day." Once in second, she lifted my same hand and kissed and licked the fingernails and tips. "If you ever remembered a poem in your life other than 'O Captain! My Captain!' or 'The Man with the Hoe,' could you recite it to me now?"

"Ummm...Roses are you, violets are me, irises I guess are just irises or irides just as daisies could be dazzlers or marguerites. No."

"Why not? It doesn't rhyme."

We got to the theater, parked in front and found we had an hour before the movie began. "Let's nosh somewhere," Mary said, "but not one of those swinging East Side hamburger joints where the French-fried onion rings come to the customer kitchen-unfrozen and factory-made."

We settled on a small luncheonette because its door was open to let in the air, the door was being held open by a beveled wood block, this stop seemed to have been chopped by a non-axman's whacks, a cat sat at the window, an old bladed fan revolved on the last stool, lottery tickets and Bromo-Seltzers were sold, Greek music was playing on a radio and it looked like an eatery out of the early American forties, which was the period, despite its great war and other collapses and aftermaths, that Mary would most love to have lived through other than late Olmec and seventh-century Damascus under the Omayyad caliphs.

We sat at the counter. The man on my right read a scratch sheet and actually said to a counterman "Who do you like in the fifth?" The two countermen looked Mary up and down, crossways and cornerwise, then tried to eye each other hugger-muggerly to say they liked what they saw.

Mary said "Ah, Greeks," and said something like "Kalimara" to them and shook their hands.

One of them said "Ah, you speak the Greek," and spoke back to her in Greek. She said something else in Greek and they looked impressed and spoke to one another in Greek, and to me she said "What I just told them meant 'You speak much too fast for me in Greek and I can't understand a word you said.'"

"See anything that looks good?" I said.

"Let's see. You make the soup here?" she said to one of the countermen, and he said "Yes, soup, straight from home."

"You mean you or someone else makes it home and brings it here or you make it here yourself?" and he said "Yes, I make it here—we, my brother and I. Good soup. Lentil, plenty of lentils."

We ordered one bowl of soup with two tablespoons, a side dish of French-fried onion rings, because they also came from home and along with the cheese blintz were Mary's two quests for food perfection in life, and a Western omelet, though on a wall sign it said San Diego omelet. I told her that in California the Western was called a Denver. "I don't know what it's called in Denver—maybe an Albuquerque. Though maybe by some luck a Denver's called a Denver in Denver and Albuquerque, and the naming journey for this kind of omelet could end."

"Now that's what I meant the last time we split about your intellectualizing the hell out of almost anything. Why can't you just accept their San Diego for our Western or at least stop at what it's called in California?"

"I don't want to mislead you or go any further with this when it's obvious I shouldn't, but as far as I know it's only in San Francisco that it's called a Denver. In Oakland it might be called an Orange County and in Whittier or Sierra Madre, let's say—but you're right," when she gave me a look to stop, "I'm probably only playing these word games to draw attention to myself. And maybe now talking about drawing attention to myself because I want to draw attention away from the countermen to myself." But she was speaking in Greek to the younger counterman again, who was beating our omelet eggs into the sautéed vegetables as he sang along to the radio song.

"What?" he said and she asked for the call letters of the radio station and hours it plays Greek music, which she jotted down in her memo book, and also "Where can someone like myself go dancing and drinking in a real Greek place in New York? I was in Samos last summer and haven't found anything like those tavernas they have there."

"In Astoria, that's where all the best Greeks live." He gave her the names and addresses of three places in Astoria where she could eat good Greek food at no unfair prices and dance on a big floor to the best live Greek music in America—"I swear to you. You like retsina?"

"No."

"The wine? No? Ah, retsina," and he kissed his spatula. "To me it's the best."

We got our food and shared it. Mary said the onions were only so-so. "At most a C plus. I have no money," she said, and I paid.

"Thank you," she said, shaking the hands of the countermen and the man sitting beside her, still doing arithmetic and circumscribing and scratching out horses. The younger counterman said to her "My brother, he's married. But me, I like to have fun and dress up and go dancing. So maybe I see you at the Delphi one Saturday night. If I do, my name's Ted and I say hello."

"Please do."

We went to the movie theater. Mary had to go to the ladies' room and I went into the theater to get two seats. It was like walking into a funeral chapel minutes before the service began. The room was small and crowded, the recorded music low and funereal. A black curtain drooped over the screen to the floor. The audience was on an average much older than in any movie theater I'd been to recently and conservatively dressed and groomed and most had serious expressions and spoke in hushed tones.

"Joan?" a man said, looking for a seat and spotting a woman he knew sitting in the seat next to the one I was holding for Mary.

"Bud, how are you?"

"Great, and you?"

They talked for a minute, about last winter on the Island, Rhona and Tony and Bud's baby and Joan's kids. Everybody was fine. He wasn't renting the same cottage this summer. Business as in all retail stores these days was slow. The White House? Don't even mention it. She was doing the lighting and costumes for a new show this fall and in every which way had spent the happiest six months of her life. "Is that seat available?" he said to her.

"I don't know," Joan said. They both looked at me.

"It's taken," I said. "And I know what you're next going to ask me, and I'd rather not." I just didn't want to move over one seat and be against the wall and possibly out of sight of part of the screen, which I still couldn't see because of that black pall.

Bud said he hoped to see her later and got a seat up front. Mary came down the aisle waving at me waving at her just as the lights began to dim.

"Lots of women with urinary problems and only one stall. And looks like you might have had a tough time saving my seat," and I went into the incident about not moving over one.

"You should have. For how do you know you'll miss part of the screen?"

"I just feel it."

The curtain rose on an award-winning Slovakian cartoon. It seemed everyone found it funny but us. "Looks like you were right about the screen," Mary said. "But you still should have moved over one, as at the time you didn't know you were right and they wanted to sit as a deuce. But no big thing," and she took my hands, rested her head against my shoulder and stayed that way throughout the show.

Walking up the aisle, she said "When have we seen an audience like this? They all look like the radicals and revolutionaries of the thirties and forties who are now very to excessively successful in whatever they never set out to be." The film was by Jean Renoir—his last, we overheard.

"I have to make a phone call," she said outside. I remembered the Greek place had a pay phone on the wall. It was on the next block. We went back. The chairs stood on the tables and the brother was gone and Ted was mopping the floor. He saw us looking at him through the outside gate and waved. Mary made motions of dialing and speaking into a receiver and cupped her hands in prayer and looked heavenward. Sure, Ted said. He unlocked. The music was blues-oriented rock. She went inside and he relocked the door and she made her call. A couple walked by, with the woman saying "The truth will always surface if you let it," and the man said "Yes?" and she said "Yes," and darted into the street to flag down a bus. "Let's take a cab," he said, but she was already in the bus and he followed her.

After the phone call, Mary talked with Ted for about five minutes. They laughed, he took a pencil off his ear, put it back without using it, patted her arm as she left. "Ciao, Mary. Hello," he said to me, shutting the door.

"He wants me to go to the Delphi with him any day I will please myself, as he put it, though it has to be in the next three months. Otherwise, he'll be unfree."

"You consent?"

"He's cute, though too much the smoothie for me, but I said let's leave it to chance. I meant it, for I never know."

"Get through your call?"

"I had a date at ten but had to break it."

"Two people passed when you were in there," I said, but she cut in "Where'd we leave the car? I always forget."

I pointed. We walked. She said "Your two people before," and I shook my head. I was thinking about her phone call and Ted. Other than for a long-standing friendship, I hadn't seen another woman in the year and a half I'd known Mary. No, once, when she was in Greece and a week or so after she wrote me from there saying she wanted to continue to be unattached from a man, but both that woman and I were drunk and didn't much care for each other before we met up again in the bar or even in bed. "This is one of our main problems," Mary had often said in different ways. "Your external world is too small for me"—a few months back. "I shrink from the pressure of your intensity," or the other way around, "and need to find space alone for myself and for others," she wrote a while ago. Last night I wrote her a postcard that said "It now seems clear to me what you want for yourself and from me and what you want me to want for myself and from you, and I now finally know there's no solution to it and so no future for us and I also regret it took so long for me to find all this out." I wrote this, in slightly different versions, on six postcards before I was satisfied with the writing and the way the words looked, and mailed the sixth card and dumped the rest when I went for my morning run.

We reached the car. It was still light out. "You drive," she said. "I'm tired of the wheel."

"Let's walk along the river first."

"I like your idealism."

We walked down to the East River, found there was no way to walk along the river. A raised highway. Nothing for pedestrians. A high chain-link fence with garage-parked cars behind it giving us a broken-up view of the river but blocking our way. "Let's go back," I said. At the time she was talking about shirts. Walking down to the river we had talked about the revival of cuffs in men's pants. I think the conversation had started with her remarks about being tired of the steering wheel and pleased with my old-fashioned idealism. She said that when she was married she had to iron five shirts a week for her husband, more if he was covering a weekend story out of town. "It also depended on the season. Savannah during one week was worth twelve. That was before wash-and-wear shirts that really looked and felt like broadcloth. I mean oxford. Myles was never a broadcloth man."

"You must have hated ironing."

"No, it was kind of peaceful. Mandolin music on: I could really think."

Just then a man walked by, stopped, turned to her. "Aren't you," he said, pointing, "Mary?" She didn't recognize him. "We went to high school together. At least my boys' school went to dances at your girls' school and vice versa. Rick Hallmark." He put his laundry bags down. "Where Myles used to go."

"Now I know. I was just talking about him. How I used to iron his oxford button-downs five to twelve times a week. Don't ask. He's fine. Writing books, caulking boats. Don't say. You haven't seen him since you both graduated high school."

"Right. I'm still friends with Lance Boyle though. Remember the Terrorful Trio—L, M and I? You were like our mascot."

"Thanks lots."

"Well you were the only girl who was a steady attachment to our trio."

"That's what most men think women and children are. Attachments."

"Steady," I said.

"I'm sorry. Newton Leeb: Rick Hallmick."

"That's right," he said, winking at Mary. "Gave you me wrong name." We shook hands.

"How come you didn't shake hands with me?" she said.

"I will." They shook hands. "And no offense meant before. All I was saying was that Myles was the only one of us who had the same girl for three years."

"You mean he was the only one getting steadily laid. And sixteen years, not three."

"Sixteen? Well, if you see Myles, give him the mick's regards." He picked up his bags and left.

"I hate bumping into people from the gay olden days," she said. "Those times were too great. Race race race," and she ran off and let me catch up and we raced back to the car and she let me win. "You're getting too leaden. What you need like Mick had is a quick marriage, child and divorce in three easy lesions with someone else. That'll take off a big load."

We got in the car. "Where to, my lovey?" she said. "I'd like someplace I've never been before."

"Let's scout." I drove. "There's Maxwell Plums."

"I've never been there. You? Then let's." We parked a couple blocks away and started to walk back. We passed a candystore with a newsstand outside. She picked up a copy of *Screw*, opened to a photo of a woman on her back with her mouth taking two men, who you couldn't see—just their penises from two sides—and her vagina another man, who also couldn't be seen except for his penis. "God, there really is no censorship anymore," and she paid for the paper and turned to the personals. "Three other things I've never done before is read and buy one of these rags and answer one of their ads. Now what's my pleasure? Gentle genital massage? Group climax control?"

We went to Plums. "Too crowded and gaudy," she said. "Look at those obscene goblets."

"It is a bit flashy, but let's have one beer at the bar."

"I don't want to. And why should you when nine out of the ten men there are men. Let's leave."

"You can be too bossy sometimes."

"I was born under the sign of the lioness, so what do you expect?"

"Leaving?" a man coming in with some other men said to Mary and she said "Yes we are" and he said "Sorry about that."

We looked for another place in the neighborhood. They were all too crowded or smoky and seemed like Plums, though less gaudy and no goblets. Through the window of one of them I saw the couple from a few hours ago. The T.A. and the man. Sitting at a table, drinking beers, his hand over hers. He spoke. She pulled her hand away and put it on her lap, but didn't look annoyed. He laughed, lit a short stogy and spoke. She smiled, put her hand back on the table and stroked his wrist. I tapped the window from the street. They looked. I said "Hi," and waved. You know him? their expressions asked of each other.

"You know them?" Mary said.

"From your school before. But only to overhear and watch."

Mary, with her index finger, made a screwing motion at my temple for them and they laughed.

"That wasn't nice," I said.

"I'm sorry. I also make mistakes." She made the same screwing motion to her own temple and the couple laughed and made screwing motions to their temples and the waiter picking up the empties after he set down two new steins made the motion to his temple, but I kept my hands at my sides and only watched.

In the car Mary said "Let's drive over the bridge to the Brooklyn Boondocks."

"Too far."

"Then the Boondocks downtown. Then the old place." That was a bar on the West Side three blocks from where I lived. We'd been there a hundred times together. We got a table in the glass-enclosed patio that jutted out onto the sidewalk. Mary wanted sangria for a change. But the only sangria they had came in big pitchers, the waitress said. "I still want sangria but not a pitcher of it," Mary said.

One of the two women sitting at the next table said "Why don't you take some of ours, as we won't be drinking through more than half of it. We didn't know we were getting so much."

"I got a great idea," Mary said.

"Good," the woman said. "I love great ideas."

"Why don't we order a glass of red and white wine and then you can sit here with us and we can add our wine to your pitcher and we'll all drink wined-up sangria together."

"That is a good idea," the woman said. "Done."

Our wine came. "Come on over," Mary said to them. We also ordered an avocado salad and a cheese, fruit and bread board. "Now you have to take some of these too."

"Honey. See this waistline?" the woman said. "Or this clothes-line? Well, that isn't slimness. That isn't even unpleasant plumpness. That's big blubbery fat, so thanks but no."

We poured our wine in their pitcher and toasted to "continuing great ideas and camaraderieship." We talked about politics, city and federal. Then Lucille, the one who wouldn't take any food, said to Mary "Okay. You sound like a liberal and that's good, I'm not saying no. But what would your folks say to seeing you sitting here with two blacks?"

"I didn't know either of you were black," Mary said.

"I don't quite get the point of what you said, or rather why you're saying it," I said to Lucille. "It doesn't seem to relate to what we were speaking about."

"It's a point, can't that be enough? Now you know, period. But what would your folks say, Mary?"

"Probably nada. Or my father would say 'Pour your mom and I a glass of that fruit punch, M and M. We want to partake a taste of it.' And if they were here, then realistically there would have been enough of us to order a pitcher just for them and Newt and me, and then the four of us now would never be sitting here like this. So you win and lose."

Terry, the other woman, said "Screw color. Screw all race relations except the sleepytime kind." Lucille looked reprovingly at her. "That's right, baby. Screw all that crap. I say have fun, have fun. And these are young people. They don't define you by your shades and hues."

"I'm not young," I said.

"So, your girl's young. And you look young. Don't give me a hard time. You look good. Accept it." She got up. She'd gotten up every five minutes or so to phone someone. When she came back she said "That son of a b's still not home. Where in hell is he? He knows I'm not stepping a foot in our flat unless he's there first."

We talked about street and building crime, cities where there was street peace. About what an exciting, occasionally harrowing but always diversified city New York was. As an example Mary mentioned the Continental Baths, which was a few blocks from here. "You two should go," she told the women. "I was there this Saturday. That's the one night they open it for both sexes. But everybody there was so into him- or herself that it turned out to be almost antisex, despite half the guys being gay."

"Did you take a bath?" Terry says.

"A swim. They have a big pool. You sit around it in your bathing suit or clothes and eat and drink and watch the entertainment, which can be good: a very Great Gatsby singer type and female comedienne. But it gets so stuffy inside that we stripped down and dived into the pool nude."

"They don't mind?" I said.

"They don't encourage you. But nobody there was going to be so un-twenties to admit with mouth or glance to being concerned. You ought to take an overnight or weekend room there just to see what goes on. I would if I were a man and especially one in your profession."

"I don't think I want to."

"What do you do?" Terry says.

"Nothing much."

We got into the subject of romantic love. Men and men. "Sure, lots of them seemed like they were in love and really making it," Mary said. Women and women and then women and men. Lucille said she was a heterosexual to the nth degree and then some, "but never in my life, and I'm over forty, honey, have I ever felt what it is they say is love at the exact time a man was feeling it for me. That high feeling like too much caffeine in your too many coffees, but softer—like rolling. Either he's up there and I'm not or I am for him and he's somewhere else, but never love with any of its most extreme advantages."

I said "We've had that high-flying feeling lots of times together," and Mary looked at me and then nodded and said "You're right, we have."

"Then you're lucky," Lucille said. "But I've been married and with live-in lovers and the best of men and everything, but not once. I never told you this," she said to Terry.

"No, and I'm really flabbergasted to hear it."

"It's the truth. I don't lie."

"I know, dear, which makes it more amazing. You wouldn't say it 'less it was."

"I can't lie either," Mary said. "I try but find it impossible to lie to anyone about anything, even to my own daughter when it's damn well the best thing for her."

"You've a daughter?" Terry said. "You look too young to have a child."

"I've two children, a daughter and a son. The girl's twelve."

"Twelve? That's unbelievable," Lucille said.

"Her son's fourteen," I said.

"Now I absolutely don't believe it."

"Why? It just means I married young."

"Honey, if they were sitting next to you now and both of them had your puss stamped on them and were calling you mommy, I still wouldn't believe it."

"They yours too?" Terry said to me, "or you two aren't married?"

"No, by somebody else," Mary said. "The son's with the father and Linetta's with me."

"That's too bad."

"It works out. We exchange them weekends and then some long weekends and two weeks a summer each of us gets them both. It also forced me to get my own digs and job and hack it out on my own."

Lowell, my closest friend, came into the bar. "Hey, schmoozer," I said, and his eyes bounced back and forth between Mary and me. He came over, eyes raised translatably for me, as a few days ago I drank at this same table with him and said that Mary and I were "this time really through," and he said then "Nah, you two are never really through. You're a pair: Tom and Jerry, Biff and Bang. You just tell yourselves you're through to make your sex better and your lives more mythic and poetic and to repeatedly renew those first two beatific weeks you went through."

He sat, we shook hands, he kissed Mary's cheek. I introduced him to Lucille and Terry and straightaway he was talking about shares and losses, that platinum was the best investment bet for today and silver the worst but in the long run it was still gold. Lowell was deeply into gold. He bought gold coins and whatever else there was to buy of gold and sold them when the market went up or down or both, I forget which. And I never knew what market he was talking about because he'd said the gold market was controlled by the oil and stock markets, which were influenced by the grain and livestock and cotton markets, which in turn controlled the fish, farmers and flea markets, and so forth. "Buy it," he said of something now, "and you'll double your dough in a month or maybe two. But while your savings are losing, my gold shares are soaring." After about fifteen minutes of his almost nonstop lecture on investments and the interconnection of the world's economy right down to a Berber's dung stove, Mary tugged at my sleeve and looked at the door and I paid up. Lowell stayed behind with the two women. Before I left, Lucille whispered to me "I'm flashing on your cat. He's a whiz."

"I better be getting," Mary said outside. "I don't want to leave Linetta alone too long and there's my job tomorrow."

"I thought we might have an hour in my apartment before you left."

"Drive up with me then. But you can't bring anything except what you have on."

"If I'm staying for a day or two I've got to take my jogging sneakers and work materials along."

"But no shopping bags filled with bagels and food. Linetta and I buy groceries too. Just one bag with everything in it to wear and work with and the only thing for your mouth being your toothbrush."

We drove to my building. I went upstairs, packed a few clothes, work materials and a bread my cousin Harriet had baked for me and I'd frozen and went back to the car. "Could you drive?" she said. "I'm bushed." On the West Side Highway she said "Mind if I sleep?"

"No, sleep, please. Just take it easy, you're tired." I stroked her forehead. She rested her head on my lap, tucked up her legs, rubbed her cheek against my penis through the pants leg. The lights of the bridge woke her up. "I don't know how I could have said I was no longer in love with you that last time we drove in. I want things both ways. Tide's turning again—I swear. Though I still think we need a long separation. Maybe half a year."

"Before you said only a few months."

"Maybe even a year. I need that time to be out on my own and in the marketplace to see what I'm valued at there."

She went back to sleep. Half an hour later I pulled up in back of the house she rented and shook her. "God," she said, "it's like being a kid again and waking up when we arrived after a long drive with my parents and grandma."

There was a note from Linetta: "Peter, Buzzy and a clown named Schnitzer called. Peter said save all day Saturday, Schnitzer said when I told him what Peter said, DISCO FRIDAY NIGHT? He told me to write that in capital letters and his name in a Switzerland accent."

Linetta came downstairs. "I'm hungry, tired and thirsty and I don't feel too well."

"Hi, Linetta," I said.

"Hi. I didn't think I'd see you again."

"Things happened."

"What happened?"

"I'm here."

"Yeah, I can see you're here, but how come?"

"Things happened. And I missed your sweet face."

"Yeah, and if it makes you feel any happier, I missed you too."

"What's bothering you, darling?" Mary said. "Stomach?"

"Oh yeah, I said I was sick. All I need is a glass of milk and something."

I poured her a glass. "Want me to warm it for you?"

"She knows how to warm it," Mary said.

"No, not warm. But I'd like some powdered chocolate in it."

"We don't have any," Mary said.

"You didn't bring any of that Dutch stuff with you this time?" Linetta said to me.

"No, and no bagels."

"Then just toast, please." I made her toast. "Tell me a story?"

"You can't go to bed without stories yet?" Mary said.

"Come on, Mom, I read. But you know I still like stories read to me sometimes."

"Sure, I'll read you one," I said.

"And carry me to my room?"

"What is he, your slave?" Mary said.

"Yes, my slave."

"I'm her slave," I said. I got down, grabbed her around from behind to carry her piggyback.

"Not that way. On your shoulders."

I hoisted her to my shoulders, carried her upstairs. "Watch your head, chickadee," I said as we passed through her doorway.

"Now throw me on the bed, slave." I dropped her on the bed. "I said throw, slave." I picked her up and threw her on the bed. "Now cover me, slave." I covered her. "Now tell me a story, slave."

"You said read."

"Tell. I'm afraid you don't read well, slave."

I told her a story about a cat that its owner tried to get rid of by leaving it in New York and then flying home to California. But the cat walked and ran all the way back across the country. Took several months to make the trip. But it found its way home.

"That's exactly the Lassie story," she said. "Though Lassie was a collie."

"No, Lassie was a cat that only looked like a collie. You see, Lassie was so big and looked so much like a collie that its owner, after many protests from neighbors and city officials about having this big scary cat around, told everyone that Lassie was really a big collie, and then quickly taught Lassie how to growl and defile the streets and slop up its food like one. But someone got wind of the truth and that's why the owner flew with Lassie to New York and abandoned her at the airport there and hopped the next flight back to California. Anyway, when Lassie the cat finally reached its home in California, there was a note left it by the woman which said 'Dear Pussydog. I knew you were too clever and persevering and devoted a cat not to make it back here, so I decided to emigrate to Australia. Tough lucky, baby, and goodbye.'"

"Lousy owner. But at least the story's better."

"But Lassie wasn't upset or even discouraged. She just jumped into the Pacific and swam to Australia."

"That's ridiculous. Cats can't swim that well."

"This one could. Remember, she's Lassie. But actually, she got on a log a couple miles out in the ocean and stayed on it, for food scooping up fish from the sea again like a real cat would, till it reached Australia."

"Where she had a reunion with that former lousy owner."

"No."

"Good. Goodnight. I'm tired."

I kissed her, shut off the light and went into Mary's room. She was in bed.

"Can you do one more small favor for me, please?" she said. "Give me a mini midnight special?"

I started to massage her back. "Anybody able to give you as good a massage or back rub in the last few weeks?"

She shook her head.

"You've asked?"

"No more questions."

"They volunteered?"

"That part of my private life's my own, sweetheart. Please?"

I massaged her neck, feet, arms, each of her fingers, her buttocks and thighs. Then we made love and after that got under the covers.

"It's so warm in here," she said. "But I just can't part with the comforter you gave me."

"I can open the windows."

"Good idea."

I opened the windows. I got back in bed, under the comforter, shut off the ceiling light by pulling down on the string with my big and second toes. Then we made love again and held one another till the alarm woke us the next morning and I shut it off and Mary jumped out of bed.

Parents

I say "What do you say we see my father today?" and she says "Your father?" and I say "Yeah, don't worry, you want to see him?" and she says "Okay by me, where is he?" "Downtown." "Where downtown?" "Just downtown." "You want to lead me blindfolded or like a blind person, that it?" "Just cover your eyes. That'll do."

She covers her eyes with her hands. "I can't see."

"Just keep them shut then."

Takes her hands away but keeps her eyes shut. I don't know if they're completely shut. I remember. I recall. As a boy I used to say I'd keep my eyes shut tight, but opened the little slits very slowly to see things finally blurredly but to see them and no one who asked me to keep them shut seemed to realize I could see when I said my eyes were tightly shut. They'd say "Eyes still shut tight?" and I'd say yes. Then they'd hide something while I watched through opened slits. "Now open your eyes and tell me where it is," or if it had been placed in front of me, "how you like it." I'd pretend to look for it, find it, be surprised.

"Eyes still shut tight?" I say.

"You want to take me there without telling me exactly where, that it?"

I nod.

"That it?"

"You didn't see me nod?"

"Yes, since I can't tell a lie to any small extent. Blindfold me. That's the only way I'll keep the truth."

I tie a hanky around her eyes. "Can't see?" She nods. I swish my hands across her eyes. No wince. She can't see. Or else there's something I found out about her I hadn't till now known. "I know you whisked me," she says, "though I don't know with what."

We leave the apartment. Hand leading hand always two steps in front of her going downstairs. "Maybe you ought to pull up the blindfold for the steps."

"No, I want this to be a real blind person's trip all the way. Lead."

I lead. Outside, my landlord's pulling in the empty garbage cans.

"She burned?" Mrs. Rorng says.

"Blind, though we're not making fun."

"Morning, Mrs. Rorng," Mary says.

"Can't see but she can hear, huh? Cute. Two lovebirds. Two cute kids. Really, two cute lovebird kids." I'm thirty-eight. I don't know how old Mary is but her oldest child's fourteen. "Though I'm glad it's not two indispositions. But it's in the air. Lovebirds and lots of other birds flying all over and sometimes through my hair. Go. Have a find."

Trying to upset Mary's sense of direction, I spin her around several times, then point her toward the park and give her back a push. She walks. "Park's smelling nice," she says.

"Already other senses taking over," I say.

Puts out her hands. "Feels like it's going to snow."

"You can really tell?"

"The cold. The wet. Yes," though middle of June. We go into the subway station. She pulls out a dollar, gets two tokens and change. "You gave her a fiver." "No I didn't. I only had on me one one." Puts the tokens in two turnstile slots and we go through. Downstairs to the downtown trains.

"Maybe for safety sake you should take off the fold or at least push it up a little and open your eyes to seeing slits. Nobody has to know you can see. I'll even try and believe you can't. I'll tell myself she's blind, poor child, can't see, what a shame. Repeatedly till we reach the station and walk up the stairs from the platform my dad always gets off at and walks up from to get to his dental office."

"Just lead." I lead. Hand in hand we stand on the platform waiting for the train. "Snap snap," from a platform bench. Person chewing gum. "Smell the gum?" Mary says. "I can almost taste it. Wrigley's.

Spearmint. Two sticks. Freshly stuck in mouth. Pack recently made and wrapped."

Person reading *Photoplay*. I also read the story in that magazine. "Famous Actress Unwet." No, Unwed. Mother. "Famous actress unwed mother," I tell Mary.

"Who is this unwed famous father?" famous actress says. "Possibly a Hollywood actor? I will tell you who it is. It is none of your business."

"Pity you can't read, Mary. Good article here."

"Newspaper?"

"So you are blind as a bat."

"Bats aren't blind."

"Bats haven't eyes."

"Bats have eyes."

"Bats have eyes?"

"And are insectivorous and the only true mammals capable of true flight."

"Sure you're not mistaking them for batboys? Batons? The ists who toss those ons?"

"My being blind has perhaps given you bats in your belfry, sir. But hold me. I hear something." "I don't, except for your talking." "Long train coming our way on the nearest track." "I see it now too. The local." "Can only be the local at this only local stop." Local stops. We get on. Nearly full car. Reading, standing, sitting, looking the way people usually do in a subway car at a certain hour on a certain train heading in a certain direction from certain areas on a weekday during a regular workday which Mary didn't take today because she called in sick to be with me and which I didn't take as I no gots. Several stops. Nobody seems to really notice her. "Head wound?" someone says. "Joking?" person with him says. But they're speaking about a war photo in a newspaper. We get off. I lead her out of subway and station.

"That's where the old Met used to sing," I say.

"I can hear the conductor conducting, the orchestra orchestrating."

"Across the street: my dad's office."

"How you think he'll react to your going out with a blind girl?"

"People's afflictions never bother him much. He deals with them all day. Bad tooth, he fixes it. Can't: extracts. That's not to say another dentist couldn't fix it, and if he couldn't, would extract, and if he wouldn't, send the patient to another dentist who could, and only as a last resort, to a dental surgeon to extract. But if my father can't fix: extracts. So he deals with people's afflictions all during his working day and at night at home when he talks on the phone to patients with dental problems, such as why their teeth were extracted when it's possible they shouldn't have been or at least not before he took X-rays to see that they positively couldn't be saved. But he makes up for it in the long run I heard his waiting room patients say by making great plates for them they can be proud of, or as proud as people can be of their plates, no matter how great. But here's his building entrance, there's his mailbox. Two-story run-down structure with his office on the top floor. Long steep flight up and then left twenty average-length steps to his door. Somewhere beyond it my short father, round of stomach and head. Soft face, lit-tle hair, legs thin, strong arms and chin, soap-scented hands, pruned nails, greatest pride is in his wrists. Usually of good humor, shined shoes, saggy socks, urine-stained fly and food-tainted tie and shirt smelling from hard work and in a dental smock, which more than likely not has several blood drops on it if in the last week he came up against a patient with a tooth or teeth he couldn't fix, which more than likely not he had."

We start upstairs. Halfway there I say "I forgot his coffee and cake. Usually I bring him a schnecken or Danish and light container of coffee. Not light container, but container of . . . I'm going down-stairs for it. If I don't, he'll send me downstairs for it. It's a dairy cafe-teria, known for its pastries and free seltzer, only a couple of blocks away."

"Isn't that carrying things too far? No? Yes? All right. I'll wait here. In the dark. Sitting on the spitting steps. But no guarantee I'll be here when you get back."

"Soviet."

"So?"

"So take the so out of Soviet and you don't get USA."

"But that's yesterday and today. Tomorrow we don't know. But you're much too apolitical a person to be making attacks and state-ments like that anyway. Viet."

I go to Dubrow's. Same counterman of years ago still works there. Or maybe he's been away for the same number of years, days and hours that I have and only started reworking here a minute ago today. "Hi," I say.

"Hello."

"You don't remember me?"

"Come to think of it, not completely."

"Newton Leeb, Dr. Leeb's boy. He treated you. Gave you first-class dental service at third-class prices and second-class sanitary conditions and pay when you want to, my pal, and advice that you walk downstairs from his office very slowly after he's filled one of your teeth for fear the filling will pop out."

"Now I know."

"So how are your teeth?"

"My teeth are doing fine, thanks, and yours? Come to think of it, nobody ever fixed them like your dad, the old Doc, or at least for as cheap."

"He was a great dentist, right?"

"Wrong. Only so-so. But we had great times up there. All those kibitzers in his office. Bookies, cardsharps, horseplayers, thieves, talkers, con guys, cops on the take, the works. A real place. A real place. You got a number? Forget it. What'll you have?"

"Light container of coffee and schnecken to go. No, container of light coffee and Danish. Sorry again. Container of light coffee and schnecken."

"Just like Doc. Always either schnecken or Danish but coffee light. Years and years when I went to his office I brought him one on the house and also a couple coffees and container of seltzer, because that's what he liked best for his thirst and which we never then sent out. Manager would see me and say 'Two for Doc, both Danish and schnecken both and tell him with my compliments,' just as he always did except for the seltzer as he was a patient of your pop's too."

"That must be when Dad brings home with him a schnecken or Danish wrapped in the wax paper he took his sandwich in that morning that he'd made the previous evening out of leftovers for tomorrow's lunch."

"You mean must have been when, for both your mother and Doc drove or dove over some cliff overseas is what I heard, though it wasn't in the obits themselves."

"I can't tell a lie to even the smallest extent: that's not true."

He gives me the schnecken and coffee in a bag with a look. Everyone knows that look. Maybe babies don't but most adults do. It must be the same look in every language, all societies, round the globe, maybe on other planets also and perhaps even chimpanzees and orangutans and every anthropoid ape give that look too. That hey what's with this guy or ape kind of look.

"So long," I say. His answer: still the look.

Mary waited. Blindfold's off. I say "Maybe it isn't necessary now to go." She walks upstairs. "Blindfold," she says, "I had to use for my nose, eyes and mouth during a sudden sneezing and coughing seizure. Besides, after everything you said about your father, I thought I'd go over better with him if I uncovered my sight." I say "Mary, I said maybe it isn't necessary for us to go see him and his office now." She pats her ears, sticks her fingers in to pop them, says "Me thinks my hearing's gone plop. Lose one, gain another, or vice versa." I follow her. Top, we go the twenty average-length steps. Electrolysis, the office door says. I knock. Same tiny sign under the jamb bell says ring bell and walk in, but the bell never worked and the door's locked.

He's changed. Pencil-thin mustache. Who'd believe it from him? But all for the better I'd say. Grown too. Lost weight. Nose job and new shoes. But same white smock, no blood, no extractions this week or just put a clean one on. Lots of hair now too: wavy black combed straight back. Woman in the waiting room reading a recent issue of a woman's magazine. Must be hers because he never had anything before but dental journals and religious tracts religious people dropped off. He says "Yes?" and examines my face, Mary's face. I hand him the bag and he says "I didn't order anything," and I say "I thought I'd bring you something nevertheless." He opens the bag. Little to the right is the alcove where he eats and phones and a couple of his bookie friends phone and diplomas and pictures of his parents and wife on the desk and walls but no radio now or it's off with its tinny sounds of semiclassical music and news. Treatment room facing it with his dental chair and revolving bracket table and foot pedal drill and foot pedal sink I liked to play with with my feet or on my knees with my hands and which was always in need of a washer and so always ran.

Mary elbows me. I say to him "I want you to meet." She sticks out her hand. They shake. Also kisses his cheek. "Well now," he says, "nice to meet you." Then a stern look at me when I'm looking at him and Mary's looking around the room. Later at home he'll say "Is she not of our faith?" I'll say "No, Father, she's not." He won't say that in those words and neither will I. He'll say "Don't be a schnook. Only go out with girls who are rich and Jewish." He'll say that. He's said that. I've brought girls here before. He'll say "Beautiful girls also come rich and Jewish." He'll say "I know lots of beautiful rich Jewish girls who'd love to meet you. Their mothers tell me. Their fathers too. What do you think I've so many photos on my waiting room walls for, all showing my girl and boys at their very best. You're a good catch.

Handsome, tall, nicely built, college educated, bright, you got brains—you should begin realizing all that. And you wear clothes well, so you ought to dress better. I'll buy you a two-pants suit. It'll be a good investment for me. How much you need? Actually you should work for it yourself just like I always did and you used to even when you were a kid. But I'll find you a nice beautiful rich girl who's Jewish. What's the difference if she's rich? Somebody's got to marry them and you can't imagine the idiots who do. Follow my advice and you'll never have to work another day in your life, or at least not hard." Tool still in his hand.

"Doctor." Masculine voice from the treatment room. "Will you come on? I'm in a rush."

"Just a second," he says. Later he'll say "Open . . . open . . . open . . . little wider . . . wider. That's good, stay." Has hair now. Once bald and gray. Must have been all that massaging my mother said she started doing to his head on their honeymoon night to save what little hair was left. He closes the bag. "Thanks very much but I had my snack," and hands me the bag.

"I don't want it." I give it to Mary.

"Don't want it either," and she gives it to him.

"Now if you'll please excuse me," he says, "but I'm kind of tied up today."

"See you later, Dad," I say and we go. Mary waves. Door shuts. Locks. "Who was those two?" woman in the waiting room says.

"Think I know, Ma? Crazy. Crazies."

"I don't know," I say to Mary. "He never kicked me out like that before. He always enjoyed having me around no matter how many kibitzers and waiting patients were there. Only with prostitutes. He drew the line. With others he'd say 'Sit, Newt, stick around, stay.' And when I worked in the garment center at various belt firms and dress houses, all jobs he got for me throughout high school, he always had me stopping by after I finished work, hanging around for him to finish up and close. It wasn't a good waiting room to read and do homework. Lots of dust. Peeling paint. Bad light. He loved company though. About to go—lights off—I'm starving—in would come some guy and say 'Take out this tooth, Doc, right now, it's bothering me, but don't freeze me up as I got to chew food tonight.' Tooth out without Novocain, he'd recommend a teabag on the root holes for the tannic acid in it if the lesion starts bleeding, and if it continues, ring him at home. And in'd walk another patient, crony, his passerbying sister with stuffed cabbage gifts and asking financial advice, fidgety bereft junkie nephew wanting to be fitted for plates then and there on the cuff. And I'd be waiting, waiting, wanting to get home, hungry, but knowing dinner never began without him. And then the subway ride home with him with his stacks of ratty rubberband-wrapped filled manila envelopes with their mixed medley inside. Newspapers and clippings from them pulled out of trash baskets along both ways. Individual toilet tissues for his saliva and nose removed in clumps from men's room dispensers and which only he also used for his behind at home. Samples, dental tools, upper and lower molds, prosthodontic parts—"

"Hey? C'est enough now, nu? And what about your meeting my folks? We're right by the bus terminal. They live an hour and a half away upstate. Express bus. Seven bucks. One stop. We can be there in at the most five minutes after two and a half hours from now, as the bus leaves once an hour on the same minute after the hour sixteen straight times a day and their home's only a five-minute trot from their bus terminal."

We go to Port Authority down the block. Bus tickets. Get on it. Goes, arrives. Her father admiring the hundred different kinds of daffodils and jonquils he planted last year for his wife when he sees us jogging up and says "My, what a surprise." Her mother sitting behind the porch window waving at Mary, face thinner than in her pictures, afghan covering her lap. Dinner that night à l'americaine: measured out shot of whiskey and soda and corn bread baked in iron molds and mutton gumbo and napkin rings and real whipped cream and Jell-O. White-haired couple. Loquacious gentleman, sedate lady. Father invents. Mother composes. He dominates the conversations and has to be quieted by his wife. She dexterously steers the talk to great authors and books and the family silver Mary and then Linetta will inherit and cupboard of Limoges. Charades later. Then Mother plays the piano for us while we have postprandial cheese and cognacs. Delicate soft-pedally pieces of hers on the high keys reminding me of Ravel and fields of breezy flowers and Mary cycling to the store for powdered doughnuts Sunday mornings and clouds and Debussy. I applaud and say bravo and her husband Nicholas says "That was very very lovely, my dear." Later some discreet whispering from the cleanup kitchen and Mary confesses her father thinks I'm intelligent though partial to the wrong party and not born to the right religion for his darling girl and her mother thinks I'm whimsical and adores looking at my smile and strong neck and back. I love them immediately and they seem to like me. Love them partially because Mary looks and except for her breasts is built like her and acts with the alacrity and peppiness of her father and just because they are her parents and because Mary tells them she loves me.

Her mother's sick with a killing illness, has to retire early but first breathe on her nightly breathing machine. Just before she's walked upstairs she takes my hand, brings me close to her ear as if to say goodnight but only to whisper "I want you to leave here convinced of at least one thing. I love my husband and grandchildren but Mary means more to me than my own life. Take good care of her," and I hug her and kiss her cheek and say "Me too, Louise, me too, and I'll take as good a care of her for as long as she needs and wants me to, I swear."

Mary and I walk through her hometown. Ancient history all around. Rebuilt fort. Colonial church. Huguenot patentees. Apple tree Nicholas proposed to Louise under. Their original stone home the town dispossessed them from to include in a historical street to draw tourists. Cellar where Mary's ancestors escaped from the Indians. "One didn't and that's why I've this thick black braid and raven eyes and no hair on the soles of my feet."

When we get back the downstairs bed is ready to be slept in: coverlet turned down, pillows plumped up, kerosene lamp wick ready to be lit. "Think they mind my sleeping here much?"

"They mind. I asked. But since the last bus back to the city has already left and they don't see how anyone can afford the local motels and they want me to stay put another day with or without my kiddies and couldn't give up one of their own beds upstairs, it's okay."

We undress, wash, light the lamp, Mary unbraids and brushes and gets in bed.

"In this bed my father and I were conceived. Not everyone's so sure about my grandmother, though my father says she was, but she told me her father and grandfather definitely started here too."

"I feel ghosts in the room. Some presence or force."

"You do? This place used to be their storehouse. Could be they've come in from the old stone house down the street to be with their relatives and bed and quilt. Blow out the lamp. Maybe they'll really come alive. I've questions to ask them, patches of family history that could be cleared up. And maybe, if they're privy to it or know anyone there who is, if they see any extensive future for us."

Lamp out. We're quiet. And hear nothing. I touch her. "I've never done it in this house," she says. "Even with Myles all those times we were here legal or not."

"Will it be all right?"

"It'll be different."
"Still, let's try."
"Though no noise."
"I won't."
We don't.
Outside: crickets and cicadas or katydids.
Early morning: birds, birds, birds.

Man

of

Letters

Em—

I don't want to see you anymore. There's a lot else that can be said about this decision of mine, but I don't want to go into it. So that's it then. Don't come by. And I won't be coming up there again. Much love, Newt

Em—

I think we need a nice long rest from each other. You're aware yourself that things haven't been going well with us for a while. Thing that most elicited my decision was that I just didn't like the way you set the relationship for us. The "week" together this summer. On a "beach." Perhaps you have to act like this. What you are, want to become, your history. But it's now too much for me. I won't be coming up. I don't want you coming by. I want no communication between us of any kind. I can't say "Maybe some other time perhaps." I just don't feel like that. I'm sorry. Love, Newt

Dear Em:

I won't be coming to Stonehill anymore. I don't want you to come to my flat again. I just don't want to go on with our relationship anymore. It's not going to change: the relationship or my decision. At least it doesn't seem so to me. Most of all, I'm tired of you setting our pace. That "week" in the summer. On a "beach." It's usually your way. It's a shame you can't just let things happen between us without always analyzing it, trying to control it, putting me to tests, being worried that everything will pass you by and too many things will never be tried out by you if you stay only with one mate.

I do think about you sweetly. Fooling around. Holding you close. Talking. All that. But the other disturbing things that have happened between us, if they're not already embedded in my head, just don't creep in anymore, they rush.

I don't feel responsible for this break. For a little, all right. But it does seem it has to go the way you want it, without any give and take, and I find I can't exist in an atmosphere like that. Especially when it's coupled with your repeatedly turning me on and off and I think your serious remarks about how you look forward to the day when you'll be able to manage two and maybe three successful love affairs at one time, so I just don't want to see you anymore.

I don't say that what you're proposing for yourself is impossible or wrong. Maybe I am "rigid," "superannuated," as you said—whatever, but it just isn't my way. And I do love you very much, but for the first time in my life that doesn't seem to be enough to make me want to stay. So, cheers then—En

Dear Mary—

I won't be coming to Stonehill anymore. I don't want you to come by my place. I just don't want to go on with our relationship anymore. I'm tired of you always setting the pace. The "week" this summer. On a "beach." And I don't think it's because I'm "indecisive" or don't like to make "any decision" that this is the case. You take over because you want to, have to, whatever's the force. If you tell me once more it's partly astrological, I'll have to yell at you again "That's asinine."

I went along like a "dud" because I don't like to direct a relationship based on love. It's a pity you can't let it happen without dashing it to dust every time it goes well. We've gone on for hours about the reasons for all that: the history. But to me there really aren't any explanations.

I also can't get the bad things out of my head. I think about you sweetly. Fooling around. Joking. Holding you close. Talking. Walking. Working. All that. But the other disturbing things just don't creep in, they rush. And a lot else about what's happened between us just hasn't been etched out of my head yet. Your turning me on and off. Blowing me up. Indifferently letting me go. Separating "for the time being" because you thought it was the "wrong time for us" or it was just "bad timing when we met" and soon after that your returning and for a while staying and being open and loving and then re-going when you thought it was the wrong time for us again or just thought that for yourself it was best. I always felt when you returned "Well that's the last time for that, folks," but it never was. Now I think "How in hell could I have thought any of those times after the first few times could have been the last time?" And after the last last time I suppose I was just holding on. Like a kite. No, a kite doesn't hold on, it's held, and I was held, though not tight like a kite. Oh, I was held tight like a kite sometimes, but we're talking about my holding, not being held. Maybe the kite holds on to a tree. But you're no tree, though you do have roots. But so do turnips, teeth and attributes that lead to actions and decisions, but as you can see I'm the worst at analogues, metaphors and similes. Yes, you can so be a tree. But no, I wasn't a kite that way except maybe in my becoming entangled in you and not being able to fly freely or sail away or something because of the string. But a kite becomes entangled around something, not in it, except if it maybe got blown into a window or cave. But even there it would probably only get entangled around a table or chair in the window or a rock in the cave, and not entangled around the window or cave it got blown in. Anyway, now I'm letting go.

I don't feel responsible for causing this break. Or, maybe a little. But I'm not going to rationalize it away by saying, as you hinted the last time we drove in, that what we both probably have wanted for the last few weeks is for the relationship to quietly and unemotionally end. Maybe that's the way you want it, but I really don't care. I don't care anymore what you want or what you'll do. Honestly, I'm saying that what we had eventually went the way you wanted it, without any compromising on your part or give and take, and I couldn't tolerate it, so I just don't want to see you anymore.

I still love you, but for the first time in my life the existence or reality or whatever it could be called concerning this love for you just doesn't seem to be enough to make me want to stay. I'm sorry. I hate writing letters like this, like less to get them, but there's no other way I see to express what I must say, short of calling you, and I don't have a phone, it's a trudge through slush and snowdrifts to reach a booth, and you know I'm even more uncommunicative, befuddling and in the end agonizingly battological when I try speaking on one. So, best ever then—Newt

Dear Em—

I won't be coming to Stonehill anymore. I don't want you coming by my place. Simple as I can say it: I don't want to go on with our relationship anymore. It's not going to change. The relationship won't.

You talked a lot about "growth," both as individuals and as a couple. But we didn't grow together after the first few months, only repeated the same mistakes and agonies endlessly rather than understanding and correcting them and moving on.

I'm also tired of you always setting the pace, the distance, how high we could climb. That "week" in the summer. On a "beach." Why didn't you also suggest what color bathing suit I could bring along and how many hours in the sun I'd be allowed a day? It's usually been your way, do you agree? I went along like that because I don't like to direct a relationship of any kind—love, business, professional, familial, matrimonial, you name it: none. It's a pity you couldn't have let things sail freely without always dashing and mashing them against rocks every time it went well.

You said you were afraid of getting trapped. Well maybe the reverse is the trap. The trap could be what you think it's not. Maybe. In other words, the trap might not be the one you think you'll get in with me, but the one you go to to avoid getting in a trap with me, which then wouldn't make it a trap. Wouldn't make the anticipated trap with me a trap. The trap would be the trap you divert to to avoid that anticipated trap. No, the trap is trying to establish here what is and isn't a trap.

We've gone on for hours and ruined too many weekends discussing and discovering the reasons for our inability to sustain a preponderatingly smooth relationship—our histories and also the irreconcilabilities built into any more than casual comings together of two people: professional, familial, amorous, etc. (see above). But to me, either a couple make it or they don't. Deep endearing feelings and mutual respect keep them together, and the theories and therapies and the rest of it regarding love are at the most temporarily satisfying but usually stultifying and ultimately desolating and worthless. Even here, the more I think of it, the more I'm giving some theory about it, and the more doltish I am but bombastic I sound and perplexed I get. The hell with it.

I also can't get the bad things out of my head. I think about you sweetly most times. Fooling around. Holding you close. Working. Walking. Talking. Laughing. Jogging. Hogging. Joking. Just dancing to some dumb radio tune together or silently reading different books on the same couch or challenging those boys to a two-on-two basketball game or chasing away those oafs that day who didn't know there were two of us who could bite and bodychop with the best of them to protect old winos and not one. All that. But the other disturbing things just don't creep in, they rush. A lot else about what's happened between us just hasn't been carved out of my head yet. Turning me on and off. Blowing me up. Flying me like a kite or balloon. Popping me when need be or letting me hang or cutting the string whenever you wanted to and letting me go. I always thought "Em won't do that again." I was always so hopeful. Optimistic. See the bright flashing lights in his naive eyes. After that last time—your last break—I suppose I was just holding on. What in the world was your need for always wanting to come back to me after you broke us up "for the benefits of us both" and after I'd finally felt "Good, I found I can live without her again. Took me four days which is a day more than the last three times but two days less than the first, so maybe in my twenty years of developed sexuality or so I've actually grown some." Now I'm letting go. Nothing much to hold on to anyway, so it isn't hard, and I don't mean to sound tough.

I also don't feel that responsible for any of this. Not at all responsible. And I'm not going to rationalize my decision to disband by saying, as you suggested, or more accurately, kidded around about as we drove in last time (and to pinpoint the spot: on the big bridge at the bistate halfway marker which you only then discovered and pointed out after having passed it a few hundred times and my having remarked about the marker to you at least twice), that a quiet uncomplicated indestructible separation is what we've both probably been wanting for the last month. I'm saying that what we had eventually went the way you wanted it, not me, and without any give, take or faint nod toward compromise on your part, and I couldn't tolerate it, though for a while deluded myself that I could because one great day your attitude would change to me and us and my acceptance and sufferance would have been worth it. But now when I think about it I can't stand it and can barely tolerate myself for being such a shortsighted simp and slave.

So I just don't want to see you again—it's important that's clear. I love you very much, that's too damn true, and still do, I'm saying that, no matter how foolish or even gain-making that must now sound, but for the first time in my life the existence or fact of my love just doesn't seem to be enough to make me want to stay. Isn't enough—absolutely—so that's it, I'm afraid. Love, Newt

Dear Emmy—

I won't be coming to Stonehill anymore. I don't want you to come by my place again. I just don't want to go on with our relationship anymore. I'm weary of you always setting the pace. How high we should climb, far we can go. Let's sprint, rest, fall back, on our face, scrape our knees, break our ankles, spurt, zip, lunch, get lost, make it a marathon, two marathons, three. That "week" this coming summer. On a "beach." And "always" is an emotional word you said and I said "It's just a much abused one," but you know what I mean. I went along as I did because I don't like directing a relationship of any kind, personal or professional. What a waste you couldn't let whatever it was between us happen without your customary dashing it to dust every time it went well.

You said you're afraid of getting trapped. But maybe the reverse is the trap. Maybe the trap's what you're moving to now. We've gone on for weekends about this—our histories. That I met you after not being close to a woman for years. That you met me a few months after you left the man you were close to for years. "That the cross-purposes and inconciliabilities of our aims, outlooks and maybe our natures are monumental." I said "What do you mean?" You said "The most ignorant men are those who feign ignorance." I said "What do you mean?" You said "The most ignorant men are those who continue to feign ignorance." I said "What about women?" You said "The most ignorant of the most ignorant men are those who continue to feign the same ignorance that classified them among the most ignorant of men." I said "What do you mean?" You said. I said. You said that being tied down to one man over a period of sixteen years was enough and that instead of pinning into a second you wanted a rest. I said "I won't keep you back or hold you down." You said "Right now just seeing only one man is keeping me back and down." I said. You said "Truthful as the pain must be to you, I want to explore other relationships, lifestyles and professions." I said "I suppose I really couldn't tolerate seeing you if you were at the same time seriously seeing other men or casually allowing them to slip it in." You said "If that arrangement doesn't suit you, Newt, then maybe after a few years, if either of us is still available, which sounds impossible, we can try as a single couple again." I said "That would probably be impossible." You said "We revolve undolved without resolve." I said "What do you mean, what do you mean?" You said "From paddle to pedal to piddle to podel to puddle again." I said "Don't I know. But why'd you always, unpsychotherapized always, come back to me after all those times you told me to go or you picked up and went, and never after more than five or six days?" "You mean I never came back to you after more than five or six days?" "Yes," I said. "Five," you said and I think I said "I think the maximum was six."

Though I do think of you sweetly most times. Holding you close. Joking, jogging, nuding and screwing around. Sleeping, seeping, eyes uttering, nares stuttering, walking, talking, doing ludicrous things. Precious and energetic and hilarious and creative things. Holding you close. Just playing those boys two-on-two basketball that playground day. Fending off that pack of oafs in front of Oscar's with our hoofs, cuffs and butts when our wits didn't work. Quipping, unzipping, being comfortable and rumpled while silently reading side by side on your settee. Holding you close. Nuzzling. Puzzling. All of those. More of these. Unstrapping, while lips lapping— But the other disturbing things that happened just don't flip in, they flush. A lot else just hasn't been excised out of my head yet. Those four to five times you dropped the relationship cold. Wanted to go back to Myles. "Go if you got to go I sometimes say another way about something else," I said, but when he wouldn't do the bee's dance for you you devised some other plan. "Cancel your plane reservation overseas with me as I want to go alone. Timing, poor rhyming, but we're just never going to materialize, Newt." Your loving letters, each one better, till the last one when you said "When you come to the airport for me could you only come to return my keys and cars?" Then after an exhilarating night and day at the terminal and home you gave me the boot again and three days later got into my building somehow and through my peephole said would I be dumb and daft enough to have you back? "Of course— I'll open the door." Well enough, I'm tired of being turned on and off. Hot water today?—okay. Tepid?—you bet. What's that: boiling, hyperborean?—no sweat. Of being your straw man, tin man, wrong man, enough. Blowing me up. Letting me fly. Like a balloon or kite: piping goodbye as you cut me loose. You: "Howdy-do again, you undrownable goose." Each time my feeling that time's the last. Emotional always so hopeful I was—my eternally gyring eyes, or what you twice called "The naively cherished long overromantic view." Well now I'm letting go. Hip, hip, and nothing much to hold on to anyway, so it's not that hard. And I don't mean to be mean with these remarks, and why couldn't I ever resist your returns long enough till I had become fully unglued?

I don't feel responsible for any of this. Maybe a little. And I'm not going to rationalize my decision away by saying as you hinted when we drove in last time that if we both had the courage to say it, a complete break is what we've been wanting for the past two months. You did, I didn't, and now I don't care what you want or do. I'm saying that what we had eventually went the way you wanted it, with little give or take, and I couldn't tolerate it, though for a while blinded myself that I could—deluded myself was what I was thinking of now and wrote in the previous letter to you that I'm typing this from—and now when I think about it I can't stand it. Can't stand the thought of it all. I don't want to see you again. Don't want you ever to come by here again. If you do—so much as ring my vestibule bell or let yourself in some way and come up and rattle your baby tap on my door—I'll drag you downstairs by the hair and throw you into the street. I will. So don't!

I love you very much, which has to sound ridiculous and suspicious and quite peculiar after all I said above, but for the first time in my life the existence or whatever it is of this love for someone just doesn't seem to be enough to make me want to stay. Isn't enough. So that's it then: never again, and there'll be no other word more. Newt

Dear Em:

I've tried writing you about something that's sitting very heavy on my mind. A series of letters so far. They're all in front of me, one on top of the other, till the last long one I just finished and am looking at now. Nothing useful, sensible or insightful came out of any of them, and at their very best they were a lot of drivel, bad gags and rhythmic rot. Even this one, I can see, still trying to rhyme and alliterate to impress instead of saying simply what I want to express, though no matter how wretched it is I'm going to send it off. What I intended saying in each of the previous letters today was that I don't want to see you anymore. I still feel that way. It just isn't going to work. We aren't. So please don't come by, I won't be busing up, and there'll be no further communication between us of any kind from now on. Very best and my love, Newt

Dear Em—

There's only one thing I want to say here. I won't be busing up, I don't want you coming by, and we won't be seeing each other again. So that's it. There'll be no other communications, explanations, letters, calls, nothing else between us from now on. Thanks for understanding that and much love, Newt

Dear Em—

I've decided we shouldn't see one another anymore and that there'll also be no explanations or communications about it either. Love, Newt

Dear Mary—

No more, and no explanations either. Thanks. Newt

Dear Em—

No more and no explanations. Newt

Dear Em—

No more and no explanations. En

Dear Em—

No more.

Em: No more. En

Em: no more

Dear Mary—

This weekend, instead of my busing up, why don't you drive in and stay here? I think we've some things to discuss, and just for a change let's spend an entire weekend in the city. The snow's supposed to be gone and the sky clear and weather relatively mild.

I wanted to write you about what's been on my mind lately concerning our relationship, but decided against even trying to put it down in words, as I thought it best to just talk things out. We always did that pretty well and I'm sure that this problem too will be resolved. If you can't come in, could you call Harriet? I'll be dropping by her place Thursday night and will get your message and then take the bus up Friday afternoon—probably the 4:55, as that one skips several towns and takes the upper route rather than the river and is less crowded, and as long as I have the choice I prefer shorter more comfortable trips and climbing down to crawling up. If you do come in I've already selected the perfect restaurant for our undutch dinner Friday night and "beeg talk." We haven't had dinner alone together in a quiet good place for a long time and that was always a nice experience for us and lots of fun. As a dining celebration excuse we'll make it your teaching snow day this week, all right by you?

So, if I don't hear from you I'll know you'll be driving in. If for any reason you want to phone me, tell Harriet. Otherwise: my love, drive carefully, have a pleasant end of week and no matter what I'll be seeing you Friday night. Newt

The
Franklin
Stove

—➤

My story's burning. As I write this. Just a short manuscript. I looked at the first page of this first draft of a story and thought no, this will only be another one I'll keep in a box by my typewriter for about a year and look at from time to time but never rewrite and later stick in my file cabinet with about a hundred more. I always thought I'd take one out of the box or cabinet one day and get an idea for it and rewrite it or just sit down without any idea of even rereading it and finish it and it would turn out to be a story I like and maybe as good as any I've written. This one might have. It's still burning. I threw it in the stove only a few seconds before I started writing this.

A certain amount of time's elapsed. About two minutes since I threw the story in the stove and fifteen minutes since I came into this studio after breakfast, did fifty push-ups to immediately get warm and started the stove to stay warm while I wrote. But about a minute ago I opened the door on the Franklin stove to retrieve my story, with the idea of blowing or stamping out the fire, rewriting the burnt parts from memory if I could and putting the story in the box with the other first drafts I might one day rewrite. But too late. Already burnt. Too far back in the stove to poke up front and save even a page of. Mostly ashes. Now while I watch it burn it becomes all ashes. Black clouds. Lit city. Burning city. Burnt unlit city on a starlit night. Stars gone. Sky demooned. Black alligators crawling out of swamp mud on an eclipsed starlightless night. And now I'm miffed at myself for burning it. I always wanted to destroy at least one story. I've spoken to writers who've burnt the only draft of a novel or sheaf of poems and they said it freed them somehow. This one didn't me. My file cabinet's in the city. So I should have, for lack of a much older story, combed through the box for the story I liked least instead of grabbing the last story I put on top. And now I forget what page one and the rest of it's about if I'm to rewrite it and possibly get a better story than the one I burnt—a finished story, one to send around. A story that would dash my dumps and lift my spirits a bit and maybe even make me ecstatic as some of my finished stories have and in fact could only have been written because I burnt the previous piece.

So what happened in that burnt story? I don't write from notes. I go right into a story once I begin it, finishing the first draft in a single stint. But I can't think of anything but the first word of the story: The. But so many of them have started off with that. The what? The boy? Man? The lit city burns? The black ashes disintegrate? The story's gone? The Franklin story burnt my stove? The quick Franklin stove jumped over the foxless story? I slam the stove door shut. I throw my typewriter through the window in a crazed state of dejectedness. Of course I don't. Too cold to break windows and I'm still typing on this. And what would I say to the director of this colony? "I tripped rearwards through the window while excitedly typing the final line of a new draft"? "Were you hurt?" he'd ask, scanning me worriedly, "or any damage to your work?" Always so much forgiveness and bigness and forbearance to the artist here, which I think is overgenerous humaneness to the humanities and possibly even pity for its practitioners and can't take. "Stand on your own twos," I like to urge myself. "Tell the truth." So I'd explain "It was really a chipmunk who jumped through the window to get at the sandwich on my desk. I'd opened my lunchpail three hours before noon. Most mornings I finish off my two sandwiches by the time I get to the studio. And he didn't see the pane. Chipmunks are notoriously jumpy and strabismic and walleyed. To make amends I'll take care of his medical bills if he isn't covered and see that his winter granaries are filled if he has to be hospitalized for a long time." But start the story. Forgot the line and plot, show you're a pro and think up new ones. A story, to really make up for the destroyed one, that would have in it the burning and writer's reasons why and subsequent regret and dejection and then that he couldn't recall any of the story line. I can title it "The Burning Story" or just "The" for the only word I can remember in its right place in the destroyed story and also as a sort of testimonial to that article or adverb that's begun so many of my stories and titles. I'll even put in the chipmunk jumping through the window and possibly getting hospitalized. The ashes, images of singed cities, dawdling alligators, starlit eclipsed nights. But start it before you get too tired typing what you plan to put in. There was a story. (This is the story.) Rather: My story's burning. And the title before you forget it.

The

The story's burning. It's in the Franklin stove. It was in a box. The box is on my desk. I'm sitting at the desk next to the stove. I'm at an artists' colony. In a studio in the woods. Woods on the colony's grounds. Grounds in upper New York State, etcetera: America, Earth, Universe, and I came to this studio from the main building they call the Mansion where I had breakfast at eight. Time now is nine. It's actually ten after, but nine rhymes with time. So I must have sat at the desk a few minutes after I lit the stove, read the first pages of the top story in the box and remembered it was about a man who returns to his native city and rings the doorbell of his parents' flat whom he hasn't seen in ten years—his parents, their flat too. Maybe even their dog. No dog. Too many dogs in the city as it is.

But the story's coming back. In the original he rings the downstairs bell to their apartment. A voice says "Yes?" and he says his name over the intercom to his mother whom he hasn't seen, spoken or written to in twenty years.

"Hank who? I don't know any Hank." He says "Maybe you won't know me, and sorry for the surprise. I'm your boy from way back. Hank B. Stritin, or Stritinitinvitivitivitch before it was changed." She says "Henry? Oh my God," and there's this mad scramble—no, mad scramble came when she ran downstairs—a noise, like a lamp crashing, something breakable breaking—and he says "Mom, you okay?"

Footsteps. Hers? Or his dad's. One of them scrambling downstairs. Then through the vestibule door he sees her rounding the second flight—girdle, open housedress flowing, slippers slipping loose and preceding her downstairs. She trips on the last step, jumps up and opens the door and hugs him and bawls, head wedged under his chin, body growing limp, arms sliding off. He drops his knapsack and holds her, afraid she'll fall.

"Dad's dead, you know," she says. "We couldn't reach you. How could we? We started thinking you were maybe dead ten years ago and five years ago gave you up either way for hopelessly lost. What you put us through. If you ever came back, your father said to tell you to go hang."

"I'm sorry." Walking up with her he sees himself thirty or so years ago bounding up and down these stairs. Walloping the walls. Stick, bat or pencilcase slapping the balustrades. Singing. Whistling. Such a happy kid with his Indian whoops and war cries. "Hey, shorty," a neighbor would shout, "you got a real sweet voice but someone in here can't stand canaries and also works the night shift."

Resting on the next landing because she's breathing uneasily, he asks after his sis. "Doing great. Two adorable babies, both twins. Fine intelligent provider of a husband, and resourceful to boot. Flusho-meter breaks, he climbs right in the toilet bowl. Car falls apart, he ends up a greaseface. Kids that bright and filthy too. Three-year-old one's my sweetheart. Naturally they're both three, but the second's not so keen on me and in fact beats a retreat each time she sees me and prefers her other grandma. She's Peony, my lovey's Penny. I'm always getting their names and looks mixed up, which can lead to loud screamfests when you rush up and try cuddling a girl who hates your guts. I've tried to get Ida to have one of the twins grow a mus-tache so I won't make those mistakes, but your sister can blow stacks too. But how are you? You look like I feel. Bald also, but you were fast losing that straw when we last saw you, which was how long ago? Seems like 1919. Remember? 'Folks, I'm driving my honey across country and will be back in a month.' You dropped us a card from Wyoming. 'Having a ball,' you said. Then another from Wyoming, sent the next day but arrived the same. First card a close-up of a mon-key on a bronco horse. Second of the same rodeo scene taken from far off so we could also see the crowded bleachers, and the message 'Still having a ball.' I remember your father saying 'Got a good mem-ory, your son. Remembers what message he wrote the day before and also his address.' I still have them. Magnets hold those cards to the inside of the kitchen cabinet above the phone. Same black and white Scotties you used to get mesmerized with endlessly as a boy. They made them toys well then. In a Fabulous Forties antique store down the street they sell that pair for twelve dollars, so when things really get sticky for me economically those'll be the first of my holdings to go."

They go in the apartment. No new furniture and all in the same spots. Bedroom, living room, bathroom and that's it except for a walk-in closet and Pullman kitchenette. Folks slept on the convertible for twenty years behind a Chinese screen. View through caged windows now of caged rear windows of other brownstones and ailanthus trees covered by tent caterpillar canopies. He sits.

"Sleepy? I'll make you coffee. . . . Then soothing spiked tea." Can't drink. Too tired. She makes up a bed for him in the bedroom. Ida and he slept in these twin beds. Then Ida got too woolly and bumpy to undress in front of him, so he had to cover his eyes and turn over or sleep in the walk-in closet. When he still couldn't stop peeking, she moved in with an aunt. His mother comes in.

"Just give me a brief rundown on what's gone on with you for the past two centuries and I'll never busybody you about it again."

"Married, assaulted and battered, jailed and unmarried, drafted, wounded and deserted in war, worked on a number of assembly lines and produced two more marriages and boys. Then started writing at night to pay alimonies and child supports, and so impressive were the number of stories and novels I sold that I got loads of selling jobs in department stores, working myself up to phone orders and 'Hello, Little Kids Shop, Nom de Magasin speaking.' But seems I lost my memory somewhere along there. Because of reading books, I always wanted to grow up a siblingless orphan. Or to be a foundling left on a rector's step or a tot gobbled up by the woods and raised by wolves. Childhood fantasy finally fulfilled in middle age when I walked into the woods, stuck a rattle in my mouth and went waa waa till wolves devoured me. No I did. Cannot tell a fib. After you and Pop it was skunks who brung me up, Ma. I don't know why I never contacted you. Thought I had. Once from Wyoming. Then another time from Wyoming. Both picture posts but I thought better than no photos at all. Plain unvarnished truth is that the first day I reached the West Coast I fell asleep for twenty years. Woke up last week and asked who I am and how come I have such a long beard? So I shaved and bathed, mooched enough loot to bus and subway to the address on my old draft card and here I am, wit as a riddle and right as a slum. Forgiven?"

She tucked him in. He had a bad dream. Something about a beard strangling him to death. What happened next? Forget. Should have read the story through before chucking it in the stove. But something about a Henry, a Hank. Goes home. Long time no see mom. Girdled and housedressed, she falls down the stairs and lets him in. Plate-glass door breaks. Nah. She's stoned. Nope. He's. Nuh. Holds and hugs her as she cries "Dad died. We tried to reach you. I had to take care of him alone the last five years. Bet you had lots of fun though."

Walk upstairs. She mumbles. He says "You've addled since I last saw you." She says "And you look younger. Living the soft life I guess. Off women and their brats I bet. You were always no good. That's what Dad used to say and at first I objected, saying 'Hank's okay. Not the refined English frog by any means, but don't make him worse with your blames and insults.' Later I had to agree. Bike thieving. Car stealing. Pickpocketing relief people and batting old hags to the ground for their handbags. And no grades in school and relieving yourself in church hallways and Jewish shuls and all the teachers and shopkeepers and girls' parents phoning us about how you tried pinning their Mary Ellens and Sues to jump and hump on and force to screw. Lucky for them they combed your eyeballs with their fingernails and kicked in your nuts. One didn't. Couldn't reach. Tinier than I am, that's why. Overpowered her, ya bastard, though without your father's good looks and charm. One time. Boom. More harm than an A-bomb. Marion Broombie, remember her? Son old as you were when you left."

"What's he called?"

"Henry. Big slap at you. Only other breathing creature named your name by people who knew or heard of you since you were three are their pet spiders and Venus's-flytraps. I can't stand the boy. Comes over here only to sponge off or torment me. Inherited your mean sneers and grubby ears. Told me if he ever sees you he'll kick the shit out of you for what you done to his mother and for the raw deal you did with him with your genes. Which reminds me. Know what your father's last words about you were? 'That stinking kid. You ever see him again, Kay, spit in both his eyes for me for all the crosses he caused us, you swear?' I told him 'You know I never swear, Hal,' and he said 'Then vow,' which I did."

Spits in his eye. "Thought it'd be bad luck and irreverent if I didn't. Now I got the other to do."

"Let me snooze first. I'm pooped."

Goes in his old room. Twin beds. One his sister slept in, other his. Used to watch her undress when she didn't know it, powder her puff and check her own breast rise. Knockout, his sis. Tried jumping her in her dreams once when her covers were off and sleepshirt wasn't working, but she screamed for the folks and his father beat his back bloody with a strap while his mother held him down. "That'll teach you," his father said, "or at least with her." Didn't. She got married soon after anyway and was in a plane crash coming home from her honeymoon. End of Ida. Now he's the only child. His mother comes in. Hot tea for both of them reeking of rum.

"How'd Dad die?"

"Young age. Everything functioning past perfection. Blood vessels so clear you could send salt shakers through. He died. What do you want to hear? That you weren't around to help out those last years? Even your rotten son came to the funeral. He, me, your Uncle Ted and two of your father's business cronies, Crazy Louie and Manny the Bum. At the cemetery it was only Henry the Second and I. Other three the limousine had to drop off for the eighth race at the Big A or they'd die. Your son. For one week he was a dreamboat, can't deny. Did all my shopping and talked to me till way late. Then my week's grace was up and he said 'Mourning period's over, Grandma,' and emptied my changepurse and fruitbowl and left. Last time I saw him was a month ago. Stopped by with his new young chippie. Cheap. Bleached. Bracelets up to her armpits and cheeks working on six gumsticks at once. You would've loved her. No better than his mom. Ah, Marion wasn't that bad. Goodlooker at least when you took her but now pussed out like a hag. Got married, you know. To a light heavyweight who beat the bags out of her morning and night. So she hit him with a hammer. Claw end square in the nog. He went down for the count of a million. Came home a cripple for nine years when he died. She took care of him good during that. Cleaning up his piss and shit. Spoonfeeding him baby food she made and mashed herself. It changed her life. Now she's working in a hospital as a nurse's aide. Night shift. Tough job. Very nice girl. Taking care of him wore her out. But she was guilty over it. She phoned once. I said 'You're killing yourself physically for that pig. If he deserved it, be another thing. Park him in an army nursing home for the duration of his war.' She hung up. Maybe I was wrong. But I felt pity for her. What's been with your last twenty-two years?"

Doorbell rings. She says "Don't tell me anything till I get back," and leaves the room. Loud voices, then someone rushing in. Young man. Looks just like Hank so who else could he be? Lamp in his hand. Raises it high and says "Crapper. I've been waiting for this. I knew you'd be back one day no matter what this old fart said."

But he talks too much. Still jawing on about how he's going to make mincemeat of Hank's head. Hank rolls out of bed and socks him in the nose. Splat. Everything goes. Kid drops to the floor cold. She's screaming. Hank wraps him in a blanket, drags him down the three flights of stairs and lays him out on the sidewalk next to the garbage cans. Police car's coming. Fast service. She must have called them. Policeman steps out. "Hey, buddy, what you got there?"

"My son. Yapped back to his papa, so I gave him the ole heave-ho."

Policeman questions Hank and seems he knew him in school thirty years ago. "I thought you'd never come to any good."

"That's what my dad said and he's dead. But you're a cop now. Got your own car even. Big deal."

"Don't wise on me. I got the badge."

"Oh, the badge now, the badge. Stick that tip on another patsy. I was right in busting the kid's beak. Just as I'd be in breaking anyone's face who threatened me including the police."

Hank's handcuffed, sat in the car's rear seat. His mother's taking care of his son.

"Put him away for life," she says.

"Thanks, Mom," Hank says, "though you can be sure to your flophouse I'll never come back."

"Bastard," his son says.

"Oh, I'm the bastard?"

Ambulance comes. "I don't need no ambulance," his son tells the attendant.

"Any ambulance, you moron," Hank says, middle finger up to them as the car drives off. Then something happened. I forget. Car crash. His car crashing another police car going the wrong way. No, I'm only making that up now. And his son never came to the apartment either. Hank was lying in bed. And not such a tough guy either, nor his mom. She was asking him where he'd been the last twenty-two years, when the phone rang. "Excuse me," she said, went for it, returned. "You won't believe it but it's for you."

He picks up the receiver. "Hello?"

"Hankie?" It's a woman who says she knew him twenty-two years ago and a half hour before saw him walking up the block. She's taking care of her folks as she does once a week. Stays the entire day. Cleans, shops, sews, launders, cooks enough dishes for them for the week. "They're practically helpless now so I do about everything you can think of including bathing them and paying their bills. And after I wash a week's dishes and sit them in front of their favorite eight o'clock TV show, I kiss them goodbye and go home to my husband and son. But there I was. Staring out the window. Truthfully to distract myself from one of the hundred chores here today, when lo and behold. It's him. Spitting image of himself. Still the same tall handsome dark rangy rascal you were when I last saw you, though built even stronger and with longer curlier hair."

"Who is this?"

"Still don't know? You were my first lover, lover. Same place you're in now. Your folks were out. You conned me up. Though I knew what I was doing. And we shared a couple of beers and then you stuck it in, you devil. Broke me good. I couldn't walk right for a week. We were thick lovers for a year after. You even gave me a heart for my neck. No initials or loving inscription, but inside was a set pearl. And every time one of our apartments was free, we'd make it like hogs. Bags we used then. What laughs when I'd help you put them on, though they stunk. You bought them by the gross and I don't know how many times you must've bought a gross. Three? Four? How many hundreds in a gross? You devil. Know my name by now?"

"No."

"Lie. You even once said you loved me. I finally tore that confession out of you soon before you left. Never saw you again. For years I asked your folks about you and they said for all they know, you died. Then five years ago your dad died. I loved that man. So smart, sweet and kind. I still see him sitting out in the sun. Bundled up. Fedora down. I used to wheel my dad over to him. We could've done that together if you'd've stuck around. Both of us wheeling our dads. Maybe on our dads' laps our kids—twins, one for each of theirs. But they'd talk. Politics. Economics. The old days and full-time jobs after school till late when they were eight or nine and how they'd walk the five miles home from work to save the nickel trolley ride. But you devil. Come on now. Who am I? Could it be Marilyn?"

"Marilyn, Marilyn. No, no bell. We were once together though, right?"

"What about three hundred sixty-six times times once? And then double and triple that for all the nights, noons and afternights and very early in the days when you or I or both together couldn't wait. You broke me, you bastard. My gorgeous virginhood. Deflowered a prize flower—one that could've won best of entry awards worldwide. Tons of blood. We brought the sheets to a laundromat. Then you said 'Screw that,' and trashed them and bought a new pair and we went back to put them on your bed. But instead went at it again and there was more blood and you said 'Now we've really done it, as I have no money for new sheets or even to clean these.'"

"I said that? Doesn't sound like me."

"Almost the exact words. I know. Diaries don't lie. I came across that scene a week ago when I was poring over my entire fifteenth year. Icy freezing February day it said. 'Deflowered when there are no flowers out by an amateur gardener name of H. Taken by a big boob with a small tube.' "

"Now I know you don't know me."

"Aha, got you in the heart then, right? Still the same egotistical heel you were at sixteen. But you know what we did with those sheets?"

"Oh yeah, the sheets. What?"

"We stole some newsstand coins, washed the sheets in the laundromat and put them back on the bed and then you started getting hot again. I said I was sorry but I hurt too much. All from my diary. You said 'But it's bad luck the first time not to do it at least three times in the same room on the same bed with the same guy on the same day. If you don't, your sex and reproductive life will be ruined for all time.' I didn't believe a word of it but said 'Okay, let's have another try at it. Maybe this time I'll feel a little something in there but a scrawny itch.' "

"Bull. I can tell by the way you're speaking of it, with whoever you first did it with, that it was great for you all those times too. But tell me more about those twenty-two years ago. It's interesting."

"So we did it again. Kissed. You showed me tricks. Then I showed you some I developed on my own on just that first day. We became lovers. Gross after gross. But we should've gotten warranties, because I had two abortions through you. Both up in the Bronx and butcher jobs. Phone calls from the corner booth nearby. 'You can come up now, babies,' telephone voice said. El train screeching by as she D and C'd. 'We gotta hold it, wait'll it passes,' she said, spoon between her teeth. Big butch. Room clean like a latrine. You squeezed my hand, more scared than me. Second time she sliced me like meat, but by then you'd disappeared. Okay okay. Long time ago. Since then I've married three times, got that one kid. According to your prognosis that first day, I should have by now nine and at least three thousand great comes. And I hate my third husband as much as I did my second and first. Even when he catches too few fish on a picnic day, he takes it out on me. And I thought, just for sentimental time's sake—hell, because I'm horny and want to get laid—if you knew of a spare bed with clean or bloody or just no sheets where we could have one more whirl around before I say goodbye or you do or whatever for forever for good. Right now, H. Your mother's there, send her away. Or ask her. She's cool and we're of age. So how about it—chicken or game?"

"Sure. Your talk's got me climbing the wall." Hangs up, tells his mother "A woman's stopping by who might be spending time in my room, okay?"

"That idiot from across the street? She could use it. And I like her. Takes care of her folks. And that sonofabitch husband of hers beats her silly I heard. Bet she still loves you. Play dumb and they always do. Well good for her, fine for you, okay by me, so I'll leave. I never cared for that huffing and puffing fanfare of two people renewed after twenty-two years."

Vestibule bell. He ticks back and lets her in. They shake hands. His mother says "It'd be nice to see you two settled already," and leaves.

They go in the bedroom. Marilyn says "Haven't much changed in the body, have I? Except about twenty poorly placed extra pounds and this wig."

"Look, I've had blackouts before. But far as I know I've never seen you nude or with your natural hair."

"You've seen me, darling. Think I'd get in bed with a perfect stranger? Oh, if he was perfect, maybe, but let's begin. Mind if I put my hair on the chair?"

Doorbell rings. Front door opens. Loud voices. "My husband," she says. "Lock the bedroom door. Long as he caught us we might as well try and get one good bang in."

No, doorbell doesn't ring. And I already had his mother leave the flat. She could've come back. Be sitting knitting in the living room when bell rang. Husband barges in. Kicks open the bedroom door when Marilyn's atop. "Hi, dear," she says. "Home so soon from work?" Husband pulls a gun. Points it at her. She jumps out the window. Or Hank jumps, so it'll have to be the second or third floor, landing on an awning below. Naked and knocking on a garden apartment door. "Excuse me. You won't believe this." But Hank didn't go up that street. His mother's been dead for five years, father for thirty. Hank remembered him putting a shotgun in his mouth. Pow. Nothing left but the lips. No gun. They were in a car. Hank screamed. Father tried dodging a truck. No luck. No crash. They were on this same sidestreet. Hank's hand in his. He was eight. Walking to his grade school his father also taught at. Telling Hank about the sun. Will eventually die as many stars have and all suns must. When wham. Car jumped the curb and came straight toward them. His father shoved him. That was the wham. Hank bouncing off an ash can. Too late for Dad. Saved Hank's life. But no curb or car smash. Father didn't save but did die. They were in a boat. Sunny beach day. Hank languidly steering with a twig in back while his father rowed. Motorboat coming too close with two skiers in tow. Father shouting for the boat to get away. Big splash and crump and his father flying through the air in a crash dive. Hank woke up ashore. Uncle pumping water from his lungs while his mother blew air in. He vomited back. Wiping it away she said "He couldn't've done that if he wasn't alive." "Dad?" he said. "He the shouting man with you in the boat?" "Yeah." "Then they think he died." "No." "Yes. They don't see how he could've survived." "Yes." "No. You got to start facing it, son: your dad done died when your boat capsized."

No, not in the boat either but a plane. Of course. That's where it took place. Father and Hank flying back to California where they'd gone to see his grandfolks. Sudden fluttering of cabin lights. "Captain to passenger area: got a small touch of turbulence up ahead for the next hundred miles." Bam. Minute later. Plane nose and mountaintop meeting face to face. Hank sole survivor. Also a girl and her doll for a while, dragging them from the flames and later burying them in a double grave. "Doll's name is Delilah," wrote in the snow. "Girl's about six and never said what hers was." Found his father up in a tree like a bat. "Hey, Dad." No reply. Shook it. Came down on his head but seemed already dead. Buried him upside down where he fell. Nobody came to rescue him. And no more shoes, belts and briefcases to eat, he started consuming himself. Starvation is a loss of about one third normal body weight. Death when he's down to his last sixty pounds. Legs better, started crawling down from the wreckage site. Days later, sheepman found him. "Where's your kin, boy? They don't feed you so you run away? Don't you know you also need shelter and clothes?" Rode him home on his horse. Sad tale: wife died at childbirth with their only son. So he raised Hank as his own. Hank was an orphan now anyway and always wanted to live and work on a ranch out West with his dad top ranch hand. Later went to college. Ran for Congress. Served in the Senate. Married a blueblood Blackfoot who gave him many moons and suns. Never happened. Hank walked up that street. Into his building. Mother answers. Slaps his face and slams the door. That's all. Goes downstairs and there's a man standing out front who says "Stritin?"

"I know you?"

"Sure: Tulie Moore. Geez if you haven't changed one bit. Still the spitting image of spit." Tells Hank what's happened around here the last twenty-two years. "Your dad died. Next your sis. Then your teenage sweetie Marilyn in a car crash with your bastard kid. And war, death, famine, etcet, though the ole block survived, now filled with litter and dog shit." No, there wasn't a Tulie or story or Franklin stove. I had nothing to burn. I've this manuscript now, but no stove to stick it in. I could throw it out the window. Because it's not exactly a piece of words that will help me change careers. Story starting off with a man who's written enough stories to file away about a hundred of them and burn one? A man, if I can recall, who's been writing them for twenty years, compared to the real-life me who's only written this uncompleted one? If I had a Franklin stove I'd burn it. Not the stove, the story. Probably the studio also, because I don't know about working those stoves. In other words, if I'd been writing for twenty years or so, then I too would probably have by now produced a body of work that would make me eligible to get in that free artist colony upstate that a writer friend of mine was recently at and where among the many things they give you, besides elegant living and dining and a swimming pool, is a studio in the woods. But really in the woods. With foxy red foxes sometimes limping past the window his writing desk overlooked and plenty of morning rabbits and cute chipmunks always going chick chick and cack cack as they zigzagged around the colony grounds.

"Actually it's an artists' paradise, not a colony," my friend said. "Because you should have seen my studio. Cot. Old-fashioned oak desk. Even clean blankets and a pillow and a Franklin stove." I asked what's that, "besides obviously being a stove, if it really is one." "Oh, it is one. Stove devised by our own Big Ben. And you run out of wood for it, just sign your name at the Mansion message table and lickety-split a pickup truck whips you up a woodbox more. Paradise, right? So I just spent my working day tending fire and fiction. Story I didn't like or inoperative page I'd typed both sides of, I'd throw in the stove." My friend running on about arting and this artistic paradise. He's who I mean where I got the idea to begin my story from. Maybe that's how it's sometimes done. See someone intriguing on the street or sadly trudging through a subway car dragging a dozen stuffed shopping bags: you write a story about them. Person you know well and talk to: better. Yourself: well I'm not so sure that's a good idea unless in the most objective and impersonal aspect possible. But then I met him. After Paradise. Subbing in the school where I teach science at. I was on hallway patrol and passing the room he was supposed to be teaching language arts in when I see him through the door window wrestling a girl to the floor. I ran in, pulled him off, her blouse torn and one of her clogs being hot-potatoed around the room and the class shouting "Rape! Rape!" Then as the girl's crying and this guy who I'd seen around and knew his name was Newt is explaining to me why he wrestled her to the floor—something about trying to disarm her when she instead of answering a grammar question pulled out a saber-toothed comb to scratch his eyeballs—a boy rushed him from behind with a wastepaper basket filled with books and smashed it on the back of his head. Bang. He went down. Class went wild. Jumping on desks and overturning chairs and flowerpots and running out of the room and down the hall, pounding on other class doors. I yelled "Everybody! Shut up and sit down!" and got on one knee. "Can you hear me, sir?" He wasn't dead but unconscious. The class was still uncontrollable. Other teachers came in and I grabbed the boy and girl and marched them to the dean of boys. As I was marching her to the dean of girls, the comb neatly back in her hair, she slammed her foot down on my toes and kneed me in the groin and ran past the uni-formed guard to the street. "Hey you, girl," he said. She didn't belong in the school anyway we later learned. Came to sit with her lover, the boy who assaulted Newt. The guard finally got off the stool to help me but I said "Let me just rest here till the pain stops."

When I got back to the classroom the assistant principal already had an icepack on Newt's head and salts under his nose, which he kept pushing away because the smell was making him nauseous. Then an ambulance came. The hospital people thought he'd been stabbed and seemed a little put out that he hadn't been. An attendant said that Newt should at least get on the stretcher so they can take him in for X-rays for a possible fracture. "If you want to get accident leave or compensation, just going in for X-rays helps."

"It's okay," Newt said. "Just a little fracture. Probably just linear. That's me all over. No bother."

"Take him for tea at least," the AP said to me.

"I said it's okay," standing up, whole body buckling, what looked like sweat but I guess was the icepack seepage trickling down his neck.

"Hey," I said, "I get to get out of hall duty and you your class, so let's go."

We went to the teachers' cafeteria. I'd say that day we became not acquaintances but friends. I liked him right away. A funny guy and not much bushwa. Similar background. Same age about. Never mar-ried but said he now wants to be. Biggest difference between us was our lifestyles and work. He'd gone everywhere and done just about everything it seemed and not just on chartered teacher flights for Easter week in Crete, and at the time and now again was deadlocked in a love-hate relationship with this superenergetic and to me very beautiful divorcee who he calls La Mare that will surely in the end sink them both I think, but that's another story.

Because he was a sub, Tuesday through Thursday so the rest of the week he could just write, he had a rough time in school, while I at least knew how to handle a class and was the only teacher there who admitted I was in it as a career. Newt's students ran him ragged in figure eights. Never shut up or came to attention and they threw things at him throughout the day. Once, for instance, he entered my class and his clothes were dripping red and blue and his hair covered with yellow and behind him a trail like a rainbow I was sure all the way to his art room and he said "What do you think of my new suit, Mr. G—bit too flashy?" and I laughed so hard in my chair that I fell backward and bumped my head on the blackboard. Incidents like that make for lasting friendships. I also invited him to our home for dinner a few times, with or without La Mare. Always lots of fun there too. But what happens? In a month he starts making it with my wife on the one weekday he doesn't sub or she nurse and both our kids are in preschool and I teach: Monday. It was also during the time he and La Mare had permanently split up for the third time in a year.

This May my wife even went to see him at that artists' paradise, where he'd gone a second time. Asked would I take care of the chickadees while she drove to the Cape for a much needed solitary rest. "Sure, anything you want, honeybun." Then surprised him in his mansion bedroom at one in the morn and stayed the weekend with him in his studio, which as far as paradisiacal taboos are concerned is comparable to defecating in the pool just before the colony's trustees are about to wade in. Still, my wife and I worked it out. How? First I had to learn of the affair. That took the type of initiative and curiosity I don't have. Newt avoided me when he returned from the colony and immediately started subbing somewhere else. When I told my wife this and how weird it was that he just left like that to an even worse school that he had to go to by subway while to mine he walked three blocks from his house, she told me why. I said "Guilt, huh?" and something like "Well, what is life anyway, dear? A lot of sadness and a lot of boredom and a lot of mistakes and a lot of fun. Also a lot of sleep," and I went to bed for three days. They went camping on Fire Island for two weeks. That was my suggestion. "Better you two see if you got something going besides sex," I told her. "If you do then maybe you belong together and I take or don't take the kids, dog, car, but definitely go my own way." What can I say? I may sound indifferent and cold. But my personal ethic is love but don't push it or try to figure out its mystery and you'll be a lot better off.

Though set for the worst, it worked out as I thought it might. I didn't pick Paris for them, that's for sure. Sun was too hot, tent like a furnace, almost no privacy or shade, flies in their food, dug clams condemned, beer and wine twice the price than on the mainland, they argued, felt like grubby hobos, barely screwed. Perfect. Ice cold showers to get the sand out of their ani and ears. Couldn't be better. She came back to me. Not so much to me, though eventually she did. Couple of months later I said "Is it all right?" and she said "Go ahead, I don't dislike him anymore," and I said "I never did," and she said "Well we all know what a prince you are," and I said "Who knows but you?" and called Newt and said "How's subbing?" and he said "Worse than it ever was anywhere," and I said "Look, don't be a dunce. The appointments secretary's crazy for you and I hold no grudges and my punches I don't even pull, so come on back and sub at my school, I could use some laughs," and he did.

In time I invited him for dinner too. Since then it's been like a ménage à trois without the trois person directly participating and he's also now more of a friend with my wife than not liking her or her him and so between them it kind of worked out too. My wife and I are again pretty close and she says if she ever does take another lover she'll tell me this time or at least soon as she can without aborting the new relationship and Newt's back with La Mare and for the time being they seem tighter than tight too. But all this is getting away from the Franklin stove. As I said, he's who I got the idea from. And this story would also be thrown in the stove if that stove was here or I was in that paradise studio and had the stove to throw the story in. Though if I was there, this wouldn't be my first story, or it could be. I could be a novelist. Three under my belt, up there to write or revise a fourth novel when I get an idea for my first short story. So I write the first draft, don't like it and throw it in the stove. But would a novelist do that with his first story? Doubt it. But enough fantasies. Just finish the draft of this one, put it away and maybe go over it with the idea of making a final version of it another day.

Dear?

That was my wife. Just got home. Mary I'll call her, to save her face. She works Saturdays in a hospital as a registered nurse. Three nights a week also and one other day. She's in the next room. Our kids are outside with the sitter.

"Dear?" Mary again.

"I'll be out in a second, love." That was me.

"What are you doing?"

"Writing a story."

"I can hear it. Never heard you typing so fast. What kind of story?" All this from the next room.

"Short story."

"Short sad story to our creditors or fake short story to pay a million bills?"

"Fiction. First time. I'm really only trying."

"You? Fiction? Let me read it?"

"Let me finish it."

"Then you'll let me read it?"

"How was work?"

"You didn't answer me."

"Yes I'll let you read it if I don't throw it away or burn it in a Franklin stove."

"What kind of stove?"

"The stove that could have been in the studio at that paradisiacal colony you and Newt were at last May."

"Newt who or just who this Newt?"

"Don't try and pull the wool, dear."

"What do you mean?"

That's where my story should end. End: "What do you mean?" Bringing us right back to the beginning. Or this is where the story should begin. She comes into the room.

She comes in the room.

But she does come in the room. She's standing behind me. Over my shoulders. She gets a chair behind me and tries standing on my shoulders so I can write while she's standing on my shoulders that she's standing on my shoulders, but she can't. She doesn't fall. Just gets down. Slides away the chair. She wants me to stop writing. She's come from a tough day and long week at work she says. She wants a little play too. She's tugging at my erm. Tht's why the tupings all messed up. She's saying #Some on, finish that story, I want to heve a lirrle fun too, im tired. Leta8f go to bed." "What kind of fun can we have in bed if you're tired?" I say. "And how do they correspond: fun and bed? Or tiredness and fun?" "They correspond through love letters," she says. "Très touching. You go to bed and I'll join you. In your dreams. Right now I don't want to finish but begin a story. I have the first line. Your walking in here gave it to me. I suppose that's also how it's sometimes done. 'She comes into the room.' That's the first line. And I'm going to call you Mary in the story." "But my name is Mary," she says. "I'll call you Mary nevertheless." "Mary Never Theless?" tuggink on my arm agaon frying to gew me awry from this typewriter. I'm joined to it though. It's a new experience. My first extramarital affair. I like it. She can't draw us apart. "Don't make me abort," I say. "You had one, I can have one too." I was only able to get Newt and her apart by putting them together in sandland for two straight weeks. She reads that. "What do you mean Newt and I together for two weeks? Who's this Newt? Somebody I'd like? Who'd go for me? You going to fix me up? That'd be a nice change." "You were in love with him." "Was I?" "You admitted making love to him behind my back you she-eviltress." "Did I? Am I?" "When I was teaching and Newt was separated from his La Mare and subbing in school but not on the one weekday you weren't nursing then and the children were at nursery or postnursery or preschool or whatever that kind of school for posttoddlers is called—writers know the words of things, the names of things and how and where to use them and how to fool around with them to make even more use of them and and—and then what?" I'm no longer saying these things to her but just writing what I think I'd say and while she's reading them. "He'd come here and you'd go to bed with him in our bed and make lovely love and noises with him I suppose and fell in love with him you never said but I suspect and he with you too though he never said but because you're lovely and make noises and lovely love so I suppose and then you brought it out when I didn't suspect it and I suggested you two go off together but not Paris, etcetera—I didn't suggest you not go to Paris but didn't suggest it either, but it's all in this piece."

"Show it to me."

"Part of it you're reading. The part you haven't read and the part I haven't written you'll get after I finish."

"Then you won't burn it in your Franklin stove?"

"Oh, you now remember the stove."

"You only spoke or wrote or spoke-wrote about that stove a couple of minutes ago. Don't you remember?"

She takes off her clothes. Nurses don't have much on. Maybe some do. No, some definitely do. Some of Mary's colleagues say for possible rape protection they wear lots of underwear and body hose or both under their white pants suits. But not my gal. Panties. With holes in them. Sheer where you can see her hair through. Shoes and stockings already off in the next room. Likes to patter around the apartment barefoot. Sits on my lap. She's making it quite tough for me to tupe. Again: misepllings, typogripical eras, wife in my xlap. In my lap I mean. Slip of the slip that one. Her slip also on the floor. Unbuttoning my shirt.

"I am unbuttoning his shirt, folks," she says.

"Hey," she says, "this is like being on radio."

Sticks her tongue in my ear. "Or on TV," she says. "Candid Chimera. Or one of those vinegar vérité flicks. This is a cinema cerité story. No, can't be. Your typogryphical eras are making me say things I never said. A vérité story. A veritable vérité story. A veridical verifiable verisimilous veristic—"

"Why are you looking up those words in the dictionary under veri to put in my mouth?" she says. "You know I don't speak like that. You know nobody does. Maybe some people, but we don't know them. Me, I'm plain-speaking." Mary. My wife. Unbuttoning my life. Shirt unbuttoned: kissing my globes, my lobes. Taking off my tie.

"You don't even own a tie," I say.

"I said it, not he," she says. "Or him," she says.

"Ho ho ho hum," I say.

"I said that too, chief," she says. "You know I said thief," she says.

Nibbling my shoulderblade. Licking my chest. Sucking my nips. Making me want to leave the typewriter to go to bed with her in this room. Or to the floor on her slip. We're carpeted. Gift of the previous tenant who wanted to sell it to us but we told him to pick it up as we wouldn't pay a cent. But I won't go. I've a story to write. "One piece at a time," I actually say. And the first line of the story is "She comes into the room." Or "She comes in the room." "Which do you like?"

"Which one of what?" she says, lips on my eyelid giving me what she calls her butterfly kiss.

"Of opening lines."

"What are they?" Neck, nip and blade. Dezippering me. Feeling me. Playing with me. "Up Johnny up Johnny up Johnny whoops."

"Read the page. The two lines are on this page."

She reads while she continues to hold. "You mean between she comes in or into the room?"

"Those."

Opens her legs. "You want to do it here or there?" she says. "I can take you where I'm sitting right now. I've been thinking about doing it all day. All those patients. The old man. The one from two nights ago? Poor guy. Oh, now I'm turning myself off. Hot off. Well he talked about sex today. Suddenly he starts relating in detail about how great were those days with his wife and only up to a month before she died they used to do it all the time. Almost every day for forty years. And how they had the richest love and sex life creatable and how they first did it four times a night and then week after their honeymoon they broke it up into four times a day and then three and then two and over the years just once a day but that once, oh boy, he said. 'What we learned about sex in forty years couldn't be put in a book, which is why I'm telling you this, miss. So you'll know it can't be told,' he said, the old guy, this Mr. Stritin, a very nice man."

"Stritin? That's the main character's name in my piece."

"Because I spoke of him before. I had to. But I'll read it later. Anyway—is this talk making you less excitable? It's not for me any-more—just the reverse. He told me when they were past seventy they would take an hour or so to do it but they'd do it. If not an orgasm then for sure gobs of fun getting close to one, with all sorts of kiss-ings and fondlings he said, and it made me think of you. Not your face. Your thing. Of this thing. This thing I hold here, folks. Of us. Of our doing it. Loving it. Of my munching and you mine and tonguing our hips and thighs and all the positions we do it in and all that we haven't tried and all the flawless highs I've had through you with it by you with it together. All that. And all day after I left Stritin—no, it was Silbit. Stritin was the old guy who was declared spontaneously remitted today and left the hospital singing and polkaing and carrying an open champagne bottle and attended by a multitude of children and grandchildren and friends, when we just about kissed him off forever two years ago. Well Silbit, not Stritin. He made me think of you and all we do and I've been thinking of it on the crosstown bus and then the number ten here and walking from the bus stop and seeing the kids on the street and not home I was so happy I gave them each and the sitter two bucks and told them to go to the movies and then another two bucks for the three of them to buy candy there, something I hate doing because of their teeth and because I know our kids are too young for the movies and will fall asleep there after they eat their sweets. But I wanted to be with you alone here and here I am with you alone and what are you doing with me alone but holding back from me when I want to do it so much, and all because of this piece you're writing. Well okay," she says, getting off me, "that the way you want it, dandy by me," and she slams the door and I write everything she said since she said "Well Silbit, not Stritin," or as best as I can remember it. And now I hear something behind me and it's she standing there when I didn't know she was there and for all I know she never left the room.

"I didn't."

And so she didn't. She was there all the time watching me write what she said. And now she pulls my chair back from the typewriter a few inches and sits on my lap again and is playing with me there again and she never had to unzip me as I never zipped myself up again and she has me going again and she's kissing me, as she sits on my lap facing me, and I'm leaning around her left side to type with one finger the rest of this and what she's doing to me now to make me stop typing. She is making me stop writing this story which isn't yet a story or whatever it isn't yet but which at least has a first line which is "She comes into the room" or "She comes in the room" or even "Mary comes in the room." "Which do you like best?" I say, all typed with one finger, Mary nude, Mary naked facing me, Mary holding herself up a ways so she can get me inside her, Mary sitting down on me again with me inside her, Mary bouncing up and down, Mary making noises. Mary's eyes closing. Mary's mouth opening. Mary bouncing harder and harder on me. "Mary Mary Mary," I say, her two hands on my shoulders as she goes up and down on me, "which do you like best: 'Mary comes into the room' or 'Mary comes in the room' or 'Mary came into the room' or 'She came in' or 'comes in' or 'comes into the room,' which?"

Em

So it happens again. Does it never end? "Dearest," she says, "I love you but feel I really need to be free and away from you for a while. I think we should part for two months." "Separate" was the word she used. "Maybe through June." That would make three. "Then we'll see." Telling me all this in my single room. She on the only chair, me sitting on the bed. Hands folded in my lap. I remember that. There's no reason I can see that I made those two sentences almost rhyme. The lap and the that. But there we were. Chair: bed. Two pieces of furniture existing opposite one another about four feet apart. Chair with its coat on, bed in its bathrobe. The chair had previously knocked. The bed said "Yes?" The coat said "It's me." He opened with glee. The rhyme there was done intentionally. All this taking place two nights ago. Last night was something else. But she knocked on the door. Waited for him to open it though she had her own set of his keys. They kissed. They pressed up tight. Me: she. He held her face in his hands. He was going to say "He held her face in his." Now he does. There's a long corridor from the front door to his room. Actually his flat has three rooms: small kitchen with a window, large bathroom with a chest of drawers and a window, each off the main room. But they walked through the corridor holding hands. He walked first. No reason except one of them has to as the corridor's too narrow for them to walk two abreast. But could it also be called a hallway? Or does a hallway, when it's in an apartment, only join up two or more rooms, while it's the corridor that connects the apartment building's public hallway to get to the interior of the flat?

But let me get on. They go in the room. He says "It's been too long." They last saw each other the night before. They'd gone to a party. She lives thirty miles upstate, teaches in a high school, lives with one of her two children in the community she teaches English in. They'd met five months ago and have gone together since. Many times he stayed at her house for an extended weekend or week. He can stay that long, as his rent and expenses are cheap and for income he subs when he wants to in a New York City junior high school. He didn't go back with her the night of the party as he had a nine o'clock appointment the following morning with a New York internist. She was coming in the next night anyhow to see her family therapist. She's presently breaking up with her husband. No, they're separated, been separated for almost a year, and once a month they meet with the therapist to discuss such things as how they can make their separation easier for each other and their children and to resolve problems revolving around money, mutual property and support and custody of the children. He's not sure if that's why they meet. She's told me several times, but on the subject of her husband, therapist and child custody and support I look at her interestedly but don't listen well. Anyway: she'd pick him up after her session. One or the other of them would drive her car to her place upstate. Usually he drove. He was the better driver. That's not why. "A better driver," he once told her, "is one who directs almost his entire attention to his driving, and unless it pertains to his driving performance, disregards most of what's occurring in the car." So she was there. They are there. "It's not that I don't love you or love you any less that I don't look at you when I talk," he thinks he said that same time in her car, "but because I think it best for both of us if I give my full vision to the road." They walk through what I'll be a little perverse about now and settle on as the passageway. But I've done that move. Done their sitting on the chair and bed, she in her coat, he the bathrobe. She came earlier than he expected, so though he had his things packed to leave, he was still reading in his robe on the bed. The only other furniture in the room is a night table with a lamp on it by the bed and an end table next to the easy chair (if it was by the bed it'd be a night table) with a lamp on it and soon a bottle of beer. Neither of them smoke. So there'll be no smoking or sharing of an ashtray or lighting or putting out matches and cigarettes. The coat speaks: There's something I want to tell you.

The bathrobe replies: It's obvious you got something bothering your mind.

The chair: It is?

The bed: I don't want to be sidetracking you, but you seem a little depressed yet anxious—

She: I am.

He: I was going to say "anxious to get it out, to tell me."

Mary: Well, I am depressed, though not anxious to tell you what's causing it.

Newt: Just say it. Everything now hurts.

Ms. Em: I can't just come out with it outright.

Mr. TS to his friends: Want me to say what I think it is for you?

My stringbean casserole: No.

The man she once said he'd have to guess or figure out why she semioccasionally likes to refer to him as her prince of priests: I mean say for you what I think it is?

Darling Diana Monkey: Don't worry, I'll shpill. By the way, what the doctor say about your back today?

Dearest Douroucouli: I knew I shouldn't have sidetracked you. And I didn't go to today's doc for my back. That's what I saw yesterday's osteopath for and he went snappery crack with my neck, shoulders and back and fixed me up one through Z. Want a beer?

The coat nods. The bathrobe gets off the bed and goes to the kitchen for a beer. Or the bathrobe got off the bed and went into the kitchen for a beer. Or the bathrobe goes into the kitchen for a beer. Or the bathrobe got off the bed and in the kitchen got a beer. Or the bathrobe gets a beer. Or the bathrobe got a beer in the kitchen. Or in the kitchen the bathrobe gets a beer. Or the bathrobe, in the kitchen, got a beer. Or after the bathrobe got off the bed and went into the kitchen or just got off the bed or just went into the kitchen, it opened the refrigerator for a beer or got a beer out of the refrigerator or got a beer. Or the bathrobe went (goes) into (in) the kitchen (and) got (gets) a beer out of (from) the refrigerator (icebox) and yelled (yells) "I've also some ale ("I've also some ale.")."

The coat says "Beer, dear." That rhyme was unintentional on my part. I mean that out of the many remarks I've written so far that are free renderings or near, or maybe for some of the shorter statements exact quotes (my memory of things said isn't the equivalent of photographic of things read), that last one is the only one I'm sure of that was just as the person said it. He said "Beer, dear?" He also said "You're a poet and you don't even know it." "Yes I do," she said. "If you say you do then you do," he said, "but I think I'll have an ale."

She said "What?" and he said "Nothing, I was only talking to myself out loud. I said I think I'll have an ale instead of a beer. Actually, I said if you think you're a poet then you are one, but I'm going to have an ale. Actually, I didn't even say that but something pretty close to it." "Oh," she said, another exact photographic equivalent, and unless there's an important reason I see for citing another one, which is not to say that this one was important, which is not to say it wasn't, the last I'll name. He sticks his head past the kitchen entrance (there's no door to the kitchen, which is why I call it an entrance, though I suppose it could just as accurately be called a doorway since I don't think a doorway has to have a door on it to be considered one) and said "Like something to eat?" "Will you please?" she said, beckoning him back into the room and with the same finger pointing to the bed. "Right," I said.

He opens the bottle of beer and with the other end of the church key, the can of ale, and goes into what I'll from now on call the living room. He sits on the bed, leans forward to hand her the beer (I can't be exact about any of these actions, as my memory of movements and especially gestures and expressions made is even less the equivalent of photographic of things read to things said. Though I can say that if he did give her the beer without his standing up again and moving a step or more toward her, he would have had to lean forward if she at the time didn't lean forward to take the beer out of his hand or stand up and move a step or more toward him while he was still sitting on the bed holding the beer, neither of which he thinks she did), sits back on the bed (he also can't recall just coming back into the living room and handing her the beer before he sat down), drinks some ale (he's simply assuming he did, since it's what he thinks he'd normally do before he set a can of ale down), sets the can on the floor (he'd have to do that to fold his hands in his lap, which is the one action out of all that went on there then that he almost definitely remembers doing: perhaps it's almost always, when he can get his hands free, part of his listening pose when he's not only preparing to look at someone interestedly but to listen well), folds his hands in his lap (I don't like confusing things even more than maybe they already are in this long sentence with its many parentheses, and which I no doubt did even more so by saying before that I don't want to confuse things even more, and now even more so with that last phrase explaining the first one and then this third one explaining the second, but if the night table had been on the side of the bed he sat on, he probably would have put his ale on it instead of on the floor) and looks at her and waits.

They'd planned to bike around the Benelux countries this summer and he now questioned her about it and she said she still wanted
to go but he said "No, I'm sure that's off," and she said "Maybe
we should cancel it then if that's how you feel," and he said "Me?
How I feel?" but he said he would, since he was the one who put
the deposit down for both of them on the flight, as she was going to
pay the balance of the fare when the charter company asked for it
in June.

It's now April.

She said she knows she's being a big jerk about the whole thing
and was thinking today how she could really be blowing a good relationship with him by her actions, but he must see by now how much
she needs to have the freedom she doesn't, and not because of him,
have with him or has had with any man since she left Myles and
which she can almost say she almost never had with Myles either, and
he said he understands.

"And I do love you, my toots sweet, and you're the most understanding man I've ever known in this way and the more I talk with
you the more understanding you seem to be to me and so the more I
love you and think of you as my azygous toots sweet however regret-
table or unintelligible or whatever able or ible you said that endear-
ment sounded like to you. And I do think if we stayed together we
could go on ento uternity as you once said and which is still to me too
construable to fully understand, but I don't like that feeling about
myself that right from Myles I jumped to someone else who I loved
and who I can say truly busted my cherry as we diddled jills used to
say before we became janes but who never really satisfied me no matter how contradictory those two statements might seem to you said
successively like that. And then three days after him I started in with
someone else who satisfied me even less, and this has nothing to do
with sex, than the previous man or Myles did during the last months
of our marriage, but who I also thought I loved and then to you without even a week's breather from the man after the man after Myles
after sixteen years," and he said "I think I understand."

"There's really nothing about you I don't like" and he satisfied her
in every imaginable way "and it's never been anything with anyone
anywhere anytime as it has been with you in bed or wherever we
did it—"

"On the floor one time," he said, "standing up."

"You caught me unawares."

"You mean I caught your unawares."

"You what?"

"Or your unawares unawares when you also weren't aware you weren't wearing your underwear."

"My what?"

"I'm not quite sure. But it still sounds like a passable depiction of both the act and place of contact and even our correlative parts we made contact and then concurrence with, though I'm not quite sure as I said and have said so many times about so many things I've said so many times."

"I'm shtill shtumped."

The fact is she was in his living room slipping on her shirt when he caught her unawares unawares, or to be more direct without rebeginning this set, happened upon her with her body bent slightly forward over the bed spreading her shirt out so she could more easily slip it over her head when he etched in behind her, both naked from at least the waist down, and suddenly he was erect and within when all he intended with his caress was to put his arms around her chest and kiss her neck, and it was morning, a Sunday, shortly after they'd shared one of his Instant Dairy Screams as she liked to call his invariable daily breakfast mixture of creamed cottage cheese, wheat flakes and grated fruit and were planning to bike to Prospect Park and had only been done making love some twenty minutes before during some song to God and Earth and Praise the choir of the church a few backyards away had sung. Let me also say, concerning that time, that they both on their individual quake gauges registered their highest readings than with anyone else before, and it was so accidental. A fluke, she said. Whatever wit was, he said. Whatever what weans, she said. When they both thought they were through conjoining for the morning, he thinks she said, or at least neither thought the other wasn't. And let me say they've tried reduplicating those sussultatory shocks as she called them, on other mornings and afternoons and evenings, he standing up and she leaning over the bed though without their going through the prelims of planning a bike hike or spreading a shirt out or sharing his IDS or winding up making love shortly before—the initial intercourse as essential foreplay, as one of them put it—the absence of all or some or one of these conceivably accounting for their failure to not only reproduce even once that so far inimitable exquisite physical thrill at the end but of even coming close to matching the memorable intensification or the dizzying alignment of their respective connective parts during the act, which could also be the single or principal or contributory reason for their repeated failures. But let me finally say that this has all been said, over and over and over again.

But that was that day some two or so months ago, but two days ago the coat sat huddled up in the chair and the bathrobe was taking another swig from its ale. Or at least he's assuming it took a swig. But the coat said. But I forget what the coat said. But the bathrobe said to the coat in response to what I forget the coat said "Well, do what you want, as whatever you decide on I'll go along with and without any big emotional scene or difficulties to you either. If you don't know whether you want to go back to Myles or not, then maybe now, in the time you'll be by yourself—those two months you mentioned, the three months I refigured—the time you'll be away from me I mean but of course with your daughter. But if you asked me what I think about your going back to Myles, I'd say, if you asked me right now that is, as I don't know what I'd say if you asked me a minute from now, although I might say the same thing I'd say right now, word for word even, though I'm sure that would be less apt to happen than my saying the same general thing in different words. Anyway, what was I saying? I was about to say what I'd say to you if you asked me what I think about your going back to Myles, which is close to a minute after I would have answered you if I hadn't gone into that business about what I'd say a minute from now to the same question. Though if you did ask me now the same question that you might have a minute ago about your going back to Myles, and I didn't start speaking about what I'd say to the same question if you asked it a minute from now, then I'd say that I think a lot of things about your going back to Myles and many quite different from some of the other things, so what I really think about it would be unworthy of regard, of little interest and in the end counteractive to any decision you might hope to make with the help of what I'd say. That's what I'd say right now to that question. Now if you asked the same question a minute from now or even right now, which is about a minute from the time you hypothetically asked the question and I answered it, and I didn't start speaking about what I'd say to the same question a minute from now, if you asked that question right now, or two minutes from now if you asked it a minute from now, then I don't think I'd say anything much different from what I just said."

"But he's all wrong for me," she says. "I never got along with him. Well, of course sometimes I did, but mostly never. Never is perhaps too expressive and confining a word. And expressive is perhaps too emphatic a word and confining not expressive enough. But maybe you get what I mean. His assessments of things are so different from mine. I don't even think I like him that much."

"Do what you want. But I make myself clear. I say I love you.

That's not important. I give unequivocal evidence that I do. Our relationship's been a good one. We haven't fought once, and not because either of us isn't temperamental or holding back what we want to say. We just haven't. And I am temperamental, you are temperamental. We've been good for one another like that. I don't know what that means. Everything's been good. Let me think now. I've never seen another couple like us who kiss in the street and on stairs and in museums and restaurants and even between courses and during courses and between sips of wine or beer. Any drink. And maybe other couples do kiss between and during courses and even with forkfuls of food in their mouths. Or spoonfuls or even handfuls or at least one handful. And even male couples, female couples, and all over the world perhaps. In Vatican City. At the Londonderry barricades I bet. Even in foxholes. Even foxes, in or out of foxholes, theirs or anyone else's, including other foxes'. Even fox terriers and fox sparrows. All birds. Even pigeons. Especially pigeons. I've seen them pecking away at one another in the park. And on sidewalks and streets in New York and Vatican City and Londonderry and probably at or on the barricades there also and also in foxholes there if there aren't any foxes or fox terriers already there or wherever there are foxholes, barricades and pigeons. Not with forkfuls of food in their mouths, unless they're being force-fed, but possibly with some food. What I'm saying is all couples kiss, all sexes, all animals. Maybe even parameciums too. I don't know. But if they do, then probably with some food in their mouths or with whatever they kiss with, though I'm sure none of it force-fed with a fork. In other words: everything. From fox moths to foxgloves and maybe bathrobes and beds too. Twin beds. Maybe they do kiss. In their own way. Even on the barricades, if that's what the barricades are partly made of and the beds are close enough. And coats and chairs too. Chairs on the barricades also and coats kissing one another in dark closets perhaps. Or maybe their best kissing's done when they're suddenly thrown together on beds. But I was talking about what a great couple we were. Maybe we'll be one again. But now you want to be off on your own for your version of a couple of months and where it might work out with your returning to the man who, one, right now you're quite sure doesn't want you back, and, two, who you don't even think you like that much and you almost never got along with and who you think is all wrong for you besides, which is three and probably four. Well, fine. Settled. Now finish your beer and go."

"Don't be mean," the chair says, she does, Mary, Em, the coat.

"I said that last line about the beer and for you to go because I thought it would be so melodramatico. But what I was really thinking is that what we both now might be thinking is that we could go to bed now and end it that way for a couple of months. Not to go to bed for a couple of months, as that would hardly allow you the time to be alone for your two months, but just once and until it ends or even before it ends, if that's what either of us wants, or until we want to get up to dress, if we undressed before we got or once we got to bed, or just to get up to straighten out our clothes, if we kept our clothes on in bed, if we even do it in bed, if we even go to bed, if we even do it. And then later you can leave with me accompanying you to your car, if you came by car."

"I didn't come by train."

"Then you're saying you had to have come by car?"

"I don't know about the bed idea, Newt."

"Bad idea my bed idea?"

"Linetta expects me home in an hour."

"You can call her up."

"You don't have a phone."

"We can go to the corner store."

"Once I get outside I'll want to drive straight home."

"Then it probably wasn't a good idea."

"It wasn't a bad idea."

"But not a good idea?"

"Well, not a very good idea."

"Then it certainly wasn't a great idea."

"I think we'd have to see how it turned out to be called a great idea."

"I think it would turn out to be at least a good idea."

"It never once turned out to be a bad idea."

"How, in percentages or whatever proportions or comparisons you want to use, would you rate this subject as an idea?"

"You mean in bad, good, very good and great?"

"No inexpressible after the great?"

"I think we've had a couple of inexpressibles and one time after a great."

"That time you were putting your shirt on and I came up to you from behind?"

"I don't think that time could be said to be beyond the inexpressible once I said it was such. But no bads, lots of goods, quite a few very goods, several greats and a couple of inexpressibles."

"Shouldn't we even try now for a good?"

"I've got to go."

"I'll get dressed."

"That'd be a good idea."

"You know what'd be a very good idea?"

"A really great idea?"

"Maybe even inexpressible."

"Please express yourself."

"Right." He quickly dressed. They left the apartment. He thought about asking for his keys back, but decided no, as one of the things they'd just talked about was that she could come by anytime, call him if she knew where to reach him by phone and send letters to him whenever she liked. He'd probably get one soon, mailed or dropped off by her, and like most of her letters it would be a poem. She'd sent him a poem by mail or personal delivery, as she wrote on the envelope whenever she stuck it in his mailbox or shoved it under his door, about once a week since after the first month they met and twice a week before that. One he remembered she wrote went And now years have gone by / remember that? / when each hour represented a day / or was the day a week / that weekend several months? / I forget. / I forget that your eyes aren't black but brown I think / why is that? / I remember where you live though. / Simple things (such as how I feel about you) / a name, let's say (I only forgot yours once) / an address (Newton, Newton, the pleasure of your arms and our embrace) / I don't forget, though I probably do. I forget.

There's more and she called it "To the night of know things from the lazy who can only give shpace." He remembers it ended— Actually, he only remembers that first part and has been looking for and just located the poem in his desk. So he also has a desk, a lamp and typewriter on the desk, a dictionary of international slang on top of a thesaurus on top of a dictionary on top of the desk, and right beside the desk an old dental cabinet he uses as a file cabinet that belonged to his father the doctor the dentist and which is still filled with the chemical residues and minuscule mineral remains of his forty-year practice along with a few blackened cotton alcohol balls his pincers after his fingers must have pinched and several real or false individual teeth in the drawers' corners. The poem, written while she sat against a car fender waiting for her therapist and Myles to show up, was shoved under his door after that session, though he was in and heard the envelope sliding on the floor and ran after her down the stairs and in the street yelled at her double-parked car pulling away for her to stop while he stood on one and then the other foot trying to get the backs of his tennis sneakers over his heels. But the rest of the poem goes

I think squirrels forget
(their nuts, I mean)
where they leave them: that I didn't forget
even if that little animal life fact might not be true.
I won't go into elephants, and not because I can't fit.
I also forget that with my last so-called poem to you
I was to be finished with them for good.
Oh I forget. My way to you: will I also forget that?
I thought of it, but forgot what I thought of course
and no doubt I should forget this entire piece too.
I forget the reasons for what I do
soon after I've contrived them, or through
serious contemplation: oh, forget it
as I forgot what I was going to say
why I was going to say it
and my long-thought-out conclusion too.
Perhaps all I don't forget is that I forget
though I can't be too sure on that point too.

They also agreed in his flat that he would call, write or drop by her place anytime he liked. But he didn't think he would. This was her show. She wrote and staged it, so he'd just watch, maybe applaud to be polite and possibly review. How was that for whatever figure of speech it was? The audience and stage walk downstairs holding hands. The figure of speech falls apart when he realizes they both helped produce the play. In the street she says "It's very cold for April. They even expect it to shnow." "Brrr," he says, wrapping his arms around her and clasping his hands against her back while she wraps her arms around his and maybe clasps hers. "You've got to keep me warm," he or she said. Or "We've got to keep me more than wee warm," she or he said. Or "wee-wee warm." No they didn't. Nothing like that was said. Edit out everything from "You've got to keep" to what I'm saying till now. But they laughed to whatever one of them said, and kissed. You see: they were always kissing in the street. Not once in their five or so months did they walk for a couple of miles or in the time, if they were driving or standing relatively still, that it approximately took them to walk a couple of miles, without a kiss. Never once does he remember them even sitting in a luncheonette or at a ballet or play or any theater really where they didn't kiss. The Moorish City Center to see the Bunraku last week, for example. Which they took her daughter and son to and sat in the last row of the orchestra after slinking there during intermission from the last row in the second balcony (her son Timon, out of integrity, refusing to make the move), and where Mary was viewing the puppets and to him near invisible manipulators through her husband's grandmother's opera glasses and listening over a rented headset to the translation of Japan's most famous classical play of forbidden love and double suicide, when he got his lips in between the wires and under her arms and opera glasses and kissed. She put the glasses down and worked one of the earphones around and kissed him back. Then they placed the glasses and headset on her lap and embraced, is the only word I can think to use for what they did and he, inside her blouse from below while she stroked his chest, got one of her nipples erect—probably the right one as he was sitting on her right with Linetta on her left—by lifting the nipple up with the backs of his middle and index fingers and rubbing and skimming the top of it with his thumb, a habit or procedure he thinks he picked up by giving his dad insulin shots twice a day for two years. And where Mary later said "Linetta saw us and put her program over her lids and insinuatively said ohhh. If she lets on to Myles he's liable to accuse us of corrupting her and maybe use it in court to get full custody of both Timon and Lin if we get divorced. Can a child, like one's spouse, be barred from testifying against one of her folks, if that is the way the law goes?" But everywhere. That's what I've been saying. That's the kind of couple we were. Though what does all this talk about physical activity mean when she also said in his flat "Are we supposed to be beyond saying things like 'Lots of times when I'm sleeping with you I make believe you're Myles'? for if we are, I'm not." And "Intellectually and sexually we're very close but emotionally you won't let us go all the way," which he said to some could seem like a contradiction coming so soon after what she said about making love to him through Myles or the other way around. And which he also "out-and-outedly" denied, saying that his remark about what can she really ever do for him? and which likely invited her previous remark that he won't emotionally let her in "didn't mean you could never do anything for me, but what can anyone do for anyone else to stop the deepest and ultimately least problematical realizations from seeping in about the betrayal of time and boundaries of being and self-deceptions that we'll ever find fulfillment and self-knowledge and the well-meaning lies and myths of all our customs, codes and social and emotional tricks. Saying all that while even here, right after I said it, I probably don't believe more than a word of it and just said it as a cop-out of some kind, just as just what I just said to you could be a cop-out, just as just what I just said to you could be a cop-out too," but now they're heading to her car.

"Where's it parked?" he says.

"I always think it's parked where I parked it the last time I was here."

But it's not a hard car to spot if it's not parked too far down the block and she puts the key in the passenger's side door and when he says "But I'm not driving back with you, right?" she says "Belief and doctrine, my head," and goes around and unlocks the door at the driver's seat.

He comes up beside her. Maybe they briefly held hands. They did or didn't quickly kiss. That pick-peck goodbye when he or she's going to the grocery store and the other person's staying home. But he definitely remembers slapping her back a couple of times, patting it really, like a good-time Joe to a good-time Sally, and said "Well, so long," and she said "That's it?" and he said "I don't know: what do you expect me to say?" and she said "It really doesn't take you long to make the end or separation of these things a total blank in your mind," and he said "Maybe it's like my father used to say to me when I'd really start bitching," and she said "What was that?" and he said "No, it's got to be too corny, a man saying what his father used to say to him when he was a kid," and she said "You mean if he can lose his father and mother he can lose you too?" and he said "I didn't think I told you that," and she said "So, now that you've lost your parents can you lose me too?" and he said "I don't want to speak about losing my parents or anything related to that yet, please," and she said "I'm sorry, I forget. But I told you I always forget. I even wrote a poem to some man I liked about forgetting which I now forget not only whom it was to but what it was all about," and he said "To me," and she said "My poem called 'Forget Me Snot'?" and he said "No and it was about your remembering those first weeks after we met when we were so close and felt that each hour represented twenty-four times that in time," and she said "You see?" and he said "Dumbhead, dumbhead," and tapped her forehead with his knuckles and said "So I'm shoving off now, okay?" and she said "Godshpeed, matey, and how does she head?" and he opened the door and removed the keys from the lock and gave them to her and as she was getting into the car he walked further down the street, though he didn't know to where. For a beer? Movie? Someone's house? Something to eat or to a store to buy food and drink? But what? Whose? Why did he go that way rather than straight home? Or at least pretend to go home by walking in that direction, even down the steps to his building's landing or into the vestibule if she still hadn't driven away, and then back on the street toward Columbus Avenue once she was gone. For if he now made a right at Columbus she might think he was going to see a woman he once went with who lived a block north off that avenue, and if he made a left at the corner at Columbus she might think he was going to the bar three blocks away he so often went alone or with her to and for some reason he didn't want her to think, if she was watching him, that this separation or end, as she said, was driving him to a bar where he just might get crocked or cockeyed drunk and stinko, as his father also used to say.

He ran across the street. This man was a runner let me add. Let me also add he ran four to eight miles a day just about every day and only heavy snow slowed him down and reduced the miles of his run to about one and torrential rains and paths and walks coated with ice meant he ran in place in his apartment or inch by inch through the passageway and rooms for twenty minutes twice a day. I'll add too that he even had his running shoes on. Or running sneakers or whatever real runners like the runners who run in marathons and belong to a certain running club in the city called the Roadrunners Club I think it's called call these sneakers or shoes. But he ran down the north side of West 75th Street to Columbus Avenue. He sprinted across Columbus and then walked in a brisk manner, as some people used to say, farther west along 75th toward Amsterdam, the next avenue. Every time a car passed he turned to his left to see if it was hers. Because this would be the street she'd logically drive down. For she lives upstate as I said and to get to her house, if she was parked on West 75th anywhere between Central Park West and Amsterdam or even on Central Park West between 73rd and 75th facing north, she always made a right at Amsterdam and 75th, or first a left down 75th if she was parked on Central Park West, drove to 79th and made a left and crossed Broadway and West End Avenue and Riverside Drive and got on the West Side Highway and continued north on it or Henry Hudson Parkway as the highway's also called or only called once a car passes a certain unspecified landmark farther uptown or down, to the George Washington Bridge and then to the Palisades Parkway and then onto another road or highway or parkway to her town that's within sight and earshot of the traffic on the Tappan Zee Bridge and then up a hill to a street and lane to her house, which isn't.

So he walked in the manner he said. Three cars passed in a row. None was hers. All were larger. Every car's larger than hers except the tiniest Fiat and Honda and whatever that Fiat's called when it's made in Spain. The small car was perfect for her. She was small. Her voice, mannerisms and aspirations were small. Her body was lean and small. Her buttocks weren't that small and her thighs were kind of large in fact, though not that large as it might sound when someone says "her thighs were kind of large in fact." He adored her small body. Worshiped it he used to say. She used to say "I have a short awful body," and the first night they met and were taking off their own clothes after each had removed the other's shoes and socks and he had untied her blouse bow on top, she pointed to and then covered up a long scar below her navel that furrowed perpendicularly through the middle of the hair to the vagina and said "This is the ugliest part of me you'll see. I had something even uglier inside but the medicine men cut it out," and he remembers thinking Oh my God, she has a long scar on her body. And fairly large thighs and chubby knees and kind of big buttocks. It will affect my relationship with her. It'll never work out. And she's really not that pretty when I get a good look at her full face. With little bumps and a couple of chicken pox pits and a bleached mustache and jaw mole with a hair or two in it and small teeth and conspicuous gums and a wide fleshy nose and nostrils that stayed flared. And I need to have a pretty woman. It's always been a pretty woman. She's got to at least have an almost beautiful face from all three seeable sides if she's small and her body's only halfway attractive to me or marred with a long visible scar, or have a beautiful body if she only has a very pleasant though not exceptionally attractive face. That's what he actually thought that first night and could quite conceivably, though again with subsequent self-reproach and avowals not to think that way again, think the same thing about another woman in the future, though he never again thought that way about Mary. Because he quickly came to love that face and buttocks and thighs and scar and height and all her extrusions and holes and folds and pits and hairs and sounds and drools and rheums and even her smells. Even the intestinal ones. No, not the intestinal ones, though they hardly bothered him anymore. "If you can take mine then I can take yours," he once said in a hurry to get to the bathroom she was coming out of and she said "Why even mention? Who even cares?" though when she was around he still tried to conceal his own smells by opening the bathroom window, if it wasn't too cold out, and lighting a match above the bowl and twirling around the room with it after he flushed: so there was a lighting of a match in this piece. But the cars. They passed. Maybe she made a left at Columbus to avoid seeing him and being seen and got on the highway at Seventy-second.

He was nearing Amsterdam when he heard another car behind him. He turned and saw Mary in the front seat of her car, crying hysterically. Throwing her head back and forth uncontrollably. The windows were closed. He couldn't hear her. She wasn't looking at him. He knew she must be making loud sobs in there. He thought she'd bump her head on the dashboard or the back of the seat. "Mary," he said. She didn't hear. He didn't say it loud enough. Didn't shout it out. "Emmy, don't cry," he said just as low. The car drove past. She might never have even seen him. The car stopped for the red light. He walked past the car. His hands in his pants pockets. His body hunched up from the cold. His jacket was too thin. He'd lost the fleece lining two winters ago. He should have worn a sweater. He didn't look at her. He stopped at the corner. He thought she'd make a right at Amsterdam when the light changed. He ran across the avenue against the light and was near Broadway when he heard her car coming along. She was driving very slowly. She wasn't looking at him. She was still crying hysterically or had resumed crying that way from the time he last saw her till sometime just before now. "Mary," he yelled. A lady across the street turned around. The car drove by. Mary never looked left or right. The lady was looking at the apartment windows above. "Em, you shouldn't cry," he said. He held out his hands. He wanted to cry. He was smiling. It wasn't a malicious smile. If Mary saw it she might think it was. The smile wouldn't go away. It was out of embarrassment and helplessness. Out of sadness and pity. Out of lots of things. Out of wonder. Concern. Nobody bawling and tossing her head around like that should be driving a car. She stopped for the light. His smile went away. He wanted to run to her car and tap on the window and say something. He walked fast on the sidewalk till he stood parallel to her car. He looked at her. If she looked at him he would wave. He would motion her to pull over so they could speak. Or just to pull over and then she would open the window or door and he could get in or stand in the street by her car and speak. He still never heard her sobs. The car must be solidly built, the convertible top double or triple lined. She was crying for lots of reasons, he supposed. She was probably thinking What am I doing? Why am I doing this? Am I crazy? An idiot? Should I be put away? Do I kill everything I love as Newt said? He'll never want me back. Do I even want to go back? Do I even want to be with a man? What do I want? Will I even know what I want? Is it just that there's nothing I want? Or what I don't want is a man who has too few or too many or just any wants? He must think I'm crazy. Nobody wants a crazy. Or just a woman who's always saying one thing to the man and then when alone changing her mind. She of course could be thinking plenty of other things and then maybe none of that. Though that's what he thought she was crying about.

The car behind her honked. The light had changed. He went right and ran to the gourmet shop a few blocks away and bought lots of goodies to console himself with: rich Jamaican coffee from the high mountains, black Brazilian espresso freshly ground, Brie cheese, Switzerland Swiss cheese, dark bread, German mustard, French mayonnaise, four bock beers from Denmark and an Irish stout, a ripe Colombian plum and ugli fruit, fresh carrots with the stems still on, three Belgian endives, an undamaged artichoke he might steam when he got home and a quarter pound each of health salad and stuffed grapevine leaves. She never passed him on Broadway. She must have crossed the street and gone to West End or Riverside and made her right there.

The next night I dropped by my cousin Harriet's place and while her daughter made a zoetrope out of the canister from the canister of clay and with the sculpting tools I also bought her, Harriet said "Don't worry. Mary will take care of Mary all right." After a couple of condoling drinks and toasts she said "By the way. There's a very nice actress type who works as a temporary at the next desk from mine and who's quite pretty and kind of bright."

"Not so soon."

After I left Harriet's I went to the neighborhood bar Mary and I used to go to. It was around ten o'clock. The bar was crowded. The hockey playoffs, someone said. I don't like hockey or TV. I stood at the back of the bar away from the television set, ordered a draft and thought I'd call the son of a woman I used to live with in California a number of years ago. The boy was eleven now and for a few years had thought of me as his father. I still sent him presents on his birthday and holidays and money when I had it to help pay for his summer vacations with his real father or to buy a special coin. I loved calling him. He always made me cheerful with his high excited voice and what he had to say about what he was presently involved in and had recently done. So I went to the phone booth in front. Someone was in it. I put down my beer, thinking I'd get back to it after the call, and took my jacket off the wall hook to call from one of the booths outside. As I opened the door with my jacket in my hand, a man with an aluminum hard hat on and who I thought had looked at me sort of contemptuously when I came in and who of course stood out among his friends and everyone else in the bar because of that hat, stopped me and said "Oh no, you're not going to steal my friend's jacket."

"Your friend's?" I looked at the jacket. Sure enough it wasn't mine. "There's mine," I said, handing him his friend's jacket and getting mine off a coatrack near the wall hook. I put my jacket on and started for the door. "Sorry. It was an accident."

"Accident your ass," he said.

"It was an accident. Why would I want your friend's jacket?"

"Because it's better and cleaner than yours."

"Better it may be, and cleaner also, but mine has my keys in it," and I patted my jacket's breast pocket which made a jangling sound.

"You thief," he said.

"Now listen. That's ridiculous. I come into this bar a lot. They know me here and they know I'm not a thief. I made a simple mistake. Both jackets are waist-length and dark suede. Mine must have dropped from the hook I almost always hang it on and where your friend's must have been and someone probably picked mine up and put it on the coatrack and that's how the mistake was probably made."

"You Jew," he said.

I don't know why. Because of the gas showers? Crematoriums? Jew-baiting and walled ghettos? Because that's the generation I was brought up in and it was an extremely emotional issue in those days? Whether I'm actually a Jew or not I don't even think matters that much. But I suddenly began strangling him with both hands. His hard hat fell off. It wasn't aluminum but aluminum-colored plastic. His friends dragged me off him. While they held my arms he punched me in the face. His friends let me go. He punched me in the face again before I could get my hands up. Was it because of the rum tonics at Harriet's place that I didn't feel the blows or any pain? Both bartenders rushed up front, one climbing over the bar and the other with the bar's team shirt on and darts in his hand, as he was one of the players in another round of the dart tournament between bars taking place, and they grabbed me and said "Go in back, Newt."

"But I didn't even hit him," I said. "I strangled him for a second, but then he hit me twice and once with my arms tied."

"In back!"

"All right." I grabbed my beer off the bar and went to the back. Then I said "But I was only going outside to call someone from a phone booth. Your booth is filled. Then I was coming back to finish my beer and have a hamburger, so I couldn't have tried to steal his friend's jacket as he said."

"Call from my phone," the bartender behind the bar said.

"It's to California."

"Then you better call from outside."

The dart-playing bartender walked me to the door. I was heading for the phone booth at the corner when someone shouted "Hey you. My friend here wants to know why you wanted to steal his jacket." It was the hard hat and the man whose jacket I suppose it was, since he was wearing it, and who must have been somewhere else when the scuffle took place. I thought of saying "Take off, will you?" and walking away, forgetting the phone call or at least from this booth. But I went back to try and explain to the friend in a calm rational way that I had grown very fond of my jacket over the past ten years and that the only set of keys to my apartment other than the ones in my jacket pocket were thirty miles upstate on the key ring of a person I didn't especially want to see now and the reasons why I think I took his jacket off the wall hook by mistake.

I started my explanation to the friend by saying "Now let's talk this out in a completely unemotional way."

"You bet," the hard hat said right beside us.

"Don't listen to him," I said. "Honestly, I never intended to steal your jacket. I go in there a lot, as I told him. My house keys were even in my own jacket. So my jacket must have fallen to the floor from the hook your jacket was also on and someone—"

"You got blood on your nose," the hard hat said. I turned to him as I felt my nose and said "Will you just go away?" Then the friend punched me in the face and they were on me from in front and back and while my head was being pummeled from above I bent down and grabbed one of their legs apiece around the knees and I swear lifted them off the ground and threw them further up in the air. I screamed something like "Yaaach," and ran after both of them and kicked one and slashed my hand down on the other's neck and then kicked that one and slashed the other across the head and was grabbed from behind by two other men from the bar, one of them saying "We're only trying to protect you," and I said "Bullshit, because in the bar while you were protecting me you let that bastard there get one off at my face," and I threw them off me and began kicking and slashing away at them and the friend who had come back to try and tackle me. And then I was free of them all and in the middle of the sidewalk and they were against the parked cars and a tree and the window of a grocery store and I said "Well come on. I'll take on all three of you. All four." And I really felt I could. I felt that powerful and aggressive. But the hard hat said "Fix your nose," and they all went into the bar. The doors closed. Some other people from the bar had been watching.

Both bartenders too. The man who had come out of his store to watch said "Crazy."

"That's right," I said.

"I didn't mean it in a harmful way."

"I know. And I didn't mean it to you in a harmful way either."

He went into the store. I started for home, laughing a little as I went. At the way those men, at first so belligerent and brave, could be beaten off by just one not too strong man, though probably strong then. For I don't like to fight. I can't remember when I last had a fight. I really would stand there and let a man hit me in the face without hitting him back and then say something like "Fine. Did it feel good? Are you through?" and walk away. I won't go into that bar again. And I suppose, which is why I brought up the incident, that my maniacal counterattack and sudden surge of unforeseen strength, as we used to say, came not so much from any flashing thoughts about crematoriums and gas showers or weariness of the continuing and probably never-ending contentiousness of men, but from something I had to get rid of concerning Em.

14

Stories

➤

Eugene Randall held the gun in front of his mouth and fired. The bullet smashed his upper front teeth, left his head through the back of his jaw, pierced an earlobe and broke a window that overlooked much of the midtown area. A chambermaid on the floor said to herself "What kind of noise is that—that sounds like a bullet. And a window being broke. But maybe it wasn't either." The bullet landed a block away on a brownstone roof, where a boy was watching mama-and-papa pigeons sitting in the sun. Mr. Randall fell over the end table, sending to the floor a lamp, pack of cigarillos and an ashtray that had been resting on the three notes he'd written regarding his suicide. The wind came in through the broken window, picked the letters off the floor and distributed them around the room. The chambermaid leaned on her cleaning cart and said "Yes sir, that was a shot all right. Someone's practicing on the windows or furniture or maybe gone and killed himself or someone he didn't like. It happened last month on the twenty-first. And a year before that on the eighth. All kinds of suicides and nuts end up in this hotel, and these drunken conventioneers and lonely Japanese businessmen the worst." She lifted a phone receiver. One letter landed on the couch. Another under the coffee table. The third floated out the window and higher than Mr. Randall's room on the fourteenth floor. The boy looked at the bullet that had rolled to within a foot of him. He thought it was a stone, picked it up, dropped it because it felt so rough, almost prickly, stared at it and said "Holy G, that's a bullet. Someone tried to shoot me with a bullet," and opened the roof door and ran downstairs. The pigeons flapped when the door slammed behind the boy, settled in the same positions they were in before. "This is Anna," the chambermaid said on the phone, "Anna from the fourteenth, and I think there's been a shooting on my floor." The hotel detective said maybe it was a loud car backfire she'd heard and Anna said "No sir, no backfire. I heard it while in the hallway, so you could be right if you said it came from a guest's television screen." He told her to wait for him by the center elevators and she said "Make it snappy, sir, as who's to say there isn't a lunatic loose."

Mr. Randall lay groaning on the floor. Bad shot, bad shot, he thought, he tried to say. That note out the window—which one?—he hoped not to his ex-wife or mother.

"Where's the fire?" a neighbor said, grabbing the boy's arm as he raced around the second-story landing.

"Someone tried to kill me up there—with a bullet. I was sitting watching the pigeons, minding my business, when wham, it's shot, a bullet, not an inch from my eye. If I'd been sitting where I always sit, I'd be dead, I swear."

"Now what kind of story is that?" the neighbor said, and the boy said "You want to come and see?" and they went up to the roof. The neighbor pushed open the door slowly, said it was safe, no sharpshooting assassins from what he could see, "that is, if you're telling the truth," and stepped onto the roof.

"There it is," the boy said, pointing to the bullet between their feet. "Don't touch it. The police will want it for evidence." The man picked up the bullet. "I said not to touch it. You're going to get in trouble. The police don't like people fooling with their evidence."

"Don't worry." The neighbor inspected the bullet. "This is a bullet all right. No little air pellet either. It's a real bullet, real meaning from a real pistol or rifle, probably a .22. You're lucky you're alive." They went downstairs to phone the police.

"Right this way, sir," Anna said to the hotel detective who came out of the elevator. "Right down here somewhere down this hall's where I heard the bullet sound." The detective said he would check out her story with some guests on the floor and knocked on the first of the twenty rooms in this wing of the hotel.

"Yes?" a male guest said through the peephole, and the detective identified himself, said don't be alarmed but wondered if the guest had heard anything around here in the last fifteen minutes that sounded like a gun being fired.

"A gun? No, not since breakfast. No, let me correct that—not since a few seconds after the boy wheeled in my breakfast. I shot him for bringing me three two-minute eggs when I had explicitly called down for two three's."

"Thank you very much," the detective said and Anna and he went to the next door. Nobody answered. He let himself in with a passkey. No smell, no bullet, no disturbance here, he thought. And nice neat person who's renting the place also—pants hung so evenly over the back of the chair, the orderly way he put his toilet and personal articles on the dresser, all lined up like a column of soldiers. "Let's try the next one," he said.

Head, pain, help, quick, Mr. Randall thought. He tried to scream. He tried to crawl. He tried to reach for a part of the broken lamp to throw and smash so someone would hear the noise and come. But his arms and fingers wouldn't move. His lips did, but nothing came out but more blood and pain. Better in a hospital. Better under sedation. Anything better than this, this pain, this killing pain.

"Maybe I ought to tell my mom first," the boy said, stopping on the fourth floor. He didn't know whether to ring the bell so his mother could have time to fix herself or open the door with his key and maybe surprise her nude or in panties, which she didn't mind when they were alone, but with this man with him and all.... "Maybe I better ring," the boy said.

"Don't you have a key to your own place? You seem old enough."

"Who said I didn't?" He unlocked the door, parted it an inch, yelled "Hey Mom—you home?" though he knew she was, reading or asleep. She only went out on Fridays, to shop.

The wind died and the note drifted for a while over a busy street before it landed on the hood of a parked car. A young woman walking arm in arm with a man said "Look, Ron, a message from heaven just came." She started for the car but the man, keeping their arms locked at the elbows and spreading his feet to anchor his weight, jerked her back to his side. "Let me get it," she said. "Maybe it'll tell us where a secret city fortune is."

"Uh-uh," Ron said. "We're chained like this for life."

"For life—that's nice." She kissed his lips. "Though it also sounds horrid, like a prison term. But please let me see what it says."

"Well...why don't we kind of slide over there together." They moved sideways, arms still locked, the woman leading, till she got close enough to stretch for the note with her free hand, but it was blown over the car hood. "This is getting exciting," she said, and they waited for the traffic to pass so they could follow the note across the street.

Mr. Randall couldn't move his body from the waist up. He was able to dig his knees into the carpet and push himself a few inches a minute that way, but even if he reached the door he wouldn't be able to unfasten the latch or turn the knob. He would be able to draw attention by banging the door with his feet, but it might take him an hour to get there. He didn't want to suddenly get stiff in his haul across the room and then suffer this pain for hours till he died. Better the telephone on the end table at the other side of the couch. He could knee himself there, knock the table over with his feet. The operator would know something was wrong when no one answered. And if he got his mouth right on the receiver she would hear him breathing.

"What is it, love?" the boy's mother said, coming out of the bedroom. "Oh, excuse me," and she turned and quickly buttoned up her bathrobe. "You should've told me you were with someone, Warren."

"It was sort of emergency—that's why I forgot."

The man was thinking And I always thought she was so flat and skinny, I don't know why. Seen her on the stairs maybe three four times in a year and always thought she had a body like a boy and even looked like one with her short hair and always sneakers and slacks. But good Christ what a figure.

"I was up on the roof watching the pigeons when someone tried to shoot me, Ma."

"Something like that, Mrs. Lang. I was climbing the steps when Warren was running down, and I asked what was wrong and he said the same thing he told you. Here it is," and he opened his fist and showed her the bullet.

"You sure he didn't just plant that thing up there? You didn't, did you, Warren?"

"Well, because of his frightened look when he was running down, I tended to believe him. Nobody could impersonate such a scare—not even an actor. You think you should call the police?"

"My God, what a neighborhood. Boys being shot at on roofs. Shopkeepers hiring police dogs. Addicts, these filthy addicts making us all fearful to walk into our own homes. Are you sure that's a bullet—what's your name, please?"

"William Singerton. I'm a neighbor, one floor right below you. In fact, we have the exact same apartment layout I see, though your stove and refrigerator are bigger."

"If you think his story's authentic, Mr. Singerton. I mean, even if someone was only shooting the pigeons, I suppose you should still call the police." Mr. Singerton dialed Operator.

"Hear that?" the hotel detective said.

"Hear what?" Anna said.

"Phone falling. I heard the short tingling like from the bell inside a phone when it falls. Came from one of the rooms down there," and they walked to the three doors at the end of the corridor.

" 'Dear Mom,' the letter starts off with," the young woman said. "It's to this Gene fellow's mother, and the writing seems very legible and intelligent."

"Let me see," Ron said.

"First you got to let go of my arm."

"I told you, Loey: we're locked like this forever and ever no matter what adversities we face. Now let me see the letter."

"Not till you release me."

"I'll release you if you kiss me once on the cheek, once where my eyebrows meet, and once right here, smack dab on it," and he touched his lips.

She kissed him on all three spots. "Now release me."

"Not until you hand me the letter. Because what I failed to mention about me is also your main disadvantage: you're linked for life to a liar."

"Then neither of us is going to read it," and she stuck the letter into her coat pocket.

"Hello? I said, hello? I said, this is Mrs. Vega, your hotel operator, may I help you?" She signaled the operator seated beside her to remove her earphones. "What should I do? 1403's breathing pretty heavy into the receiver but not answering me."

"Maybe they accidentally knocked over the phone while they were making love. That happens. Check with Desk if it's a couple staying there, or someone with a small child."

"What should I tell the breather?"

"Say 'Hold on,' that's all. 'Hold on,' and then call down and ask who's in 1403. Also ask if the guest's got a dog or cat, which could also be the problem."

"Thanks, Andrea. I only hope I can be as much help to the girl who takes over from me when I go."

"The girl who takes over from you is going to be a machine, dearie—a computer with a recorded sweet voice and perfect brain. Why do you think I'm leaving the profession after so long? Not only because you never meet anyone but the janitor, cooped up in this cell, but for another reason that the job's getting extinct. For you it's fine because you need a couple years' wages till your husband says 'Let's have a baby.' But for me, a lifetime worker—I know that, there's no family or man in my future—this profession's dying out quickly. Like the ink pen. Like the elevator operator."

"Like the elevator operator. That's true. They haven't any in this hotel, do they?" and she rang the desk clerk.

"A phone drop?" the woman guest in 1402 said. "Since when does management have to send up a detective to see about a phone being dropped?"

"It's related to something else—a possible accident on the floor."

She called out "Leonard? Did you recently drop a telephone on the floor?" and a man yelled back through the closed bathroom door "Not unless I did and didn't know about it."

"What's the trouble if I may ask?" the woman said. "I'm worried now."

"Don't be. It's only that Anna here—"

"How do you do, ma'am," Anna said.

"Anna thought she heard a noise like a gunshot go off before, though it could have been a car backfire or sound effects from a TV show."

"Leonard," she yelled, "did you hear anything like a gunshot before? Something that wasn't a car backfiring or from a television show?"

"I did," Leonard said through the door. "From right where I'm sitting. But I didn't know what to figure with this town, so I forgot about it. Why, is someone hurt?"

Over the phone the desk sergeant took down the name, address, apartment and telephone number of Mrs. Lang. "You sure someone will be home when we get there?" he said.

"We'll stay here till the police come," Mr. Singerton said.

"What's your connection with the mother and the boy?"

"A neighbor."

"A neighbor around the neighborhood, in the building or a roomer in Mrs. Lang's apartment?"

"In the building, though I don't see what bearing that has on the matter. When the questions get that personal I sort of feel I shouldn't have gotten involved."

"All right," the sergeant said. "Just stay where you are and a man will be right over. And don't touch the bullet. Leave everything in its place."

"He said not to touch the bullet," Mr. Singerton said to Mrs. Lang, opening his fist and showing her the bullet. "What do you think they'll do when they find out I did?"

"Why don't you put it back where you found it?" Warren said.

"With my prints all over it? Besides, if they find out, I'll get in more trouble that way."

"Wipe them off why don't you, but I told you not to touch it."

"Thank you. *He told me.* If I'd been smart I should have let him pass when he came flying downstairs. I never should have left my flat for cigarettes—never should have been smoking, in fact. Cancer I'll get, and also a jail sentence. In fact, I never should have taken my first puff when I was young and everyone said don't take your first puff, Willy, because it will lead to bad things. Little did they know. Do you smoke, Warren?"

"Me? I'm only ten."

"Well don't, you hear? Don't even experiment. Take my troubles with the police now as an example why not to."

"'Dear Mom,'" Loey read. "'I'm sorry for what sadness to you and disrespect for the family my death this way will cause you, but all I ask is that you try not to be too sad and try to understand me. I've thought about killing myself for more than a year now. I tried to work things out for myself many other ways, but everything I did always made things even worse, which you know for me is really not too hard to believe. After the business went, Sarah and the kids went soon after that and it was just too much for me. And then all my so-called friends went. I suppose they thought I'd sponge on them or else be too maudlin a person to be with, now that my business and wife and—' I can't go on," Loey said. She gave the note to Ron, began crying. He unhooked his arm from hers and said "Maybe this letter isn't a joke at all."

"You mean you still think someone could think up a joke like that?"

"Yes."

"But the letter writer even put his mother's name, address, city, state and phone number on top of the page. Now why would a joker go to that far extent in making a joke?"

"To make the joke seem more real?"

"He'd write a long letter like this and put all that information about a woman on top of the page and then sail it out the window hoping that someone he had never seen before and would never see unless he's now looking at us from one of those windows, would find the note and think the suicide story is real?"

"I didn't say I was positive it was a joke. I only said I maybe still think it is." He read the note: "'. . . too maudlin a person' etcetera, 'children were gone,' period. 'I don't know. I can't explain anything anymore. I'm sick. Blame the whole affair on my emotional sickness. I'm sorry, Mom. I love you. I hate for the pain I know I'm going to inflict on you. You've been the dearest person in my life. Of course Greta and Zane are dear, but they're across the country and too young to help. This note's too long. I love you, Mom. It's silly, but if I could live it would be most to spare you the pain of my death. I was almost going to say "To help you live through the pain of my death," which is why I said before "It's silly." And now I'm getting too silly for a suicide note, besides too long. Always my love. Your devoted son, Gene.' "

"The note's real," Ron said. "I feel awful feeling it wasn't. I think we should call the police about this, as that mother should get her note."

"No she shouldn't," Loey said, and grabbed the note from him and tore it up and threw the pieces in the gutter. She ran across the street and around the corner.

"There's a Mr. Eugene A. Randall in 1403," the desk clerk told the operator on the phone. "It's a double occupancy he's in, and though he's renting it as such, he's a single."

"Well, I hate to be a busybody, Mr. Hire. But 1403's been buzzing me for some time now, and when I said 'Hello, may I help you?' all I heard was heavy breathing."

"Is that room still on the line?"

She switched 1403 off Hold, heard the same kind of heavy breathing, said "Hello? Mr. Randall? This is Mrs. Vega again, your hotel operator. Is anything wrong? I said, is anything wrong?" She switched 1403 to Hold and said "Still on it, Mr. Hire, breathing just as regularly. Being new here I don't want to be advising you your business, but I really think something's the matter."

Mr. Hire dialed the hotel detective's extension, but nobody was in. He checked in his book of private listings, called Operator and told her to page Detective Feuer on his pocket pager and have him contact Mr. Hire on extension 78 regarding a possible hotel accident.

"Hello?" Mrs. Vega said in his head, "is anything the matter, 1403? If it is then say so. Say 'Help' if you can't say anything else. If this is Mr. Randall and anything is wrong with you, then someone's coming right up, Mr. Randall. I'm sure they'll be right there."

Someone knocked, rang the bell. "Mr. Randall, you in?" a man said. "Better use the passkey," another man said. "What did he look like?" the first man said. "I don't know," a woman said, "I never saw him. When I brought him his towels, he was in the bedroom. When I brought up glasses and ice for whiskeys, he was in the bathroom. He left a good tip both times, though. And never any noise from him till now, sir." The door opened. Lots of legs and stockings and shoes. "Oh God," the woman said. "Oh God, oh God," and she ran screaming down the long hall. She knocked over her cleaning cart. Doors in the corridor opened, heads looked out. "What's all the commotion about?" a woman guest said. "What's with this hotel?" a male guest said. "Noisy—the worst," and he slammed his door. "The doctor will be here shortly, Mr. Randall," a man kneeling beside him said. "I'm the hotel manager. Try and rest. Don't speak."

"Now you say you picked up this bullet on the roof here?" the policeman said.

"I didn't pick it up," Warren said. "He did," pointing to Mr. Singerton. "I told him not to, but he wouldn't listen."

"You should have known better, Mr. Singerton."

"I probably did, but got overeager. I wanted to see if the boy was telling the truth. If the bullet was warm, recently fired."

"The sun—lots of things could have warmed it. Not hoping there's a next time—please be more careful? For now I'll report it, and if anything comes in about a shooting here around the time Warren mentioned, then your phoning might be some use." He got up. "Thanks for the coffee, Mrs. Lang."

"Not at all. You finished also, Mr. Singerton?"

"Finished." He handed her his mug, gave a dirty look to Warren.

"I'm sorry," Warren said to him. "I forgot."

"Forgot what?" the policeman said.

"Oh, I forgot I wasn't supposed to say anything about how I wasn't supposed to tell him how I told him not to touch the bullet on the roof. That it was evidence."

Ron caught up with Loey in a drugstore. She was sitting at the counter spooning the whipped cream off a hot chocolate into her mouth. He sat beside her, showed a handful of pieces of torn note. "I think I got every one of them. And I still believe his mother should get it."

"Let's forget we ever read it, Ron. Ever found it?"

"How? Just by pushing it out of our heads? And why try and forget something that maybe really is a joke and now an even bigger one on us because we took it so seriously. And then maybe the man who wrote it was telling the truth but hasn't killed himself yet. I just thought of that. Maybe he's right this moment planning to kill himself tonight or tomorrow morning and this note fell out of his pocket and by phoning the police we can still stop him. That is, if it isn't a joke."

"It isn't a joke."

The fountain man said "Did I hear you say something about someone's suicide note?"

"Not mine or hers, or maybe nobody's. We're not sure. You have a phone we can call the police on?"

"Go through the rear door there into the hotel lobby. They got plenty, all supervised. Ours have all been ripped or kicked out."

"A man, you should've seen him," Anna said in the female employees' washroom. "Room an ugly mess, blood all over his face, a black hole in the side of his cheek, half his ear off as all chewed through. I saw it once and ran as I never did. A Mr. Randall."

"Randall?" a typist in Accounting said. "No, I didn't see his bill today. What room number?"

"1403. Such a clean nice man. I never saw him once since his two days here, but he gave me big tips all the times I came in his room. Once for extra towels. He yelled out to me from the bedroom he liked to bathe a lot. And a second for glasses and ice for whiskey. And one more time just now I remember. What was it again? He called Service to bring up two real down or no-rubber pillows, and he tipped me for that also. Left the money right where the used whiskey glasses were."

"That's something I've always been curious about. Because I can't see how you girls can know for sure what change lying around when you're cleaning up is for a tip and what change was left by mistake."

"We don't. But if you want to make enough living at our job, then you have to think all change lying around except on the bed or dresser, if all his other pocket things are there also, is yours. That is, if there's only one pile of change and it doesn't come up to a lot more than a dollar for one day let's say, but just to around fifty to a dollar in cents. But if it has odd pennies in the change, meaning one to four but not five or ten exact, then we also don't take. Then we think the change was left by accident, because no tipper leaves odd pennies."

Easy, *easy*, EASY, Mr. Randall thought as he was being lifted onto the stretcher. He wanted to say they were handling his head much too roughly, wheeling the stretcher much too hard. "Easy," he finally said, "or I die."

"Were you planning anything for dinner tonight?" Mr. Singerton said.

"Same as always: something nothing for Warren and me."

"Like to eat out then? This might seem strange—how it started off I mean—though I have seen you on the stairway."

"Seen you also. You must work nights, because the only times I've seen you is during the day."

"I write technical brochures, so I can work home as long as I hand in my copy at the specified time."

"To work in your apartment and get well paid for it would be the best kind of work I'd like to do. But I don't know anything about writing except for letters. Plus a journal I've been keeping on and off since Warren was born."

"To me the worst thing about other people's journals is that I can't read them. I'm a born snoop."

"That's probably why you picked up the bullet when Warren told you not to."

"I knew it had to be something," Warren said.

"You still want to go out?" Mr. Singerton said. "I can pick you up at six."

"That's foolish," she said. "If I lived below you then I could see you coming to my door, but not when I'm one floor above. I'll ring your bell when I'm ready."

"But that wouldn't be proper," he said.

"First saw it on the car hood," Ron said on the phone, "just laying there. It's a bit ripped up now, but I got all the pieces and with Scotch tape I think you could read it. My girlfriend just didn't want to believe the note. Did the guy die?"

"Last we heard, he was living," the detective said. "You stay there and I'll have a man get the note."

"He's still alive," Ron said to Loey. "Shot himself right in the head. I wonder what kind of gun he used."

She grabbed most of the note which Ron had assembled on the counter, and ran out of the drugstore. Ron ran after her, shouted "You crazy? You want us both thrown in jail? The cops have my name. They're coming now to get the note. Bring it back, goddamn you," but she got in a cab and one by one threw the pieces out of the window as the car drove away.

"Goodbye, Mr. Randall," the intern said in the ambulance, and covered Mr. Randall's face with the top of the blanket.

"You were right, Bonnie," Andrea said, removing her earphones. "Desk phoned for me to locate fourteenth-floor service to clean up 1403. That Mr. Randall. A suicide."

Bonnie closed her eyes, was silent, tears came, said "I knew it. That breathing wasn't natural. It didn't sound like sleep or sex or dogs, cats or anything. It truly sounded like someone dying," and she imitated the sounds she heard on the phone. "Like that."

"If you ask me it still sounds like sex," Andrea said. She rang fourteenth-floor service and got Anna on the phone. "Anna, this is Andrea. Mr. Hire wants for you to go to 1403 and clean up the room. I'm sorry, but there's been a suicide there, love." Anna hung up. Andrea called back. "Anna, you feeling sick from what I told you? You see, Mr. Hire wants the room cleaned up immediately. He tried reaching you himself but you weren't in. There'll be police up there, so he wants you to try and do your best and clean around them. The fourteenth is your floor, isn't it?"

A policeman was looking at the two suicide notes when the chambermaid walked into the room. One was addressed to "Mrs. Sarah Randall, my former wife." He read: "I have nothing unkind to say to you, Sarah, nor anything that is kind. Do what you think best in disclosing the news of my death to the children. Word it any way, I don't care. You were always good with them—with words. I hate writing letters like this. Any letters. I haven't much money left and only a few questionable stocks and the insurance policies, and they are of course all for you and the children. Also, every thing I can't think about right now, like the car. It's parked in this hotel garage in my name. The parking spot is row L, space 16, if I recall correctly. And everything in our old apartment which might turn out to be more trouble in disposing than they are monetarily worth. Always my love. I'm also sorry for the difficulties my death will most naturally cause you, and for the fact that I am leaving you theoretically impoverished because of the cutting off of my monthly payments. As for the children's shame and/or grief and/or realization later on in life as to the kind of maniacal blood that might be running through their blood if yours isn't hopefully dominant; I am of course absolutely despondent about that too. I love them. I pray they get a more sensible father. Love, Eugene."

And the letter to his friend: "I've informed Sarah that everything I own, including cash, stocks, policies and apartment possessions are hers to do with as she wishes. My bank is City Central. I don't remember the account number for either my savings or checking accounts, but I'm sure a bank official will be able to provide them to you without much trouble. The savings should be all of $150, the check account balance possibly twice that. I've neglected to keep my bank records straight this past week, but I'm sure that figure ($300) is close. The car's all paid up as of two months ago and has a bluebook value of $425. It's in this hotel garage, row L, space 16. The hotel, which you probably know, is the Continental. I suppose all this makes you the executor of my vast estate. Sorry, for that burden, Harris. My best to you, Whitney, the children. Things were good and not so complicated for me when they were going good, but I think you'd be the last person in the world to ask or even desire an explanation, right? Always my best for our many years of friendship and my regrets for our recent falling-out. Gene."

"It's all yours, miss," one of the policemen said, and they left the room.

"Why me?" Anna said in the empty room. "Of all people, why me? Why not the maid on the twelfth, for instance? Why couldn't they bring her here for the job instead of asking the one maid who already saw that poor man? It'd only be one flight up for her, and she has a strong stomach for everything she's always said and she didn't have to see that poor man. That dumb man. Shooting himself like that. Causing everybody else who comes after him all these troubles and heartaches and extra work. Like cleaning up after him. Always I have to clean up after these kind. Never a suicide yet. Thank God never one before on this floor. And shooting out a window, which makes no sense. It's crazy."

She called up the hotel repair shop. "Could you please send up a window man to put in a new window in 1403? And hurry, please."

She wrote on a list: "New ashtray, new lamp." These she could get easily from Stock. She swept up the pieces of broken window glass and china and dumped them in the can on her cleaning cart. But the blood? "Oh you unfeeling man. What do I do about getting rid of your blood? Soap and water won't work. The stain's been on the carpet too long. I know. I don't have to test. You need something else to get it out."

She phoned Mr. Hire. "Please, Mr. Hire, I don't like the job you told Andrea to give me in 1403. I can't clean up this room. I can't even stay in this room. Just the thought of that poor man lying where he was on the floor where I saw him before, me first with the detective and Mr. Reece, is enough to make me sick. Please take me off. Call Harriet who works on the twelfth or that new girl on the fifteenth. They can come up or down on the elevator and use my cart. And I also don't know how to clean up dried bloodstains. Maybe that makes me a very bad chambermaid, Mr. Hire, but I never can stand the sight of blood. I can't even stand the sight of my own blood. I can't even hardly take care of my daughter when she gets hurt and spills lots of blood. Please take me off, Mr. Hire. I just can't do it."

Milk Is
Very Good
for You

———

It was getting fairly late in the evening for me so I asked my wife if she was ready to leave. "Just a few minutes, love," she said, "I'm having such a good time." I wasn't. The party was a bore, as it had been from the start. Another drinking contest taking place in the kitchen, some teachers and their husbands or wives turning on in the john, Phil somebody making eyes at Joe who's-it's wife, Joe trying to get Mary Mrs. to take a breath of fresh air with him as he said while Mary's husband was presently engaged with someone else's sweetheart or wife for a look at the constellation she was born under, and I felt alone, didn't want to turn on or drink another drink or walk another man's wife through the fresh air for some fresh caressing. I wanted to return home and my wife didn't as she was aching to turn on or drink with some other man but me and most especially to walk in the fresh air with Frank whatever his name was as Frank's wife had just taken that same stroll with Joe after Joe had learned that Mary had promised herself tonight to the dentist friend accompanying her and her husband to this house, so I decided to leave.

"Goodbye, Cindy," I said.

"Leaving now, love?"

"Leaving now, yes, are you going to come?"

"Not right this moment, Rick, though I'll find some way home."

"Take your time getting there," I said, "no need to rush. Even skip breakfast if that's what you've mind to—I'll see to the kids. Even pass up tomorrow's lunch and dinner if you want—things will work out. In fact, spend the weekend or week away if you'd like to—I'll take care of everything at home. Maybe two weeks or a month or even a year would be the time you need for a suitable vacation, it's all okay with me, dear," and I kissed her goodbye, drove home, relieved the babysitter who said "You needn't have returned so early, Mr. Richardson, as the children never even made a peep. I like babysitting them so much it's almost a crime taking money for the job."

"So don't," I said, and Jane said "Well, that wasn't exactly a statement of fact, Mr. Richardson," and pocketed her earnings and started for the door.

"Goodnight," I said on the porch, "and I really hope you don't mind my not walking you home tonight. I'm really too beat."

"It's only two blocks to the dorm, though I will miss those nice chats we have on the way."

Those nice chats. Those tedious six-to-seven-minute monologues of Jane's on her boyfriends' inability to be mature enough for her or her inability to be unpretendingly immature for them or more likely she telling me about her schoolwork, no doubt thinking I'd be interested because I teach the same subject she's majoring at in the same school she attends. "Tonight," Jane said, "I especially wanted your advice on a term paper I'm writing on the father-son if not latent or even overt homosexual relationship between Boswell and Johnson, since it's essential I get a good grade on my paper if I'm to get a B for the course."

"Bring it to the office and I'll correct and even rewrite a few of the unclearer passages if you want."

"Would you do that, Mr. Richardson? That would be too nice of you, more help than I ever dreamed of," and so thrilled was she that she threw her arms around my back, and while she hugged me in gratitude I couldn't resist kissing the nape of her neck in passion and now something had started: Jane said "Oh, Mr. Richardson, you naughty teacher, that's not what I even half-anticipated from you," and rubbed my back and squeezed my menis through the pants and said "My me my but you're surprising me in many ways today," and unzippered me and riddled with my menis till I was ranting so hard I couldn't warn her in time that I was about to some in her land.

"What funky rickety gush," she said. "Do you have a hanky?"

"I'm sorry. And I think I also spoiled your pretty skirt."

"This dinky old thing? Here, let me clean you off properly." And still in the dark of my porch she squatted down and wiped me dry with a hanky and then wobbled up my menis and before I could say anything rational to her, such as this was an extremely indiscreet setting for a young woman from the same college I didn't as yet have tenure at to be living read to the man whose children she just babysat for, I was on the floor myself, her south never letting go of my menis as I swiveled around underneath her, lowered her panties, stack my longue in her ragina and began rowing town on her also, slowly, loving the gradually increasing pace we had tacitly established when Jane said "Go get the flit, Mr. Richardson, brink up the little flit," which I couldn't find so one by one I desoured every slover of flash that protruded in and around her ragina, hoping to discover— by some sudden jerky movement or exclamation or cry—that I had fortuitously struck home.

"That's it," she said, "right there, that's the little devil, you've got him by the nose," and after several minutes of us both without letup living read to one another, we same at precisely the same time.

"Now for the real thing," Jane said, "though do you think we're in too much light? Screw it, nobody can hear us, you and Mrs. Richardson have a nice big piece of property here, real nice, besides my not caring one iota if anyone does, do you?" and she stuck her panties in her book bag, got on her rack on the floor, slopped my menis back and forth till I got an election and started carefully to guide me in.

"Rick, you imbecile," my wife said. "I can hear you two hyenas howling from a block away."

"Good evening, Mrs. Richardson," Jane said, standing and adjusting her skirt.

"Good evening, Jane. Did the children behave themselves?"

"Angels, Mrs. Richardson. I was telling Mr. Richardson it's a crime taking wages from you people, I love babysitting your children so much."

"I told her 'Well don't take the money,'" I said.

"And I said 'That wasn't exactly a statement of fact, Mr. Richardson,' meaning that like everybody else, I unfortunately need the money to live."

"And what did you say to that?" Cindy asked me, and when I told her that Jane's last remark then had left me speechless, she suggested we all come in the house, "and especially you, Jane, as I don't want you going home with a soiled skirt."

We all went inside. Cindy, getting out the cleaning fluid and iron, said "By the way. You two can go upstairs if you want while I clean Jane's skirt."

"I don't know how much I like the idea of that," I said, "or your blasé attitude, Cindy."

"Oh it's all right, Mr. Richardson. Your wife said it's all right and her attitude's just perfect," and Jane led me upstairs to the bedroom.

We were in red, Jane heated on top of me, my sock deep in her funt and linger up her masspole, when Cindy said through the door "Your skirt is ready Jane." "Is it?" Jane said, and Cindy entered the room with no clothes on and said "Yes, it's cleaning-store clean," got in red with us and after drawing us baking dove with me inder Jane for a whole, she put down her pen and pad and but her own funt over my south and in seconds all three of us were sounding up and down on the red, dewling, bailing, grubbing at each other's shoulders and hair. "Oh Rick," Cindy said, "Oh Mr. Richardson," Jane said, "Oh Janie," both Cindy and I said, "Oh Mrs. Richardson," Jane said, "Oh Cindybee," I said. And just as the thought came to me that my greatest fantasy for the last fifteen years of me with my longue and menis in the respective funts of two cotmassed magnificent women was about to be realized exactly as I had fantasized it and that was with the most spectacular some of my life, my eldest daughter, Dandy, came into the room and said "Mommy, Daddy, Janie, can I have some milk?"

"Go back to bed," Cindy said.

"I want some milk too," Beverly, my other daughter, said.

"There is no milk," Jane said. "I drank it all."

"You did what?" Cindy said. "You did what?"

"Drank it all."

Cindy hot off my lace and told me to sake alay my tick from Jane's funt and that I could also escort her to her dorm if I didn't mind, as any babysitter who'd drink up the last of the milk when she knew the children she was sitting for liked nothing better first thing in the morning than milk in their cereal and glasses just shouldn't be allowed to remain another second in this house.

"How much milk was there?" I said.

"A quart at least," Cindy said.

"Two," Jane said, "—but two and a half to be exact. I simply got very thirsty and drank it all, though in several sittings."

Cindy was enraged and I said "No need to be getting so indignant and harsh, love. So the young lady got thirsty. So it was an act of, let us say, imprudence."

"I want some milk," Dandy said. "Me too," Beverly said. "Drink some water if you're thirsty," Jane told them. "Drink water nothing,"

Cindy said. "Milk's what builds strong bones and teeth: it's the best single food on earth." "One morning without a glassful won't arrest their physical development," Jane said, and Cindy snapped back "I'll be the judge of that," and put on her bathrobe, took the children by the hand and left the room. She was saying as she went downstairs: "The nerve of that girl. Two quarts. That cow. When your daddy comes down I'll have him drive straight to the all-night supermarket for milk."

"I want some now," Dandy said. "Me too," Beverly said. "I have to go," I said to Jane.

"You don't think we can just finish up a bit?"

"The girls want their milk and Cindy's about to explode even more."

"You realize it was only this seizure of thirstiness I had. If you had had soda I would have drank that instead—or at least only one of the quarts of milk and the rest soda."

"Cindy won't have soda around the house. Says it's very bad for their teeth."

"She's probably right." Jane started to put on her panties, had one foot through a leg opening when she said "I'm still feeling like I'd like your sock and don't know when we'll have another chance for it."

"I have to go to the market, Jane."

"Your wife has a nice funt too. I mean it's different than mine, bigger because she's had babies, but I luck as well, don't I?" I said I thought she was very good, very nice. "And I know what to do with a menis when ic's in my south. I think I excel there, wouldn't you say?"

"I really don't know. This is kind of a funny conversation."

"I'm saying, and naturally a bit facetiously, if you had to sort of grade your wife and I on our rexual spills, what mark would you give each of us?"

"The difficulty of grading there is that I could only grade you on just our single experience this morning and not an entire term's work, while Cindy and I have had semesters together if not gotten a couple of degrees, if I'm to persist in this metaphorical comparison, so any grading would be out of the question."

"So grade on just what we'll call our class participation this morning."

"Then I'd give you both an A."

"You don't think I deserve an A plus?"

"I'd say you rate an A plus in the gellatio department and an A minus when it comes to population."

"And your wife?"

"Just the reverse, which comes to a very respectable A for you both."

"I was sort of hoping for an A plus. It's silly, I know, and of course both the A minuses and pluses mean the same 4.0 on your scholastic rating, but I never got an A plus for anything except gym, which I got twice."

"Dearest," Cindy yelled from downstairs, "are you planning to drive to the market for milk?"

"In a second, love. I'm dressing."

"Daddy," Dandy said, "I'm starving, I want milk," and Beverly said "Me too."

"Those are precious kids," Jane said. "And even though Mrs. Richardson is mad at me, I still like her a lot. I think she's very knowing, if not wise."

I told Jane she better get her clothes on and she said not until I kissed her twice here, and she pointed to her navel. "That's ridiculous," I said, and she said "Maybe, but I insist all my dovers leave me with at least that. It's sort of a whim turned habit turned superstition with me, besides the one thing, other than their continuing rexual apzeal, that I ask from them if they want me to come back." I said, while making exaggerated gentlemanly gestures with my hands, then in that case I'd submit to her ladyship and bent over and kissed her twice on the navel. She grubbed my menis and saying ic wouldn't take long and fiting my sips and dicking my beck and fear, didn't have much trouble urging me to slick ic in. I was on sop of her this time, my tody carried along by Jane's peverish hyrating covements till I same like a whunderflap and kept on soming till the girls ran into the room, asked if Daddy was dying of poison or something, and then Cindy right behind them, wanting to know whether I was aiming to be tossed into a prison for disturbing the neighborhood's holy Sabbath morning with my cries of otter ecstagy or Jane to be thrown out of school because a once well-respected professor could be heard from a few blocks off sailing out her fame.

"A plus," was all I could answer. "Milk," the girls said. Cindy threw the car keys on the red.

"What a luck," Jane said, "what a sock, what a day."

"Jane and I will have to run away for a month," I told Cindy. "I'm serious: there's no other way."

"And the milk?"

"I'll go to the market first."

"And your job?"

"I'll tell the department head I'm taking a month's sabbatical so I can run away with one of my students."

"And Jane's studies? And the children's sitter? Who'll I get now?"

"I'll provide you with a few names," Jane said. "Some very sweet, reliable girls from my dorm."

"It's useless arguing against you two. Just do what you want."

"You're a love," I said to Cindy, and hugged her. She sissed my boulder, right on the slot that excites me most and that only Cindy seems to be able to do right, so I mugged her lighter, clitched her mute rutt, and she began dicking my fear with her longue, holding my fair, pickling my falls, and said "Let's go to red. Last time for a month, let's say."

"Milk, Daddy," Dandy said. "Milk, Daddy," Bev said.

"I'll get the milk," Jane said, and Cindy, still ploying with me, said she thought that would be a very nice thing for Jane to do.

Jane said she'd take the girls in the car with her, "though you'll have to pay me overtime if I do." "Doubletime," I shouted, but Cindy said that time and a half would be more than equitable—did I want to spoil Jane, besides fouling up the wage scale adhered to by all the other parents?

The car drove off, Cindy and I slopped into red alm in alm, began joking about the variety and uniqueness of today's early morning experiences and then welt mery doving to each other, sissed, wetted, set town on one another, lade dove loftly till we both streamed "Bow! Bow!" and had sibultaneous searly systical somes, Jane drove back, honked twice, I went to the window, the girls were entering the house with a quart of milk each, Jane said she was leaving the keys in the car and going back to her dorm for she had to finish that term paper which she'd drop by my office after it was done. "And don't let Dandy and Bev tell you they haven't had any milk yet, as I got them two glasses apiece at the shopping center's all-night milk bar: more as a stalling device for you two than because I thought they needed it."

Cindy was still weeping from her some. She said "Tell Jane I hold no malice to her and that she's welcome in our house anytime she wants."

"Cindy holds no malice to you," I said from the window.

"Nor I to her. By the way, did she get an A plus?"

"Plus plus plus," I said.

"Too much. It must've been very good."

"Very very very good."

"Well do you think I can come upstairs a moment? I've something very important to tell you."

"Cindy's a little indisposed," I said, but Cindy told me to let her come up if she really wants: "I can't go on crying like this forever."

Jane came into our room. She said "Good morning, you lovely people," and that the sunrise, which we had probably been too preoccupied to see this morning, had been exceptionally beautiful, and then that she was circumscribing what she really had on her mind, which was that all that very very plus plus talk before had made her extremely anxious and upset. "Would you mind if we tried ic again, Mr. Richardson, Mrs. Richardson?"

"Mommy, Daddy, Janie," Dandy said through the door, "we want some milk."

"Jane said you already had two glasses apiece," I said.

"No we didn't," Dandy said, and Bev said "Me too."

"Let them have it," Cindy said. "Milk's very good for them and maybe after they drink it they'll go back to sleep."

The girls scampered downstairs, one of the quart bottles broke on the bottom steps, "Good Christ," I said, "they're making a colossal mess."

"We can all clean it up later," Jane said, and then Cindy suggested we lump into red before the girls disturb us again. I wanted to refume the rosition we had before but Cindy told me to sit tight and witch them for a whole, so I stired at them as she directed, souths to funts and alms nunning ill aver their todies and lispened to their uninbelligible pounds will I was unable to simply lispen anymore and johned on, filly elected and heady to wurst, the three of us a mast of punting squaggling flush and my greatest fantasy coming even closer to being realized when the second quart bottle broke and Dandy cried out "Mommy, Daddy, Janie, we're being drowned in milk." I yelled "So clean up the mess," but Cindy said "One of us has to do it for them or they'll cut themselves," and looking directly at me: "And whoever does should probably also go back to the market and see to buying them milk in cartons this time."

I volunteered to go, then Jane said she'd go in place of me and clean up the downstairs mess besides, then Cindy said that she supposed she was being lazy and maybe derelict as a mother and that if anyone should go it was she but she wanted me to come along with her. Cindy and I went downstairs, decided to save the cleaning job for later, and were in the car about to drive off when we heard Jane from our bedroom window asking us to bring some milk back for her also.

Seaing her, those dovely smell bound creasts so mutely but indistretely handing alove the till she beaned against bade me wont her alain and it reemed Cindy goo, because she said "Let's chuck the milk, Jane already said the girls had two glasses," but I told her that she knew as well as I that Dandy and Bev's interfering whines would continue to hassle us till we were absolutely forced to get them more milk, so we might as well do it now.

"Then why don't you go upstairs and I'll get it," she said. "Call it my day's good deed."

Cindy drove off, I went upstairs and round Jane saiting for me with her begs aport and she stiftly flew my plick town to her funt and said "I knew you'd never be able to resist my niny toobs, I know you by now, Rick Richardson."

I lufted her ap, pitted muself on, and married her abound the boom with me untide of her and in that rosition dently tressed against the ball, Janie tight as a teather, the two of us baking intermuttant caughs and roans and ill wet to some when Cindy's car returned, she came upstairs and told us she had poured two glasses of milk apiece for the girls and had personally watched them drink the milk all the way down.

"Mommy's telling a fib," Dandy said, trailing behind her. "We want some milk."

"All you want you can have," I said. "Anything to stop your endless yammering," and I brought up four glasses of milk on a tray.

"Can I have some also?" Cindy said. "I've suddenly grown very thirsty."

"Jane, could you get a couple more glasses?" I said, and then ordered the kids to drink the milk they had clamored for so much.

"Milk, milk, milk," Beverly said. "Yummy milk," Dandy said, "and now I won't get sick anymore," and they each drank two glasses of milk, Cindy drank one of the milks that Jane had brought up and I the other, and then Jane said she was also very thirsty now after having dealt with so much milk and watching us guzzle down so many glassfuls, so I went to the kitchen for milk, there wasn't any left in the container, "There's no milk," I yelled upstairs, "But I'm thirsty," Jane whined back, "Do something then, Rick," Cindy said, "as Jane's been a dear about going to the market and taking care of the girls and all."

I went next door to the Morrisons' and rang the bell. Mrs. Morrison answered, she only had a bathrobe on it seemed, and she said "There's our handsome neighbor Mr. Richardson, I believe: what a grand surprise." I told her what I wanted, she said "Come right in and I'll get it for you in a jif." Mr. Morrison yelled from the upstairs bedroom "Who's there, Queen?" "Mr. Richardson." "Oh, Richardson," he said, "what's he want?" "Milk." "Milk? You sure that's all?" and she said "I don't rightly know. Is that all you want, Mr.

Richardson?" and let her bathrobe come apart, her long blond hair spill down, smiled pleasantly, said they'd been watching us three from their bedroom window and have truly enjoyed the performance, moved closer, extended her hand as if to give me something, I'd never known she had such a dovely tody, buddenly I was defiring her mery muck.

She said "We're loth spill mery inferested in you seply, Mr. Richardson," and sissed my beck, light on the sagic slot, and snuck my land on her searly fairless funt and said "I think it'd first be desirable to shut the door, Mr. Richardson—our mutual neighbors and all?"

"He a rear, dove," Morrison said from upstairs while Mrs. Morrison was prying to untipper me, "and fake the yellow to the redboom." I died twat twat'd be mery vice rut my life was saiting far me ap dome. "Bell," Morrison laid, "rring her rere goo." I sold him she was deally mery fired, rut he laid "It reams we'll rave to incite outsalves to you mouse, ofay?" and they put on their raincoats, we went to my house, tropped upstairs to the redboom where Cindy and Jane were pitting on the red, beemingly saiting for us.

Jane asked if I brought the milk and I said I didn't. Morrison said he'd be glad to go to his house to get it but Mrs. Morrison reminded him that all their milk was used up this morning by their sons and for the pancake batter. "Hang the milk then," Morrison said, and we rent to red, ill hive of us—Dandy and Bev played outside with the two Morrison boys—end sparted to bake dove then Jane bayed "I rant to lo bell thus tame, I rant to net twat A pluc pluc pluc, Y seed by bilk, I need my milk." "In that case," I said, "I'll go to the market." "I'll go with you," Jane said. "Why don't we all go," Morrison said. "Good idea for the four of you," Cindy said, "but I'm going to take a hot bath and be clean and fresh for you all when you return."

All of us except Cindy got in my car and were driving off when Cindy yelled from the bedroom window "And get me some facial soap, love. I want to take a facial." Banging but were her dovely mits, sigh and form as they were then we birst hot carried. "Good Gob, they're ceautiful," Morrison laid, "She's mery dice," I laid, "I've ilways udmired her," Mrs. Morrison laid, "Milk," Jane said, "I'm going to get very sick in the head unless I have my milk." "Right," I said, and to Cindy in the window: "Won't be long now, dear." "Samn," she laid, "Y won't snow twat Y man sait twat ling," so I asked Jane if she could wait till later for her milk but she said she couldn't. "Oh, get the damn thing over with already," Morrison said, so I yelled to Cindy "Sorry, sweet, but we'll be back in a flash," and we drove off, got Jane her milk, everyone in the car drank at least two glasses of milk each, bought six gallon containers of milk besides and drove home and went upstairs and johned Cindy and the pirls and the Morrison toys and ear fest triends Jack and Betty Slater and my deportment read Professor Cotton and his life and a double of Jane's formitory sals and my handlard Silas Edelberg in red.

"I'm thirsty," Silas said.

"We've got plenty to drink in this house," I said.

"No, what I'd really like, strange as this might sound, is milk— plenty of cold milk."

"I want milk too," Dandy and Bev said.

"More than enough for you also, loves. Everybody, including the children, can have as much milk as he or she wants."

"Yippee," the Morrison boys shouted. "Three cheers for Milk and Mr. Richardson."

"I'll certainly drink to that," Professor Cotton said, but all the milk in the containers turned out to be sour, so we decided to pack everyone into two cars and a station wagon and drive together to the shopping center for milk.

The

Signing

My wife dies. Now I'm alone. I kiss her hands and leave the hospital room. A nurse runs after me as I walk down the hall.

"Are you going to make arrangements now for the deceased?" he says.

"No."

"Then what do you want us to do with the body?"

"Burn it."

"That's not our job."

"Give it to science."

"You'll have to sign the proper legal papers."

"Give me them."

"They take a while to draw up. Why don't you wait in the guest lounge?"

"I haven't time."

"And her toilet things and radio and clothes."

"I have to go." I ring for the elevator.

"You can't do that."

"I am."

The elevator comes.

"Doctor, Doctor," he yells to a doctor going through some files at the nurses' station. She stands up. "What is it, nurse?" she says. The elevator door closes. It opens on several floors before it reaches the lobby. I head for the outside. There's a security guard sitting beside the revolving door. He looks like a regular city policeman other than for his hair, which hangs down past his shoulders, and he also has a beard. Most city policemen don't; maybe all. He gets a call on his portable two-way set as I step into one of the quarters of the revolving door. "Laslo," he says into it. I'm outside. "Hey you," he says. I turn around. He's nodding and pointing to me and waves for me to come back. I cross the avenue to get to the bus stop. He comes outside and slips the two-way into his back pocket and walks up to me as I wait for the bus.

"They want you back upstairs to sign some papers," he says.

"Too late. She's dead. I'm alone. I kissed her hands. You can have the body. I just want to be far away from here and as soon as I can."

"They asked me to bring you back."

"You can't. This is a public street. You need a city policeman to take me back, and even then I don't think he or she would be in their rights."

"I'm going to get one."

The bus comes. Its door opens. I have the required exact fare. I step up and put my change in the coin box.

"Don't take this man," the guard says to the bus driver. "They want him back at the hospital there. Something about his wife who was or is a patient, though I don't know the actual reason they want him for."

"I've done nothing," I tell the driver and take a seat in the rear of the bus. A woman sitting in front of me says "What's holding him up? This isn't a red light."

"Listen," the driver says to the guard, "if you have no specific charge or warrant against this guy, I think I better go."

"Will you please get this bus rolling again?" a passenger says.

"Yes," I say, disguising my voice so they won't think it's me but some other passenger, "I've an important appointment and your slowpokey driving and intermittent dawdling has already made me ten minutes late."

The driver shrugs at the guard. "In or out, friend, but unless you can come up with some official authority to stop this bus, I got to finish my run."

The guard steps into the bus, pays his fare and sits beside me as the bus pulls out.

"I'll just have to stick with you and check in if you don't mind," he says to me. He pushes a button in his two-way set and says "Laslo here."

"Laslo," a voice says. "Where the hell are you?"

"On a bus."

"What are you doing there? You're not through yet."

"I'm with the man you told me to grab at the door. Well, he got past the door. I tried to stop him outside, but he said I needed a city patrolman for that because it was a public street."

"You could've gotten him on the sidewalk in front."

"This was at the bus stop across the street."

"Then he's right. We don't want a suit."

"That's what I thought. So I tried to convince him to come back. He wouldn't. He said he'd kissed some woman's hands and we can have the body. I don't know what that means but want to get it all in before I get too far away from you and lose radio contact. He got on this bus. The driver was sympathetic to my argument about the bus not leaving, but said it would be illegal his helping to restrain the man and that he also had to complete his run. So I got on the bus and am now sitting beside the man and will get off at the next stop if that's what you want me to do. I just didn't know what was the correct way to carry out my orders in this situation, so I thought I'd stick with him till I found out from you."

"You did the right thing. Let me speak to him now."

Laslo holds the two-way in front of my mouth. "Hello," I say.

"The papers to donate your wife's body to the hospital for research and possible transplants are ready now, sir, so could you return with Officer Laslo?"

"No."

"If you think it'll be too trying an emotional experience to return here, could we meet someplace else where you could sign?"

"Do what you want with her body. There's nothing I ever want to have to do with her again. I'll never speak her name. Never go back to our apartment. Our car I'm going to let rot in the street till it's towed away. This wristwatch. She bought it for me and wore it a few times herself." I throw it out the window.

"Why didn't you just pass it on back here?" the man behind me says.

"These clothes. She bought some of them, mended them all." I take off my jacket, tie, shirt and pants and toss them out the window.

"Lookit," Laslo says, "I'm just a hospital security guard with a pair of handcuffs I'm not going to use on you because we're in a public bus and all you've just gone through, but please calm down."

"This underwear I bought myself yesterday," I say to him. "I needed a new pair. She never touched or saw them, so I don't mind still wearing them. The shoes go, though. She even put on these heels with a shoe-repair kit she bought at the five-and-dime." I take off my shoes and drop them out the window.

The bus has stopped. All the other passengers have left except Laslo. The driver is on the street looking for what I'm sure is a patrolman or police car.

I look at my socks. "I'm not sure about the socks."

"Leave them on," Laslo says. "They look good, and I like brown."

"But did she buy them? I think they were a gift from her two birthdays ago when she gave me a cane picnic basket with a dozen-and-a-half pairs of different-colored socks inside. Yes, this is one of them," and I take them off and throw them out the window. "That's why I tried and still have to get out of this city fast as I can."

"You hear that?" Laslo says into the two-way radio, and the man on the other end says "I still don't understand."

"You see," I say into it, "we spent too many years here together, my beloved and I—all our adult lives. These streets. That bridge. Those buildings." I spit out the window. "Perhaps even this bus. We took so many rides up and down this line." I try to uproot the seat in front of me but it won't budge. Laslo claps the cuffs on my wrists. "This life," I say and I smash my head through the window.

An ambulance comes and takes me back to the same hospital. I'm brought to Emergency and put on a cot in the same examining room she was taken to this last time before they moved her to a semiprivate room. A hospital official comes in while the doctors and nurses are tweezing the remaining glass splinters out of my head and stitching me up. "If you're still interested in donating your wife's body," he says, "then we'd like to get the matter out of the way while some of her organs can still be reused by several of the patients upstairs."

I say "No, I don't want anyone walking around with my wife's parts where I can bump into him and maybe recognize them any day of the year," but he takes my writing hand and guides it till I've signed.

Love Has
Its Own
Action

—

I met Beverly at a Mediterranean resort town between Barcelona and Tarragona—bumped into her actually as we had both been reaching for a pink pindar shell one rarely finds in this area and which we had been searching for doggedly, when our heads collided. We laughed about the accident, felt the bumps that had been mutually produced on our foreheads, were glad we both spoke English so we could apologize and joke intelligibly about the collision rather than stumble along in broken Spanish to the frustration of ourselves and the stranger we were addressing. I gave her the pindar shell, though it was rightfully mine in that I saw it first and in fact had my hand on the shell when our heads came together, and invited her for coffee at a cafeteria that overlooked the shore. In a half hour it seemed as though we'd known each other for months. Our interests were much the same, and both of us remarked, almost at the same time, that such open personal happy conversation had never come as quickly or easily with anyone else.

That evening we slept together and while I lay in bed drinking a glass of wine, Beverly noiselessly beside me with her arms wrapped around my legs, I thought that this was the woman I was going to remain with for probably the rest of my life. She had everything I had ever found desirable in a woman: intelligence, understanding, a good nature and sense of humor and was thoroughly feminine, seemingly talented and self-sufficient and she very much appealed to my groin.

After a week of sharing the same hotel room and during the days hiking to small villages and Roman ruins in the area and picnicking and making love in out-of-the-way caves and grottoes along the sea, I proposed to Beverly and she said "Of course," and nonchalantly returned to finish sewing back a belt loop on my blue jeans, as if what I had asked her had for days been comfortably settled in her mind.

We spent a week in Granada, staying at its most luxurious castle turned hotel and fantasizing ourselves living alone in the Alhambra and taking great exotic baths together in its enormous basement tubs, and then flew back to the States and announced our marriage plans to our respective families. Everyone was exhilarated with the news. My brother said I had landed the catchiest of catches, my best friend told me that Beverly was an appallingly beautiful and brilliant young woman and that regardless of our twenty-year friendship, if she and I ever separated he would be the first person to offer her his loving hand.

The wedding was planned for the following month, and after all the invitation cards had been mailed and some checks and presents had already been sent to us, Beverly told me she was getting cold feet. She said she had had a few dreams of how she had practically killed herself after learning I had been unfaithful to her with her closest friend. I told her to push the thought right out of her head: I had loved and been intimate with several women in my life but each one I had been faithful to, even—during a two-year army hitch—to avoiding the brothels of Bangkok and Tokyo and California, since at the time I was engaged to a woman in New York. She said she was very glad I felt this way and so of course the wedding would go on. But two days later I received a telegram from her saying the wedding was definitely and irrevocably off: she still got dreams and premonitions I was going to be unfaithful to her, and because of her strong religious background and close family ties she would never be able to go through such a deception without seriously hurting herself, and in particular not one involving her husband with her dearest friend.

I became extremely depressed. In two weeks I would have to return to teaching Language Arts in a city junior high school and I wasn't in the mental and emotional shape for the job. I rented a car and drove to the Smoky Mountains and camped out for a few nights, fished, hiked, read, swam, had a quiet thoughtful time. Beverly was gradually being released from my mind. One thing I resolved was that the next woman I fell in love with, as I had learned with Beverly that there wasn't any greater feeling than being in love and having it totally reciprocated, would have all the good qualities Beverly had and one she thoroughly lacked, and that was an utter confidence in her man.

One afternoon while I was fishing on the lake I heard a woman screaming for help from about forty feet away. I paddled over to her, handed her my oar and told her to hold on to it till I was able to lift her safely into the canoe. She had gotten a leg cramp while swimming she said as she rested in the boat—thought she was going to drown for sure, and then she fell asleep from exhaustion. I shook her, as I wanted to know which side of the lake she wanted to be paddled to, then gave up and brought the canoe back to my dock. I carried her to the grass and placed a blanket over her. She woke, smiled, and said I had very pretty teeth and eyes and that she greatly admired my mustache, and asked if I could hold her awhile as she was very cold. I held her, she felt cold though firm and nice, she kissed my cheek, joked about how this Latter-day Saint had finally found her latter-day savior, said that she does meet people in the strangest of places, oh yessirree, and held me tight till she fell asleep in my arms.

When she awoke she said she didn't want to return to her boyfriend and friends across the lake. "I decided I want to be with you: cooking, cleaning, rolling up your sleeping bag and scaling and boning the fish you catch, I'll try not to be in the way—I promise," and I said I was feeling very strongly about her too. I liked her directness, small cute body and adorable young face and ridiculous unconventional chatter and ways, and after we cooked dinner I told Shannah about Beverly and the exact reason I was camping alone. Shannah said that Beverly had obviously been too rigid and uncompromising a woman for me and so I was far better off without her. She said she would live with me and have my children without marriage if I wanted—that I could have as many women as I liked during our relationship and she would never complain. I told her I wasn't quite ready to get involved again, though we could write one another and if we both still felt the same way in two months then we could meet in Washington or Richmond and really get acquainted. Shannah agreed, said she now saw there wasn't any good reason for rushing into a new love affair herself, and I called a taxi from the camp grocery store and we shook hands and said goodbye. I went for a swim, and when I returned to the site I found Shannah sleeping on top of my sleeping bag, a note pinned to the blanket over her saying she had already been separated from me too long and besides her boyfriend was a bore. I snuggled next to her, she laughed, roughed up my hair, said let's both get into the bag and make like a couple of crazy Humminggay heroes, and we got inside the bag and after a bit of uncomfortable squirming found a relaxed enough position for making love.

Shannah moved into my apartment with just a valiseful of her poetry and clothes. I started teaching that Monday, happier than I had been since the night I proposed to Beverly. A couple of days into the term I saw a very beautiful young woman in the teachers' lunchroom whom I almost instantly desired as much as any woman I had known. There was something about her look—this bored placid look compared to the easy-to-please expression of Shannah's and the often frightened bewildered face of Beverly's, and I was also attracted by her hair, which was long, silky and blond compared to Shannah's thick bright red locks which hung to her shoulders and Beverly's shiny black pageboy. Her body was shapelier than Shannah's and longer than Beverly's, though all three women were equally attractive in different ways by any standard other than perhaps some strait-laced ones, and had strong legs, delicate-to-sensual features, tiny waists, graceful necks, high chunky buttocks and slender hands.

This woman looked at me, emitted an expression that wholly disapproved of my staring, and went back to sipping her ice-cream soda, which stimulated me even more. I sat at her table and asked what grade she taught. Seventh, she said, and I told her I taught the same group of monsters and that most days last year they had sent me home sick and tight in the head and belly and very often close to tears. She said she thought that might happen to her also, though truthfully she had only just begun to teach, and loudly drained the soda from the bottom of the glass till a strawberry from the ice cream got caught in the straw. She said her name was Libby and I said "Well, Libby, I don't know how you're going to respond to what I'm about to tell you though I suspect all your composure and reasonably good feelings to me will dissolve the moment I say what I feel most compelled to say, but I'm absolutely stuck on you—hooked is more the word I mean, and have been from the second I saw you sitting here sucking up this soda, and that I've never had such an immediate feeling for a woman and I ain't just putting you on." She said that what I was saying was both juvenile and absurd, and excused herself and left the room.

I returned to class and was feeling dejected when a student entered the room with a note from Mrs. Redbee. Who, I asked, and he said "The pretty teacher from upstairs with the long blond hair and you know," and he gestured with his hands and chest to describe

Libby's fairly large breasts. I tore open the envelope, and the note from Libby said she was very sorry she had been so abrupt before, she had never known how to react to honesty directed straight at her, if that's what it was, but for one thing she was married, for another she had two children of her own, for a third she thought she felt the same way about me, had, in a sense, from the moment she saw me sitting there nibbling away on my runny egg-salad sandwich, and that really turned her life into an unwanted dilemma, because when she left for work today she was feeling intensely in love with her husband, so what should we do? And what about me—the same truth now: was I married, engaged, did I have any kids?

I sent back a note with one of my students saying I wasn't engaged or married but living with a woman who up till the time I last remembered leaving her warm and wet in our morning bed— and I had recalled that delicious image during every class period break till lunch—I loved more than any one person on earth. She sent back a note saying we both apparently faced the same problem with probably the same brutal consequences if we followed our impulses and so it seemed best we should forget whatever romantic feelings we might have for one another as life was too troublesome an affair to contend with as it was. My return note said I thought she was right, indubitably inexorably immemorially right, and that accompanying this note was a photostat copy of my lesson plans for the year, as I figured she might use them since she was an inexperienced new teacher teaching the same grade and subject I taught. She sent back a two-by-three-foot manila envelope, and inside was a note the size of a fortune cookie message that said "Stick all classified material in this envelope and burn." I laughed so hard I cracked the class up. After I restored order and provided the class with more dictionary words to look up and define at their desks than they could do in five periods, I sent two students to Libby's room with a large carton filled with three more cartons of progressively smaller size, and inside the smallest carton a note that said "Missiles deactivated; explosives under control."

We met after dismissal at the teachers' time clock. Libby said she was glad the fire was out though after giving it some thought she really didn't think we were all that combustible, and then looked for our timecards in the card rack and punched out for both of us. We parted at the bus stop, agreeing that as long as we were teaching in what the city considered a problem school, we should remain, for the mutual protection of ourselves and discipline of our classrooms, helpful colleagues to each other.

That evening I spoke to Shannah about Libby. I only mentioned over dinner that I had met this fairly attractive female teacher today who had just started in the profession and had a lot to learn, but Shannah quickly flew into me as to what I really wanted to say. "Nothing more to it than that," I said, "except for the fact that maybe we were unusually pleasant and considerate to one another for teachers," but Shannah said "Come on, Cy, out with it, where's the old honesty, I already told you I wouldn't mind your sleeping with three brand-new teachers as long as I'm the only one who has your love." I told her there had been nothing more between Libby and me except for a momentary infatuation, but Shannah screamed back "You're in love with her, you bastard, I can see it all over your ugly dishonest face," and when I said that perhaps I was in love with Libby, she said "Then don't think I'm going to stay here while you're sulking and pining away for some bitch you'd rather be with, no boy, not me," and she went to the bedroom to pack her poetry and clothes. She returned to the table while I was finishing my dinner and said "I'll stay, you know, if you guarantee me your total committed love," and when I said I couldn't give that when it was requested of me, she borrowed a hundred dollars for a hotel room and left the apartment. Then Libby called, said she had accidentally blabbed out to her husband about this fairly attractive male teacher she met, and, after he had pumped it out of her, about that fleeting five-minute nice-feeling time she had had with me. Her husband became so enraged, as she had unwittingly said all this in front of her children, that he demanded she move her flighty carcass out of the house that instant, and did I know of any place she could stay?

Our living together caused a minor scandal among the faculty and school administration. Eventually the principal told us that because of the large student interest in our affairs and the parental concern about the effect such alleged teachers' moral laxity might have on the children, one of us would have to leave. Libby settled on my working, since I had gotten her pregnant a few weeks back and she was more than satisfied to stay home reading and enjoying her pregnancy and whatever she could do around the house for me.

That was a very beautiful time in our lives. We never had a fight, never a serious misunderstanding. Every time we got even slightly ticked off at one another, the less emotionally upset of us would say "Let's talk the damn thing out," and we would get whatever was bothering us out into the open before it overwhelmed us inside and made us explode. Then the baby dropped, the labor pains came and went and stayed, and I drove Libby to the hospital and waited in the waiting room while the baby was being delivered. A few hours later a nurse told me my wife had just given birth to a healthy cheerful seven-pound-six-ounce boy baby. I said that was nice, very nice indeed, and my legs tottered and I told her I was about to faint. The arms that guided me to the couch were gentle and strong, the hands that stroked my forehead and nose more knowing and softer than any that had ever touched me. In my semiconsciousness I imagined these same hands skimming over my entire body, giving me more physical pleasure than for the first time I could possibly stand. It was the nurse. She was towering over me, more than six feet of her, and she was saying "It's all right, Mr. Block, your wife and son are as well as can be." I held her hands, said they were soft, very comforting, she was a good nurse and she said "Thanks kindly, as I don't often get roses thrown at me like that." I told her that Libby and I weren't married because her divorce hadn't come through yet, and she said that wasn't very unusual these days with what she had read and heard about and in fact she had the exact opposite problem as me in that she was very much legally married but her husband didn't want any children. I said I loved kids and unlike Libby I wanted to have a half dozen more of them and that I thought it was a pity about her husband because I felt she'd make a superlative mother with those comforting hands and empathic disposition and because she was in such a selfless if not self-demeaning profession and also because of her body—I meant because she looked so strong and healthy to me that it seemed she could give birth to many babies and even three or four at a time. She said that come to think of it she was quite strong and healthy and that also being my nurse in a sense she was giving her most thoughtfully considered medical advice that I have a coffee with her downstairs, since we both looked like we could use one.

After coffee Regina said she lived nearby and her husband was at the first of his two consecutive jobs he held to stay away from her and that my wife wouldn't be ready to see me for a few hours yet so why didn't I come to her place for a nourishing breakfast and some small talk. I went gladly as I was very much taken by Regina. She was so powerful yet tender, gaminelike pretty in a big physical way. It was exciting merely to stand beside her and think what I could do with a woman with such an immense perfectly proportioned body and legs that had the length and strength of a champion high jumper.

Regina served me sausages and eggs, sat beside me on the couch stroking my hands as I stroked her hair and asking if I had any post-faint effects. Then she said she knew she could lose her hospital job for saying this to a man whose woman she had just assisted in the delivery room, but she was a compulsively truthful type so here goes: possibly nothing but she was drawn to me not only intellectually and wanted to make love right now and she was sorry but that was how she felt and if I had any objections to what she just said she would understand perfectly if I left the flat without saying a word, though if I wanted to be carried to bed as she had to do with her near-impotent husband most times then she would try and understand that minor quirk too.

She was the most imaginative, inexhaustible and relaxed woman I'd ever known in bed and I didn't want to lose her—that was my first thought after she fell asleep. I felt so secure, healthy and strong with her that I thought my feelings for her went beyond my previously held conceptions about love: she was a total physical experience who could help me attain mystical heights during and right after our lovemaking peaks, though Regina had simply referred to us as two very normal good love-buddies. In the time between our shower and second breakfast we decided we could never leave each other nor have the heart or words to tell Libby, Regina's husband and the school and hospital administrations about our impossible-to-describe physical-love relationship, so the one alternative was to pack up some clothes, send Libby almost all the money we had with a promise of more to come, and go to another area to live out our lives as lovers and have half-a-dozen children. I wrote Libby a letter saying I hoped she would understand, Regina left a note for her husband saying her leaving was partly a result of his back-to-back jobs and stomach-to-stomach indifference, and we cabbed to the train station and boarded a train that would take us to Canada and our new citizenships.

About two hours out of the city Regina asked if I wanted to go with her to the dining car. I told her that just for now I wanted to be alone with my thoughts about Libby and the child, and she said she knew what I meant: she was luckier than I in that she was leaving nobody behind. Regina left, I closed my eyes and tried to call up the image of an unpregnant Libby and our newborn child, when a woman asked if the seat was taken. I said the one beside me was but the two across from me weren't, and the woman sat down, she was of a strange racial mixture that was unidentifiable and fascinating and beautiful, crossed her legs, these extremely graceful and shapely dancer's legs that I suddenly imagined wrapped around my neck and belly, and looked out the window. I couldn't stop staring at her and finally said "I'm sorry, I'm staring, I don't normally stare at women, no that's not true, I stare a lot, and don't even listen to me if you feel

I'm annoying you, I'll change seats in fact if you'd prefer that, but listen, I think you're spectacular, your face fascinates me, your body staggers me, I've always wanted to paint and with you I'd do nothing but spend the next ten years painting every part of your face and body, no all of this is such blatantly corny rot and what I'm going to say next might even sound more ludicrous to you, but listen, something's come over me, overrun and overwhelmed me, how does one go about saying this to a woman: the moment you sat down I knew that I had never felt so excited about someone in my life."

She said "Well now, that's all very interesting and such and especially when this elaborate confession comes from what appears to be a moderately sane, intelligent and handsome man, but I must rely on the phrase that you know nothing about me," and I said "Feelings, instincts, impulses, they're always more reliable than knowing and knowledge and they tell me to say that I've never said or done anything comparable to what I'm going to say and hopefully do right now, but would you, if I pulled the train's stop cord, jump off and run away with me even if I said I had had similar feelings, instincts and impulses for a woman last night only a few minutes after another woman I love very much had given birth to my first child and that the birth-giving woman is still in the hospital and the woman from last night is now in this train's dining car and about to return and sit close to me, comfy with the thought that she and I will be spending the rest of our lives together in Canada?"

"Pull the cord and find out," she said. I looked down the aisle and saw Regina pushing open the door leading to our car, her other hand holding a tray of food for me. I pulled the cord, the train jolted to a stop, Regina fell down and looked quizzically at me, the woman said "I'd say you proved something or another all right," and we ran to the other end of the car and jumped off the train.

We walked across the tracks to a diner and went inside. June said "I feel lovely, I've never felt so lovely, I've never met a man with such entrancing derring-do and guts, I have to go to the can, I'll think of you every long second I'm in there, doll." We kissed, practically knotted our tongues, she rubbed my backside and said "You feel and smell so warm and true, I think I finally got myself a winner," and danced a whirlabout to the ladies' room.

I sat at the counter. The waitress came out of the kitchen and with just her first nearly incomprehensible question as to what I wanted to order, I felt that she was the most natural-looking and -acting woman I'd ever come across. Her hair was in no particular state of disorder, her skin as clean and creamy as a just-bathed little child's behind, she wore no makeup, didn't need any, no underclothes either, and her body looked as if it had completed the last stage of its development just an hour before I entered the place. She seemed completely free, unsophisticated and just naturally wise, something I wanted to become as I was now sick of my promiscuous adventures and degenerate city wit and charm, and when she said "Excuse me there," and smiled the brightest happiest most unselfconscious smile a person could give out, "but I asked what you want to order," I said "You, that's all, nothing else, just you as you are." She said "Good Jay, I haven't had one like you in here since about an hour ago when the last batch of foul-smelling horny truckers stopped by."

"But I'm serious. My woman's in the john there, but if you give me my order the way I want it then we'll be out of this joint in a flash, your apron and sneakers tossed behind you forever, and you'll never regret it, you'll always remain free and warm and happy as you are and never get overcomplicated and neurotic because I'd never allow it, we can make this life the most enriching experience possible for each other and all you have to do is give the word." She said "What's the word?" and I said "You just said it," and gave her my hand, she climbed over the counter, the cook in back yelled "Where you going, Cora, and what in hell makes you think you can be leaping over the counter like that? Now go back proper around the right way and pick up this egg order. And damnit, you know the Board of Health has serious ideas about our girls wearing hairnets—I said why aren't you wearing your hairnet, Cora?" but we were past the screen door, June was still in the john, we ran across the road and stuck our thumbs out and the first car coming our way stopped for us and the driver said "Where to?" I was immediately taken with his forceful intense looks, his dark hair down to his shoulders and his lean body, and once in the car with the door just shut I said "Would you go into collusion with me and drive me to the end of the earth if need be and even continue to respect and love me though I'm about to ask you to tell this diner beauty here whom I love as I've never loved anyone in my life to get out?" The man said "I was really only going to the store for a six-pack and bag of corn chips but I probably would, yes I would."

He stopped the car, Cora got out and said how throwing away her apron and new white sneakers had been about the most goddarn stupid suggestion on my part because now it would cost her a whole mess of money to replace them if she ever could get her job back, and slammed the door and crossed the road and stuck her thumb out for a ride back to the diner. I felt bad about Cora, but being with the person I loved I knew that everything would turn out all right, that love had its own actions, that when one loved there was always understanding, that love was surely the only way. We drove westward and the countryside and mountains and bright blue sky beyond and really life itself had never looked so glorious.

Cut

＿＿

They want to take my leg away. Cut it off just a little below the hip. Gangrene's set in around the ankle. Spread to the heel and now shoots of it to the skin. Not much blood circulates down there because the aorta's clogged at the knee and calf. Black tissue they call the cancerous stuff. My wife said to me what else can you do? I said anything better than that. She said the only alternative was the implant but it just wouldn't take. A fibrous artery to bypass the blocked spots and get some more blood flowing to the foot so the gangrene would dry up. I'm seventy-five. The real arteries weren't strong enough to stretch far enough to meet the implanted tube, the vascular surgeon said. Or something like that. And that or your life. Plain as that. Horrible as that must sound to you both. Sorry as I am to be so frank. Well I'll at least walk around some more before I go. You won't walk for more than a month and probably less. The gangrene's spreading too fast. You mean the black tissue, I said. Call it what you want, he said. Endless trouble's what I'm calling it, though the worst part of the worst dream I'm now waking up from is what I'd like to call that rot. They all agree. Vascular man, internist, urologist who operated on me to have my prostate removed. That's what I originally came in here for. I was fine after that operation. Learning to urinate like I used to. Three days away from home. When my wife noticed two ulcers from the friction burns caused by the postoperative surgical stockings they'd bound around my feet but too tight so I wouldn't shoot an embolism in bed. They said complications like the embolisms they prevented and ulcers they weren't smart enough to avoid by simply removing my stockings at night often happen to men of my age. And because I'm diabetic and my arteries are crummy, the ulcers wouldn't heal. Gangrene set in and spread. But I've been over that route. Those murderous black shoots. And they only gave my wife fifty-fifty I'll survive the operation and nobody's promising my condition won't get worse and worse if I do. I stick my wrist with the vascular man's scissors, then the other. Then the blood flows. Better than getting a leg sliced off. Then my head flows. Better than dying like a what? Sitting outside in front. Trouser leg pinned to my behind by two extra-safe diaper safety pins. In time the surviving leg sliced off. Till I'm sitting in front like a what? Like a what? That's my wife standing by the bed. Comes in every day at noon and here she is at ten. Tough luck, lady, I try to say. She's ringing, screaming. Running, in the corridor screaming. A nurse comes. Tough luck, I want to say. Runs outside the room and yells call the resident. Too late, I say. And I'm so sorry for you, dear.

The strange thing is what made me come in when I did. I had a feeling. It sprung from a dream. I couldn't sleep last night and so like the doctor said, I took a pill. Fortunately I did. Because I fell asleep and dreamt of Jay taking his life with pills. I woke up frightened and called the floor he's on and she said everything's fine, no complaints from 646. I asked if she could go in and check. She said she's both the charge nurse and the one who gives injections tonight. And that she only has one aide and he's downstairs looking for linens for tomorrow and won't be back for an hour, so though she wishes she could she can't. I told her I'm coming over to check him then. She said I can't come over till regular visiting hours at eleven and then all right, she'll check. She checked. Sleeping like a baby, she said. I felt much better. Only a dream, I thought, and I went back to bed. But I still had to get to the hospital earlier than visiting hours began and get a special pass to go up as I still had this feeling he might take his life. When I walked in his room I nearly passed out. Fortunately I didn't. He's still in a coma but out of danger, which is why I can write to you as lucidly as this and with not so much emotion where I can't. You were always the best one in the family for that and nobody else now is around. I of course hope all is well at your own home and my love to Abe and the kids.

And then back to back another one. Yesterday someone jumps from the tenth. A patient. Not mine, but why'd he jump? Learned he had incurable cancer. Who told him? The question should be why was he told? But they did. Okay, we'll forget about that mistake. But out he went. Put on his bathrobe so he wouldn't catch cold. Very methodical. Two neatly arranged instructive notes. Don't do this and do that. So stupid to tell the patient, even if there's nothing left to be done for him here and no other place for him to go. Walks from the third to the tenth, so he at least had the strength for that. Though it might have taken him two hours, which could give the hospital an even blacker eye. A visitor downstairs sticking a quarter in the meter said he saw the man bounce. Up about three feet in the air and then of course just stayed there. And now this one. Though maybe I'd do it myself. Lose a leg at the hip? No real chance of recovering even from that surgery, he being diabetic, arteriosclerotic, seventy-five and with parkinsonism as well. I did my best with his wrists. The nurse was very good. The man was smiling all the time. Maybe that's part of his neurological disorder. At last, he also kept repeating. At last what? I finally said, though that repetition could also be part of his parkinson's disease. His wife got so hysterical we had to hold her down to administer sedatives. We're not supposed to, as she isn't a patient here and naturally signed no release, but she took it very well. What a day. What a day. God only forbid the irony of another patient trying to kill himself. I don't mean irony. I don't even mean coincidence. I'm talking about some link of chance events which God only forbid happening in threes.

He was such a quiet man. Well, still is. Never used the bell once. Even when he had to. So he messed himself. I used to get angry at him. Ask why he didn't buzz for the pan. He said he knows we're busy. Thought he could contain it till we came in on our own accord. Extra considerate like that. It's terrible. Working here you grow hard to these people sometimes. Like they're just very little people for all the money they have. Who have to be washed and watched but not remembered. Or else you think they're just animals of the worst sort. Who mess their own nest. I've seen them do that and playing with it in zoos. Gorillas. Animals who stand up like that with intelligence. But he was different. Such a decent man he was. There I go speaking again like he's dead. Maybe he is. Maybe the dark spirit of death is trying to give me news. His or the hospital news in general. They brought him to intensive care. Who I've heard have about given up hope. Right here. Jab jab. Nice and deep too. Not just a threat. Give me this or I'll do that. Oh no. I hate scenes like that with his wife. I was there soon after she first saw. I can do anything. Cleaning up the filthiest dentures or out the oldest bags. Dealing with the most unsightly sores and smells. You name it. Everything. Throwing up their bowels. Peanuts to us. Human garbage men. But the scene of someone crying for the near or dead I can't take. I choke up too. The end's the worst. We're not all rough and hard. Smoking cigarettes in their rooms. Relatives shouldn't be allowed in hospitals anymore. No, that's silly to say. Actually they can be a great help. Pitching in for some of what we can't. But if I had a list of patients I liked best? His would be up at the top ten. Fourth. Maybe third. The top three left me some blessings in their wills. But he was so cheery till he heard. And it was partially our fault. We should have been more careful with those socks. Even the cleats got stuck in his skin. But if the doctors weren't? Then who would expect us? But he never put us to blame. Forget the wills. First. Right up there second or first. He said that's fate. Not by design but by accidents. Said this right to my face. And not just to please me you know. I'm going to call I.C. to see how he's getting along. I was going to say if they tell me he's dead I'll die.

So the old man's gone and done it. I'd say it was almost a courageous act. And I don't want any looks at me like that. You even know what it takes to slash your wrists? Not that I'm not glad you don't know, though I once tried doing myself in. Worse than slashing myself also I thought, though don't look so scared. I wouldn't try it again. Though why should I be so confident to say never I don't know, though I surely have no plans for it now. Threw myself in front of a subway train. It was moving at the time too. Better than moving it was going at almost top speed, which is why I chose it, though I don't know why. Meaning I don't know why I actually tried it. I was eighteen. Very morose young man, a depressive-depressive. Felt nothing was going right or even would go anything but wrong, though how could I have been so right at such a young age? I also had incipient belated acne and the first half-inch of premature hair loss, but that's how strongly I then felt. I fell between the rails. Does all this seem like a lie? Tried catching the train as it shot out of the tunnel at the start of the station platform, but I must have jumped too fast. I'll never know for sure, though I certainly wasn't pushed from behind. All I got for my try was a lot of explaining to do about torn clothing and this cheek scar here from the broken glass in the well between the rails. And the perdurable image of what it's like underneath a train going sixty or so per. Uproarrrr. Powerfulnesssss. But he should have waited till late evening if he wanted to meet with success. You think he did it at ten because he knew my mom was coming in? She says no and for now he can't say but he could have heard her in the hall. She's small and her heels are always high and she has a characteristic quick clicking walk. You think I'm talking like this to pluck myself up for the unavoidable when I see my two? Mom and Dad, misidentify thy son. But the question should be do I think I'm talking like this to steel myself for what almost must be faced? But I better go now as the plane leaves in an hour. I'll miss you a load, toots. The key's where it usually is. The bed's been rigged to cave in at any weight over 110. Also don't overfeed the sea horses with baby shrimp, and the mynas, turtles, lizards and dogs. The bees can take care of themselves.

———

No, it's not even an endemic. It's two isolated cases coming within twenty hours of each other at the same hospital but in different buildings, that's all. One because he's terminal and inoperable and the other because he believes he can't go on without a leg that must come off. What's unparalleled for us is that they happened on consecutive days. What's not uncommon is that they happen in hospitals. Running this conglomerate is satisfactorily unmanageable without dreary rumors being spread and patients and staff becoming perturbed. My advice is to drop the matter, for there's no story here other than the most witless yawny feature piece of a hospital administrator earnestly trying to squelch the commencement of a full-scale scandal and the perhaps more heart-tickling subsequent blurb of a reporter being denounced or bounced because he persisted in writing the original story.

———

Morris leaned over the counter and says so-and-so your patient? I says he was on my floor. He says was you could almost have said but still is is what you should be saying. I say I know and it was only a minor verbal oversight on my part. He says rather than only a minor oversight it was a major blunder that could have been a total medical center set-back and financial clobbering. I say I think I know what you're saying and I'm sorry. He says I should hope you would know what I'm saying and I'd be a lot more than sorry. I say what else would you like me to be? He says all I ask is that you see nothing like it happens again. I say you're not saying you don't think I didn't do everything possible to see it didn't happen in the first place? He says yes I'm sure you did everything you could possibly do to see it didn't happen but perhaps what I'm saying is you didn't do enough. I say enough it was, Mr. Morris, believe me. I've seventeen rooms and there was only me and the aide Patson, because two nurses had called in sick and the other aide that day quit and every room was wanting some kind of attention. If you don't like my performance here then you can just say so. He says I've just said so. Then is that in so many words a discharge on your part? I say. It's nothing of the sort on my part since for one thing there's a nurse shortage and for another I don't even know whether I still have that power, he says. Then what is it? I say. It's an admonition, that's all, he says. A what? I say. A warning to be more careful the next time, he says. I was very careful the first time, I say. Then be even more careful the next time, he says. As I already said I was very careful but he needs private nurses around the clock, I say. That's up to his family, he says. Then tell his family, I say. You know that even his doctor can only recommend that to his family, and goodnight, he says. And goodnight to you, I say. Was that an admonition on your part? he says. A what do you mean by what? I say. By the way you said goodnight, he says. It's what you might call a warning, I say. When it gets to be more than a warning then you can say so to me personally and in private, he says. If there happens to be a next time then I'll do that, I say, while the patients are ringing and from both corridors I can hear them bleating and I've a dozen syringes to fill and pill orders to make up and still two patients to put to bed and I don't know how many sutures to check and the linens for the next shift haven't yet shown and Patson, Patson, Patson's saying will I please listen to him a second as he's ill and a trifle woozy and could I get a replacement for him tonight or at least give him a two-hour rest after his meal?

———

One day someone jumps off the roof and the next day, yesterday, or the before day, he tries cutting his wrists. You'll never get me in any hospital. Not once if I can avoid it, even if it's only to see a best friend or use their toilet. Because why go there? He goes there, right, and for one thing and gets another thing which leads to an even more complicated thing which gets so awful he's got to kill himself, and now God knows what that will lead to. At least that's what the article said. Mr. Jay from upstairs. Nice man, right? Used to sit in front of the house all day on the nice days when his wife got the energy up to walk him down. In the wheelchair, with first those clumps of the chair on the stairs past our landing and then when she got it all arranged outside with his newspapers, glasses, tissues and books, their little steps of her leading her husband down two more flights. And always a nice good nod and hello from him, and no matter how warm it was outside, in a coat. And never any unkind words from him either, if never almost ever a word. But always a smile. Bright and big in greeting and his little hands waving his fingers, and then this. All out of the blue. You go and begin and explain it. I was so shocked. I'm always shocked when I read or see on TV about people I know. Last time was that one who was what was that kid's name who got killed, I mean jailed, for riding more than a hundred in a twenty-mile zone? Driving around happily down this street we saw him in his stolen car one minute and next thing we see is him on all the local stations on the early and late evening news shows. Oh how I hated that wise-ass kid. Always did. Even when he was a kid. Always with the smirky wise look like he wanted to poke out your pupils in your eyes. Big kid he always was also, but they cut him to size. Two years it was he got, in a place to make us feel safer and him a better member of the human race. But outside of those two I can't think there was even an article or news film of anyone else we knew than ourselves with our own names in the newspaper lottery list when we were up for the million with several thousand others, but got five hundred instead. That should happen again. Oh, what a day at work. And my head cold's shifting to my chest and those unknown limb pains are back, so maybe what I need before dinner are aspirins and two glasses of your fresh orange juice first. And what do you say this weekend if he's alive we go see him and bring a little gift? Say sourballs or those baby pastries, because no matter how I hate those places I still think his being our neighbor these amount years it'd only be right.

—

Next door's a man dying from too many cigarettes. On the other side of me to the left's a lady who doesn't know she's having half her insides taken out tomorrow at eight. Across the hall's a boy who's spent the past year in a coma and every other hour on the hour only cries mummy mum mum. Next to him on one or the other side's a man who tries suicide and I overheard his wife say in the hallway still has to lose his leg. In the next room to his is a woman who no specialist knows what's the matter with other than for her losing weight at an unbelievable speed. Can't eat. Next she can't even speak. Down to seventy pounds for a hefty frame and they don't think she'll last the week. Positively no visitors allowed it says on her door. I feel so ridiculous being on this floor. With only a couple of benign polyps to be removed and a little fright, though I might catch something worse from being around all these sorrowful people and horrible news. Is it at all possible to get my room switched to a less sickly floor?

—

Hello, Dad. I'm glad you're feeling better. Listen, don't try and speak. Even if you can. They say you can hear. Can you hear? You can let me know by smiling a lot at what I say. Not that anything I'll say is funny, but I love seeing your smile. My favorite father. You're looking real well. I would've been here sooner but the weather in our country's been so bad the planes couldn't go. When they did and the kids and I got here, your airport was on strike so we had to land three hundred miles out of the way and bus in here slowly overnight because it snowed. Then I heard what happened to you. But let's forget about going into that. My husband Lanny sends his best and says he wishes he could've also flown here, and the kids their love. They're right downstairs, and after all this traveling by trains, planes, buses, cabs and subways and now only an elevator ride away, it's frustrating for them not to be let up, and unfair. The youngest I wanted to sneak in here under my coat, as he's never seen you, but if they saw him they might not let me see you again. You're their one grandpa and what they know of you is only from what I tell them and old snapshots. I don't know—but am I speaking too much or too fast? Just relax. But nod if you want me to slow down or shut up. I was saying that I don't know if you knew that Lanny's folks died in a car crash together when he was a boy. He was in it too but thrown into some soft bushes so somehow survived. Though he did get a broken neck at the time which he still gets headaches from when he stretches too far. The neck too far. Don't try it again. All right. There it is. Off my chest. But please don't make me. I mean please don't, please make me a silent promise and to yourself you won't ever try it again. I've got to know before I go. It'll also be a stigma for the kids later on. Worse than anything it'll kill Mom for sure. And you and Jay Junior never got along too well, but you should see how he feels about you now. He's even postponed going back to his children and job and the new girl he's going to marry, so if for anything get out of here quick for another wedding. And when Mom's here we often get calls at home from all over from people who are concerned about you. Relatives, friends, and don't worry about the leg. Whatever happens you'll still always have your good heart and head and your life. Think of new interests you can develop you never had. Music. And if I was in your position I'd read more and draw. I'd draw the doctors and nurses and how I feel about them and what I see in the room and aides and also my leg. And also my face in the mirror, looking like how I felt about myself in such a state. And in the background I'd get the pills and food and needles and curtains and even this blue urinal here. I'd make a study of it, in fact. A whole portrait devoted to it and whatever else is on the table at the time. I'd draw it all. I'd use my ambition, which you always had plenty of for that, and believe me anybody can draw. You're smiling. Is it what I'm saying's so funny or do you agree? Anyway, good. And get out. Your body's still strong. Your internist only wishes he'd be as healthy as you at your age other than for the other things and says they'll have to both run you over and then beat you to death to finally get you to go. To go from life he meant. And don't give Mom any more pain. Consent to whatever the doctors say. Then everything will be all right. You'll be all right. We're not leaving from Mom's till I'm absolutely sure you're all right. I'm going out for a smoke now so you get some rest. And don't pinch, oh, just sleep, just rest.

You can't believe it, Jay. When they heard at the office they all nearly cried. First the prostatectomy. That wasn't so bad. With fifty percent of us supposed to get it, no man should think he'll be exempt. But that other thing. Hospitals. When I was in. Not this one, the V.A. downtown, good God what a mess. Same thing, only different. Good hospital, I'm not saying that. Our taxes have at least gone for something and our soldiers are getting treated right, but one thing always leads to the next. Went in to get a few boils on my butt cut off and what happens after that? One week is three. Pneumonia it turns out. You're telling me pneumonia from boils? Then a bad reaction to the antibiotics to cure up the pneumonia. Then I trip over my roommate's walker—an ex-major—and he breaks his other wrist and me an arm. Get me out of here, I yell, hand-to-hand combat was never as bad as this. Of course my arm's set wrong and the boils begin to return. Double pneumonia's on the way, I begin thinking, and even spare me the thought of what's following next. You think I don't discharge myself to have my new boils taken off somewhere else? Just got dressed, packed my gear, slipped down the stairway past the guards and reception desk and went to a private doctor in his office, where in a day he did it for me one-two-three. Also reset the arm and sent me home in an ambulance with a free air cushion and all the drugs in my life I'll ever need. But how they treating you, Jay? Your wife says they're making up for all their past mistakes by giving you extra-special food and service. Whatever it is you rate, I've never seen better-looking nurses. All Orientals it appears, which I think they'd make the sweetest and most competent. Everyone at work's optimistic that things are at last working out right for you. They're also getting you up a plant. Chipping in as if you never retired a hundred years ago. Even half the new help who never heard of you, and a box of chocolates as well, though I'm not supposed to tell. I told them but he's diabetic and one scimpy bite might mean so long our dearest old pal Jaysie, but Betty the great arranger there said, so, he can give the chocolates to his guests. But you suddenly look tired, as if falling asleep on me. Just go ahead, it's probably what your body most wants you to do. Their chair's very comfortable, so I'll sit here and read my paper and maybe take a nap myself.

Good evening. Your operation's scheduled for tomorrow morning at eight. It'll take from two to three hours, and naturally you'll be totally anesthetized the entire time. After the operation you'll go to recovery room for several hours and then be returned here. You'll be getting the best after-surgery treatment available, and at home the hospital's best physical therapists and homecare nursing staff. I also understand you have an excellent nurse in your wife. I would have preferred getting your written permission, but because there isn't a day to lose with your leg, I'm satisfied with your wife's okay. I want you to know I'd never operate if your internist didn't say you're a thousand times improved since you were admitted with your urine retention and had your prostate removed. And then your self-inflicted development, which you've healed faster than expected and have sufficiently recovered from. Let's be frank. You were here when your wife asked what would happen if the implant didn't take. I said we'd discuss that bridge if we had to come to it. Well, we're there now and must cross.

I told you both at the time that we were one run behind with two out in the ninth with your leg and what I wanted to do, but unfortunately couldn't, was hit a homerun with a man on. Now it's a brand-new ball game, one much simpler to win and with negligible trial and risk. I can't think of anything else to tell you, other than you'll be shaved tonight, wakened at seven and fed no food or fluids till tomorrow's IV. If there are no further questions, I'll see you in the morning when they bring you up at eight.

Come on now. Breathe deep. Breathe deep. Take a deep breath. I said deep breath. Deeper. More. More. That a boy. You're all right. He's okay. Only a little scare.

It's the anesthesia. He'll be less groggy tonight. What we'll have to check daily is how his diabetes affects the thigh's healing. The Parkinson's pills we've taken him off till he's well on the road to recovery. Closest I can pinpoint for you for a discharge date is a month or so, most likely more. One thing I never like doing is sending my patients home with dressings or packings or where they still must use drugs, drains or pills.

You think he looks bad now? You should have seen him when he was wheeled in. I was the only person in the room. Your mother was having a cigarette in the lounge. Dotty was down in the cafeteria getting coffees and teas for us all. His face was greener than your shirt. We thought for certain it was going to turn blue. The man who wheeled him in didn't know what to do. I rang for the nurse. The orderly came in and slapped his face around and called for the doctors and oxygen tank. His color's about back to normal now, but for a few minutes we thought your father was gone.

Dear? Jay darling. What a morning we had. I'm so glad you slept through it all. Last night I couldn't get a single wink's sleep. Right now I'm so exhausted I could pass out on my feet. But I won't leave. Not at least till the night nurse comes. She called in saying she'd be an hour late. Something about her car stuck in the garage. But isn't it all so grand? You'll be home by the end of the month, maybe less. More than likely less. The doctor says it was a complete success. But sleep then. Close your eyes if you can. Tomorrow they'll try and give you real food.

———

They're all excited, Jay. With flying colors you passed the test I tell them whenever anyone asks. I reported in sick for the day. Though if they want to know the truth and dock me, then I was right here. I see all the candy's gone. What kind of vultures you got for guests? And I don't see the plant and Mrs. Jay says none was delivered. Since Betty said they said it was sent a day ago, maybe I should call her to check.

———

Now that you're well on your way to health I'll be leaving. I'm sure the person I left my fishes and animals with has glutted them to death. And my boss is beginning to ask what's up with me. And the kids are screaming Daddy, Daddy, and my ex-wife Sondra is writing oh, some terrific father you make. Next time I fly in it'll be good seeing you sitting up again. So goodbye and best wishes and I'll be phoning Mom periodically to hear how you are.

———

Lil Bird from number ten. I would only drop by when I knew you were feeling well. Now that I know you are, I came over. The whole building misses not seeing you in front, as on the sunnier days. You were a pretty good watchdog against people who shouldn't be coming around for things that aren't theirs. Whether you knew that or not, and my husband sends his hellos also. I don't mean watchdog in the dog sense but as a watching human protector. Seeing someone there might be just what a thief needs to make the wrong person turn around. My husband likes hospitals worse than I do but thought it was our duty. I was undecided at first but happy I did and if you want anything, or the lights turned off, you tell me to tell your wife and I will.

I was your aide on the fifth when you had your prostatectomy. I always like to keep posted on my old patients if they're still around here, my little boys and girls. It's fabulous what one higher floor can do, so much extra light making the room so much more brighter. And your chart reads fine and your aides tell me you've been good as gold. I'm a bit rushed today but if there's anything you ever think I can do for you, just holler. Ask for Mrs. Lake from floor five, floor five, and goodnight.

You don't know me. I'm a patient across the hall. Only some polyps removed. Now that I'm here they're giving me the round of tests. I only wanted to pop in when nobody was around to wish all the good luck to you. And also to say you got one raw deal and have every right to sue. Not that you'll collect a cent from suing hospitals. Though you will get the satisfaction knowing they might think twice about being as careless with the leg of someone else.

This must seem so very silly to you. My writing a letter like this almost a week to the day after I wrote a similar letter about almost the exact same thing. What's different this time is that instead of using a pen I'm typing on my machine. The portable I treated myself to ten or so years ago and which has almost never been touched, which accounts for it being so stuck, though it's probably also in need of a cleaning. Somehow the dirt must have seeped into it through the portable case. I'm typing to you because I have to. I can't read and writing by pen is too slow and games like solitaire and needlework and talking to strangers here just won't help. I suppose I'm making a lot of noise. Not noise like complaints but typewriter noise. Sitting here in the visitors' lounge on Jay's floor, I'm sure it must only be my mind where I think they can hear me in the patients' rooms and hallways and at the nurses' station, though the nurses have assured me they can't. And there are closed doors to this room and the walls are padded with soundproof squares and the typewriter is supposedly a silent. I haven't checked with any of the other patients, though Jay I know can't hear me as last time I looked he was fast asleep with enough drugs to keep him that way for a while. The only visitors in here I've asked said go ahead, type all you want. As you know from your experiences with Abe in hospitals, people here are much more tolerant and kind. The typewriter is on my lap. It doesn't weigh more than six pounds. The way I've balanced it I can type without discomfort and with ease. The children, thinking the worst had come and gone with their father, had gone back to their individual homes. Jay has done it again. This is the story. He tried killing himself again. He's recovering now. I caught him as I had the last time. This time lying on the floor instead of in the bed, tubes winding every which way around his arms and legs, and a needle from one in his hand with which he just managed to give himself a pinprick. I had got this strange feeling about him as I had before. I called his floor. The nurse said she couldn't check since she was the only one on duty, but when she looked during her rounds the hour before he was doing fine. I begged her to check again. She said all right, maybe she would. Everything is still fine, she reported back to me, he's sleeping well. But like the last time I couldn't take her even rechecking him as a suitable enough answer, and certainly not since that last time, and I took a cab over. It was around 4 A.M. The woman at the hospital reception desk asked what did I want? I said I only wanted to wait in the waiting room on the first floor till the regular permitted visitors' time, which is 10 A.M. She said do as you like as long as you don't go upstairs before. I waited for about five minutes. She couldn't see anything that was happening behind her except through a small mirror. Then when she wasn't looking I climbed the five flights. A nurse followed me down Jay's floor asking what did I think I was doing going to his room? There he was. She knew now what I had come for. Saved again. He looked at me crossly. If he could have spoken I'm sure he would have insulted me and scorned. Not for long though, as they soon gave him sedatives to sleep. The nurse and I lifted him onto the bed. The tubes and needle were easy for her to replace and stick back in and the hand wound just took a Band-Aid. The doctors were called, but it wasn't that necessary. All they did was strap his wrists to the bed rails with bandages and assign an orderly to his room as a guard. Jay at first refused all sedatives by mouth, so they had to give it in his veins. He had done it by taking down the bed rail and rolling off the mattress onto the floor. I can understand how he feels. But the doctors told him what about your wife if you try it again or were even successful at it one of the last two times? I think he understands now. He promised to everyone he'll never try it again. But who can say? What's a promise worth these days? But once he's medically released from here I've been told to institutionalize him for life. In a nursing home or a good asylum if there's one. The government will pay the whole cost or close to it I've been told. Doctors, nurses, my friends and his few old friends and even his own children have urged me to do it. They've said Mom, you can't handle that man. It'll be too much for you and ruin your own health. He has to be watched all the time. And you have the authority now, everybody tells me, as his past two attempts gave you that. But I could never be that cruel.

The

Intruder

I go into our apartment. She's being raped. They're both naked. He's on top of her but not inside. He holds a knife to her neck. I say "All right, get off." She says "Tony—don't." He says "Just stay where you are, buddy, and your girlie won't get hurt."

"I said to get off."

"Tony, don't do anything. He'll kill me. He means it."

"You want your girlfriend killed?"

"No."

"What's your name?" he says to her.

"Della."

"Della doesn't want to be killed," he says.

"Just get off and dressed and out of here and we won't make any complaints against you."

"First I get my satisfaction and then I think about going."

"Then I'll have to kill you," I say.

"Tony, don't try anything. Let him do it to me. It'll be all right."

"The lady's got a good head," he says. "I'm going in. You just stay where you are."

"Stay there, Tony."

"Get off," I yell.

"Open up," he says to her.

She opens up.

"Don't do that," I yell at him.

He sticks the point of the knife to the side of her neck. She says "Ouch, that hurts." I say "Leave her alone. What did she do to you?" He says "Then just stay there and don't leave the room or I'll cut her throat and then go after you."

"I don't care about myself."

"Be a hero, big boy, but the lady dies if you step a foot nearer."

"Please stay there," she says to me.

"I can't stay here and watch."

"Then turn around."

"Better you turn over," he says to her. "My neck's beginning to hurt from trying to keep an eye on him while I make it with you." He gets up.

"What do you want me to do?" she says.

"Get on top of me." He gets on his back. She gets on top of him.

"And now?" she says.

"Don't do anything," I say.

"Just be quiet, Tony. It'll be quick."

"It'll be great," he says to me. "And now I can have my fun and watch him both. Now put it in," he says to her.

She tries. "It hurts," she says.

"Bullshit."

"But there's pain," she says. I turn around.

"Don't you go anywhere," he says. I go into the next room.

"Tony," she says. "Come back or he'll kill me." I go back. I watch. They make love. He says "Bounce." She bounces. "Go slower," he says. She does. I put my hands over my eyes. I hear noise from both of them. Panting. Then him screaming. She screams too. I think she's hurt. I look. He's clutching her hard to his chest, squeezing all the air out of her. She's still on top of him. He holds the knife to the back of her neck. His eyes are almost closed, but he's looking at me. "Over for now," he says. He falls out. She says "Can I get up now?"

"Get up and clean yourself and then we come back," he says. "And you just stay there," he says to me, "or Della gets killed." They go into the bathroom. "Let's take a shower," he says to her. "I like them with girls. Turn on the water." She turns the water on. "Make it lukewarm." She turns the spigot and says "It's lukewarm." He sticks his hand under the water. "A little warmer." "That's lukewarm," she says. "Warmer!" She turns the hot spigot. "It's warmer now," she says. He feels the water. "Good. Now let's get in." They get in under the shower head. "Wash me," he says. "And you stand by the door," he says to me. I stand by the door. She washes him. "Now get behind me and scrub that back." She scrubs his back. "No washrag?" he says.

"Do we have one, Tony?" she says. "No clean ones," I say. "Your hands will do then," he says to her. "Now wash my hair but no soap in the eyes." She washes his hair. "You got shampoo?" "Yes," she says. "Not in the eyes, though." She suds his hair with shampoo. He rinses himself off. "Wash my thing." She does. "Now yours." She washes herself down there. He gets out. "Now turn the cold water on all the way and the hot all the way off." "I don't like it cold," she says. "All the way." She turns the hot water off and the cold water on. She's shivering. He's loving it. She says "It's too cold. I can't take any more."

"Jump out of the shower," I say.

"Does and she's dead. Now turn it all the way hot after you turn all the cold off."

"I can't." She turns the cold water off. "I'll scald myself."

"I said hot."

"No. Cold's enough." She's still shivering.

"If you make her turn it on hot I'll jump and kill you," I say.

"Remember, I still have a knife."

"And I got a table leg," and I knock the lamp off the end table next to me, take the table in the air and smash it against the wall. It breaks. A support piece is still attached to one of the legs. The other three legs are still attached to the table top. I snap off the support piece and now have my table leg. "I can split your head in very nicely with this, very nice."

"Don't, Tony," she says.

"Only if he forces you to stand under the hot in there."

"I won't mind. I mean, I'll mind but I'll at least be alive."

"You don't know if he'll let you live after that."

"I'll take my chances with him. Don't do anything. Let him do what he wants."

"No," he says. "No hot water. I was only kidding. She'll be of no use to me later on with burns. Get out of there." She steps out of the shower. "Dry me." She does. "Especially my thing." She does. "Dry yourself." She does. "Now back in the bed. And you step a few steps aside," he tells me. I do. They go back to bed.

"You," he says to me. "Get on the floor and lie on your stomach right at the side of the bed. I want to make sure I see you when I get on top of her."

I stand where I am.

"Do it, Tony," she says. I lie down parallel to the right side of the bed.

"You get on your back this time," he says to her. She does. He gets on top of her. "And you keep your arms under your head and your eyes on the floor and don't move from there," he says to me. I look at the floor. "Now make me big again," he says. I don't see anything. I hear him getting excited. "That's nice. You really do a job," he says. I hear the bedsprings. I hear them both making noises. Pants and groans. He screams. She doesn't. "Move it some more," he yells. I hear the bedsprings rattling louder. Then they stop. He says "That was good. First class. You're really good. You're really a piece I wish I had always. I wish you was my girl for a long time. I'd do it to you all the time, baby, I mean all. You'd never have complaints."

She doesn't answer. "You all right, Della?" I say.

"I'm okay. I'm getting sick of this, though."

"You want me to jump him?"

"Hey, where'd you put that club?" he says. "Look up." I look up. "I'm so stupid. I forgot about your club. Where is it?"

"I left it in the bathroom."

"Tell him the truth," she says.

"Under me."

"Throw it out," he says. He has the knife on her throat.

"I can also use a lamp. One of the other table legs. My hands."

"Throw it out."

I throw it under the bed.

"Now you get up and come here and make me big and strong again," he says.

"No thanks," I say.

"I was kidding again. You think I'd want a man touching me there? You're crazy. But if I said your girlfriend dies if you don't, you'd do it."

"I wouldn't."

"Your girlfriend dies if you don't."

"Do it, Tony," she says.

"You see, she wants you to." I stand up. I grab him. It's like my own. I know what to do. He stays soft.

"Put it in your mouth," he says.

"Nothing doing."

He puts the point of the knife to her Adam's apple.

"Do it," she says to me. "Soon it'll be over."

I do it. I close my eyes. He gets hard. "This isn't bad," he says. "Never did it before with a guy, but not bad. Now you run it up and down with your hand while he's doing it to me." She does that. I feel her hand brush against my lips every now and then. As if she's trying to comfort me with her touch. Brushing up against my lips and under my nose and against my nose. I know her touch. I concentrate on that.

"Hey, this is even great," he says. "What kings had I bet. What every man should have at least once in his life. You should have it too. Except I'd never do it to any man. Except if my girl was being threatened with a knife. My girl or baby. Only then." He comes. "Oh crap. I meant it for her. You did it too well. Both of you. My congratulations, but that's it." Her hand stops. I spit on the floor several times. "Can I go in the bathroom?" I say.

"No, just stand there."

"Let him go," she says.

"All right. Go because your girl asks for you to go. But I'm watching, so no tricky stuff in there or she gets killed."

"I know." I wash myself in the bathroom.

"Take off all your clothes and come on out now," he says. I take off all my clothes. I come out of the bathroom and he motions me to stand by the bathroom door. They're still in bed. Knife against her throat. "I suppose I should go now," he says. We say nothing. "You'd like for me to go of course." Nothing. "Well say it, goddamnit."

"Yes," she says. "We'd like you to go."

"No reason to stay here anymore," he says. "Three times. In how many minutes do you think? Not that anyone's counting. But it's enough anyway. But maybe I can get hot once more if you two do it. I'd like four times. I'd like five but I got to be realistic. But with four I can say it's really been worth it. Go on. You two do it." He gets off the bed, stands by the bed with the knife at the side of her neck. I get on the bed. "Do it with you on your back," he says to me. "That way I'll have the advantage."

"I don't feel like doing it," I say.

"Neither do I," she says.

"I said do it."

"I can't just do it like that," I say. "I'm not like you. I have to want to and I don't feel like it."

"Neither do I. Just go," she says to him. "Please?"

"I said to do it," he yells at me. "Now do it. Try. Get big. Do it to her. Then if I'm big I'll take over for you."

"But I don't feel like it."

"Rub him," he tells her.

She rubs me. Nothing happens.

"When he doesn't want to he can't," she says. "I know him."

He grabs me. Rubs me. Nothing happens. He puts it in his mouth, the knife against my penis. Nothing happens. "What do you expect?" I say. "It's impossible. Nothing, you see?"

"If I didn't have the knife it wouldn't be nothing," he says.

"Then put away the knife," I say.

"You do what I did," he tells her. He gets up, holds the knife to her neck. She does it. Nothing happens. He rubs me while she's doing it. Nothing.

"Say nice things to him," he says.

"Tony, I love you. Tony, I love it. This. What we're doing. What I'm doing. Do it. Get big. I want you to make love to me. I'm going to do it again now, so get big."

She does it. Nothing happens. "It's impossible," I say.

"It's impossible," she says. "Believe him."

"If you don't get that thing going I'm going to cut it off," he says to me.

"I'll try." I concentrate. Nothing. "Maybe it will. Wait."

"Get hard," she says. "He'll kill you if you don't. Then he'll kill me. Put your mind to it."

I concentrate. I shut my eyes. Nothing. "I'm sorry," I say to him. "I can't. But don't do anything rough. Maybe I can. Just wait."

"Don't do anything to Tony," she says. "We were nice. We did what you asked. We won't make any charges against you to the police. We won't even call them."

"Bull," he says.

"You're right," she says. "Of course we'll call them. But don't do anything now. Tie us up. Then leave."

"I want to do it once more," he says. "Four's my lucky number. Not my lucky, just a good number. And I've never done it four times in a row in so short a time. And I feel cheated. That one with him doesn't count. So I haven't even got my three yet. And three's my minimum. The absolute must. And I can't get big either. Make me big," he says to her. "Do what you can." She tries. "Everything." She tries everything she used to do to me. Nothing happens. "Both of you try on me." We both try. Things I've never done before. Knife at her neck. Nothing happens though. He stays the same way. "You're both screw-ups," he says. He stands up. "You come with me." She stands up. "You stay there," he tells me. I stand up. "I said stay."

I walk towards him. He has the knife at her back. I bend down and stretch under the bed and get the table leg. "I don't care about her life anymore," I say. "I just want to beat your brains in."

"Bull," he says.

"Tony, drop the club."

I drop it.

"You didn't mean what you said," he says. "Too bad. It would have been nice sticking it in her and then pulling it out quick and fighting you off with a couple of feints and slices or two and then sticking it in you. Maybe not nice. But different. And I could do that. I'm ready. I hope you believe that. Sure you do. And I'm very very good with this knife. So maybe you should try," he says to me. "Come on. Pick up your club and try and get me."

"Don't, Tony."

I don't. "I wasn't going to hit you with it anyway," I say to him. "Just go. Leave us alone."

"No, come on," he says. "If you don't come at me with the club I'm going to stick the knife in Della's neck."

"No." I sit on the bed.

"You want me to stick it in her neck?"

"No."

"Where then?"

"No place. All I want is for you to go."

"Just stay there like that, Tony," she says. "This will be over soon. Or in an hour. Or a day. Then it'll be over. But you're being smart. Even if he knifes me don't attack him and risk your life. Only attack him if he comes after you. But now just leave him alone. He'll eventually go."

"Don't be too sure," he says. "Come on, big boy, come try to get me with the club."

I lie on the bed, head on the pillow, arms over my chest.

"Then I'm going to put it in her back or neck."

"Please don't," she says.

"Even if you do, it'll be her neck and she'll be dead. So what's the sense of risking my life for her as she said?"

"Because you'll have a better chance to come get me and beat me over the head in the time I stick it in her neck and try and pull it out to get you. You have to think like that."

"That makes sense," I say. I stand up.

"Sit down," she says. "Lie down, Tony."

I lie down.

"You two are just no fun," he says. He gets dressed. "Don't move," he tells her. "Just stand by my side." He sits down. "Put my socks and shoes on and tie them tight." She does that. "All your money now," he says, "and his." She collects it with him following her right behind. "Now walk me to the door. And you stay in bed or try and come after me with or without the club," he yells at me.

"Stay in bed, Tony," she says.

They go to the door. I can't see them. "Now kiss me goodbye," he says.

"Oh stop the crap already and go," she says.

"You're right. You're much smarter than him. Who needs a kiss? Kiss him. He needs it." He opens the door and goes.

We don't have a phone. I go next door to call the police. Della says "I'm going to take a shower for an hour and don't want to be bothered by anyone," and goes into the bathroom. The police come. "Come out when you can," I yell into the bathroom. She comes out. Lots of questions from the police. We tell them everything. One policeman says to Della "You should go straight to a doctor." She says "No, I'm okay. I can take care of myself." We go to the police station and answer more questions and look at photos. None are of him. I say to the police we're exhausted. They say sure. We go home. That evening a circular from our police precinct is pasted on the mailbox in the vestibule and slipped under every tenant's door. It's a warning about that man today who's been raping and robbing women in their apartments in the neighborhood lately. It has a good description of him, ours along with others. Several different outfits and hats. The outfit and hat he wore today are there. The circular says he gets into the apartments mostly by telling the woman over the downstairs intercom that he's a delivery boy from a local florist with a box of flowers for her.

"Did he tell you on the intercom he was a florist delivery boy with a box of flowers for you?" I ask her.

"No, at the door."

Streets

⌒

Two people stand on the street corner. Or rather she stands on the corner. He's gone into the corner store. She looks up. A jet plane passes. She waves at the plane and laughs. She looks at the cars passing on the avenue. A bus. She waves at the people in the bus. A young boy in the bus waves back. She sees me waiting at the bus stop. She smiles. I smile. The man comes out of the store. He holds out a package he didn't seem to have when he went into the store. She takes the package and puts it in her pocketbook and runs. He walks after her. She sees him walking after her and runs faster. He starts jogging after her. She sees him and begins to run as fast as she can. At least it seems like that. She's sprinting. He's now running after her. She turns around as she runs and sees him gaining on her. She seems to try to run faster than she was going, but she can't. She's in fact slowing down. She's getting tired. The pocketbook she's holding might be heavy. I'm running along the avenue behind both of them. People turn as we run past. They look at the couple and then me as if I know what's going on. I don't. As if I'm part of a threesome—this woman, man and I—but I'm really not. I was just watching them on the corner. Then just the woman on the corner. Then the man leaving the store and holding a package out to her and the woman taking the package and putting it in her pocketbook and running away with it and the man following her, and now he catches up. He tries to take her pocketbook. She pulls her pocketbook back. I stand and watch this from about fifteen feet away. Other people watch. He pulls the pocketbook from her. When she tries to get the pocketbook back, he pushes her. She falls. A man steps over to them and says something to the man who pushed her and holds out his hand to the woman and pulls her up. The man with the pocketbook tells him to mind his own business. The helping man steps back but continues to watch them while sitting against a parked car. The man he's watching pulls the package out of the pocketbook and puts it in his side jacket pocket. The woman reaches into the pocket. He slaps her hand. She slaps his face. He punches her in the face. She falls, this time on her back. Her head hits the ground hard, and she seems unconscious. The helping man rushes over and begins arguing with the man who hit the woman. The man swings the pocketbook at him and catches him in the face. The woman was only stunned or maybe unconscious for a few seconds. The helping man has a cut on his cheek from the bag. He pulls out a knife. The other man tries to knock the knife out of his hand with the pocketbook, but the strap breaks and the pocketbook drops to the ground. The woman takes a handkerchief out of the pocketbook, presses it against the back of her head and stands. The two men are facing one another and shouting, the helping man waving his knife in the air, the other man his fists. "Use it. You just try and use it," he says to the man with the knife. Several people come over, and others from across the avenue, and almost all of them crowd around the two men and the woman, though giving them plenty of room to move around. I still haven't moved. The crowd forms quickly and so densely around the trio that I can no longer see what's going on. I hear screams. From women and men. One woman turns around from the crowd with her wrist to her lips and looks at me and walks away. Her space is taken immediately, so I still can't see what's going on. I go over to the crowd, try to get a place in the circle by squeezing between two people, then look over a couple of shoulders to see what's going on inside. The man who tried to help the woman has his own knife in his chest and is lying on his back. The woman is lying on her front, her face on its side. Blood frames the back of her head, though it could be from the second fall that I saw. The man who hit her then is on his knees. Blood seems to be blotting his dark shirt around his stomach where he's holding himself.

"What happened?" I say to a man.

"Don't you see?"

"But how'd it happen?"

"What's the difference how? It's happened."

"Someone should go for the police."

"Good idea. You go."

"And the people there should be helped."

"That's what someone else said. You help them."

"How can I if I'm going for an ambulance and the police?"

"That's true. And an ambulance. You're right. They need one."

"Will someone please go for an ambulance and the police while I try and help these people?" I say.

"I'll go," a girl says. She doesn't look older than eight.

"Someone older?" I say.

There are about twenty people around the trio. Nobody responds to anything I say with even a head shake. I push through the crowd. The man's shirt is soaked now and he's groaning. The man with the knife in his chest looks dead. The woman is still bleeding from the head.

"Will someone please go for the police?" I say.

"Let the girl go," a woman says. "I know her. Know her mother, I mean. She's a smart girl. Rather, her mother says she's smart."

"She's smart," another woman says. "Go, girl. Call the police."

"I need the money," the girl says.

I put my hand in my pants pocket. Everyone watches me go through all my pockets for change. I look at the crowd nearest the girl. "I thought I had change," I say.

"Sure," a man says. He gives the girl a dime.

"Give her two," a woman says. "She might lose the first."

"I won't lose the first," the girl says. "I know who to call and how. I dial. I put the dime in."

"You put the dime in and then you dial," the woman says.

"I know, I know. I only need one dime." She goes.

I get down on one knee. I don't know whom to help first. Probably the woman. The knifed man looks dead. If the knifed man is dead, and he didn't by some accident fall on the knife himself, then the man who stabbed him would seem like the last person to help. I'm not sure about that. All I know is someone has to be helped first. So I pick the woman. Maybe because she is a woman. Though if she's the one who stabbed the man, then I probably should first help the man who I thought stabbed the man in the chest, though only if I'm sure the stabbed man is dead. If he isn't dead, then I wouldn't know which man to help first—that is, if the woman is definitely the one who stabbed the man, but not out of self-defense. If she stabbed him out of self-defense or to protect the man who chased and hit her before, then the last person to be helped would be the stabbed man, dead or not, and the first would be either the woman or the man holding his stomach.

"Who stabbed who?" I say.

"Who stabbed who?" a man says.

"Who's responsible for all this?"

"I didn't see it."

"I did," a woman says.

"Who stabbed who?" I say.

"Why you want to know? You a cop?"

"No. I just want to help these people."

"You a doctor?"

"I'm a passerby, just like you."

"No you're not. You were running after them before."

"I was running after them because I saw the man chasing the woman, and I thought something was wrong."

"Something was," a man says.

"What happened?" I say.

"You're the one running after them, and all of a sudden you didn't see?" a woman says.

"No."

"Like hell you didn't."

I decide to help the knifed man first. At least I can find out quick enough if he's dead or not. If he's alive then there can't be much I can do for him except put a support under his head, and then I can go right to the woman or other man.

"Will someone please do what they can to make the woman and that man comfortable while I see to this one?"

"Best medicine and treatment in these situations is to wait for professional help," a man says. "Real doctors or hospital aides, but someone ignorant of medicine can do more damage than someone not doing anything."

"He's right," several people say in different ways.

"But I know what I'm doing. I'm not in the field of medicine, but I know how to stop someone from bleeding to death."

"How?" a man says.

"Tourniquets, for one thing."

"That's for arms and legs, not the head."

"I said 'for one thing.' Another way is pressure points. The neck. There's one there. They're all over the body. Or you stick your finger on the wound or in the blood vessel that's cut if you can't find the right pressure point. At least let me try."

"Sure, we can let you try, and watch you finish off all three of them before our eyes. Just stay off them."

"I'm sorry, but I still think it's best I try." I feel the woman's forehead. Put my ear next to her mouth. "She's breathing."

"We said stay off her," the man says. "Wait for help."

"What I think is someone else ought to call the police for help. That girl might have met a friend or someone and just forgotten about it."

"She's a good trustful girl," the woman who said she knows the girl's mother says.

"I'm not saying she's bad or distrustful. But younger people—particularly around her age, eight or nine or so—do get distracted more than adults."

"She's ten," the woman says.

"Ten-year-olds probably get less distracted than eight- or nine-year-olds, but still get distracted a lot."

"So do adults," a woman says.

"I know. But children more so."

"Children more so. You're right. Maybe someone ought to go as he says. You go, why don't you?" she says to me. "You seem so interested and reliable."

"I want to stay here and help these people now."

"I think you'd best be giving help by phoning for it than touching them," a man says. "And out of all of us, you're the one who seems more liable to do the most trouble if you stay."

"I agree," a woman says.

"I don't." I feel the stabbed man's temple. "He's alive."

"Too bad," a man says.

"What are you saying?" someone else says.

"What I said. Too bad he's alive. He started it, didn't he?"

"No, the other man did."

"It was a woman," a woman says. "She stole something from the man with the knife in him. That's why he chased her. The other man just happened to step in. And she took the knife out of his hand, which he only pulled out to protect her, and put it in the stabbed man's chest."

"I think the woman and the man holding his stomach did know one another," I say.

"You know them?"

"I saw them together. They were standing on the corner of this same avenue three blocks away. The man went into a corner store, and the woman waited for him outside."

"What kind of store?"

"I forget. A jewelry store. I was waiting for my bus. Then the man came out and held the package out for her, or just held it out without any intention of giving it to her. Anyway, she took it and put it in her pocketbook and ran. The man walked after her. She ran faster. He started jogging and then ran after her. She at first ran faster than him when they were both running, and then, because she was tired or her pocketbook had become too cumbersome to run with or something, she slowed down and he caught up. Right here. I was standing over there. Next to the hydrant. The one where the two dogs are."

I'm still on one knee and now pointing through someone's legs. Almost all of them turn to look at the hydrant and dogs. "Then the man took the pocketbook from her, and she tried getting it back. He pushed her and she slapped him. Rather, he hit her hand and she slapped his face and he punched her and she went down. That's when the man who was knifed stepped in for the second time. Most of you must have seen that. The first time he stepped in he was told to mind his own business and he did. This time I don't remember him being told anything. They just argued. And he pulled out a knife—the knifed man did—after the other man hit him in the face with the pocketbook. Then the other man must have taken the knife away from him and stabbed him with it, though I'm only assuming now, since that's when you all suddenly encircled them and I couldn't see what happened."

"That's not at all what happened," someone says.

"Then what really happened?" someone says.

"You didn't see it?"

"I just got here."

"Remember that little girl who went to phone the police?"

"I told you, I just got here."

"Well, there was a little girl of about nine or ten or so who we sent to call for help."

"Ten," a woman says.

"Ten. Well, she knifed him."

"Don't be ridiculous," several people say in different ways.

"I thought we needed a bit of, I don't know, levity here, what with the grim sight of them lying there and waiting for help taking so long. But I guess it was in bad taste."

"Very."

While they were saying all this I took my jacket off, rolled it up and put it under the woman's head.

"Here it comes," a man says.

We hear an ambulance siren and look in the street. The ambulance and police escort preceding it pass.

"Must be for someone else."

"I really think one of us should try and get the police now," I say. "Just to remind them, if the girl called, or to let them know, if she didn't."

"Maybe he's got a point," the woman who said she trusts the girl says.

"I'll go," I say.

"You've already done enough damage," a man says.

"What do you mean? You wouldn't let me do anything, which is why I'm volunteering to go."

"You picked up that woman's head just before. Maybe they didn't see you, but I did. And in her condition you might have done just enough damage to kill her, when if you hadn't touched her she might have been saved."

"You don't know that."

"I say we make sure he stays here and we send someone else to call."

"Send anyone you want, but I'm also phoning for help." I push through the crowd. I look back. The circle's together again around the three injured people. I go into one of the stores nearest the crowd and ask the hardware-store man if I can use his phone.

"There's a public booth a block north of here," he says.

"I haven't a dime and this is an emergency."

"All I get every day are people with no dimes and life-and-death emergencies."

"Let him use the phone," a woman at the cash register says.

"I said no."

"But it's real important. Can't you look outside yourself and see?"

"Just keep looking for your register-tape error and don't butt in."

"Don't you talk to me like that."

"I said shut up," he says to her.

"And I'm telling you this is as much my store as yours and even more so, as it's in my name. And I want him to phone for the police for whatever it is that happened out there."

"I better go somewhere else," I say.

"You're damn right," he says.

"No. Go no other place. Use our phone. It's mine—in my name—and in the back there, right down that aisle."

"Use the phone and you're flattened," he says, his hand in a tray of wrenches on the counter.

I head for the door. The woman runs after me. "I said you can use the phone."

"But I don't want to cause any more trouble and also get killed for it."

"Trouble between him and me is nothing new. Besides, he's a blowhard—all wind and words. So use the phone."

"No."

"He's smart," the man says. "Here's a dime, sonny. Now get the hell out of here." He throws me a dime and I catch it.

"Coward," she says to me. "Idiot," she yells at him.

He picks up a wrench and comes over to her. "Don't be calling me an idiot."

"All right. I apologize. You're not an idiot." He relaxes both arms to his sides and walks away. "You're a big moron and stupid son of a bitch."

He rushes at her to hit her with the wrench, or it at least looks like that. She runs. I freeze. But I just about froze before and watched and now three people are near dead out there. The man runs past me after the woman. I grab the hand that holds the wrench. "Get his other arm and we'll trip him," I yell at her. He hits me on the back with his other arm or hand. I fall. He lifts the wrench over my head and yells "Meddler, meddler," and comes down on my shoulder with it and then my neck. Both times it seemed he aimed for my head. Something in me broke both times. He lifts the wrench again.

"Don't," she yells.

He turns to her. I start to crawl to the door. He comes after me.

"Leave him," she yells.

He turns to her. I'm still crawling. He steps over to me with the wrench raised.

"Stop," she yells.

He rushes her and hits her across the face with the wrench at the same moment she sticks a chisel in him. I don't see where she got him. Somewhere high up. They both fall. They don't make sounds. I crawl out of the store to the crowd. The ambulance and police still haven't come. I grab a man's ankle and shake it. He turns. "Oh my gosh," he says. "What happened?"

"In there." I can't point. "The hardware. Two people are hurt. Maybe dead. The man hit me twice with a wrench and then the woman with a wrench, but she much worse than me. She stabbed him to protect me and herself. Take care of her. Then me. The man should come third. Or rather, call the police, for I never could. Help for all six of us. I'm sure that girl never called. They would have been here by now."

"He wants us to phone for help," he says to the crowd.

"You go," a woman says to him. "He told you."

"I haven't any change."

"Use the phone in the hardware store," I say. "In back. Straight down the middle aisle."

"You don't need a dime?"

"Maybe you do. I thought it wasn't a pay phone, but maybe it is. But they must also have a regular business phone that doesn't take dimes."

"I better take a dime just in case."

"Two," I say.

"Two dimes then."

"Two ambulances. For the trio in the street and the couple in the store and me."

"The stabbed man doesn't need help anymore."

"The one in the street?"

"Maybe the one in the store also," a woman says.

"That would mean only four people need help," the man says.

"We'll still need two ambulances if they're the triple kind," I say.

"The lady doesn't seem to need help either," a man says. "The one in the street, I mean. She doesn't seem to be breathing."

"Check," I say. "No, just go in the hardware store and call the police. Don't tell them how many ambulances we'll need. The ones I'm thinking of they might be out of. Just say six people are seriously hurt. Also, if some of you would turn me over now and put something under my head. A jacket. But gently. Rolled up, and not the jacket that's under the head of the woman in the street."

"I wouldn't touch him," a man says. "You might do more damage than not."

"Don't worry," I say. "I'm uncomfortable, in pain, and know what I need. I give you permission."

"For his own good I wouldn't touch him. His shoulder seems broken. So does something with his neck the way he's keeping it."

"Wait for the ambulances," several people say in different ways.

"Phone," I say to the man.

"I don't want to go in the store. The man with the wrench might be up and ready to clip the first one to come in. For all we know, you could have been the one who provoked him into using the wrench, and he might think the next person to come in his store is the same."

"I didn't provoke him. I only went in to call."

"Maybe you're right. The courts will decide if it has to come to that. But I'm not going in there. Anyone know where the nearest phone booth is?"

"Three blocks south on this avenue," someone says.

"One block north," I say.

"The dime," he says. "I'm all out."

Several people search their pockets and handbags.

"In my shirt pocket," I say. He takes out of my pocket the dime I was going to call with before and goes. "I think someone else should go in the hardware store to also phone the police and see about the couple."

"You think he's going to get distracted like that ten-year-old girl?" a woman says. "He's a grown man."

"I know. But I'd like the double assurance that help will come."

"Look. I know him a long time, that fellow who went. When he says he'll do something, he does it."

"That's not the way I see him," a man says. "He's owed me ten dollars for two years now and always says he's paying up and never does. I've given up on him and don't even ask him anymore."

"Well, I know him as a very dependable honest man," she says. "Always pays his rent on time. Never a bill due on anything for more than a day or so."

"Not him. Two years he's owed me. For supplies."

"Then you better go in the hardware store and call the police," I say to this man.

"Right." He goes into the store.

"You know who you just sent to call the police?" a man says to me. Several people laugh. "The worst thief of them all. He's going to steal from that store everything that isn't held down."

We hear sirens. It seems the ambulance is going to pass. A man runs into the street and waves at the ambulance to stop. It's gone.

"Someone else again must be sick or in trouble," a woman says.

"Or that siren's on just so they can get through the traffic quicker," a man says. "They have that advantage over most of the other cars and use it."

I turn myself over on my back.

"You shouldn't do that," a man says. "You can hurt yourself worse."

I put my good arm under my head. Everything hurts. "You know, it's possible those people who went to phone could all be unreliable," I say. "I think someone else should call."

"How many do you want?" a woman says. "If they are reliable and too many people phone the police, they'll think we're cranks or crackpots and never send anyone to help. Three's enough."

"Three are plenty," a man says.

"Three for what?" someone new in the crowd says.

"Three people have gone to call the police for these four people in the street here and a couple who are seriously hurt in the store."

"Three calls are more than enough," the new person says.

I shut my eyes and wait.

Movies

He says "Hey, where you going?" and she says "I told you before, the movies." He says "Wait for me" and she says "Can't, or how long you going to be?" "Couple of minutes" and she says "Please make it snappy." "That's what I said, couple of minutes, quick, zip and snappy, I'm already on my way." "I won't delay you any further by talking about it or encouraging you to. But kind of make it even snappier than you're doing, as you know I hate getting to a movie even half a minute late." "What about a quarter minute late?" he says, putting on his shoes, and she sticks her arms through her coat sleeves and says "Ready?" and he's looking at her, untied shoelaces between his fingers and she opens the door and he says "Hey, wait for me, I was only sitting here wondering why you're acting like this, but I'm ready, I'm ready," and he ties his shoes and grabs his coat off the hook just before he shuts the door.

He's locking the door while she's already down one flight of stairs and rounding the second for the first floor. He runs downstairs and catches up with her at the corner where she's waiting for the light to change or the heavy traffic to pass. He says "You don't have to run, do you? What time the show begin?" "Any minute" and he says "We'll make it. It's only a three-minute walk to the Embassy." "It's at the Symphony, what gave you the idea it was the Embassy?" "Because you said yesterday there was a movie there you wanted to see. But if it's the Symphony let's take a cab." "You have the money for one?

Because I don't—I was thinking of a bus." "You can think of a bus while we're in the cab where I'll be a sport for a change. I mean, how many times has that happened with us?" "None?" and he says "Don't be a wiseguy," and flags down a cab.

They drive to the theater. The line for the box office runs along Broadway and then down Ninety-fifth Street past the Thalia Theater and halfway to West End Avenue. She says "I bet the line only started forming like this a few minutes ago. I should have hurried you up more. I'm sure there won't be any tickets left, and if there are, the movie will probably begin while we're on line and I was told especially not to miss the beginning of it." "Don't worry," he says, "it's a big theater with I think a balcony and orchestra both. They'll never start the movie till all the ticket holders are inside; they want our money and not our howling or demands for our money back, right?"

The line begins moving. People in front and back of them are talking about what a great movie they heard it is. "One of the best . . . nothing like it in five years . . . ten . . . the directing . . . you won't believe it I heard . . . a new woman director . . . worked under what's-his-name, the famous German one whose name I just forgot, or is he French with a German-sounding name? Now he's calling her his master with just her first full-length movie and most critics consider him one of the two or three greatest in the world . . . and the acting . . . editing . . . photography . . . color . . . even the sound . . . something totally new, but no tricks like wraparound or wallaround or whatever it is sound . . . also not that avant-garde a movie where it's unintelligible or intentionally obscure to make up for all its deficits . . . it's the real thing . . . a work of art . . . a classic . . . has animation and real acting and mime and puppets and footage from old films separate and combined and sometimes all five going at one time . . . will definitely win most of the awards, I understand . . . already won the three major foreign festival awards for best acting, direction and movie . . . even the screenplay . . . supposed to be truly original . . . better than any fiction book when read . . . going to be published as a book and is being fought over now by the two big book clubs . . . and the costumes . . . makeup . . . incredible things they did with subtitles streaming out of the actors' mouths in a dozen languages and in several layers all over the screen. . . ."

"I don't want to hear any more," she says, putting her hands over her ears. "And I'm going to be one disgruntled lady if we have to sit way on the side or the back row somewhere or right up front." "I know. I'm really glad we came now." "What?" He takes her hands off her ears and says "The movie sounds great and I'm glad I came along. Where'd you hear about it?" "This? I thought everybody knew about it. Big ads. Posters all over town. And these great film buffs at work have been talking about it long before it hit the States and maybe a half-dozen reviews and articles I read, all raves." "Nobody mentioned a thing about it to me and I can never get through movie reviews. My loss I suppose. Good thing I know you."

She puts her head on his shoulder. They turn the corner and get closer to the ticket booth. "Have your money ready please," an usher says. "How much?" he says and the usher says "Four dollars." "For two or a season pass?" and the usher says "Per ticket." "I know, but that's highway robbery, four dollars." "It's because of the high cost of the print or something," a man on line says and he says "That's their problem," and to her "I don't think I'm up to paying four for any movie." "Then I'm going in myself, because look at the line behind us and down the block. Probably most of them for the show after this and they'd give their right arm to take our place." "But it's usually two-fifty here, at the most three." "So go home then," and she opens her shoulder bag. "Next," the usher says and he says to her "All right, put your money back, it's big sport all the way tonight," and shoves a ten-dollar bill through the window, holds up three fingers to the cashier and gets a pair of raised eyebrows, two tickets and change.

They go in. "Candy?" "Let's just find seats," she says. There are few seats left and none together it seems and it also seems more people are looking for seats than there are seats. "We're going to be out if we don't split up fast," she says. "There's two," he says, pointing to two seats with clothing on them and a woman sitting between them. "Excuse me, miss," he says, "but if those seats aren't taken, would you mind moving over one either way so we can sit together?" "I like the one I'm in," the woman says, "no tall heads in front like the free two. As to whose these coats are," taking her own off one of the seats, which still left coats and sweaters on both empty seats, "maybe the people on the other side or behind me know, but not me." The houselights begin fading. She says "You sit in the first seat you get and I'll find one on my own." "Wait. Maybe these two aren't taken and we can sit a seat apart from each other," but she's already down the aisle. He yells into the row "Excuse me, you people in there. Is one of the seats with the coats on them not being reserved?" The whole row except the three people sitting beside the empty seats look at him. He finds a seat two rows back. He looks around where she might be sitting and sees her in the third row or so, moving past several people to get to a seat. "Pardon me, pardon me, pardon me," she seems to be saying. The movie begins.

It ends. There's quite a lot of applause for a movie and in a theater that's not known for being patronized by cinemaphiles. Not a very good picture though, he thinks. The houselights go on. Most of the audience get up to leave. He doesn't see her where she was sitting before. Maybe the row became too close for her and she changed seats during the movie. He makes his way up the aisle. "I don't get it," a man in the aisle says and the woman with him says "What can I tell you? If it had any faults, complexity certainly wasn't one of them." "It isn't I don't understand it. It was a travesty." "So? Suddenly travesties can't be profound?" "I mean it was stupid, juvenile, ridiculous. It ridiculed our intelligence it was so jejune and dumb." "Let's just say we have different opinions about that." "Let's say that for sure," one of the three young men behind them says. "Okay, then one of you explain to me its meaning and appeal," the man says to them, "because outnumbered like this, maybe I'll admit I didn't get it after all." "Explain it in just one quick shot up the aisle?" the younger man says. "Let's save it for outside when we're not getting so pinched and pushed," the woman says. "Good idea," the man says, "we can talk about it over coffee or beer. You guys game? I am. Enid?" "Yes," the woman says. "Why not," one of the younger men says.

He waits for her in the lobby. Just as many people seem to be waiting in line to see the movie as leaving the theater. She doesn't show. The doors open on the other side of the lobby and the waiting line moves in. The doors the people who were leaving came out of are shut and he tries but can't open them from the lobby. He climbs over the rope that separates the two lines and goes back to the theater and looks around for her. Almost every seat is filled and again more people seem to be looking for seats than there are seats. He goes down to the first few rows where she was sitting before. "Bud? Up here." She's about halfway up the aisle, sitting right in the middle of the theater. There's an empty seat next to her with her coat on it. "Joan, what are you doing? Aren't you leaving?" "I want to see it again, all right with you? I didn't see you leave but thought you'd figure out my plans and come back. I didn't want to lose these two seats together." "I'm not staying a second time." A man behind Bud says to her "That seat taken?" "Bud?" "Yes," he says to the man, "she was holding it for me," and moves into the row, hands her her coat and sits down. "You have to be kidding," he says, "because never was a movie more overrated in my life. What's so worth sitting a second time around for?" "Everything. Acting, directing, editing, screenplay and God knows what else." "What do you know about editing?" "I can tell. The way the film was cut. More. The quick cutting, intercutting, beautifully spliced sequences and frames. Animation into reality and back again and the superimposition of those two and splitscreening and the sound editing too. Tripling and quadrupling the soundtrack with voice overlays and overlays of previous overlays. It moved so quickly, the whole film. You saw it. That surely had to do with both types of editing and lots of other cinematic stuff that I'm of course not aware of. Hundred-twenty-two minutes running time that felt like half an hour." "For me it was like ten half-an-hours. Twenty." "If you think you'll be bored seeing it again, leave. Really. Go home or for coffee and pick me up after the show if you want or I can take the bus. No problem." "But I want to stay with you now that we finally got two seats together. Whose hand am I going to hold in the coffee shop, mine?" "If you stay, don't grumble, will you? I want to enjoy it."

The houselights fade. A little applause. This time the film is preceded by a preview. "I want to see that when it comes here," she says and he says "I heard it's a bomb." "You said you never read reviews." "Someone told me. Two people in fact. Not buffs but in the buff." "Come on." "It's true. At the Y, in the sauna." "Well I heard it's great." "The editing, acting, writing, directing, sounding, coloring and the rest, I know." "God, you're cynical. You didn't want to stay, why did you?" "Quiet please," a woman behind them says. "I guess what it comes down to is I just don't like movies," he whispers to her. "Shh," she says. "Will you two please be quiet," the same woman says. "It was only me speaking this time," he says, turning around, "and besides, it's only the previews." "It's a trailer of a movie I'm particularly interested in seeing," the woman says, "and a very interesting trailer if you gave it half a chance." "Oh please, what are you talking about, making this trivial commercial movie ad into a major art form." "Do you want me to get the usher?" "Bud, turn around and be quiet." "Excuse me," he says to the woman. "I'm sorry. It is a well-done trailer and truly artistic," and sits back in his seat and Joan says "Good, at least you didn't slug her. Now let's just enjoy the movie." "Will you two can it already," a man behind them says, "the picture's on." "Only the credits," Bud says and someone in the same row as him says *shush* and he looks over to the shushing person and sees a woman with her finger over her lips and the man next to her nodding at him.

The movie begins. "Hello," a man's voice says, on the black

screen, then just a pair of small moving lips on the black screen, then two lips as the movie continues, both on the black screen saying *hello*, then three, four and five lips, all saying hello, and the audience loving it, laughing, saying "Fantastic . . . too much," some applause, six, seven and eight lips, then the entire screen quickly taken over by lips, a hundred, two hundred lips, all looking like different people's lips, male and female and children's lips, even a few gorilla or some kind of anthropoid or monkeys' lips, all saying *hello*, though not necessarily at the same time, when the screen goes black, no lips and suddenly just a pair of lips in the middle of the screen, which opens wider and gets larger till it takes over almost the entire screen and these lips growing two short legs with knobby knees and big feet and after doing a quick softshoe routine, walking off the screen saying *hello, hello, hello* as it goes, leaving behind the mouth's tongue in the middle of the screen, a wagging, fluttering and then gagging tongue, which sends most of the audience into hysterics and applause, Joan included, the man behind them kicking Bud's seat he's breaking up so much, then the tongue licking the black screen around it white till the entire screen except for the tongue is white and then licking itself till the screen is nothing but white for a few seconds, when the story begins. A single bed appears on the white screen, then disappears and a double bed appears. Then walls, furniture, floor, paintings, ceiling, all sort of flashing on the screen but staying there. Then a door in the wall and a doorknob and the doorknob turns and a man and woman enter the room through the door and sit on the bed. She puts on stockings, he a pair of different-colored socks. She puts on several pairs of stockings one over the other in increasingly rapid speed and he several pairs of socks, all different colors and sizes. They hear a door knock when they're trying to get on their third pair of shoes. "Hello," a man's voice behind the door says, the same voice that opened the movie. "It's him," she says. "No, her," the man on the bed says. "No him?" "Him her." "Him her she?" "Her his he." "Jest opium," she says. "He ha who," the voice behind the door says. "Who he has?" she says. "Just injun I think," the voice behind the door says. "Oh what's the dif for angst?" she says; "come in then." The sound of a whistling and hooting audience comes from the screen. The theater audience responds with whistles and hoots. The couple on the screen get up and bow, then throw the shoes they were trying to get on at the camera and Bud ducks, for suddenly that sequence is in 3-D. The door disappears and a man crawls through a large painting of the outdoors, which for a moment had moving birds and clouds in it, rolls his eyes and says "Eve ya, folks, and hello." "Hello," people in the audience and on the audience soundtrack say. "Muh-ruh-puh and luh tongue too, fuhtykes." At the bottom of the screen while he's saying this the words read "*Sous-titres*," then "Subtitles," then "Lights, camera, action!" He takes off his coat and underneath is a spangly dress. He lets down his hair to his waist and his body is shaped something like a thin shapely woman's. "Is that a woman or man," Bud whispers to Joan, "or is it not important?" and she says, "Shh, I'm enjoying." "Oh, closing hello," the couple say in unison. The woman-man jumps on the bed and they all start tearing at each other's clothes, hose and shoes till they're all nude, the woman-man never exposing the front part of his body as the other two do.

"I'm afraid I'm bored," Bud says to Joan. The screen trio have become a fidgeting, shifting mound under the blanket, making no sounds now but ouches, grunts and shouts. Part of the audience soundtrack is booing and snoring and a few of them chant "We want our money back . . . lynch the producer." The real audience is laughing and applauding, and when the mound grows to the size of about ten to twenty people under the blankets, parts of both audiences yell "More, more." "I'm leaving," Bud says. "Quiet," the man behind him says. "Now . . . oh nothing. Enjoy the unenjoyable. The deplorable. The I-don't-know-whatable. Just enjoy." "How can I do any of those with you yakking all the time?" "Why don't you say something to the people shouting and clapping?" Bud says. "That's different. I'm sure you know the difference." "This is where I came in, Joan. You coming?" "I'll meet you after," she says.

"Excuse me, excuse me please," he says to the row as he leaves. "Why didn't you think of that before?" a woman says. "Don't worry, I'm not going out for what you think. It's only for a few bags of popcorn and soda and I'll be right back." "Can't wait." "You giving up that seat?" a woman says, rushing down the aisle. "Yes." "Pardon me," she says, getting into the same row he came out of, the seat he vacated. People are standing at the back of the theater and crowded at the end of the aisles watching the movie. "Oh my God, they're eating it," someone says. All are laughing. One man covers his eyes.

He gets a beer at a bar, buys a paperback at a bookstore, reads part of it in a fast-food place where he has onion rings and tea. The first story's about a man who "once and for all, decided to find out whether he was actually going to be a survivor or victim of this impersonalized and alienated industrial society" by sitting at a busy city intersection during a cold spell for a few days, without food or drink. Nobody offered him anything but advice. "Find a job . . . clean yourself . . . go back to India . . . get something to eat." "The civil authorities finally took notice of him" and Klaus died in an ambulance on the way to the hospital. "This story," the author says in a postscript, "is based on a true event that occurred in West Germany several years ago during its greatest modern economic boom. The gentleman in true life happened to be a very successful and talented writer of television documentaries on the physically and mentally afflicted, but for my own unknowable, though I hope not objectionable, reasons, I made him intensely religious, creatively impoverished, and monetarily poor."

He gets up. Skip her. She's a big girl. Let her go home alone. "You like to read?" "Mucho." "Then here's a book you might like." The busboy begins reading the first story. Bud walks downtown, goes into a twenty-five-cent peepshow place just to see what it's like. Filthy. Fetid. Signs on the wall saying "Please don't piss in the booths. It's unsanitary and some of us have holes in our shoes." There are about twenty booths. Above each one is an obscene photograph and the title of the movie being shown. His has a naked woman hugging a big sheepdog. A man's behind the woman. The handwritten caption underneath says "Just in from Sweden: Reddest stuff yet about knockout blonde and a dog with one like King Kong and does he get his? No, she does!" He sticks a quarter in the slot and looks into the viewer. A man on the small screen spends the first minute of the movie rubbing his finger in a jar of Vaseline. Long shots of the man, close-ups of his finger in the jar and then just the jar. A woman comes in the room, gives him a big kiss hello, drops her skirt, kicks off her panties, gets down on her knees and he applies the Vaseline to the woman from behind. There are foreign words for subtitles but they're being shown backwards. He can't figure that out since the movie is running forwards. The movie is about three minutes long and ends with the man still applying Vaseline to the woman while unzippering his fly. During the movie men pass his booth and look in through the space where the door won't close. He thinks about sticking in another quarter to see what happens to the couple and Vaseline jar, but the smell inside the booth is too much and so are the eyes that keep looking in.

He leaves the booth. "Go right in," a man says. "No loitering around. Plenty to see. Three booths right there are free. Oriental films and exotic filmstrips upstairs. Postcards and telescopes as souvenirs over here." Leaves the peepshow. Thinks of sitting through an hour or two of a seven-hour all-night porno festival for three dollars across the street, takes a subway back uptown. Joan's standing in front of the theater, talking to a woman. "Where were you? Bud, this is Holly." "Hi." "Hello, Bud." "We were just discussing the movie. Holly's seen it sixteen times." "Seventeen, I think. I don't ever expect to see a better movie, more experimental and real and superincredible and everything else exceptional in every way all at the same time. Not ever. *Children of Paradise* even. Not even *Citizen Kane* or *Les Enfants* Cocteau. You know the one. Or even *8½*, which up till this moment I thought the best. I can never believe what I saw and then see each successive time. I think I might even see it tomorrow night. Yes." "I'll meet you if you don't mind. Bud didn't like it. Twice. Hated it, right?" "It was a big put-on." "I don't see how you can say that." "Bud says a lot of things to be outrageous." "Look, I just went to a twenty-five-cent peepshow downtown—" "That's more your style." Holly laughs. Holly, he now realizes, is the woman who got his seat beside Joan that last time. "Wait a second, Joan. It's not a question of being more my style or to bring it up as any form of comparison. I only wanted to see one once in my life, and you know what? We could have saved ourselves the eight bucks and two hours for that *Big Mouth and Other Things.*" "*The Big Mouth and Udder Flings.*" "*Swings*, I thought," Holly says. They all look at the marquee. "*Swings*. Okay. My mistake. But it wasn't much different from that garbage downtown for a quarter." "From put-on to peepshow. I'd say you've had quite the visual night though haven't come a long way." "But you still can't compare the two types of movies," Holly says, "even if you say, a bit unconvincingly for me, that you're not comparing them aesthetically or any otherwise." "What do you say we forget it for now and go somewhere for a bite." "Right now I don't want to do anything but talk about that movie," Joan says, "and you know for the next hour you're not going to be anything but a sourpuss and a drag." "That's not true." "It has been, Bud." "And you're not being very nice. Maybe I'm not either. As for Holly, well, she seems reasonable, but who can ultimately tell? But I'll see you both. Bye bye, have fun." He kisses Joan, shakes Holly's hand. "Nice meeting you." "Same here," Holly says. "See my smile, Joan? Not sour." "I see." The women walk away. "Is he really your husband?" Holly says. "My husband." "Her husband," Bud yells.

He goes home, turns on the TV. Movie about miscegenation and rape, abortion and murder. Same uninteresting movie that was beginning in the bar before and which none of the drinkers took their eyes off of except to reach for their cigarettes and steins. Then a commercial about a bad-tasting mouthwash. Several more awful ads and promos and an announcement that the movie's conclusion will follow station identification, and then two more commercials and a promo and the movie again. He turns the television off. One day I'm going to throw this set out the window. No I won't. Someone below might get hurt.

He goes to bed. He doesn't know what time, but much later Joan comes home. He hears the door shut, then smells toast. She comes into the bedroom. With the light on in the hallway, he watches her undress, put on her pajama top, hears her gargle, brush her teeth, flick the light off, get in bed. "I'm up," he says. "Oh, hi. It's very late, Bud. Goodnight." "Don't you want to talk?" "Not now. Tomorrow." "I'd like to talk now." "And I want to sleep. I also think what we should talk about we should talk about tomorrow." "Let's talk about it now." "All right." She turns on the light. "I think, for the time being, that we've had it, Bud, and should separate." "Divorce is more like it." "No, not divorce, separate. Don't jump to worse than it is. I'll get my own place for half a year or maybe a full year and you can stay here." "Because of one movie?" "It's a long continuation of things. The movie incident was just one of them." "What incident?" "Incidents. Everything. You're just so inflexible and unrelaxed. It's too unrelaxing being with such an unrelaxed man who won't change. But about that movie, you mock it but it opened up something very new for me in the way of living and thinking, more than any group or wise doctor or religious person ever had." "Bull." "See? You won't even ask what. You just say bull. That's you all over, hardly ever interested in what I have to say in depth." "I am interested. Say it." "Not now." "I'm sorry. Please say it. You just can't come in here and say we should separate and call me eternally pigheaded and rigid and blame most of it on a movie and then not explain why you think that movie changed your life. Just tell me. I won't say a word till you're through and probably not even then." "All right. As I said, it didn't change my life as much as open new things up. Its ideas on women and men and relationships and sex. On the sometimes absurdity of living together as couples and the possibility of undiscovered courage and different lifestyles. It almost documented, as if it knew us, what's been wrong with our personalities together and relationship since its inception, things I've thought about but which that movie made much clearer to me and confirmed. Of the voices we hear. Not so much that. The movie said to me that if your present life is too confining and frustrating and unsatisfactory for reasons you've so far unsuccessfully tried to bring to light, then go out and discover life, that's what. Don't wait for the answers to come from the people and sources that have been most faithful and helpful to you till now, that too. In other words, what it said with that image of the woman feverishly digging around with her hands in the desert and the numerals falling off her watch and then out of her eyes was don't keep looking for water where you've already found there's a ninety-six percent chance there's nothing there but dry sand. You're more a delayer, the movie said, and will be one till you definitely decide to undo your particular personality type, which is hard but not impossible. I'm not a delayer, the movie said, and I'll be less of one—I mean, we're both of everything but you'll be less a delayer and me more the doer if I take advantage of my type and break what's holding me back and not be worried about what I can't so far fathom about my life. I see that as a separation from you and possibly my job and going out and really discovering life, which is maybe as deep as I have to fathom or anybody can. So I'm separating from you and going out and really discovering life. The enriching, fulfilling, powerful, sensual, multidimensional, interesting and creative life in all things and me. The life which at the end of one's life no matter what age as an adult you die one can say was worth living, the person living it or who lived it can say, even if she dies quote too early unquote. Life as perpetual curiosity and recurring passion and joy, and right now it isn't that way with either of us separately or together in almost every way. I'm sorry. And the second time I saw it that meaning became even clearer to me. And after speaking to Holly—well it's obvious she's gained from her sixteen to seventeen viewings of it as many insights and insights in insights about her life and outsights she also says, that her whole life has changed." "Oh please. What's she done since she first saw that movie other than see it fifteen or sixteen more times?" "No, you don't understand." She shuts the light. He begins crying. "Oh come on. Stop it. I won't accept it. Not as a way out or in," she says. "Don't you see? Just that crying proves in some way that life the way you delay it is getting you down too, and you know it'll only get worse for us if we don't separate. What do you think all those flashing yesses in every language were when that woman was all skin and thirst and bone and the sun was at its highest and so hot? That was positiveness. Affirmation and hope. That she could do it. Get up, it said. Upsy-daisy and no clothes on, no energy—hell, she did it anyway: crawled, smiled, masturbated, roared, walked and ran on. Then an oasis and one not even on a map. A little Eden, that water hole. That could be it for you and me. Edens all over the place. It sounds ridiculous but it's not. And this time I'm not going to feel sorry or sentimental or any of that for your crying and what we once were and have come to and so forth, and you should be happy about that. We have all the signs and they pinpoint the way for us and almost tell us how far we have to go. That was the point of those almost subliminal shots of landmarks and milestones, but we still continue not to want to know or see them and go off in the wrong direction when we—" He gets out of bed, unplugs the television set, opens the window wide and takes a deep breath. "What are you doing?" "Throwing the television out." "Put it down. That's my TV." "We both got it for our marriage." "My sister gave it to us for our marriage so it's more mine than yours." "Hello down there," he yells, "anybody in the backyard?" "Don't you dare." She gets out of bed and turns the light on. "I'm going to drop something very heavy and possibly lethal from one of the apartments to the backyard of One-fifteen West Seventy-third Street, so if anyone's down there in the dark below, let me know." "They might not be able to hear." "Nobody's down there." She tries grabbing the set out of his hands. He drops it out the window, she screams and it crashes below. Windows open, people look out. "Anybody jump?" someone yells. She pulls down the shade and says "You're crazy and also corny with your stupid symbolic gestures worthy of the most insipid soaps," takes her pillow and goes into the next room and slams the door. "I saw Clark Gable do that once," he yells. "Shut up." He feels bad but gets to sleep.

Next morning there's a note on the kitchen table saying "I'm moving in with Holly. For now I don't need much. If I don't stay there permanently and you don't move out of the apartment, then I'm getting my own place. I hope we can arrange this amicably. If you can't, then go off the road again, but I'm not. Please don't destroy the rest of the place till we divvy it up. Cheers."

He takes all her books on movies and movie directors and the Aesthetics of Cinema and so forth and throws them out the window. Then he realizes the mess he's made down there and goes downstairs with a broom and dustpan, gets a garbage can from the basement, goes to the backyard and cleans up the mess, dumps the broken books and television set pieces into the can, carries the can, broken television cabinet and tube to the street. Then he goes to the library and spends a couple of hours there trying to find some books or a book that will lift his spirits and change some of his ways and give him more confidence in this time of emotional and forthcoming emotional stress or at least convince him he doesn't have to have this stress or in some way bear out something of what he thinks his attitudes about life are or just distract him till he feels a lot better than he does now. He goes through the fiction and poetry and literary criticism and philosophy and biography and religion sections but finds nothing. As he's leaving, the librarian whom he's come to know here over the past few years says from behind the counter "Can't find anything you like today?" "Sorry." "There are other branches, or the bookstores—what about one of those?" "Good idea. I'll go to one now." But he was in a bookstore yesterday and to him each library branch is like the next. "See you," he says. She smiles and waves. He goes home depressed.

Layaways

Mr. Toon says goodbye and goes, keeps the door open for two men who come in. Wasn't a very good sale, pair of socks, layaways for a couple of workshirts. Two men look over the suits.

"Anything I can do for you, fellas?"

"Just looking," shorter one says.

"Harry, mind if I go to the bathroom?" Edna says.

"Why ask? You ask me almost all the time and I always say yes.— You don't see anything you got in mind you're looking for, just ask me. We got things in back or different sizes of those."

"Thank you," same man says.

"Why do I ask?" Edna says. "Because I like to ask. Because I have to ask. Because I'm a child who always has to ask her daddy if she can make."

"You're my wife, talk to me like my wife, not like my child."

"You don't get anything I say. You're so unclever, unsubtle."

"What's that supposed to mean?"

"You don't pick things up."

"I pick up plenty. I picked you up thirty-two years ago, didn't I? One pickup like that, I don't need any more."

"Well that at least is an attempt at cleverness. What I meant," she says lower, "is those two men. I don't want to leave you out here with them alone when I make."

"They're okay."

"I don't like their looks. They're too lean. No smiling. One has sneakers on."

"So they're lean and don't smile. Maybe they got good reason to be."

"They're swift, they do a lot of running, I don't like it."

"They're okay I'm telling you. You work here Saturdays, you think you know everything. But I've been in this neighborhood for how many years now, so I got a third eye for that."

"Your third eye you almost lost in the last holdup."

"Shut up. They might overhear."

"And get ideas?"

"And get scared out of here thinking we always get holdups."

"We do get holdups."

"But not always. You want to go to the bathroom, don't be afraid. You got my permission. Go."

"Call Joe out first."

"Joe's on his break."

"Let him take it out here."

"He's taking it in back because he wants to get away from out here.—Sure nothing I can do for you, fellas? You're looking for a suit, sport jacket? Just what size are you exactly?"

"If we see anything, we'll tell you," shorter one says. Taller one's holding a hangered suit to his chest.

"Big one doesn't talk much," Edna says. "He I think we got to be especially leery of."

"You're paranoid, you know what it is?"

"No."

"It means you're paranoid. You know what it is."

"I was just testing to see if you do, and you didn't. You couldn't define it."

"I can too. You're paranoid. *You.* That's my defining it. To every lean-looking man not smiling if he has sneakers on you're paranoid."

"So what's a man with sneakers buying or looking at a suit for?"

"To buy for later. If he buys a suit from us, he'll go to Clyde's or Hazlitt's and buy a pair of shoes to match. He's in a buying mood. These guys, they get a paycheck Friday, they spend it all at once the next day and mostly on liquor and clothes. What do you think you're here for? Leave me alone with your being paranoid. One robbery this month—"

"Two."

"One. That second we didn't know was a robbery."

"The one last week? Call Joe out and let him tell you how much a robbery it wasn't. That was a knife that man pulled out of his newspaper on Joe, big as your head."

"But he was crazy. He carries the knife and makes threats so he can feel like a big man. He does it to lots of stores around here and they just tell him 'Sure, here's a penny, all we got, it was a slow day,' and show him the door."

"Okay, that one doesn't count. But what does? When they stick it in your heart?"

"Shush, will you? They'll hear. You're going to the girls' room, go like I said, but don't worry about bringing out Joe."

"No, I'll stay here. I don't want to leave you alone with them."

"Do what you want."

"At least say thanks."

"Why should I? I don't think you're right."

"My heart's in the right place."

"Okay, your heart. You're a dream. You saved my life. You made me live twenty years younger, oh boy am I lucky. But scare these two away with your knife talk just before my antennas say I'm going to make a big sale with them and I'll be mad as hell at your heart because we need every cent we can get.—That one's a real good buy and a beauty. Want to try it on?"

"Yeah, that's a good idea, where can I?" shorter man says. They come over to the counter Edna's behind and where I've been talking to her and he holds out the suit to me. "How much?"

"Tag's right on the arm cuff. Sometimes they're hard to find. Size forty-four? This is for you? I say that because it's more a size for him. You can't be more than a thirty-six, and besides, this one's a long and you're a regular."

"I'm regular, thirty-six, you're right, you really know your line," and from under the suit he's still holding he points a pistol at me. Other one opens his jacket and aims a sawed-off shotgun at Edna and cocks it. "Don't scream. Whatever you do, don't. You'll both be nice and quiet now, and you call out your friend Joe. But call him out nice and quietly, don't startle him. Just say—"

"I know, I know how to say it," I say.

"Quiet. Listen to me. Just say 'Joe, could you come out and help me with this fitting for a second, please?' Exact words. Got them?"

"Yes."

"Repeat them."

"Joe, could you come out and help—"

"Okay, say it."

"Do as he says," Edna says.

"I will, you think I'm crazy? Joe, could you come out and help me with this fitting for a second with this gentleman, please?"

"I still got ten minutes," Joe says.

"He's a nice boy," Edna says. "He's my son. He's his son. He won't do anything. Don't touch him."

"We just want him out here, lady. Now call him too, same kind of words but harder."

"Joe, will you please come out here a second? Your father— Harry's got two customers at once and it's too much. For a fitting."

"You can't do it?"

"I don't know how like you yet."

"You don't know how. You'll never know how. I worked my butt off on stock today and want to rest. Oh hell," and he comes out holding a magazine and a coffee container.

Taller one holds his shotgun behind him, other one inside the suit.

"Which one needs the fitting?" Joe says.

"Just keep it quiet, baby," shorter one says, pulling out the gun and aiming it at Joe. Other one has the shotgun on me, Edna, then keeps it on me.

"Don't hurt him," Edna says about Joe.

"I won't if he does everything we say."

"Everything," Joe says. "Give them it all, Harry."

"You think I won't? Look, gentlemen. Come behind here and take everything, please, take it all. Edna, get out and let them in."

"No, lady, you dish it out for us in one of your stronger bags."

"As you say," she says and rings "No Sale," he looks over the counter into the bill and change tray and says "Okay," and she starts putting the money into a bag. They keep their guns on us, their backs to the store windows. Joe has a gun on the shelf under the cash register but deep in back. He got a permit for it last month because of the three robberies so far this year when each time we got cleaned out. Edna drops a few change rolls and bills on the floor.

"I'll get it," Joe says.

"You'll get nothing," shorter man says. "Pick them up, lady."

"She's too nervous. She went through a robbery here just last week with a guy with a knife."

"I am very nervous," she says.

"Then you pick them up and empty the rest in the bag, but make it quick."

"Just be careful, Joe, and don't do anything silly," I say.

"Like what?" shorter man says.

Man taps on the door, shorter man waves at him, holds up one finger and the man goes.

"Like not making any wrong moves which are innocent but you might think suspicious," I say, "that's all. We're not armed or anything like that, I wouldn't allow it here, and no trip alarms to the police. We'll only cooperate. Do only what they say, Joe, and nothing more."

"I know."

But I can see by his look he doesn't. "Let me get the money."

"Why you want to get it?" taller one says.

"Because Joe seems nervous too. He went through the war. He still has tropical diseases."

"I'm not nervous. I want to give them all the money and for them to leave right away with no trouble."

"Why you two talking like you're up to something?" taller one says.

"We're not," I say.

"They're not," Edna says.

"No, we're not," Joe says.

"What do you have back there?"

"Nothing," Joe says. "Come and look."

"Pick up the money, old man," shorter one says to me. "You come away from there" to Joe. "Go into the middle of the room. You stay back there, lady."

Joe goes to the middle of the room. People pass on the street. Two look our way as they walk and I guess don't see anything but don't hesitate or stop. Radio music from in back is still playing. A dog's barking nearby and from somewhere far off is a fire engine siren. I bend down and pick up the money and put it in the bag and empty the rest of the tray money into the bag and lift the tray and stick the big bills under it into the bag and say "I guess you want our wallets too," and shorter one says "And her pocketbook money and all your watches and rings."

"My purse is under the counter," Edna says. "Can I reach for it?"

"Go ahead."

"You want the personal checks from today too?" I say.

"Forget the checks."

We empty our wallets, watches, rings and purse into the bag and shorter one says "Good, now go in back. The two men, right now. Lady stays here. We're not taking her so don't worry. Just want her standing here between you and us so you don't do anything stupid, now go."

We go in back. Joe looks through the tiny two-way glass to the front he had me install last month. I say "They taking her? What are they doing? Joe?" I hear the door close. Joe runs out and goes behind the counter and gets his gun and yells "Both of you, flat on the floor" and Edna shouts "Don't, let them go," and I shout "Joe, what are you doing?" The men aren't even past the store yet. They're in the street flagging down a cab with that tapping man from before when they see Joe opening the door and turn all the way to him and shorter one fumbles for something in the bag and taller one reaches under his jacket and Joe's yelling "You goddamn bastards," and the two from before have their guns out and Joe's shooting the same time they're shooting or almost, I think Joe first, and our windows break and Edna screams and blood smacks me in the face and across my clothes and the two men fall and Edna bounces against the wall behind the counter and falls and glass is sprayed all over the store and clock above me breaks and Edna's jaw looks gone and face and neck a mess and Joe's alive and the tapping man from before gets up from where he dived and starts running across the avenue and Joe fires at him and runs over to the men on the ground and I yell "Joe, stop, enough," and kicks their guns to the curb and runs a few feet after the man and then back to the store and jumps through the empty window and sees his mother on the floor and screams and drops to his knees and says "Mom, Mom," and I hold his shoulders and cry and mutter "Edna, Joe," and he throws my hands off and runs to the front and opens the door and shouts "You bastards," and one of the men on the ground raises his head an inch and people who have come near them now scatter every which way and Joe puts two bullets into the man who raised his head and grabs the pistol and shotgun from the curb and puts the one shotgun round left into the taller man's head he just put two bullets in and about five bullets from the pistol into the already unconscious or just dead shorter man and then he kicks their bodies and whacks the shotgun handle over the shorter man's head and throws the broken gun away and pistol-whips what's left of the taller man's head and gets on his knees and sticks the pistols into his pockets and pounds the ground with his fists and some people come over to him and the bell from the door tells me someone's coming into the store while I get a pain in my chest that shoots from it to all four limbs and sudden blackness in my head that's only broken up by lightninglike cracks and fall on Edna and feel myself going way off somewhere and in my blackness and lightning and going away I feel around for her hand and find it and hold it and pass out from whatever, maybe the chest pain.

I ask to be in the same room with her but they say we have to stay in two different intensive care units at opposite ends of the hall, one for serious gunshot injuries and other for coronaries and strokes and the like. Joe sits by my bed for the five minutes they give him and says "I hope Mom dies, it's not worth it to her or you if she lives. The bullets went—"

Nurse puts her finger over her mouth to him and I nod to Joe I understand.

"How's the store?" I say and he says "I think I better go in tomorrow. We got all those layaways for Easter. The customers will be disappointed last day before the holidays start not to get them and they won't want them after and will want their money back."

"You better go in then."

"I'm not afraid to."

"Why should you be?"

"People say those two men got friends who'll want to get revenge."

"What do the police say?"

"They say what I did will act as a deterrent against revenge and more robberies, but what am I going to be a deterrent with? They took away my permit and gun."

"For the time being?"

"They got to investigate if I couldn't've not used it. But who knows?"

"Don't go in then. I don't want you getting killed."

"But those customers. They got layaways and it's our best two days."

"Do you have to talk about business now?" nurse says to him.

"It's okay," I say. "Store talk relaxes me and I feel all right. Don't go in," I tell Joe. "Go back to college. Stay away from business. I just made up my mind for you."

"I like the business. I got my own family to support too. I want to keep the store."

"We'll get insurance from the robbery and the sale of the merchandise later on. You can have half of it. You deserve it. You have to go back into business, open a store in a quieter neighborhood."

"In a quieter neighborhood the store will die."

"Go into another business."

"What other business I know but men's clothes?"

"Once you know retailing you can open up any kind of store."

"I like men's clothes."

"I don't think your father should be discussing this now," nurse says.

"I feel much better, miss. Anyway, it wasn't a heart attack I had."

"It was a heart attack."

"It was, Dad."

"It was indigestion. It was that, doubled up with nerves. I didn't deserve them? My own wife? Him? That whole scene?"

"You'll have to go," she tells Joe.

"I'll see you later." He kisses my forehead and leaves.

"Could you call him back?" I say.

"It'd be better not to."

"I want to ask him something I never got an answer from. If I don't get that answer I'll be more worried and heartsick than if I do."

She goes outside the room and Joe comes back. "What?" he says.

"You going back to the store?"

"I guess I have to."

"You really aren't afraid?"

"A friend of mine, Nat, has offered to stay with me. He's a big guy and will take care of the register and look after the door."

"Call Pedro also. He called me just a week before the accident and asked if business was going to be good enough to hire him back. Call him. His number's in the top drawer of the counter."

"I know where it is. We have money to pay him?"

"Even if you have to take it out of my pockets. The glass fixed?"

"They put it in yesterday. We had to. Cops didn't want it boarded up if we're going to still occupy it and other store owners complained it looked bad for everybody else."

"They're right. Don't keep more than three hundred dollars in cash there any one time. You get one dollar more, deposit it—it's worth the walk."

"I know."

"I still have to tell you. Two guys like those two come in, even one who looks suspicious, don't take unnecessary risks. No risks, hear me?"

"I won't."

"Give even a ten-year-old boy who's holding up the store whatever he wants."

"A ten-year-old I'm not giving in to."

"If he has a gun?"

"That's different."

"That's what I'm saying. But any older person who says this is a holdup—even if he or she doesn't show a gun, give them what they want. Remember, you're only going back to be nice to the layaways, right?"

"I'm going back because I also need the money, me and my family, you and Mom, and to tell the goddamn thieves they're not shoving me out."

"They know that already. Listen to me, don't be so tough. I can tell you stories about other tough merchants. I'm not saying what you did caused your mother like she is. But if you didn't get so crazy so suddenly, not that you could help it—well right?"

"Don't make me feel bad."

"I'm not trying to."

"Don't blame me because I got excited. Sick as you are, I'm telling you this now for all time."

"I understand you. In your own way that day, you did okay."

He waves.

"Where you going? Give your father a kiss goodbye. He needs it." He kisses my lips. He never did that before. I also never asked him to kiss me anytime before. My own father asked me to kiss him hundreds of times and I always did. But only once on his lips did I kiss him and that was a few minutes after he died. I start to cry. Joe's gone. Nurse asks me what's wrong. "Got any more news on my wife?"

"You know we're not allowed to speak about her."

"What am I supposed to think then, she'd dead?"

"She's not. Your son told you. She's holding her own."

"She isn't much, right?"

"I can't say. She also has the best equipment to help her. You can talk about it more tomorrow with her doctors when they move you to a semiprivate."

I'm released three weeks later and go back to the store a month after that. Joe's had another robbery. He gave them what he had without a fuss. Pedro was there that day and later said he'd never let anyone take anything from him again, even if it wasn't his store. Pedro got a gun. Two of the merchants on the street stood up for him for the gun permit. Because Joe's not allowed to apply for one again for two months, he told the police Pedro needed the gun to take the store receipts to the bank. Pedro keeps the gun in back. He told Joe it's no good keeping it under the counter or in the register for where's the first place they look? They find it, they just might use it on you. He's been robbed three other times besides his twice at our store and in back's where they always send you or want to either tie you up or lock you in the men's room so they have as much time as they can to get away.

Edna's in the nursing home now paralyzed from the neck down. Even if she comes out of her coma she'll be paralyzed like that for life. She'll never be able to speak and if she gets out of the coma she'll hardly be able to think. She should've died in the hospital or in the store but more in the hospital because there's more dignity to dying there. The doctors say she won't last another few months. So I go back to the store just to get my mind off her and have something to do, though my own doctor says I shouldn't. I say hello to Pedro and he says "I'm really sorry what happened to you, Mr. Sahn."

"It was a long time ago."

"It's never a long time for something like that and it's still happening with your wife, right?"

"Maybe it isn't too long ago at that. But you've been a great help to my son and me and if we could afford it, we'd double your hourly salary and also put you on for all six days."

"I'm glad I got what I got, so don't worry."

"But we'll give you forty cents more an hour starting today."

"Hey Pop," Joe says, "what are you trying to do, rob us? We haven't got forty cents more to give."

"Twenty cents will be fine," Pedro says, "and I can really use it."

"Twenty then," I say.

I go to work every other day and on Saturday of that same week two men come in when Pedro and I are reading different sections of the newspaper and Joe's taking care of the one customer in the store. The men take out their guns before the door's even closed and thinner one points his at Pedro and me and heavier one at the customer and Joe and says "Holdup, nobody go for anything or step on alarms." Customer says "Oh my God," and Pedro says "We freeze, fellas, no worry about that, we're no dopes," and heavier one goes to the register and starts emptying it into a briefcase and thinner one says to me "You there, owner, hold this," and gives me another briefcase and says "Your wallet and everything else in it and get the same from the rest," and we all dump our wallets and watches and rings in it, but I don't have a ring because mine was taken the last time and for some reason never recovered though everything else in the bag outside was. Heavier one comes around the counter and runs in back and comes out and says "They got no storerooms to lock themselves in and the bathroom has no door," and says to us "All right, you all go in back but way in back and don't come out for five minutes minimum or I swear one does you all die" and Pedro says "Don't worry, we've been

266 The Stories of Stephen Dixon

through this before and we all go in back for ten minutes not five, I'll see to that," and we go in back and Joe goes to the two-way and says "They've left," and Pedro reaches behind a pile of shirt boxes and pulls out a gun and I drop the phone receiver and say "Pedro, don't," and he says "I'm not letting them get away with it, Mr. Sahn, I told your son," and the customer sticks all his fingers into his mouth and says "Oh no, oh no," and Joe says "Let me have the gun," and Pedro says "No, I'm licensed for it and get in trouble letting anyone else use it," and Joe says "But I know how to use it," and Pedro says "I know too, the police showed me one day in practice," and Joe says "One day? You crazy? Let me have it," and I say "None of you, let them go, nobody goes after them," but Joe reaches for the gun and Pedro shouts "Watch out, it's cocked," and jerks it back before Joe can get hold of it and the gun goes off and bullet into Pedro's chest and we hear shots from outside and windows breaking and duck to the floor, customer already there bawling, and Joe yells "You goddamn bastards," and grabs the gun and runs to the front but the men had only shot out the windows because I suppose they thought they were being shot at by us and by the time Joe gets to the street they're in a car and gone.

I close the store and sell the entire stock, Joe goes back to pharmacy college for the next year with me paying all his bills, Pedro dies from the bullet through his lungs, Edna lives on in a coma for another month before she succumbs in her sleep the doctors say, I have another heart attack and move South into a single room by myself among a whole bunch of much older people in the same crummy hotel, living off my social security and Edna's life insurance and our savings and maybe not in a better hotel till Joe graduates and can earn a salary large enough not only for his family but to begin paying me back. Then I get a phone call from his sister-in-law who says Joe got in an argument in the park with three men who were mugging a young couple and they beat him in his kidneys and head till he was dead.

I return for the funeral and because I don't like the South much with all that sun and beach and older people having nothing to do but wait for death and me with them, I move back for good and open another store, but a much smaller one for candies and greeting cards and things like that in a much safer neighborhood. I ask Joe's wife Maddie if she and her kids want to share an apartment with me to save money and because I'd also like to be with them more and she says "Actually, I don't want to, not that I don't like you, Dad. But with us not having much money and all and the kids for the time being so small, maybe for the next four years and if I don't get remarried or move in with some guy, it's probably the best of ideas."

So we live like that, me not making much in my store in a neighborhood that only rarely has a robbery, my grandchildren asking me questions and wanting me to play with them like I'm their dad, Maddie working part time and going out with different men and sometimes staying overnight in their apartment, but not really being attracted to any of them just as I think they're not attracted to her. Some days we go to the two graves in the plot for eight I bought thirty years ago and that's the only time we all just hold one another, the kids not understanding it too much, and say some prayers from a little book the cemetery provides and cry and cry.

The
Watch

~

Man on the street says "Spare me a quarter, sir?" I say "No, really, I haven't much myself." He says "That's all right. Thanks." I walk a few steps and think "What the hell, I had a pretty good day and can spare a little," and go back to the man and say "Sure, I can give you something," and put my hand in my pants pocket for a dime or quarter, but he looks so sad and sickly that I pull out the largest coin among all the change in my pocket and give it to him. It's my watch. I thought it was a half dollar. It felt like it, thin and round, but it's my pocketwatch. "Excuse me, I gave you that by mistake," and reach for my watch, but his hand closes on it.

"You gave me your watch. Thanks a lot," and sticks it in his pants pocket and starts walking away.

"It was a half dollar I wanted to give you."

"You wanted to give me the watch," and he keeps walking.

I run after him and grab him by the shoulder.

"Let go or I'll call a cop."

"I'll let go when you give back my watch. I didn't mean to give it and you you know that. I was being absentminded, just pulled out the largest coin in my pocket because I was feeling extra generous, or what I thought was the largest coin, forgetting my watch was in that pocket too. Now give it back, please, or I'll have to make trouble for you."

"You don't take your hand off me, I'll make even bigger trouble for you."

I take my hand off him. "You don't understand. That watch was my father's. It's the only thing he left me. He got it from his uncle, who bought it somewhere overseas. It's the one valuable thing I own and my father owned. Now give it back. It has tremendous sentimental value to me."

"And to me it has money value."

"It has money value also, but I'd never sell it no matter how broke I was."

"I'm going to sell it because I'm broker than you ever were. Broker than your father and mine both. Dead broke. Thanks for the handout," and he walks away.

"Police," I shout.

No policeman's around. It's night and on a busy downtown street and people are around and they stop just as they stopped when I was arguing with him at the corner before and now they listen and some ask among themselves what's happening but nobody asks me or the man or tries to step in.

"Listen, people," I say. "I gave that man my valuable watch by mistake."

A few people laugh. The man's past the crowd by now. I run after him. People follow. I grab his arm. He's smaller than me and thinner, much thinner. He's all bone it seems. Dirty too. His coat smells. He has two coats and a jacket on I now see. His hair coming out from his cap looks like it hasn't been washed or combed for weeks. He has two sweaters on too. People have crowded around us again but several feet away. "People," I say, "please listen. Help me get my watch back. It's a long story. This man asked me for money for coffee—"

"I didn't say for coffee," the man says.

"He asked for money. 'Spare a quarter,' he said. I felt sorry for him and thought I was giving him a half dollar, but it was my watch by mistake."

"That's what I asked him," he says to them. "And that's what he gave, but not by mistake. Get your hand off me," he says to me.

"I will if you don't walk away."

"Okay. I won't."

I take my hand off him. He walks away. The crowd opens up so he can get through. I run to the man and grab him with both hands and say "I'm not letting you go again and I might even throw you to the ground and by mistake break your head if you walk away again."

"I won't then."

I let go of him and say to the crowd "Will someone please get a policeman to straighten this out?"

"There'll be one around soon," someone says. "There always are. What happened? You gave him your watch by mistake you say?"

"I thought it was a half dollar I was taking out of my pants pocket."

"How come you keep a watch in your pants pocket and not on your wrist?"

"It's a pocketwatch and I lost the chain on it a few years ago, so I keep it in my pants pocket instead. It's very old and valuable. I'd never just give it away. It's my only good possession, my only possession of any worth. I'm a poor jerk. I've a job that doesn't pay well at all."

"You think I make a lot of money?" the man says to the crowd. "I asked him for money. He gave me his watch. I thought that was really generous, but it's not the first time people gave me things valuable like that. Once a man gave me a hundred-dollar bill. He knew it was a hundred. He even said 'Here's a hundred, pal,' and that was more than twenty years ago. Ten years later a woman came up to me when she saw me with my hand out and gave me a brooch. She knew it was a brooch. She unpinned it right from her jacket lapel and handed it to me without a word and walked away. I thought it was glass but I got two hundred for it. I bet it was worth a thousand then. People have done that over the years. A new radio here, a twenty-dollar bill there. So now, ten years after that lady, this guy gives me a valuable watch. I believed that he gave it to me because he wanted to and I still believe that. Only he, unlike the man with the hundred and the brooch lady, went back on his giving me it. But that's too bad for him. Once you give, you can't take it back. You make a mistake like that, you have to pay for it."

"He has a point," a man says.

"Only if he's telling the truth," a woman says, "which he isn't."

"How do we know?"

"You saying you believe a pig like that?"

"Pig though he may be, and I don't think it's for us to judge just because our clothes and appearances are better, he could still have a point. The watch-giver might have changed his mind. Should the beggar be penalized for that?"

"Yes, people have a right to change their minds."

"Not where I come from," the beggar says.

"They do have that right in most cases," I say, "not that that has anything to do with the situation here. I never intended giving him the watch. But if you people are only going to talk and talk about it, I'm going to get my watch back in my own way."

I try to get my hands in the pants pocket where he put the watch. He pushes my hand away and I grab one of his arms and start twisting it behind his back.

"Leave him alone," a man says. "He's so frail you'll kill him."

"But I have to do something," I say, letting him go. "That watch is worth over five hundred dollars."

"It is?" the beggar says. "Then I bet I'll be able to get a hundred for it."

"Why don't you just give him a hundred for it," someone says to me, "and be done with it. You pay for your mistakes like that man said."

"I don't have a hundred. Who carries a hundred on him these days? Maybe plenty do, but I only have a twenty on me, maybe less."

"I won't take twenty when I can get a hundred," the beggar says.

"What's this all about?" a policeman says.

I explain my story. The beggar explains his. The crowd stays around us. The policeman says to the beggar "Why don't you take the twenty and let the guy off light? You see the sentimental attachment it has for him."

"I'm starting to get sentimentally attached to it too," the beggar says.

"Twenty-five," I say, counting the money in my wallet. "That's all I have besides my fare home." I hold the money out to him. "I shouldn't even be giving you this, but I just want it back without any more fuss."

"Take it," the policeman says to the beggar.

"Take it," a few people say.

"I think he should hold out for fifty," a man says.

"Mind your business," the policeman says.

"Fifty I'll hold out for then," the beggar says.

"I don't have fifty," I say. "I have twenty-five and change when I didn't even think I had that."

"Someone here you know who can loan you another twenty or twenty-five?" the policeman says.

"Why should they? What I'm offering's more than fair. And I

don't know anyone around here. It's not my neighborhood. I went to that movie theater there, because it's cheap, but I live uptown."

"Then I don't know what to say. Take the twenty-five," he says to the beggar. "I've work to do. This man wants his watch back and to get home."

"Take it," some people say.

"I still think he should hold out for fifty," that man says again.

"Keep quiet about what you think," the policeman says.

"I know my rights. I can open my mouth when I want to except when it's to yell fire in a theater when I know there isn't one."

"But you're making it worse for the watch-owner."

"What do I care for him?"

"No, I decided," the beggar says. "I can't give it away for just twenty-five."

"Then I'll have to take the watch and the two of you to the station so this man can file a complaint against you for his watch, and you, if you want, against him for breach of giving you it, or whatever that's called."

"Okay by me," the beggar says. "I've nothing much doing tonight and that watch is worth it."

"Nothing I can do about it," I say, "and at least the watch will be safe."

"The watch," the policeman says, holding out his hand.

The beggar puts his hand in the pocket the watch is in. Puts his other hand in his other pants side pocket. Feels through all the pants pockets and then all the pockets in his jacket and shirt and one of the sweaters with pockets on it and his coats. "I can't find it," he says. "I don't know what happened."

"Oh no," I say.

"You have holes in your pockets?" the policeman says to him.

"Sure I have holes. But I didn't think in the pocket where I put the watch. That one I had change in. So I also lost all my change." He feels in that pocket again. "Yeah, I have a hole in it. Must have been coming on for a long time and then all of a sudden tore apart."

"Oh no, oh no," I say. "My watch," and I run back to the place where I first met the beggar, looking at the sidewalk along the way. No watch. I go back to the beggar and the crowd and walk all around them and then walk back to the place where I first met him, looking at the sidewalk along the way. No watch. Some people from the crowd follow me the second time. The beggar and policeman follow them. Everyone seems to be looking with me including the beggar. "If anyone finds a watch," I yell, "tell me. Please tell me. A pocketwatch. No fob chain. A silver watch, roman numerals on the face, no inscription or design on the back and it's all by itself, not in a case."

"If I find," someone says.

I don't find the watch. Nobody does, or if they do, they don't say anything. "Please search him," I say to the policeman. "He might be lying."

"I'm not lying," the beggar says. "I have holes." He pulls his pants pockets out. He has holes in them. Then the side pockets of his outer coat. Holes.

"Please search him," I say. "He might be hiding the watch. He could have dropped it through the hole in his pocket to some place deeper inside the coat."

"I didn't," the beggar says.

"Do you mind a search?" the policeman says to him.

"Yes, I mind."

"If he minds, I can't search him. I can take him to the station and you can press charges there just as he can press them against you later for having him brought there if your charges turn out to be untrue, but I can't search him here just on your word. I can there, but he does seem to have holes in all his pockets."

"Let the cop search you," someone in the crowd says. "That way they'll know you have nothing to hide."

"Look, I'll give you ten dollars to let the policeman search you," I say to the beggar. "If the watch isn't on you I'll know it was really lost and then I can maybe do something about getting it back."

"Ten dollars? I lost everything else tonight, so what do I have to lose? Okay."

I give him a ten.

The policeman searches him. "No watch," he says, "unless he has a hiding place in all the clothes he has on that I can't find."

"Find it then," I say.

"I searched him. He doesn't seem to have anything on him but clothes."

"Now you're a watch and ten dollars out," someone says to me. "Try for more. Give the bum another ten for nothing and then your last five."

"That's all right," I say. "After the watch, nothing hurts."

"Excuse me," the policeman says to me. "Unless you want to

press charges against this man, though I can't see what you'd gain by it, I'll have to go."

"What about me?" the beggar says. "How come you don't ask me the same thing about him?"

"All right," the policeman says to him. "Do you want to press charges?"

"No. I was only saying. As if you thought I didn't have something to complain about too."

"Sure," I say to the policeman. "Go. I'll continue to look for it. And honestly, thanks a lot."

I look at the sidewalk around me. The policeman goes. Most of the crowd goes. I walk to the place where I last grabbed the beggar and then back to the street corner again. The beggar's still there and says "If it's all right with you I'd like to help you look for your watch. I really don't have it on me. Not hidden. Nothing. If I did I'd be gone by now, wouldn't I?"

"Unless you want to prove something to me or yourself that I'm unaware of, then I guess so."

"I swear I don't want to prove anything."

"Why not then? Four eyes are better, but you have to understand that I'm not paying you to look, though I will give you another ten if you find it."

We search together and in different places for more than half an hour. During that time the beggar tells me his name and I tell him mine. Several people come up and ask us what we're looking for. Either Tom or I or both of us tell them. A few of these people join in the search for a while. We don't find the watch. Finally I say to Tom "It's not here. Someone must have picked it up or I don't know what. Maybe I'll put a notice in the paper for it. I'm going though."

"I'll look around a while longer. If I find it where can I get hold of you?"

"You won't find it." I leave.

I hear someone running up behind me a minute later. "Say Gene," Tom says. He's holding out a ten. "I didn't think it's fair to keep this. I should have let myself be searched for nothing. You were right. I shouldn't have kept the watch in the first place. If I had to for a few minutes, then I shouldn't have put it in my pocket. I knew I had holes in most of my pockets. No reason why I wouldn't have gotten holes in the rest of them or at least one more of them. I'm sorry for causing you so much trouble, because if anybody knows how you feel, it's me. My dad once gave me his gold cigarette case and I had to hock it when I needed money. I waited too long and when I went to get it back it was already sold and I still feel that loss today."

I still hadn't taken the ten. "Keep it," I say. "I just feel too lousy to care."

"No, you take it. Help pay for your newspaper ad with it, because that's a real good idea," and he puts the ten in my hand.

I go home. I phone the newspaper the next morning and put a notice in for the day after. Several people call about finding a pocket-watch, but none of them are mine. I put a second notice in the paper a few days later. This time nobody calls.

A week later Tom calls. He says "I saw your ad. You said you'd put one in, so I looked for it. Any luck?"

"No."

"That's too bad. You said in the ad you'd give a reasonable reward. Would you have considered three hundred reasonable?"

"That's twice as much as I wanted to give, but I probably would have."

"Would you still consider three hundred reasonable if you learned I'm the one who has your watch?"

"You were hiding it?"

"Whether it was hidden or I found it, what's the difference? You'll never believe me anyway. But three hundred. Say yes or no. If it's no, I won't bargain down and I'll also never bother you about it again."

"Yes. I'll get the money up some way. I'll borrow it from friends."

"Don't fool with me, Gene. I might not look it, but you got to believe that just staying alive the way I do I can handle myself okay. So don't bring cops when you come meet me. Do, and I'll either toss the watch across the street on the sly or say I found it after you stopped looking that night, and phoned you today for your newspaper reward. You can't deny I was still looking."

"I won't bring anyone."

He gives me the time, day and place. I tell him I can probably get the money by then. I borrow two hundred dollars from several friends and also take the last hundred out of my bank account.

I meet him on a busy street. He says "The money." I say "The watch." He says "Let's meet each other's hands halfway." I hold out the envelope of money. He says "Open it." I open it. He sees the money. He puts his hand in his pants pocket and feels around inside. "Oh my God," he says.

"Don't give me that."

"No, this time it's for real. It's gone."

"Come off it."

He smiles. "Of course it's not. You think for three hundred I wouldn't make sure the pocket's sewed?" He takes out the watch. It's mine. I give him the envelope same time he gives me the watch. He immediately turns around and walks away. "You bum," I yell after him. "You bum. You bum."

Stop

A car stopped. Man got out. "You there," he said. I dropped my package and started running. "Hey wait, where you running to?" He knew. He knew I knew. Car stopping, man getting out, motor still running, driver inside with his hands on the wheel, car door left open so the man outside could jump right back in. And the look. If I could see the driver's face, probably both their looks. But I didn't have the time to speculate on all this. Just keep running.

The car caught up with me a block later. They drove alongside for a few seconds, pointing and talking about how good a runner I was, seeming to enjoy a joke, for they both broke up. Then they parked about fifteen feet in front of me. I stopped. Both men got out. Motor still on, doors left open. "You there," same man from before said, approaching me, driver staying behind. "We only want to speak to you about something, so what's the rush?"

Standing in the middle of an intersection I had four ways to go. Back, to them, either sidestreet. Back they probably had another car coming by now. Left sidestreet ended in a school ballfield with a chain fence around it with the exits at the other side of it locked sometimes. Right sidestreet I'd never been on before and I ran down it. "Oh for godsakes," the driver said, "do you have to? We just ate." They got in the car. Drove slowly behind me. Then accelerated past and made a sharp turn onto the sidewalk in front of me right up to the building's steps, cutting me off. I couldn't stop in time and slammed into the car door, went down, got up, legs gave and I fell down again. The man in the right seat seemed shaken too.

"Did you have to turn so fast?" he said to the driver.

"I didn't want to be chasing him all day. Anyway, I immobilized him."

I jumped up. Both doors opened. I was stuck in a triangle made by the car door and front of the car and the steps. Two possible ways out were to climb over the hood—but the driver suddenly stood there with his arms out as if to catch me—or down the steps.

"Now please, just a minute of your precious time," the driver said, climbing over the hood. Other man shut his door and reached his hand out for me. I ran down the steps and pushed past the vestibule door. Door to the hallway inside was locked. "Hold up, already," the driver said. "My stomach, my feet." I rang all the building's bells. The men started down the steps. I braced one hand against the hallway door and foot against the vestibule door so the men couldn't get in. A woman on the intercom said "Yes?"

"Let me in."

"Who is it?"

"Just let me in please. It's an emergency."

"Not until I know who it is."

"Police. There's a man we're after who just ran into your building and we want to get in without breaking down the door."

"That's still not saying who it is." The men were trying to push their way in. "I need proof. For this building, in this neighborhood, you have to."

"Look out your window. That's our double-parked car on your sidewalk. Now would we park like that if we weren't after somebody?"

"I have the back view."

I rang all the bells, keeping my hand and foot braced against the doors. The men were caving in my foot. I kept ringing the bells with my free hand. The woman kept saying who is it, she needs proof, will I please stop ringing if I can't give it as she's old, too lame to be walking back and forth like this, till she or someone else rang me in. The driver threw open the vestibule door and rushed to get to the hallway door with the man behind him practically falling on top of him, but I got it shut. The other man got up and rang the bells. I ran to the back of the first floor looking for a rear exit. There wasn't one. I ran upstairs. The men were in the vestibule. "Yes, police," the driver said into the intercom. "Precinct Seventeen, ma'am. Officer Aimily. Your local patrolman's Grenauer or Pace. Pace, then. But we're after a man who just came in your building. That's our car outside." Someone rang them in.

"There's a back entrance?" he said to the other man.

"No, all the buildings on this side face the river."

"What do you mean—right on it? I thought we were a block away."

"Flush up against. From some of the back flats you think you're floating in the ocean."

They started upstairs.

"The roof," the driver said.

"Oh damn, I forgot. They're connected."

"You stay on the street. I'll follow him."

"But your stomach. And you said your feet."

"I'll live. Call in for more. He comes out, grab him. Bat him to the ground if he won't stop. I've had enough."

The driver continued upstairs. I knocked on the rear doors as I went up. The roof was out of the question. Unless someone was working up there on another roof or sunbathing in this cold. For all the roof doors were locked from the inside. Once up there you had to keep the door open with something to get back in. Way it was in my own building and all the roofs I'd been on in this neighborhood and by fire law all the roofs in the city. But if someone in one of the rear apartments opened up I could run past him, throw open a back window and jump out and try to swim away. I'd jump from two stories up at the most. That would be about three to four stories up because there must be at least a floor or two between the ground floor and water. The fourth floor was a little too high to jump from though I might give it a try if I really felt lucky. But from the fifth floor I didn't think I'd survive.

Nobody on the third-floor rear opened. The driver was panting as he climbed the stairs. I had youth on him, energy, not as much fat, no recent meal in me, not that any of that would help me much unless I jumped and swam. Nobody on the fourth floor answered my door-pounding either and I climbed the last two flights and unbolted the roof door.

No stick or anything to wedge under the doorknob to keep the door closed. Now the driver was climbing the last flight. "Boy," he said, resting halfway up and seeing me looking down at him, "you're the biggest pain I've had all week. I could throw you off that roof—I'm not kidding. Throw you off without thinking much about it for what you're putting me through."

I looked around. "Anybody on one of the roofs here? Hey, do you hear me, anybody around?" Nobody answered and I couldn't see anyone. I ran to the next roof. They went on for a block. The last roof looked down on the street I'd just run on, the avenue where I'd first seen those men, and the river. The man stepped out onto the roof, put a brick he found inside between the door and jamb so the door wouldn't close all the way. I ran to the last building, hurdling the dozen or so two-foot-high parapets separating each roof.

He followed me, stepping over each parapet very carefully so he wouldn't dirty his pants. "Don't make it so tough for me anymore," he said from five roofs away. "Meet me at some halfway point. Or, if you want, I'll go back to the door we came out of and you can meet me there."

"I don't know what you want," I said, "so why do you keep coming after me?"

"You don't know, then why you so quick to run?" from three roofs away.

"I see two big men chasing me, I run, wouldn't you?"

"We didn't chase. We walked. We drove. We said where's the rush? We were very polite and showed no harm. You smacked into our car, we didn't smack into you. But let's talk about it downstairs. It's filthy up here and the air stinks from the incinerators and exhaust chutes."

He was on the last roof with me. I tried opening the door. Locked. What a fool I was not to have tried the doors on all the roofs I ran across. They were probably all locked but I shouldn't have been so sure. Though even if I got in one of them, probably nobody in the fourth- or third-floor rear apartments in that building would have opened up for me and there was still that other man on the street and by now probably a few more. I looked over the roof to the street.

"Don't jump. You say you don't know what we're after you for— well okay, maybe you're right and we're wrong."

"Who's jumping?" There were lots of men down there, most looking up, and double- and triple-parked cars. The street had been blocked off.

The man came up to within ten feet of me. "How about it now?"

He was getting his wind back but maybe I could run around him. Left or right—where did I have the most room to get by him?—when another man came out of the door held open by the brick and then other men came out of several doors. I ran to the side of the roof overlooking the river. A liner was out there. *Olympia* it said. Ocean liner. Going for a cruise. All white. People on the outside decks, probably with drinks in their hands and bundled up in warm coats and furs. It must have just sailed. Tugs at both ends of it pulling away from it now, so it was probably starting to get out of the harbor on its own. I waved to it. Took off my sweater and waved it. A yellow sweater. Probably easily seen. Someone waved back to me. Now several people were—more. I was sure it was me they were waving at, probably some with binoculars looking at me too. I waved harder at them and yelled "Hey, hey, have fun, a great journey," even if I knew they couldn't hear me from where I was. Then a whole long railing of them at the bow were waving and then another railingful at the back and it seemed people from the other side of the ship were coming to this side to wave too. They were happy to wave to someone at the start of their trip, even if it was maybe only for a week south to the isles. I know I'd be.

"You're not going to be rushing me and doing anything silly with that sweater now?" the man said. He stayed where he was but the closest of the other men was now only a roof away.

"I wouldn't," I said, still waving. "I don't want to hurt anyone and least of all myself when I know I didn't do anything wrong."

"Then let me put these on you and you'll come along. Because really, I'm getting more mad at you all the time."

"Granted." I put out my wrists. He handcuffed them. The closest man was almost right behind him now. I broke away and jumped over the roof on the river side, my hand holding the sweater which trailed above me. From the liner I heard this loud single human noise.

That should have done it but they had a couple of launches below in case I jumped. Biggest surprise was popping out of the water alive. All it took for them was a long pole with a hook at the end of it which they got around the chain of my cuffs. They dragged me to the launch, lifted me out of the water gently and rolled me over on my belly and two men sat on opposite ends of me as if I was a very dangerous but prize rare whale.

Cy

      ———

One look at me, they turn away or run. All I have to do is step out-side. Even leave my flat. Even begin to unlock my door and turn the doorknob: people in the hallway, they make tracks. Even the kids. Even the brave kids. The brave kids as fast as the most afraid though not as far. Once they've seen me. That's the ticket. The brave ones have to have seen me at least once. The bravest of the brave want to see me again and again. The most afraid take it from hearsay. Hearsay says: "Don't ever look at him. Face like a bogeyman, body even worse. Vampire, demon, hobgoblin, spook. The worst imaginations of hell." That's what I am to the most afraid. The bravest of the brave play a different game. They've got to get their jollies from being afraid. One flick of my lightswitch, and if they're waiting for me in the hallway as they like to do on rainy days: "Uh-oh, he's going out. Beat it, scram, scat, get. Doorknob's beginning to move. Here he comes. We'll watch out for you, we'll protect. There's his sleeve. There's his shoe and leg. Oh my God what a sight. Run. Run." Often I hear them around the corners of the staircase as I hobble down. Bad face, bad leg. For each of my steps down, they make one too. Though to some adults my face and posture might be interesting. Isn't that what they say? The uglier you are, the more interesting you become. Never met a person who felt that way about me yet. Nobody that courageous so far, maybe nobody that perverse. But I'm leaving the house. I don't really know what makes people tick. I'm more than taking a walk. I'm going to try to make today a very special day.

I lock my door. "Why lock it?" someone might say. If I'm as scary-looking as I tell it, who'll want to go into my flat? Landlord, for one. With the super and a couple of drifters off the street hired as haulers for five dollars each. Maybe because it's my apartment: ten. Though each about to whiz in his pants, afraid I might suddenly return and catch them emptying out my apartment quick. Not that I don't pay the rent. I do. I've got a one hundred percent disability, which keeps me alive. Army wounds. That's where the initial disfigurement and the monthly money come from. Grenade went off near my face. Not an enemy grenade. Oh yes, the enemy, but not our country's. A soldier friend. Accused me of making it with his girl. Grenade practice. We were allowed ten duds, and then, when we had proved our aim and had been taught the safety musts of grenade tossing, one live one to heave at a target fifty feet away. He held it above his head. Said "Admit, admit," and I kind of jokingly said "I cannot tell a lie, Ed, I never so much as set a fingertip on your girl." I don't know why I didn't run or drop instead of standing there. Shock maybe. My best pal: a real grenade flying at my face? He timed it just right. Pulled out the pin, counted three seconds, tossed it at me and it exploded in midair. He was smart enough to throw himself to the ground and only got a few shrapnel bites in his ass. He learned his lessons well. But I just stood there: "I don't even know who your girl is," I think were my actual last words for several years. But the vocal cords were eventually patched up to a degree, and with a dozen plastic surgery operations, courtesy of the government, half my head and face, but there was too much to be replaced. But where was I? Can't say my mind wasn't also a little affected by the blast. Oh yes. Special day today. More than just taking a walk. Imaginary people invading my apartment to get rid of me if I don't triple-lock the door. And the explosion, head and face injuries, and the body roughed up a bit though not as much as it was in my two other accidents.

Because being blind in one eye from the grenade explosion, I didn't see this bicyclist steaming down on me in the park one day. What he was doing on the pedestrian instead of the bike path is another story: one he always avoided telling. "I've been biking this park for years," he told the policeman while I was crying for mercy on the ground, "and never hit a soul or tree. I'm a champion cyclist, I've ridden in derbies and competed in the most grueling obstacle courses—fire, moats, nails—and never got a scratch, never damaged a bike, never came in less than second or third, so it had to be this nut who jumped in front of me."

Sure. I did that. Wanted to break a leg and hip in ten places and walk like this, with a hobble to the left and after each step the right foot's left in the air so long I sometimes stumble off-balance to the floor. Sure. Add to the weird gimp the face from the grenade, mix in the results of my third accident, and anyone can get a good picture of the fine figure of a man I am today. A car: two years ago: still blind in one eye, now slow of gait, hobbling across the street with the light turning from green to amber but not yet red—and even when it does there's still a few seconds' safety margin for the pedestrian—a car jumps the light and drags me one hundred feet on its fender with my face slapping and sliding on the pavement till it stops with its front wheel parked on my chest. But the driver in court: "I waited for the light to turn green, then seeing the coast was clear, shifted into first and slowly started to drive. Suddenly this man ducked under my wheels."

That's right. Every time I see a moving vehicle I go berserk. Kids zipping down the sidewalk on rollerskates I'm at my suicidal peak. Sure. But the judge said he could well understand it: "Man as deformed as that would certainly think of killing himself." And the witnesses: backed up whatever the driver said. Maybe I ruined the meals they just had or were about to have: mate or friend slaved all day at the stove: what a waste! Case closed. From the last accident I lost my other ear—whatever sound I get comes in through two eyesore slits—chest caved in, leaving me looking like a tilted question mark when I stand, and most of the good the plastic surgeons did to my face from the grenade accident got rubbed out or mashed in irremediably, they said, when I bounced and slid on the street, besides my losing all sensation for temperature changes and pain.

But why think about it? A mess. I see it now. People I pass on the street: one look's enough, yeck! Artificial limbs and transplanted kidneys we've plenty of, but heads? An ordinary face? Doctor's final opinion: "Wear one of those ski caps pulled down to your chin with two holes cut out for eyes"—why didn't he say "one"? The doctors can look at me though. Nurses wince a bit, but the doctors have seen it all and to them I'm a medical wonder, so they've got to take more than a peek. A textbook case they say: lucky to be alive. But the landlord still wants me out of the flat. What does he care about medical history: he gets a lawyer's letter made up and drops it in my box. "A welfare worker rented the apartment for you under false pretenses, since you know the landlord would never have rented it to you if you

had asked for the place yourself. He also claims mothers in the building complain you're the cause of their children's nightmares, children
complain you're the reason they can't study, train themselves or eat,
fathers complain you frighten their wives and daughters and ruin
business in their local stores and shops, so for the sake of the building, block and neighborhood we shall begin eviction proceedings
against you, if you won't leave voluntarily, and if that doesn't work,
you'll be thrown out on the street."

I believe it. I can understand it. I know I haven't much time left
there, but where am I going to move? "Go to a nursing home," the
super's yelled through my door. Why not an old age home: after all,
I'm almost thirty-five. And I've applied. All the homes, but none will
take me unless I consent to being locked in my room and never
allowed out except when the rest of the patients are asleep, forfeit
ninety percent of my disability check for the costs of being an outcast,
and have my food shoved through a special chute built in my door.
Thanks a lot. So I put up with the threats and gaff. I walk the streets.
Today with a big purpose in mind. Today's the day I decided, yes sir-
ree. My sole enjoyments up till now and for the past ten years: going
to the park and watching the ducks quack and beg, the swans glide
on the pond, the geese overhead. And the tots. They don't mind me.
So freshly formed. They're not afraid of me at all. Their mothers are,
though: snatching the kids away from me fast. And if they're pregnant
again: afraid their unborn babies will look like me, so they summon
the police: "That man," I've overheard. "That beast! That thing!
That it!"

Who can go on like that? That's what I asked myself in bed today.
Couldn't get up: thought I might just starve myself to death. But hope
gave me courage to eat and leave the house. Hope's a doctor I insist
exists somewhere on this globe who can do my face up a bit, improve
my voice, which since the chest caved in has been hardly more than
an intelligible rat's squeak, straighten the tilt a little as it'd be so nice
to even walk just a trifle lopsided as I did after the grenade accident.
Though some people: one never knows. Maybe for a day, a year,
they'd like the power of a path opening for them as it so often does
for me when I walk down a street. As is happening now. Like a path
for a president, a czar, a great movie star, and maybe also someone
with a year's run of unwashed body smells. I've seen it happen.
Smelled is more accurate: my nose, though shaped like a corkscrew
with a single nare, still functions okay. At a library: a lady like that.
Suddenly the smell. I knew right off what it was: walking death.
That's how we'll all probably reek one week in the grave. But with her

I think it was power. Really lapping it up it seemed. So blasé. Taking her time inspecting each shelf, but out of the corner of her eye watching the impression she made on the man who just passed, his fingers gripping his nose. Then she spotted me: another one who didn't wince. Buddies under the skin, I suppose she thought. Two power-houses meeting: dictators of our own domain: she of the odors; me, the looks. But I cleared out like the rest. Face: smell: no how-do-you-do's from me. And she's got a remedy I haven't got. Few successive scrubbings and soakings and bury the clothes and she's as sweet as everybody else.

But here I am. I ring and walk in—just like the sign says—but the receptionist: one look and she gulps, gets up, turns around, pretends to file: "Sorry," she says, "doctor's not in. What I mean is . . ." still with her back: God, you'd think she'd have seen them all in a plastic surgeon's office, "he's in, but busy. Appointment book's all filled up. Filled up for a month in fact. Then he's on vacation. If there's a can-cellation before then. . . ." What's she talking about? Nobody's in the waiting room but me.

"It's urgent."

"With you it's always urgent. I know. I don't mean to be unsympa-thetic. It must be rough. But he's told me. Any new discoveries or developments about your case, you'll be the first to know. He's promised. But there isn't another case like yours. You're unique."

I walk past her. With her back to me she won't even know till I've reached his office.

"Please, Doctor. One minute's all I ask. I'm about to give up." He waves the receptionist away, points to a seat. "Surely something new must've been found in three months. Have you tried Russia, China, Africa, Japan? They're doing wonders with folk medicine now I've read. Acupuncture, then? Snake venom? Vitamin E?"

"We've tried," he says. "I've tried. There are no bones to break to correct your nose. Nothing to cover the ear apertures that wouldn't impair what hearing you have. Your missing eye socket's been leveled off. No supporting gums to sink a tooth or hold a plate." He goes on. My case history. "Half a skull . . . most of it reconstructed . . . by me . . . a special cement . . . quarter of your brains gone also . . . yet here you are . . . reasonably alert . . . fairly good motor and muscular control . . . some vision . . . perceptible reflexes . . . all the hair and cilia out . . . that can never be explained . . . isn't important except cosmetically . . . but your gastrointestinal tract's fine . . . lungs and cardiovascular system couldn't be better . . . buck up . . . you'll live a normal lifespan . . . lots of people can't even say that . . . doctors

don't know everything . . . maybe one day . . . fifty years from now the
way science's been advancing . . . they'll know not only what kept you
alive after your injuries but how to restore a patient like you to the
original . . . but for now you're a medical phenomenon, a reconstruc-
tive impossibility."

"Vienna . . . Stockholm . . .Vietnam. Surely the doctors must have
run across similar plastic surgery cases in Vietnam?"

"I've written, read all the journals, inquired at medical conven-
tions. Nothing. Try wearing a much longer cap. Maybe I've suggested
that. Or an eye patch. They can be quite chic, and I'm not saying that
for a laugh. And move into a nursing home. I'll try to get you admitted to one. A life alone like yours can be unhealthy. But what else can
I say? Get a dog."

I go home. My apartment's been broken into. All the doors are
off. Furniture destroyed, mattress and linens soiled, clothes slashed.
It had to happen one day. Landlord, tenants, neighbors: they can only
take so much. Menace to the building, economic danger to the community: I understand. I'm sure the cop on the beat provided the
know-how, the judge up the street the crowbar. What they don't realize is I can't leave. Find another place? Fat chance. Sleep on the sidewalk and get mauled by a do-gooding gang? Somehow I'll get a
locksmith up here. Maybe that welfare worker can impersonate me
again and let him in. For now, I'll curl up on the floor.

An ammonia bomb's thrown into the apartment. Then two more,
till I get up, five o'clock I figure by the sky: evening graying into day,
and yell out the window: "Okay. I know when I'm beat. Give me
another hour's sleep and you've struck a bargain." Two more bombs
are tossed in. I leave with only the clothes I've got on. And the savings
book and cash I carry with me everywhere. And who's to complain
to? Some federal agency about my civil rights? Sure thing. Mayor's
office or Bureau of Consumer Affairs? You bet. And I know where to
go now. Only one place left for me. The one I wanted to avoid most.

I knock on her door. "Yes?" she says.

"Mom, it's me. But before you open up—" Too late. "Son!" I
hear. Then the door's being unlocked. I should've called first. Don't
be surprised if I've changed a little, I would've said. The door's
instantly slammed shut. "Imposter," she says. "Cyrus is dead."

"Not that easy, Ma. If you don't want me in, that's another story,
but remember the heirloom compote I broke when I was five? The
dog called Bo I loved so much and buried in the backyard? The time
Dad took us to the aerodrome show and three planes collided above
our heads? Do you still have the souvenir that floated down from the

sky into your lap? And the old jalopy we had painted black from blue? Remember its rumble seat you wouldn't let me ride in till I was six? 'On your sixth birthday,' you always said. 'Not till Cyrus's six.'"

"Not true. We could never afford a car."

"And here's one you couldn't've forgot. Who taught me how to walk?"

"I did. I mean, I taught my son how to walk. A mother usually does."

"It was cousin Ferdie. Ferdie who was studying to be a physical therapist and got killed in the last great war. Everybody thought something was wrong with my legs. I was already three and a half and still crawling. Maybe it's his head, people said. A retard . . . a basket case. But Ferdie said 'There's nothing wrong with him. Watch,' and he said 'Cyrus want candy?' I shook my head. Nodded, rather. That's another thing. A selected short subject. You were always teaching me the difference between nod and shake. 'Shake is to no,' were your words, 'nod is to yes.' But the main feature's my first steps. Ferdie went across the room and said 'Here, Cyrus, you want to have candy, you walk across the room. One step you get one piece. Two steps, two. Walk all the way to me and you get the whole jar. All yours to eat when you want to and as much as you like.' You protested. Said I could get cramps eating a whole jar of sourballs at one time. But Ferdie said 'You want him to walk, he'll walk. But Cy's got to have your approval about the candy first.' Dad said 'If it's jake with Cyrus, it's jake with us.' I walked straight across the room to pick up my prize. Didn't falter once. That's what you said later. 'You never faltered a second, as if you were born not only to walk but to run. To skip and be a champion racer and soccer player and do anything with your feet. Even dance. You'll be a great stage dancer one day,' you said. And remember how sick I got that night with all the candy I ate and you—"

"Cyrus," she says. "I thought you were dead." She opens the door. Her eyes are shut. And lets me hug her. My first hug in how many years? Her arms stay held out behind me, as if she's still waiting for someone to come into them. But I'm there. "Oh, Ma, can you ever know what this moment means to me?" Her eyes stay closed. Her nose is pinched. Maybe she thinks everything inside me also went haywire. But it is a hug. I don't dare kiss her cheek yet. I kiss the air instead. I've forgotten what it's like to hold another human being. The feeling can't be physically or mentally reproduced. How often I've hugged my pillow. Myself, if only to embrace some person's flesh. And even though she doesn't hug back, the feeling can be the living end. Not even a dog have I kissed the nose of or hugged in ten years. Before today I would've given half my savings to hold or nuzzle a child for a minute or less. Not just to touch someone. I've bumped into plenty on sidewalks and in the subway and department stores. Sometimes on purpose to feel what they still feel like after a very long while. Most times accidentally: in their frenzy to get around me we'd clunk shoulders or nick hands. But an honest-to-god hug? It all comes back. When I used to freely hold and hug people: women, girls, boys. In kindergarten. In grammar school. Teammates hugging the daylights out of me after we won the state championship. When I was in the army. Not my friend's girl. I didn't touch her. Why couldn't he take my word? I did know her, but only to talk to as a close friend. I thought he'd get mad if I told the truth. Ed had a reputation on the base as an excitable jealous man. And what's happened to him? Married her of course. They had children, he became a famous out- fielder: peg to home like a rifle shot from three hundred fifty feet away. Then divorced and remarried to a showgirl and more children: I read about him in the newspapers and magazines. A sock on the jaw was all I deserved. That should've been the extent of his rage unless I'd raped her.

The hug's over. She turns her back, says "Come in, but quickly." Already the change in attitude, the urgency in her voice: people across the street will think she's cohabiting with the devil. "Sit here. You hungry?" She gives me a sandwich and milk. Her eyes always away or closed. Food on a paper plate, milk in a disposable glass. Will she burn the napkins I use, scour the garbage pail daily? Maybe she thinks what I've got is contagious and because we're blood her chances of getting it are twice as great. She does say, which nobody's said: "It'll take time. You have to excuse my behavior, but I'll adjust to you yet. We'll do something to change your condition. A mother can work miracles for her child. I'll see doctors."

"I've seen them all. Zero can be done. And I don't want to hurt you, ruin your life in this town. But not even a fleabag hotel would take me in. 'Sorry: all booked,' though they were starving for guests. I did have the train car to myself all night. And could've ridden free: the conductor never came in to punch my ticket. So there are advan- tages being like this. But I'll only stay the night. If you still don't mind me in the morning, then two nights. Always from day to day though, and whenever you say go, I'll go."

"Never. You're my flesh and blood. My only child. Your poor father. Good thing he's dead. I'm sorry, but good thing for you too, as he never would have tolerated your being here. Bad for business he would have said. For his heart, our community standing, the family name. But I'm glad you saw to coming home. You knew there was always your mother. Silly as this might sound to you: a mother never stops loving her child and is the only one who'll welcome him back into her house no matter what's happened to him or what he's done outside."

That's true. I say goodnight. No more hugs. I could've used one more. But my old room. Mom's kept it up. Pennants of my old schools. The trophies and awards I won. My legs were as good as she'd predicted. I excelled in all sorts of sports with my quick movements, long strides, record-breaking speed. High hurdles. Sixty- and one-hundred-yard dash. A halfback. Shortstop. Crack of the bat, my bat, and zzzing the ball went, I went, whipping around the bases, stretching doubles into inside-the-park home runs. And the pictures: me with my best girl, my graduating class, Simonizing my first car, and about to enter college, when the army stepped in. Well: who didn't it affect? And even my medical discharge framed. Army must've sent it to her at her request. So she knew something was wrong. She probably even asked after my injuries, but what could they say? Cranial disjunction? Ophthalmic dysfunction? Rhinoplasty: surgeons did their best. And the one hundred percent disability, since they knew I'd never find work. I tried. After a few hundred turn-downs, I even applied to circuses and traveling sideshows. Send us photos they said: "Grotesqueness is our butter and bread." So I got some photos in a four-for-a-quarter machine. Once stripped down in a half-dollar booth to really give them a look. Curtain drawn: nobody saw. Not that a big courtroom to-do with judge and jury and then imprisonment would have bothered me that much: but I'm sure I would've wound up in a solitary cell as in a nursing home. The few freak shows that answered my applications were very honest: "Too grotesque. There's got to be a middle ground in every profession. If you've no limbs then you've got to have a pleasant face and do a trick with the stumps like type or play the harmonica, though we don't ask for concert hall expertise. We're here to startle and thrill the audience, not infuriate and disgust them where they want to tear down the tent. Thanks for trying us though, and good luck." The ones who wrote back did so with more respect and consideration to me than anyone since the army. They know how tough it is getting jobs in their line of work and the lonely outcome and near-poverty circumstances for the applicants who are too extreme for the norm. And it wasn't just to make money and be with some understanding people and feel like I was chipping in with society as a whole by serving myself up as entertainment that I wanted the job. But also to try and have a close relationship with a woman who'd be physically equal to me, and I thought the sideshow would be the best place to meet someone like that. For there's nothing I or the doctors know of that's diminished in my erotic and emotional parts. But enough of that. Instead I make love and declare my positive intentions to the women who fill up my dreams. One can almost say I live to sleep—and for the faint hope that in the near future my physical condition can be changed. In my dreams I am always the man I was before the grenade.

My bed's nicely made. Sheets clean and smooth, pillows aired and plump: it'll be my most restful night's sleep in years. But a few hours into it something wakes me up. A movement in the room like little cautious feet. There can't be any rodents in my mother's house. Maybe a pet she didn't speak of has come to lick my face or nap in its traditional place under the bed. I turn on the light. It's my mother with an axe that's swishing down at my head. I move: it cuts into my neck. There goes another piece: thank God from the waist up I'm mostly paralyzed. I roll to the floor: her second chop slips into the sheets. I grab the axe from her and drop it out the window. Now to see how bad's the cut.

I wrap my neck with a towel. "Knot this for me please," I want to say, but something to do with my vocal cords must've got stuck. *Tie this*, I write on paper, *before I bleed to death.*

"I can't, son, don't you see? There's no place in the world for a boy like you."

Call the hospital, goddamnit!

She leaves the house. Could be to get the axe. I dial Emergency. When he says "Officer Peters: what is it?" I tap an SOS on the receiver with the pen. "Is there something wrong? Will you stop making noise and speak? If there is something the matter, how will I know where to reach you if you can't say what's the address?"

Maybe if I keep tapping SOS someone else will get on the phone and understand and start tracing the call. But here's Mom again and as I figured: going to finish the job. I cup my hands in prayer, wave for her to stop, write *Listen, let me be the one to decide when to put an end to it*, but the axe is swung at my face.

I push her up against the wall with a table and head for the door. Behind me she says "Spare him. Help him. Make him to understand the depth of a mother's anguish."

I pound on her neighbor's door. I can predict their reaction, but I've got to take the chance. On a paper I've written *Call for an ambulance: there's been a serious accident.* The door opens. From her front yard my mother yells "Watch out: that animal tried to brutalize me." The man shouts for his gun. A woman comes running downstairs. He shoots one over my head. "Out out out," he says. All the lights in the neighborhood are now on. Anyway: someone's bound to call the police. I go into the woods that face these homes to wait for them. They'll take care of my wound: policemen have strong stomachs. Then the ambulance, hospital, an investigation: somehow I'll prove I'm my mother's son and who tried to brutalize whom.

I hear sirens. A policeman: "How long you say he's been in there?" Time to come out. But my mother: "I never saw him before he attacked me with an axe. This axe. I wrenched it from his hands. He's heavily armed. Guns, knives, he talked of explosives around his waist."

What to do? Further into the woods for a mile till I reach another development with more men with guns in their homes and calls to the police? I couldn't even hobble a half block with this gash. And start for the police and they might shoot me before I could explain. Well, I should at least try. Don't want to stay here and just die. There's always the future if they don't kill me straight off. The possibility of new discoveries: I still insist. Why not plastic ears, eyes and noses in twenty years and simple injections that clear up all blemishes and illnesses inside and out? Or a sideshow that'll finally have to hire me because of a lagging, jaded audience and want of anything more grotesque. The middle ground can also change. Maybe this last blow did the trick. And there are always the tots to watch. The ducks, swans and geese overhead. I've got no pain. I don't ask for much. My mother, after ten more years of my scrounging, might even mellow toward me and take me back. I crawl to the lights I vaguely see.

"I think he's coming," a policeman says. "Throw out your weapons and leave your explosives behind."

If I could speak I'd say "Help, I surrender, dear." Something like that. But instead I stand and put up my arms and wave my pajama top.

"It's him, it's him, all right," my mother says. "And he said he especially hates policemen and will shoot them on sight."

The
Hole

—

The City Planetarium blew up. I was sitting across the street on a park bench at the time. The blast shook the area so hard that my tie and newspaper flew in my face. When I peeled them away I saw pieces of the planetarium's gilded dome dropping around me and flames shooting out of the now domeless theater, in seconds disintegrating the upper branches of the city's oldest and tallest trees.

A woman ran across the street from Planetarium Square. "Two men," she said. "I saw them myself light the dynamite and drive off in a big car. They wore hats and didn't care who was hurt, who was inside," and she beat on her temples and collapsed into my arms.

I took down her name, address and the information she gave, and tried consoling her. But the tighter I held her and the more comforting words I used, the more hysterically she sobbed.

"Excuse me," I said, "but I'm a policeman. On vacation now, which accounts for my civilian dress. But technically on duty all the time, so I have to get over there to see how I can help," and I sat her on the bench and started to cross the street.

Behind me she yelled "Don't leave—I'm afraid. Your duty is as much to protect me as to help them. Because who knows where those men might strike next. Maybe right here," and she jumped off the bench. "Or even down there," and she jumped off the subway grating and darted into the street. "Or even here, or over here, or right here," and she jumped from the sidewalk to the street to the sidewalk again before she ran screaming into the park.

The fire in the planetarium theater had leveled off to a small steady blaze. The building was made of poured concrete, so once the theater seats, carpet and wall paint went up, there wasn't much left to burn but the wood floor.

The planetarium guard told me the children now trapped in the basement cafeteria were having their lunch when the explosion occurred. "For now," he said, "they're probably safe from the fire. Their teacher and two of the kitchen help were with them. And the basement, surrounded by thick sturdy walls, has enough open air ducts to keep them alive. But once the theater floor over them goes and the smoke pours in, then the most useful thing we can do for them is step back from the heat and pray out our hearts for their souls."

The one approachable entrance to the cafeteria was in the lobby through a door completely covered with debris. I flashed my badge to the crowd there and said "Dig. We've all got to dig for those kids," but only the sickly old guard and myself began pulling away the rubble that sealed up the door. I wasn't sure what was keeping the others back. One man said there might be more dynamite behind the door and a woman said she was scared of the young human parts she might find. And there were too many people to cow with the guard's gun as he was urging me to do to get them to help.

The police and fire departments arrived with the best digging, firefighting and rescue equipment the city had. In minutes they reached the door leading to the cafeteria and pried it open. Behind it wasn't the empty circular stairway the planetarium director told us to expect, but what looked like a large hole filled to the top with sand, concrete chips and slabs and bits and twists of metal mesh.

"You'll never free them in time," the guard said. "It's too far down—sixteen steps to the cafeteria exact. I know. I've trudged up and down those stairs on my lunch and coffee breaks maybe ten times a day for the past twenty years."

The power-run excavating tools worked rapidly and well till the stair's halfway landing, then became too large and cumbersome when the stairway curved, and the digging stopped.

"Blast the stairway open," a sergeant in Rescue Operations said. He held the explosives, blasting cap and primer cord and was ready to use them the moment the captain gave the command.

"Blast it open," the fire chief said, "and you'll weaken the building's structure entirely, which will cave in the ceiling long before the fire can."

The sergeant said "No offense meant, but I know what I'm talking about also. I've been on more entombments of this kind than I
want to recall. Those seven priests buried alive in the Holy Cathedral
dynamiting last month, for example. Those forty ballplayers suffo-
cated to death in the locker rooms at the City Stadium bombing last
week, for instance."

The captain decided to dig out the trapped people with manual
tools. "That way, even if we're unable to rescue them, at least we
won't be charged and be saddled with the guilt of having caused the
deaths of those children with an unnecessary blast."

There was space for three men in the stairway. I volunteered and
was chosen to be part of the second team, which would work when
the primary team came up to rest. The one-to-two buddy system of
digging was to be used: one man dislodging the embedded slabs
while the other men hauled the freed slabs and metal mesh and pails
of fragments and earth around the stairway landing to the sling,
which when filled would be hoisted out of the hole by a tackle.

The primary team, working on their bellies and knees, dug out the
rest of the halfway landing and two of the remaining eight steps to the
cafeteria. Then our team went down and was working past a third
step when we heard children screaming.

"They're alive," we all yelled, and a roar went off above the
ground that I'm sure was loud enough to be heard by the children.
We continued to dig and load, the ground beneath us becoming
looser and studded with fewer and smaller slabs. After clearing a
fourth step I was able to poke a lance to the bottom of the stairs. I
flashed a light down the hole and saw three wiggling fingers, then a
mustache and mouth.

It was the teacher. He said there were thirty-five children and two
elderly female cafeteria employees with him and all were in reasonably good spirits and health. We sent down penlights, chisels and sanitation bags. Then we widened the hole from above while he chipped
away at it from below, till the captain came down and said the hole
seemed large enough for the smallest of the third-graders to crawl
through.

"Make the hole wider so we can all crawl through," the teacher
said.

"We'll widen it some more once the kids still down there can't fit
through the hole we've already made," the captain said. "That way,
we'll at least be sure to get some survivors, as the firemen don't know
if they can douse the fire before the ceiling falls."

The teacher said he wouldn't let anyone through till the hole was wide enough for everyone to leave. "I don't see why I should be the one who has the best chance of being left behind in this progressively expanding digging system you've developed, just because I'm by far the largest of my group," and he began widening the hole with the lance and spade we'd sent down and ordering his students and the kitchen ladies to carry the rubble to the other side of the room.

The captain said he didn't think anything would change the teacher's mind right now and ordered the primary team back into the hole.

The primary team dug the hole wide enough for their lead man to squirm through. When he made it to the bottom of the stairs and stuck his head past the mouth of the hole into the cafeteria, the teacher told him to either boost himself back to the top or get a lance in his throat, as he wanted to make sure he could get through the hole himself before he let anyone inside.

The lead man squirmed back up and crawled to the halfway landing with the two haulers. The teacher started to crawl up the stairway hole. But because he was too broad-shouldered when he tried to make it up frontways and big-bottomed when he tried to push himself up hindways, he couldn't get more than a few feet up the hole.

"The hole still needs some widening," he said. "And don't be trying to bully your way down here with any of your thinner police, as my threat to that man before holds true for anyone else barging in. But to encourage you to widen the hole further, and repay you for the good work you've already done, I'm sending up my five smallest students."

Each child emerging from the hole was immediately wrapped in a blanket and carried to the waiting ambulance. None of them seemed sick or in the slightest state of shock. All complained that the blankets were too itchy and warm for them on this hot day, especially after they'd been so long in that hot temperature and stuffiness down there, and what they wanted most was to run around on the cool grass without any shoes or clothes on and breathe fresh air. But they were forcibly held down in the blankets, strapped to the ambulance stretchers and driven to the hospital.

Our team went into the hole again. "How goes it in there?" I asked the teacher, only a few feet from him now and both of us digging away furiously to widen the hole.

He said "Sticky, stifling, nearly suffocating—what do you think? There's also a little smoke leaking through these ceiling cracks, which means we haven't got long down here if you don't get me out fast."

"Try it now," I said, convinced the hole was wide enough for him.

We edged back to the halfway landing as he told us to. He advanced a few feet more than he had the last time, then said he felt as sorry as we must be, but the hole was still too narrow for him to get through.

"Listen," I said. "What'd certainly be worse than dying by yourself in there would be to die with all those kids and kitchen ladies dying around you."

"Listen yourself," he said. "If I know anything about human nature it's that you men will dig a lot harder for me while the kids are down here than if they've all been released. And especially now when you think you know what kind of man you'd be digging out if I happened to end up being stuck alone in here. But I will let the women and some more students up, though not as a digging inducement or rewarding ploy anymore. But because nobody's going to dig a whit harder for two ancient cooking ladies, so I might as well free them to put a stop to their constant nagging and save on the little air we have. And the boys I'm letting out are the ones who always gave me the most trouble in class: puking and bawling now and inciting the rest of my children into an increasingly unmanageable disobedience and maybe a mass physical attack on me soon or total hysteria."

First the cafeteria women came up, looking very frazzled and reviling the police who helped them out of the hole for allowing what they called "that inhuman madman down there" to keep them in that inferno so long. Then seven boys came up. Their faces smudged, bodies limp, hacking and gasping from the smoke in their lungs, all of them fell to the ground when they reached the lobby. One boy yelled to his mother in the crowd. She ducked under the police barrier, clutched her son and screamed into the hole "Butcher . . . murderer . . . you'll get yours quick enough if you ever get up here alive." She fainted and was put on a stretcher alongside the one her son was on, and both were carried to the same ambulance.

"Maybe we better hold up on her," a doctor said, directing the bearers to take her out of the ambulance. "We'll need every stretcher and hospital bed if the kids still down there are suddenly let go."

The woman was lifted off the stretcher and set down on the grass. Several mothers of children still in the cafeteria administered aid to her: holding her hand, massaging her ankles, telling her how lucky she was knowing her son was alive, though she remained unconscious. Her son and the other boys and the cafeteria women were driven to the hospital in a convoy of ambulances and police escorts.

A few hundred people had gathered behind police barriers on the grassy area past the planetarium's driveway. Many of them were calling the police cowards for not forcing their way down the hole to arrest the teacher, and idiots for not shooting him in the hole when they had the chance. The captain said through a bullhorn that any policeman entering the cafeteria wouldn't have had any defense against being lanced as the teacher had sworn to do. "As for shooting him before, an off-target or flesh-exiting bullet could have easily rico-cheted into the cafeteria and killed one of the children," but he had to end his explanation because of the jeers from the crowd.

I was sitting on the grass during my rest period when a man stand-ing near me said that today's bombing might wind up producing the city's first lynching in a hundred years. A woman next to him asked if that was a historical fact. "I mean about the possibility of it being the first lynching in a hundred years. I'm a civics professor at the univer-sity here, so I'd naturally like to know."

"Two hundred years—even three hundred if you like. What do I know from how long ago the last one was? All I'm saying is it doesn't look like anything could stop this mob from stringing him up. And five gets you the same the police will even be in on it because of the threat to them before. Or at least won't do anything to hold us back—right, Officer?" and he patted my back.

I told him that I for one wouldn't take part in any unlawful execu-tion and in fact would do everything in my power to see the teacher got to jail unharmed and order prevailed. The man laughed. The pro-fessor said she hoped all the police here felt as I did.

The primary team told the teacher to try the hole again. They moved back to the lobby as he instructed. The teacher crawled to the top of the hole, said "Fine job, very well constructed, we all thank you very much," and returned to the cafeteria and started sending the children up, smallest ones first.

Tired, disheveled, but emotionally calm children were either reunited in the arms of their parents or bundled up in blankets and dispatched to the hospital. Now only the teacher remained. Our team was sent down to assist him or find out what was keeping him from coming up on his own. Near the bottom of the hole we could still hear the parents in the lobby and spectators on the grass screaming for the teacher's neck.

"Will you please halt where you are?" the teacher said from the cafeteria opening, when I told him we wanted to get him out quick as the ceiling was about to cave in. "And no matter how horrible it is for me in here, it sounds as if it'll be worse for me upstairs. But the chil-dren and ladies are all right, am I correct in assuming that? Nobody hurt. Everybody alive. A few minor eye and lung ailments which ought to be cleared up in a week. And not only did I preserve the required order down here till everyone was rescued, but my students also learned a vital lesson about life I never could have taught them in class on how to stay alive and deal with their fellow human beings in an emergency situation. Plus an auxiliary lesson related to the city's brotherhood program this week, about how no person should be discriminated against because of his or her age, sex, color, religion, thoughts, health, physiognomy, ethnic, political, geographical or employment group. What I'm ostensibly saying, Officer, is that I hope no person or assembly upstairs thinks itself justified in playing jury and executioner with me before I've had my rightful due in the proper courts of law."

"The police will do everything possible to see you get booked and arraigned without incident. Now will you please come along?"

Just then a loud crash came from the cafeteria. Smoke looped around the teacher and up the stairway hole. "That was the ceiling that went," he yelled, "so get, you got to get—I said move."

Our team scurried up the hole into the lobby. Part of the crowd had broken through police lines and were waiting for us at the door, clamoring to kill the teacher the moment he appeared. We thought the teacher was right behind us. But he yelled from the halfway landing that he had decided to stay where he was, lance in hand, till he felt certain his chances for survival were better above ground than below.

"A little gas will get him up," the sergeant in Rescue Operations told the captain, and he loaded a tear gas canister into a gun.

"Force him up before we're sure we can handle this mob," I said, "and we might be delivering him to his killers rather than protecting him from them."

We pushed the crowd back behind the barriers. Many people continued to chant for the teacher's death and threatened to bowl over any police who might try to stop them. The captain told us to let the teacher stay put for the time being. "The mob will have shot its rage and disbanded for their homes and bars in an hour, and then we can get him up without further trouble and over to jail. But if he shows before we tell him it's safe, then all we can conclude is that out of a deep feeling of remorse or something, he intentionally crawled out of the hole to get himself killed."

I was thanked for a job well done and released from emergency duty. I went home and sat for a while at the kitchen table, but wouldn't eat. My mother asked what was disturbing me so much that I couldn't even touch my favorite dinner.

I told her I didn't share the captain's optimism about getting the teacher to jail. "I know something about crowd control and collective violence, and a lot of those people didn't look like they'd leave till they had manipulated the others into helping them lynch him. And this might make me a bad policeman, Mom. But realistically, no healthy sane person wants to get himself killed if he can help it without seriously harming or killing someone else, and that teacher turned out to be the only right one among us after all. Nobody got really hurt or killed. And though I detest his threats against the police, I'm sure we did dig twice as hard because those kids were still with him, which means he would have been buried alive if he'd let them all go all those times we asked him to. And then he wasn't responsible for the bombing or their being entombed. So no matter how evil the mob thinks his motives and methods were, they should at least feel he's gone through enough mishaps and hardships to warrant getting a fair trial."

"Then go back and do what you can for him, since you'll never enjoy your food and vacation the way you are," and I said she was right, phoned the station house and was told the teacher was still in the hole, got my revolver, kept my civies on as I wasn't allowed to be in uniform unless assigned to duty and when going to and from work, and drove to Planetarium Square, hoping the incident would be over by the time I got there and the teacher unharmed and safe in jail.

He was still down there. A crowd a little larger than when I'd left it was still hopping for his neck. The fire was out and the firemen were gone and the captain had been replaced by a lieutenant and most of the police company had been transferred to City Concert Hall across town, as a bomb had exploded there an hour ago and some three hundred people were still trapped in the debris.

I asked the lieutenant if there was anything I could do. He introduced me to the teacher's son and asked if I'd mind accompanying the young man down the hole so he could try to coax his father up. "I don't want him going in alone. He might leave provisions or clothing on the sly or even stay down there himself, making it even tougher getting the teacher up later on. Now's the most opportune time to get him out too. The darkness should conceal his escape movements if we can avoid tipping off the mob with any scuffling or squabbling sounds from below. If we wait till morning I'm afraid the mob will be larger and doubly intent on getting revenge on him for his treatment of his students before and this new rash of bombings and now all those deaths at Concert Hall. But this is a volunteer assignment, you understand. You're still on vacation. I wouldn't order any man to risk facing a lance while on his chest. But since the teacher seemed to trust you most and you know the hole better than anyone else around, you're the most suitable man for the job."

We entered the hole. The son, lagging behind me, complained about his knees being scraped and brand-new sandals and slacks getting torn, then apologized for his self-centeredness and said anything was worth ripping and ruining to save his dad. We both carried flashlights and spoke softly as we crawled.

"We're coming, Dad."

"Though please don't make any fuss or objections about it," I said.

"We want you to come out quietly with us for your own good."

"I'm the officer who was the lead man for that backup digging team."

"He's very sympathetic to you and came with me only to help."

"Your son will confirm that now's the best chance you'll have for ditching that mob upstairs."

"It's true, Dad."

"I'm armed. But to show my good faith, I'll leave the gun behind me anytime you say."

The teacher never answered. We crawled to the end of the stairway without finding him. The ceiling caving in before had blocked the cafeteria entrance again. We checked and rechecked the entire hole with our flashlights till I spotted a tiny aperture in the wall where the stairway curved. We broke through the wall, enlarged the opening wide enough to fit through. Behind it was an empty basement corridor still lit by electric lights and seemingly untouched by the explosion and fire. It was about thirty feet long and had a door at either end of it.

I opened one door and found nothing behind it but soap powder and cleaning equipment. The son ran and stood in front of the other door. "Come on," he said. "What's the harm if we let him get out on his own?"

"The harm's that I was sent down to get him up safely, not let him escape."

"He'll be escaping from the mob, not the police. He'll turn himself in tomorrow when he's sure it's safe enough. I know my old man. He's extremely legal-conscious, has an unflagging respect for the law. He'll want to face up to all the charges brought against him, and if guilty, he'll gladly serve his time."

"I promise to do everything I can to see he gets to court. Now will you please let me get on with my job?" I pushed him aside, opened the door and found the room or passageway behind it packed with rubble. We searched the corridor and utility closet for an exit the teacher might have gone through, but there were no other doors, vents or tiny holes.

"He couldn't have just vanished," I said.

"What are we going to tell them upstairs?"

"That he couldn't have just vanished."

"They'll never believe us. Both the mob and the police will say we were in on the escape. And the longer we stay down here, the less they'll believe he got away on his own. We have to think up some airtight excuse right away. What about that he fell down a shaft made by the bombing before and which then crumbled apart and buried him?"

"And if he turns up tomorrow as you say?"

"Maybe his great respect for the law and its court system has finally wavered."

"No. The lieutenant will send some men down to try and dig him out."

"Then what about that he took your gun and made us dig through the cafeteria entrance and got out some way through there?"

"No. They'll want to know why we filled in the hole after him."

"So we did it at gunpoint or he filled it up himself."

"Then they'll want to know why I still have my gun on me."

"We'll say he threw it back just before he put the last stone in the hole."

"No. They'll dig through the cafeteria entrance and probably find there isn't another escape route through there."

"How do we know? Maybe there is. But the reason he couldn't find it before is because for most of his time in the cafeteria he had no light."

"The kitchen ladies would have told him of another exit when they were with him."

"Then a new hole or old sealed one they didn't know about could have been opened by the explosion."

"It's too far-fetched."

"It'll get us off the hook for now. What about that he went through that second corridor door when he saw us breaking through the wall, and which immediately caved in behind him just as he got past?"

"The lieutenant will get the floor plans. And that door might lead to nothing but a storage room and freezer locker and lavatory and another utility closet with no other way out of these rooms but the doors leading to the room with the door to the corridor that he came through."

"Then what about that he fell down a shaft made by the bombing before and which then crumbled apart and buried him?"

We gave up trying to find a plausible excuse and returned to the lobby and told the lieutenant the truth.

"No chance," he said. He sent several men into the hole to find the teacher or the exit he used. "And this time," he yelled down the stairway to the men, "shoot to disable if he won't come up nice and sweetlike by himself. We're through pussyfooting around that guy just to prevent the unlikely prospect of his getting beaten up or lynched."

The men came up an hour later saying they discovered a chute in the utility closet that led down to a small room that had nothing in it but dirty table linen and uniforms and a door plugged up with impassable debris. Other men were sent down to look for possible escape routes in the laundry room and chute, utility closet, corridor and stairway hole, but all they could come up with were two six-inch-across air ducts filled with concrete chips and sand.

"How are we going to explain this to the mob?" I asked the lieutenant.

"Very simply that he got away through an opening we've yet to uncover."

"Think they'll believe that?"

"What do I care what they believe? As long as they can mull it over for a while and I get them off my back."

"But they'll say we're still holding him till they leave."

"Then we'll let a few crowd representatives into the hole to inspect the stairway and laundry room."

"When they don't find him they'll say we knowingly let him go to avert disorder."

"So we'll tell them we smuggled the teacher through the lobby as we'd first planned to, and he's now in a downtown jail."

"They'll find out later tonight or tomorrow we don't have him. And when the papers get wind of it we'll be in even worse trouble with a bigger mob, with the jail liable to get destroyed."

"Then we'll tell them exactly what happened, because we haven't any more time to think up an excuse. There was a bombing at City Art Museum a half hour ago and we're all needed there to dig out the night guards and works of art."

He ordered his men into the police vans. Two policemen were kept behind to guard the stairway, just in case the teacher had been hiding someplace in the hole all this time and was waiting to leave through the lobby after everyone had gone. I was asked to make sure the son got home all right and then to resume what the lieutenant called my much-interfered-with-though-more-than-ever-now-well-earned vacation.

He addressed the crowd, told them of the most recent bombing and of his new assignment and that the teacher had apparently given the police the slip. "Though nobody should worry any about it, as we've excellent photos and fingerprints of the man, so it won't be more than a day or two before he's caught. So break it up, everybody. We don't want total chaos and terror becoming the rule of our city. Go back to your homes or jobs or to a quiet bar if you can find one, as there's just no sensible reason left to stick around," and satisfied the crowd was splitting up and leaving, he and his unit drove to the museum.

The crowd quickly re-formed. A group of men bulldozed its way past the two policemen and went into the hole. The son and I stood in the dark behind a parked car nearby in case the teacher turned up. The group came out and said they'd found nothing new downstairs but a trapdoor in the laundry chute that tunneled through to a sewer pipe that wasn't wide enough to fit a kitten in.

The son and I crossed the street and were hailing a cab coming out of the park when a woman shouted "Why are you letting the cop get off free? Wasn't he the one who was so chummy with the teacher, and for all we know came back here to sneak him past us and the police?"

"That's not quite true," I said, when the crowd began forming around us and the cab. "I'll admit I did come back here to see what I could do to get him past you all and safe in jail, but I had no specific plan as to how I'd bring it off. And I only went into the hole a second time because the lieutenant felt the best way to get the teacher to jail without any police and civilians getting hurt was for the teacher's son and I to quietly coax him up into a police van, though we never saw a trace of him."

"His son?" a man said. "Then he's the one we ought to be getting. He's got the same kind of blood in his veins, so he'll be doing the same thing to our kids his dad did if he ever gets the chance. We'll be doing a favor to a whole slew of people in the future by doing away with him now."

The son bolted through the crowd. I yelled "Don't run, you fool, you'll only provoke them more." The cab drove off with its back doors flapping and people pounding its sides with sticks. Some men chased after the son. I drew my revolver, was grabbed from behind, knocked to the ground and sat on while part of the crowd disarmed the policemen who tried to help me. They caught the son, dragged him back, kicked at his head and body till it seemed all his limbs, ribs and face were broken, then hung him upside down by his feet from one of the tree branches that had survived the fire. They continued to spit at him and some women pulled out patches of his hair and beat his already unrecognizable face with their handbags, till one of the policemen said "All right, folks. I think you did everything you could do to him short of setting him on fire, so why don't you go home." Someone lit a match to the son's shirtsleeve, but the policemen slapped the fire out.

The crowd broke up. One of the men who'd been sitting on me said "Just thank your lucky stars you told us the truth." Some people as they walked away from the square turned around every few seconds to give the body dirty looks.

I cut the rope holding the son: he came down on his head. The policemen put him in a canvas sack and that sack into the trunk of their squad car. No charges were brought against anyone for the son's death. The following day the newspapers said the son had died from a fall inside the stairway hole while looking for his father, who was still being sought by the police. The police, the articles said, were still trying to determine the causes and persons responsible for the planetarium bombing and other related explosions. So far they've had no success.

Joke

She takes off my shoes, gets up, goes to the kitchen with the shoes, comes back, sits next to me, takes off my pants, gets up, goes to the bathroom with the pants, comes back, sits beside me, takes off my jacket, gets up, I say "Where you going this time?" she says nothing, leaves with my jacket, I don't know where she is, comes back, looks the same, no more makeup than before, she hasn't taken anything off or put anything on herself or changed her hairstyle since I got here, sits beside me, takes off my socks, gets up, I say "What now?" she says "I've got to go," I say "Where?" she says "You know where," I say "No, where is 'you know where'—where I'm supposed to think it is, wherever that is, or someplace else?" she says "Maybe," and goes, I say "Damn, I'm getting tired of all your getting up and going and coming back and sitting and then going again," but she doesn't answer, maybe she didn't hear me, just like before she comes back in two minutes and sits beside me, takes off my shirt, gets up, I grab her hand, she says "Let go," I say "But where you off to this time if I can ask?" she says "None of your business," I say "You don't think it's partly my business or at least that I should think it odd your repeatedly taking off something of mine and disappearing with it right after and not bringing it back?" and she says "Let go of my hand first," I let go, she goes, down the hall again which could be to any number of places: the two bedrooms, the bank of closets, the front door, out of it or standing near it, the stairway outside the front door, the other apartment on the floor, the flight up to the roof or the four flights down to the ground floor or street, though probably not out there and back in two minutes unless she ran all the way, though I didn't hear the front door open or close and she wasn't breathing hard when she returned, though the door could have been open from one of the two previous times she went down the hall with my clothes when I wasn't listening as closely as I did this time and she could be in even better shape than I thought, anyway she's back, two minutes, no change, shirt gone, sits beside me, takes off my underpants, "Now I'm naked," I say, "Except for your cap," she says, "Oh I always leave my cap on," "No, this time I won't let you leave it on," "Yes I say," "No I say," "All right," I say, "take it off," "Later," she says and gets up, I grab her wrist, "I swear you're making me mad no matter how nice our conversation just was," "Tough," she says, "Don't make me even madder," I say, "Tough," she says, "You're making me much madder, Dotty," "Tough tough tough," she says and jerks her wrist out of my hand and goes down the hall with my underpants to any of the places I mentioned before, or maybe to none of them, maybe she's just staying out of sight from me in the hall to make me madder than I am, or maybe she did leave the front door open from any of those last times she went down the hall and now goes out to do something or see someone in any of the stairways or other apartments or vestibules, roof, another building or street, but she comes back, two minutes, "Where you been?" I say, sits beside me, "What are you going to take off me now?" I say, knocks off my cap, "Now there's nothing to take off me," gets up, "I'm not going to stop you this time," I say, leaves the room with my cap, "You want to know why I didn't stop you?" she's somewhere in the hall or any of the other places or one I haven't thought of yet, "Because I want to see what you're going to take off me next," comes back, I say "Well hello there, Dotty," sits beside me, "What you got planned for me now, Dotty?" puts her lips near my mouth, "That a way to go there, friend Dotty," kisses me and leaves a blob of something on my tongue, I take it out, "What did you do that for, this old prune which for all I know was in your filthy pocket first," takes it out of my hand, "Oh, still undressing me, Dotty, that's what your prune's supposed to signify?" starts down the hall with it, "Oh, going to deposit it with my other things you took down that way?" comes back, in about two minutes, "What are you going to stick in my mouth this time?" I say, sits beside me, "I'm curious, for this is quite the game you're playing—more prunes, a wad of gum? Well, I'm not kissing you if it seems like it's going to be anything like that," she just looks at my eyes, "Maybe something else you're going to stick in or on me this time so you can take it out or off me, right?" still just looking at me, "Well, I'm not going to let you even touch me till you're totally undressed yourself," just looking at me, "Then it is all right, if you're through undressing me, if I start taking off your clothes?" blank expression, eyes blinking naturally but never looking away from mine, "Then how about if I start undressing you without your permission?" still just looking at me, "Okay, I'm going to do it, now I warned you, Dotty," and I slip off one of her shoes. She kicks my hand. I start removing the other shoe. She punches my jaw. I slap her face. She pulls my hair. I swat her with my open hand. She pulls me up and knees me in the groin. I fall over. She pounds my head with the shoe I took off her. She pounds it a lot. She pounds it before I can stop her pounding it some more. She pounds and pounds it. I'm on the ground on my face. I try but can't get up. She's still pounding my head. "I didn't know," I say, maybe to myself when I want to say it aloud, "I didn't know this all wasn't to you mostly a joke."

The

Gold

Car

⟨ornament⟩

She drives up in a gold car. A crowd's in front of the house. She saw the crowd when she turned the corner. At first she thought the crowd was in front of his house or the houses on either side of it. As she got closer she knew it was in front of his. There was very little overlapping of the crowd on the lawns of the houses next to his. Groups have been in front of his house before. Either just to look at it and take photographs, just because he lives there, or to get his autograph by waiting for him in front of the house or by walking up to the door and ringing the bell. But this crowd was about three times as large as any she'd seen in front of his house, and she now sees a policewoman in it. She gets out of the car, takes off her sunglasses, puts on her prescription glasses, gets her shoulder bag and walks up the path to the house. "What is it?" she says to the first person she comes to. Several people turn to her and say "Sid Anscott died."

It was early morning when she left, she tells the policeman. "What time early?" he says. "Ten, ten-fifteen. I went to get some milk and eggs and things—fresh breads, rolls and bagels if they had any. Sid loved bagels or rolls for breakfast. I haven't known him for long so I wasn't too familiar with his neighborhood. But he was all out of everything and I thought I'd do him a favor for once. Oh, I've done him lots of favors, but you know what I mean: going out and surprising him by getting breakfast food while he slept. But I met an old friend at the market—Lucille Booth—and she said 'Let's have a coffee, I haven't seen you for months.' So I went to a coffee shop with her but called Sid at home. No answer. I knew he'd be up by now, so I thought he was either in the shower or had gone out for a run. He was overweight, as you probably know, but liked to run every single morning."

Sid was sleeping when she got out of bed. She didn't think he was breathing right and she shook him a little. "Sid, Sid," she said. He said "What?" She said "You're not sleeping right—you're breathing so hard. Anything wrong?" "No," he said. "I'm sorry for waking you then, I was just worried." He said "Leave me alone, will you—let me sleep." He never moved his head or opened his eyes when he said all this. She said "Sorry, honey, I'm really sorry—just go back to sleep." She went to the bathroom, doing stretching exercises as she went. She washed up, then went into the kitchen and opened the refrigerator. She felt like having a glass of some kind of cold juice, orange most of all. The refrigerator and its freezer were empty except for a bottle of champagne on its side, two six-packs of beer, butter, wilted vegetables, hamburger meat and rolls. No juice, milk, nothing like that. She'd get some juice and other things, she thought. She went back to the bedroom. He was still asleep. She said "Sid, Sid, mind if I borrow the car to get some groceries—you're all out." He said something but she wasn't sure if it was "Go ahead" or "Let me sleep." Anyway, she knew he wouldn't mind if she took the car. She'd done it a few times before and the last time without asking him. She got the car keys off the dresser and thought about taking some money out of his wallet, but didn't. She had enough of her own and what the hell, he'd been plenty generous with her last night, taking her to an expensive restaurant and before that to a bar where they had these great Hawaiian cocktails that must have cost five dollars each. Of course he could afford it, but she knew he'd appreciate her thinking of him as someone who didn't have to pick up the tab every time. Then she got dressed and drove to the market where, when she was paying for the groceries, she met Lucille.

"So tell me what you've been up to lately?" Lucille said in the coffee shop. "Let me phone Sid again—I don't want him to worry." "Sid who?" Lucille said. "Sid Anscott—but don't tell anyone. His wife's not supposed to know, nor, to tell you the truth, his agent, who's a good friend of his wife." "Oh I won't, sweetie, I won't. But good for you. He's very big now, very very big. Does he treat you right?" "Why shouldn't he?" "He has a reputation of not treating his women right, his wife foremost among them." "That's out of the magazines and ugly gossip papers. He's a doll. He's beautiful. I love him. He's sweet as cake." "Okay, all right, you convinced me. From now on someone asks what kind of guy he is, I'll say better than Christ and more romantic, though I won't say where I heard it from. And love, is it?" "I said so, not that I expect anything from it. He said he'd never get divorced. He's very honest about it. He tells me staying married keeps him from making the same mistake twice. I go along with it. It lasts a month more, fine; a year, better. But he says I'm special and it could go on for he doesn't know how long, and I believe him. Why shouldn't I? He treats me like I should believe him." "So, to answer my question finally," Lucille said, "he does treat you well, right?" "He got me on the payroll of his new movie. Not in acting but working with the script. Technical things, and on location. It's terrific experience. It might even get me better jobs in that line, and if it does, then the hell with acting. I'm sick of it already and it's got me almost nothing so far but a date with him which led to the script job and possibly better things after. Sure, better things after. But it's enough that I'm with him, without the job or anything, though it's certainly better with the job." "He sounds okay," Lucille said, "—much better than what I've heard of him. Maybe he's changed or maybe everyone else was wrong." "I got to go to the phone."

His phone rang. Screw it, who's calling so early? he thought. The phone continued to ring. "Bea, get the phone, will you?" he said, "I'm still too freaking bushed." The phone continued to ring and then stopped. He felt for her on the bed. He turned over. Where the hell is she? "Bea," he yelled, "hey Bea." Oh yeah, that's right, took the car, went for groceries. Good girl; I'm hungry already. He got up. Who the hell was that on the phone anyway? Doesn't everybody who knows my number know I'm not to be disturbed till twelve? Well what do you know, looking at the clock. Ten after. So someone for once was paying attention. He went into the bathroom. Oh mama, what a head. He got two aspirins out of the jar—make it three, you're a big fella—too freaking big, squeezing his belly, and ran the water awhile before he filled up a glass, let the cloud in it disappear and drank the water down. Best way to avoid ulcers from aspirins, the water, and to avoid burping from those clouds.

"Officer, this woman seems to know Mr. Anscott." She was being held up by two men. "Someone—say, someone," the policewoman said, "bring out a chair. No, inside bring her. Bring her inside. Here, I'll take over. Bram," she called to a policeman at the door, "give me a hand." The two officers brought her into the house. She was crying. She said "They said he's dead. I just left him a few hours ago, how could he be dead? I left him in bed sleeping." "You're his wife, ma'am?" Bram said. "No, his wife is in New York." "You're a good friend then—a business associate?" "Sure, both, but you want to know, it'll come out anyhow. I'm a very good friend. We've been together for more than a month now. I have my own place but last night I stayed here with him. You'll find some of my clothes in his closet and some of my evening clothes over the chair in the bedroom. Could you please tell me what happened?" "You sure you don't want a lawyer first?" the policewoman said. "We want you to know all your rights." "What do I need a lawyer for? They said he died and your looks aren't denying it. I was outside at the time. I went to the market for us. I'm absolutely heartsick at the whole thing. What do I need a lawyer for? My problem is nothing except that he's dead. What could he have died of, could you please tell me?" "Look," the policewoman said, "why don't you sit down? Yes, that's a good idea. Bram, will you get her some water, and then you can tell us what happened right from the time you last saw him here. When was that exactly and what's your full name?"

She put the key into the ignition. Boy, she thought, wouldn't it be great to own a car like this, and if she still lived where she lives, to have the money to garage it. She drove off. Let's see: eggs, milk, bread, rolls, bagels if they have, orange juice, muffins even, butter because the butter he has is probably rancid, pancake mix. Did he have pancake mix? Should've checked. But the heck with pancake mix. He said he wants to lose weight. His studio in fact insists he lose weight and I'm now working for the studio. So what do you buy for breakfast and lunch—a brunch—for a man who will wake up starved after so long a sleep and when he really didn't eat that much the night before, expensive as the food was, but who wants to lose weight? Grapefruit. The biggest pinkest grapefruit they have. Two of them. And maybe cottage cheese and plain yogurt and a jar of dietary marmalade. I know he loves it because when we went to that chalet in Arizona he practically ate the whole cup of marmalade they gave us. And maybe for his coffee I'll warm the skim milk it's going to be and serve him breakfast in bed. No, that would be too corny. A car pulled up alongside hers when she was waiting for the light to change. Oh, the dapper type—a ladykiller. Bushy mustache, shirt unbuttoned to the navel, car looking like it was polished just today. Look at the way he combs his hair. Must've taken him an hour to get it set that way. Nice looking though. He's going to say something. I know it's going to come. Here it is, folks. "A very fine-looking automobile," he said through her passenger window, "and a very attractive driver handling it as well. That's all I have to say. If you want to talk more I'll be parked on the right side just beyond the next traffic light." The light changed and he took off before her. What a character. I wonder how many women he picks up a month with that line. In this town, with those looks and that car, I bet he does all right. It's sad though—just depressing, to think that that's what relationships have come to. What do I mean by that? That it's just in and out, meet me at the light, do it in the hotel, see you, sweetface, without most times either person catching the other's name. Actually, things longer lasting can come from pickups like that. Didn't I meet Sid at that screening in almost a similar way? I'm at the refreshment stand wondering what to buy for the movie when he comes over to buy something too, or so he said, but I'm sure with his appetite it was true, and he said "Hey, you think if we buy two boxes of popcorn at the same time they'll give us a break on the price?" I said I didn't know. I immediately recognized him. He said "What about one giant pail between us, no break on the price, but we have to sit next to each other to eat it?" I'm game, I said. So we ordered a giant pail. I insisted on paying for it—after all, I told him, "you don't look like you can afford it." He got a big laugh out of that. We went home after a late-evening snack together—his home, in this car, since he wanted me to leave mine in the parking lot rather than follow him in it, and he'd drive me to it the next morning. So we slept together that night and here we are, a month later, with me minus my car because of that night, but that turned out all right thanks to Sid, and us much closer than we ever were and I think getting closer all the time. She drove past the next light—it was green—and there sure enough was that guy from before. She waved to him as she passed. He honked his horn and pulled out and at the next street made a right.

Sally rang the doorbell of Sid's house. There was no answer. She rang again and again. What in God's name is wrong with him? You make appointments, you keep them. She rang some more, then tried the door. Locked. Well, why shouldn't it be in any neighborhood in this city, and if it was open what did she think she'd do, go in? Maybe. She'd at least open the door a little and say into the house

"Sid? It's Sally. You said you wanted me to come by at noon, so here I am. I brought the publicity photos and blurbs. All you have to do is look them over and check which ones you like." Well, she wouldn't say all that. Just "Sid, it's Sally, you there?" Maybe he's in the back of the house or having his coffee on the patio. She went through the gate, didn't even see a chair out there, and knocked on the rear door. No answer. He did say one time when she came here and he didn't answer though he was home that if it happened again, just go around the house and walk in. "You see me naked," he said, "scream, but don't rip your clothes off right away, as I might be with my wife." "Oh, funny guy, this Sid," she said, "funny, funny. We're strictly business, for now and forever, got that straight?" "Straight, yes, you said it, baby, I didn't—because if I can avoid it I wouldn't do it any other way. But only kidding. I've more than my share of complications already, so why kill the hen that gave the golden goose, hey?" She said "I'm hardly the golden goose—I might work for a few who aren't so golden—so maybe at the most I'm a three-minute soft-boiled egg." He said "Good, great, write that down for me—I call you a hen, you call yourself an egg. Beautiful, what a yak; I'm going to use it next time I want to lay one." She knocked on the rear door again and opened it slightly. "Sid, it's Sally, you around? Hello? Nobody home?" He could be in the shower or sauna. She went into the house and called "Sid? Sid?" as she walked through it. "Anybody else around? One of Sid's friends?" The bathroom door was open. She went in and knocked on the sauna, but the red light was off so she knew no one was inside. She went into the kitchen, then to the bedroom. The door was open, room was dark, blinds were closed. She saw him on the floor naked, and beside him part of a hamburger roll.

Herman gets a phone call from Fritz who tells him Sid Anscott died this morning. "Probably of natural causes. Got some food lodged in his windpipe and choked to death. But that's just the on-the-scene report—he's now with the coroner. Want me to make a statement for us to the press?" "Do what you feel comfortable with," Herman says, "but be nothing but straight-out flattering. We loved, unbelievable loss, he was the greatest—that sort of stuff. But before you say anything to anybody, get hold of his wife and tell her if she doesn't know—I can't," and hangs up. Poor Sid, he thinks. And the poor studio. And the studio's even poorer insurance company if it pays up. And the poor girl he was seeing now and he asked me to put on the payroll. And his poor wife though she won't be so poor in other ways once his estate's settled. And his own poor kid and his poor mother. And all the poor kids and mothers and grandmothers who are going to be pouring their eyes out once they hear about Sid. This calls for a meeting. For how in the world are we going to finish three-quarters of a picture without him? Later. I got a few days to decide. Now I just feel too bad. He presses a button on the telephone, puts the receiver down and goes into the next room. "Willie," he says to his secretary, "get me Fritz again. I want to ask if anyone's thought about the funeral arrangements. No, I don't want to speak to anyone for ten minutes, so tell him from me, please, that the quicker we get Sid back and buried, the less time they'll have to see what a mess he made of his body. But not to lean, tell him, on the police or medical examiner, because then they might dig even deeper into that poor guy."

Fritz calls Sid's wife in New York a third time and Sid's daughter says "I told you, my mother's at a class now and won't be home till six." "It's not six now?" Fritz says. "I'm sorry, honey, I always get those California–New York time differences mixed up. But your mother comes in before six, give her the number I gave you and my name, okay?" What should I do? he thinks after he hangs up. Call up again and break it to the kid before she hears it on the radio? Because it's going to be on the radio soon or in their late-edition paper. It might even be on it now. He calls Herman and says "One or the other of us has to tell Sid's kid if we can't get his wife in the next half hour. The kid will be shocked even worse out of her wits if she first hears it on the radio or TV. Worse on TV if they have a picture of Sid, and much worse if they have one of him on the floor." "I'll do it," Herman says, "but how old you think that girl is?" "Fifteen, sixteen, by her voice." "Ten," Herman says, "if that. But so grown up. Too grown up for even a sixteen-year-old, but that's what to expect, I guess, for those California kids with successful showbiz parents, even if they live in New York. I used to hold that little angel on my knees and she once took a swing at me—innocently, I mean—and broke my glasses. Ah, maybe you should call Jenkins and have him rush over to their apartment instead."

Sausages, she thought. Why not link sausages and eggs? She'll poach the eggs even if he doesn't have a poacher. She knows how. Water boiling—frying pan, she'll have to use—drop the eggs in just right with a spoon, curl them over and cover and three to four minutes they're done. That'll at least make up for the grease and extra calories in the sausages. Or bacon. How about that? Not the most original idea, but broiled almost to a crisp in the stove and then stretched out on a paper towel and delicately patted till the bacon's dry. She wishes they had scrapple in L.A. They have everything else including better bagels than even in Brooklyn, Sid's said—"It took people like me to insist they make them better if they want to keep a colony of New Yorkers here"—and cheese better than maybe even in Italy and France and certainly as good as wines as they got there—but what's she going on about? She doesn't want wine for brunch but something very sobering after last night—coffee, the richer the better. So some dark espresso coffee to mix in with the regular coffee too. He even have any regular coffee in the house? She doesn't remember seeing it, so get a pound can of regular coffee and a half pound of espresso and maybe even croissants if they have no bagels or good rolls. No, too fattening. He'll complain about it to me after he eats every one. So just sausages or bacon, eggs, a tomato or two, grapefruit, a little low-fat solid cheese, but not yellow—too many chemicals in that one, he's said—and the coffees and yogurt and cottage cheese and that should do it. Milk and orange juice, of course. It'll be a great breakfast. And butter.

When they got back to the parking lot the next day, her car had been stolen. Sid yelled at the parking lot attendant "Didn't you have someone here all night?" "Easy, babe," the attendant said. "At midnight, it says on the sign there, the lot's closed and unattended, so the car owners keep it here at their own risk. Read it, babe. I hope your buggy was insured." "Was it?" Sid asked Bea. "I don't think so for theft," she said. "It was my sister's." "Well if it wasn't insured I'll pay your sis back whatever she would've got for it if it had been insured—bluebook value, and she can also rent one on me till the insurance comes through. It wasn't a new one, was it? Eh, what's the difference? Let's look at it positively: from now on you'll have to be dependent on me." "Maybe first thing we should do is call the police." "You're a genius. I'll drive you there and wait outside, as I don't want to get involved, if you can understand." He gave the attendant a twenty-dollar bill. For what? To keep his mouth shut, she supposed, for after the attendant and he had that little argument, the attendant said "Say, babe, aren't you Sid Anscott? I knew I recognized you, but in that hat and glasses and all, you fooled me a second. Those lenses for real?"

Sid's wife sits in the classroom listening to the lecture. What ever made him think he was interesting enough to listen to and with that squeaky voice, and me think I could go back to school after hating it all my life? "Plague, and the death of Pericles in four twenty-nine—that's B.C., B.C.—severely lowered Athenian morale," the teacher says. Someone knocks on the door. The whole class looks over to it and the teacher says "If that's anyone late again—yes? enter," after someone knocks again. The door opens. Her daughter and Jack Jenkins come in. Something's very wrong, she thinks. I bet Sid got into a car accident and died. She stands up. "Mommy," Sonya says and runs over to her and grabs her around the waist and presses her head to her breast. "Excuse me," the teacher says, "but what is going on?" Jenkins says to the teacher, while Margo's asking him "What is it, Jack, what's wrong?" "It's all right, sir, sorry for this little disturbance," and takes her arm as he rubs Sonya's shoulder and says "I've something dreadful to tell you, Margo, just the worst thing possible. I think we should step outside." "Daddy's dead," Sonya says.

The bag of groceries was beside her when she drove back to Sid's house. He's going to love what I got for him, she thought. She saw a jogger running past her going the opposite way and thought it's not beyond the realm of possibility that Sid might be jogging along here too. Twice before he was when she was driving back and both times she stopped and said something like "Like a lift, gorgeous?" He said no, but rather matter-of-factly—he was a serious jogger despite his being overweight and that he didn't jog more than two miles a day—"I better run the rest of the way home." The first time he said that, she said "If I drive you home I'll get into my sneakers and shorts and run with you for a mile." "No, really," he said, "I don't like to stop. All I want now is to finish my run, take a shower and have a big fat glass of water. See you," and he started to run. The second time she only said when he said he wanted to continue his run, "Whoops, forgot; see you at home," and drove off. Now she saw another man running in her direction from about a block away. Looks like Sid, she thought. Same red T-shirt. The shorts though—blue? He doesn't have blue shorts as far as she knows. She got nearer and saw the runner was too thin to be Sid. Then she turned the corner and saw a crowd in front of his house or the houses on either side of his.

Darling

"Darling?"

I go to her room, turn on the light, stand by her bed.

"Could you turn me over, please?"

I turn her over on her back.

"And get my pills?"

I go to the kitchen, turn the sink tap on and wait for the water to run cold.

"And don't forget a glass of water."

The water runs cold. I bring the pills and glass of water to her bed.

"I hope the water's cold."

I hold the pills out on my palm. She points to her mouth, sticks out her tongue. I put a pill on her tongue, hold the glass to her lips while I hold up her head with my hand. She swallows. Then the second pill and water. She nods. They're both gone. She opens her mouth to show me: all gone.

"Could you turn me over, please?"

I turn her over on her stomach. I turn off the light.

"Thank you."

In a minute she's snoring. I leave the room. I get the mail which has been pushed through the mail slot of the front door. Around noon she'll call me again.

"Darling?"

I go to her room and raise the shade. She's still on her stomach.
She can't turn over by herself though occasionally she still tries.
She can't walk. She can't sit up or lie on her side for more than a
few minutes without it causing her great pain. She never gets out
of bed.

"Could you turn me over, please?"

I turn her over and give her today's mail. From the kitchen I get
her soap, towel and basin of water so she can wash her mouth, face
and hands.

"And you know what else."

I get the bedpan out from under the bed. While she's on it I cook
all of today's food. I bring her a tray of food, take the bedpan out
from under her, empty the basin water into the bedpan and the bedpan into the toilet. I wash my hands. I help feed her what she can't
feed herself, give her her afternoon pills and water, go to the front
door and get the morning newspaper on the stairs of her building's
stoop. Most of the time it's on the sidewalk in front of her house
and only once a month is one of her two daily newspapers on her
front door mat. I give her the newspaper. While she reads it I take
away the opened mail, tray and basin with soap and towel, have my
lunch, wash the tray, eating utensils and bedpan, hang up the towel,
put the soap and basin into the cabinet under the kitchen sink, separate the bills from the correspondence and ads in the mail, put the
ads into the kitchen garbage pail, the correspondence into a box in
her living room desk and make out and have her sign the monthly
checks for the grocer, druggist, doctor, utility and telephone companies and newspaper delivery service and place the last check under
the doormat. I put away all the things I washed, do today's shopping
and give the grocer and druggist their checks, return to the house
and put away all the things I bought and get the afternoon paper at
the front door. It's been carefully rolled up and bound with a rub-
berband and left on the doormat. I give her the paper. After she finishes it I put both newspapers on the pile of newspapers in the
kitchen corner. Twice a month I tie the newspapers into three or
four stacks and set them in front of the house with the week's
garbage. I turn on her bedroom light and pull down the shade. I
turn her over and turn off the light. She'll sleep on her stomach till
around six.

"Darling?"

I go to her room and raise the shade. It's nearly dark.

"Could you please turn me over?"

I turn her over, heat her supper, turn on the light, give her her pills, water and supper, help feed her, take away the tray, pull down the shade, give her the bedpan, book she's been reading and needlework, have my supper in the kitchen, clean the tray, eating and cooking utensils, take away the bedpan and empty and clean it, put away everything I cleaned, put her book and needlework back on the dresser, turn her over and shut the light.

"I think tomorrow you'll have to bathe me and change the bed."

Of course tomorrow I will. She doesn't have to remind me. I sponge bathe her and change her bed every three days unless she's had an accident, and then it's every three days from the day of the accident. She hardly ever has an accident. The last was three months ago. Before that, six months ago. Before that, I don't know. I wasn't here. I never asked. She wouldn't tell me besides. I was living with my wife and child in another city at the time. Why'd I ever leave them? Because my wife threw me out. Said if I couldn't provide for them I couldn't live with them. Said they'd get more from welfare by living without me than I ever gave them when they lived with me. I tried to earn enough to stay. For a while I had three jobs at once. But minor jobs, poor-paying jobs. In the morning I worked as a life model for a group of artists. In the afternoon as a sweater salesman in the men's section of a department store, but I got fired when I tried sticking some of the store's money into my pocket. On weekends I cleaned up the laboratories of a university's science building, but lost that job when they heard I'd been fired for stealing money from the department store. The artists kept me on despite knowing of my theft, but it wasn't enough wages for my family to live on. I went to several cities to find a well-paying full-time job, thinking that if I got one I'd get a nice apartment and have my family move in with me. But I never found any other work than part-time modeling for poor artists and cleaning up labs and such for universities and churches that didn't pay very much. Eventually I landed in this city. I answered a newspaper ad the day I arrived: *Young man to help elderly woman. Room and board plus adequate pay.* I called her with one of the last coins I had. She said come right over. There were three other applicants when I got here, two not that young so they were disqualified from the job. The third was much bigger and stronger than I, but too young and good-looking, she said. She told him he wouldn't stay the month: "You'll use my place as a flophouse till you catch the eye of a pretty counter girl, then leave me high and dry without even a day's notice." I was hired on the spot, given the

room next to hers. Besides all the duties I mentioned, I do the laundry, see the doctor in and out of the house, and answer her call to me
every night around ten.

"Darling?"

I go to her room, turn on the light, turn her over on her back.

"My evening pills, if you don't mind?"

I bring her the pills without water, I don't know why. Maybe so
she'll have reason to fire me. I don't know if I want to be fired, but I
think I do. This drudgery. I've had the job for seven months. This
loneliness. If she fired me I might find a more interesting job, one that
would pay me enough to afford an apartment and send for my wife
and child. But I don't have the courage to quit, as not only wouldn't I
be entitled to unemployment benefits but there's a good chance my
next job would be even worse than this.

"You intentionally forgot the water."

I nod. She's right. Why try to fool her? I go to the kitchen, again
let the water run cold. But no. I turn the warm water tap on, and
bring her a glass. She drinks it with the first pill.

"It's warm. Now you know I like it cold. What's got into you
tonight?"

I raise my shoulders, go to the window and raise the shade.

"You know I like the shade down when it's dark."

I lower the shade.

"The cold water, please?"

I go to the kitchen.

"You forgot the glass."

I return to her room, take the glass from her hand.

"Only half a glass of cold water. I already took the first pill with
the warm."

I go to the window.

"Please don't raise the shade again."

I empty the glass onto the floor.

"Please clean that up."

I go to the utility closet for a mop, leave the glass on a shelf and
return to her room.

"Please don't forget the cold water. I want to go to sleep."

I turn off the light.

"Not before I've had my pill."

I turn on the light, turn it off and on repeatedly.

"Please?"

I leave the light on.

"The cold water?"

I begin mopping the floor.

"First the cold water."

I get the glass from the utility closet, go to the kitchen, bring her a glass of cold water and spill it over her bed.

"You did that intentionally. Now you'll have to change my bed. Also my gown. And you still have to get me half a glass of cold water. And then finish mopping this floor. That's all you have to do. Besides turning me over and shutting off the light."

I turn her over.

"I didn't mean for you to turn me over right now."

I turn her over on her back.

"And for mercy's sake, don't shut off the light now."

I shut off the light.

"I said 'For mercy's sake, don't shut off the light now.'"

I turn on the light. I mop the floor. While I'm mopping she says "All right, finish mopping the floor. At least get that out of the way. And once that's done, let me repeat for the last time what you still have to do, though I don't want you to start doing them till I tell you to. First of all, get me half a glass of cold water. Second, get clean sheets and a clean nightgown and make the bed and change me and then turn me over, turn off the light and go to sleep yourself. No, you can do what you want in your own room after you've done all those things, but first get all those things done."

I finish mopping the floor. I go to the kitchen and bring her half a glass of cold water. She drinks the water down with the second pill.

"Good. Now the linens and gown. But don't forget to return the mop."

I wring the mop out above the utility sink, hang it up in the utility closet, get a broom from that closet and sweep up the kitchen. I continue sweeping into the hallway and then into her room. I sweep under her bed.

"Please don't sweep under my bed. You'll dirty the bedpan."

I sweep the side of her bed, the blanket over her bed, the sheet across her shoulders.

"Please get the clean bed linen and gown."

I return the broom to the utility closet, get a dustpan from the closet and with my hands and feet push onto it the piles of dirt I left in the two rooms and hallway I swept in, empty the dustpan into the kitchen garbage pail, put the dustpan back on its closet hook, get two clean sheets and pillowcases out of the linen closet and return with

them to her room. I begin changing her bed with her in it. It's something she taught me how to do from her bed the first day I got here,
and I've been able to do it without her instructions ever since. After
rolling her from one side of the bed to the other to get the old sheet
off and new sheet on, I tuck in the top sheet, change the pillowcases,
lift her head, stick the two pillows underneath and gently lower her
head to the pillows.

"Finally you do something right. Thank you. Now the blanket and
my gown if you don't mind."

I raise the shade.

"Please lower the shade."

I go to the kitchen, fill a glass with warm water, go to her bedroom
and empty the glass on her.

"Now you'll have to change the bed again. It's a good thing you
didn't put on the blanket. Please get another clean set of linens.
Though before you do, lower the shade."

I lower the shade. Then I raise and lower it repeatedly till she says
"Will you please keep it lowered. Then get the linens, change the bed
for the last time tonight, get my gown, help me change into it, turn
me over, place the blanket on top, dump all the old linens into the
washing machine, shut the light and get out of this room."

I go to the laundry room with the old linens, stick them into the
washing machine, add a cup of detergent, go to the adjoining cubicle,
turn on the hot and cold water spigots of the cubicle's utility sink
which is attached by long rubber hoses to the washing machine, and
return to the laundry room and start the machine.

"Darling?"

I go to my room and sit on the bed. On my dresser is an empty
frame. Yesterday I removed the photograph of my wife and child
from the frame and tore it up. Then I began putting the photograph
back together and have half of it done now. It's like a picture puzzle
which is getting easier and easier to solve. I have most of my son's
face, none of my wife's, all of her knees, calves, ankles, both her socks
and shoes, and all the grass they're sitting on. When I get the photo
together again I'll cover it with cellophane tape and stick it back in
the frame.

"Darling?"

I throw the frame against the wall. It splits in two, the glass shatters on the floor. Of course I'll never be able to get the glass together
again, while the frame I can. I get a hammer and nails from the tool
chest in the garage and start to fix the frame.

"Darling?"

I go to her room.

"I hope you're not planning to use that thing on me."

I forgot I was holding the hammer. I return it to my room, go to the kitchen, bring her a glass of water and place the water to her lips while I hold out the pills.

"I already took my pills, thank you."

I forgot that too. I return the pills and water to the kitchen, dry the glass and put it back into the cupboard, get the mop out of the utility closet and begin mopping her bedroom floor.

"You've already done that."

That's right, I have. I raise the shade.

She shakes her head.

I pull down the shade and turn off the light.

"Darling?"

I turn on the light and turn her over.

"Not yet, please."

I turn her over on her back, get fresh linen from the linen closet and begin changing her bed.

"That's fine. Very good. You know how to do this extremely well. I'm sure you'll be able to get a hospital orderly or nursing home job any time you want, just by the way you change a patient's bed."

I finish changing the bed and shut off the light.

"Not before I'm in a fresh gown, on my stomach and covered up."

I turn on the light, sit her up, slip off her gown, bring the gown, linen and mop to the laundry room, take the washed linen out of the washing machine and stick it into the dryer, put the gown, used linen and detergent into the washing machine, start both machines, return the mop to the utility closet and get a nightgown out of her dresser. As I'm pulling the nightgown over her I look at her chest. She has many brown blotches there, a new growth, long scars on her neck and back from her last operation when she had several growths and some muscle removed. She's still very ill. The doctor told her she'll never again be able to leave a bed. She never speaks directly of her illness or incapacity, though she's often mentioned how much she misses taking walks and just being well. I hug her. I want to hug her tighter, but fear it might hurt her and even cause injury. I cry on her shoulder and she pats my back.

"There, that's okay. This job can get you down sometimes—I know. And I'm not getting any better to look at or easier to handle. And what I say can occasionally get anyone down. You're very sensitive in many ways. It's not healthy for you to be in this kind of work, though I suppose it's better for the people you take care of. You're a little eccentric at times as we all probably are, but deep down you're very kind. Just try and deal with me and my situation the best way you can."

I kiss her shoulder and cheek, finish dressing her for sleep, lie her on her back, turn her over on her stomach, cover her up and tuck in the top sheet and raise the shade.

"Please lower the shade. Leave it up then. What harm will it be but a little morning light waking me up sooner than I planned. I'll simply pull the covers over my head and fall back to sleep that way."

I pull down the shade.

"Keep it down if you wish."

I raise the shade.

"It's fine that way too."

I turn off the light.

"Goodnight, darling."

I turn on the light and lower the shade.

"Then I'll sleep with the light on and shade down."

I raise the shade, lower it slowly, tear it down and kick it around and pick it up and smash it against the windowsill.

"If you're through, I'll again say goodnight."

I tear the shade into many pieces, toss them around the room, get the broom from the utility closet, sweep up the shade pieces and dump them into the garbage pail in the kitchen, sweep up the broken glass in my room, dump the glass into my wastebasket and empty the basket into the garbage pail, bring the broom back to the utility closet and return to my room with the basket.

I work on my photograph. I find my wife's head. I haven't found her neck yet, so I've no place to put the head. In the photograph my son sits on my wife's lap, his body concealing her belly and chest. I find her neck attached to her shoulders, place this piece and the head on the bottom half of the photograph I've put together so far. The photograph's now complete for my purpose. I get a roll of cellophane tape from the desk in the living room and tape the front of the semi-complete photograph.

"Darling?"

I go to her room, reach down for the shade string, reach up for the string, remember there is no shade, turn off the light, return to my room and tape the back of the photograph.

"Darling?"

I go to her room with the roll of tape and fasten several strips over her mouth.

"Dlung?"

I turn on the light and return to my room.

"Darling?"

I go to her room, turn off the light, stand above her bed and look down at the back of her head made visible by the streetlamp light.

"Turn me over, please?"

I turn over the bed.

"Ring the doctor, please?"

I call the doctor, sit by the front door till I hear his car pull up, open the door as he rings the bell. He sets down his bag, gives me his coat and hat, goes into her room with his bag, comes out without it.

"She's had an attack. And broken a bone in the fall. I'm afraid it looks very bad." He calls for an ambulance.

I put on his coat and hat and leave the house. I stand in front of her building. The air's cold. The sky seems empty of stars. Both curbs are packed with parked cars. The doctor's is the only car double-parked, its emergency lights flashing. An ambulance pulls into the street with its siren on and double-parks behind the doctor's car. The siren's turned off. The two ambulance men run around to the back, pull out a stretcher and go into the woman's house with it. They come out bearing the woman on the stretcher. The doctor, wearing one of the woman's fur coats, walks beside her holding her hand.

"Wait."

The bearers stop sliding the stretcher into the ambulance. The doctor says push it all the way in as they have to get to the hospital fast.

"Wait."

"Okay. Do as she says. Wait for a second, but no more."

The woman beckons me to her with her finger. A bearer braces up the back half of the stretcher which extends out of the ambulance's rear door. The other bearer lights up two cigarettes and sticks one between the first bearer's lips. The doctor rests the woman's hand on her chest, takes his hat off my head and brushes it off. The woman takes my hand in hers.

"Don't forget to turn off all the lights. And shut and lock all the windows. And make sure the oven and all the stove burners are off. And the furnace is switched off. And all the electrical plugs are pulled out of the walls. And all the faucets are turned off tight. Then leave the house and lock the door. But *leave* the house. Drop the keys through the mail slot. I'll have the doctor phone the newspaper delivery service and post office to temporarily suspend service. He also took my keys and left your week's wages and two weeks' severance pay on my dresser. You may take my valise if you feel it'll be of more use to you than your own. It has my initials on it so I suggest you blacken them out. If I survive all this and am discharged from the hospital, I'm going to place a notice in the newspaper for a man needed to help an elderly woman. I'll stress that he be middle-aged and reasonably educated and strong, and this time I'll insist on references I can verify. I don't think I'll be confined so long that by the time I'm discharged you'll be middle-aged, so you needn't apply for the job if you see the ad. Goodbye."

She lets go of my hand. The doctor puts a note under his car's windshield wiper, signals the bearers to slide the stretcher all the way into the ambulance and for me to give him back his coat. He hands me the fur coat, puts his own coat on, climbs in after her, sits next to her, puts on his hat and adjusts it and takes her wrist pulse. The bearers step on their cigarettes, climb in front, turn on the siren and the ambulance drives off. I watch its revolving roof light till it's just a blinking speck in the distance. Then it disappears. I look up. The sky still seems empty of stars.

I go into her house, hang up her coat, put on my jacket, take the money off the dresser and stick it into my pocket. She didn't include half of the two-weeks-per-year vacation pay for the seven months I worked, but I'm lucky to get what I did. I remove the shade from my bedroom window and put it on hers. I lift up the bed, make it, pick the pieces of cellophane tape off the floor, pull down the shade, pull out the lamp and radio plugs, shut off the light and go to the kitchen, put the pieces of tape into the garbage pail, make three stacks out of the corner pile of newspapers, bind them with cord and cut the cord with the scissors I get out of the utility drawer, return the cord and scissors to the drawer, carry the pail and newspaper stacks outside and leave them in front of the house, go to the laundry room and take the first batch of linens out of the dryer and fold them up, take the nightgown and second batch of linens out of the washing machine and stick them into the dryer, turn the dryer on, put the folded linens back into the linen closet, turn off the hot and cold water spigots of the utility sink in the cubicle, pull out all the electrical plugs in the living room, my bedroom and kitchen, and make sure the faucets in the bathroom and kitchen are turned off tight.

I go to my room and try to piece together the top half of the photograph. The last piece I insert to make the top half complete shows a barn on a hill with part of a mountain behind it. I tape both sides of the top half, tape the two halves together to make the photograph complete, nail the frame together, put the photo into the frame, make my bed, dust the room with an undershirt, put the roll of tape back into the living room desk, get my valise out of my closet, take it outside and leave it on top of the newspaper stacks, get my toothbrush out of the bathroom holder and the woman's valise from the hallway closet, put my clothes, toothbrush, framed photograph, book and wallet inside the valise, zip it up, get paint, paintbrush and turpentine from the paint rack in the garage, shut the furnace off in the garage and lock the garage door from the inside, black out the woman's initials with the paint, moisten the undershirt with turpentine and clean the brush with the shirt, return the paint, brush and turpentine to the paint rack and hammer and unused nails to the garage tool chest, put the shirt into the furnace, take the gown and linens from the dryer and fold them up, pull out the electrical plugs of the washer and dryer, put the linens into the linen closet and gown into her dresser, shut and lock all the windows, turn off all the lights, leave the house with the valise, lock the front door and drop the keys through the mail slot.

I walk downstairs and away from the house. Halfway up the street I remember I didn't check to see if the oven and stove burners were off. I run back to the house with the valise, go around to the back and look through the kitchen window. Two burners I used to heat up her supper are still on. I put the valise down, find a large flat stone and wedge it between the window sash and sill and with all my might I try prying the window open. The window springs up and the pane breaks from the force of the window hitting the lintel. The wind knocks a napkin holder off the kitchen table as I'm pushing the glass chips off the sill. The holder lands on the floor. A paper napkin falls out, floats above the stove, lands on one of the lit burners, ignites, one part of it quickly disintegrating while the burning part flies higher and ignites a window curtain. By the time I climb through the window, a kitchen cabinet has caught fire. I spray water on it from the sink faucet, but now the wall is on fire. I leave the kitchen through the broken window, pick up the valise and am running to the fire alarm box on the street when I hear sirens and see fire trucks turn the corner and pull up in front and behind the doctor's car. A fireman pushes me aside so the hose won't be dragged over my feet. Another fireman breaks open the front door and goes into the house, comes out and yells "Nobody's home from what I can tell." I stand across the street with a crowd of people and watch the firemen try to put the fire out and the house burn to the ground. The firemen pull in their hoses and leave. The entire crowd but a next-door neighbor leaves. A policeman stands guard in front of the debris.

"Terrible," the neighbor says to me and goes into her house.

I pick up the valise and walk several blocks till I come to the avenue. The avenue leads to the boulevard that leads to the highway that takes one out of town. About two miles away the highway hooks up with the superhighway that goes across the entire country, one of its last exits being the city my wife and child live in, the one I left nearly a year ago. Maybe my wife will take me back. I'll promise to work very hard, never steal from a store, try and get three jobs again if that's what it takes to keep us going, even four if I can. A car comes along. I stick out my thumb.

"Where to?"

But what for? I've most of my seven months' wages, so I can afford to take a plane. Why lose time on the road when I can be home tomorrow and already looking for a job? My savings aren't much but enough for us to live on for a couple of months if it takes that long to find work. If it takes longer, she'll throw me out. I know her well. I wouldn't blame her one bit. A man should provide for his wife and child, no matter how tough it is for him to get and hold a job. I smile my thanks to the driver, wave him on, cross the avenue and wait for a hitch or bus to the airport. But it's late and by daybreak no other cars have come.

The
Frame

➤

I go into an art gallery and framing shop. The door's unlocked. I'm
surprised. Last time I got something framed here a woman let me in
with a buzzer. And when I came back to pick up the framed work she
let me in with a buzzer. A different woman sits behind a long table at
the end of the room. "Yes," she says on the phone, nodding at me, "I
tried to get it. . . . No, it was the wrong color but the right size. . . .
Uh-huh. Uh-huh. Yes, but lookit, a customer just walked in, so. . . .
Uh-huh." I'm comparison-shopping. There's another art gallery and
framing shop several blocks closer to my apartment. I came downtown to buy tofu at a natural foods store a few doors from this shop
and to see about getting this—what would I call it?—framed. A photocopy. A friend of mine in Maine does photocopies as art. This one's
of a heron's feather. She wrote on the matting "Feather of a Heron—
to Jay Weiss." I can't get one of the standard picture frames at an
odds and ends store for it, since the matting is a nonstandard size.

The woman says on the phone "It happened two weeks ago, I
didn't plan it. It just happened." The look she gives me says "Please
bear with me, I can't get off the phone." She's physically deformed.
Her chest. She almost has no neck. It's sunk into her chest or her
chest has risen above her neck. That's not accurate. She reminds me
of my sister. She's about twenty years older than my sister was when
she died fourteen years ago, but my sister—no. I was going to say my
sister looked as old as this woman. She looked unhealthy since she

330

was ten, then very sick, then at twenty-five, the last year of her life, deathly sick, but she never looked older than she was. The woman's deformed like my sister was. At least it seems so, in that sitting position, the way my sister would sit: top half of her body bunched up. Something. The bones of her chest way up, her back humped. With my sister it was something to do with the series of operations she had on her spinal cord and through her back and chest. I've an idea of what this woman's body will look like when she stands, if she can. My sister in her last years could stand, but only with the aid of crutches. The crutches were stretched out to the sides, like legs spreading to a split, when she just stood in place. When she walked, the crutches were thrown forward one at a time. And metal braces, not crutches. I knew the words then. I'll never forget the sounds. I still hear them occasionally in the school I teach at. The clink-clink of a disabled but not deformed young man using metal braces to walk down the hall past my open office door. Sometimes we look at each other through my door and nod or I say "How you doing?" or "Hi." "That's right," the woman says on the phone, "but it wouldn't have been like that if you'd made him sign first. . . . It's true, it's ridiculous to argue—I won't even go into how often I warned you. But really, Helene, I have to go. The customer. He's getting impatient."

"No I'm not."

She mouths to me *It's okay,* says on the phone "I'll call you back, goodbye," and hangs up. "Sorry. Can some people talk? Oh boy. That one—well anyway, what can I do for you?"

"I came in to see about a frame for this." I feel sad. I did want to comparison-shop. To see which frame store's price was the lowest for a frame of the same quality. I'm taking the matted photocopy out of my book bag. It's a snug fit. I'm doing it carefully. "It's not a drawing. I actually don't know what to call it, though I'm sure you do, but it is paper and matted and I don't want to scratch or dirty it when I take it out." She's sitting, watching me slowly inch the matting out. But if the price seems at all reasonable, even a little above reasonable, I'll pay it because the woman reminds me so much of my sister. Because she looks like Kathy—her body. Face too: slightly—how can I put it?— frozen on one side and disjointed. Because if Kathy were alive maybe she'd be working in a place like this and I'd come in, customer she never saw before, and I'd want to give her my business to keep her in business or just working at this job and making sales if the store's not hers, just as I do with this woman now. All that's pretty confused, but I'd want to do something like that. To keep her involved with people in a decent business or job. Because without this store her life must be fairly lonely and sad. That true? Kathy wasn't lonelier or sadder than most people when she could still get around. She knew people in the neighborhood. She went to block parties and meetings. People took her to movies and concerts and museums and a few times on weekend vacations at their country homes or resorts out of town. She converted to Christianity near the end of her life and was very active in the church a few blocks from where she lived with my parents, and for one year was in its choir. She had real friends. People liked her. She was nicknamed the mayor of the block. Dozens of people came to her funeral and then to pay their respects to my parents and me when we sat in mourning for several days. The matted photocopy is out. It has a sheet of white paper over it, taped to the back of the matting on top by the woman who made the photocopy. I pull back the paper. "I'd like the least expensive frame possible for it."

She looks at it. "Black?"

"Oh, yes, black, no other color. It'd be right for it, right?"

"It's what I'd choose. You don't mind a very thin frame? It would be the cheapest."

"Thin as any black frame you have. It couldn't take more."

"Let's see then." She gets up and turns around. She doesn't need braces or crutches to stand. She faces many quarter-sections of frame models hanging on the wall. Black, brown, natural, gold and silver trim, fretted, metal, plastic, wood. "I know it's here. A lady ordered two yesterday, much larger frames than yours. Two by three almost. Maps." She's fingering through several black frame models. Her back's like Kathy's. Crooked on one side, the left. I forget which side Kathy's was. Right, I think. Left. I can't picture it. She finds a thin black frame model. "That one's just fine," I say.

"Let me see it against your artwork," she says. She fits the model over a corner of the matting.

"Fine," I say. "Looks nice."

She looks at the back of the model. *1.50* it says. A foot? Square inch? Is that a dollar-fifty? She runs a pencil down the second column of a chart on the table, then two boxes across. All the boxes have numbers in them and the further down and further across, the larger the numbers are.

"Honestly, this one's fine," I say. "The matting's okay? Not dirty?"

"Just a second." She multiplies some numbers on a pad. I'm looking at her face. She's about thirty years older than Kathy was when she died. She wears large loop earrings. Gold. Hoops with a diameter of about two and a half inches. Kathy wore large hoop earrings but never that large. Her ears also were pierced. Got it done in an earring store when she was past twenty. She wanted to get them pierced long before then. I remember her saying something like "You'd think with all the touch-and-go operations I've been through, a simple ear piercing wouldn't bother me, but it did. I was absolutely petrified." "Fourteen seventy-five," the woman says.

"With the glass?"

"You wanted it with glass, didn't you?"

"Sure. It's just it's so cheap. You see, last frame I bought here was smaller and made of brown wood. An embroidery, I think you'd call it, of three horses which used to hang above my bed when I was a boy and which— Well, when I was in New York a few months ago my mother showed it to me and asked what had happened to the glass and frame on it. She'd found it in my old drawer under some things of mine when all this time for years she thought I had it or it was lost."

The woman's writing up the bill. "That so? An embroidery of horses? Here?"

"An old kind, mounted on a wood board. I think she probably got it fifty years ago. I didn't want to tell her I'd taken the frame and hid the embroidery more than fifteen years ago when I wanted to frame something I'd bought for a woman I was seeing at the time. I did things like that then. You learn. Anyway, the frame I bought here cost sixteen dollars plus tax and was about two inches shorter on each side and the wood was just as thin. There's something I'm maybe not seeing, but I don't mind. The price seemed fair then, and this one seems even fairer. Not only compared to one another, but by New York prices. I haven't lived here that long, but these frames are the only things I've bought in Baltimore that seem cheaper than the same things in New York, except the newspapers."

She finishes adding up the bill. "I don't remember that other piece. Horses?"

"Three of them only from their necks up sticking their heads through two stable windows, but seen from inside the stable. And I know how you operate," I say, taking out my wallet.

"You do?"

"The other woman who took care of me asked for half the framing price as a deposit."

"You don't have to. Your name and address?"

"You send a card when it's ready, I know, Jay Weiss. Nineteen East Twenty-ninth. But you don't want a deposit?"

"If you want. I don't care."

"Five dollars do?"

"Fine."

I put a five-dollar bill on the table between us, she writes "$5 dep" on the bill, tears the bill off the metal holder it's on and gives me the duplicate.

"In a month or so, right?"

"Yes. Thank you."

"You're welcome, and thank you."

She smiles, I smile, and as I turn to leave a man comes into the store. We pass each other. "I came back to look at that poster again," he says. I turn around. The walls have drawings and prints on them but are mostly filled with framed and unframed posters. Victorian men on bicycles, 1930s movie posters, Picasso and Miró museum retrospectives and art shows. The man's wearing a new trenchcoat and cowboy boots. The woman walks around the table to a large black portfolio leaning against a wall. She walks with a limp. Kathy did also from the time she was ten till she had to use braces to walk when she was around twenty-two. She was bedridden the last half year of her life, first at home where my mother took care of her, the last two weeks in a hospital. I was at her bedside when she died. I held her hand when she died. We were alone. The door was shut. It was a private room. I shut the door because I wanted to say things to her without anyone seeing or hearing me. Like "Kathy, you'll get better. Kathy, I love you. Kathy, don't worry. It's rough going now but I swear you're getting well. Kathy, it's Jay. Is there anything you need or that you want to say?" She said nothing that last day. I was holding her hand when she died. I didn't hear a death rattle. Someone told me there's always one, but I didn't hear it. I held her hand. The right, the left. Mostly the right because that was the one nearest the side of the bed I was best able to sit on. The other had life-supporting equipment and monitoring machines. I was looking at her face. I'm so sad now I'm about to cry. I held her hand, was holding her hand, which had been holding my hand a little when it just let go—no, I was holding her hand and felt that it wasn't holding mine when before it was, so I looked at it, squeezed it to feel if it would squeeze back. It didn't. I didn't let go of her hand. Her eyes were still half-closed as they'd been for most of the day. I looked at them. There didn't seem to be any movement in them when there was before. A dull movement before but movement. A blink every now and then when there wasn't any now. I had a feeling she had died. I put her hand by her side. I went out of the room, looked up and down the hall for a nurse, ran back into the room and got up close to her face. It was the same. Eyes half-closed. Tubes in her nose, but no sign of breathing. I went into the hall. A patient was walking for exercise. I'd seen him doing that many times before. I said "Please walk to the nurses' station and get the nurse." He said "It'll take me twenty minutes the way I go." "Stay here then and don't let anyone inside but a doctor or nurse." "I don't know if I can stay in any one place for very long." "Please," I said, "my sister. Don't be alarmed but I think she just died." "I'm so sorry," he said. "Of course I'll stay." I ran down the hall to the nurses' station.

"Is there anything wrong, sir—Mr. Weiss?" the woman says.

I look at her. The man, kneeling beside the opened portfolio on the floor, looks up at me.

"No, I was just thinking. Of my—why, don't I look all right?"

"The light isn't what it should be for this kind of store, but you look as if you suddenly lost all your color."

"No, I'll be okay."

The man's still looking at me. Then he looks at the woman and pulls a poster out of the portfolio and stands.

"Thank you," I say.

"You're perfectly welcome," she says. She holds up the other end of the poster and looks at it with him. I leave the store. Just then the elevator door opened and my mother walked out of it and started down the hall.

The
Bench

➤

Each year when spring comes I do a lot of handyman work for the
row houses that line Wilmin Park Drive on the 2900 to 3300
blocks. Across from the 3100 block is a park bench and this spring
for about a month on the nice days I see this man push a stroller
with a baby in it to the bench and stay there for an hour or two
around the same time every afternoon. Sometimes he reads for a
few minutes or eats an orange while the baby sleeps or is quiet, but
usually he has the baby in his lap or stands it up on his thighs or
holds it in the air or feeds it some bottle or baby-jar food or keeps
it sitting up on the bench but always with a wide bonnet on or its
face out of the sun and he kisses and hugs it a lot and smiles and
talks to it a lot too, words I never hear, this baby of around six to
nine months. I've never seen a man so affectionate to his baby,
maybe not even a woman to her baby too. I mention him a few
times to some of the people I work for. Several times when he looks
our way as we talk or just my way if I'm working alone then and
sees us or me looking at him, he waves and we wave back or I wave
back alone and then he goes back to being so affectionate to the
baby.

Then one day he doesn't show up, but a nice sunny day, one I'd
think he would. And not the next nice day and the next nice day after
that. When he doesn't show up on the nice days for a couple of

weeks, I mention it to the homeowner I'm working for that day. "Remember that man with the baby on the bench—he was pretty tall and had kind of sandy hair—but there almost every afternoon or at least every afternoon when I worked around here?" and she says "Most certainly do. Hasn't been around for a while, I know. Something terrible—almost unspeakable—happened." I say "Yes?" and she says "He got mad one day, but I mean stark raving crazy mad—I got this from a woman I know who lives on his street and knew he spent some time on our park bench almost every day. Anyway, he got so mad that he shot his wife—because she made him mad or as a result of his getting that way—and killed her instantly— in their home—and is now up for trial and the baby's with his wife's sister. I didn't read anything about it in the papers, but this woman friend said it absolutely happened and that everything bad like that that happens in the city doesn't appear in the news. I thought I spoke about this with you."

"No, really—I'm shocked and surprised. I didn't think he'd do anything like that to his worst possible enemy. He had so much to lose, with that baby, and seemed so peaceful and affectionate; and with those spontaneous waves of his, to other people and myself, very nice."

A week later, the man I'm trimming bushes for says "Howard, you recall that strange man who used to spend the end of almost every pleasant afternoon on the bench there?" and I say "Yes sir. I heard something awful happened to his wife and child." "Something awful indeed. For a few weeks I was wondering why we didn't see him any- more—he had practically become a fixture on the drive. Then I'm talking to Bill Schechter"—someone else I work for—"but about something entirely different, when he says that the man's wife sud- denly got very sick and died in less than a month. And the man got so upset over it that he couldn't function normally and had to be institu- tionalized, and the baby, until the authorities can find a relative of the husband and wife willing to take her in, had to be placed in a tempo- rary home."

"No," I say, "that's terrible. And the baby's a girl? I heard some- thing much different happened, but both things couldn't be worse." "What did you hear?" he says and I tell him and he says "Oh no, Bill Schechter's brother lives two doors away from the family and that's what Bill's brother said."

About a month later in the supermarket I bump into one of the people I work for on Wilmin Park Drive. We start talking general-like and then she says "By the way, do you remember the young very neatly dressed man on the bench right across from my house who used to wave to us from time to time?" and I say "The one who was so nice to his baby—kissing and hugging her all the time? I heard." "Isn't it something? Because rarely do you see a man so openly adoring and attentive to his child, so you can just imagine how he, and of course his wife, felt after. And at the baby's funeral—my God." I say "What funeral?—I didn't hear about any baby dying," and she says "Oh yes. Bertha Arnold saw it in the *Evening Sun* and over TV. She put two and two together quite easily, she said, when she saw the photo of the man and read their address and the baby's age. He and his wife and their baby were in a rowboat they rented at Loch Maiden and the man's wife stood up, it was never said for what, and the boat capsized and the baby drowned."

I don't tell her what I've already heard about the man and his family, just look very shocked when I'm really not feeling that way because I'm wondering more what really did happen.

Just a few days later I'm doing work for a couple who live a block down from Mrs. Larkin who told me the drowning story. I ask if they've heard about the man who used to bring his baby to the park every spring day for about a month and who we talked about a couple of times and Mr. Radderman says "We thought you out of anyone would have known what happened to them because you get around so much," and I say "No sir, nothing, though I am curious, because when you see a man and his baby almost the exact same time almost every day and especially when he—" "His wife left him for a friend of his and took the baby with her. They lived just a short walk from him and after he went over there a few times to take the baby back, they took off and disappeared. We heard it from our top-floor tenant, who's a graduate student in the same department the man teaches in. He knew him and in fact from his window he used to see him sit on the bench with Olivia, the baby daughter, on some of those days. It's so sad. The professor must be heartbroken—not for his wife so much but the baby. Because in your life, Howard, have you ever seen a man so attached to his child? Sometimes, I was telling Mrs. Radderman, but just a silly joke, of course, it looked almost incestuous." I say "Never," and go back to fixing their front steps, looking out to talk to their tenant who might show, but he never does.

Two months later when I'm painting the porch deck of Mrs.

Cottrell, who lives a few doors down from Mrs. Larkin, I see what I'm sure is the same man on the bench. He's alone, no stroller, a book and paper bag next to him on the bench, staring at the ground for about an hour or so or maybe asleep, because either his eyes are naturally very narrow—I forget from two months ago—or closed. When he gets up and from the park side of the street passes the house, I want to wave to him but he doesn't look my way.

He's there the same time the next day, which is around the same time he used to come with his daughter. Now the sun's higher up and much stronger than it was in the spring, which could be why he wears one of those white sailing caps today, not realizing yesterday he had to. But everything else is much the same as it was when he came here in the spring: has a book, though this time he reads it for an hour, which I don't ever remember him doing then, and takes an orange out of a paper bag instead of the tote bag he had attached to the stroller. He looks up at the sun and a passing plane a few times, but mostly just stares at the trees some distance across from him and occasionally at the cars and joggers and the few people who stop in the park to let their dogs loose.

He comes back the next day. I'm at the top of a ladder against Mrs. Cottrell's house, trimming the second-floor window frames. Suddenly she's looking out the bedroom window I'm working on, checking to see how good a job I'm doing, I suppose, or just making sure I'm working at what she's paying me for. I nod to her, she starts speaking to me while pointing to the park, then she mouths "Wait," since I can't hear her through the closed window, and leaves the room. Next she's standing at the foot of the ladder and says "Howard, excuse me for interrupting you, but what I was saying upstairs was isn't that man on the park bench the one who used to come months ago with his baby every day—the baby who I was told was in a car crash with the man's wife where they both died?" I say "Is that what they say happened, Mrs. C.? Because I've heard a half-dozen stories about what happened to him and his family," and she says "What else did you hear?" and I say "Too many to remember, but all different," and she says "Oh, if I only had the nerve to ask him. Not point-blank but around it. But pity no matter what it was, don't you think? Of course you do, because he loved that little darling. That was obvious in every one of his gestures."

She goes into the house, I go back to my trimming, but by now I'm so curious about what really did happen if anything that when the man gets off the bench and starts for the street in my direction, I put down my brush and climb down the ladder, not so much to ask him anything directly but just to get a sense of what happened by what he might say in passing or the way he looks. I take off my gloves as if I'm done for the time being, scratch some dried paint off my arms, and as he's passing the house I look up and say "Hey there, how's it going?"

"Can't complain," he says, still walking.

"And how's that lovely little daughter of yours?" and he stops and says "What lovely little daughter?"

"Well, I don't know if it was a daughter or son—all I'm saying is the baby you used to come to that park bench with almost every nice spring day for a month. We all admired you for the way—"

"I never had a baby," and I say "You didn't?"

"Never even came close to having one. I was engaged once—a century ago—but we didn't get married and certainly never had a child."

"This is really funny, but you didn't used to bring a little baby there—no more than six to nine months old at the time? In a yellow snowsuit she had when it was still a bit cool out? And then in just pants"—he's shaking his head—"or some outfit I don't know what it's called, where the feet don't come out of it and it zippers all the way up, and a sun bonnet and white sweater and maybe a little blanket?"

"Never."

"In a stroller. Rolled her there, stayed for about two hours, usually put her back in it when you were leaving or sometimes carried her while you pushed the stroller? I mean, I never saw anyone who looked after and was so affectionate to his baby, that's the only reason I'm mentioning it."

"Honestly, you have the wrong man."

"I'd almost swear it was you. I'm not saying it was now, but even Mrs. C. who owns this house and who just saw you would swear, I'm almost sure, that that man with the baby was you."

"It sounds very nice. In ways I wish I were him. But I never had a child. And since I don't plan to get married, I doubt I ever will have one, I'm afraid. Nice talking to you."

I look for him the next day and then a couple of days the next week when I'm working on the drive, and then for the one or two days a week I work around the drive till the fall, but I don't see him again. I suppose I can get the real story somehow by asking a few people on the drive what else this man's university student or neighbor or brother of a neighbor or whoever it was who knew him might have heard about him. But after that last talk with him, and because I feel I did enough damage by maybe forcing him away from this part of the park, I decide I've been nosy enough.

For
a Man
Your Age

＿

"I'm twenty years older than you," she says. "I mean twenty years younger. I don't know if it's a problem for you but for me it is."

"Isn't for me."

"That's what I said. That it wouldn't be—might not. And it's not that I don't like you."

"Or that I love you."

"See? That particularly scares me. Because I know you do. While I don't love you. Like you, yes. But twenty years. More. Almost twenty-one. You were born in May, I'm in November."

"Let's call it an even twenty-one."

"Even twenty-one. It's so much. Tell me what you really think about it."

"What do you think? That I wish it wasn't a problem with you and that we should continue seeing each other despite the difference of our ages."

"See each other perhaps but not sleep with each other."

"See and sleep both. Or only sleep with each other. We can do everything in the dark."

"Don't joke. I'm in no mood."

"No, listen. You can come to my apartment or I to yours. The lights will be out in either. Let's say you come and ring my bell. Lights totally out, place pitch black, I'll open the door and you'll come in. If you don't remember the terrain I'll take your hand and guide you in and shut the door so no light from the stairway comes in. And then kiss you or we'll kiss and talk perhaps or no talk if that's not part of the bargain and then go to bed, everything in the absolute dark as it can get. That way we won't have to see each other."

"What about the public hallway light?"

"Okay. You ring my bell and shut your eyes. I'll shut mine, we'll both put out our hands, and I'll bring you in and shut the door. Then we'll go through what I said before till it's over and you can leave in the dark or in the light with our backs toward each other. Or I will if it's your apartment where all this is taking place."

"Doesn't sound like a bad idea, for a fantasy, but it won't work."

"Why, you don't like my lovemaking anymore?"

"No, I do, I do."

"Then not in the dark."

"No. Dark, light or one of those mini-watters on with a red shirt over the globe, our lovemaking was good. But you're forty-two, I'm not even twenty-one. I'm a half year from being twenty-one. So that's actually twenty-one and a half years difference, not twenty. Why'd I always think it was only twenty?"

"Maybe because I was always referring to it as twenty. Not to make it less. Only because what the hell's a year and a half mean in all that?"

"And if you were forty-three and a half to my twenty and a half, or I was nineteen and no half to your forty-two, that wouldn't make any more of a difference to you?"

"There is probably an extreme somewhere in age differences between couples. Thirty years difference when the woman or man's twenty. Again thirty years difference when the woman or man's thirty. So I suppose thirty years difference is the beginning of the extreme, except if the younger person's fifteen, boy or girl. Then it's probably five or ten years difference, and if the younger person's thirteen or fourteen, three or four years difference, though even with any of those I'm not sure."

"I don't agree. And I think that from tonight—I know that from tonight onwards—it has to be over with us, all right?"

"What can I say to complain?"

"Then you won't phone me, write or any of those things?"

"So it's both? No sleep or see? You don't even want to be friends?"

"Friends if we really need one another—in six months, maybe more. But I won't need you. I've my parents, and good friends. And you're a very nice man, very desirable too. There must be lots of women ten to fifteen years younger or older than you or the same age who'd love to have you as their lover, husband or friend. You should even get married and have the baby you say you always wanted so much before it's too late."

"Men can be fathers into their sixties and seventies."

"Not if your prostate's removed before then. Besides, you don't want your five-year-old kid wheeling you around an old-age home. You want to get down on the floor with it, run and play sports with it, dance with it at its wedding and so on, if it's a girl, and maybe even later play a little with your grandchild."

"Don't worry about me—I'm going to stay active until I'm eighty. I'll also dance with my son at his wedding if we feel like it. It just doesn't have to be a girl."

"No matter what, I can't get married and have a baby for at least six or eight years. I've too many things to do before then. I have to graduate college first. After that I want to move to New York and get a job as an editorial assistant in a publishing house somewhere while I write myself sick on weekends and early weekday mornings and late at night. I want to do all that while I'm young. I have to. Then, if one of my books sells or lots of my stories and some money's coming in or I'm starting to get established, I'll maybe settle in with someone and have a baby. So when I'm twenty-eight or twenty-nine. But no matter what happens, certainly not sooner."

"It could happen sooner. You could fall in love and the pressures from him might be too great. Who knows?"

"I won't. But if I do, and actually I probably will several times, I still won't get married or have a baby. I'll get rid of him, no matter how much it hurts, because I want to know many men. I want to be able to say 'All right, I'm experienced, or as much as I want to be before it starts working against me.' I also want to travel, and not necessarily with a man. That I can always do ten years from now."

"If you stayed with me you could do all of those."

"You're lying to yourself."

"You're probably right."

"You're already jealous of other guys I see and sometimes when I'm just doing nothing alone away from you, and we weren't really that serious as lovers."

"We almost were. Maybe for a while we definitely were. Obviously now we're not, but what is it?"

"Excuse me, but what is what?"

"You think I look too old for you? Act too old also, or both those or more?"

"No. You act young enough. Maybe too young for your age, but not for mine. Actually, sometimes the young way you acted kind of embarrassed me, though I'm sure it didn't bother anybody else."

"So I'll act older. Not as old as your father or like your father, but just older."

"I don't want you acting any way but what you are, not that you could be any other way. As for your looks, well, you don't look forty-two but you do look thirty-six or so, though don't ask me what's the difference. And your physique is good, but for a thirty-five-year-old man. Not one twenty-five or even thirty, which I think, if you want my preference, is the maximum age I'd like my man's body to look now."

"I don't get it. What could be the difference?"

"Your upper arm muscles, for instance, are huge, as are your pectoral and whatever those muscles are in back—the ones like water wings when they're flexed. But all of them, hard as they are and maybe too overdeveloped, like your pects, which if you continue exercising as you do will in a year be grotesque, are sagging somewhat. That disturbs me, what can I say? As great a shape as you're in, your body still seems to be starting to fall apart because of your age."

"I don't see it."

"It's true. Look at any twenty-five-to-thirty-year-old man at a pool next time, or even thirty-five, but not one overweight. Their pects, even when they're not developed, are a little higher, and if you see them in the shower, so are their testes by a bit. You can't stop that."

"Say you're right, which I'm not saying you are, how come you never said anything about it before?"

"How come? You kidding? Because I didn't want to mention it. I thought of it though, occasionally. Your body's the body of a man desperately trying to stay in shape and look much younger than he is, and that makes me sad in a way. Also your hair."

"I'm nearly bald, okay, but so are lots of twenty-five-to-thirty-five-year-old men. Blame my father. Even if when he was my age, though he said it came from wearing tight religious caps when he was a boy, he was completely bald on top."

"Baldness I can live with. Though again, everything else being equal and you gave me my choice of men, why wouldn't I choose one with a head full of thick hair? Wouldn't you if you had your choice of women who were in every respect alike except one who was much more beautiful than the rest?"

"I don't see how any two women could in every respect be alike except for being very beautiful."

"For argument's sake."

"For argument's sake, yes."

"Anyway, what I was talking before about your hair was the gray."

"So I've a little on my sides, so what?"

"On your back, shoulders, chest and also around your groin. There more than anyplace disturbs me about your hair. I don't know why. Maybe because I think that'd be the last place someone getting gray would get gray. And soon you'll be totally gray all over or close to it and it would seem strange in a way going with someone who's all gray, bald and desperately trying to make his body look like the body of a young man who lifts too many weights. You'll probably even get a heart attack from it."

"Chances are a lot better that I won't. I run and enough miles a day so that my heart and lungs are probably as good as any man who's twenty-five."

"Heart and lungs I can't see, the body I can. Anyway, why would you want to continue seeing a woman who thought all these awful things about you?"

"Why? Very simple, I'll tell you."

"Don't bother, because why wouldn't you want to see me? I'm twenty, no, twenty-one-plus years younger than you. Even if I don't work out, my body is still great. I haven't a line or sag on my face or anyplace. I'm still growing in fact. This year alone so far I've grown a quarter of an inch. I haven't a gray hair. No reading glasses either just because I might've reached, say, thirty-five, nor a tooth missing besides."

"That's because your dentin's impenetrable, which you were born with, so thank your genes and stars. As for my eyes, I'm lucky that's all that's wrong with them with the reading chores I've put them through in thirty years."

"Okay. Maybe you're right there. But everything about me is young and in perfect shape—that's my argument. There's no way I'll die of a heart attack in twenty years. My liver has to be a beautiful pink and its proper size because I've hardly taken a drink to your, what, maybe twenty-five years of drinking too much wine and liquor and some years heavily you said. I'm even so young that I still get pimples about once a month."

"There. Ask me why I'd go with a woman who still gets pimples."

"Because it means I'm still physically growing and changing, my glandular system particularly, and to a man your age, that might be attractive and even exciting. But you go on about my skin, I could talk more about yours and also your hair. It's aging, getting brittle, while mine is still soft and bouncy, even if I don't brush it for days. I know all this must sound shallow to you, but I find what a person physically feels and looks like to be important. But there are other things."

"Sex."

"You're very experienced, but you're not a young man in bed. You make love the way you do because you have to because of your age. One time and that's usually it, right? But a young man, if he ejaculates too quickly, can be right back at it. Maybe not with your experience or cooperativeness, though I've known some who have been as experienced as you or acted like it, but at least he's ready for more in fifteen minutes and right now that's the type I want to be sleeping with. Young, energetic, wants to try lots of things, and more in tune with my own energy, curiosity, stamina and so forth. Does all that make any sense?"

"Sure it does. I wish you would've complained sooner. It would've made this whole discussion unnecessary."

"I'm not complaining. I loved making love with you and have gotten as excited with you as I have with any man I've made love with who I didn't love. But I've lots of years before I want to settle in with someone who makes love like you."

"Anything else?"

"What I said wasn't enough?"

"My feet? Do they stink? My breath. Is it smellier than a man's half my age or even ten years younger?"

"No. You take good care of your teeth—a plus for you compared to some of the younger men I know—and you don't smoke anything and know how to get rid of the horrible alcohol breath. Your body smells nice too. Maybe you've more hair on your body than a younger man, which can catch the perspiration more, but you're clean, so it's no real problem. But you also in a way make me feel dumb at times—at least ignorant or near to because of everything you know from books and life and just reading the newspapers for twenty-five years. But then I get sort of exuberant when I think that in ten to twenty years I'll know as much if not more than you, and maybe for one reason because by that time your brains will have started to forget."

"It's a possibility. Though if I stay active and creative and don't drown my head in alcohol and have no serious accidents up there, I don't see why my brain capacities shouldn't even grow."

"Another thing is that I sometimes feel you think you've seen and felt it all or almost. I don't want to be intermittently tugging at your sleeve and saying 'Ooh wee, you ever see anything like it in the

world?' knowing you probably have and then pretending, for my
sake, it is interesting or exciting what I'm looking at or experiencing
for the first or second time. Also—"

"There's more?"

"You said you wanted to, but I'll stop."

"No, let's finish. Honesty? Facts of life? That's what I want? Sure
I do, or at least how much can it hurt?"

"Well, all those cultural things you try to turn me on to. I wanted
to turn you on to things too, but you were so set with everything you
liked that it was nearly impossible. Music and films, for instance."

"If you mean your new music—that heavy electric guitar and tom-
tom stuff that's been increasingly crowding the atmosphere for the
last fifteen years with its untrained bombastic voices and illiterate
lyrics, most of it's worthless. Worthless."

"But I don't think it is. I think a lot of it is great, as good as the
best ever, and outside of the younger teenage music, appealing and
meaningful and even poignant to people my or any age."

"Maybe it is, I don't want to be unfair. But I'm sure you'd appreciate my music more if you'd had some grounding in the classical and
really serious modern works. But that's my preference, I don't see
why it should be yours, and obviously one of the big differences
between us. As for films, I thought our tastes were pretty much the
same."

"They are. I forgot. Though for you it's mostly just entertainment
while for me a lot of it is art. But I used to love when we were in a
theater and I'd turn to you or you to me and we'd with just a look
know we both didn't like the movie or stage show and get up and go
before it was over. That kind of silent like-mindedness happened so
many times there and the pity's that it didn't in most other things
we did."

"Like reading."

"I love writers you hate. And I know it's because they're writing
about things closer to my age and past experience, and same with
your writers to you. Some we both like, but they're masters or poets,
so easy to like, or writing about eternal questions or the few things we
both experienced or want to know more about."

"We forgot food."

"What about it? I think we both like the same kinds, except for
the meats I won't eat and you do, but that was never a problem.
You're also a lot less into the junk thing than me, though you think
it's cute that I am. Really, I was partly raised on it, while you grew up
when there was almost no junk food and your mother, you even said,

strained your vegetables with a hand strainer, which of course my mother, who's almost your age, never would."

"But junk food's bad for you."

"They taste good though. But that sort of represents another thing we disagree on. You're so much into health in your own way and I simply haven't come to that point except for my staying away from chemically filled carcasses and dead crap like that."

"I'll give up all my meat for you."

"I know you're joking. But there is some truth in it, isn't there? And that's that you'd give up things you like for your woman while I don't want to give up anything for any man yet. But another thing is your mother. Nice as she is to me, she seems like my grand or great-grand—"

"Don't go overboard. 'Grandparent' should suffice. Just 'parent' would suffice also if you considered that some adults, like the possibility of myself, have children at a later age."

"Your possibly becoming a parent I don't want to go into. But I do want my man's parent to be around the same age as mine, so she can get along better or whatever the reason. Though how can she be when the man I'm with is the same age as my father minus two years? And talking about that, people have sometimes looked strangely at us because of it. I know I shouldn't be bothered by such things—that it's so bourgeois as you say for them to think that way. But I do get bothered by it sometimes, probably because I am young and as a result still unsure of myself in some ways, and I want to avoid those looks and talk."

"Those looks you can get walking with any man. Though I can see how it could bother you if you're in no way in love with that person."

"Listen, what it comes down to is I want to give myself more of a chance and time, okay? You seem more desperate to be mated now and from everything I said today, I'm not, agreed? And it's not only what I said but all the other things I didn't, all right? And I don't want to talk anymore about it, I just don't. It was nice, different, we had some terrific times, etcetera, and I know the break will be a lot more painful for you than me, but what can I say? You feel more deeply about me than I do you, that's all. And maybe I don't or couldn't because of the age difference—well of course that's one of the main reasons because that's what I've been saying all along, true? And I know I've contradicted myself a hundred times in almost everything I said, but in a discussion like this, who doesn't? And— excuse me but what was I saying before I started talking about contradicting myself?"

350 The Stories of Stephen Dixon

"I forgot."

"Your memory's not too hot also, but I'm only kidding."

"And yours? You're the one who forgot what you were saying after you got into that topic about deep and no feelings for me."

"Oh yes. I was saying that the break, more painful for you than me, etcetera, and I know why. You think because of your age you'll have little chance of meeting someone new. But for all I know there are many women and even some my age and maybe even younger who might want to be with you because of your age. Sure there are—plenty. But to me your real obstacle in future relationships is that because you've had so many affairs and breakups, you've become cynical about them and women and so they'll never work out or almost."

"Not so."

"Believe me, it's so. And maybe you really don't want, no matter what you claim, a longtime relationship—one ending in marriage and a baby."

"How can you say that? I'd marry you today and conceive with you tonight if you wanted and we could."

"You say you would but if I said yes, I'm sure you'd change your mind."

"Say yes then. Go on, say it."

"You know I won't. Not to you or any man, as I said, for six to eight years or more. Not that when I get married a man will have to ask me to. I can just as well ask also, right? Or that person and I will just naturally slide into marriage, but a happy slide, without either of us asking the other. But what was I saying again? Oh yes. I really believe that deep inside you want to live alone for the rest of your life. That's why you've lived alone all these years and all your relationships have failed, except for a couple of unsuccessful living arrangements with women—relationships which eventually failed because of the very living-alone reason I gave."

"Okay, say what you said is true. All of it, right from since we started talking. But now I want to stop that pattern for good."

"Then do, but with someone else, not me. It will in fact have to never be me. Because when I get to that age where I only might want to get married, you'll be forty-eight or fifty-two or whatever then and so still way too old for me. So you see, it can never change. There's no reason in the world for you to think it can change. At forty-five I might not find a man sixty-six or so that unappealing, but that's so ridiculously far away and I also, if I was going to have a baby, would

have had one long before that age. So from this point on the relationship and everything we have to talk about it has to end, okay?"

"Not even as friends?"

"You know that's not all you'd want, and besides, I really have
more friends than I can deal with now, but thanks."

"All right then, goodnight."

"Goodbye."

"Right. Goodbye, goodnight and the rest of the goods. I'll see
you."

"Okay," and hangs up.

I hang up, tell myself to stay calm, it's happened before, though it
hasn't happened and hurt so much with someone in a couple of years,
pick up the receiver to call her back, put it on my lap and think what
am I going on about, because she's right, I am too old for her though
her reasoning against my age is mostly bull and my arguments against
her reasons are just as full of it, when the phone starts making its off-
the-cradle noise and I put the receiver back on.

Goodbye

to

Goodbye

—

"Goodbye," and she goes. I stay there, holding the gift I was about to give her. Had told her I was giving her. This afternoon, on the phone. I said "I'd like to come over with something for you." She said "How come?" I said "Your birthday." She said "You know I don't like to be reminded of those, but come ahead if you want, around seven, okay?" I came. She answered the door. From the door I could see a man sitting on a couch in the living room. She said "Come in." I came in, gave her my coat, had the gift in a shopping bag the woman's store had put it in. "I have a friend here, I hope you don't mind," she said. "Me? Mind? Don't be silly—but how good a friend?" "My business," she said, "do you mind?" "No, of course not, why should I? Because you're right, it is your business." We went into the living room. The man got up. "Don't get up," I said. "It's no bother," he said. "How do you do? Mike Sliven," and he stuck out his hand. "Jules Dorsey," and I stuck out mine. "Like a drink, Jules?" she said, as we shook hands, and I said "Yes, what do you have?" "Beer, soda, wine, a little brandy, but I'd like to save that if you don't mind." "Why should I mind? Though something hard is what I think I'd like. Beer." "Light or dark?" she said. "Whatever you have most of," I said. "I have six-packs of both." "Then . . . dark," I said. "I feel like a dark. Suddenly I feel very dark. Only kidding, of course," I said to Mike and then turned to her so she'd also see I was only kidding. She went to the kitchen. Mike said "Now I remember your name. Arlene's spoken of you." "I'm sure she had only the very best things to say of me too." "She did and she didn't," he said, "but you're kidding again, no doubt." "Oh, I'm kidding, all right, or maybe I'm not. Say, who the hell are you anyway and what the hell you doing here? I thought Arlene was still only seeing me," and I grabbed him off the couch. He was much bigger than I, but didn't protest. "Where's your coat and hat?" I said and he said "I didn't come with a hat and my coat's over there, in the closet." "Then we're going to get it and you're going to leave with it." I clutched his elbow and started walking him to the closet. Arlene came into the living room and said "Jules, what are you doing?—and where are you going, Mike?" "I think out," he said. "Out," I said. "I came over to give you a gift and take you to dinner for your birthday and later to spend the night with you here or at my place or even at a great hotel if you wish, and goddamnit that's what I'm going to do." "What is it with you, Jules?—I've never heard you talk like that before." "Do you mind?" I said. "No, I kind of like it. And Mike. Are you going to leave when someone tells you to, just like that?" "I think I have to," he said, "since if there's one thing I don't like to do in life it's to get into or even put up a fight, especially when I see there's no chance of winning it." I opened the closet. He got his coat. I opened the front door and he left. I locked the door. Bolted it, just in case he already had the keys. Then I turned around. Arlene was standing in the living room holding my glass of beer. She came into the foyer with it. I didn't move, just let her come. "You still want this?" she said. "No, the cognac," I said. "It's brandy but good imported brandy." "Then the brandy," I said. "How do you want it?" "With ice." "Coming right up," and she went back to the kitchen. I followed her. She was reaching for the brandy on a cupboard shelf above her, had her back to me. I got up behind her—she didn't seem to know I was there—put my arms around her, pressed into her. She turned her head around, kissed me. We kissed. I started to undress her right there.

That's not the way it happened, of course. The way it happened was like this. I did come over with a gift, it wasn't her birthday, a man named Mike was there when I thought she'd be alone, she said he was a good friend, "in fact, the man I'm sleeping with now." "Oh," I said. "Well, I still have this gift for you so you might as well take it." She said "Really, it wouldn't be fair." Mike came into the foyer, introduced himself. "Mike Ivory," he said. "Jules Dorsey," I said. "Maybe I shouldn't stay." "No, Jules, come in and have a drink. What'll you have?" "What do you got?" I said. "I don't know. What do we have?" he said to Arlene. She said "Beer—light and dark—wine—red and white—scotch, vodka, rye, bourbon, gin, brandy and I think a little of that cognac left, and all the mixers to go with them, besides other nonalcoholic stuff if you're suddenly into that." "Come on, Jules drinks his share," Mike said, "or at least will with us here." "I drink, all right," I said, "though not that much. But tonight I'd like a double of that cognac you said you have, if you've enough for a double." "Why not—right, Arlene? Want me to get it?" "It's okay, I'll get it," she said, "but what's a double?" "Just double whatever you normally pour," he said. "If there's so little in the bottle that you don't have enough to double what you normally pour, empty the whole thing in his glass." "I just usually pour, I don't know how much," she said. "So do it that way," he said, "but double it." "Fill half a regular juice glass," I said, "and then put some ice in it, if you don't mind?" "Ice in one of the best cognacs there is?" he said. "No way, sir. Sorry." "Then make it your worst cognac," I said, "but ice in it, please. I feel like a cognac and I feel like a double and I feel like I want that double cognac ice-cold." "Sorry—really," he said. "We only have one cognac and it's one of the rarest there is. Gin, vodka, bourbon, scotch, even the beer, light or dark, I'll put ice in for you, and the wine, either one, too. But not that cognac or even the brandy. They're both too good. I'm telling you the truth when I say I couldn't sleep right tonight if I knew I was instrumental or helpful in any way or even allowed it, just stood by and allowed ice in cognac or brandy when I knew just by saying something I might be able to stop it." "Listen, you," I said and grabbed his neck with one hand. He swung at me. I ducked and hit him in the stomach, he fell forward and I clipped him on the back. He went down. I put my foot under his chest and nudged him with it and he turned himself over on his back. I looked at Arlene. Her hands covered her eyes but she seemed to be peeking through the finger cracks. I said to Mike "Probably Arlene won't like this but I'm going to give you to ten to get your coat and hat and—" "I didn't come with a coat and hat," he said. "Then ten just to get the hell out of here." "Jules, this is awful," Arlene said, not looking alarmed or frightened or really upset or anything like that. "I don't care. It's what I suddenly felt like doing even if I didn't feel that right about doing it, so that's what I did. Now get, buddy," I said to Mike. "One, two, three . . ." He got up, held his stomach as he went to the front door. By the count of eight he was out of the apartment. She said "I hate when anyone does that to people, but I think deep inside I loved it when you did it to him. Not because it was Mike. He's very nice. It's just that you were, well—I've never seen you like that before. I don't know what that makes me, but come here, you rat." I came to her.

She mussed my hair, with her other hand slipped off one and then the other of her shoes. "Shall we do it here or in the bedroom?" "Here," I said, "or the opening part of it, but first let me lock the front door."

That's not the way it happened either. It happened like this. Arlene's my wife. We've been married for three years. We lived together for two years before that. We have a nine-month-old son. During dinner Arlene said she wanted a divorce. Our son was asleep in his room. I'd just put the main dish and side courses on the table. I dropped my fork. I was in what could be called a state of shock. I don't like that term but for now it'll have to do. Figuratively and maybe in some way literally—technically, scientifically—I was in a state of shock. I didn't move for I don't know how long. A minute, two, three. Just stared at my fork on my plate. Till the moment she told me this I thought that though we had some problems in our marriage, they were manageable and correctable and not untypical and that we were serious at working them out. All in all I felt we were very compatible in most ways and that the marriage was a successful one and getting better all the time. Arlene had said it several times—many times—too. About once a month she used to tell me that she loved me and loved being married to me, and about once a month, and not just after she told me this, I'd tell her the same thing. I meant it and felt she meant it. I had no reason to believe she didn't mean it. This is the truth. Sometimes out of the blue she'd say "I love you, Jules." Sometimes I'd answer "You do?" and she'd say "Truly love you." We could be in a taxi and she'd turn to me and say it. Or walking to a movie theater or in front of a theater during the intermission of a play and she'd break off whatever either of us was saying to say it. At that dinner, which I cooked—it was a good dinner, a chicken dish, rice cooked to perfection—something she taught me how to do—a baked zucchini dish, a great salad, a good bottle of wine, crabmeat cocktail to begin with, two drinks with cheese on crackers before we sat down, we had made love the previous night and we both said later on that it was one of the best acts of lovemaking we'd ever had, our son was wonderful and we loved being parents though admitted it was tough and tiring at times, both of us were making a pretty good income for the first time in our marriage so as a family we were financially sound, nothing was wrong or just about nothing, everything or just about everything was right, so that's why I say I was suddenly in a state of shock. "You want a divorce?" I finally said after she said "So what do you have to say about what I said before?" "Yes," she said, "a divorce." "Whatever for?" "Because I don't love you anymore," she said. "But just last week or the week before that you said you loved me more than you ever have, or as much as you ever have, you said." "I was lying." "You wouldn't lie about something like that." "I'm telling you, I was lying," she said. "Why don't you love me anymore?" "Because I love someone else." "You love someone else?" "That's what I said, I love someone else." "Since when?" I said. "Since months." "And you stopped loving me the minute you started loving him?" "No, a couple of months earlier." "Why?" "I don't know. I asked myself the same thing lots of times and all I could come up with was that I felt rather than knew why. You fall in, you fall out. You fall out, you fall in. Though this time I'm sure I've fallen in forever, since the feeling has never been stronger." "I can't believe it," I said. "Believe it. I've been having the most intense affair possible with a man I met at work—someone you don't know—and he's married but will get a divorce to be with me, just as I'm going to get a divorce to be with him." "But the children, I mean the child," I said. "We'll work it out. We were always good at working things out in the past that most other couples never could, and we'll work this out too. I'll take Kenneth for the time being and when he's completely weaned you can have him whenever you like for as long as you like so long as it doesn't disrupt his life too much." "But just leaving me, divorcing me, breaking up this family, will disrupt his life," I said. "I'm sorry, I didn't want to, I in fact tried not to, but the force of the feeling I have for this man and he for me—" "What's his name?" "What's the difference?" "Just tell me his name? Maybe I do know him." "Even if you did, which you don't, nothing you could do or say—" "His name, please, his name? I just want to know what and whom I'm up against." "What could you know by just his name? If it was Butch or Spike or Mike, would it make you feel more or less confident that I'm not very much in love with him and that I'm not going to divorce you to marry him?" "Is it Mike?" "It isn't, but you know that wasn't my point. —All right, it is Mike," when I continued to stare at her as if I'd caught her fibbing, "but so what? Mickey, Michael or Mike, it's just a given name." "Mike what?" I said. "Now that's enough, Jules. I don't want you starting trouble." "I won't start anything. I just want to know the man's full name. That way I can begin saying to myself you're leaving and divorcing me and breaking up our family for Mike So-and-So and not just a shadow. I'm not sure why, but it'll make it seem realer to me and so will be much easier to work out in my head." "Spiniker," she said. "Mike Spiniker. "With an 'i,' 'a' or 'e' or even a 'u' on the second half of his last name?" "Now you're going too far," she said. "Anyway, good—I have enough." I got up, got the phone book off the phone stand in the living room. "What are you doing?" she said. "Can't be too many Mike Spinikers in the book with an 'a,' 'e,' 'u' or second 'i.'" I looked up his name. "One, a Michael, with two i's, on Third Avenue." I dialed him. "Stop that," she said. "He lives in another city, commutes here." A woman answered. "Is Michael Spiniker in?" I said. "Who's speaking?" the woman said. "Lionel Messer. I'm his stocks and bonds man." "Mike has stocks and bonds? That's news to me." "He has a huge portfolio of them and I've something very urgent to tell him about them if he doesn't want to go broke by midnight tonight." "I'll get him, hold on." She put down the phone. "Stop wasting your time," Arlene said on the bedroom extension. "Hang up. It can't be him. I'm telling you, he lives fifty miles from here." "Hey what's this about stocks and bonds?" Mike said. "Hello, Mr. Spiniker. Do you know Arlene Dorsey? Arlene Chernoff Dorsey—she goes professionally by Chernoff." "Sure I do. We work in the same office building. But anything wrong? Because I thought this was about some stocks and bonds I don't have." "You seem very concerned about Ms. Chernoff. Are you?" "Sure I'm concerned. By your tone, who wouldn't be? What's happened?" "You sound as if you're in love with Ms. Chernoff, Mr. Spiniker. Are you?" "Listen, who is this? And what kind of jerky call is this? You either dialed the wrong Spiniker or you're crazy and not making any sense, but I'll have to hang up." "This is her husband, wise guy, and you better stop seeing her or I'm going to break your neck with my bare hands. If that doesn't work, I'll put a bullet through your broken neck. I have the means. And I don't just mean a weapon or two or people to do it for me—I'll do it gladly myself. I can. I have. Now do you read me?" "I read you, brother. Okay, fine. You have the right number and you're not crazy and you're probably right on target in everything you said, so my deepest apologies for getting excited at you. But let's say there must be two Michael Spinikers in this city, because I have no stocks and bonds broker and after what you told me, I don't ever plan to do anything with my money but keep it in the bank, okay?" "Got you," I said and hung up. Arlene came running back to the living room. "You'd do that for me? You'd really go that far?" "I wasn't just threatening for effect or because I knew you were on the line. The way I see our marriage is that until it's clearly impossible to stay together, we're stuck together for life. Of course I only feel this way because of the kid." "I bet. You know, awful as this must seem about me, I think my feelings have come around another hundred and eighty degrees. What a husband I now realize I have. And what a weakling and pig that guy was for taking it the way he did, even if you weren't all bluff, after all he swore the other day about how he'd stand with me against you and his wife when it finally came down to this. I'm sorry, Jules. So sorry, I want to beat my brains in against this chair. If my saying I love you very much isn't enough, what else can I say or do to prove what I just said is true and that I never want to stop being married to you?" "You can take my clothes off and carry me to bed." "Will do if I can." She put her arms around my waist and tried to lift me. "Oof, what a load. Instead of carrying you, which I no can do, what would you say to my just taking your clothes off and we do whatever you want us to right here on the floor or couch?" "Fine by me," I said and she grabbed my shirt by the two collar ends and tore it off me.

That's ridiculous also and never happened. Why not say what really did happen and be done with it? It was all very simple and fast. We were eating dinner when she said she was leaving me for a man named Mike. We had no child, we'd been married for eight years. I said I wouldn't try to stop her. I could see it'd be useless and I did only want her to be happy. If she couldn't be happy with me, I was glad she was with someone she could be happy with. She said she was thankful I was taking it so well and in such a decent civilized way. I asked about him. She said he worked in a law office on the same floor as hers. They'd been carrying on for six months. He was divorced, had two children. That night Arlene and I slept in separate rooms for the first time in our marriage, or for the first time when one of us wasn't very angry at the other or wasn't so ill that he or she needed to sleep alone. We just thought it best to sleep separately till she moved out. They rented a new apartment together the following month. I helped her pack and bring her belongings to the van she rented and drove. I told her I wouldn't mind if Mike came and helped, since she had several vanfuls of stuff to move. She said she felt I shouldn't meet him till much later on: when they were married, perhaps; maybe a year into their marriage when I could come by with my new woman who she said she knew I'd have by then. "You'll be as much in love with someone else in a few months as I am now with Mike." I said "I hope you're right. It'll certainly be what I want." So she was gone. I thought I was taking it well but I wasn't. I couldn't take it, in fact. Every night I'd get drunk thinking about her. I read her old adoring notes and letters to me and looked at her photos and would slam the wall or table with my fists and shout and cry. I couldn't stand thinking of her being with another man, kissing him, whispering to him, making love with him, doing all those private things with him, confiding to him, telling him what happened to her at the store that day, asking him if he'd like to see such and such movie or play that week, meeting him for lunch, going away with him some weekend, visiting friends, maybe even planning to have a child. It also distressed me that they were in the same profession. I knew that'd make them even closer, all those professional matters they could discuss and look up and share. A month after she left me I showed up in front of their office building at around the time I knew they'd be finished for the day. They walked out of the building fifteen minutes later, holding hands, chatting animatedly. I had a wrench with me. I pulled it out of my jacket, ran up to him and screamed "Meet Jules, her husband, you bastard," and hit him in the hand he threw up to protect his head from the wrench. He grabbed that hand, turned to run and I hit him in the back of the head with the wrench. He went down. I kept yelling "I'll never let her be with anyone else, you bastard, never. I love her too much. I'll love her forever," and swung the wrench over his face but didn't hit him again. The police came. I didn't try to get away. I don't know what Arlene was doing at the time. I was arrested. Mike was taken away in an ambulance. Later he pressed charges against me. I pleaded guilty and was sentenced to five years. That means I'll serve around three and a half years if I don't cause any trouble in prison. Arlene visits me every day she's allowed to and stays the maximum time. It's six hours by bus for her round-trip but she says she doesn't mind. Twice in my first half year here we were allowed to walk around the prison garden for an hour. She broke off with Mike and he's already moved in with another woman. "So much for his professed eternal devotion," Arlene said, "not that I would want it now." She's said several times that she'll never again be with another man but me. She hated my hitting Mike with the wrench but sees now it was probably the only way I could ever get through to her how much I loved her and wanted to get her back. "In some oddball way," she said, "it made me fall for you all over again. Maybe also because what I did and the way I did it forced you to lose control and try to kill him and I'm trying to make up for that too. But it'll all be different from now on. I can't wait to be back home with you, my arms around you, in bed with you, I can't wait." At certain designated spots in the garden we're allowed to hug and kiss for a half-minute, which we always did past the time limit till one of the guards ordered us to stop.

That's not it. This is it. There wasn't a wrench. There is a Mike. My wife fell in love with him and told me this at breakfast, not dinner. She said she didn't want to tell me at night because she wanted to give me plenty of time to adjust to it before I went to bed and also time for her to get her things out of the apartment and move in with a friend. We have no child. We tried for a while but couldn't. Then I had a corrective operation and we could have a child, but she said the marriage wasn't as good as it used to be and she wanted to be sure it was a very good marriage before we had a child. That was three years ago. She's had several affairs since then. She told me about them while she was having them. I didn't like her having them but put up with it because I didn't want her to leave me. I don't know why I mentioned anything about a gift. Maybe because her birthday's in two weeks and I've been thinking recently about what to get her. A bracelet, I thought. But that's out. This morning she said she realizes this is the third or fourth serious affair she's had in three years. She's had one or two others but they were quick and not so serious. She doesn't want to continue having affairs while she's married or at least still living with me. It isn't fair to me, she said. She also said I shouldn't put up with it and shouldn't have in the past. Not that if I had told her to stop she would have, she said. But I should tell her to get the hell out of the house and should have told her two or three years ago. Since I won't, she'll have to leave me. That means divorce, she said. The marriage isn't working out. What she's talking about? she said. The marriage is so bad that she doesn't think it'll ever work out—it never will, that's all, never. And because she wants to have children, maybe two, maybe three, but with someone she's very much in love with, she'll have to end our marriage and eventually get married to someone else. Maybe it'll be with Mike but she doubts it. He's married, but about to separate from his wife, and has indicated he never wants to marry again. He also has two children from a previous marriage and has expressed no interest in having more. Anyway, she said, it's fairer if I stay here and she goes, since she's the one breaking up the marriage. Of course, if I want to leave, she said, then she'll be more than happy to stay, since it's a great apartment and one she can afford and she'll never be able to get anything like it at twice the rent. "If you don't mind," I said, "I think I'd like to keep the apartment. Losing you and also having to find a new place might be a little too much for me." "I don't mind," she said, "why should I mind? I already said the apartment's yours if you want. So, do you mind if I start to pack up now to go?" "No, go right ahead. I'd love for you to stay forever, naturally, but what could I do to stop you from going? Nothing, I guess, right?" "Right." She went to the bedroom. I brought the dishes into the kitchen, washed them, sat down at the small table there and looked at the river. She came into the living room an hour later with two suitcases and a duffel bag. "This ought to do it for now," she said. "If it's okay with you, I'll arrange with a friend to come by for the rest of my stuff some other time." "Sure," I said. "You moving in with this Mike?" "No, I told you, he's married, still living with his wife. I'll be staying with Elena for now. If you want to reach me for anything, you can get me there or at work. You have her number?" "I can look it up." "But you won't call me at either place for very personal reasons, will you? Such as saying how much you miss me or things like that and you want me back? Because I've definitely made up my mind, Jules. The marriage is finished." "I understand that. I mean, I don't understand why it's so definitely finished, but I do understand that you definitely feel it is. But I can't make just one more pitch? There's nothing I can do or say or promise to help you change your mind?" "Nothing." "Then goodbye," I said. "I'll miss you terribly. I love you tremendously. I'll be as sad as any man can be over a thing like this for I don't know how long. But that's my problem, not yours, I guess, and eventually I'll work it out." "I'm glad you're taking it like this. Not that you'll be sad—I don't want you to be like that—but at least that you see the situation for what it is and that in the long run you'll be able to handle it. Because it'll make it much easier—it already is—for both of us. You'll see. You'll get over me before you know it." "Not on your life," I said. "Yes you will." "I'm telling you. Never." "No, I know you will. Goodbye." She opened the door, put the suitcases right outside it, said "I'll be back for these in a minute," and carried the duffel bag downstairs. "I'll help you with the suitcases," I yelled down the stairs. "No need to," she said. "It'd actually be better if you closed the door so we won't have to say goodbye again." I shut the door.

Come

on

a Coming

"So come on up," and I say "Okay," and start climbing. But not enough what for my feet and hands? Places, ledges, perches, niches, nooks, holes or whatever they're called to put my feet in or on and my hands to get a good grip on to climb up more than eight to ten feet on this wall. My hands are holding on but I can feel them about to slide off.

"I can't make it up this way," and one of them says "Sure you can, don't give up now. Climb. All you got to do is climb."

I try to but can't find anything higher to stick my foot in or on or anything also for my hands to hold on.

"No, I can't make it up another inch," and one of them says "Then drop down and we'll throw you a rope."

"I might break an ankle or something if I drop," and one of them says "From that height? Don't be a baby. Just drop."

I drop, landing on both feet and hurting one around the ankle. "I knew I shouldn't have," and one of them says "Shouldn't have what? What happened, you hurt your foot?"

"Not the whole foot, just the ankle. What I said before. What I told myself not to. From now on I'll stick to taking my own advice."

"Could be you didn't fall right. But watch it—here it comes," and the rope drops from the top of the wall to the ground.

I pull on the rope. Seems a bit slack. "You sure you have it real tight up there—I mean, where it won't fall down when I climb? Secure, I mean."

"Secure, sure—you think we'd take someone's life in our hands?"

I pull on it again. It still feels slack and I say "I don't know. It doesn't feel that secure. What do you have it tied around?"

"We have it around this and that and something else. Not only do we have it secure but this rope's the best you can get for climbing. You coming or not, for if not we'll pull up the rope and leave."

"But it's secure," and one of them says "Secure as it'll ever be. I'm telling you, it's taut."

I grab hold of the rope with both hands. I've climbed ropes before. In high school: not very well but it was a start. In college, where we still had to take, at least in my college, four physical science courses they called them then to graduate. One of those courses had rope climbing in it. Twenty feet to the ceiling I think we had to climb. Maybe thirty, because it was in the same gym the college basketball team played in—and then with our feet wrapped around the rope in some way, we slid down. I remember the physical science teacher saying when I got down "You ought to be a genie." I remember saying to him—

"Hey, you coming or not? We only have so much time."

"Coming, coming," and I start climbing. It all comes back to me as I hoped it would. As my hands pull, my feet and knees push. Something like that. I'm about fifteen feet up when the rope suddenly feels loose in my hands and I yell "It's coming loose," and someone on top says "Where? What?" and just then the rope comes off whatever it was around above and I fall.

I come down hard. This time I know I sprained a foot, maybe broke one. It certainly hurts.

"Didn't I tell you to check the rope?" and someone says "You didn't say to check it. You asked if it was secure and we said it was. Anyway, we did check it. You must have been too heavy for it. What do you weigh?"

"You said that was the best rope around for climbing, so what does it matter what I weigh? If I weighed three hundred pounds it should've been able to hold me."

"You weigh three hundred pounds?" and I say "No, but that's not the point."

"It would be if you weighed that much. This rope might be the best, but it only holds till around two-fifty, maybe two seventy-five. What do you weigh?"

"Less than two hundred, way less. Oh, forget it. I'll never be able to get up there no matter what I do, and certainly not with a broken or sprained ankle, so I'll be seeing you all."

"Sure, give up. That's what you do. That's what almost all you guys who want to come over do, though it hardly seems the attitude to take if you're sincere about being in here. Look, if you want, we can throw you a rope ladder."

"Rope ladder attached to what? No thanks. You have a regular ladder—wooden, aluminum? But wait. What do you mean 'all us guys'? That rope wasn't my fault but yours. What were you giving me, some kind of test?"

"No. And I was only talking for all of us here about hundreds like you. 'I want to come up.' 'I want to be over.' 'I want to be in there,' and so on, right? But give them two good shots at it and when they fail for their own reasons—"

"My own reasons?"

"—then that's it, they give up, but don't you worry about it, because when they get home they'll complain we're keeping them out, we don't want them in, we're only playing with them, and so on, right? You wait and see. You'll be just like the others."

"Okay, throw over the rope ladder. But secure it, will you?" and he says "Don't worry, it'll be secure. We want you here. We've nothing against you or the others. But we can't just let everyone in, can we? People who don't even want to make an effort? Believe me, you get in, you'll feel just like us. So make the effort. Climb. We might be serious but we don't play tricks," and he throws the rope ladder down.

I pull on it. It's tight. "It's tight," and one of them says "You mean good and tight. Start climbing."

"Because of my foot it might take me a little longer than usual, but I'm on my way. You have someone to fix a foot there?"

"We have everything. Someone to fix a foot, someone to make a new foot if you want. Anything you want with feet, arms, head—any part or any one thing in the world. Maybe the one thing we haven't got so much of right now, or at least for you, is time, so come on."

"Right," and I start climbing. The foot really hurts, but what they said makes it seem worth the pain. Once on top they'll probably give me something to ease it, and it also should be much easier getting down the other side. Who knows how they work it? Maybe they've a sliding pond. Or more rope ladders or wooden ladders or steps, even. Probably steps. They take good care of themselves. They have the means and ingenuity. Whatever it is, they got. Probably steps or maybe even some motorized car. An elevator or funicular or seat car or whatever it's called that's used in skiing to go up and down a mountain—a chairlift. Anyway, they want me now. Want me? I'll say they're still interested in having me, but if I don't make it now, then that'll be the end of their interest for a while. It first came in the mail. "You're invited," it said. To such and such place, "which you'll have to get out to on your own. We know you want to be with us and will be excited at receiving this. Now we're inviting you to be with us. It won't be easy for you, but we also don't think it'll be that hard. In other words, you've more than proven to us because of your past deeds, industry, sincerity, perseverance and honesty that you're the kind of material we want and could even use here, so come on a coming." That's what the letter said. "Come on a coming. We'll be waiting," and it gave the directions, time and date and said to wear my work clothes. So I came. When I got here and looked around and didn't see anyone or anything but this wall, one of them said from on top of it "You there—up here." "Where's the door?" and one of them said "Door? You have to climb up, old friend, up up up." "With what?" and someone else said "Your hands." I tried, couldn't make it. Tried the rope, couldn't make it. So now I'm climbing the ladder. Seems easy enough despite the ankle pain. They didn't make it that tough for me. Probably some sort of initiation, those first two. Though I just about knew I couldn't make it by hand or rope. I went through both figuring that falling ten to fifteen feet each time would prove even more to them how sincere and persevering and so on I am. It worked. I'm not sure that's how I felt those two times, but they have given me a third chance and this ladder is relatively easy to climb.

The strut—no, what's it called?—the ring, the rung, though maybe also the strut, or even the crosspiece, beneath my bottom foot feels loose. I climb a step higher and the next strut, rung or crosspiece is loose, so now both feet are on loose crosspieces, I'll say. I climb a step higher and that one splits in two, so now one foot's on a loose crosspiece and the other's dangling in the air. I'm twenty feet up and have about fifteen feet to go and the crosspiece in my top hand is loose too. I climb a step higher and the crosspiece above the broken crosspiece splits in two and the next crosspiece my top hand grabs is loose, so now I'm dangling there, two feet in the air, hands holding on to two loose crosspieces I'm sure are going to split, and I don't know what to do.

"Help, please, the ladder crosspieces are breaking or coming loose," and someone yells "Hey, what's happening down there? We know you've a bad ankle or two, even a broken one, but we got to get down our side of this thing one of these days too."

"Do something, I'm about to fall," and one of them says "Fall? From where you are? You'll be hurt. Look, you've fewer feet to climb up than down, so I'd advise, and I think I can say this for everyone here—yes, they're all saying I can—that you just come on a coming, because there's nothing else we can do for you now."

"You can quickly pull the ladder up," and one of them says "Okay, good idea, that's what we'll do, that's really thinking, sorry we didn't come up with the idea ourselves," when the crosspieces I'm holding split in two and I fall to the ground, my feet breaking every crosspiece along the way.

"Hey down there, how do you feel?"

I'm lying on the ground, hurting all over, and for all I know I was out for a few seconds or even minutes.

"Hey, hello down there, I said how do you feel? Any broken bones? You alive? Answer us. Anything we can do?"

"I think I definitely broke a foot this time and I think also my arm which I landed on. Yeah, it's limp, won't move. What kind of ladder did you give me?"

"The best kind," and I say "If it was the best it would've had secure crosspieces or rungs or whatever you call those damn bars."

"Both will do. In fact, all three are good. And they were secure till you started going through them. How much you say you weigh? Less than two hundred? Don't try to fool us. Anyway, you can't do anything. Okay, you followed our directions and got yourself out here, but what have you done since? You can't scale a wall on your own. You don't know how to use a rope. We give you a perfectly good rope ladder a child could climb, a person twice or even three times your age could climb—"

"Nobody could be three times my age. And anyone twice my age who could climb it would have to be in extraordinary shape and have a ladder whose bars are strong. But the bars on my ladder were weak, once I got up around twenty-five feet—"

"Twenty at the most. Don't exaggerate."

"Twenty, then. But after I got up that high, all the bars were either very loose or splitting the second I stepped on them, and I didn't step on them hard, nor pull on them hard either. That ladder was defective."

"If it wasn't, it certainly is now. Look, I'm sorry, we like you and you're a nice guy and all that—sincere too, which I think is what we said in our invite to you. And you come with good recommendations, though maybe in the future we'll have to check everyone's recommendations a little deeper, seeing what yours came to. But it just doesn't seem you really want to be in here."

"What are you talking about—I do."

"You still do?" and I say "Sure, why not? I heard great things about the place, and it'd be a terrific achievement for me and I think a big improvement over what I have now. So yes, I absolutely still do."

"Okay, then you're in. We only wanted to see how much you'd take before you quit. But it doesn't seem anything's going to break you, which is just the kind of material we want and need, so come on in. Door into here might look like part of the wall from where you are. But if you look close about ten feet to your left, you'll see it and a latch to pull, which will let you in easier than any other way. Congratulations."

"You mean it?" and one of them says "Mean every word we just said," and I say "Why thanks." I get up, fall, my right foot is useless for the time being, and I say "You sure you have someone to fix a broken, or if that seems like an exaggeration, then a badly sprained foot and arm?" and someone says "Everything, just like we said. We have every kind of doctor and profession and healing art and all the other disciplines and arts and whatever you want and the very very best. But show us again how much you want to come in, by not having us come out to get you, though if you're really that hurt, we will."

"I'll show you, don't you worry," and I crawl to the place they said the door was, but don't see any outline of one or a latch. "Say, you said ten or so feet to my left, correct? So I'm here, looking at nine and eleven feet to my left also, and I don't see any kind of anything that looks like a door or a latch, handle, lever, button or whatever it might be to open it."

Nobody answers. I can't see anyone on top, maybe because I'm so close to the wall, and I say "Any of you still up there?" Nobody answers. I crawl around, cover every inch of the wall I can see from one to twenty feet to the left and right from where I fell, but always crawling because of my broken foot, and I'm sure it's broken. Crawling's made even more difficult because of what I'm also sure is a broken arm, but there's no latch, door seam, nothing but a wall.

"Say, I don't see anything resembling what you said would be here, so give me some more instructions how to get in, though don't forget to take into consideration my bad foot and arm."

I yell and look for another half hour. By this time it's dark. I wouldn't try to make it to the road to get the bus back the way I am, so I just sit against the wall, roll down the sleeves of my sweater and shirt, and to help keep out the cold, roll my socks up far as they'll go and button the top shirt button and buttons of my shirt cuffs. In the morning I should probably be rested and strong enough to not only yell to those people inside what I think of them, but to limp or just crawl to the bus stop.

Time

to

Go

My father follows me on the street. He says "Don't go into that store and don't go into the next one you might want to go into either. Go into none, that's what I'm saying." But I stand in front of the door of the jewelry store I heard was the best in the city and am buzzed in. My father's right behind me, and I nod to the guard and say to the saleswoman after she says "Can I help you?" "Yes, I'm looking for a necklace—amber—I mean jade. I always get the two mixed up. But jade's what I want: long-lasting, forever, is the symbol, right? This might sound funny, but I want to present the necklace to my wife-to-be as a prenuptial gift."

"Doesn't sound funny to me and you've come to the right store." She takes out a tray of jade necklaces. All have gold around or in them, and when I ask the price of two of them, are too expensive.

"I don't want any gold in them, except maybe for the clasp, and these are way too expensive for me."

"Much too expensive," my father says.

"I'll show you some a little lower in price."

"Much lower in price," my father says.

"Maybe a little lower than even that," I say.

She puts away the tray she was about to show me and takes out a third tray.

"These seem darker than I want—to go with her blue eyes and kind of pale skin I mean—but how much is this one?"

"You can pick it up," she says. "Jade doesn't bite."

"Just the price," my father says. "But go on, pick it up. You'll see how jade's as cold to feel as it is to look at."

I pick it up. "It feels nice, just the right weight, and seems"— holding it out—"the right size for her neck."

"Is she around my height?"

"Five-five."

"Then exactly my height and this is the size I'd wear."

"I'm sure it's still too expensive for me."

She looks at the tag on it, which seems to be in code: $412xT+$. "It goes for three-fifty but I'll make it two-seventy-five for you."

"Way out of my range."

"What is your range?"

"You're going to wind up with crap," my father says, "pure crap. If you have to buy a necklace, go somewhere else. I bet you can get this one for a hundred any other place."

"Around a hundred, hundred-twenty-five," I tell her.

"Let me show you these then."

"Here we go again," my father says.

"I have to get her something, don't I?" I tell him. "And I want to, because she wants something she can always wear, treasure—that'll remind her of me. That's what she said."

"Fine, but what's she getting you?"

"How do I know? I hope nothing. I don't want anything. That's what I told her."

"Oh, you don't want anything to remind you of her?"

"She'll remind me of her. I have her, that's enough, and besides I don't like jewelry."

"You thinkers: all so romantic and impractical. I wouldn't get her anything if she isn't getting you anything. Listen, I like her, don't misunderstand me: she's a fine attractive girl and you couldn't get better if you tried for ten more years. But tit for tat I say. He who gives, receives, and one should be a receiver and giver both."

"You're not getting my point. She wants something and I don't. I accept that and I wish you would."

"Sucker," he says. "All my boys are suckers. None of them took after me."

"Some people might say that was an improvement."

"Stupid people might, just as stupid people might make jokes like you just did. If you took after me you would've been married sooner, had almost grown-up children by now, a much better job, three times as much income and been much much happier because your happiness would've been going on longer."

"Look at this batch," the saleswoman says, putting another tray of jade necklaces on the counter. I see one I like. A light green, smaller beads, nicely strung with string, no gold on it except the clasp. I hold it up. "I like this one."

"Hedge, hedge," my father says. "Then ask the price and offer her half."

"How much is it?" I ask her.

"A hundred-ten."

"Fifty-five or sixty—quick," my father says.

"Sounds fair, and this is the first one I really feel good about."

"That's the only way to buy. Janine," she says to a younger saleswoman, "would you try this on for this gentleman?"

Janine comes over, smiles and says hello to me, undoes the top two buttons of her blouse and starts on the third.

"It's not necessary," I say.

"Don't worry," the older woman says. "That's as far as I'll let her go for that price."

Janine holds the necklace to her neck and the older woman clasps it behind her. "Feels wonderful," Janine says, rolling the beads between her fingers. "This is the one I'd choose of this box—maybe even out of all the boxes despite the more expensive ones."

"Who are you working for, him or me?"

"No, it really feels great."

"Don't fall for their patter," my father says. "Sixty-five—go no higher. She says seventy-five, say 'Look, I'm a little short what with all my wedding expenses and all, can't you take the sixty-five—the most, seventy?' But you got to give them an excuse for accepting your offer, and no crying."

"How much is this one again?" I ask her.

"One-ten," the older woman says, "but I'll make it a hundred."

"That's just fine. I didn't mean to bargain down, but if you say it's a hundred, fine, I'll take it."

"Idiot," my father says. "You could've had it for seventy easy."

"Terrific. Janine, wrap it up special as a prewedding gift. Cash or charge, sir?"

"You'll take a check?"

"Janine, I don't know this guy, so check his references. If they're okay, let him pay by check. Thank you, sir. What about calling Michaels now?" she says to a man at the end of the counter and they go in back. I take out my wallet.

My father sits in a chair next to the guard. "My son," he says to him. "Nothing like me. Never learned anything I ever taught him and I tried hard as I could. He could've been much more successful if he'd listened. But he was stubborn. All my children were stubborn. Neither of my girls had the beauty of their mother and none of my sons the brains of their dad. Health you'd think they'd have had at least, but they didn't even have that. Oh, this one, he's healthy enough—strong as an ox. But two I lost to diseases, boy and a girl, and both in their twenties, which was hard for my wife and I to take, before I went myself. So, there you have it. And I hope his bride likes his present. He's paying enough. Though why he doesn't insist on getting something in return—hint on it at least if he doesn't want to insist—or at least insist her family pay for the wedding, is a mystery as much to you as to me. To everyone including his bride, who I admire—don't think I was just buttering him up there—he says he's too old to have anyone but him pay for the wedding, and she makes it worse by praising him for what she calls his integrity. Make sense to you? Doesn't to me. Since to me integrity is great in its place but is best when it pays. All of which is why I hound him the way I do—for his benefit and his only. So. Think it'll stay as nice out as it is? Ah, what's the difference?"

I get off the train from Baltimore, get on the subway for upper Broadway, suddenly my father's in the car standing beside me. "Welcome home," he says. "You still going through with giving her that present and making the wedding all by yourselves? Anything you say. I won't interfere. I can only tell you once, maybe three times, then you have to finish digging your own grave."

"If that's really the last time, fine by me," and I go back to reading my book.

"Just like when you were a boy. You didn't like what I said, you pretended I wasn't there. But I'm here all right. And the truth is, in spite of all the mistakes you made with your life and are still making, I'm wishing you all the luck in the world. You were okay to me at the end—I won't deny it. I can't—who could I to?—the way you took care of me when I was sick—so I suppose I should be a little better to you now. Am I right? So do you want to be not only family now but good friends? If so, let's shake like friends. We kissed a lot when you were young—in fact, right to when I went and then you to me a few seconds after that, which I don't think if the tables were turned you would've got from me—but for a first time let's just shake."

The car's crowded. Late-afternoon Christmas shoppers returning home but not the rush-hour riders yet. I'm squeezed right up to him. "Look," I say, "we can talk but don't remind me of how sick you were. I don't want to think of it now. I will say I respected you for a lot of things in your life, especially the way you took the discomfort and pain then, something I told you a number of times but I think you were too out of it to understand me. But you also have to realize, and which I maybe didn't tell you, how much you screwed me up, and I allowed you to screw me up—whatever the causes or combination of them. I've worked out a lot of it, I'll try to work out the rest, but no real complaints from me for anything now for I'm going through absolutely the best time in my life."

"Good, we're friends," and he shakes my hand.

I get off at Magna's stop. Today began my school's winter break. I head for the revolving exit gate at the end of the platform. A boy of about sixteen's between me and the woman exiting in front of him. But he's hesitating, looking around and behind him, at me, the downtown platform across the tracks, the woman who's now through the gate and walking upstairs, back at me sullenly. I don't know whether to walk around him or go to the other end of the platform and the main exit. Maybe I'm wrong. He might just be an angry kid who's hesitating now because he doesn't know which exit to take, this or the main one. I walk past him but keep my eyes on him. As I'm stepping backwards into the gate he turns to me, sticks his left hand into his side jacket pocket and thrusts it at me, clamps his other hand on my shoulder and says "Give me all your money." I say "What? What?" and push backwards and revolve around the gate to the other side and he has to pull his hand away or get it caught between the bars.

"Hey, wait," and he revolves around the gate after me, rips the satchel off my shoulder and runs upstairs. It has the necklace, my writings, student papers, a framed drawing I bought for Magna, some clothing. The boy's already gone. I yell upstairs "Police, police, catch that kid with my satchel—a canvas one," as I chase after him. On the sidewalk I say to that woman "Did you see a boy running past?" and she says "Who?" but he's nowhere around. A police car's across the street and I run to it. The policemen are in a luncheonette waiting for

374 The Stories of Stephen Dixon

their take-out order. I go in, say "I'm not going to sound sensible to you, believe me, but I was just robbed, he might've had a gun or knife in his pocket, a kid, boy, around sixteen with a gray ski cap on his head with the word 'ski' on it, down in the subway exit there, he took my satchel with some valuable things in it and then ran upstairs. I'm sure if we—" "Come with us," one of them says and we rush outside and are getting in their car when the counterman raps on the luncheonette window and holds up their bag of food. "Later," the policeman shouts out his window as we drive off.

We drive around and don't find the boy. The policeman says "There are so many young thieves wearing the outfit you described. Parka jacket, fancy running sneakers, hat sort of extra tall and squeezed on top, sometimes with a pompom, sometimes not. Tough luck about your necklace and painting though."

"I could've told you," my father says, seated beside me. "Fact is, I told you—a thousand times about how to be wise in New York, but you always got your own ideas. You think I'd ever exit through a revolving gate when there's no token booth there, even in what they call the better days? That's where they leap on you, trap you against the gate on either side or on the stairs leaving it, but you never want to play it safe. Now you've lost everything. Well, you still got your life and it's not that I have no sympathy for you over what happened, but it seems you were almost asking for it it could've been so easily avoided."

"Lay off me, will you? I already feel bad enough." I get out of the car in front of Magna's building. "Thanks, Officers."

"As I say," my father says, going in with me, "I can understand how you feel. But this one time, since your life depends on it, I wish you'd learn from your mistake."

I go upstairs and tell Magna about the robbery. My father sits on the daybed she uses as a couch. "Every week closer to the wedding she gets more radiant," he says. "You got yourself one hell of a catch. She's smart, she's good, she has wonderful parents and she's also beautiful. I don't know how you rate it but I'm glad you did."

"It had your special present in it," I tell her, "plus some drawing for you I know he's going to just throw away. I won't tell you what the special gift is. I'll try to get something like it or close to it. God, I could have killed that kid."

"That wouldn't have helped," she says.

"It certainly wouldn't've," my father says. "Because in the process you could've got killed in his place, and those kids always got ones working with them or friends for revenge. This is what I tell you and hope you'll remember for all time: stay out of other people's business, and if something like a robbery happens to you, shut your mouth and give everything you have. Twice I got held up by gunmen in my dental office and both times my advice worked. They not only didn't harm me but gave me back my empty wallet."

Magna and I go to the Marriage License Bureau. The line for applications extends into the hallway. "I hate lines," my father says. "I've always avoided them by calling before to see what time the place opens and then trying to be the first one there."

"It looks like the line for food stamps," the woman in front of us says to her mate.

"To me like the one for welfare," another woman says.

"Unemployment insurance," Magna says to me. "I've been on them. Didn't want to but had no choice. Have you?"

"Him?" my father says. "Oh, he was too pure to take unemployment. He deserved it too but you know what he did? Refused to even go down to sign up for it. He was living home then and I told him he was crazy. I said 'I always want you to have a job, but if you're fired from one or laid off, well, you paid for that insurance, so take it.' But him? Always too damn pure. That can work against you as much as it can for. Must've got that trait from his mother, because he certainly didn't get that way from me."

"I could have got unemployment a few times," I say to her, "but I always had some money saved and so thought I'd live off it and write at the same time. To sort of use the time break to produce some writing that might earn me some money but not intentionally to make me money—"

"There he goes again with his purity bent. Look, I never encouraged my children to take anything that wasn't theirs. Oh, maybe by my actions I occasionally did, but I never encouraged them personally to take like that. But he wouldn't listen about that insurance. We had terrible fights over it. Of course he never would've had to reject or accept any unemployment insurance if he'd've become the dentist I wanted him to. I pleaded with all my sons to and each one in turn broke my heart. But he out of all of them had the brains and personality for it and he could've worked alongside me for a few years and then bought me out of my practice. I would've even given him the practice for nothing if that's what it took to get him to become a dentist, though with maybe him contributing to my support a little each month, mine and his mother's."

"I wasn't good in the sciences," I say to him. "I told you that and offered my grades as proof over and over again. I used to almost regurgitate every time I went into the chemistry building and biology labs. I tried. I was pre-dent for more than two years."

"Regurgitate. See the words he uses? No, you didn't want to become a dentist because I was one. You wanted to go into the arts. To be an artiste. The intelligentsia you wanted to belong to. Well, now you're able to make a decent living off it teaching, but for how many years you practically starved? You almost broke my heart then, seeing you struggle like that for so long, though you still have time to become one. Dentists average even more money than doctors today."

"Next," the clerk says.

Magna gives her our blood tests results. She gives us the application to fill out.

"Can we come right up to the front of the line after we fill it out?" I say.

"You have to go to the back," she says.

"Why aren't there two lines as there are supposed to be? Why's the other window closed?"

"We're a little shorthanded today. You think I like it? It's double my usual load."

"There are three people typing over there and two putting away things in files. Why not get one of them to man the other window till this line's a little relieved?"

"Shh, don't make trouble," my father says. "You can't avoid the situation, accept it. It's the city."

"I'm not the supervisor," she says, "and the supervisor can't just tell someone to do something when it's not that person's job. Next," she says to the couple behind us.

Magna pulls me away. "Wherever we are," she says, "I can always count on you to try to improve things."

"Am I wrong?"

"You'd think at the Marriage Bureau you'd tone it down a little, but no real harm. It'd be too laughable for us to break up down here."

"He was always like that," my father says. "Always a protester, a rebel. Nothing was ever good enough in life for him. He'd see a Broadway play that maybe the whole world thought was great and which'd win all the prizes, he'd say it could've been much better. Books, politics, his schools, the banks—whatever, always the same. I told him plenty of times to run for mayor of this city, then governor, then president. He never took me seriously. I suppose all that does mean he's thinking or his heart's mostly in the right place, but sometimes he can get rude with people with all those changes of his he wants. He doesn't have the knack to let things roll off him as I did. Maybe that's good. I couldn't live with it if that was me. You'll have troubles with him, young lady."

We go to the Diamond Center for wedding bands. "How'd you find us?" the man behind the counter says.

"We saw all the stores and didn't know which one to choose," I say. "So I asked this man who looked as if he worked in the area 'Any one place carry only gold wedding bands?' He said 'Nat Sisler's,' who I suppose, from the photo there, is you, 'Four West, down the middle aisle on the right. There are forty other booths there but you won't miss his. He's got the biggest sign.' "

"Just like me on both my office windows," my father says. "Biggest the city allowed for a dentist. If they'd allowed me to have signs to cover my entire window, I would've."

"Too bad you don't know this man's name," Nat says. "We always like to thank the people who refer customers to us. But he was right. We've nineteen hundred different rings, so I promise you won't walk away from here without finding one you like. Anything particular you looking for?"

"Something very simple," I say.

He holds up his ring finger. "Nothing more simple and comfortable than this one. I've been wearing it without taking it off once for forty-five years."

"That's amazing," Magna says. "Not once?"

"I can't. I've gained sixty pounds since I got married and my finger's grown around it. Maybe he'll have better luck with his weight. He's so slim now, he probably will."

"More patter," my father says. "Then when you're off-guard they knock you over the head with the price. But remember: this is the Diamond Center. The bargaining's built into the price. Here they think it's almost a crime not to, so this time whatever price he quotes, cut him in half."

"Single- or double-ring ceremony?" Nat says.

"Double," Magna says, "and identical rings."

"Better yet," my father says. "For two rings you have even greater bargaining power. Cut him more than half."

Nat brings out a tray of rings. "What do you do?" he asks me. "You look like a doctor."

"I teach at a university."

"So you are a doctor, but of philosophy."

"I barely got my B.A. I write, so I teach writing. She's the doctor of philosophy."

"Oh yeah?" he says while Magna's looking at the rings.

"Turn your ears off," my father says. "Next he's going to tell you you're a handsome couple, how great marriage can be, wish you all the luck and success there is, which you'll need, he'll say—all that stuff. Though they love bargaining down here, they love making money more, so act businesslike. Ask him right off what the price of this is and then that. Tell him it seems high even if you don't think it is. Tell him you're a teacher at the lowest level. Tell him you make almost zero from your writing and that she won't be teaching next year, so you'll have to support you both. Tell him any other time but this you might have the money to pay what he's asking, but now, even if it is something as sacred as marriage, you're going to have to ask him to cut the price more than half. And being there are two rings you're buying—"

"What do you think of this one?" Magna asks me. It looks nice. It fits her finger.

"You have one like this in my size?" I say.

"That's an awfully big finger you have there," Nat says, holding my ring finger up. He puts several ring sizers on my finger before one fits. "Ten and a half. We'd have to make it on order. When's the wedding date?"

"Ask him how much first," my father says, "ask him how much."

"The fourteenth," Magna says. "But I'm sure these will be much higher than we planned to pay."

"That a girl," my father says.

"Hey," I say. "You'll be wearing it every day of your life, you say, so get what you want. I happen to like it."

"How much are they?" she asks Nat.

He puts the ring she wants on a scale. "Seventy-two dollars. Let's say seventy. The professor's, being a much larger size—and they're both seamless, I want you to know. That means they won't break apart unexpectedly and is the best kind of craftsmanship you can get—is eighty-five."

"Sounds okay to me," I say.

"Oh my God," my father says. "I won't even say what I think."

We go to the apartment of a rabbi someone told us about. His wife says "What would you like to drink? We've scotch, vodka, white wine, ginger ale—"

"Scotch on the rocks for me," I say.

"Same for me, thanks," Magna says.

"So," the rabbi says when we all get our drinks, "to your health, a long life, and especially to your marriage," and we click glasses and drink. He shows us the certificate we'll get at the end of the ceremony. "On the cover—I don't know if you can read it—but it says 'marriage' in Hebrew."

"It's a little bit gaudy for me," I say. "You don't have one with fewer frills? Oh, I guess it's not important."

"It is so important," my father says. "That certificate will end up meaning more to you than your license. And it's beautifully designed—good enough to frame and hang—but of course not good enough for you."

"You'll have to provide two glasses for the ceremony," the rabbi says. "One with the red wine in it you'll both be drinking from."

"Dry or sweet?" Magna says.

"What a question," my father says. "Sweet, sweet."

"Whichever you choose," the rabbi says. "You'll be the ones drinking it."

"A modern rabbi," my father says. "Well, better than a modern judge. Ask him what synagogue he represents."

"By the way," I say, "do you have a congregation? George said he thought you'd given that up."

"Right now," he says, "I'm marketing a wonderful little device that could save the country about five hundred thousand barrels of oil a month, if the public would just accept it. I got tired of preaching, but I'll get back to it one day."

"What he's not saying," his wife says, "is that this gadget will only cost three and a half dollars retail, plus a slight installation fee, and will save every apartment and homeowner about fifty dollars a month during the winter. The oil companies hate him for it."

"I wouldn't go that far," he says, "but I will say I haven't made any friends in the oil industry. But the effectiveness of the device has been proven, it'll last without repairs for up to fifteen years, and someone has to market it, so it's almost been like a crusade with me to get it into every oil user's home. Wait, I'll show it to you."

"Wait'll he comes around to telling you the cost of his ceremony," my father says.

"The other glass," I say, after we've passed the device around. "Is that the one I'm supposed to break with my foot?"

"Scott has the most brilliant interpretation of it during the ceremony you'll ever want to hear," his wife says. "I've heard it a dozen times and each time I'm completely absorbed. Actually, except for the exchange of vows, I'd call it the highlight of the ceremony."

"Would you mind if we don't have the breaking of the glass? We've already decided on this. To us it represents the breaking of the hymen—"

"That's just one interpretation," he says, "and not the one I give. Mine's about the destruction of the temples and other things. I use biblical quotes."

"Wait wait wait," my father says. "Did I hear you don't want to break the glass?"

"It's also just a bit too theatrical for me," I say to the rabbi. "Just isn't my style."

"Isn't your style?" my father says. "It goes back two thousand years—maybe even three. You have to break the glass. I did with your mother and her father and mine with our mothers and their fathers with our grandmothers and so on. A marriage isn't a marriage without it. It's the one thing you have to do for me of anything I ask."

"I can wrap a lightbulb in newspaper if it's only that you're concerned a regular glass might cut your foot," the rabbi says. "But if you don't want it . . ."

"If they don't, they don't," his wife says.

"We don't," Magna says, "but thank you."

"Then no second glass," he says. "It's your day."

"That's it," my father says. "Now you've really made me mad. That she's on your side in this—well, you must've forced it on her. Or maybe not. Anyway, I'm tired of complaining. From the man's point you'll be missing the best part of the ceremony, not the second best. I won't even begin to advise you about anything about the rabbi's fee."

"I know what your advice will be," I say, "and I don't want to bargain with him, is that so bad? Because what's he going to charge—a hundred-fifty? two hundred? So how much can I cut off it—fifty, seventy-five? What's fifty anyway? What's a hundred? And he's a professional. A professional should not only do his work well but know what to charge. You always let your patients cut your dental fees in half?"

"If I thought they'd go somewhere else, sure. Because if I wasn't working on them I'd be sitting around earning nothing in that time. But if your rabbi asks four hundred?"

"He won't. You can see he's a fair guy. And I'm not a complete jerk. If I think his fee's way out of line, I'll tell him."

"That's not the way to do it, but do what you want. I've said it a hundred times to you and now I'll say it a last time. Do what you want because you will anyway. But I'll tell you something else. Your mother didn't give you three thousand dollars of my insurance policy benefit to just piss away."

"That money was nine years ago. I didn't ask for a cent of it but she thought I deserved it because of the four years I helped her with you. And I used it to good purpose. I lived off it and worked hard on what I wanted to work on for one entire year."

"Oh, just pay anything he asks no matter how high. In fact, when he says his fee, say 'No, it's too little,' and double him. That's the kind of schmo I sometimes think you can be."

—

We're being married in Magna's apartment. The rabbi's talking about what the sharing of the wine means. My mother's there. My brother and sister and their spouses. My nieces and an uncle and aunt. Magna's parents and cousins and her uncle and aunts. A few of our friends and their children. My father. He looks tired and ill. He's dressed for the wedding, has on his best suit, though it needs to be pressed. He sits down on the piano bench he's so tired. The rabbi pronounces us married. I'm crying. Magna smiles and starts to cry. My mother says "What is this? You're not supposed to be crying, but go ahead. Tears of happiness."

"Kiss the bride," my sister says. I kiss Magna. Then I kiss my mother and Magna's mother and shake Magna's father's hand while I kiss his cheek. I kiss Magna again and then my sister and brother and brother's wife and my nieces and aunt and uncle and Magna's aunts and uncle. Then our friends and Magna's female cousin and I shake the hand of her male cousin and say "Oh what the hell," and kiss his cheek and the cheek of my sister's husband and the rabbi's cheek too. I look over to the bench. My father's crying. His head's bent way over and he dabs his eyes with old tissues. He starts making loud sobbing noises. "Excuse me," I say and I go over to him, get on my knees, put my arms around his lower legs and my head on his thighs. He's sitting up straight now and pats my head. "My boy," he says. "You're a good sweet kid. I'm actually having a great time. And there was no real harm meant between us and never was, am I right? Sure, we got angry as hell at one another lots of times, but I've always had a special feeling for you deep down. It's true, you don't have to believe me, but it's true. And I'm so happy for you. I'm crying because I'm that happy. I'm also crying because I think it's wonderful you're all together today and so happy, and I'm glad I'm here. Your other sister and brother, it'd be grand if they were here too." I look around for them. "Maybe they couldn't find the right clothes," I say. I get on one knee and hug him with my cheek pressed against his and then he disappears.

Eating

the

Placenta

Class is over, I go to my office and call Magna.

"Will, listen, you must come home. I think it's started."

"What do you mean?"

"I've had contractions since five o'clock and bleeding. There— there goes another one. I'm not in pain, just a little uncomfortable, but please hurry."

I look for a book to bring to the hospital. The doctor said the whole process might take fifteen hours, might take thirty. Two books, just in case. I slip into my jacket pockets two books I've been wanting to read for a long time.

"Mr. Taub, may I speak to you a minute?"

"I'm sorry, Gene, I'm in a rush—my wife. She just called. I mean I called her. We were supposed to go swimming at the gym, but she said her labor contractions have started. Today might be the day we have the baby."

"Oh, that's really something. Really, congratulations. They're premature congratulations, but I know everything will turn out all right for you both. But this will take only a few seconds. It's about what you said on the story you handed back to me today."

"Honestly, Gene, whatever I said doesn't mean anything right now. It means a lot to you—that's not what I'm saying—just that I have to go."

"I understand, but I just wanted to know—"

"What? Please, I said I have to go. My wife's gone into labor."

"Of course. I shouldn't have stopped you. I didn't know, and now I shouldn't still be stopping you. And regular office hours would be better. Could I see you here Friday at your regular two o'clock appointment time?"

"If I'm here, Gene, if I'm here. Excuse me, I have to lock up." I look for my keys.

"Your keys. Over there on the desk."

"I'm a little nervous, you can see that. So forget anything I say or do from now on."

"Sure, the baby—who wouldn't be? Mind if I walk part of the way with you? We live in the same direction. You are heading home, am I right?"

"Home. I'm going to have to walk fast."

"No problem, I'm a fast walker."

I lock the door, we leave the building. "Maybe along the way," he says, "you can explain to me what you meant on the second page here, third paragraph"—he holds out his manuscript—"that my narrative 'shows no movement forward.' I thought the point of my story—the point I wanted to make, at least, and whether I did it successfully isn't for me to judge, I think you once said. That the judges are the readers, not the writers. That the writer's job is just to—"

"Did I say all that? If I did, I don't know what I meant, at least not now."

"Still, my point wasn't to show plot but style, not to move forward in the story but to remain stagnant, not to—"

"Look, I can't talk about it. You're holding me up, and I have to hustle. I'm in fact going to run."

"Because your wife's in labor?"

"What do you think?"

"Was this the first time she called to say she was having contractions?"

"Yes."

"Then I wouldn't worry. I know something about it and the first time or two is usually a false alarm. It was with my mother when she had me and my older brother and my younger sisters, but the last two she didn't overreact on. False alarms all four times. I think they call them false contractions."

"She's had those false contractions for months."

"I didn't mean false contractions. I know what those are too. But false alarms. Or false labor. When the contractions can actually be timed. With the false contractions they can't be timed—the stomach just stiffens up. So I wouldn't run if I were you because sooner you get home, sooner you'll probably want to go to the hospital. And I bet after the doctors examine her they'll send her home. That's what they did with my mother the first two times till she learned. And my older brother's wife too. But only once with her. A week after she went to the hospital with that false alarm or false labor, she got real labor pains and that's when the hospital admitted her. She lost the baby though."

"I'm sorry."

"It practically devastated her. My brother took it badly but okay. Anyway, I hope I got my point across before about this thing," waving his manuscript. "That my story wasn't supposed to move forward at all. It was supposed to—"

"I know. It's clear to me now. And if you don't mind I'm going to go."

"Not at all. I hope I haven't detained you too long."

"To tell you the truth, Gene—yes, why not? To tell you the truth I'm kind of surprised that—well, just that I think you have kind of a nerve detaining me as long as you have and I've been kind of stupid or remiss or something in letting you."

"I don't think that's fair. What did I do? Actually, if you take what I've said about labor pains seriously, I'm probably stopping you both from rushing to the hospital and then being sent right home."

"Stopping us? Hey, babe, maybe my wife is in pain right now, did you ever think of that?"

"I'm sure she isn't, if these are her first contractions, but I'm sorry—you should go. And I just hope this isn't going to affect your attitude to me in class and my grade."

"You know what I think about grades in my class."

"Then just your attitude to me."

"I don't see how it can't, but I'll try not to let it."

"Thank you, because I didn't mean any harm. And I certainly don't have anything but the greatest respect for you as a teacher and also as a—"

"Forget your respect and telling me how much you have. You know what I think about that too."

"Right. 'Don't you praise me, let me just praise you.' A bit one-sided perhaps, but I'm sure your line of reasoning in that area is valid and very fair. But could I—as long as we're thrashing it out—mention one more thing about my story and then let you go?"

"What are you—"

"It's a minor point. You said at the end of your critique—and I appreciate every one of them, especially for their thoroughness, despite what I've said about anything else here—that my story has no ending. I think I discussed with you in our last conference that one of my principles, if you like, about my writing is not to write stories with endings. That life—though we as creatures die—has no ending, and that stories, when I finish them—ah, let's scrap that 'life' business for the time being, since it's weighing it down too much and I think complicating my argument unnecessarily. Just that my stories or longer fictions have no endings, period. I just don't like the contrivance of endings and I doubt I'll ever write—"

I take his story from him. He points to the second page of my critique and says "Right here you said it."

"Do you have a copy of this original?"

"This is the copy of the original. You told us to make at least one—that you wouldn't be responsible for losing a manuscript turned in, though you've never lost one in four years of teaching."

"You know where the original is?"

"Sure, in my writing desk, why? What are you going to do, tear this copy up?"

"That's right, I am." I tear it in half and throw it in the air. "Did I make my point or do I have to go after your pen and pad?"

"Sloppy," he says, looking at the pieces on the ground. "Who do you think picks them up, God? An angel? Hardworking workmen pick them up. Or concerned passersby, if we're lucky, who don't like seeing messes like this blowing all over the campus. It's unaesthetic." He picks up the half still stapled and some of the other pieces. I grab the stapled half from him and tear it into smaller pieces and stick half of them into my jacket pocket and try stuffing the other half into his shirt pocket.

"What are you doing?" he says, pushing my hand away. "You're crazy, did you know that? I'm dropping out of your class."

"Good," and I walk away.

"Besides all that, I hope your wife has a very safe delivery."

"Oh, thanks," I say without turning around, and start running the five blocks to my apartment building. I'm three blocks from it when a bicycle pulls up beside me and continues moving at my speed.

"I had to steal this bike to catch up with you," he says. "I'll get it back before the owner finds out. Stupid guy, just had a chain wrapped around it with no lock."

"How do you know it's a guy?" I say, still running.

"It's a man's bike. But you're probably right. A writer should be an acute observer of the most seemingly trivial things in life, you once said, but also shouldn't make summary judgments or general statements in his fiction without providing the reader with the correct facts."

" 'Correct facts'? 'Summary judgments'? No, no. Again, you either misquoted me to some incredible degree or are mixing me up with another teacher. Anyway, I'm going to stop saying things that sound anything like a quote or maxim or whatever if students are going to start repeating me."

"That's what I like about you and the way you teach—that you don't pretend to know all the time why things in writing work. That's what everyone likes about you in class."

"Good. Look, you stole a bicycle, so it must be important what you have to say."

"I wanted to apologize to you. I can understand why you tore up my story, and I don't want to drop out of your class."

"Tearing it up was dumb of me—overwrought, sensational; and you want to stay, fine, stay."

"Do you know if it's a girl or boy yet?"

"No."

"I thought because of your age and your wife's you would have had an amniocentesis done."

"We did but didn't want to know the sex."

"While your doctor knows? That's interesting. But I can also understand why you wouldn't, though I'd want to know."

"Hey. It's difficult to talk and run at the same time. And even if I'm going at a good speed, I think I could run faster if you weren't right next to me and scaring me that at any moment you'll lose control of a bike you're unfamiliar with and swerve into me."

"How about if I pace you then? I'll stay a few feet in front and in that way provide a service to your getting home sooner."

"I'd feel safer if I did it alone."

"Okay. Just wanted to be helpful. And if I haven't said it a million times, I think you're a terrific writer, Mr. Taub, whatever I think of your teaching—which is good but not as good as your writing. And much luck to you and your wife—if not today, if you don't have the baby, then whenever when."

"Thank you." I wave. He turns around.

I reach the building, run up the three flights and unlock the front door. "Magna?"

"In here." She's in the kitchen making a pesto sauce in the blender. Big pot of water's coming to a boil on the stove. "Salad's already prepared, though you might want to do a dressing."

"What's this? Contractions stopped?"

"No. Here." She points to her lips and I kiss them. "Since we probably won't have to leave for hours, I thought you should have dinner. I can't. Then we might even read or you read to me, and if the contractions still aren't regular, we'll go to sleep and see what happens."

"Great, fine, but I thought we had to go to the hospital now. And I'm sorry, I would've been here much sooner, but this student—Gene Kyplie?—I've mentioned him before."

" 'Big mouth Gene'?"

"I can't believe this kid. Today he—"

Phone rings. "If it's one of our parents," she says, "say nothing. That I'm okay, everything's the same—resting now—but let's not tell them things have started or they'll never stop worrying."

"Got you." I run to my workroom. "Hello?"

"It's Gene. How is Mrs. Taub?"

"She's fine."

"I was thinking. If you need a ride to the hospital—and I'm not saying on a stolen bicycle—or feel too nervous to do the driving yourself, I could—"

"We're not leaving yet."

"False labor?"

"No, seems real enough. Just that we're going to spend the first hours of it at home."

"That's smart. That's what my mother did with my two sisters. Why go unless the contractions are coming regularly? That's it, isn't it?"

"Yes."

"You'll just get bored to death there and then have to come home, just as I said. It's going to be a long haul. The first one always is. But let me give you my phone number in case you do need a driver. I can drive you in your car or mine. I'm only a five-minute walk to your place, and by car, less than two."

"Gene, we'll be all right. Thanks for your thoughtfulness."

"No problem. You've been more than thoughtful to me in class.

And your long written critiques and some of the office discussions we've had—"

"Good, I'm glad, but I have to go."

"Before you do may I ask one more thing? I mean, since there's no emergency now."

"What is it?"

"It's about my story. Is it okay to speak of it now?"

"Go ahead. One thing. What?"

"You once said that every first line of a story should get the reader right into the story. Should sort of pull him right in. That's the same thing, I realize. But you said the first line should usually be brisk, brief, with almost no adjectives if we can help it, and be something like the first line of a news story. To get the how, why, what—"

"I didn't say like a news story. I said—"

"Anyway, it's been one of the greater points of our disagreement. Since you also said that there are no rules to writing except one which really isn't a rule and that's to write as well and as honestly and uncompromisingly as one can. Terif. I go along with that. What's not to? So why the rules that a story must have an ending and that the first line should get the reader right into the story? Because I don't believe and never have and maybe I never will, though I admit I'll change some of my attitudes about writing in the future and maybe this will be one of them, that a story should grab the reader from the start. I believe the first line should show the style of the writing rather than the content of the story. Should stamp the writer's mark on the page rather than the narrator's. Should say to the reader 'Okay, pal—or enemy, or whatever you are to me—I the writer—' "

"I got to go, Gene. Seriously, something's changed. My wife, she just came into the room and—oh my God, she's having the baby right now. Hold it, honey, wait—there, my arms are out, let it come—push, push—holy God, I can see the head."

"If your arms are out—since one of your other big points about writing is plausibility, something else I can argue against strongly—how are you able to hold the receiver?"

"Lots of ways. It could be one of those receiverless phones you can talk to from any place in the room. But it's between my shoulder and neck—how could you have missed that?—and now—hold it, Gene. —Okay, honey, here comes another contraction. Push, push—one more should do it—got it. What do you know, a boy. What do you want to name it? Gene? Nah, I don't like that name. Here, let's get the mucus out of its nose and mouth before we do anything. There—great—and sponge its top and then in a blanket and under the lightbulb to keep it warm. Want me to bite through the cord now?"

"I'd wash its eyes first. That's almost the first thing they do after the birth—to prevent infection, I think."

"Right. Eyes. Clean. And boy he's a big beaut. I'd say around nine pounds. And why don't I like the name Gene? You relaxed now? Yeah, baby's just fine. Well, you know, you just about always associate the name you're going to give your kid with the people in the past who had it, and I once had a Gene in my class—that's right, the—"

"I'm still in your class. I haven't dropped out but I am thinking of it again, though it wouldn't be the courageous—"

"Well, this kid Gene—all right, not a kid—a student—was kind of a pest. Not just extrapolating too much in class and hogging a lot of the talk. But lauding me one minute, damning me the next. And on the students' evaluation reports of their teachers last year—for the course guide they publish for themselves? I got one comment that was so nasty and cheap—that I was only in teaching for the money? Remember that one? 'Mr. Taub says he can't teach writing, that we can only teach ourselves. So why is he at this university then? I'll tell you.' That my chairman wanted to speak to me about it, because he said one of the deans had called him—not that I gave a goddamn— and you know who I think wrote that report?"

"I hope you're not saying it was me. I know who wrote it—or at least have two good possibilities, since I think it was a combined effort—but I of course can't give their names."

"Not only that, this kid Gene likes to take his shoes off in class, and he doesn't wear socks. And he occasionally picks his toes or plays with them during most of the class, which wouldn't be so bad if he sat at the other end of the table—bad for me I mean—but he always sits a seat or two away from me. I've hated this habit of his but never said anything. Okay, I've given plenty of reasons why it can't be that name, so enough complaining. And baby's nice and comfy now. Cord's neatly tied, face and body thoroughly sponged. He's as clean and healthy as can be. What a kid. Want to feed him now?"

"I don't think your wife will have much luck feeding him so soon, with a bottle or by more natural means. And what about the placenta? Has it come out yet? If it hasn't at the next contraction you should get her to push."

"The placenta, honey. Has it come out yet?"

"You'd know if it had. It looks like the raw horsemeat they feed the lions in the zoo. I was there when my mother had my youngest sister. I watched the entire delivery—special permission for siblings sixteen years and over—she was a change of life baby, in case you're wondering—and my parents also told the doctor I was pre-premed. And she couldn't feed Ramona for two days, till the milk came. Even after that it was rough for weeks."

Magna's standing by the door. "What are you yelling about a placenta for? Who's that?"

"Gene you-know-who. Here, take the baby and see if it will feed, honey," and lodging the receiver between my shoulder and neck, I pretend to give her a baby.

"Are you really talking to a student that way? You don't want him to think you're insane. You shouldn't get so close to your students. Dinner will be ready in three minutes. Spaghetti's already in and you like it al dente."

"Make it softer tonight."

She leaves. "But you were saying about me, Mr. Taub?" Gene says.

"Whatever it was, I got to go. Nice talking to you."

"But if you had the baby and she's feeding it or is trying to, you have time to talk a few more moments, right?"

"About your work?"

"More about the principles involved in writing and technique overall. Because, quite truthfully, not once have I ever fully agreed with a thing you've said about technique, as much as I admire—"

"Oh stop that nonsense and leave me alone. I'm busy and I wish you'd see that and I shouldn't have joked around with you on the phone in the first place and I'm hanging up now, Gene."

"Oh say, a real conclusion. A hanging-up. My teacher is going to hang up on me. What finality."

"Not *on* you. I'm simply putting the receiver down. My dinner's ready. I'm very hungry."

"You're right and I guess I have taken enough of your time. Too much, probably. You'll have to excuse me."

"Sure."

"And my offer still stands, despite all the things that went between us. You need a driver of your car or someone to drive you in his car—"

"You return the bicycle?"

"Yes, why?"

"I don't know. Didn't want you to get in trouble or the bicycle owner to think his or her bike was stolen."

"Very kind of you. You were always a very kind guy. You always have something nice to say about everyone's work in class. I'm not sure if that's good or bad, but there it is. And come to think of it, since we do disagree so strongly about the principles of writing and because I did take you already for one term, maybe I should drop out of the class while I still have time."

"Maybe that's a good idea. Do what you think best."

"You do want me to drop, though, don't you?"

"No, you're okay. You cause a little excitement in class that I kind of like. And also having you there as an adversary sort of—my countering your ideas as much as you countering mine. Something like that. You can understand if I'm not too articulate to-night."

"I don't know if I like being used in class like that."

"You aren't, entirely. Listen—"

"And if you really didn't like my playing with my toes, as you called it, why didn't you just say so? I'm not addicted to the practice."

"I was hoping someone else would before me. But the class is too damn tolerant."

"Except for me."

"Dinner's on the table," Magna says at the door.

"That was my wife. She says the placenta's ready to come out but she wants to do it in the bathroom where it'll make less of a mess than in this room. So, must go, Gene. Goodbye."

"I'll wear socks from now on and won't take my shoes off once. I'm staying in your class, in other words. I also like the exchange of ideas we have and—"

"Anything you want." I hang up. "You okay?" I say to Magna.

"No, there's another one," holding her stomach. She looks at her watch. "The last three have come more regularly. I think we should go soon. First eat up. You'll need the food. I'll be resting in the bed-room."

I walk her to the bedroom, then go to the dining room and start eating. Phone rings. "I'm not going to answer it, Magna," I yell out. "Don't answer it either." Phone keeps ringing.

"I'm all right enough to get it," she yells back and she goes down the hallway, picks up the receiver, says "No, Professor Taub can't be disturbed, Gene. He's eating the placenta and it's bad luck to stop the father in the middle of that rite. . . . I'm feeling fine, Gene, thank you, and you're wrong—I'm telling the absolute truth."

The

Letter

He goes to a corner of the room and reads the letter. "Dear Stanley. It will never be the same. It never really was. One day. That's all I can say. Enough. So long. Louisa."

He folds the letter in half, puts it into his side jacket pocket, looks at the ceiling, shakes his fist at it, shoves his hands into his jacket pockets. One hand touches the letter. He pulls it out, sits in the easy chair, turns the floor lamp on, and reads the letter. "Dear Stanley. I don't know. Can you say why? Can I? Some things just happen. This did—we both know that—so it's why I have to write this. But I can't write any more. It's too tough to. Goodbye. Louisa."

He crumples up the letter, throws it across the room, gets up, stamps on the floor, stamps again, goes to the window just to do something other than think of the letter. His foot kicks the letter as he walks to the window. He looks at it, picks it up, sits in the couch, turns the side-table light on, reads the letter. "Dear Stanley. Did you have to say it? Did you have to act like that? Did I have to? Is it possible to answer these questions? More important, is it necessary to? Forget it. I don't even know why I try to explain. What I'm saying is these things you can't. See ya. Louisa."

He drops the letter behind the couch, gets up, punches his palm till it hurts, walks to the door, feels for his keys, leaves, walks to the elevator, turns and goes back into the apartment, reaches behind the couch, fingers around till he finds the letter, pulls it out. It's not the letter. It's a rug-cleaning bill from he doesn't know when. Two years ago. Paid in full, it says. He looks at the rug. It could use a cleaning after two years. It could also use a vacuuming or at least a good sweeping. He puts the bill on the side table, fingers around behind the couch but can't find another piece of paper, pulls the couch out, sees the letter among other debris: a ballpoint pen with its cap gone, a coat button, two coins. He pulls the couch out more. A beer-bottle cap, movie ticket stub, ballpoint-pen cap, lots of dust balls. He picks up the letter and coins, puts the coins into his pants pocket, looks around for a place to sit, sits on the rug, and reads. "Dear Stanley. Remember when? Remember the bridge? Remember the bridge's lights? Remember the do-not-walk-on dunes? Remember the wren? Remember when someone said that? Remember when someone said, 'I'm not poetic, but life is'? Remember the response? Remember when someone's eyes lit up someone's eyes with the bridge's lights? All remembrances. Or memories. If only. I'm saying, 'If only.' I'm saying, 'IF only.' I'm saying, 'IF ONLY, IF ONLY.' Oh God, goddamn. I'm sorry, Stanley, I'm sorry. No. Each try at this makes it worse, for you, me—us both? No. I have to go. Louisa."

He puts one corner of the letter between his teeth and rips it in half. He stands and takes a half in each hand and throws them up and watches them float down. He kicks one half just before it hits the ground, and it flips over and comes down almost on top of the other half on the floor. He puts his foot on both halves and mashes them. He goes to the closet, hits a row of his hanging clothes with his fist. Several of his pants slide off their hangers to the floor. He takes off his jacket and hangs it up, holds one of its sleeves to his face and rubs it against his closed eyes. He runs back to the center of the room, picks up the two letter halves, flattens out the creases as well as he can, holds the two halves together, and reads. "Dear Stanley. Even Mother said. Even Father said. First yours and then mine. Even Jack and Babs and Albert and Treat. They all said. They all felt. They all hoped but knew. Still, it continued. Will we never learn? That might sound trite, but try for a moment to say it another way. It's what I'm going to sit down and think about later today: why we don't ever seem to learn—not necessarily us but just people in general. Excuse me. Because as someone also once said, 'You do go on.' Or 'You can go on.' But now I'm going out. I have written myself

out, completely out. I must stop. I will and now. Dear Stanley, goodbye. Louisa."

He tears the two halves into halves. He opens the window and
holds his hand with the letter pieces in it outside the window. A car
passes one way, a bus, another. Several vehicles—cars, trucks, a bus,
and motorbike—are waiting at the corner for the light to change. He
hears a propeller plane, looks up. Clouds and, behind one, sun, but
no plane. He pulls his hand in, closes the window to about an inch
from the sill, sits on the bare floor directly below the window, fits the
letter together, and reads. "Dear Stanley. Someone phoned. You
know who. It was"—he turns each piece over and fits them together—"almost four. But in the morning. I didn't know the time
when the phone first rang. I knew it was late. Or early. I'd gone to
sleep around twelve at night. The phone rang and rang. Rang and
rang and rang. I wanted to answer it. I didn't want to. I told myself to
answer it. I told myself don't. I put my hand on the receiver. I took
it off. I kept it on. I kept it off. Rang and rang and rang and rang.
What did? The phone! Forty or fifty times? Sixty, perhaps? Then it
stopped. That was the one call to me that night. Or morning. At least,
the one call while I was awake or the only one that woke me. We both
know whom from. We both know who rings like that and who has a
tendency to call very late at night but never that late. We both know
why too. Why that person rang like that and so late. Why why: all
questions. Ring ring: all rings. Letter letter: all words. Goodbye goodbye: all goodbyes. Louisa."

He puts his mouth right up to the bottom of the letter, takes a
deep breath, and blows. The pieces scatter one or two feet. He puts
his mouth up to the two pieces that are closest together and blows
harder this time. They separate one or two feet. He puts his mouth
up to the piece he's blown farthest from the original spot, takes an
even deeper breath, and blows. It flies up a few inches. He tries to
grab it in the air but misses. He crawls around collecting all the
pieces, stands, tears them into little pieces, and throws them into the
air. They come down on his head, some of them. One stays on his
head. He can feel it. Right in the middle, very light. He takes it off
and reads it. "Someone phoned." He turns it over. Blank. He mashes
it between his fingers, drops it on the floor, picks up another piece,
and reads. "My love for." He reads. "My love for." He turns it over
and reads. "Remember when?" He turns it over and reads. "My love
for." He picks up all the pieces, tries to put the second side of the
letter together on the floor. He has to flatten out most of the pieces.

Some of the pieces keep curling up after he's flattened them out, and he has to flatten them out several times. It takes him a while to put the letter together, but he does it. He reads. "Dear Stanley. Now is not the time. My love for life is great. Forgive me for what might appear to be confusion here. This will be the last of these, I swear. Adieu. Louisa."

He gets up, kicks the couch, kicks it several times till his foot hurts, kicks it with his other foot till his shoe falls off, slams the couch against the wall so hard that the wall cracks where the couch hit it, picks up his shoe and throws it across the room. It barely misses a print hanging on the wall. He grabs a couch pillow, throws it at the print. It misses. He grabs the other couch pillow, throws it at the print. It hits it. The print falls off its nail to the floor. The glass breaks, the frame splits. He stamps across the room, picks up the largest piece of glass and throws it at the couch. It hits the wall above the couch. Glass flies back at him, a piece nicking his cheek, another piece cutting his leg. He smears blood from his cheek on the floor-lamp shade. He puts his hand back on his cheek, but the bleeding seems to have stopped. He drops to the floor, rolls up his trouser leg, runs his hand over the blood there, slaps his hand down on the letter on the floor. He lifts his hand. Some of the letter pieces have stuck to it. He looks at the bottom of the second side of the letter still on the floor and reads. "Dear Stanley. What more? Can't think of anything more. Can't think of anything at all but to say that I can't. Can't can't. This will have to be all, then. This will have to be all. This is all. Because there is no more. There can't be. There is not. There really isn't. I keep saying that in various or different ways, but do I mean it? Do I know it? Dear Stanley, I mean it and I know it and I believe it. Dear Stanley, there isn't. You shall see also there isn't, because there won't be anything else under my last 'Louisa.' Under my last 'Goodbye, so long, see ya, adieu, Louisa.' Bye. Louisa."

There's nothing else after that. He collects all the letter pieces on the floor and puts them on the grate in the fireplace. Several pieces fall through the grate. Other pieces are still stuck to his hand. He gets a section of newspaper off the bookshelf to the left of the fireplace, rolls it up very tight, sticks it under his arm, gets a book of matches off the same shelf, lights a match, lights the rolled-up newspaper with it, puts the newspaper roll under the grate, throws the lit match and the book of matches on top of the grate, watches the letter pieces burn. The letter pieces under the newspaper roll will probably burn too. He picks the letter pieces off his hand and flicks them into the fire. One piece drops on the tile part in front of the fireplace. It's all red with blood. He turns it over and looks at the other side. Red. He leaves it in front of the fireplace, turns the easy chair to face the fireplace, sits in it and watches the fire.

Change

Now I must change. She said I had to change. "Enough with your cynicism, scorn, arrogant egotism and unsociability, and overall unfriendliness." So I'll change. I've thought about how to change. Starting from the most elementary human intercommunication and gradually working myself up to the most complex. For one thing, no more disapproving looks or under-the-breath comments about people on the street I don't even know. For who did I think I was? And don't cross the street and walk with your head turned or pass on his or her side of the street with your head down when you see a neighbor you could momentarily be civil to and perhaps eventually get to know. Look up and say something next time, and whatever you say, don't ever again be supercilious. One's coming. "Hello," I say.

"Good morning."

Say something else. "And a nice morning also."

"It is a nice morning, you're right, though the radio said it might rain."

"The radio? The weatherman inside your radio said that? I got one inside mine too."

"You do?"

"A little weatherman inside my radio."

"Very nice."

"Several, in fact. When I switch radio stations, I mean, and when I go to FM, several more."

"I see."

"Don't you also have FM?"

But he was gone. I don't think I did very well. His expression and the way he waved his hand down at me when he left. Too screwy, he must have thought. Though what did he expect me to say: that drivel to drug him that he so likes to hear? No, that was more cynicism and scorn. Be more receptive and even appreciative of different lifestyles and personal values. To everyone: a readiness to listen to and lots of understanding and respect. They might want to engage in drivel till what they think is the right moment in a conversation with a relative stranger, when they can become intelligent and imaginative, if not deeply insightful and profound.

Another neighbor. Seen her around often enough too. She's across the street, heading in the same direction. I cross over and catch up with her. In time I would have had to get over to this side of the street anyway.

"Good morning," I say.

"Good morning."

"Nice day today."

"It is."

"Very pleasant out."

"Yes. Breezier. Be seeing you."

"Lovely. Just a lovely day today."

"So I've heard." She speeds up, is gone too. Why did I persist? Once or twice is enough. If I want to say anything other than a greeting or what kind of day it is, make it different but not screwy or repetitive or initially too complicated or forward where I drive them away.

A boy approaches. Neighborhood kid. Try it out on him. "Good morning, young man."

Doesn't say anything. Walks right past, head intentionally averted, just as I used to do.

"Cat caught the old tongue, kid?"

Continues on.

I run up to him, tap his arm. "Hey, I said good morning to you."

"I heard you. And don't touch."

"So why didn't you say good morning or at least a hello back?"

"I'm only supposed to speak to people I know."

"You can always say good morning to someone. That's just everyday good manners, which I'm sure your parents would be happy to know you have."

"My mother's said if I don't know the person who even says he has an important message from her to me, don't stop. She also said to get someone to call the police if any stranger is bothering me."

"I'm no stranger. I live on this block. Have for years. I know you. I've seen you since you were in your baby carriage and just the other day playing wall ball."

A man passes. "Mister," the boy says, "could you do something against this man or call the police? He's bothering me."

"No, I'm not. All I did was say good morning to him, and he didn't answer, so I asked him why he didn't say good morning or at least something like hi or hello in return."

"I don't believe anyone's compelled to return a good morning or hello to anyone," the man says. And to the boy: "You really think he's annoying you enough for me to call the police, Robert? I will if he is."

A young woman stops. "What's wrong?" she says. So now something was wrong. I'll work it out. Sensibly, even good-humoredly, won't get overemotional.

"Nothing's wrong," I say. "As I told this gentleman, I said good morning to Robert, whose name I admit I just learned. But Robert didn't answer me, so I asked him why, and he said his mother told him not to talk with strangers, though like him I live on this block and have for years. Then he stopped this man and asked him to do something about me or call the police because I was bothering him, which I wasn't."

"He grabbed me."

"I touched his arm to gain his attention."

"It could have been one way or the other," the man says, "as I wasn't here when it began."

"Good morning," I say to the man.

"Good morning?"

"Not 'Good morning?' as if you're questioning whether the morning's good, unless you are."

"He was questioning you," she says to me.

"Good morning," I say to her.

"I'd just walk away from him, Robert," she says.

"Anything the matter?" a mailman says, pushing his cart, first deliveries of the day.

"Good morning, mailman," I say.

"Good morning."

"There, you see how simple it is to say good morning?" I say to the three others. "Thanks."

"You're welcome," the mailman says, "though I hardly know for what. What happened? The boy?"

"No, him," the man says. "Bothering Robert for not saying good morning to him, Robert said. That's why we stopped. Robert asked me to do something about the man or to call the police."

"No police," I say. "Not necessary, and certainly none of this would have been if Robert had responded with a good morning just as the mailman did. Good morning," I say to the mailman.

"Good morning, good morning, good morning," the mailman says.

"I was only trying to demonstrate how easy it is to say. Good morning," I say to the woman.

"He needs an ambulance, not the police," she says.

"Both," the man says.

"Well, I have to get on with my deliveries."

"And me to school," Robert says.

"Then we'll forget about the police?" the man says.

"I'm late," Robert says.

"Forget it, then," the woman says.

They all go in different directions. Deliveries, school, work. For the woman, school, job, shopping, newspaper, or home—I just didn't know. "Heading for work?" I say, walking beside her, going to that corner too.

"What's it your business?"

"Just talking. Everyone has a place to go and something to do most of the time, I was just thinking. Me? I was getting the newspaper and also trying out the new changes in myself. The way I deal with people. To be friendlier, warmer, more considerate and sociable, not to always have the heavy face and critical word."

"Am I going to be allowed to walk in peace by myself?"

"Of course. And good morning."

"You mean goodbye."

"No, I mean good morning."

"You know, you didn't ask me, but you're doing a very bad job on yourself, really. People hear you like this, they won't take to it. I don't know what you conceive of as new changes, but if this is supposed to be one for the better, I hate to think what you were like before."

"Good morning."

She goes.

"Good morning, everybody," I shout. "Good morning, good morning. And all of you have the very best of days."

A man on the third floor of one of these five-story row houses opens his window all the way and says "Hey, buddy, it's still a little early, and some people work later than others and even at nights and sleep days, so keep it down, okay?"

"I'm sorry. I didn't realize. Part of my self-absorption and insensitivity and lack of understanding about people. So thanks for telling me, and you can be sure I'll know next time. Goodnight. I mean, have a good sleep."

"I didn't say myself. Someone else here. And probably other people on the street too. But drop it."

"Right. Then good morning to you." He shuts his window. "I said good morning to you." I shout "Good morning. I'm saying good morning to you." He opens his window and throws a garbage bag at me. His aim's good, but I step out of the way.

Moving

On

—❦—

I'm despondent. For one thing, I've no money. For another, I don't know how or where to get it anymore. I've looked and looked for work and run out of people to borrow from till I find a job. I've gotten my full share of unemployment insurance and refuse to put my family on welfare. My wife's begged me to take welfare money, but I said that's not how my dad did it or grandfathers would have done it and so not the way I'm going to do it. I owe on my telephone, utilities and several months' rent. My landlord's been patient and kind with me but for the last few weeks has been saying he might be forced to evict us unless I pay up right away. My—a paper's slipped under the front door. It's a court order saying we have to vacate the premises in three days or a city marshal will put all our belongings on the street and get a locksmith to change our door locks so we can't get back in.

I wake up my wife. She's been ill for months. Our child's in a free nursery school. I show her the court order, and she says "I thought you said you paid the rent."

"Not in full."

"Did you even pay any of it for the last few months?"

"If by 'few' you mean the last four, then the answer's no."

Suddenly the lights go. "What's that," she says, "the fuse?"

I check the fuses. Both are okay. "It's probably—no, it has to be, and you're not going to like this—the utility company shutting the electricity off because I also didn't pay that bill."

"I've had enough of this. Sick as I am, I'm leaving you till you get things back for us in much better shape."

She starts getting dressed. She's really too weak, and I help her on with her clothes and pack her suitcase and an overnight bag for our boy. She makes a phone call, asks me for my last few dollars so she can cab to our son's school, pick him up, and then cab to the apartment of her best friend, whom she's going to move in with for the time being. I grab and hug her, say "Please stay."

"Let me go. I don't want to make a ruckus and cause my illness to get even worse."

I straighten her hat, see her to the street, and hail a cab. She says "If you get a job or work it all out some way, call me, and I'll come right back," and blows me a kiss as the cab drives away.

I stay in the apartment for the next two days, phoning the same people who couldn't give me a loan or help me get a job in the past, eating only cold food because the gas has also been shut off.

The marshal comes early the third day. I open the door, and he says "You leaving voluntarily, or do I have to do it by force?"

"Give a guy a break. My wife's already left me and taken the kid. And this is my only home. These are my sole possessions. I couldn't sell them when we were living here and eating and sleeping on them, and now I've no money or place to store them and nowhere to go or money for a hotel."

"Does that mean you're not leaving voluntarily?"

"Give me just two more weeks to find a job or borrow enough money to pay part of the rent or to leave here with my belongings to a rented room."

"Mind if I use the phone?"

"Sure. I won't be able to pay the bill anyway."

He lifts the receiver, listens to it, and says "Did you know your phone's dead?"

"No, but I feel lucky it didn't happen sooner."

"I'll call from your landlord's." He goes downstairs and an hour later rings my doorbell. I don't answer it. He says "I've got two assistants with me, and there's no way you're going to stop us." I stay quiet. They break my lock and force the door open. "You leaving now?" the marshal says.

"Please, you can't just throw a man and all his belongings into the street, and I'm sure if you wait a while longer something will turn up.

Maybe a nice-sized check in the morning mail from my uncle or a friend."

"I can't wait. I've other people to dispossess. All of my pay and, through me, my assistants', comes from the number of cases we complete a day." The three of them pick me up in the easy chair I'm sitting in and carry me this way to the street.

"I feel bad about this," my landlord says, while the marshal and his men pile up my furniture and things around me on the sidewalk. "But I've my bills to pay too. Heating oil, for example, has practically doubled in two years, and I was only allowed to pass a little of that extra cost on to my tenants."

"I understand," I say and continue to sit in the chair, protecting my property and waiting for the mailman to come.

An hour later the mailman enters my building's vestibule. I wait till he finishes depositing the mail before I go inside and open my mailbox. Just a few store ads and notices for my wife. I go into the next building's vestibule, where he's delivering the mail, and say "You sure you didn't forget anything for Crin in number seventy-nine?"

"If it's not in your box, I don't have it," he says. "Maybe tomorrow it'll come."

The landlord follows me into the vestibule and says "Could I also have your mailbox key? It's already going to cost me plenty with your new door locks and also repairing what was once just a little scratched door and frame."

I give him the mailbox and door keys and go outside. The sanitation men are putting into their truck what furniture and things of mine that the scavengers aren't picking through and carting away. I start to protest, then wave everybody to just go ahead, and walk to the phone booth at the corner. Maybe my wife and her friend will take me in. I don't think so, but maybe if I give them a real sob story, they will.

I stick my last coin in the phone and am about to dial her friend's number, when I see a sign right above the coin slot that says "Are you flat-out poor, down on your luck, and, let's face it, just plain damn hungry for an honest job and some good hot cooking? Is this coin you're dialing with one of your last, if not the very last change you got? Are you in one of the worst, if not *the* worst bind of your life, and you don't have a single other clue what to do? Well, friend—and you'll call me your friend if you follow these directions and turn out to be a winner—this is no gimmick, swindle, or illusion

you're reading here. I am a bona fide extremely rich and generous
lunatic but not a con artist or liar by any means, so what I promise to
do in this notice I will. The first person to phone me with the right
answer to the following question will have five thousand dollars in
cash delivered to him or her at this booth within ten minutes of the
phone call. 'What is the one end unly ful pruf race to the luggin
botm kur?'"

I get so angry by the message on this sign that I dial the phone
number below the question. A man answers by saying "Question or
answer?"

"Probably eventually an answer. Is this the person who put the
sign up in the phone booth at Ninth and Grand?"

"That's a question. And I'll answer your question with a question. The message about answering my question for a specified
sum?"

"You're the one. Well, I'll tell you what my answer is Mr. Rich or
Just Crazy Rotten Lunatic. My answer is, How dare you insult poverty and deprivation that way," and I hang up.

I lost my last coin, but I feel good about what I did with it. I look
around the floor for another coin, don't find one, and go outside and
look around the booth. It's been my experience that people lose more
coins around telephone and subway-token booths and also automatic
toll-collecting machines, though those are much tougher to pick up
because you're in a car, than anyplace else.

I don't find any coins around the booth. As I start to walk away, a
car pulls up, stops with its motor running, and the man in back rolls
down his window and says "Question. Are you the gentleman who
phoned me a few minutes ago from this booth with the answer to my
question about what is the one end unly, etcetera?"

"You're damn right I am. What of it?"

"Answer. You won, my friend. Feel good." And he drops a package out of the window, and the car drives away.

I open the package, just out of curiosity since I don't believe
there's anything inside but more wrapping paper bound real tight,
and see a stack of fifty-dollar bills. I go into the booth, shut the door,
and huddled against the phone, count the amount of money in the
package—it comes to around five thousand dollars. I hail a cab and
give the driver the address where my wife is, but after a few blocks I
think, Suppose the money's fake? I don't want to build up her hopes
or have her think I'm a complete idiot for being so taken in by some
man's elaborate prank.

I tell the driver to stop in front of the next bank, hold out one of the fifties and say "I think it's real, but if it isn't, you still willing to accept it as my fare?"

"If it's not real, I'll know what to do with it," and he takes the bill.

"Listen, I don't want you deceiving anyone with it if it's counterfeit."

"Listen, yourself. Want me to call a cop on you for trying to beat the fare and maybe even passing a fake fifty-dollar bill? Just get out of here."

I get out of the cab, go in the bank and ask to see the manager. I'm brought to her office. I put the money on her desk and say "Excuse me, but is this money stolen or real or stolen and real? Someone gave me it, and if it's real but not stolen, I want to put it in your bank."

"I'll have to check." She jots down some of the money's serial numbers and makes several phone calls. She repeats the serial numbers to each of the persons she calls. After her last call she presses a button on her desk. Two guards come in, and she says to me "So far they're all fake. I'm afraid you'll have to wait here for a federal officer to speak to about them."

She leaves the office with the money and one of the guards. I stay there with the other guard and say "Someone gave me that five thousand."

"Sure someone did," he says. "I'm not protesting."

"But it's true. I had no money of my own—that you can almost tell from my appearance—when I'm in this phone booth—"

"And you see a sign on the wall that says 'Call this number for five thousand free dollars.'"

"Then the guy who does this has a reputation for signs and phony bills, that it?"

"What guy?"

"The one who put the sign on the phone-booth wall. 'Call this number with the right answer to my question,' the sign said. But I didn't answer the question right or even call him for that. I called because—"

"Whatever you called him for, he zipped over with the money, gave it to you and disappeared."

"Then you do know of him?"

"Know of who? Because I've nothing better to do, I'm just making up your story as you go along."

The federal officers come, take down my statement about how I got the money and say that it's inconceivable that anyone but a crazy person would bring money into a bank and ask the manager if it was real or not if he already knew it was counterfeit and that I was probably the victim of a very bizarre practical joke or hoax. They ask for my IDs, run a check on me over the phone, find I'm clean and never been in for anything and ask where I'll be staying the next few days, in case they want to get hold of me. I tell them I've no place to live right now, though I hope my wife will put me up at her friend's home. One says, "We'll drive you, and on the way you can show us this sign, if it's still there, in the phone booth."

We drive to Ninth and Grand. There's no phone booth there, but there is a newsstand. I say "This stand was never here before. I know this neighborhood. Nothing's been here for the last ten years but a phone booth."

He says to the newsdealer inside the stand "How long has this stand been here, ma'am?"

"This one or the one my family had here before?" she says.

"This one."

"First my dad had it, and when he ran away, my mother took over, and when she got sick, I got it and am supporting her with it, besides my own children and my sister's kids. It's impossible earning a living just by selling newspapers and magazines, so against my mother's better wishes and, you can also say, the memory of my grandparents and the law, I take numbers and sell cigarettes. You look like a gambling and smoking man. Like to buy a carton or two and put down your lucky number for today?"

"No thanks," and he walks back to me.

"Oh, come on, ask anyone around here. You there," I say to a woman passing, "ever see this newsstand on the corner before they put it up today?"

"Today?" she says, then goes up to the newsdealer, and says "I'll have the *Star* final, Marilyn—so don't try and slip me the early city edition this time—and also a pack of Ours."

"All right," I say to the men, "I won't lie anymore. I found the money in a garbage can. I was hungry and looking for edible food or for things to sell to secondhand stores so I could buy some food, which is why I didn't tell you the truth where I actually found it: I was too ashamed, besides feeling you'd never believe I found the money in a garbage can."

They drive me to the place where I say I found the money: one of the trash cans in front of my old building. They search through all the cans, find nothing of any use to them, tell me I wasted a lot of their time by not admitting from the start where and how I got the money and I should feel fortunate they're not taking me in, and drive off.

I go back to the newsstand. A man's inside it, and I say "Where's that woman who was working here before?"

"What woman? Nobody but my wife from twenty years ago has ever been inside this stand."

"Now you listen to me," I say, grabbing him by the shirt.

"Okay, okay, take it easy. I was just still having a little fun with you, but you don't want to play, that's your privilege. Allow me, please." He pushes my hand away, takes off his mustache, sideburns and glasses and says "You recognize me now, don't you? Clothes a bit different, though you don't expect me to change into my real ones right on the street. But I'm going to make up for everything I did to you so far—and doubled. Ten thousand legal dollars to spend as you like, since you really earned it."

He comes out of the booth, gives me a package twice the size of the one he dropped out of the car earlier today and snaps his fingers. A truck pulls up. Six men get out of it, quickly dismantle the newsstand and put it on the open bed of the truck, just as a second truck pulls up behind it with a phone booth. The men take the booth off and start installing it where the stand was. The man climbs onto the bed of the first truck and waves to me as it pulls away.

"I'm going to get those officers back to show them the booth," I shout.

"See who's got what to lose," he shouts back. "Not me, for sure." The truck turns the corner.

"Who is that guy?" I ask the man smoothing out the new cement around the booth.

"Think I know? He gives my boss money, my boss gives me a job to do and I do it, and that's all."

"Who's your boss?"

"Forget my boss. That guy before likes to give away money, take it."

"Fake money he likes to give away. You want it, it's yours." I hold out the package of so-called money.

"I'd like to, believe me, because I know it's real, since I've seen this happen in different ways a few times before, but I'm not allowed to take it. See those windows?" He points across the street to an office building with about two hundred windows facing us. "In one of them, I don't know which, we're being watched. If they saw me take this bundle, I'd be in big trouble. So keep the money. Have a terrific time with it. And any day after this if you see me walking down the street and you still want to give me the money with no questions asked, do it. But starting tomorrow, when it's by accident and they're not watching. Today, I'm very sad to say, I can't." He goes back to his work.

"So you think the money's real?"

"Don't take just my word. Check it with a bank."

I open the package, see about ten thousand dollars in fifty-dollar bills and go to a different bank and ask to see the manager. This manager goes through the same serial number and phone process. "The money's real," he says after several calls. "But I've been told to ask you to wait."

"What for? The money's not stolen. I didn't do anything wrong."

"You say that someone gave it to you and that you have no known address. Well, the federal people I spoke to are contacting an Internal Revenue officer to come here and bring you to his office so he can attach a certain amount of this money for income taxes. Gifts have to be declared, you know, except for a few thousand a year from each parent. If you don't earn much this year, you'll probably get most of it back when you file your tax returns. Meanwhile, the government, because it might not have as good a chance to catch up with you later, wants its share."

"I'm not hanging around for anyone to take part of this. I need every cent right now."

"Guard," he says into the phone. I grab the money and run out of his office for the front door.

"Stop," a man shouts. Several customers drop to the floor around me, and in the window reflection I see a bank guard pulling out his revolver.

"Don't shoot," the manager says. "It's not our money he's taking."

I run out of the bank, around the block, take a cab to my wife's friend's building, pay the cabby with a fifty-dollar bill and have to give him a lavish tip so I can get back some change.

I ring the friend's intercom bell. Nobody answers. I ring it several times and then sit on the stoop steps. A couple of hours later an elderly woman walks up the steps. "May I help you?" she says. "I'm the landlady."

"I'm waiting for my wife and child. They're staying with Lisa Monobin."

"They all went to Lisa's parents for the week."

"You know where that is?"

"I do, but I'm not going to say."

"Is it all right if I stay in Miss Monobin's apartment till they come back?"

"It most certainly is not."

"How about if you phone her and ask if I can stay here?"

"I'm sorry, but I also don't want a stranger in the building while the tenant's away for so many days."

"Thank you."

"I don't see for what."

"For looking out for their interests. Know where a nice hotel is around here?"

"Two blocks north to Dinmore, then left one block and you'll find the Dinmore Arms."

I go to the hotel, get a room, shower, have supper and wine sent up, eat and drink till I'm stuffed and almost drunk, and fall asleep on top of the covers. The phone rings a few hours later.

"This is the desk clerk, sir. I know it's late and I wouldn't have disturbed you, but the gentleman on the line says it's most urgent."

"Put him on, I guess." He does.

"Mr. Crin?"

"Yes?"

"It's me, the money giver. Having a swell time? Things going well? Nice hotel? Did the money prove true, and are you using it well? Didn't I just say something like that before I said that about the nice hotel? How are your wife and son? I'm certainly having fun with you and can afford to, and why so? But what am I trying to say, Mr. Crin? Would you—and this I suddenly remember is it—like another ten thousand dollars of false or real bills?"

"What do you mean false or real?"

"You take your chances. I have ten thousand in false before me and another ten in real. I will shut my eyes, turn around several times on the spot I'm standing on and with my eyes still closed pick one of the identically wrapped and weighted parcels on my desk. It might be the false or the true. I swear I won't cheat, so it's a fifty-fifty chance that the package I pick for you will be the one you want. But first you must answer my question before I grab either parcel."

"Go ahead. As you said when I last saw you on that truck, what do I have to lose?"

"I said that? Hackneyed of me if I did and platitudinous to you too. Excuse me while I sneeze. *Kerchoo!* And you could have lots to lose. For instance, if the bills are bogus and you're caught, try to explain it again to the bank or the law. But the question. Still want it?"

"I'll take my chances and try to get around the bank and law some way."

"Great. Now who in due time is the incidental chieftain of a very special excessive place going on forever till death to us party of the first lark or what?"

"Not that this will be news to you, but I don't understand."

"Did you say 'Dr. I. Don't Understand'? *I* standing for Alain."

"That's a ridiculous old kiddish joke, and besides, Alain starts with an *A*."

"Yea, you win. Congrats. Or as I also sort of said, it might be years you'll lose, though you're still young. Anyway, I'm shutting my eyes, turning around. The phone cord's getting wound around my arm and chest, something I didn't expect, and I reach out an extricated hand for my desk and blindly select one of the packets. The money will be delivered to your hotel lobby in the morning. Goodnight. Or good morning. Or just good good, not?" He hangs up.

Early in the morning I go down to the lobby, sit in a chair and wait several hours for someone to deliver the package. I give up just before noon and am heading back to the elevator when that man runs in, looks at his watch, then at the clock above the hotel desk, and is about to hand a package to the clerk when he sees me.

"Mr. Crin, as long as you're here, take the parcel yourself," and he throws it at me and runs out. "Sorry for being so late," he says, coming around once more inside the revolving door, "but I had another lark to attend to, which also worked," and back on the street he jumps into the rear seat of a car, which pulls away before his door's closed.

I go to my room and open the package. Ten thousand dollars exactly, which look real to me—or as much so as the first batch of bills that turned out to be fake.

I dial the desk clerk. "Anything I can do, sir?" he says.

"Clerks are supposed to know a lot about city life and where to get and do what and such—you know what I mean. So I'll stop being cagey and say that what I'm asking is in strict confidence, and see if it doesn't benefit you. I closed a deal in cash today and now think I gave good legal merchandise for counterfeit bills. Do you know anyone who can tell a real from a fake fifty-dollar bill, though not someone in the service of any law-enforcement agency?"

"I have a friend who might, but how much will it benefit us?"

"Three hundred to be divided between you in any way you like, half now and half after it's done."

"Bring down the bills in question and also half our three-hundred-dollar fee."

I bring several of the new bills to him and for his payment three of the real fifties that man gave me at the newsstand. He says "Stay in your room till my friend comes. If they're real, I'll call you to come down and pay the rest of our fee. They're fake, I'll slip them under your door, and we'll call it even."

I wait in my room. Half an hour later someone knocks on my door.

"The desk clerk?" I say.

"You bet. Let me in."

"I'm sorry, it doesn't sound like him. You better leave the floor fast because I'm calling the police."

I run to my phone. Someone puts a key in my door and opens it. I try to force it closed, but it's pushed back, and the door chain's snapped. Two men I don't recognize come in, shut and lock the door and order me to give them all my money and not to talk above a whisper or make any dumb moves.

"What money?" I say.

"You know what money." They twist my arms behind my back, and I tell them that all my money's in the tissue box in the bathroom.

One of them gets it and says "Now the other package."

"What other?"

They twist my arms back again. "Wedged behind the dresser," I say. They get that package, take my wallet and change from my pockets and leave.

The phone rings just as I run to it to dial the desk clerk.

"It's Josh," the clerk says. "My friend says your money's real, so come on down with the other one-fifty."

"I was just robbed. Two men who just left. You can still get them if they're leaving through the front."

"Are they kind of stocky guys wearing felt hats and short dark coats, and one has red-tinted glasses on?"

"That's them."

"They just went through the door. I wouldn't have wanted to tangle with them, and neither would our security guard, who's on his break. They took all your money and things?"

"Cleaned me out. And you know damn well they did. You probably sent them up."

"What a thing to say. But if they took all your money, you don't have any to pay your hotel bill, do you?"

"Except what I left with you to find out if it was real or not."

"That my friend and I will have to split up for the second half of your fee. And you, sir, since you can't pay your bill, will have to be out of your room in fifteen minutes, or I'm getting our security people to bounce you."

I try to phone the police through the hotel switchboard, but it doesn't answer.

I take the elevator to the lobby and say to the clerk "I'm getting the cops here about this robbery."

"Go ahead. What proof you have? I had nothing to do with it, and as for the fee you gave my friend and I, I'll deny it. But wise up. A man carries around so much cash, he has to expect to get robbed and bumped on the head. Goodbye."

I leave the hotel. If I go to the police, they'll ask where I got all that money. If I think up a plausible enough story and they do believe me and eventually find the thieves and money, they'll call in federal officers who will want me to pay taxes on the twenty thousand. If the police only find ten thousand or so, I still might have to pay taxes on the entire twenty. If I had earned fifty to sixty thousand this year and the money's not found, I could claim the stolen money as a loss on my income taxes at the end of the year. But the police aren't going to find the thieves or believe me. The clerk will have a good excuse, if he was involved. And I've been in too much trouble the last few days, have no identification papers or residence, and I'm also beginning to look like a bum.

I go to my wife's friend's building. Maybe they returned earlier than they thought they would and will put me up.

"No," the landlady says, "they haven't come back and aren't expected till I won't say when. You can't stay in their apartment, either."

I sit on the stoop and wait.

"Please," she says from the second-floor window, "no loitering. This is a respectable building, and I won't allow it. Besides, how do I know that woman friend is actually your wife or that you even know Miss Monobin?"

"You have to take my word."

"That's not enough. Get off the stoop, or I call the police."

"You think they'd come these days, with all the other crime going on in the city, just to tell someone to stop sitting on a stoop?"

"They would for me. My son-in-law's on the force. My husband was on the force before that, and his father before them."

"One part of me believes you, but another part says you're not telling the truth."

"Try me."

I stand up and start down the stoop.

"And stay away from my building from now on. If I see the woman you say is your wife, I'll describe you to her, and if you are her husband, I'm sure she'll know where to come looking for you if she wants to. To me, though, you look dangerous." She shuts her window.

I walk down the block to I don't know where. A car pulls up beside me, its back window sliding down, and moves along with me as I walk. The money giver's in the rear seat, smiling at me and extending his hand out the window to shake.

"Go on and take it, Mr. Crin. I've nothing tricky inside it, and the car won't suddenly surge forward or, if you don't, suddenly stop. Okay. No hand. Keep walking. But how are you? Not so good it looks like. You're finding life isn't as easy as you thought it would be, isn't that so?"

"That, my friend, I knew long before I met you."

"Ah, I'm your friend. You see what I said we'd become? And terrific. You just answered my question correctly, so you win again. I can't say you're lucky, and I can't say you haven't been played with, and I can't say you didn't earn—"

I stop. "What are you talking about? Why don't you make sense for a change or just level with me for once? Like those two thieves in my hotel room before. They were yours also, right?"

"I can't say."

"And the clerk. He's in with you too, true?"

"No, I don't think so, though come to think of it, I can't say."

"Then you tell me how those thieves could have gotten my hotel-room key if not from the clerk. And how they could have known how many packages I had if not from you or through you from the clerk."

"You think so? That what happened? Was all your money taken? But that was so much. It certainly looks like it happened—you're still in shabby clothes and wandering around aimlessly on this rather unseemly street. But answer me only one more thing, and I swear that what I have for you won't be taken away. What is the state of the state in the state by the—"

"Please! No more questions, answers or games. I won't win when I win, so what's the sense of my playing them anymore. Go away. Leave me in peace."

"That's the answer. Just that. 'Go away. Leave me in peace.' For a moment I didn't think you'd make it when you began going on about 'Please, no more questions or games.' But you just won back everything you lost, plus another five thousand. An additional ten would be out of the question, I'm afraid, which I'm sure you understand."

"I don't want it. All I want is a job. You have a job for me, an honest one, enough to keep my wife and child and me living frugally but decently till she gets well and can also work, I'll take it. Nothing crazy, I want you to know. Driving your car for you on your chauffeur's day off. Cooking your meals or answering your mail or painting your rooms. Any of those will be okay, something I can do. Come on, you must have one or know somebody who does. Look at this long expensive car and all the money you toss around. You must employ plenty of people."

"You want a job more than you want to play this game?"

"Definitely."

"End of game then. But you won't earn in three years from me what you'd have right now if you consent to taking your winnings."

"It'll do. I want benefits, though. Medical insurance for my family and me."

"I give it to all my employees."

"Vacation days. The regular ones, nothing out of the ordinary. The normal holidays every workingman takes unless you need me that day."

"If you have to work on a holiday because my entire staff can't take off, I'll give you time and a half, and if you work more than eight hours that day, double overtime pay."

"Fine. Sounds more than fair. Hire me, please. And give me enough money to get a good meal tonight and sleep in a cheap hotel for a couple of days till my wife returns."

"I'll do that. I will." He snaps his fingers at the chauffeur, and the car drives off.

I wait for him for several hours to give me the hotel and food money and tell me where and when I can start work, but he doesn't come back. I sleep in an alleyway that night and beg for food money the next day. After I eat, I go back to the same spot I last saw him and sit on the curb, but he doesn't come all day. When it gets dark, I go to the building my wife's staying at and ring her friend's bell. Nobody answers. I sit on the building's stoop.

"I warned you," the landlady says from her window. "Now get off."

I stay there. I'm too tired to go anyplace else.

"For the last time," she says.

A police car parks in front of the building a half hour later. "Don't give us a hard time," one of the policemen says.

"Who says I would or could or anything," I say. "I just need a place to sleep and eat tonight."

"How about for the next few nights?"

"If that's the least I have to take for a place to stay tonight, fine by me."

I'm booked for loitering and put in a cell for three days. When I get out, I go to my wife's friend's building and ring her vestibule bell.

"Yes?" the friend says on the intercom.

"Dana, please."

"Yes?" Dana says.

"It's me. How do you feel? You won't believe what's happened to me the last week. Please let me in."

"Michael, I have to tell you something you're not going to like. I had a solid week to think it over. I heard what you've been up to. It's clear to me we're never going to work it out anymore, and I'm filing for a divorce."

"I said let me in," I shout. "The landlady doesn't want me out here, and her son-in-law's a cop."

No answer. I ring and ring. I bang on the lobby door and try to kick it in. Then I hear a police-car siren. I run down the stoop stairs, trip on the last step, get up, fall—it feels like my ankle's broken or badly sprained—get up much slower and limp around the corner and for several blocks, till I reach the park. I hide in it behind some bushes and try to think what I should do. I can't think of anything that will help me, and I fall asleep.

"Wake up, buddy," a policeman says a few hours later. "For your own protection, nobody's allowed in the park after midnight, so you'll have to move on."

"Sure, sure, I don't mean to cause any trouble." And I leave.

The

Rescuer

➤

He hears people screaming, looks at them, looks at where they're looking and pointing, and sees a child standing on a chair next to a balcony railing about ten stories up. The child's trying to climb from the chair to the railing. It puts one foot out, brings it back. It holds the railing with one hand and puts the other foot out, brings it back. People are screaming "Go back. Young girl...baby...young boy... get off the chair. Go to your mommy. Go to your daddy. Go inside. Get back into your apartment." The child gets off the chair, pushes it against the railing, climbs back on it, stands up and puts its hands on the railing. It lifts a leg. Henry wants to scream at it to get off the chair and get into the apartment, but everyone on the street seems to be screaming at it. He shouts "Everyone, be quiet. Let only one person—and that person with the strongest most authoritative voice— yell up to the child. I'll go into the lobby and try to call up to the apartment. If an adult's there, he'll get the kid off the balcony. If no one else is home, then I'll somehow get into the apartment myself. What floor's it on?"

He starts counting. Someone shouts "Seven stories up. The eighth floor." Someone else yells "Baby, go back. Go to your mommy. Get off that chair. Get off the balcony and go inside your apartment this second."

Henry runs to the building's lobby. The crowd screams. Henry stops. The child's on the railing and seems about to fall. He's almost directly under it. It looks like a boy. I have to catch him. It might kill me, but I have to try to break his fall. The baby falls off the railing and comes straight down, sideways, then feet first. Henry tries to stay under him, but the child hits the ground a few feet to his right.

He doesn't look at it. He puts his hands to his ears to keep out the sound he heard. He gets on his knees and starts crying, his hands still over his ears. He lies facedown on the sidewalk and scratches at the ground. He draws his legs up under him and covers his head with his arms. People pat his back. He hears a siren. Someone rubs his head. He hears a different kind of siren, then the motor of a fire truck parking very near. Someone takes Henry's arm away from one of his ears and says "Sir, you should get up. I don't want to say this, but you're in the way." His eyes are shut tight. He says "Let me stay here a while longer. Is the child gone?"

"The child's dead, yes, of course."

"I mean, is it gone from here, taken away?"

"Not yet. They're doing measurements. There are some technical things, police things, that have to be done on the ground before they take her away."

"It was a girl? I thought it was a boy. Was she alone in her apartment?"

"Her older brother was with her, but he was playing in his room."

"What, he was very young?"

"Five or so. Why don't you get up? You don't want to look, that's fine. In fact, you shouldn't look. No one should who doesn't have to. I'll take you wherever you want to go. I'm a police officer. I'll take you to a hospital if you think you have to go there, but I'll also take you home. One of us will."

"I just want to stay here for the time being. You can understand."

"It's just that—oh all right. For the time being, I can understand."

Henry continues to lie on the ground, his eyes closed. He doesn't want to see anything. Not the balcony, street, the building, even. He wants to go to sleep. He thinks, Try to sleep. They'll see you asleep, and they'll carry you away from here to someplace. Or if you're still here when you wake up, maybe the girl will be gone. The building won't, but time will have passed, and you can go home then. You'll be stronger—something like that. Anyway, let everyone walk around me for now. I deserve it.

"Do you have anyone at home?" a different man says. Henry pretends to be asleep. "Sir," the man says, speaking right into Henry's ear now, "I asked if you have anyone at home."

"A wife and child." His eyes stay closed. "But an infant child, maybe a couple of years younger than the one who fell."

"She was two and a half. We still haven't located the parents. The father's in a plane, the mother went out shopping, the son said. Did you ever hear of such a thing?"

"My child's a year younger. More: he was just sixteen months. When I saw that child up there, I saw my own. Not that my boy can climb up a chair, but he can climb down one, backward, just as that girl did. I doubt he'd know to push the chair up against the railing to get nearer to it, and I'm sure he hasn't the strength to push it. But I could be wrong. It could be a very light chair. And when I say that when I saw that child, I saw my own kid, don't misunderstand. If that girl had been five years old, ten, twenty, not a child but a grown adult, an old woman on her last leg, even, a ninety-year-old man, I'd still feel the same, but I probably wouldn't have tried to save it. A young child I thought I could catch or break its fall. Anyone older than five or six would probably kill me if it hit me from that height."

"The two-and-a-half-year-old would have killed you also. She was going sixty miles an hour, one of the experts here said. Something of that speed."

"It seemed fast. I still think I could have saved it if the wind hadn't taken it out of my reach at the last moment. It was almost in my arms—she was—I swear to you, when whoosh, she was swept away. Right now, if there's anything I wish for in life, it's that I could have saved her somehow. Even with a major injury to both of us—but one quickly repairable for her and, of course, for me too. But preferably where she could have just dropped or rolled out of my arms and walked away, and I could have walked away after her. But no more talk. Let me sleep. Or try to sleep. Please."

"If you wish. It's really no problem for us if you stay here."

Henry thinks, Go to sleep. Just go, now, to sleep. He can't. He thinks about the fall. He sees the girl falling once, five times. He sees ten babies falling from ten stories up, first one at a time, then all at once. He sees a fire in a building and one child after the next jumping out of all the front windows, some of them yelling before they jump, "Catch me, save me, help me, please." He sees a building falling down with hundreds of children in it. Falling on him, the children tumbling out of it just before it lands. Then the sky dropping children: head first, feet first, sideways, face down and face up. Children falling from planes, helicopters, falling at speeds of a hundred miles an hour, two hundred miles an hour, so fast he can't see them till they hit. He opens his eyes. I'm worse off down here than if I were standing up and away from here, for away from here maybe I'd be able to sleep. He tries to stand. He can't. "Someone help me," he says. He's helped up. "Please lead me away but not in the direction where that poor child is."

"She's gone, if you mean the one on the ground," someone says.

"Still, lead me away from where she was."

"That was quite the fall," says one of the two people holding him up. "And that was quite the thing to do, trying to stop the fall with your body. You were smart, though, to get out of the way at the last instant. I know you didn't want to, but the girl had no chance to live, and you were putting your life on the line. Do you know what it'd feel like if just a pebble dropped from that height and you tried to stop it? It'd go through your head or three inches into it, if it landed there, or all the way through your hand, if you tried to catch it. Nothing survives from that height in a free fall, and the same goes if that free-falling object strikes any vital part of you. Can you stand on your own now?" They're across the street.

"I think so." They let him go. He falls down.

He tries to stand on his own several more times in the next hour. He can't. He's taken to a hospital. Doctors test him, diagnose him, say his legs are temporarily paralyzed, something psychological, but they'll be back to normal after he rests awhile. His wife's there. She says her mother's with their son.

"Did you lock all the windows?" he says.

"How could I? It's too hot to keep them all locked and when the only air conditioner we have is in our bedroom. The windows, as usual for the summer, are open at the top."

"He might suddenly be able to climb onto a chair and stand up high enough on it to pull the top part of a window down."

"He hasn't the strength to pull a window down, and Momma's watching him."

"Momma might fall asleep or go to the bathroom, and it could happen then."

"Even if he had the strength, he'd never be able to reach the top part of any window from a chair."

"Then he could try, by standing on a chair next to a window, and lose his balance and fall through the glass. Call Momma and tell her to lock all the windows and keep all the chairs away from the windows."

"I'll call her."

"Call her now."

"There's a phone down the hall. I'll call when you're napping."

He knows she won't. He gets out of bed to call Momma and then to go home and see that all the windows are locked and all the chairs are across the rooms from the windows. He looks around for his clothes. "Where are my pants and shirt?"

"You're walking."

"So I am. They said it would only be temporary. Are my clothes in the bathroom?"

He gets dressed and phones his mother-in-law. "Bertha, lock all the windows and push every object Timothy can climb on away from the windows—far away. We're coming right home. How is he? In fact, don't let him out of your sight till we get there, because for all we know he might push a chair back to the window or stack a pile of books by a window and climb on it."

Outside, he looks up at the twenty-story hospital. "We have to move to the country," he says. "Not the suburban country but to a real rustic area where no building's more than a story or two." Then he sees a child falling from the solarium terrace about ten flights up. He closes his eyes, shrieks, drops to his knees. His wife helps him into a cab, and he cries the entire ride home.

That night he sleeps on the floor beside his son's crib. The next day he moves the guest bed into his son's room, so he can sleep beside him every night. He stays close to his son for the next few days. Finally his wife says she thinks Timothy needs a rest from him and he from Timothy. "Just stay in bed—our bed—and try to get some sleep." She takes Timothy to her mother's house across town.

He tries to go to his office the next two weeks, but most of those days he just walks by tall apartment buildings, looking up for children on terraces or balconies or hanging out of windows. If he sees one, he'll do what he can to stop it from falling. If one falls, then this time, from no matter what height it comes, he'll try to break the fall with his body.

One morning, after being out for a couple of hours looking up for children, he sees one leaning out of a sixth-floor window. He yells "Stop. You there. Go back, back, or I'll come upstairs and beat you black and blue." The child's pulled in by an adult. Henry follows the flight path the child would have taken and then looks at the spot around where it would have hit and sees a huge bloodstain on the ground. It starts to rain, and he sees tiny children falling from the sky and running down his face. He suddenly screams when a child lands a few feet from him in the street and disappears into the hole its fall made. He looks down the hole. It goes so deep he can't see the end of it. Then he sees liquid rising in the hole. It's blood, he smells, when it gets within about ten feet of him. He dives into the hole to pull the child out. He finds himself diving off the bridge that connects this city with the one across the river. He closes his eyes and waits for this image to change into another one, but it doesn't. He tries to imagine himself being caught in his son's arms.

Love

and

Will

⟶

Say about an hour ago she said well I don't want to beat around the bush, Will, I'm deeply in love with this man. She wasn't being cruel or rude. What was she being? Of course not cruel or rude. It's starting to snow. When I was in her apartment just before, she said when you were outside did it seem as though it might snow? I said why, does she want to go out? She said she just wants to know, that's all. I told her I was never in my life able to tell. But truthful is what I suppose she was. I don't know. But certainly truthful is what she came closest to being to me at the time. I don't know anything right now except right now I'd like nothing better than to be on top or underneath or at the side or moving at intervals all around her but inside her and with our tongues tied and playful and bodies tight. But there she was. After a while rather tired of me and wanting me to go. Though looking so calm at first. Kissing me when I entered the apartment though now instead of a whole mouth I got the tip of her lips. The peck. And stepping back from me when I put out my arms to hug. And when I finally got her into my hug, placing her arms around me weakly and patting my back as if to console me for my loss. Then holding my hands mother to child. Speaking to me man to man. Looking so sorrowfully at me as if for the pain she was causing me which she couldn't help me get out of or over or undo. It's done. She's in love.

Listen, she said, trite, ridiculous or whatever this might sound to you, I'm in love with my entire being. So am I, I said. She said she doesn't believe me. I said did I say it was with you? Anyway what you say doesn't sound ridiculous or anything else to me because I too strongly believe in love. That's good, she said. Or believe strongly in love—they both sound right. That's good, she said. Or I just believe in love, I said, why should I refer to strength? But me she could easily dispose of. The lesser of two loves. Rather the one she said she was growing to love. Or at least could have grown to love. Or whatever it was she said about love. But what she did say was that for a while she felt she might have liked to learn to live with me but could now only afford from a distance to like. The one she loved deeply was the other whom she'll be flying to during her Easter break in two weeks. In London where she said he says he has a large and lovely Victorian-like flat. Saying things to me like that. And that she's so sorry it had to come to this. Her one-way bliss. Because she was really quite content with me till she met this new man. It was all such a fluke. A girlfriend called her up. She said she knew this English fellow about to leave for England whom she wanted her to meet before he went. He came over for tea for an hour and stayed with her for a week before he took his flight last night. For a few days during this time she kept telling me on the phone she's sick and very tired and thinks she's coming down with the flu. Tonight she said she was fairly sick and tired but seems to have escaped the flu.

She also told me she thinks I'm a bit off. That she didn't want to say it. That she in fact at first didn't believe it. She said she thought when I said certain things she didn't understand that she was being obtuse. Now she's certain that many things I say are a bit off. I said off? She said off. I said excuse me but off to where? To China? To the provinces? Off to the outer regions of our solar plexus or the inner legions of hell? She said off like that. No not like that. Now I was being belligerent, defensive, reactive, if maybe a little off. What she's talking about off is when I say things she thinks I think come to me from faraway places or just pop presto magically in my head and which she said I repeat with total confidence without really knowing what I said. Because aren't people obliged to understand what they're saying to other people aloud? she said. What they say to themselves or too low for anyone to hear is another story—she supposes anything goes there. I said I suppose so unless what the person's saying to someone is said more for the poetry of the words—the sounds. She said these off things she thinks I say don't sound poetical or anything else to her except off. I said I didn't say they did. And that she's right. I often say off things simply because I think they might or do sound metaphysically comical or epistemologically profound or just plain bright or yuk yuk funny and she'll enjoy my company more for my having said them than if I hadn't or some such stuff. Then you agree? she said. I said cross my hope and heart to die. She said that's the first time we agreed on anything since that first time we ever agreed on anything which was when we agreed that her sister's Great Dane puppies we were watching suckling their mama were performing a very sensual act. I told her we didn't even initially agree on that. That I didn't think the puppies were doing anything especially sensual in their suckling till later that night when I dreamt of those suckling puppies and in my dream became one of those puppies nuzzling my face between the back legs to get at the two hindmost nipples and that instead of suckling a nipple it was like being with my tongue and lips down in there doing it to a woman which I did to her when we woke. She said she doesn't remember that. I said I'm sorry but it was only as a result of my dream and between the time of our waking up and making love that I agreed with her that those suckling puppies had performed a sensual act.

It's snowing harder. Where oh where in my pocket is my collapsible green felt emergency harsh weather hat? I'm walking to my parents' apartment of thirty-three years. People scurry past all four ways. Ahead a block away a figure slips and trips before he can get himself upright to flip over again. I pull down my hat tightly so it won't blow off. If Dana were with me now she might walk right behind me holding my waist and then say she sees she can't be protected from the snow and cold this way and can we take a cab? If I said let's walk a little more, as I like a strong wind with lots of curlicuing large flakes, she'd probably say she'll pay. It's eleven blocks south along Central Park West from her building and then a right turn down a sidestreet to a brownstone halfway down. I pass the statue I passed with Dana a few weeks ago when I said remember the time I told you I once saw one of the museum's custodians polishing the bronze testes of Theodore Roosevelt's horse? She said then that as she said before she thinks the experience has to be experienced to be appreciated though not visualized. Tonight she said her scalp had mercifully stopped itching during the time David was with her though resumed a few minutes after I came in. I said I suppose that's reason enough for falling deeply in love with him, seeing how she's compared her up till then irremediable fungus to thousands of microscopic devils trying to claw their way out of each of her hair follicles and then getting lost in her hair, but why doesn't she come right out with it and say she thinks I'm the main cause of her itchy scalp? She said she thought she just did. No she only looked at me teasingly as if to say she thought she just did.

I'm sure my mother's asleep. She usually reads in her room while sipping from a half glass of sweet wine for a half hour after she puts my father to bed at nine. He'll be asleep in his hospital bed in the living room, the room closest to the kitchen and bathroom, where during the colder months he spends most of his waking day. He'll be facing the window. The floor-length curtains inches away from him will be fastened together by safety pins. I'll turn him over as I do every night I sleep home. About once a month I must rush him in his wheelchair to the bathroom so he can make two. He can't turn over by himself. We've been warned he can get bedsores if he isn't turned at least once a night and that in the morning his muscles and bones on one side will most likely ache. And he can develop red spots on his ankles from the pressure of one foot lying too long on the other and his having dislodged the pillow placed between his feet. And because he's a diabetic the red spots can lead to open wounds which can lead to a foot being cut off. Before I turn him over I'll say urinate first. I'll place the urinal between his thighs and stick his penis inside if he's too tired to do so or can't locate it. I'll hear the splash against the plastic and then say through now? and he'll say no or yes. If it's no I'll take the urinal away a minute later and empty and wash it out. Then I'll turn him over and place the pillow between his feet. Two Chux between his penis and thighs in case he has an accident overnight. Cover him up with the top sheet folded a few inches over the blankets and place the urinal beside the Gelusils and bell on the table-tray beside his bed. I'll say comfortable? and he'll say yes. I'll kiss him on the forehead and say goodnight. Maybe touch his cheek or run my hand across his face or pat his shoulder or head and shut out all the lights and say sleep well and he might murmur thanks. I'll close the louver doors to the kitchen. Get a glass of wine from the refrigerator and read in bed with another glass of wine. Maybe return to the kitchen for a third or fourth or fifth glass of wine before I feel sleepy enough for sleep.

Tonight she said that's your problem when I said I'm sure if I had showed her more affection and attention this past month she never would have become interested in this English guy. She had placed on the table a plate of different French cheeses she had picked up at the same store she bought the closest American bread to a baguette. I said I'll get a knife. She said break it with your hands. I said it isn't easy breaking butter with your hands unless the cubes are frozen solid and it also gets very messy smearing it on bread with your fingertips. She said she'll get it but I said stay. I got up so I could get behind her. Her back was to the kitchen. I leaned over her from behind with the knife in my hand and kissed her lips. She let us linger there but when I tried opening her mouth it wouldn't budge. Maybe you better go, she said. I spoke about passion. I forget whose. Maybe hers, mine, ours. She said must you yell? I was putting my shoes on at the time. I said when I speak about passion I sometimes have to do it passionately. And passion to me is the essential, Yeats said, I said. I told her that was in a letter he dictated or wrote. I know because I read it yesterday. And I know I read it yesterday, I said, because if I had read it the day before yesterday I wouldn't have remembered the quote and if I read it today I would have remembered if the letter had been dictated or written. She said someone else once said. I said Shakespeare always said. She said Shakespeare isn't the one she's thinking of although one of his characters did say give me that man that is not passion's slave, which she thinks applies to her here. My shoes, coat and muffler were now on. She said she forgets which play it's from though it was in one of the textbooks she taught from last term, but let's call it a night, Will, she said. I said I can't and I'm not going to transform into the little boy she says I sometimes become when I don't get what I want. Hamlet, she said. Act scene, seen act, I should have said. But I said my stomach hurts and I'm feeling awful and I don't want to be alone tonight. She said well what do I expect her to do? I said her sleeping with me now would be a very considerate thing to do. She said not tonight. But you don't even know, I said. Didn't one time in bed you didn't want to do it when I did and I stirred you up into wanting to and later you said you were glad I hadn't let you fall asleep straight off? She said she'll call me at the end of the week and we'll meet. I quickly calculated. Today's Monday. Four days. Too long. Maybe the end of the week meant Sunday to her. I said we can simply sleep beside one another if she likes, arm around arm, not even that if she doesn't like. Just in the same bed if she likes. Or if she likes I'll place a board between us if she has a board or a column of thumbtacks down the middle of the bed if she prefers. I said do you have any tacks? She said no. I said what if I just sleep on the living room couch surrounded by thumbtacks and broken glass and you in your own bed in your room? No that won't do, I said. What have I come to? I said. What about the time she was so warm to me when I was sick? It started in a movie house. We had to leave before the picture was over but she said she didn't mind in the least. Not if I was sick. She gave me medicine, a back rub. I had fever and chills. She tucked me in, made me mint tea. Paid for the cab. Untucked me, got in beside me. No clothes on. Oh what a sight. I wore her shirt. She turned down the electric blanket. Warmed me with what she for the first time out of many called her hot box body. And next morning I was well. The infamous ten-and-a-half-hour virus had passed. Doctor Dana I said when she gave me tomato juice in bed. Just old Doc Dan to my friends she said when she took the glass. I don't know if it was when she took the glass. I do know it was tomato. I think she that night stirred me up to doing what I originally didn't feel like doing though I'm now not so sure. I think I said you'll get sick. I think she said don't fret about me. Did we come? Was it fun? Tonight I said passionately that I won't speak about passion passionately anymore tonight or even dispassionately or even the word passion or passionate or passionately or passional or even passionless or -ateness or passion fruit or flower or week or -tide or play or Sunday or even pass in or passing or pass sing or passengers sing or passenger pigeons used to sing or any words like that. None. I promise. Heart my cross and die to hope. I'll be passionless. No words even near to passion. Not even passive, passage, passport, Passaic, passe-partout or even passe or partout.

By now I was at the door. At the door I said I'll stay a while longer if she still wants to talk. I'd like to talk. Stay then, she said, but please not for long. So I again thought there was still some hope. What I wanted most was to get us both into bed. But that I already said. But that I still want to do. Just to get this horrid night through. Because tomorrow, she said, I think tomorrow we both have to go to work. But how am I going to get through work? Should I call in sick and lose a per diem day's pay? She gets paid when she phones in ill. She teaches at college, I'm at junior high. She works one-third of my hours and gets twice as much pay. Her work's more than not intellectually stimulating and emotionally satisfying while I come home physically exhausted and emotionally and mentally drained every workday. But she takes the subway to work while I walk the three blocks to school and run home for lunch. I shut the door. Close call I think I thought then. And sit at her table without ever again removing my muffler, coat or gloves. In the movies we used to hold hands. Tonight I said I bet in a month this piggy finger of hers will have rings. In the street it was arms around waists and also hands. And one night at Ray's place she fell asleep with her head in my lap. I petted and played with it as I would with a cat. Lights were out, logs were on. Later she said she didn't much care for my friend and his girl but liked their fire. She also had this bad habit of bugging taxi men. You're taking us too far out of our way she used to say. Shhh, I told her, better gypped than dead. She said in the cab I looked quite strong but wasn't that brave. But then another time she spoke about my courage but said I lacked common sense. And then a third time she feared how physically weak I sometimes appeared and that—

"Beep beep yourself. I said beep beep it up your nose. I said the pedestrian's got the right of way. Especially in a snow and sleet storm and even if the red light's against him which it wasn't. Oh don't give me that hand over the ear you can't hear. Go on, go on, before you miss your precious light. Then open your window a tinkle if you want to understand." There they go. Waving goodbye to me as if departing for across the States. Bye-bye now mama and papa and all the relatives, afraid for a little chill. Your door's open I should have yelled. Your back lights aren't working, muffler's hanging, fender's dragging, tire's flat or very short of air. I'm sure they thought he's a crack. Nut job to say the least. Looks so dopey in his nitwit Pinocchio hat. La la—listen to your tape deck and stereo set. Turn up the heater some more you Cadillac people, cushy as you are in your own mushy homes. But what do I know what kind of people they are? Besides it was a Buick. Be by me now, sweet, and I wouldn't rage at all. Die my heart and cross to hope. I'd laugh. Ya ya. Out loud. Ha ha. We'd nip from my mouthwash flask of gay sherry.

Four days ago Thursday I like an idiot called. How's your flu faring along? Health and energy sufficiently restored to have dinner tomorrow night, tonight? Clown, fool, greenhorn, tool. French or fish at Oscar's Salt of the Sea I was about to say. She said this iniquitous illness and inexplicable exhaustion and she'll call me in a few days. I came over anyway. Rang her bell. First a how do you do to her doorman who doubles at suddenly starting and short-stopping her elevator up. Five, but he says he knows. Flowers under my arm. Brushed-breath sweet, dentin and cementum dehypersensitized. I wanted a yes or no or whether in her indispositions she was giving me the ole heave ho. I also had the collected shorter works of Wordsworth she once wanted to reread. David? No, Will. Just a minute and in a minute she opened the door. Clothed only in a body hose from the belly button down. Didn't think you'd come. Putting a top on she said she doesn't want David finding her naked with another man. David's the English fellow she's been wanting to tell me about who's staying with her this week. She asked what I'm doing and I said looking for his luggage to throw into the backyard. I threw her the flowers instead. For David, I said. She laughed. I started for the door. But why'd she laugh? Wordsworth I must have let just slide down my leg to the floor. The meaning of my flowers-for-David remark was unknown to me then but could now be made to seem clear. Garlands for the victor? To the swines goes the spoiled. Pearls before oxen. Rich gifts wax poor when givers prove unkind. I don't know. Truer sayings have been said but none as known—no. Say it with flowers. All work and no play makes Will a dull boy. She wants to explain things about David and herself but I'm already two flights down the service stairs. Don't ever try to contact me again is what I yelled.

I called her tonight and she said sure if you want to come by. She didn't know how it had happened with David so fast—would I like a beer? She's grown addicted to Heineken's this past week. A girlfriend rang her up. But I've been over all that. Maybe I'll ring her when I get home. Hello, London calling. Oooh our mouths. Our attacking genitals. I liked us best when—no. The one post she lost her mental self in most was—no. In the Brooklyn Botanical Gardens last month—no. Same day we watched the bonsai grow and she zipped us through the Van Gogh exhibit, afraid I might faint from the crowds. Ballet, dinner parties, never a stage play or sporting event, long park walks, and when it was nipping cold, backwards short runs. Do you also dance to records and thumping FM while you're both undressed? and she said yes. Next thing you'll say is he's as loving and rutty as I when you're both entangled and compressed and she said she's afraid even more so yes. I told her I never quite felt I was good enough for her anyway and she said she was surprised she got to like me as much as she did. My moral code and standards were usually too rigid and high, too many times she felt compelled to concur with me or be browbeaten, there was something disquietingly revealing about the fact that I never got along with any of her male or female friends. Before we met, she never before told me, she vowed never again to date a psychologist or any man too analytical of himself or critical of her. No, David's a psychologist, though she thinks they're called another name in England as lawyers and lorries are, and maybe too self-analytical though not at all critical and like her a bit weary of the supersensitive and inordinately cautious and just plain brilliant and creative types and loves lots of dumb horsing around. Baby powder's what she used to put on in the morning if we made love the evening or hour before and she was late for work. What could her fellow subway riders and her students be thinking, she said, when she sits down and up comes clouds of scented smoke. Besides everything else I was too caliginous and morose. Can't stand that in a man. I can't stand it in myself so we also agreed on that. And also how good we were feeling those days when we were so often laid so well. And that the bed was our preferred mediating place in case anything between us went awry. And that there was nothing wrong with a lifelong streak of vanity, that this summer we'd try two months of northern Maine sanity, that philosophers are not doctors of philosophy who teach and lovers are not people who preach and Blake's binding with briars my joys and desires the most novel last line we knew in a non-twentieth-century poem. I'm home.

"Will?"

Let me at least remove my guaranteed waterproof shoes, my sopping socks. Why'd I throw away the guarantee? Why do I usually speedily discard vouchers, contracts, receipts, invitations, instructions, stubs, phone numbers, directions, warranties and guarantees and whatever else relevant to me in this category and rely on my time-attested incompetent memory or good luck or the buyer or seller's good faith or will?

"Junior?"

Why don't I keep a record of the checks I make out? The poems, drawings and picture-poems I send out? Where they are, how long, and if they've ever been there, how much money I've still in my account or owe or am owed and who the owers are?

"Will?"

"Coming." Why won't I wear a watch? Why do I avoid health checkups yet see my dentist twice a year? Is it only money that keeps me from buying a reliable pair of waterproof shoes or shoelike insulated boots? How come I've never been able to resist chocolate, have always hated the flavor of coffee, can't pass a day without munching several carrots, have never wanted to smoke? Why have the girls and women I've fallen in love with dumped me in a maximum of three months? Why have I always reacted to these one-sided falling aways or breakups in the same hurt sorrowful mawkish way? Why am I always so much of the same? Why are things so permanent? Why can't I tease instead of torment myself for my seemingly eternal limitations? Why can't I take my satisfactions in just the barely perceptible change? Why have I been so consistently contradictory and thus contradictorily consistent? Why is it such a struggle to lift a toilet seat when I pee when by nature I'm so unlazy? Why do I usually get nauseated in art museums and libraries and end up making runny movements in their johns? Why have I always been a whiz at mathematics and picking up languages and a dunce at any subject scientific or doing anything with a typewriter except two-finger typing and clogging the keys with eraser flecks? Is it the stars, God, gods, my hormones—

"Junior?"

—genetic code, parents, theirs, our great and grand great-grandparents and what we and all the plant and animal life we've come in contact with have breathed or ingested or something or ings or body or bodies else? Other influences influencing these influences with still even more influent influences which some people have or might have spoken or written about but which I generally find too tedious to listen to or want to learn about or have simply forgotten about and which in fact might be too complex or mazy or lost in space, time or imagination for any man in this or any of the past thousand centuries to know about if any of those or these are or is the reason or reasons I am the way I am or am what I was or am what I will probably always be?

"Will, please."

"Got you, Dad. The bows and knots in my shoelaces got shrunken tight. And I've got to get rid of these drenched socks and turn on the kitchen lights first. It's snowing outside."

"Well, come on."

"Take it easy. You've got to hold on at times too."

"Oh go take the gaspipe."

"What? Just screw yourself."

"And you take the gaspipe."

"And you go screw yourself."

I leave him holding the filled urinal. In the kitchen I open an ale. He must have used it when he heard my keys in the locks or while I was untangling my shoelaces' knots. But I don't want to be teaching lessons tonight. With his arms reared high and jug in hand he looked like a proffering trodden servant-slave in a hieroglyph. Nor if possible to Dana tomorrow about her unattractive brusqueness with cabbies and waiters or even where her fondling and positioning with me had been remiss. Some days while walking it to the john I thought I might suicidally take a swig of his piss. And morning he'll badger Mom about my conduct and she being what she is will take the brunt. She'll say I know he can be rough on you at times but he's a sick helpless man who if we want to help we've got to give in.

"Finished?"

"Yeah."

I turn him over, empty, wash out and replace the urinal on the table-tray. When he said go take the gaspipe I should have clutched my throat, gagged, fallen to the floor and played dead for a few seconds as if one of his curses had finally worked. I cover him, kiss his forehead, pat his back. "Goodnight." From what I've seen and my mother's said and said his mother's said, he's always been the same too.

"You drink too much."

"I should have left the glass inside."

"Not the glass, your breath. From alcohol. It stinks."

"Anyway it's only ale."

"Ale now, what before? Some more later. For ten years at least. From what I can imagine, longer. Your liver."

"My liver's okay. Though maybe it's not. What do I know? That a man starts off at the place where he's born and ends at the place where he dies. Sound bright? It's what the priest or anti-priest said in a movie on television I recently saw. But I should get it checked out. By an expert on foie gras. I'm the goose, take a gander. No, but maybe a bad report will give me a good scare. Though I do like to drink. But only wine with my evening mess, beer with my friends more or less, ale for what ails me, never cider cept on salads, hardly the hard stuff anymore, but you used to drink."

"I got smart. Be like me."

"Why should I be like you?"

"Because you're not as smart."

"Well, by the time you wake up tomorrow I'll try to have become as smart as you."

"Not a chance."

"Why so sure?"

"I'm tired."

"Ah the goods are, when we get down to the nitty-gritty, beyond all the flimflamming hunky-dories and icy-nicies to the heeby-jeeby really trulies, is that you only tolerate me as much as you do because you think I might beat it out of here and leave you both stranded or stay and start selecting the insulin needles I inject you with daily for their barbs."

"Go to sleep. I'm tired."

"Pleasant dreams."

"The pills?"

"They're here. Two of them, one for each stomach. Tissues in your pajama pocket. Urinal within easy reach. Bell. Chux. I forgot. Your teeth?"

"Your mom."

I place the Chux between his penis and thighs. "Now you're set. Sleep well."

"Thanks."

I kiss his forehead and shut the light. In the kitchen I open another ale and dial Dana's number.

"Hello," she says.

"Hello, London calling."

"Yes?"

"Sorry there, Miss. Can't hear you my very best. Must be a bad connect. Transatlantic tubes must have become untied or innerpacific allied." But I can just as well imagine our conversation and I hang up. She'd say Will? I'd say the tubes are retied now, miss. Called in London's leading gynecologist for the job, pronouncing gyn as gin. She'd say aren't they called cables instead of tubes and I'd say fables instead of cables and maybe then hang up. Maybe she'll call back. Twice before when I hung up she did and both times I said we'd been disconnected and we talked about the continually declining phone service in New York till she said didn't we discuss this same subject last time we were cut off? My continually declining glass. Star fright, snow blight, I wish tonight for tomorrow an empty class. Maybe stout rather than ale or sour mash straight up or with water and or ice. Perhaps a sketch of her in bed on her back in her bedroom on the back of an ordinary white postcard will suffice. Or a story drawn in two strips of four boxes apiece on a postcard showing scenes of my life serially from the start of a standard weekday. Jiggling alarm off at eight, pastry shop clock on my way to work late, teachers' punch-in clock, wall classroom clocks accompanied by students' mocks and socks and then three o'clock schlock and clock store clocks on the block and maybe Dana's shock and my father's pocket tick-tock and again me in bed behind locks beside my Baby Ben clock drinking bock from a flock of crocks. Or a long amusing letter. Sent several and she said there's almost nothing about you I like better. I'll write I'm leaving the city forever as I can't endure being in it without her. Kissing the folks adios on the avenue I stick out my thumb. Plans are after I get out of the city to make it cross country on the bum. Hop in, a shopper holding open a shopping bag will say. Hop aboard, a boy on a skateboard will say. Hop off, says the bus driver when I can't cough up the exact fare. Hop to it, says the motorcyclist after slicing off my thumbing thumb with a razor blade and breezing away with it leaving my thumb base bare. I swaddle the hand in a rag, flag down a cab, say tail that motorcyclist who's copped my thumb, as I read if you've lopped off a digit you've no more than an hour to get it sewn back on. I find the thumb on a manhole, rush with it to a hospital, the receptionist sends me to the toe-finger section, I get lost in the many corridors and wind up in the room for cadaver dissections, at the hospital pharmacy I ask for digitalis, for I also read doctors adhere fingers back to hands with it along with a dash of Vitalis, the pharmacist asks for my prescription slip, I say are you kidding and bleep bleep your blip blip, she says no prescription no digitalis, but no female pharmacist could be that callous, so I show her my severed thumb, as I figured she faints and lies numb, I leap over the pharmacy counter, just reprisal might be for me to savagely mount her, but I'm losing time all the time so I look for shelf D, find the digitalis and help myself to some Vitalis on shelf V, blend the two ingredients together with pestle and mortar, as the directions suggest add three tablespoons of tepid water, guzzle down the entire mixture, press thumb to hand till it again becomes a fixture, but maybe another letter or continuance of this one where in the digitalis section I also find shrinking powder, though because it's on the D shelf it's here called drinking powder, which makes me so small I can sit up in Dana's hand, after having tumbled out of the same envelope I sent her this letter in from a foreign land. But instead on the bottom of a postcard I draw my face frontwards from chin dimple to dome, and inside the word balloon above me write in wee letters the following poem. Skin of stone, rock for a heart, dead glaze and gaze for a look that once leaked longing, loving, sapless tree about to fall, cold dusty remains of burnt charcoal, bones found in a hundred-year-old grave, thousand-year-old grave, ancient Mesopotamian tomb, empty hospital room, pencil lead, desert of dead, polished ball of solid steel, endless wheel, nothing but space in a carapace, sealed airless Plexiglas box, doors opening on doors and each with numerous locks, vacuum, exosphere, or whichever atmosphere where there's no breathable air, lightbulb with broken filament, lightninglike cracks in buckets of hardened cement, wall of unshatterable glass I exhaust myself trying to smash, moldy lace, unalterable obdurate face, stiff plastic, what was once elastic, but didn't I, hint I, that just seeing a woman steadily for a month is for me a torrid love affair?

I address the card to Dana, drop it in the street's mail container, dogfight, lamppost light, make everything turn out all right.

And then that Will who became Guil who wrote *si jamais revient cette femme, Je lui dirais Je suis lui content.*

My old man's snoring, the snow's now pouring.

Will's tight, his poems trite, maybe sleep will shorten his half-wit's height.

To her living room ceiling's attached a double-sized hammock, first time I met her she wore gobs of blue eye shadow but no other makeup.

Losing sight, nighty-night—oh one other thing she said was will you go fly a kite.

Falling, stalling.

Grace

Calls

Grace calls. Grace called. I stand. I sit. I go to bed. I dream. I dream about my childhood. I dream about my birth. I dream about being an old man. I wake. Grace calls. Grace called. I make breakfast. I eat. I go to the bathroom. I read. I wash. I make lunch. I eat. I drink a glass of water. I read. I listen to the radio. I make a sandwich. I eat. I drink a glass of milk. I put water on for coffee. I read. I smell something burning. It's the teakettle on the stove. I open the window to let out the smoke. I watch a pigeon feather float in and land on the floor. I close the window. I throw away the burnt kettle. I sit. I read. I make supper. I eat. I wash the dishes. I put the trash outside the front door. I run in place. I shave. I bathe. I read. I drink a glass of beer. I read. I listen to the radio. I make a snack. I eat. I read. I undress. I go to bed. I think about what I did today. I think about what I dreamt last time I slept. I think about my father. I see him waving at me and saying "Juney boy." I think about my mother. She's in an evening gown coming downstairs. She's sitting on the sill washing my window. She's in a suit going to work. She's in her doctor's coat examining someone's ear. A boy's ear. My ear. I'm sitting on her examining table and she's examining me with that instrument that has a light. She says "No good." She says "Stick out your tongue." She says "Just what I thought." She says "Sit still while I make a call." She comes back with her receptionist and says "You must be a brave boy now, you mustn't be afraid." I fall asleep. I dream about eggplants. They're purple, with faces, and my size. I'm running down a steep hill with a slew of them on my way to see our housekeeper Anna. We cross a country road. One eggplant stays on the other side of the road and all the eggplants and I move our heads for it to cross the road. It bounces across the road on its bottom and gets hit by a big car. The car keeps going. Hit and run, I say. We drag the eggplant off the road and form a circle around it and talk about its qualities and weaknesses and cover it with dirt and most of us cry. I wake. I go to the bathroom. I wipe sweat off my face and back. I drink water from the tap. I go back to bed. I think about what my eggplant dream could have meant. And where is Anna now and what hill was that I ran down? I fall asleep. I dream. I dream of my father treating me in his office. His waiting room's filled as it was always filled with patients and friends. He says "Say ah." He says "Spit it out." I lean over the dental bowl and spit out pieces of an old filling and blood. He says "Now sit back and open wide." He says "Wider." He says "Wider." I watch him look through his thick bifocals at what he's drilling and picking at. He says "All done." He sticks cotton rolls in my mouth and says "Keep it open till I fill it." He mashes and mixes my future silver filling in his porcelain mortar with his porcelain pestle. A man comes into the treatment room and says "Doc, got a moment?" I wake. Grace calls. Grace called. I dress. I run in place. I put water on for coffee. I go to the bathroom. I read. I smell something burning. I see smoke passing the bathroom door. I flush the toilet. The water pot burnt. A kitchen wall's on fire. I try putting the fire out with water I spray from the sink tap. The doorbell rings. Several neighbors come and help me put out the fire. The landlord comes. He speaks to the neighbors. I mop the floor. The neighbors leave. The landlord says "That's your third fire in five weeks. The other two weren't that serious, but this one is. I'm going to get an eviction notice out on you immediately, so don't bother paying next month's rent." The landlord leaves. I hang the mop and rags out to dry. I close the window. The landlord returns. He says "Forget what I said about not paying next month's rent. You pay it, all right, and all the other months till I get you thrown out." He leaves. I read. Grace calls. Grace called. I put water on for coffee. I throw away the burnt pot. I stand by the stove till the water boils. I make breakfast. I eat. I read. I drink coffee. I get the newspaper off my doormat. I read. I reheat the coffee. I stand by the stove till the coffee's reheated. I drink coffee. I read. I make lunch. I eat. I drink a glass of water. I brush my teeth. I look out the window. A boy kicks a can into the street. A car passes. A taxi drops off its passenger. The postman delivers mail. A woman walks her dog. A delivery boy rides by on a bike. A man walks past holding an opened umbrella over his head though it isn't raining or sunny. It's cloudy and the temperature's mild. A sanitation truck picks up garbage. A man yells "Hey you. Stop thief." Another man runs up the block toward the park with the first man's brown paper bag. A police car comes. The policemen talk to the man who lost the bag. The man gets in the police car and the police car goes. A man and woman walk by holding hands. They stop. He ties his shoelaces. They kiss. They go. They stop, kiss, go. A woman dressed in white with white makeup on her face and neck and her hair powdered white and shoes polished white and everything on her like her nail polish and hands and ears painted or made white though she's black, walks past. Only the shopping cart she's lugging behind her isn't white. It's aluminum, though its one wheel and all the wheel's spokes and the axle are white. The two filled shopping bags in the cart and material and packages she has over the bags are white. I don't know what she means. She has breasts so large and round that it could be she isn't a woman but is a circus clown with balloons or whatever they use to make it seem like they have enormous breasts stuffed under their costumes. But she's a woman, or she isn't a woman. Sparks fly from the sidewalk where the wheelless side of the axle drags. The postman watches her and smiles to himself as he unstrings a bundle of mail. I still don't know what she means. There could be several meanings. I have to go to the bathroom. I get a glass of water. I return to the window. Two motor scooters go past. The drivers ride side by side and the two helmeted passengers holding on in back talk to one another. The woman of white is now at the avenue end of the block, still dragging the cart. I recall the intense look to keep going that never left her face. I still don't know what she means. A black woman. Or perhaps not a woman but a man made up to look like a woman. But a black man made up to look like a white woman, but a woman in white leotards and white walking shoes and enormous breasts and possibly a stuffed enormous behind and lugging a filled shopping cart with only the basket part of this one-wheeled cart not painted white and with light panties under the leotard and a white undershirt over it and with every visible part of the cart's contents and her body except the irises made or being white. Grace calls. I don't answer. I drink the water. I go to the bathroom. I pour milk into the water glass. I sip once from the glass and pour the milk back into the container and return the container to the refrigerator. I read. I feed my plant. I listen to the radio. I run in place. I sweep the rug. I dust some shelves. I sit. I read. I nap. I dream of something that actually happened when I was three. It was my birthday. I was very small for my age. Too small to climb onto my parents' double bed without someone's help. I thought they must use a ladder to get on their bed. I visualized a ladder against the side of the bed. I ask them to help me get up on the bed. They don't understand my words as I wasn't able to make a single word understandable to adults till I was past four. I put out my arms in the direction of the bed. My father picks me up and drops me on the bed. He takes a pillow and swipes me lightly on the head. As far as my memory goes, the real incident ends. The dream goes on. My mother complains my father's messing up the newly made bed. He lifts me off the bed, looks for a place to set me and puts me in my mother's arms. He folds the bedspread back over the pillow, straightens the bed, goes to the kitchen, puts his sandwich and tangerine into a manila envelope, kisses my mother and I goodbye and leaves for work. My mother says "Happy birthday, sweetheart, you're three." She says "From your father and me." She gives me a wrapped present. I can't get the ribbon off. She opens it. It's a dog doll. She kisses my ear and goes to work in her office at the front of the house. I play with the ribbon and wrapping in the room Anna's ironing in. The dream ends. I wake up. Grace calls. Grace called. I go to the bathroom. I read. I shave. I clean the toilet bowl and tub. I look in the mirror. I tweeze the hair out of my nose. I part my hair in the middle and pretend I'm someone else. I brush my hair back the way I always wear it. I work on the crossword puzzle. I check the movie listings. I put water on for coffee. I stand at the stove till the water boils. I make lunch. I eat. I drink coffee. I make a snack. I eat. I peel a carrot. I eat. I look through the cookbook. Grace calls. I don't answer. Grace calls. Grace called. I look out the window. Across the street a woman in the second-story apartment directly opposite mine is looking at an oil truck delivering oil to her building. The oil man reels in the hose and the truck leaves. I stare at the woman. She looks at me. I smile and wave. She leaves her window seat. I look up and down the street. I can't see a person, animal or vehicle moving on the block. Curtains move in one of the buildings across the street and now a sheet of newspaper moves in the street but nothing else. The leaves on the block's tree move. A sparrow flies out of the tree and disappears over the row of buildings on my side of the block. A man comes out of a building reading a magazine. He pats his pockets. "Darn," he seems to say. He goes back into his building. Several children on rollerskates and with hockey sticks pass. A car passes. A bus. I've never seen a bus come down this sidestreet. Maybe the street the bus usually goes down is blocked up. The man leaves the building again carrying a briefcase and with the magazine under his arm. The bus stops a few doors down from my building. The car in front of it is double-parked too far from the car parked adjacent to the curb and the bus can't get past. The bus driver honks. His passengers read, talk, look outside, one's asleep. The bus driver and the drivers of the two cars and a truck behind the cars honk. A woman comes out of a building. She jiggles her keys to the bus driver. He honks. She points to her watch and raises her shoulders and hands. The bus driver and the drivers of the cars and the truck behind the cars honk. She gets in the double-parked car and drives off. The bus starts for the corner right after her but has to stop for the light. The woman just made it through the light. The bus and car and truck drivers honk and honk. Grace calls. Grace called. I drink a glass of water. I go to the door. The afternoon paper's on the mat. I throw the paper away. I reheat the coffee. I do exercises and run in place. I wash my hands and face. The pot's burning. I put out the fire. I throw the pot through the window. The police come. One policeman says "Your landlord called to complain. First fires, he says. Now deliberately destroying his property." I hear honking from the street. I go to the window. The policeman says "When I'm talking to you, you don't move." The driver of another bus is honking the double-parked police car in front of my building. I point to the street. The policeman says "What now, for godsakes?" He looks outside. He says "I'll take care of our car, you take care of him." He leaves. The second policeman says "Why you do these things we don't know. You've a nice place. Nice and neat. Plenty of room. It's a good building. Your landlord seems like a nice enough guy. It's a nice street and good neighborhood. You're lucky to live here, believe me, and from what I hear, you're getting it cheap. So no more fuss now, please." He leaves. I go to the window. The bus is gone. The police car's backing into a parking spot. The policeman who just left my place taps on the police car's roof. The car stops. He gets inside. The car drives out of the spot and goes through the red light. Several people across the street have come to their windows. Some are looking at me. I smile at the woman sitting on the window seat. She lets down her venetian blinds and flicks them shut. I drink water from the kitchen tap. I let the water run to get cold. Grace calls. Grace called. I see water trickling out of the kitchen. In the kitchen I see I've caused a small flood. I shut the water off. The fire department comes. They drag a hose through my place. The fire chief says to these men "No need." He says to me "For the safety of all your neighbors, you ought to be locked up." They leave. I get the mop from outside the window. Someone knocks. I mop. The landlord says "This is your landlord, Mr. Lingley, open up." I mop. He says "I said open up." I open the door. He says "I've called the police and department of buildings and mayor's office. If you aren't out by tomorrow morning I'll be very much surprised." He leaves. I lock the door. He says from the stairway "Remember what I said last time about your paying next month's rent? Don't." Grace calls. I drink a glass of beer. I hang the mop over the bathtub. I cut my hair. Grace calls. I run in place. I eat a celery stick. I hear music. I go to the window. A street band's passing. I haven't seen one in years. I throw a ball of aluminum foil at it. The flutist salutes me. He opens the foil and shakes his flute at me. I forgot to put money in the foil. I throw two quarters at him. Both coins roll under a parked car. The banjoist says "Thank you, thanks a lot." The violinist hands his violin to the bass player and gets down on his knees to retrieve the coins. A car drives by and nearly sideswipes him. The trumpeter blasts his horn at the car. The car honks back repeatedly and makes a turn at the corner. The band resumes playing and walks to the end of the block. I'm leaning out the window to watch them and nearly fall off the ledge. The landlord says from the sidewalk "Don't tell me. You're going to jump. That'll save you the trouble of appearing in court. But jump from someone else's building, as what I don't need now is my insurance rates going up." I climb back inside and slam the window down. It's the window I threw the pot through and it completely shatters from the impact and the glass crashes below. The landlord says "That's it. Out you go today." He runs into the building. I make supper. Police come. I go into the bedroom and eat and drink. Police knock. I lock the bedroom door and try to nap. A policeman yells "Come on now, sir, you've got to unlock." I throw my hairbrush and shoes through the bedroom windows. The landlord yells "Break down the door before he destroys my house." I set fire to my bed and toss the chair and lamps into the flames. Grace calls. The police are banging on the bedroom door. Grace calls. The fire department comes. They enter through the bedroom window this time. They put out the fire on my clothes. They put out the fire in the room. I'm put on a stretcher. Grace calls. I'm carried downstairs. In the street I look up at the window where that woman usually sits and see her leaning outside at me and shaking her head. I'm driven down the block. I see that black man or black woman made up to look like a white woman peering into the ambulance as we go through the red light. I hear the street band play. I pass out. I wake up. I'm in a hospital. I'm in a hospital bed. A tube's in my arm. Another tube takes my pee. Several machines and monitors are at the foot of my bed. One doctor says to another that I've third-degree burns over fifty percent of my body and I'm not expected to live. A hospital aide says "Someone by the name of Grace called." A nurse says "You really in great pain?" She gives me something to sleep. I fall asleep. I dream of my parents and my dog Red. My mother says "Red's been taken away." I say "Where away?" My father says "No use lying to you. Big Red's been run over." I say "Where over?" My mother says "She was run over by a steamroller and won't be coming back." I cry. The dream ends. I wake up. That incident never happened in real life. I once did have a dog named Red. She got old and bit me in the face. They had to kill her. I remember when they took her away. They came to our house and put her in a cage. I remember hoping Red would bite them. There was something about her viciousness so late in life that I really liked. But Red was put away. "Where away?" I said. "You still don't know what we mean when we say she's been put away?" my mother said. "No," I said. "Not in a trunk or chest of drawers," my father said. I cried then. I'm lying on my back now in the hospital bed. The food and antibiotic tube's been taken out of my left arm and put in my right. The catheter's still taking my pee. With all the painkillers the nurse says they're giving me, I'm still in great pain. The doctor says "You're improving." The aide says "That person named Grace called just before. What message you want me to give should she call again?" But I can see by their faces that it's hopeless and I fall asleep.

Dog
Days

⟋

I was crossing Broadway in the Eighties when the light turned red and traffic sped past. I waited at the crosswalk on one of those islands in the middle of the avenue when a dog rushed at me from the benches and sunk its teeth into my leg. I tried shaking it off. It growled but wouldn't let go. I swatted its head with my book and it snapped at my swinging hand and then put its teeth back into my calf. I yelled "Goddamnit, whose dog is this, call it off."

Three transvestites were sitting on the row of benches with two more normally dressed homosexuals. They were all looking and laughing. I kicked the dog with my other foot and it yelped but ran away this time as I fell to the ground. The five men laughed much harder, seeing me on my behind. I got up. The light turned green. My pants were ripped where the dog had bit me and I felt saliva or blood or both leaking into my socks from the wound. The dog was sitting between two transvestites, licking himself. One of the transvestites tied a tattered cord to the scarf around the dog's neck and patted its head where I'd hit it. I limped over.

"That your dog?" I said.

"I'm not talking."

"You just talked, Jersey," one of the more normally dressed homosexuals said.

"Why you going and tell this nice man what my name is, you pimp and a half?"

"I didn't tell him. I was only addressing you by what I thought was your name. It isn't?"

"Why didn't you call your dog off?" I said to Jersey.

"That's my business and when I want it to be yours, I'll tell you."

"But he bit me."

"I thought he just psyched you out."

"He sunk his teeth into my leg twice."

"Oh yeah? Show me. I got to have proof."

I pulled up my pants leg to the calf. Blood was dribbling out of both sets of bites.

"Whoo whoo," one of the other transvestites said. "Show us some more leg, honey. You're getting me hot."

"Oh God," and I let my pants leg down.

"God had nothing to do with it," he said.

"Who said that before you just said it?" Jersey asked him. "Some famous old movie queen."

"Beulah."

"That's it—the grape. Oh, she was so funny and great."

"Your dog been vaccinated?" I said to Jersey.

"People are vaccinated. And for smallpox and polio, not animal bites."

"Then dog shots. Has he had them?"

"Hundreds of times."

"Where's his license?"

He looked at his nails, buffed them on his thigh. "I don't like this color," he said to the transvestite next to him. "You?"

"How do I know he hasn't rabies then?" I said.

"How do I know you haven't rabies?" Jersey said.

"Don't you think it's important I know? Be reasonable. If he has rabies, all I have to do is get treated for it."

"Now listen you. Either give us some more gam or make tracks. You're becoming a nuisance."

"He has nice legs though," the transvestite next to him said.

"Too fat," the third one said.

"Those are muscles, not fat."

The other two men were laughing behind a newspaper. Jersey was opening a bottle of nail polish. I said "You're all nuts and I'm calling a cop," and crossed the avenue.

"Bye, toots," a couple of them said. I turned around. The two other transvestites were standing and waving handkerchiefs at me. Jersey was polishing his nails.

A block away I saw two policemen talking to a man. The man was gesturing with his hands in a way I'd never seen before and when I came over, speaking a language I'd never heard.

"Excuse me, Officers, but I have to report something."

"Just a second," one of them said. "This guy's trying to tell us something that's obviously pretty important to him but we can't make out a word he says. That's not some Caribbean form of Spanish or South America, is it?"

"Habla Español or Portuguese?" I said to the man.

"Caper hyper yoicher," he said.

"Die Deutsch. Sprechen sie Deutsch or Français?"

"Yoicher caper hyper."

"We are trying to find out what language you are speaking or you can understand," the policeman said very slowly to him.

"Hyper yoicher caper," he seemed to say, "caper yoicher hyper."

Then he shook his head and rolled up his trouser leg and pulled down his sock and pointed to a set of teeth marks on his ankle and dried blood around it and made barking sounds and imitated an animal or human being baring his teeth and biting down hard with them.

"You've been bitten?" the policeman said.

"That's what happened to me just now," I said. "By a dog."

"It did?—Dog? Chien? Cane?" he said to the man. "Mange cane?"

"Yoicher hyper caper yoicher," the man said. "Yoicher. Yoicher."

I showed the man my own bite marks and pointed to his ankle and he nodded and smiled and said "Ya ya ya ya."

"Where?" I pointed to our bites and then to the island a block away and made barking sounds and said "There?"

"Ya ya ya ya. Caper caper hyper yoicher."

"You've both been bitten by dogs then," the policeman said. "You think the same one?"

"I think we ought to go and find out," I said.

"What do you say, Kip?" he said to his partner.

"Let's go over and see," Kip said.

We all went over to the island. The five men were still sitting there. "Officer," Jersey said, standing up as we approached them, "I want to make a complaint against this man," looking at me.

"Just a second," the policeman said. "These two men have a complaint against you. This your dog?"

"That's exactly what my complaint's about. The foreigner I've never seen till before. All I know is I'm sitting here when suddenly he's yelling and babbling at us and then left. But this one," pointing to me, "tried to accost me last night along the park side of Central

Park West. When I refused to go into the park with him or do what he wanted me to right there against the park wall for the whole city to see, he said he'd come back to get his revenge on me. Well he didn't last night. But ten minutes ago he tried to attack me on this bench. That's why my dog bit him. Out of protection for me."

"That true?" Kip said to me.

"It's so ridiculous I won't even answer it," I said.

"See?" Jersey said. "Now if you don't mind, I'm exhausted and going home." He started to walk away with his dog. Kip stopped him and told him to sit.

"Why? This man only proved who's right."

Milos, the foreigner, started to shake his fist at Jersey. Jersey told him to stick it up. He shook both fists at Jersey. Jersey said "Maricon!" and turned around and shook his behind in Milos's direction. Milos jumped at him and had to be pulled away by the policemen. He shouted at Jersey "Hyper hyper yoicher caper. Caper!"

"What language he speaking?" Jersey said.

"We're trying to find out," Kip said. "Any of your friends, maybe?"

"Foreign language," one of the transvestites said, sewing a button to his shirt. "I hate them. They should all be sent back on the boats tonight."

"Has your dog a license?" the policeman said to Jersey.

"What's your name, Officer?" Jersey said.

"John."

"My dog has a license, John, but it must have fallen off in the scuffle with this man," meaning me.

"There was no scuffle," I said to John.

"You've already proven yourself a liar," Jersey said. "Now you should shut up."

Just then a derelict walked over and asked me what was wrong. "Dispute," I said.

"Got a quarter?" he said.

"Will you please leave me alone?"

"Just give me a quarter."

"Get out of here," Kip said, giving him a dime and shoving him off.

"I'm really at a loss what to do for you guys," John said to me. "Kip?"

"You could press charges and we could take him in if you want," Kip said to me.

"That won't do any good," I said. "His dog should be picked up by the ASPCA and tested for rabies. That way we won't have to take the shots ourselves."

"You're not taking my dog there," Jersey said. "He can't even stand being cooped up in my apartment."

"I'll call in," John said. He tried his two-way radio. It didn't work.

"Don't look at me, buddy," Kip said. "Mine's in the repair shop."

"I'll call from the pay phone." I went with John to the drugstore across the street. While he phoned I bought a bottle of iodine, applied it to my wounds and then, back on the island, to Milos's ankle.

A squad car came with its siren going and emergency lights twirling. "You buzzed?" the sergeant said from the car.

"We want to know what to do about the dog," John said.

"You should have asked the desk for that." He contacted the station house on the car radio. The station house said "Normal procedure, with or without a dog license, is for ASPCA to take the mutt and quarantine it for seven days. I'll get them over."

We waited. The station house called back a few minutes later and said the ASPCA drivers were on strike. "You fellows will have to bring the dog to the pound yourselves."

"He's not getting in my car without a cage," the sergeant told the station house.

"Hold on." Later: "No cages. All borrowed at one time or another, since no real need for them till now. We can get one by tonight. Take the dog owner's name and address and tell him we'll pick up the dog at nine sharp tomorrow when we have a cage."

"He won't give the right address," I said to the sergeant.

"Also get the names and addresses of an immediate family member and his present employer," the sergeant said to Kip.

"They'll all be phonies," I said.

Jersey said to Kip "I don't work now but I'll give you three genuine addresses which I have the papers to prove them: my own, my mother's and my best friend's where I usually stay."

"Which one will you be at tomorrow at nine when we come to pick your dog up?"

"My mother."

"You be there now, you hear?" the sergeant said from the car.

"I promise. My mother's a good woman. Not like me. I swear by everything holy and her name that I'll be there at nine with my dog."

"Bull," I said.

"Faggot," he said to me. "You'll never get anything from anyone around here from now on. I'll tell them. 'Pull in your asses when you see him,' I'll say. 'That faggot's dangerous and mean.' —Can I go now?" he asked Kip.

"Let him loose," the sergeant said.

Jersey walked away with his dog. His friends remained on the bench, talking about movies now: which ones they liked or disliked. The sergeant had said he'd drive Milos and me to a hospital, but suddenly his twirling lights and siren were on and he drove off.

"They were supposed to take us to Emergency," I said to John.

"I could get another squad car for you, but it might take a while. You'll be better off by bus."

"We have to go to the hospital and be treated now," I said to Milos.

"Yoicher hyper caper."

I jabbed at myself while I nodded, made a cross in the air and pointed downtown. He looked confused. I hailed a cab and urged Milos to get in with me. During the ride I asked the driver if he'd ever heard this language before and I said to Milos "Say something. Speak. Hospital. L'hopital, Milos," and I pointed downtown and to my wounds and his bad ankle and nodded and he said "Yoicher caper hyper hyper," and the driver said "No, I never have."

Milos and I went to the admitting window of the emergency room of the hospital and I told the man there "We were both bitten by the same mangy dog and would like to be treated for possible rabies right away."

He gave us forms to fill out and bring back to him when we were finished.

We sat in the crowded waiting room. One man waiting to be treated must have been in a razor or knife fight. His cheek and neck were slashed, blood was all over his head and clothes. Seeing me looking at him, the man beside him said "Window fell on his head. No joke. Second-story window, smash, frame and all down on us both, but it got him like in a horseshoe game and only grazed my arm." Another woman must have run into a nest of bees. I don't know where in this city. Maybe she kept her own hives. And a baby with a swelled-up belly and a young girl with towels wrapped around both hands. I filled out my form, took my wallet out and removed some identification papers and pointed to Milos's pocket and he did the same. All his papers were written in letters I didn't recognize. Then I saw a business card of a Hungarian restaurant on the East Side. "You Hungarian?" I said.

"Hungarian."

I said to the waiting room "Anyone here speak Hungarian?"

A woman stood up. "I don't," she said.

Several people laughed.

"But I'm Finnish," she said.

This time even a few of the sick and injured people laughed.

"But the two languages are somewhat alike. They're both branches of the Finno-Ugric."

"The Finno-whatwik?" a man said and just about everyone laughed.

"Then I need you here, ma'am," I said when the noise had died down. She came over and talked to Milos and they seemed to understand many of the words the other one spoke and she helped him fill out his form.

Two men came in holding up a third. They sat him down. One of the men went to the admitting window and said "My friend there's been shot."

"Have you seen a policeman?" the admitting man said.

"It happened right in front of the hospital just now. Didn't you hear the blast?"

"No. You should have summoned a policeman before you came in."

"Hey Jack," he yelled, "they want us to get a policeman first."

Jack, sitting beside the wounded man, said "They're crazy. First treatment, then a policeman."

"First treatment, then a policeman, my friend says."

"Can the person who's shot fill out the admitting form?"

"He's bleeding to death, probably dying. He got it in the stomach. We thought we were lucky that it happened in front of your place."

"You can fill it out then, but you'll be responsible for the twenty-dollar admitting fee."

"I don't write but Jack does, and between us we don't have twenty cents."

"Fee temporarily waived then," and he stamped something on the form. "But your friend Jack must put his address and signature here so we can mail him the bill."

A woman came in with a burnt arm and back. Her hair was singed. A path was cleared for her when she walked to the window and a few people held their noses as she passed. The admitting man said "Yes?" She tried to speak. She fell to the floor. He called for two aides over the public address system. They came out of the swinging doors in back and put her on a stretcher and carried her inside.

"What about our rabies?" I said, giving the admitting man our completed forms. "For all we know we can be getting it now, and once you do you've had it I understand."

"Excuse me." He took the form from Jack and told him to take the man who was shot into the examining room. Jack and his friend helped the man in and then left.

"Now," the admitting man said to me, "were either of you bitten on the head or face?"

"No."

"Splenius, sternocleidomastoid, anywhere near the larynx or voice box?"

"I was bitten twice on the calf and the Hungarian man once on the ankle. And the skin broke in all three bites and the dog's saliva got in."

"The incubation period for your types of bites is rarely less than fifteen days and I guarantee you'll be in the examining room by then."

I asked the Finnish woman to tell Milos what the man had just said. She again left her father in the care of a stranger sitting beside him and spoke to Milos. He shook his head and began repeating something to her.

"He's apparently saying the incubation period might be for fifteen days. But you have to take virus injections in the stomach for fourteen days starting from the day you were bitten, which leaves you both with only one day left, he says, and conceivably he about ten minutes fewer than you."

I told the admitting man what Milos had said.

"So you have one day left. You still won't be waiting here that long. Even the chances of a dog getting rabies in this city are practically nonexistent, so please sit down."

We waited another hour. The child with the swollen belly and the man with the cut face and the father of the Finnish lady were taken before us. Then the beebite lady and Milos and I were called. We sat in one of the examining rooms with four other patients, all on stools in a circle, my knees touching the knees of the Finnish man whose daughter, standing behind him and holding his hand, said he'd come in to get a splinter removed that she had dug and dug at but couldn't even reach. A woman was telling a man with a bad cough of the beautiful mad golden retriever that had bitten her this morning.

"That's a coincidence," I said, "for I was bitten too."

"Same here," the beebite lady said.

"Both of you by golden retrievers?" the woman said.

"No, a pack of bees."

"Mine was a mutt. But yours couldn't have been on Broadway in the Eighties, was it?"

"Connecticut."

"I wish I only got bit by a dog in Connecticut," the beebite lady said, "or at least only by one bee. But hundreds. Right on West Fifty-first in the heart of the restaurant district when I'm out dumping my garbage bag."

The woman said she was driving in on the thruway when she saw a car ride off the road right in front of her and turn over a couple of times before it came up on its wheels. "I parked. A few cars got there before me and someone said the driver looked dead but that there was a dog on the seat who wouldn't let them open the door to help the man. All the windows were shattered. I tried coaxing the dog out. I've a way with them and especially retrievers—I've two myself. When it wouldn't come with words I held a strip of beef jerky through the window to get him to sniff it and eventually follow it out of the car with me, but he bit my hand."

A nurse asked each of us our medical problems and assigned the beebite lady and the cut man to special rooms. The man with the cough was given a throat swab and a prescription and told to come back tomorrow for the results. A doctor came in, gave the rest of us tetanus shots, washed our wounds and while the nurse prepared the Finnish man for minor surgery, bandaged us up and asked about the dogs that bit us.

Mina, the woman, said she'd phoned Connecticut just before and was told the retriever was licensed, had had all his shots and was now quarantined, and the doctor said the vets there will know if the dog shows any clinical signs of rabies within seven days. "What about your dogs?" he asked Milos and me.

"It has no license and probably never had any shots or will ever be found," I said and he told me if the dog isn't confined in two days we should return to this hospital and begin taking our fixed virus shots.

"I hear they can be very painful," I said.

"And possible severe reactions to the treatment can happen, so in actual fact we don't recommend them."

"But if we get rabies we can go into convulsions and die."

"There hasn't been a reported case of rabies bite in the city for over thirty years."

"Maybe this is the one. Or the man and his dog were from out of town and only visiting here for the day."

"There weren't a hundred reported cases in the entire country last year and most of those attacking rabid animals weren't dogs."

"What would you do?" I asked him.

"I'd take the injections," Mina said.

"I wouldn't," he said. "Though in the end that comes down to a personal and not a professional decision, so I know how tough it must be for both of you."

"I'll make up my mind in two days." I got Milos's phone number and said to the Finnish woman "Tell him I'll call in two days to report if the dog's been found. If it hasn't, say he'll then have to speak to his own people and make up his own mind on whether he wants to go through with the virus shots."

Mina, Milos and I went to a coffee shop nearby. I told Mina I'd like to take her out for dinner one night this week and she said "I don't think it'd be too good an idea as I'm sort of seeing someone now."

"But we've had too inauspicious and eventful and coincidental a beginning not to see what develops next."

"I wouldn't go that far. But I don't suppose a single dinner with you can matter that much and we can also learn how we all made out with our bites." She gave me her phone number. The three of us shook hands and took separate buses home.

I called the police station the next day and the man at the desk said the first address Jersey gave was fake and they're now trying to run him down at either his own apartment or where he said his friend lives.

"This is a real emergency," I said. "As even the injection treatments for rabies can sometimes be fatal, so this other man and I want to avoid them at all costs."

I called the station the next day and the policeman said "All three addresses were fake and we don't know what else to do for you now."

"I know where Jersey and his type hang out."

"You one of them?"

"No, I just live in the neighborhood and walk around a lot. And I see that on the island across from Loews Eighty-third is where a lot of the transvestites like to hang out these days, though every other month or so they switch to another island a block or two north or south."

"If you see him let us know," and he gave me a special number to call.

I went to the island on Broadway. One of the transvestites of two days ago was sitting alone on a bench.

"Excuse me," I said, "but do you know where I can find your friend Jersey?"

"I've no friend Jersey. She a friend of yours?"

"Jersey's dog bit me the other day and I'm trying to find it to see if it has rabies."

"Oh sure, now I remember. Bad scene. Too many police."

"Can you tell me where Jersey is?"

"She and her dog are dead."

"No, really."

"No, really, dead. Hit by a car."

"Both killed by the same car? Around here?"

"She didn't die, just her dog. Ballpark, she called him. The dog. Jersey went to California. Picked up on this very corner here by some new queer who stops his car and says 'I love you, darling, what's your name?' And they made it—just like that."

"I could still find out if the dog had rabies if you knew when and where the accident took place and what they might have done with the dog's body."

"Her dog didn't die either. He ran away. Ballpark. Jersey let her go when she got in that rich queer's car. 'Freedom,' she says to Ballpark, 'that's your new name,' and Ballpark runs off."

"Is that the truth now? It's kind of a life and death situation for me that I know."

"I don't know Jersey anymore. I don't want to. She's a mean mother. You saw. Lie and cheat, cheat and lie. I hate them all. And all her friends too, rich or poor."

"Can you at least tell me where she was staying or give me the name and address of someone who might know?"

"No. No one knows. And if I see her I don't speak to her or say hello. I'll say nothing. I'll walk past. Besides, I hear she's gone to Las Vegas for good with a gambler who gave up his wife and kids for her and now only likes gays. A laugh. Because Jersey's no gay. That's true."

I called Mina that night.

"I'm sorry," she said, "but Lewis who?"

"The fellow who was bitten by a dog the same day as you."

"Of course. You know, I told that story about us to my roommate and she said that only happens in movies where we get married the following week and a month later regret racing into it and have major calamities and breakups together but live happily ever after for life, though of course she was only kidding. How are your bites?"

"They haven't found the dog."

"That's terrible. Mine's healing nicely. And so far the dog seems okay and I'm even planning to adopt it, since that poor car driver was crippled and can't take care of it anymore. You going to take those treatments? It's been two days."

"I think I'll wait it out. Would you like to have dinner with me tonight?"

"I'm afraid that person I said I'm sort of seeing I'm sort of engaged to now, so I don't think I can."

"I'll call back next week to find out about your dog and you. Maybe by then you'll also have changed your mind about me."

"I don't think so, but thanks."

The police never found Jersey or the dog. I called Mina again after our incubation period for rabies was over and her roommate answered and said "Mina? That rat skipped off on her honeymoon to Bermuda and left me with her two stinking retrievers and a third one that bites people, coming any day. Who is this?"

"Lewis."

"Of the dogs?"

"Yes."

"She left a message for you, Lewis, that she told me to read to you if you call again. It says 'I didn't know your phone number nor last name so I couldn't call you with what I forgot to remind you about the last time you called. I was also in too much of a rush to get off on my honeymoon trip to wait the two days the hospital said it would take to locate your records. But I want to make sure, if that dog that bit you isn't found, that you phone the Hungarian man to tell him a lot of people would think it advisable for him to take the ten- to fourteen-day vaccine treatment for rabies.' That's it. So long."

I'd completely forgotten about Milos. I called the restaurant number he gave me and the man who answered said "No Milos, sir—tonight. Can't speak English please. Tonight."

I called back that night and the restaurant owner said "Milos is in the kitchen now washing the dishes. He's doing a fine job here and not suffering any rabies or illnesses we can see. Want me to have him phone you back?"

"No thanks."

In
Time

—

I'm walking along a street when a woman from a building nearby yells "Help, save me, they're trying to kill me in here right now." I look up. She's waving to me from a window on the fourth floor. Then it seems she's being pulled into the room by her feet, holds onto the sill a couple of seconds, is pulled all the way in and the window closes, shade drops. I look for a short while more but there's no further activity from there.

It's evening, around nine, beginning of summer so still a little light. Nobody else is on the street or looking out of any of the windows on the block. Couple cars come. I run into the street to stop them to get some help for the woman. First car passes me before I get there and second swerves around me, driver sticking his fist out the window and cursing me, and at the corner both cars go through a red light.

I look back at that building. Shade and window are still down. I look around for a phone booth. There's none on this street and all the stores and businesses are locked up for the night if not the weekend. I could walk several blocks to the main avenue and try to get help there, or call the police from one of the public phones that could be along the way. But the woman's in immediate danger it seems, so I go into the building to do what I can for her without getting hurt myself.

There are ten buttons on the bell plate and I ring all of them. Nobody answers. Most are businesses. Arbuckle Ltd this, Tandy &

Son that, except for a nameless bell on the fifth floor and Mrs. Ivy Addison in 4F. That has to be her: fourth-floor front. I ring her bell several more times. If anything is happening to her, maybe this will distract the person doing it.

I yell through the door "Someone, come down or ring me in, a woman in your building's in trouble." No response and I try the door. It's open. I go outside, look up at her window. Everything's the same there and there are no cars or people on the street or lights on in any of the building's windows. I go through the vestibule, hesitate on the bottom steps, say to myself "You've got to go up and try to help, you wouldn't be the same after if you just left here," and walk upstairs, knocking on all the doors I pass till I reach the fourth floor.

There are two doors at opposite ends of the hallway: 4F and 4R. I knock on 4F, step back to the stairs, ready to run down them. No one comes to the door. I ring the bell this time and knock, get back to the stairs, even a couple of steps down them. Nobody answers. Then I hear the vestibule door close and someone coming upstairs. I look down the stairwell. The hand on the banister seems to belong to a woman. She passes the first flight and is walking up the second.

"Hello?" I yell down the well.

"Yes, you speaking to me?"

"Do you know who lives in Four-F? Because before when I was on the street—"

"Excuse me, just a second, I don't hear too good: my ears. Wait till I get to your floor."

She walks up the second flight, around the landing and is now at the bottom of the stairs I'm on. An older woman, around seventy, old clothes, hearing aid, holding onto the banister for support, limping upstairs. "Now what it is you want to know?"

"You see, before, I was on the street, few minutes ago at the most, when I heard this woman in Four-F here yelling 'Help, save me—'"

"Oh her. She always does that. You must be new in this neighborhood."

"I don't live in this neighborhood. I was just taking a walk."

"A walk around here?" She's two steps from me now. I get against the wall so she can pass. She stops. "Why would you want to take a walk in this neighborhood? There's nothing to see or do once the stores and factories close for the day and they been closed for three hours. She's the only excitement we got on the block, and her racket like she screamed to you almost every day. 'Help save me' my eye. She's crazy, you know."

"No I didn't."

"Crazy as bedbugs. Ever see a bedbug?"

"No."

"Neither have I. My homes, even as a kid, poor as we were then and am, have always been spotless clean, though I bet hers haven't. But that's the expression they use. Bedbugs must be crazy or move in a crazy motion, wouldn't you say?"

"I think that's it. They sort of dart round and round when the covers are suddenly thrown off them or lights go on, or maybe that's only roaches. Anyway, if she's that crazy, I guess I better be going. Flase alarm as they say."

"False what?"

"Alarm. An old expression also. Like a fire. Someone puts an alarm in, firemen come—"

"Oh yeah, I remember. Okay, nice talking to you."

I start to walk downstairs. She steps in my way. Door opens above me. 4F, where the crazy woman is. I turn to look. Another older woman, looking much like this one, same features, same kind of old clothes, though one on the stairs has on a coat and hat.

"Hello there," woman above me says.

I look back at the woman on the stairs, thinking 4F's talking to her, but she says "I think she's speaking to you, dear."

"Me?"

"Hello there," 4F says. "Won't you come in and help me, save me. I'm quite calm now."

"Why don't you?" woman on the stairs says. "She's very nice. Give you a good cup of coffee or tea if you prefer and interesting talk. I know. I've heard it over and over again till my head aches."

"No thanks," I say, and then trying to pass her: "Excuse me."

"Where you think you're going?"

"Outside for sure."

"Oh, you must be crazy as bedbugs also to think you can. You go straight upstairs, dear. Me and my sister have great plans for you."

"The hell you do," and I push past her. She hooks her foot around my ankle. I try catching myself but can't and as I start falling downstairs she shoves me hard from behind and I fly over a few steps, stick out my hands and land on them and slide the rest of the way down, my head bumping on every step. I lie there awhile, whole body hurting, head and hands bleeding, several of my teeth out and lips split I think, and then try standing.

"You coming quietly or need help, dear?" she says above me.

"No, I got to go," and make it to one knee.

"Last time," and I say "I already told you," and she comes down on my head with something like a stone a few times and I drop to the ground.

Next thing I know they're carrying me into an apartment. Next thing after that I'm sitting on a couch, arms and legs bound, head wrapped with a bandage, the two women washing my hand wounds. The one who yelled out the window to me says "Listen, why you giving us such a big fuss? We just want you to hear our little story, and then if you're a good boy and hear it all without squawking, we'll let you go. Now here's two aspirins to take care of the pain that must be in your head and mouth."

She puts them on my tongue and her sister gives me some water to swallow them and after a few minutes of watching them bandage my hands I fall asleep.

They don't tell me any stories or let me go. They just keep me there and go about their regular routine it seems, shopping and cooking, ironing and cleaning, embroidering and watching TV, when they're not taking care of my needs.

They give me their bedroom and I'm always bound in ropes, even when I sleep, usually my arms and legs both, and carried to the various places I have to be carried to to eat, bathe, sit, rest, go to the toilet and other things. At first I shout and complain a lot about my predicament, calling them crazies, harpies, sadists, and they say "Don't use such ugly words around the house," and slap my face and hands and gag me and a couple of times wash my mouth out with soap. I shout and complain much less over the next few weeks because the slaps and gags hurt and the soap tastes awful, but every so often I have to let it out of me and I get more of the same.

They never talk to me or treat me like an adult. "Want some more foodie, Charles?" they say and I either nod or shake my head. If I shake my head they still put the food on a spoon and jam it against my lips till I open them and eat the food. Once a week they sit me in a bathtub with my arms and legs tied and bathe and shampoo me. "Close your eyes or they'll burn," they say, and I do because if I don't they'll let the suds run into my eyes till they burn.

Otherwise they mostly ignore me. They turn the TV on and we all watch it or just I watch it while they put away groceries or read or play cards. If they talk about the TV show or what they read in the newspapers that day, they never include me in the conversation. When I try to get in it, just to talk to someone as an adult and maybe pass the time faster, they say things like "You know the old adage, Charles: Children should be seen and not . . . what?" If I don't answer them they say "And not what, Charles, and not what?" and hold their hands above my face ready to slap it and I say "And not heard," and they smile and pat my head. If I still try to get in their conversation they always slap and gag me.

Once a week or so I ask "When will you tell me your story so I can go?" and they say "Be still."

"Then when will you just let me go?" and they say "In time, dear."

"How long is that?" and they say "In time means in time, now you want the gag or to get slapped or maybe both?"

If I then say "Then just tell me what the hell you're keeping me here for," they say "Now watch your tongue, Charles, or you really will get gagged and slapped and maybe more."

Twice I yelled after they said that "Okay, slap me, gag me, you old crabs, you hags, you crazies, you homicides," and they ran over to me and shoved the gag into my mouth and slapped my face and pulled my hair and knocked me off the chair and kicked me in the chest and head and then carried me to my bed and said "You'll be let out and fed when you get to have better manners to people in general and respect for your elders in particular, which might be only one of the reasons we brought you here," and locked the door and didn't open it till around the same time next day.

If I could escape I would. But my bedroom window has a double gate on it and in all the times I've tried I've never once freed my arms or legs from the ropes. After three months of this I say to them "I can't stand it anymore. Either you release me immediately or I'm going on a hunger strike till you let me go."

"All right," they say. "Cut your nose off to spite your you-know-what," and carry me to bed and leave me alone there for three days without anything to eat, drink or listen to and nothing to look at but the ceiling, walls and window shade. I get so hungry, thirsty, dirty and bored that I shout "Ivy and Roz?" They come in and Roz says "No false alarms?" and I say "None. From now on I'll be a good little boy and eat and drink regularly and won't ask again when I'm leaving here." They pat my head, clean and feed me and sit me in front of the TV, but only to programs they want.

A few times I plead with them to give me some physical work to do. "Anything, even for eight to ten hours a day straight without pay. Just to do something to get my body back in shape and spend my time some other way but watching television and wasting away here."

"If we free your arms or legs you might swing at us or gallop out of here," and I say "Then give me something mentally stimulating to do, like a crossword puzzle to look at and work out in my head or a newspaper or a book with words in it on pages which I can turn with my nose."

"Concentrate on improving your personality and conduct further. Because for someone of your incorrigible willfulness and stubbornness, that'll be work and time spent well enough."

"Please, you've got to, I'm going nuts here," and they say "Want to go on another hunger strike though this one organized by us?" and I shut up.

It takes a few months more before I do everything they say or what I figure they want me to, except every third week or so when I have to scream out my frustrations about staying here and having nothing to do, and I get gagged and slapped and strapped to my bed without food and water for a day.

Fall goes, then winter and spring, then summer and fall again, seasons, years. Because my behavior's tremendously improved they say, once a month I'm allowed to sit by the living room window for an hour during the day and look through a slit in the blinds to the street. It ends up being the event I look forward to most in my life, other than getting out of here. I watch the old buildings being renovated and pray that the owner of this one sells the building and it gets gutted and renovated too. I watch the styles of cars and clothes change, new tenants move in, old ones move out, neighborhood kids get taller and fuller and rowdier year after year.

While I sit behind that slit I often crave that someone will notice my eyes somehow—maybe through a roaming pair of binoculars or just from above average eyesight—and discover that I'm almost constantly blinking the SOS signal with my lids for the hour a month I'm there. Or maybe someone will think how odd it is that once a month only, a pair of twitching eyes looks onto the street for an hour, at least odd enough to wonder about it to the point of perhaps one of these months phoning the police to check out this apartment.

The only outsider who ever comes to the apartment is the building's super, who every other year or so is called in to fix a pipe or light switch. When that happens I'm gagged, strapped to the bed and locked in my room and the super comes and fixes whatever's the matter without knowing I'm here.

Once, two years ago, someone else did ring the bell. It was the only other live-in tenant in the building, the nameless one from the fifth floor. I was quickly gagged but overheard her say through the door that she was going out of town for a week to a funeral, so if Ivy or Roz hear anyone lurking around upstairs late in the evening, to call the police. "Will do," Roz said and the woman said "Thank you and have a good week," and that as far as I know was the last time she came by.

After being here for several years I long for something like a tornado to sweep through this part of the city and destroy every building in its path, though without anyone getting hurt except Ivy and Roz, but especially this building. Or that only this one catch fire somehow, when the factories are closed and the nameless tenant's out, but really anytime if it has to come to that, just to give me some small chance of getting away or being found alive.

I hope for a disaster like one of those for about a year and then decide to make one of my own. Twice a year on their birthdays they put a candle on the dinner table and the sister whose birthday it is blows it out at the end of the meal. I make my plans during Ivy's birthday dinner, rehearse it to myself day after day. When Roz's birthday comes several months later and they're in the kitchen preparing a special dessert and I'm sitting at the table with my arms and legs tied, I manage to stand and roll my body across the table and knock the candle to the floor. The rug starts to burn, just as I intended it to, and I get on my knees and blow on the fire to make it spread. The sisters smell the burning rug, run in, douse the fire with water before it becomes anything more than a small blaze, then gag me, light the candle and hold my hand over it till my skin sizzles and the gag almost pops from my soundless screams.

"That'll teach you never to play with fire or spoil my party for Roz," Ivy says and they take the gag off and I tell them I won't try any tricks like that again.

"You do and you'll get worse, much worse, maybe twice as many years with us than we planned for you," and I say "I promise, never again."

That's the first definite hint that my stay here won't be forever, unless they're lying. But it does get my hopes up somewhat that I'll be released eventually and I don't question them on it or make any trouble in the next three years. I become the model prisoner: courteous, obedient, uncomplaining, silent except to their questions and demands, always responding how they want me to and keeping out of their way. In that time I grow bald, my skin and body hairs turn gray, muscles continue to atrophy, I get so thin and weak from no exercise and their inadequate food that I can no longer turn myself over in bed, and my teeth ache night and day from my years of untreated cavities here, which they don't give me anything for but two aspirins a week.

Then, eight years to the day I got here, they take my ropes off after dinner and say "All right, you can go." I say "Thanks," not believing they mean it, and sit there at the table, taking my pleasure in being free of the ropes for the first time in eight years and wondering how many minutes it'll be before they're put back on.

"What are you waiting for," Roz says, "another eight years? You'll get it, though we sure as shoot don't want you around for that long again, if you don't move your behind out of here now."

Maybe they're not kidding, and I try to stand but am so unused to it this way that I drop back in the chair and it falls over with me to the floor. They help me up and say "This is the way to do it: spread your legs apart—rest—then one step after the next—rest . . . you'll get the knack back in time," and walk me to the door.

"My things," I say. "What I came here with and probably all I got left in the world," and Roz says "If you mean your wallet, watch and ring and stuff, all those are partial but final payment for your room, board and care these years. You're getting off cheap, Charles," and they push me a few inches past the threshold and shut and lock the door.

I still think they're playing with me and will suddenly throw open the door, knock me to the ground and carry me back inside. I only begin to believe I'm really free from them when I reach the bottom landing and open the vestibule door.

"Fresh air," I say. "The moon and stars—they're really there." My legs get wobbly and I sit on their building's stoop and take lots of deep breaths and then stay there because all my energy got used up making my way downstairs. It's almost dark, about the time of night when I was first on this block, nobody on the street or at the windows, no passing cars. "People—help me," I want to shout, but my voice is too weak for even the next-door first-floor tenant to hear.

Someone must have seen me and phoned the police—maybe even the sisters—because a squad car comes especially for me a half hour later. I put my arms out to him and he says "Too much to drink tonight, eh pal?"

"Not it at all. I've been kidnapped by two sisters in this building for the last eight years and was only just now released."

"Eight you say. Good story. Why not ten years?—let's go for twelve. At least yours is a little better story than the next wino's, though you're in a lot worse shape than most," and calls for an ambulance.

In the hospital I tell the police I'm no drunk and never was. "The doctors can vouch there's not a drop of alcohol in my blood or on my breath, and if you phone my best friend, if he's still alive, he'll tell you how I all of a sudden disappeared from this city eight years ago today."

The police call Ben and he comes right over with his wife. At first they don't recognize me and Ben says "This guy isn't Charles Kenna. Did he have any papers on him?" and the policeman says "Not one."

"Ben," I say, "remember the fountain pen complete with ink in it no less that I gave you for your thirteenth birthday? And Jill, you can't forget the swanky dinner I treated you both to on your fifth wedding anniversary and the pram blanket I gave for Tippy the day she was born."

After they finish hugging me I say "Now tell the police if I was ever a liar or drunk in my life."

"One glass of wine at dinner," Ben says, "and one only. He always said he had to have a clear head and settled stomach for the next morning if he was to do his best at work, which he also took home weekends."

"And his word?" Jill says. "He never uttered anything but the absolute truth, just like his actions: a moralist not to be believed. He used to make me ashamed of myself just for breathing, till I realized what a burden of unexamined guilt he must be carrying on his head, and then I began feeling a bit sorry for him."

The police go see Ivy and Roz. They deny everything, I'm told. "Charles Kenna? We've never known a Kenna or Kennan or any kind of name like that in our lives. And the only male to enter our apartment in thirty years was the super and he only to fix things."

The police tell me there's no proof I was ever in their apartment. "The sisters are known as eccentrics in the neighborhood, mostly because they keep so much to themselves, but they've never been in trouble with us or the city or anyone. Far as visitors go, they said nobody but that super and a lonely spinster friend from childhood who came twice a year for tea till she died recently and a few times the upstairs neighbor who they said came to the door for this or that, but no one else."

"I don't remember the friend at all. As for the neighbor and super, when she was at the door, I was bound and gagged behind it, and when he came inside, I was locked in the bedroom."

The police won't investigate further till I come up with more evidence for them. My lawyer tells me if I take the sisters to court I'll not only lose the case but be countersued for slander and in both cases I'll have to pay their legal fees.

So I don't pursue it. I never had much savings, so have to borrow from Ben and Jill to move into a hotel, get my teeth fixed and keep myself going till I get back my health and buy some clothes and find a job in my old field. All my belongings were put on the street eight years ago after I didn't pay my rent for three months.

A month after I'm released and when I'm still recuperating, I get a phone call in my hotel room.

"Surprise, it's me," Roz says. "We only today got a telephone put in after all these years and I wanted you to be my first personal call."

"Oh boy, thanks loads, but how'd you find me?"

"There are only so many Charles Kennas in hotels, you know. How are you?"

"I'll tell you how I am, you witch. I'm getting stronger every day, so don't try to mess with me again, you understand? If I didn't think you had a lethal weapon of some kind or I'd get in serious trouble for it or at least could do it in a way where the police would never know, I'd club you both over the head till you woke up in hell."

"For what, dear?"

"For what? Hey, I know you're both out of your skulls, but this much?"

"Who you speaking to, love?" Ivy says, picking up what I suppose is the extension.

"Oh, some nice wrong number I got by mistake when I dialed the hardware store."

"If he's that nice ask him to come over for lunch and a chat. That's the main reason we got this contraption for, isn't it: to widen our social life?"

"I already did. He said no."

"I didn't hear you ask him."

"You were in the other room."

"But I was listening at the door."

"All right, maybe I didn't. My mind might be slipping, just like yours. Excuse me, sir, but could you? My sister and I are two extremely lonely though I think reasonably intelligent and interesting elderly ladies and would love to have male company for a change. We're quite honestly bored with each other and ourselves, which you must have picked up during our harmless hostile exchange just now."

"Maybe another day," I say. "But Ivy, you know damn well who this is, so how about an explanation from you or Roz as to why you put me through so much for eight years?"

"Explanation?" She laughs. "Oh you poor love. We thought it was obvious to you. And this is who I suggested we invite for lunch?"

"It wasn't obvious," I say. "Maybe my mind suffered some irreversible comprehensive damage or psychological breakdown or whatever it was while I was with you two, so explain to me slowly and clearly so I can once and for all understand rather than just rack my brains and guess."

"Explain what?" Roz says. "Why I dialed the wrong number? People make mistakes, that's all," and they hang up.

After that they phone me once a week at the hotel, always asking if this is that nice man they got by mistake a week ago . . . a couple of weeks ago . . . a month ago and so forth, and each time I say no and hang up. Then my health is back to normal. I find a job, rent an apartment, get an unlisted phone and stay away from their neighborhood and never hear from them again.

Said

He said, she said.

She left the room, he followed her.

He said, she said.

She locked herself in the bathroom, he slammed the door with his fists.

He said.

She said nothing.

He said.

He slammed the door with his fists, kicked the door bottom.

She said, he said, she said.

He batted the door with his shoulder, went into the kitchen, got a screwdriver, returned and started unscrewing the bathroom doorknob.

She said.

He said nothing, unscrewed the doorknob, pulled the doorknob out of the door, but the door stayed locked. He threw the doorknob against the door, picked it up and threw it down the hall, banged the door with the screwdriver handle, wedged the screwdriver blade between the door and jamb and tried forcing the door open. The blade broke, the door stayed locked.

He said, she said, he said.

He got about fifteen feet down the hall and charged at the door.

She said.

He stopped.

He said.

She said nothing. Then she said, he said, she said, he said.

He got about ten feet down the hall this time and charged at the door.

She said.

He crashed into the door with his shoulder, bounced off it and fell down. The top hinge came out of the jamb, the door opened on top, hung on its bottom hinge for a few seconds while he was on the floor screaming from his shoulder pain, then came out of the bottom hinge and fell on his head and bad shoulder as he was getting up.

She said.

He pushed the door over, fell down on his bad shoulder. The pain was so great now not only from the first crash and then the door falling on his shoulder but the shoulder hitting the floor, that his body did a kind of automatic reflex movement where his legs shot out and his head and shoulders hit the baseboard. He screamed even louder.

She said.

He kept on screaming.

She said.

He held his breath, started crying. His head was bleeding but didn't hurt. He looked at her sitting on the bathtub rim, got up, kicked the wall, kicked the door, screamed from the shoulder pain he already had and now more so from the kicking.

She said, he said.

She came out of the bathroom, looked at his head, looked at his shoulder, looked for a towel in the bathroom. The towels were on the rack now under the door on the floor. She grabbed the handkerchief sticking out of his pants pocket, put it in his good hand, put his hand with the handkerchief to his head wound, sat him on the toilet seat and went into the bedroom and phoned their doctor.

The receptionist said, she said, the receptionist said.

The doctor said, she said, the doctor said, she said.

She came back. The handkerchief was soaked with blood and he was whining and groaning. She ran down the hall, got a bath towel out of the linen closet, wrapped it around his head, put his coat over his good shoulder, got her wallet and keys, got his wallet and made sure his hospital insurance card was in it, held his good arm, walked him out of the apartment, down the three flights and out of the building and hailed a cab.

She said, the cabby said.

They got into the cab and started for the hospital. A few blocks from the hospital a car ran a red light and smashed into her side of the cab. The cab turned over and ended up on its wheels on the sidewalk. She forced his door open and the two of them stepped out of the cab, shaken but not hurt. The pain in his shoulder was gone. The towel had fallen off his head in the crash and the wound was no longer bleeding. The cabby's head had gone through the windshield and was bleeding a lot.

They forced open the cabby's door.

A pedestrian said, she said, the pedestrian said and ran to a public phone booth and dialed.

They carefully broke the glass around the cabby's head, pulled him back into the cab, rested his head on the man's coat. She took off her sweater and wrapped it around the cabby's head. A crowd had gathered around them.

The crowd said, she said, the crowd said.

The pedestrian came back and said.

The police came in a few minutes and right behind them, an ambulance.

The police said, she said, the crowd said, the police said, the doctor and the ambulance attendant said, the police said.

The doctor examined the cabby, signaled the attendant to put him into the ambulance.

She said, the doctor said, she said.

The doctor looked at her husband's head wound and shoulder while the attendant and a policeman put the cabby on a stretcher and then into the back of the ambulance.

The doctor said, he said, she said.

The doctor got into the ambulance and the ambulance drove away.

The police said, they said, the police said, he said, she said.

A tow truck from the cab company pulled up. The tower hitched the cab to the truck, held up the bloody sweater and coat and said.

She said, took the sweater and coat and put the sweater into a trash can.

The tow truck drove off, the police drove away and the crowd broke up.

She said, he said.

He swung his arm and his shoulder still didn't hurt. She touched his shoulder gently and it still didn't hurt. He said, she shook her head. He touched his shoulder a little harder than she did and it still didn't hurt. He shook his head and smiled.

She said.

He nodded, looked sad and said.

She said, he said.

She took both his hands and kissed his cheek. He kissed her lips.

A passerby said.

He said.

The passerby laughed, waved his hand at them and walked on.

She hailed a cab.

She said, the cabby said, he said.

The cabby shrugged his shoulders and drove off. They started to walk home. A scavenger picked her sweater out of the trash can, held it up, said, dropped it back in and wiped her hands on a rag. She picked the sweater up with a stick this time and dropped it into one of her two bags.

The
Postcard

—

He goes into the apartment. His wife's waiting for him at the door. "I got this postcard today." She holds it out. He takes it and reads. "Your husband is in love with me, what can I say? Leave him, he doesn't love you. When he makes love with you, it's all sham. That's what he tells me. He pretends to have a good time with you in bed. Oh, all right, maybe he still has a good time with you—at the very end, but every man is like that then. But he has a good time from beginning to end when he's with me in bed. Or on the floor. Or against the wall. Or on the coach. Or even under the coach, and once, I kid you not, in the bathtub. It's me he loves, me he loves making love with, me he wants to be with when he sleeps with you or is just with you. Let him go. Let him be with me. Make him happy, no matter how unhappy it might make you. Are you still reading this? So, what are you going to do? Sincerely, Cecile Strick."

"I never heard of her," he says. "It's some postcard. How can anyone write so small? Must take a special pen or at least a special fine or extra-fine point on a pen. What's this word mean—coach? Couch? Has to be couch. But under the couch? Whoever heard of that? And who has a bathtub so large? I suppose some people have, and that it could be done in just about any size tub. But I've never known a Cecile in my life. My Aunt Cecile. Forget her. She's been dead for twenty years—no, more like twenty-five. I was still in college then."

"You never told me about her."

"Sure I did. I had to. My Uncle Nate used to beat her up. It's my feeling, but maybe I got the idea from someone in the family, that he beat her up on the head so much that he was the cause in some way of her getting brain cancer. That's what she died of. She was only around fifty. Maybe fifty-five. She died, actually, more than thirty years ago. I wasn't in college yet. So maybe she wasn't even fifty. I can't believe she'd be around eighty now if she had lived. He hit her on the head with a chair a number of times and once or twice knocked her out. I remember my father telling me about it. I even remember the calls he used to get from Cecile that Nate was trying to kill her again."

"You never told me about him or her."

"Never told you about Uncle Nate? I don't see how I couldn't have. My father's only brother. Or only one that lived past the age of five. Whenever we'd see him he used to give us a fifty-cent coin each. I remember wanting to go over with my brother and sister just to get that fifty cents. And they were always shiny—mint condition, almost. As if he got them straight from the bank and had asked for them to be brand-new. After he gave us the coin, or just me if I only went with my father, I'd show it to my mother at home. She was never impressed. They didn't get along. But poor Cecile. He once tried to throw her out a window, from maybe ten stories up. They lived on Riverside Drive, around Seventy-ninth or Eightieth."

"What number?"

"Ninety-eight."

"That's on Eighty-first, southeast corner. Didn't Bill live there for a year? Sublet somebody's apartment—Dan Freer's?"

"I think you're right."

"He called today—Bill did. I was going to tell you. He wants you to call him back."

"Did he say about what?"

"Nothing. Just to call back. He sounded loaded. Two o'clock. Loaded. He's never going to be able to finish it."

"Don't worry. He starts it, gets into it, gets loaded for a week or so, and then he finishes it. I've been through it with him before. I'll call after dinner. But Cecile and Nate."

"You're making them up. It's impossible for you to have had an uncle and aunt I never heard of."

"No, I must have told you about them. If you forgot it's because I probably only mentioned them once or twice in five years. Why would I mention them more? I saw Cecile maybe twenty times in my entire life, and only brief visits—maybe once a dinner at their home and they at ours. Nate was a bookie, worked out of his apartment, so we didn't, I think, for that reason—the kids at least—go over there much or stay very long. He usually had, maybe ten hours a day, someone in the kitchen manning the half-dozen phones, and sometimes two to three people working there and in the master bedroom for very big races and sports games. And policemen coming over to get paid off or make bets, and things like that. But I liked going over—and they were only ten or so blocks from us—for the good snacks, and Cecile was always very kind to me, and that half dollar. But when he tried to throw her out the window—well, after that my mother didn't want us to go over there at all. If she disliked him before, she hated and maybe even feared him now. Cecile was two-thirds of the way out the window—head first and face down and he was holding her by her legs and shaking her, shaking her, maybe just to scare her or I don't know what. That's what the doorman saw and told my father and my father told my mother and I overheard. Then some people on the street screamed—or maybe they were in the park, because most of the apartment faced the river—and he pulled her back in. He also shot her once—after the window incident—or shot at her, missed, or just grazed her arm—burned her. Whatever the bullet does. I know she was hurt but not that hurt. Nate said the wound came from the broken bottle the bullet smashed, but Cecile always claimed she'd been shot, not just shot at. Or not, as Nate told my father, that he shot at her clothes closet ten feet to the left of her, but because he was such a bad shot, the bullet hit a perfume bottle, I think it was, ten feet to the left of the closet. Once when we were there I asked my father to show me where the bullet went. He showed me a hole in their bedroom wall. The bullet had been dug out but the hole was still there."

"Maybe he was kidding you."

"About the hole?" She nods. "He did do that. I forget now where the hole was—by the dresser, the closet, whatever."

"Not that I'm saying there wasn't a shot. But I think it would have been patched up. By the way, you don't think you should call Bill now? If he was heading for a big drunk before, the later you call him, the more incomprehensible he'll probably be, if he does pick the phone up."

"Maybe I'll wait till tomorrow—around ten; noon, even. Or see if he calls back tonight. Whatever it is, I know it can hold. But last time I saw Aunt Cecile was a day or two before she died. Or a week or two, but she looked so bad—or that's my memory of it, and I probably only saw her for a few seconds—that I think of it as a day or two. I don't know why my folks brought me there. And my mother came this time. I suppose they thought I was old enough. Fifteen, maybe fourteen. Maybe they wanted me to play with my cousins Catherine and Ben—distract them."

"Catherine and Ben? Since when do you have cousins with those names?"

"Catherine's since died. She got the same brain cancer her mother had, but the doctors said it wasn't hereditary. 'Coincidence,' they said. I remember the figure of one out of five thousand that two people in the same family would get it. That was about the same as for two people living on the same city block. For a while she was my favorite cousin. We played together a lot, or at least once a month. But hardly ever at her apartment. Almost always at ours or in Riverside or Central Parks. Nate used to beat up his kids too. Ben didn't get it as much. He locked himself in the bathroom or screamed hysterically if he thought he was going to get hit, or ran to the neighbors, or just wasn't a target for Nate's violence as much as Catherine and Cecile were. Maybe because those two yelled and fought back. Catherine lost a front tooth to him once. And he hit her head too. Once with a teapot. Picked it up to throw at her and when the water came out of the spout and top—or tea did. Maybe it scalded him and he got even madder because of that, but he hit her head with it. She had to go to the hospital. Had several stitches—maybe thirty. He was a madman. He died by walking into a streetlamp."

"How? He was knocked unconscious, got a head injury—you know, swelling of the brain's membrane from it or a blood clot—and died?"

"It's a mystery. He hit the streetlamp, went down, but it wasn't enough to kill him—just knock him out. In other words, he didn't die from the blow. He died of a heart attack. There was some connection—maybe only a doctor could tell us what it was—but he got the attack while he was lying on the sidewalk. But this is the odd part. A policeman came, tried to revive Nate, searched his pockets for identification, found a whole bunch of bookie slips, and somehow got hold of a policeman friend of his, or something, because in about ten minutes two other policemen showed up at Nate's building, got into his apartment and cleaned out every cent he had stored away there. What's odder is that my father knew some policemen would do that once word got out that Nate had died suddenly on the street. Apparently every policeman knows that if you're a bookie, and Nate was a very successful one, you've lots of cash stashed away in your home to pay off big winners and such, and also because most of your income is never declared for taxes. In fact, when Ben called my father to tell him Nate had died an hour ago on the street, my father's first response was to tell him to rush right over to Nate's apartment and clear out all the money in two shoeboxes in the bedroom closet. Ben didn't want to. He said that as much as he hated Nate, he still had at least a day's grief and mourning in him for him. But my father told him 'Don't be a moron. I've got grief for him too. But there must be twenty thousand dollars there, and if you don't get it, the cops will.' How'd my father know what the cops would do? He knew lots about city life, that's all. So Ben rushed over to the apartment, but the police were already long gone. He couldn't press charges. For what? Their stealing illegal money? If he did get the money back, the government wouldn't let him keep it anyway. They'd look at all of Nate's reported income over the last five to ten years, and Ben and Catherine, to pay back Nate's owed taxes, would probably have to dig into their inheritance. Ben was also afraid the cops would kill him if he went to the city against them. Nate still left a lot to his kids. Jewelry, gold. But Catherine, married and with a child by then, died a year later from her brain cancer. And Ben's in jail now, my mother says. She saw it in the newspaper a few months ago. Maybe he's out by now—but for running a gambling operation in his home. In fact—well didn't I tell you I met him in an apartment building elevator a year ago?"

"No. I would have remembered. Because it would have been the first time I ever heard of your cousin Ben."

"I don't know why I didn't tell you. I know I wanted to. Reminded myself to tell you, after I met him. Anyway, I hadn't seen him for ten years, probably more. Maybe not since Catherine's funeral. And I heard this guy, running from the lobby, yell 'Hold the elevator. Press the "Door open" button.' So I pressed the button and in comes Ben. We were both so surprised we even kissed each other's cheeks. I was on my way up to see Hector Lewis. Ben then lived in that building. But according to the newspaper, my mother says, he has another address now, or maybe he gave a phony one to the police. But he was on the top floor, Hector on the eighteenth, and Ben said, as we're going up, 'Guess what I've become in life?' I said 'Well, according to Aunt Ruth you went into the dress business, so I suppose you've become a millionaire.' He said 'A bookie, isn't that amazing? I hated the guy, but I end up doing just what he did, and I think I'm going to do even better than him.' Maybe, after taking a beating in the dress business, he took what experience he'd learned just from watching Nate all those years and started taking book, running gaming tables, which I don't think Nate ever did, and also numbers and stuff, my mother said my cousin Holly told her. Or maybe he was never legit—

a word my father liked to use—before he became a bookie. I know that as a teenager he was thrown out of a few boarding schools for causing trouble and then in this city got arrested for drunken driving, without a license, but I don't remember hearing of anything worse."

"No wonder you never talked about them. Actually, that's not fair. Because though I can't picture Cecile very well from everything you've said, Catherine seemed very nice."

"She was. And to me, son of a bitch that he was, Nate was still kind of interesting in a way. And look what that poor kid went through—Ben. If I'd had his life as a kid, would I now be much different than he? No matter what—why I also never mentioned Catherine, I don't know. I was never closer to one of my cousins. Then, when she was around fifteen, she got big and fat, and stupid, it seemed, when before she was always curious and perceptive, and I couldn't talk to her about anything except our playing together as kids. Last time I saw her she was so sad she made me cry. She'd lost about a hundred pounds, but it wasn't, and I don't say this to be funny, an improvement. No, forget that. She had no hair. She was wearing a wig. Her speech was slow. She'd gone through operations and one chemotherapy session after the other. My heart bled for her. She acted retarded. But she was so sweet. I don't ever remember her being as sweet as she was then, though she was always a very kind person. Generous. She had about a month to live. In fact, all this took place at one of Cynthia's daughters' weddings. And it's not that she got big and fat and stupid. She got heavy, that was her business, but after everything she went through as a kid, and then was still going through as a fifteen-year-old, you could understand why. She was pretty smart too, in her own way. She was a good businesswoman till she got sick. And whatever I might have suggested, I don't think her sickness was Uncle Nate's doing—hitting her on the head. Or if it was his doing for Cecile's cancer either. I don't know about such things. But what that family's gone through is unbelievable."

"It's still difficult for me to understand how I never heard about any of them. From you, from Ruth. But this card. What's it mean? Who's it from? Who is this Cecile?"

"I don't know. Someone's playing a joke. What's the postmark say? It's this city. Sent yesterday. The mail's faster than I thought. I don't know any Cecile. My Aunt Cecile is the only Cecile I've known. Or that I can remember having known. But certainly no Cecile for years. And this Cecile is talking about today, isn't she? Someone's cracked. Someone's trying to start trouble between us. You're the only person I love and love being in bed with and the only person I go to bed with and there isn't any other woman, and hasn't been since maybe a week or two after I met you, whom I've known in that kind of way."

"I'll accept that," and she tears up the postcard. They kiss. He says "No, a long one, not just a hello, back-from-work kiss." They hug and kiss. Then she says "Like to split a beer?" and he says "Why not?" and follows her into the kitchen.

Windows

Nothing's on his mind. Can't read, doesn't want to sit around the apartment and snack anymore. If he stays here any longer he'll uncork a bottle of wine and drink it down while he looks out the window, stares at the walls, ceiling light fixture and the floor. He gets up to go out. But if I go out, he thinks, where will I go? Take a walk, see what you'll see. Don't stick around here doing nothing, ending up sleepy from all the wine, overstuffed from all the snacks, asleep by seven or eight so up around four or five in the morning and then what'll you do? More staring, eating, drinking. Maybe try the newspaper again.

He sits down, opens the newspaper. Explosion someplace. A woman shot. A woman raped. Two boys find a decomposed body on a beach. Milton Bax wins Endenta Prize. New movies. Spy grabbed. Two dozen pregnant whales run aground. Famous physicist dies of mysterious disease. A young woman crossed the ocean in a canoe. Television listings. Sports. Ads. Juniper Holland's "perfect brownie" recipe. He crumples up the paper, sticks it into the fireplace. Lights the paper, watches it burn. An ash floats through a hole in the fireplace screen and he grabs it in the air. His hand's smudged from the ash. He rubs his hand on his pants. Now his pants are smudged. He brushes his pants till only an indelible spot's left. He sits in the chair. Think about something. Let something just come to mind. Daydream.

He remembers a real event. It was a number of years ago. Three. He was married then and was changing the baby's diapers. Esther. "I peepee," she liked to say, and he or Jill would change her. "If you know when you peepee," he used to say, "then you should try to peepee and kaka into the toilet." "Toilet?" she used to say. "Potty," he used to say. "Potty and toilet, same thing." "Same thing?" she used to say. "Sweetheart, don't repeat everything I say." "Don't repeat?" she used to say. Though it only sounded a little like "Don't repeat." Like her "toilet" only sounded a little like "toilet." "Potty," she could say. "Dough repee," she used to say. "Toyet. Same sin." She didn't peepee into the toilet till she was three. People said that was very late. He and his wife didn't mind her not using the toilet till then. Some things one gets used to. And he liked changing her most times. The softness of the diapers, patting her crotch and bottom with a warm washrag, drying her, pinning the diapers on her, the rubber pants, the long pants or stretchies or shorts. She would be on her back on the changing board and he would be sitting in front of her on the same bed and he would often lean over and kiss her forehead or the top of her head or her cheek. Sometimes he'd say "Kiss Daddy," and she'd kiss his cheek. Then he'd finish dressing her, if he hadn't already finished, and stand her up on the floor or just lift her off the board and put her into or back into bed.

But he was changing her, he remembers, when the phone rang. He looks at his hand. Still a little dirt. He picks at it with his fingernail, then spits into a handkerchief and rubs it into his hand till the spot's gone. It's not that I mind dirt, he thinks. He smells his hand. It smells from spit, but that'll go away quickly enough. And an ash really isn't dirt. I could, in fact, almost any other day, walk around with my hand smudged like that or even worse. Not the whole hand smudged, but a much larger spot than there was. Anyway: walk around or just stay here without paying any attention to the smudge till it disappeared through nothing I consciously did.

He turns around and looks out the window. About fifteen feet from his window are two windows in a brick wall. Above the wall— his apartment and the apartment or apartments he's looking at are on the top floors of their buildings—is some gray sky. Maybe I should stare at that slit of sky till something passes in it. A bird, helicopter, sheet of newspaper, a plane. Rain, even. Stare till it rains. It can't snow. Not the season for it. What else could be in the sky that might pass, drop, stay there awhile, float by? A cloud, of course. Hailstones would be unlikely. A balloon. On the other side of the building he's looking at is a street. Someone could walk on it holding a balloon.

The balloon could be released, accidentally, intentionally, and float past that slit of sky he's looking at. He looks at that sky for around two more minutes, tells himself to look at it another minute and if nothing passes in it, to stop. He looks at it another minute. Nothing passes. He faces forward, rests his head back against the chair, remembers.

The phone rang. He yelled something like "Jill, would you get it?—I'm changing the baby." She yelled she would and ran to her studio from wherever she was and picked up the phone. "Oh Randi," she said, "hi," and that's all he remembers hearing from that phone call. That was all he heard. Because he remembers that maybe an hour later he thought about why he hadn't heard more of the phone conversation than just "Oh Randi, hi," and decided it was because she must have started speaking very low after that or else had shut the door. He never asked her about it, though once or twice had wanted to. But she came into the baby's room a few minutes later, while he was on the floor putting away Esther's books and toys and Esther was sitting on the floor trying to string beads, and looked very sad. She was very sad, but when she came into the room, or rather, stood inside the door with her shoulder against the jamb, as if, if she didn't lean against it she wouldn't be able to stand, all he could tell was that she looked very sad. What he thought then was that she was sad because of something she'd learned over the phone or something that had happened to her since she put the phone down. Because, he thought, what could Randi have told her that made her look so sad? And how come she didn't let him speak to Randi? She was his niece. They were quite close. Maybe Randi had called to tell him something about his sister, but something so terrible that she was now relieved she wouldn't have to be the one to tell him. "What is it," he said, "something wrong?" She nodded. She brought her hand to her mouth.

He hears a plane, turns around to that slit of sky but doesn't see anything. Then he sees it for a couple of seconds. Flying west. A jumbo jet. It could be going to any number of places. California, Tahiti, Japan. It could be going, eventually, east. If it is, it'll soon turn around. But chances are much better, not that he really knows what he's talking about, that it's going west, or west now but north or south soon. He looks at the two windows. He's never seen anyone in the right one. The shade's always down. Never even seen the room. He's seen artificial light behind the shade. In the evening, very late, maybe five or six times. But he's never seen the shade raised even an inch from the sill in the year and two months he's lived here. The fourteen months since Jill asked him to leave their apartment, which he did and got this apartment that same day. In the other window— it's much smaller—he's seen a woman showering maybe fifteen times. Showering or just shampooing, if one doesn't always shower, meaning clean one's body, which he's never seen her do, except for her face and neck, when one shampoos. He wonders if the shaded window is part of the same apartment as that bathroom. The bathroom door is at the end of the left wall. If it was in the right wall, then the bathroom would have to lead to the shaded room. Though maybe the shaded room is a hallway in that apartment or a public hallway in that building. If he steps up to his window he can see four windows on the same floor to the right of the shaded window, two with blinds, two with shades, all opened or closed or lit or unlit at various times of the day, but none, except for the one next to the shaded window and there only a little, can he see inside. Not the right angle or too far away. But a public hallway wouldn't have a shaded window and artificial light only now and then. Makes no sense. For the last two months the bathroom window has had a shade on it. Almost to the sill. Possibly because she caught him watching her showering several times. Sometimes it was by accident. He'd be slumped below the top of the padded chair when he'd hear a shower go on, look around or above the chair and see her showering. Or he'd enter his apartment, shut the door and see her showering. Hear and see at the same time sometimes. The shower part of her bathtub is right by the bathroom window. For a while at night when he came home he wouldn't turn on his apartment light till he found out if she was showering or not. If she was, he'd watch her in the dark till she left the bathroom or put her bathrobe on. If she only put on her underpants or bra, he'd continue to watch her till she left the room. If she put both under- clothes on, he'd crawl away from the window to one of the lights, turn it on and stand and go about the apartment as if he just came home. But he only caught her showering once in the eight or so times when he came home and went through this routine, so he gave it up. She's a woman of about thirty-five, somewhat plump, somewhat pretty, who spends a great deal of time lathering her long dark hair. Sometimes he's seen her entirely covered with lather, which would start at her hair and slide down on all sides and sometimes in large clumps to the rest of her body, or the parts of her body he could see above the bathtub rim. He's gotten quite excited sometimes when

484   The Stories of Stephen Dixon

he's seen her showering or drying herself and then putting on her
underclothes. Once when she saw him looking at her while he was
standing in the middle of the room and pretending to flip through a
magazine, she slammed the window down and pulled the single
shower curtain around her where he couldn't see her showering anymore, not that he would have been able to see much through the
smoked glass. Once when it was night and he was reading in this
chair, he heard her singing in the shower. He doesn't know if he had
been so absorbed in the book that he had missed the shower going
on, or else if the shower and singing had started at the same time.
Anyway, he stood up, with his back to her put the book on the chair,
shut the light, opened his door, slammed it, crawled to the far right
corner of the window and raised his head just above the sill to watch
her. By the time she was drying herself while standing in the tub, he
had his pants down and his handkerchief out. He wonders about a
woman who'd shower in front of an open window, one that faces
another open window, especially one in which she must have known
a man had caught or watched her showering several times. Maybe
she has a let-him-look attitude about it, all he's seeing is a body, one
not much different than any other woman's body her age, and if it
does anything to him, it has nothing to do with her. Or maybe she
liked showering in front of him, showing off her body, so to speak,
the pleasure it might give him, let's say, maybe even showering more
times than she normally would because he was there, but then felt
the situation had possibilities or ramifications she hadn't thought
about, so she stopped. He can't see her toilet or sink from his window. They must be on the right side of the bathroom.

Jill took her hand away from her mouth. He forgets what Esther
was doing at the time. She was probably just lying peacefully or
squirming a little bit on her back. But why'd he pick this particular
memory? It's the one that came to him, that's all. It could have been
one of any number of memories that came to him when he just sat
back and let things enter his head. The time his mother died. (He
was in the hospital room.) The time Esther was born. (He was in the
delivery room.) The time he and Jill got married. (It was in the living
room of the apartment she and Esther now live in.) The time he
learned his brother's plane had disappeared. (He was in his sister's
living room.) The time Jill ran into the bathroom with her nightgown
on fire. (He was on the toilet. She had said from the kitchen only a
half-minute before "Do you smell gas?" He had said "No, why—you
mean real gas? Do you?") The time Jill accepted his marriage pro-

posal. (He was on his knees in her living room, his arms around her legs, crying, while she was rubbing his head with one hand and with the other trying to get him to stand.) The time an ice cream Popsicle stuck to the top of his tongue. (He was standing on a busy street corner, pointing to his mouth and gagging. The ice cream vendor got in his truck and drove off. A man said "Don't pull on it, kid. It's the dry ice it was packed in. Pull on it and you'll take off half your tongue. Just let it melt a few minutes and it'll come off on its own.") The time Esther fell, though it actually seemed she had flown, down a flight of stairs. (They were in the summer cottage they rented and which Jill still rents. He was in the main room, working at his desk. Something made him look to his left and he saw her flying headfirst down the stairs. The staircase was in the hallway around twenty feet away, but he missed catching her by just a couple of inches at the bottom of the stairs. He doesn't see how that was possible. He must have seen her on one of the top steps, about to fall, and jumped out of his chair and ran to the stairs.) The time they took Esther to the hospital. (They were in their car, minutes after he'd missed catching her at the bottom of the stairs. He was driving. Esther was in Jill's lap in the reat seat, a compress on her nose, towels around her bleeding head. A rabbit jumped across the road and he swerved but hit it. The rabbit flew over the car and landed about fifty feet behind them. He'd hit it while it was in midair. Jill screamed. Esther was unconscious.) The time they waited while the doctors and nurses treated Esther. (It was outside the hospital examination room. They thought she was going to die. One of the doctors had said a few minutes before "I don't know if you know it, but she may die." Jill said "Listen, you imbecile. I know we were negligent, but now's the stupidest time in the world to remind us." The doctor said he didn't mean it that way. Jill said "You did too." Carl pulled her into him, said "Don't argue, don't bother, don't worry, it'll all turn out all right. It's got to be all right. I'll go crazy if she dies.") The time they buried his father. (Cemetery.) His mother. (Same cemetery.) The time he came home from summer camp and his parents said they'd given away his dog.

Jill said to him "—died." He said "Who?" "—Kahn." "What? I'm not hearing you for some reason. Who?" "Gretta Kahn. Gretta Kahn. She died two days ago, Monday." "Oh Jesus, that can't be. It can't. What are you talking about? That was Randi on the phone, right? So what's she got to do with Gretta?" "Not your niece, Randi. Gretta's oldest son, Randy. He called from Charleston. Gretta died in San Diego. A massive heart attack, he said. She was visiting Mona. And because he knew she was such a good friend of ours—" "Her daughter?" "Mona, her daughter and Randy's sister, yes. They're having the funeral in San Diego—something about it's easier to, not the expense—and just wanted us to have the option of coming. I told him I didn't think we could. I was right, wasn't I?" "Come on," he said, "she was too healthy. Anyone but her. Besides, it's too ridiculous. For it was just around this time of year last year—" "That's right. It's like a medical prophecy come true, except it's the reverse of what frequently is supposed to happen in that frequently it's the husband who dies a year after his wife." He remembers she cried, they talked a lot about Gretta that night, neither of them slept well, and this went on for two or three days. She was one of their best friends. And of their best friends, she was just about the nicest of them and the one they loved most. Or else it seemed that way at the time. Was it so? He thinks it was, and if it wasn't, then she came as close as anyone at the time to being the nicest of their best friends and the one they loved the most. They didn't have many friends that both of them considered their best friends. He had best friends, she did. A few they shared. Or he had several fairly good friends, she had several very good friends, and a few of her very good friends he considered fairly good friends of his. What's he talking about? Gretta was a very good close friend of them both. They talked about deep serious things together, all three of them or just when he or Jill was with her. Sometimes. Sometimes they just had a good time together, when not a serious subject or mood came up. Jill and he didn't go to Gretta for advice, either separately or together, and she never came to either of them for it, but when they were with one another, separately or together, they often talked about the most important things in their lives, past or present, including what was bothering them most. When he or Jill was alone with Gretta they also occasionally talked about their respective spouses, something they didn't do with Gretta's husband Ike and Ike didn't do with them, talk personally about Gretta or about anything deep or serious that might interest either of them, though they still considered him to be one of their dearest friends, because he was so generous and warm and Gretta's husband, though maybe not one of their closest. He remembers trying to bring Gretta back then in his thoughts. Three years ago. He remembers that a day or so after Gretta died he said to Jill when the phone was ringing "Maybe that's Randy again, saying it was only a joke and Gretta isn't dead." He remembers Jill saying "That's crazy" or "too bizarre for me." "I know that was crazy or too bizarre," he remembers saying after he or she finished talking to whomever it was on the phone, "what I said about Gretta before, but it was what I wished most. That it had been a joke. To lose Ike one year, Gretta the next? To lose them both? All a joke. For Randy or Mona or whatever the other son's name is—Gene—to say on the phone 'Gretta and Ike are alive. They said they'll explain everything when they get to New York and see you all.' " He remembers lying in bed the next few days thinking of the various ways she could be alive. That it was a seizure of some kind where she appeared dead but wasn't. Or she had been dead but was revived. Where they'd get a letter from Gretta the next day or so explaining why Randy gave Jill that message and why she had to send this letter instead of making a phone call. That it was a bet. That it was part of a plot. That it was a chain of almost inconceivable false and incompetent medical reports from hospital to doctor to Gretta's children. It took him a while to get used to her death.

He hears a shower turned on behind him. He turns around. The shade's down, woman's singing. Both their windows are open. The weather's been gray and unseasonably cool the last few days but has warmed up in the last hour and the sun's now out. He looks at the sky. He recognizes the melody she's singing but can't make out the words. He shuts his eyes and listens. She's singing in French, but he's almost sure the song's American. She has a sweet voice. Professional, almost. For all he knows about singing voices, professional. Dulcet was the word Jill used for a voice this sweet. Jill knew about voices. She listened to opera, lieder and madrigals a few hours a day, once wanted to be an opera singer, sang in several languages in the shower sometimes but would never do it with the window open or so loud. "Sweeter than sweet," she said, "is when you use 'dulcet,' or at least when I use it." He doesn't know if he'd recognize this woman if he saw her on the street. For one thing, it's been a long time since he's seen her in the shower. If he saw her and recognized her would he introduce himself? He doubts it. Of course not. Would she recognize him if she saw him? He doubts it. Maybe she would. Maybe she's already seen him on the street and recognized him several times while all to some of those times he might have looked straight at her but didn't recognize her. He wouldn't mind meeting her. He knows no woman to go out with. He hasn't been to bed with a woman since Jill, though he has been out with a number of them but never more than once or twice each. The third or fourth time is when you often get to go to bed together. He wonders if he should call Jill. He'd ask how she is. She'd say fine, probably, but why did he call? "To find out how you are and to find out, of course—how could you even ask that?—how Esther is." "You spoke to Esther this morning," she could say, "you'll see her this weekend. She's having her supper now." It's around that time. He looks at his wrist. His watch isn't on it. Where'd he leave it? This could lead to a minute or two of panic. Watch, pen and wallet, all quite valuable when one considers the wallet's contents, and all given to him by Jill. Sentimental value then? Not only. But when they're out of his pockets and off his wrist, he likes to keep them together. The dresser. He goes into the bathroom, sees the three of them and his checkbook and keys on top of the dresser, looks at the watch. He should buy a clock. A small one, that doesn't tick. It's five after six. Just around the time she'd be eating. He used to like feeding her. "Baby eat meat," she used to say. "Baby eat corn and peas, no beans," though she used to pronounce them "con and peats." Used to like putting the bib on her, making sure her hands were clean and if they weren't, washing them with a little warm water on a dish towel and drying them with the towel's other end. Now she feeds and washes herself, though sometimes when she insists he lets her eat with slightly dirty hands. Now she tucks the napkin into her shirt or spreads it out on her lap, though sometimes he lets her use her sleeve. He used to like feeding her spoonfuls and forkfuls of food, touching the cereal with his tongue before he gave it to her to make sure it wasn't hot. Squeezing orange juice for her almost every morning, every so often squeezing quarter of a grapefruit to add to the glass. He was usually the first up. Around six. Esther around seven. Jill around eight. Putting her to bed—he liked that too. Bathing her first, though the one who bathed her usually wasn't the one who then read to her and put her to bed. And after he washed her but while she was still playing with her water toys or the soap in the tub, massaging and brushing and flossing his teeth and gums and then applying that sodium bicarb–peroxide paste. He didn't like giving her shampoos. Liked rubbing her back to get her to sleep. Making love with his wife while the baby slept in the same room. She was always so receptive. His wife was. They loved each other, and he thinks the baby, as much as a one-to-two-year-old could, loved him then too. What went wrong? Why did it have to go wrong? Were there several or many things wrong or just one main one? He still loves Jill but she no longer loves him. That's what she's said so that's what he has to believe. He should go out. Take a walk, see what he sees. Not a movie. Maybe step in for coffee someplace, regular or espress. Maybe a beer. No beer. He doesn't like drinking in bars alone. Doesn't like eating out alone. Coffee in some stand-up place or on a coffee shop stool is still okay.

The shower's turned off. The singing's stopped. She's probably drying herself but she could also be shaving her underarms or legs. Saw both of those once or twice too. Today she left the shade up a couple of inches, but it's not dark enough outside yet to look. Not dark at all. Anyway, he shouldn't be sneaking looks. Maybe he should go out to buy a men's magazine. One with naked women, but which still has serious articles and maybe serious fiction in it. Photos showing everything, but of women alone or together rather than with naked men. He doesn't like to buy that kind of magazine, give a clerk money and sometimes have to get change back for it, walk home with it rolled up if he doesn't have an envelope or newspaper to put it in, or have it around the apartment. But about every three to four months, maybe two to three months is a closer estimation, he buys one, uses it in his own way, then tears it up after a couple of days and sticks the pieces deep into a garbage bag, makes sure they're covered with garbage, and drops the bag in one of the trash cans in front of his building. But he doesn't want to go out just to buy one of those magazines, though he wishes now he hadn't torn up the last one he bought.

He turns around and looks at the sky. Go out. See what's out there. Call Jill. Ask to speak to Esther. Go to a movie. Go to a bar. Go to a bookstore and buy a book whatever it costs. For the first time in your life, find a book you want very much to read but any other time you'd think way too expensive for you. If you haven't the cash, write a check. If they won't take a check, ask them to put the book aside, leave a deposit for it, go back to the apartment, and next day, or even tonight, if the store's still open and not too far away, get that book. Or just walk along the street. Walk to walk. Walk for exercise. For fresh air. To tire yourself out. Walk all the way downtown. Through the theater district. Past the Village to Lower Broadway. Go to several bookstores and bars and then cab home. Or call Jill and say you're sad and lonely and want to come back to her. "I want us to live as a family again," say. "I love you," say. "I love Esther. It's not that I can't live without you. It's that I don't want to. Living alone's killing me in a way. I sneak looks at the bathroom window across from my apartment. A woman showers there and I want to see her nude. I have seen her nude, she's bought a shade just to keep me from seeing her nude, but I often quickly turn my head to her window hoping the shade's up and she's standing there nude. I have these absurd fantasies about meeting her on the street and going to bed with her. I think about buying those awful men's magazines just to use the photos of naked women in them to alleviate my excitedness. My sexual frustration. My pent-up whatever it is that keeps getting more pent-up every day. I have bought those magazines, maybe every other month. I thought of Gretta today. I think of her a lot. Not in a sexual way. I'm sorry I linked those two subjects up like that. One coming after the other. Gretta and sex. Or rather those magazines and Gretta. But I think of her a lot. Those were good days then, the time when we knew her and she died. I mean, we were sad for her. It crippled us for a while. But we were happy with one another then, the time when we knew her and a little after the time she died. The two of us and the three of us, meaning the two of us when that's all there was of us and then with Esther, and you can't say we weren't. I know I had a bad temper. You can't say we weren't happy then. I know I was impossibly moody at times. But I'm getting to understand the reasons why I had those sudden swings of mood and also how to prevent them and I doubt I'll ever get like that again or at least as much." Call and say all that. Or walk or take a cab acrosstown and ring her bell from the lobby and ask to come up. Then say it to her or as much as you think she can take for one time.

A plane's overhead. He looks out the window. The plane passes but not in the part of the sky he's able to see. Jill has a lover now. She's in love. They'll probably get married. That's what she's said. He's met him. Seems like a decent fellow. And tall, handsome, rugged, smart. Esther likes him too. Loves him in a little girl's way, Jill's said. He's wonderful and attentive and devoted to both of them, Jill's said, and when the three of them are together they get along exceptionally well. Go outside. Take that walk. Exhaust yourself walking so you'll sleep eight to ten hours straight. Have an exotic coffee outside, have brandies and beer, have a good dinner outside and then buy a book, or buy it before you have dinner, you never would have bought for yourself before and come home. He gets up to go. He hears a shade snapped up. Bathroom's? He looks at his ceiling, floor, slowly turns around to look at that woman's bathroom. It's the shaded room's shade that's up. It must have snapped up by accident. No one seems to be in the room. It's unlit. He goes up to his window and sees a mirror at the end of that room reflecting his building's roof and the light from the sky above it. Someone goes over to the mirror and looks into it. From behind it looks like Gretta. That's the way she looked from behind. He saw her walking away from him, from them, down her road, picking a blossom off a tree, berries off a bush, going into rooms, working in her kitchen, cooking there, putting away dishes there, putting seeds into the bird feeders around her house, snapping pictures, serving hors d'oeuvres, many times. Kind of short, round, hair like that. Shape like that. Way she's fussing with her hair now like that. Then a man, both are fully dressed, comes into view and walks up behind her and hugs her while they both look into the mirror, the man looking over her shoulder. He can't see their faces in the mirror. Their images are entirely blocked by their standing in front of the mirror. Then they turn around and come up to the window, the man with his hand on her shoulder. It's Ike and Gretta. Ike raises his hand to pull the shade down and sees him looking at them. Ike points to him, they stare at him. Gretta seems shocked, Ike amused. He says "Gretta, Ike, oh God, this is too wonderful. Tell me what apartment you're in and I'll run right over. I'm so lonely. I was till I saw you. On and off, I mean, and sad—you can't believe how much—on and off too. Jill and I are divorced. She's going to remarry, while I love her as much as I ever did. That was a lot, remember? but that's not news. Esther's just great. A truly exemplary child. Intelligent, beautiful, generous, precious, good; a real dear. We missed you so. We were devastated by your deaths. The untrue news of them, rather, for here you are. We both loved you so. Love you so, love you, and I know I can still speak for Jill on this. Seeing you now is the best thing that's happened to me in a year. In two, in three. Or come over here. I'm in number nine, apartment five-D. But I'll run over to your place because I know I can get there faster than you could here. Or maybe, with this shade business of Ike's—raising his hand to pull it down, it seemed like—and the look that was on both your faces, you had something else in mind and want me to wait here a half hour or so. You can hear me through your closed window, can't you?"

He didn't go over to his window. He stood almost at the other end of his room, looking out his window from there. Shade on the window of the once shaded room did snap up, bathroom shade stayed down. He didn't see a mirror in that room. If there is one, and in the place he said there was, then he imagined it before he saw it, for so far he's been too far away from that room to see anything inside. The room's unlit, though. That he can see from where he stands. He goes over to his window and looks inside that room. There's a double bed, made, in there. A night table beside it. A lamp on the table. Ashtray next to the lamp. Radio beside the ashtray. Cup in a saucer on top of the radio. That's all he can see in the room. Spoon in the saucer. Maybe a crack in the wall but nothing's hanging on the part of the wall he can see. What will the tenant think when he or she, if there's only one, sees the shade up? That it snapped up on its own? That a stranger was in the room and let it up? But how will she or he pull it down? Will he or she allow him- or herself to be seen from a window across from that building? It's worth waiting for. Just to see the reaction of that person, if it can be seen, when she or he sees the shade up, and what kind of person lives there.

He moves the chair from the left side of his window to the right. He turns the chair around to the window and pushes it within inches of the window. He opens a bottle of wine, sits in the chair and drinks while he faces at an angle the now unshaded room. The day gets darker. He can see a big chunk of the sky from here. His phone hasn't rung, when he's been in his apartment, for almost two days. Stars come out. Two, three, then a few of them. The bathroom window shade stays down. The light in the bathroom goes on and off a few times in the next two hours. Twice it stayed on for only a few seconds, once for almost a half hour. He finishes three-quarters of the bottle of wine, has to pee. It's now night. Many stars are out. He can see the moon's light but not the moon. The bathroom light hasn't been turned on for about an hour. If the bathroom is part of the same apartment as the bedroom, he's sure the woman who likes to shower would have walked into the bedroom by now. Or at least a door would have opened from the bathroom or some other part of the apartment—a hallway—into the bedroom and let some light into it by now. But no light's come in. A little light from the moon per- haps. But now the bedroom's almost black. He can't see anything inside it. He finishes off the bottle. Now he really has to go to the bathroom or he'll have to do it in his pants right here. Maybe into the bottle, but that would end up being a mess. He tries to hold it in. He doesn't want to miss that person or persons, if there is more than one person living in that apartment containing that room, discover- ing the shade up and then pulling it down. And he's certain it'll be pulled down. But he can't hold it in anymore and runs to the bath- room. He takes his watch off the dresser while he's there. The shade's still up and the bedroom's still dark when he gets back. An hour later he has to go to the bathroom again. He runs to it, pees, runs to the kitchen and gets a beer out of the refrigerator, runs back to the chair. Nothing's changed in that room. He opens the beer, sips, puts it down, wakes up in the chair and finds the shade down but the room still dark. He doesn't know how long he's been sleeping in the chair. He should take a walk. He looks at his watch. He can't make out the luminescent numerals and hands. He squints. Still can't make them out. He gets up and turns on the side table light. It's past two. That's hard to believe, he thinks. He should go to sleep. Maybe have a bite to eat from the food in the refrigerator and a slice of bread and then go to sleep. No, just take off your clothes, pull out the bed and go to sleep.

A

Sloppy

Story

"Listen to this," I say. "This guy comes in and says to me and I say to him and he says and I say and the next thing I know he does this to me and I do that to him and he this and I that and a woman comes in and sees us and says and I say to her and he says to me and she to him and he says and does this to her and I say and do that to him and she doesn't say anything but does this and that to us both and then a second time and he says and she says and I say and we all do and say and that's it, the end, what happened, now what do you think?"

"It won't work," a man says. His partner says "It will work, I know it will," and I say "Please, gentlemen, make up your minds. Do you think it will work or not?" The first man says no and his partner yes and I clasp my hands in front of my chest hoping they'll agree it will work and give me money for it so I won't have to be broke anymore or at least not for the next year, when the phone rings and the first man picks up the receiver and says "Yuh?" The person on the other end says something and the man says "You're kidding me now, aren't you?" His partner says "Who is it, something important?" and the man says and his partner says "Just tell him to go fly away with his project, now and forever," and I just sit there and the man hangs up the phone and says to us "Now where were we?"

"I was," I say. "He was," his partner says. "Okay," he says, "let's continue where we left off from, though quickly, as I got a long day," and we talk and he says "I still don't go for it," and his partner says

"I'm starting to agree with you, now and forever," and I say "Please, gentlemen, let me tell the story over. Maybe it will be more convincing the second time around and I promise to be quicker about it," and I start the story from the beginning: guy coming in, says to me, me to him, does this, I do, woman, what we all said and did and then the partner, not agreeing, phone ringing, call ending, my retelling the story. After I finish I say "So what do you think? Will it work?"

"No," they both say and I say "Well, no harm in my having tried, I guess," and the first man says "No harm is right except for our precious lost time," and sticks out his hand and I shake it and shake his partner's hand and say "Can I use your men's room before I go? It might be my last chance for a while." His partner says "Second door to the right on your way out to the elevator," and I say "Which way is the elevator again, left or right when I get out of your office?" and he says and I say "Thanks," and they say and I leave, wave goodbye to the receptionist, go to the men's room on their floor, take the elevator down, go through the building's lobby to the street. It's a nice day, finally. It was raining heavily when I came in. My umbrella! Damn, left it upstairs, should I go back for it? No. Yes. What the hell, why not, it's not an old umbrella, it's still a good serviceable umbrella. And if I don't get it I'll have to buy a new umbrella at probably twice what the one upstairs cost me three years ago the way inflation's going crazy today.

I go back through the lobby, elevator, get on it, upstairs, their floor, past the men's room, into their office and the receptionist says and I say "I know, but I," and point to it and the partners come out of the room we were talking in before just as I grab my umbrella and look at me but don't say anything when I say hello but just walk into another room and I say goodbye to the receptionist and she nods at me and starts typing rapidly and I leave the office, elevator, lobby and see it's raining heavily again. Rain coming down like, streets filled with water like, people running out of the rain like, sky like, traffic like, I open the umbrella and walk in the rain totally protected because of my umbrella, long raincoat and boots and think "Well, I at least did one thing right today and that's going back for the umbrella, and maybe one other thing and that's wearing the right rain clothes," when someone ducks under my umbrella, a woman, hair soaked by the rain, and says "Mind if I walk with you as far as the bank on the corner? It closes in a few minutes and I have to put in some money by today."

"Sure," I say and we walk, I hold the umbrella, she her coat together at the collar, and talk, she "Can we walk faster?" I say sure, she asks where am I going, I say to an office building a block past her bank, she asks, I tell her, she says "Well what do you know," because it seems she's a good friend of the very man I want to see most about the same story project I spoke to those partners about, but whom I haven't been able to get an appointment with for more than a month. So I suggest, she says "Yes, but let me get done with my bank first," goes in, comes out, we have coffee at a coffee shop across the street, she asks, I tell, starting with the guy who comes in and says and I say and we do and the woman and all we said and did and then the partners, men's room, lobby, sunshine, umbrella, should I? shouldn't I? upstairs, receptionist and partners again, I retrieve, I leave, typing rapidly, raining heavily, everything looking like something else, open the umbrella, woman ducks under, though at first I didn't think it was a woman, I thought it was a mugger, walk, talk, faster, she asks, I say, well what do you know, she knows so and so, I suggest, she says yes, bank, coffee shop and coffees. "So what do you think?" I say. "Your friend will like it or am I fooling myself?"

"If he doesn't like it he ought to change professions," she says and borrows a coin from me, makes a phone call, comes back, "He says to hustle right over," we do, elevator, office, receptionist, secretary, big how do you do from her friend who I tell the whole story to from the beginning, he says "Better than I expected even from what Pam told me it would be over the phone. I'll take it," and we shake hands, sign a contract, he writes out a check, we drink champagne to our future success, Pam and I leave, downstairs, lobby, sunny outside. Oh my God, I think, I forgot my umbrella again. "Oh my God," I say, "I left my umbrella upstairs."

"Leave it," she says, "since you now have enough money to buy ten umbrellas. Twenty if you want, though I don't know why you would." "True," I say. "Want to go for another coffee?" "Coffee?" she says. "I think a drink's more what we deserve. I know I sure do after what I just did for you." "True," I say, "and we'll go to the best place possible," and we start walking. Sun goes, clouds come, we walk faster, looking for a classier bar than the three we pass, but not fast enough, as the rain suddenly comes, drenching us before we can find protection from it.

"I knew I should have gone up for my umbrella," I say. "So we're wet," she says. "So what? It'll make the day more memorable for you. In fact, what I'd do if I were you, just to make the day one of the most memorable of your life, is—" but I cut her off and say "I know, I might," and she says "Not you might, you should," and I say "I know, I will," and she smiles, I smile, we take each other's hands, put our arms around each other's waists, "Let's," she says, "Let's," I say, and run out from under the awning into the rain. "Dad, look at those crazy people getting wet," a boy says, protected by his father's umbrella.

"You know what I want most of all now that I've sold my story project?" I say to her, standing in the pouring rain and holding and hugging her and looking over her shoulder at the boy being pulled along by his father because he wants to stay and watch us and she says "What?" and I tell her and she says and I say "And also to eventually walk in the pouring rain with an umbrella over my future wife and me and future daughter or son, but with the child being around that boy's age." "Why an umbrella?" she says and I say and she says "Silly, you don't get colds that way," and I say and she says "No," and I say "Oh." Just then a cab drives by too close to the curb and splashes us up to our waists and I start cursing and shaking my fist at it and she says and I say "You're right, raincoats and all, we're already slopping wet," and we laugh and go into a bar a half-block away and order a glass of wine each.

"What are you two so happy about," the bartender says, "besides getting yourselves dripping wet and probably catching your death?" and I say "Really interested?" and he says "Interested," and I say "Then I'll tell you," and do, starting from the time the man came in, woman, partners, office, men's room, lobby, sunny again, umbrella and rain, woman and bank, coffees, what do you know, so and so, deal, champagne, check, no umbrella, mixing the story up a little here and there, sun goes, rain falls, running through it, father and son, my thoughts and wants, bar, drinks, bartender and he says "That story rates a drink on the house if I ever heard one," and pours some more wine into our glasses, we toast and drink, he holds up his glass of soda water, people coming in ask what the celebration's about, I tell them, from beginning to end, leaving a little out now and then. "Very interesting," one of them says and buys us another wine each. By that time the rain's stopped but we're not dry yet and I say to Pam "Let's make it a perfect end to a great day," and she says "No, really, I've had a change of mind, besides my boyfriend waiting at home," and goes.

Just then a man comes in and I say "You wouldn't believe—" and he says "Wouldn't believe what? Because if you think you've something to say, listen to my story first," and he tells me about his wife who suddenly left him last week same day his dad got a coronary and his dog ran away and I say "Excuse me, you're right, and I think I better get home before it rains again," and I get off the stool. "Wait," he says, "you haven't heard the worst of it yet," but I'm out the door, rain's started again, I hail a cab, feel in my pockets, no wallet, wave the cab away and walk the two miles to my home. Phone's ringing when I enter the apartment. It's the man who bought my story project. He says "Tear up that check and contract as I just received a cable from overseas that says our company's gone bankrupt." I shout "Liar." He says "Not so." I slam down the receiver, am shivering, sneezing, want to get into a hot tub, but for some reason the water only runs cold.

The

Painter

—◆—

So the great painter dies. Within minutes of his death the colors disappear from his paintings, the canvases crack and come apart, the frames fall to the floor. Millions of dollars' worth of paintings, perhaps a billion dollars' worth, are gone. Museum curators summon the police. Private collectors of his work—

No, the painter dies. The great one. Nobody would dispute that. Nothing happens to his paintings after his death. What does change is their value. One painting up for sale that day with an asking price of close to a million dollars suddenly has an asking price of two million. A private art collector, interviewed on TV that night, says "When I bought this red one ten years ago for a hundred thousand, friends in the know said I paid twice what it was worth. Just a month ago an art dealer offered me five times that amount. Now with his death—not that I don't grieve for him like the rest of us and think, if he was alive and healthy, what he could still do—I could probably get—"

No, the painter dies. The great one. Almost every artist and art expert agrees with that. The paintings he had in his studio will be exhibited this year in a major European museum and then travel to five of the top modern museums in the world before being put on the market. The heirs, to save on paying an estimated hundred million dollars in taxes, have made arrangements with the government where half the paintings—

No, the painter dies. We all know who. The great one. The greatest or second greatest painter in the last fifty years. Certainly one of the five great painters of the century. At least one of the ten great ones in the last hundred years. Definitely one of the ten great ones, of this century, and one of the most influential painters of all time. What modern art movement in the last sixty years hasn't been influenced by him? Maybe some haven't. There have been so many. But five, maybe ten of the major art movements in the last sixty to seventy years have been directly or indirectly influenced by his work. He died in his sleep last night at the age of ninety-one. Ninety-one years old and still painting. The painting he was working on for the last two months was to be one of his largest. Art dealers say the asking price for it, though it's little more than half finished, will be around three million dollars, which will be one of the highest sums paid for a modern painting if it's sold at that price.

No, he's dead. The painter of the century. Or one of them. The day he died—he knew he had little time left, his wife said—he asked her to destroy the painting he was working on. He also asked her to write down his last words. They were "I didn't paint any of the paintings that bear my signature, nor any painting that is said to be mine but doesn't have my signature." All his paintings bear his signature. He then gestured that he wanted to sign his name to the words she wrote down. His son held his writing hand as he wrote his name. Then he said he'd like a glass of his best champagne and some cherries. His wife went for them. By the time she got back he was dead.

No, he died. In his sleep. A peaceful death. Painting he was painting on before he got sleepy and had to be put into bed was of a man sleeping in bed. A dead man, it looked like. Didn't look like an ordinary sleeping man. That's what just about everyone said when the painting was later viewed at an auction house before it was sold for more than three million dollars.

No, he's dead. His paintings aren't. They live on on whatever walls they're on. The colors haven't faded. Nor the themes. They're still alive.

No, they've all faded, colors and themes. The painter for the last week was fading, now he's dead. Died in his sleep. He was drinking champagne at the time. No, can't be.

Dead. The painter. Had a glass of champagne in his hand. He was awake when the glass dropped out of his hand. Or was awake just a moment before the glass dropped out of his hand. His wife, who had her back to him at the time, turned when she heard the glass smash on the floor. Her husband was slumped across the bed, hand dangling just above the floor. She called for her son. "Jose!" He ran into the room. He'd been in bed with the housekeeper in her room a floor above. Two floors above.

No glass broke. He did die while he was in bed. He was put there for a nap, but could have been awake when the accident happened. A painting hanging above the bed, one he did four years ago of his wife and him copulating and which he said he'd never sell for five million dollars, ten million, "all the money from all the countries in the world," fell off its hooks on the wall and hit him on the head. "It probably killed him instantly," the doctor said. The frame alone weighed two hundred pounds. The painting doesn't weigh more than a pound or two. "He painted that one thickly," his wife said, "night after night after night for months, and it's one of his largest, so maybe it's three pounds, even four."

No no no. He was killed in an auto accident. He asked his wife the day he died to take him back to the land of his youth. She said he was too frail to go anywhere. He then asked his son to take him there. His son agreed with his mother. "Then I'll get there myself," he said. He tried to get out of bed. They stopped him. He said "I will die of a heart attack tonight if I don't make a quick journey back to the land of my youth." They called the doctor. The doctor said he might be able to survive the trip. So they dressed him and got an ambulance to come. They put him in back of the ambulance on a cot. The ambulance hit a truck three miles from the house and turned over and the painter died. So did the ambulance driver and the attendant in back. His wife broke both arms in the accident. His son was in a car behind them.

No, the painter died in his sleep. In his sleep he was journeying back to the land of his youth. He got out of bed, in his sleep, did half an hour of the same vigorous exercises he used to do thirty years ago, showered and dressed himself, went downstairs, kissed his wife on the lips, patted her backside, kissed his son's forehead, drank a cup of the very strong black coffee he always used to drink in the morning but hadn't been allowed to for ten years, had a large breakfast, more coffee, said "Goodbye, I'll see you both in a few days," went outside, got into his sports car and drove down the hill and past the gatehouse. In his dream a truck hit his car just as he was crossing the border. Just after he crossed the border. Several hours after he'd crossed the border and was driving into the small village of his youth. While he was approaching the farmhouse his family had lived in for more than—

No, in his dream he gets on his horse, after his morning coffee, breakfast, kisses and goodbyes, and rides back to the land of his youth. The journey takes him three days. The horse is the one he had as a youth. He crosses the mountains on it, fords several streams. The border guards of both countries wave him on without asking for his passport. They yell out "Maestro . . . great one." They say "Hail to the liberator of our unconscious . . . emancipator of our imaginations . . . of our dreams." He salutes them, rides for another day to the two-room farmhouse he lived in as a youth. He ducks his head and rides through the front door right up to his old bed. He jumps off the horse, hugs it around the neck, brushes its coat, walks it outside to the grass.

No, he brings grass and water into the house, puts them on the floor, has the horse lie down by the bed. Then the painter gets into his old bed and covers himself up to his neck with his coat. His hair comes back to his bald head. It turns from white to gray to black. His pubic hairs disappear, his chest and back hairs, his wrinkles, illness, clots, most of his scars. He's smaller, shinier, slimmer, solider. His sheet's clean and cool, the bed newer and he has a blanket over him. The horse snores. The young man becomes a boy thinking about becoming a great painter. "I won't be great, I'll just be as good as I can. I'll do things no one else has. No, I'll just paint without thinking what anyone else has done. No, I'll just paint, that's all, and not even think about not thinking of what anyone else has done with paint."

No, the old painter's in bed. In the two-room farmhouse of his youth. His eyes close, he falls asleep. Colors, shapes, patterns, move around in his head. Scenes from his past, from his future. His wife twenty years ago, forty years ago, as his bride. His son as a young man, as a boy, then being born. The painter making love with his wife, with the woman he lived for years with before his wife, with women before that: models, other men's wives, an actress, a princess of a principality, other painters, a young woman he met at a cafe and went to a hotel with, a young woman he met on a train and slept the night in their compartment with, prostitutes in his adopted country, a girl in his native country when he was a schoolboy. In the bed he's in now. His first time, hers. Scenes of his parents working in the fields, his horse drinking from a stream, nudging its dead foal. Sunrise, sunset, nighttime, full moon on top of the chimney of this old farmhouse. "Wake up," his mother says. "Get to work," his father says. "Do you love me?" the young woman on the train as it's pulling into his station. "Do you love me?" his wife says. "Daddy," his son says. "Papa, dada, fada, ba." Pens, brushes, palettes, tubes of paints. Newspapers calling him a mountebank, defiler, the greatest painter of them all. He tears the newspapers up, pastes them on his canvases, paints over them.

No, the painter's born. We all know who. His mother's legs are open. The doctor says push. Out he comes, brush between his gums, tubes of paint inside his fists. The doctor slaps his behind, cuts the cord. His father gets down on his knees and says "At last, a son," and prays. The painter, no more than eight pounds, starts painting on the soiled sheet. The doctor cleans and dries him, puts a canvas on the floor, the painter crawls on top of it, paints a big circle and then a small circle inside. The outside of the big circle's white, the inside of the small circle's black, the space between the two circles is red. The doctor puts the painter to his mother's breast, blows on the canvas till it's dry, rolls it up, rushes to a gallery with it and sells it for a half a million dollars. It's now worth ten times that. The painter sucks at his mother's breast, nothing comes. He cries, his tears act as a warm compress on her breast, milk comes, he drinks and soon falls asleep. His father goes outside and plants a tree in his son's name. The tree's now ninety-one years old. Once a year till around five years ago the painter returned to the farmhouse to paint that tree. He's kept all of those seventy or so paintings. As a series, art dealers say, the tree paintings could be sold for a quarter of a billion dollars. If sold individually the total sale should be around half a billion. The tree has a fence around it, a plaque embedded in the boulder inside the fence which says "This tree was planted on the day of birth of the greatest painter our country has produced in five hundred years. Any defacement of the tree, enclosed area and fence will bring swift prosecution to the full extent of the law." The painter gets out of bed, goes outside, kicks down the fence, pulls an axe out of a tree stump and chops down the tree, has his horse defecate on the boulder and eat the grass in the enclosed area. When the horse is full it lies down and goes to sleep. The painter lies down, rests his head on the horse's neck and falls asleep. In his sleep he's a newborn child. He floats backwards into the house and up his mother's birth canal. It's dark, it's light, he fingers around for his paintbrush and tubes, the dream explodes.

No, he's an old man riding a paintbrush in the sky. The sky's a clear blue. He seems to be flying around aimlessly. Far below is green farmland, terraced hills, olive orchards, a farmhouse. A boy's sleeping beside a horse. The painter's father is digging a hole. His mother's nursing a baby. His wife's making coffee. His son's playing with the wood toys he carved for him. His infant daughter holds out his eyeglasses to him. She seems to be the only one below who sees him. She drops the glasses and holds up her arms to him. She wants to be picked up. The brush drops out from under him and he floats to earth. The horse stands, shakes itself off, flicks its tail. The painter lands beside it, holds out his arms, someone lifts him and puts him on the horse. He rides to the top of the hill, looks at the brush flying around. His hand reaches up till it's able to snatch the brush out of the sky. He looks around for his paint tubes and a canvas, doesn't see any, and sitting on the horse, starts to paint the sky. Whatever color he wants comes out of the brush. One time he paints the sky five different shades of red, another time a solid gray with a thin yellow line through it, another time it's a combination of fifty different colors. Then he paints it the original blue and flings the brush down the hill.

No, the painter dies. The great one. In the middle of the night. Everyone in the house was asleep. The nurse who was sitting beside him had just fallen asleep. She said she heard a sound in her sleep. We all know what sound. It woke her. Most of the world's newspapers the next day carried the news of his death on the front page.

Takes

Man's waiting in the service elevator right next to the passenger elevator. Someone comes—a woman, hopes it's a young one, through the front door or from one of the apartments upstairs or on this floor— he'll step out behind her with the knife, threaten her with it, take her in the automatic elevator rather than this hand-operated one to the top floor, walk her up to the roof, knife always on her throat, he always behind her and threatening softly but with a real scary tone in his voice "One scream and I'll use it; make even a move from this knife or to see me and I'll kill you," take her to a good dark out-of-the-way spot on the roof—all depending what lights from the other buildings' windows are on it—and rape her. She'll never see his face and his voice won't be his own. She doesn't put up a fuss, he'll leave her there gagged and tied up. He's scouted out the building. Not many tenants come in or leave their apartments this late, but it's worth the wait. Someone will come. Lots of single women in this neighborhood, so has to be a few in this building too. But on Saturday night, most, he bets, will be with men friends. One won't though and that's who.

Tenant on the eighth floor. Can't sleep. Something's up. Hasn't always been right when she thought something bad was going to happen, but enough times she has. It's not from any crazy imagination she's thinking this. The winos were really loud tonight. Few more bottles and things smashed on the street or whatever they're smashed against than usual too. And a couple more souped-up cars and motor-cycles than she's used to racing past her building too. Why don't the police do something? If it's because they don't know of these things going on or they're too lazy to patrol or can't because of cutbacks, then why don't people call them more? This city. She turns the TV off. Get some sleep.

Young woman's mother in Connecticut. Thinking about her daughter. She went to New York to do graduate work in painting. Took an apartment with another young woman, a friend from college. But the building's bad. Filthy, poorly maintained, bell system that doesn't work; a firetrap, she's sure. Even if some of the neighbor-hood's okay, and some of the river buildings even elegant, and as co-ops or rented apartments, quite expensive, much of it's very bad. Welfare hotels. Cheap rooming houses. Awful-looking men and women on the street day and night. Little park nearby where men drink and some of them dope and urinate in the open and make vul-gar remarks to passing women and all sorts of other things. Beggars. In the *Times* she's read of break-ins and muggings and seen a city crime statistic chart that put her neighborhood near the top. Worried.

Man in a cab going acrosstown. Should have got out of the cab and escorted her upstairs. Didn't like the looks of her building and block. But then he hardly knows her. She might have thought he was being funny in a way—forward, not funny. And he had this cab, was in it, did only promise to take her to the street door, or rather: just see, while he sat in the cab, she got inside that door, and then he might not have got another cab after he left her building or not so fast. Could have asked the cab to wait while he saw her to her apart-ment door. Now he thinks of it. But she said she'd be all right. He did ask. And he's sure that no matter how hard he insisted on taking her to her apartment door, she would have said no. *Still.*

Woman's in the lobby, presses the elevator button. Light above the elevator door says the car's on the top floor, the eighth. Slow ele-vator, takes days to get down. She doesn't like waiting in this creepy lobby. Anyway, her friend Phoebe will be upstairs and they can talk about tonight. The man she met. He was nice. Took her home in a cab, wouldn't let her share the fare with him. She wishes she had accepted his suggestion and let him walk her to her door. But then she would have had to invite him in. And offer him a coffee or a beer, when really all she wants to do, if Phoebe's up—she'll be up—is talk a little with her and go to sleep. Elevator's about here. It's here.

Man thinks now's the time. She's a good-looking one. Long legs, big ass. She'll screw well. He'll screw her well. He'll screw her till she cries for more, more. He steps out. She turns around. Knife's out. Damn, she saw him. "Don't say a word or I'll kill you right here." He gets behind her and puts the knife to her neck. Opens the elevator door, knife always against her neck. "We're going to the roof. I know this building. Don't say a word, make a peep—nothing—don't even sneak a look at me again or you're dead. I know how to get out of this building easily so I'll be out of here before you hit the ground. Now get in."

She gets in. She doesn't believe this. What should she do? This is a dream. A nightmare. It's the worst thing that's ever happened to her. Think, think. That knife. It pricks. They go up. He pressed eight. He said "roof." Maybe someone will stop the elevator on the fourth floor, fifth. There's only one outside button for each floor. No down and up buttons—just one, and if you press that button when you want to go down and the elevator's going up, it stops. Please. Someone.

It's too late to call her, her mother thinks. She'd like to. She wants very much to speak to Corinne, tell her how worried she is about her. Tell her that Dad and she will give her a hundred dollars a month extra to find a better building to live in. Two hundred. It'll be a sacrifice for them, but it just shows how anxious they are about where she's living now. If she's going to live in that city, she'll tell her, then it has to be on these terms. Of course she could say no, she likes where she's living now, took months to find and then paint and set up, doesn't want to take any more money from them than she already is and so on, and they really wouldn't be able to do anything about it. It's too late to call. But it's Saturday. She dials. Corinne's phone rings. If she answers it, or if Phoebe answers it—she hasn't once thought of Phoebe, for instance how she'd take to Corinne's parents subsidizing most of their rent—she'll apologize for calling this late, but both will have to know she only has their best interests at heart. That's not enough. She slams down the receiver. She can wait till tomorrow? Has to, since Corinne will see her anxiety at this hour as bordering on mania. Just another nine or ten hours. Eleven's okay to call on Sundays for women that age. Even if they're with men friends who stayed the night, which, let's face it, could well be the case. She goes upstairs to wash up for bed. Her husband says from the bedroom "What've you been doing? I heard you slamming the phone down, picking it up, then slamming it again." "I only slammed it once. I was worried about Corinne. Worked it out in my head though, so it's now all okay."

Roommate at a party downtown. Wonders if Corinne's home by now. She's sure she's expecting her to be there when she gets home.

Note she left will explain it or should. Something like "Aaron called. Sudden invite to big bash at a south of SoHo artist's loft and wanted me to join him. I know. Swore I'd grind away at the books all weekend and maybe never see Aaron again, but what, dear, can I say?" They have a phone here? If so, she'll call Corinne and say she doubts she'll be coming home tonight, and she should try to do that before two. She's just about never seen or heard Corinne up after two. "Excuse me," to a woman she thinks is one of the three people giving the party, "but is there by any chance a phone in this place I may use?" "As long as it's not to out of town," the woman says. "Positively not." "Actually, if you're a good friend of either of the other hosts, you can make that call to as far west as Columbus, south as Washington, and as far north as Boston, let's say."

She's also a very pleasant girl, man in the cab thinks. Attractive. Even pretty. He'd definitely call her pretty, even beautiful in some ways, though he doubts a couple of his friends would. *Still.* And she had spark. Bright, besides. Far as he could make out, bright as any woman he's met in a year. He's definitely phoning her tomorrow. Monday night, not tomorrow. Doesn't want to appear too eager. Why not? She seemed like she'd like eagerness. Directed at her, but not just to score. She complained how most men she meets these days don't really care or get excited about anything but making money and getting ahead. Don't really read, don't think much about serious things, aren't interested in much art other than movies and music. She didn't say he was different than they but implied he was. She also gave him her phone number willingly enough. He likes her name. She seems to come from a good family: intelligent, moral, involved, well-off. He thinks she sort of took to him too. Maybe that's why he should act fast: so she doesn't forget why she was attracted to him, if she was. Tomorrow night. No, Monday's soon enough. He hopes she paints well. If she doesn't, he could always say at first—later he could level with her more—"Hell, what do I know?"

Top floor. Roof stairs and door. Always trying to get a look at him to see if he means it—seemed he did. Had one of the most maniacal faces she's ever seen, when she saw him just that one glimpse. Slim, young, smelly, wiry, ruthless, cagey-looking. He's crazy. He's going to kill her. If it was just robbery he would have taken the bag from her downstairs and fled. Knife isn't on her neck anymore. Rape and possibly kill her. She has to find a way to get away. She has to scream, run, kick, maybe on the roof. Now she's thinking. Roof, where there's space. Stairs he's got her trapped. This building's attached to the corner one and unless there's barbed wire or something separating the two roofs, she can make a run for it yelling all the time. Pick up a brick if one's lying on the roof and he's cornered her against something like a wall or by a roof edge and throw it at him. Anything: teeth, knees and fists and then down a fire escape, but to escape. There's one that goes all the way past her bedroom window to the narrow alleyway on the ground floor. Corner building must have one too. If not, down her building's fire escape screaming, knocking, banging, breaking all the windows along the way if she has to till someone comes, wakes up, shouts, whatever, but helps chase the man away.

Tenant hears footsteps on the roof right above her. Who could be up there this hour? Trouble. Either some junkies got in the building or corner one next door and got to the roof that way and are shooting up. Or winos or runaways or just plain bums making a home for the night up there? Why can't it rain now or snow? Get them off. She just hopes the roof door's locked tight so they don't start walking down the building's stairs and making noise and throwing up in the hallways as what happened a couple of times or trying all the doors. What else could it be up there but something awful? She hopes not someone forced to go for the worst of purposes. That's happened on one or two other buildings around here but never hers.

"Now you know what I want," the man says. "I want to screw you but I want it without holding the knife to your face. That way it'll be better for me and easier and quicker for you. Then if you're good to me and a good little girl all around and give no trouble I'll let you go. You're a real piece of ass, you know? I could tell right away you screw well and that you've screwed around a lot. You got the face for it. Saucy. Sexy. So, you going to do it like I say? You don't, you're dead."

"No, I don't want to do it with you," the woman says. And then louder: "Now let me alone. Let me get by you and downstairs. Now please—I'm asking—please!" He stabs her in the chest. She raises her arms. He stabs her several times. She goes down. She screams. She says "Help, I'm being murdered." He gets on one knee and stabs her where he thinks her heart is.

"Stop that, stop that," the tenant shouts out her window. "Whoever it is, leave that girl alone. Help, police, someone's killing someone upstairs. On the roof. Stop that, you butcher, stop that, stop."

"Help me, I'm dying," the woman says. "Stupid bitch," the man says. He jumps up. Lights have gone on in some of the apartment windows in buildings that overlook the roof. "Shit," he says. "Hey you there," a man says from one window. "What is it, what's going on?" a man says from a window right next to that one. "I've called the police," a woman shouts from what seems like the building he's on. "They're coming. They're on their way. Everybody call to make sure they come. Girl, don't be afraid. They're coming. People from this building will be up there for you too." "Shit," he says and leaps over the low wall to get to the next building's fire escape.

Her mother thinks about the dream she just had. All the apartment buildings around hers were falling down, one after the other. She lives in a suburban townhouse and has never lived in anything but a private home, but in the dream she was in she lived in an apartment in a tall old apartment building in a large city that looked more European than American. The buildings collapsed straight down as if heavy explosives had been set off under them. For a while it seemed the window was a TV screen and she was watching the buildings fall in slow motion in a documentary. She was with her three daughters, all about four to eight years younger than they are now, and her husband and mother, who's dead. Then her building was falling. She held out her arms to her family and said "Here, come into me." Her arms became progressively longer as each person came into her. She kissed their heads in a row—they were all as small as little children now—and started crying. Then they were at her family's gravesite behind her grandparents' farmhouse, burying her mother. "This proves life can go on," she said to her husband, daughters and grandmother. She doesn't know what the last part of the dream means. There is no farmhouse or family gravesite. Her parents and grandparents are buried in three different enormous cemeteries. Where was her son in the dream? She gets out of bed, goes to the kitchen, writes down the dream and what she thinks the end of it means. "That everything will be OK with C (living in her city hovel)? That I really needn't be anxious about any of my kids or really about anything in life (how'd I come to that last conclusion?)? That if people stay in mind & memory (just about the same thing; I realize that) they're never really dead? That living, dying, illness, frailty, tragedy, mayhem, mishaps, madness, revolutions, terrorism (from inside & out) and the rest of it are all quite normal? (Was that all you were going to say?) That we're all basically entwined &—now stop all that; it was never in it. Then what? Time for God? Not at any price & why'd that idea pop in? (To interpret it theologically, that's all.) An important dream though, start to end, no matter what I don't make of it. Read all this back tomorrow. Underscore that: read, read! Maybe then."

Her father can't sleep. He feels for his wife in bed. She left it before but is there now. "Hilda, you up? I can't sleep; want to talk."

No answer or movement. Why'd she have to worry him so? Not that he can't handle it, but— He gets up, goes to the bathroom, drinks a glass of water. That was stupid. Meant to take two aspirins first. He gets the aspirins out of the medicine cabinet, puts them in his mouth and washes them down with another glass of water. Now he'll feel better. In about fifteen minutes. And his dreams are usually more vivid and peaceful in theme when he takes aspirins. His doctor thinks he should take an aspirin every other night to reduce the fat or plaque on his blood vessel walls. He doesn't mind, especially for the side benefits of a more peaceful sleep and dreams, but usually forgets to.

The woman's being treated by paramedics. She gives a description of her attacker and details of what happened. "Honestly, try not to talk," one of the paramedics says. "Yes, you probably shouldn't," a policeman says. She says "No, I want you to know what happened. If I go over it enough times, you'll get everything. I came into the building. We're still on my building?" "Yes, of course," the policeman says. "I meant, he didn't drag me over the parapet to the next building?" "If he did, he brought you back or you got back here on your own." "No, what am I talking of?" she says. "I came into the building. I'll proceed chronologically, no digressions. I came into the building." "I really don't want her talking," the paramedic says. "You heard him, miss. Don't talk." "I came into the building. He was waiting for me in the service elevator. That elevator ought to be locked at night, not left open. People can hide there. I'm digressing, but so what? The lobby door should have a better lock. Anyone, with a little force, can push the door open when it's locked. The building should have better lights. Look at the lights when you leave in the lobby and hallways. Thirty watts, maybe. One to a hallway if you're lucky. There's a city law. My roommate's checked. She's studying to be a lawyer. Where is she?" "If you mean Miss Kantor," the policeman says, "she's not home. We've been inside your apartment. To look for your attacker. I hope you don't mind." "There's a city law saying the wattage should be higher, Phoebe said. Minimum of two lights too. In case one goes out. He had a long knife. Said he'd kill me unless. Well, he nearly did. Maybe he will have. No he won't. I should say that. No he won't." "You shouldn't say anything," the paramedic says. "This officer and I say *don't.*" "But I wouldn't have sex with him. Why would I? It would have been worse than anything. He was filthy. A beast. A jungle. I thought I could escape on the roof. I should have tried to break away sooner. In the lobby. That way I would have had a chance. But I was so scared. I couldn't think. I got my wits about me going up the elevator. His knife seemed shined. Maybe he shines it with polish. He was sick enough. Maybe I should have let him do it. Screw me, he said. Maybe it would have been worth it, filth and all. When you can't do anything." "Now that's enough. Absolutely no more talk." "This has all been very valuable, Corinne," the policeman says, "but this man is right. Save your strength. I insist. For your own sake." "All right."

He's in a bar about ten blocks away having a beer and scotch. He got about twenty dollars from her bag. He's standing a man he just met to a drink. He says "Oh boy, did I have a good one tonight. Met a chickie on Broadway. She hadn't been laid for months. She just looked at me and said 'I'll give you a twenty if you lay me in a basement I know of—it's the only place we can go. If you don't want to, just say so and I won't say another word about it.' No bullshit. Under a bus shelter. We were both waiting for the number four and she turns to me and says this. 'My husband's home,' she says. 'He never lays me. He likes men only now. You don't like men,' she says, 'do you? I hope not.' That's what she said. I told her I like women only. All parts of them, not just the ones that count. And I can do it all night. This is what I tell her. 'Or at least I used to. Now only half the night which is fine for most ladies, okay?' So we went to this basement. I was so hot by now I could have done it to her right on the street. She gave me the twenty. It was cozy down there. Even had a mattress and nice little table lamp on the floor. She took me into an alleyway and made me shut my eyes the last minute of walking so I wouldn't ever find the place alone. Even turned me all the way around a few times so I'd be all mixed up in my directions. I bet she did it with lots of guys down there. But twenty. For laying her. She was great. Clean. Wet. Smelled good. A Mother Earth, no Miss Twiggy. Big hips. Big tits. Big everything. I felt I was swimming in her. I would've paid her if I had a twenty and she asked. If I'd known how good she was, is what I meant, for I don't pay anyone for sex. Things are free now, free now, you don't have to pay. Women walking around without panties and bras, kids doing it before your eyes in cars—man, it's all over the place. But to get paid for it? Hey, I'll take it! But that was it. Twice. That was all she could take, and to lay it on the line to you, me too. She was too much. She nearly killed me. Then we got dressed and left together and she made me shut my eyes again till we got into the street. She never gave me her name or phone number or address, but I bet she lives in that same building but higher up. You think she had a husband?" Other man raises his shoulders. "I don't. I think that's just her line so you don't think of going to her apartment right after to rob her. You know, some guys could just get her address from her bag while they're even balling her. 'If we meet, we meet,' she said when I said what about us doing this again sometime? 'You were the best,' was the last thing she said to me. Even if I wasn't, what do I care? All I know is she gave me a great time and made me twenty bills heavier."

The other man says "That's a fantastic story—unbeatable—I only wish it was me," and thinks if ever a guy was full of it, this one's it. He downs his drink, says "Got enough for a refill?—I'm a little low." "I think I can make it." "Thanks. I'm going to hit the pisser. Tell Rich for me to put a soda in back of mine this time," and goes to the men's room.

Her parents' phone rings. He looks at the clock. "Who can be calling so late? Probably a wrong number. You answer it, please, or just let it ring. I can't even move off the bed." Which one of her children? she thinks, going to the phone. It can't be anything but bad. It's rung too many times.

Her sister's sitting in a movie theater in Seattle. The phone's ringing in her apartment. Another sister's working in the sun on an archaeological dig in Egypt. This work is harder than she ever thought it would be, she thinks, and no fun. She wishes she was back home. Face it: she's homesick. She never would have believed it but she is. Her brother's sleeping in his college fraternity house. The person calling the house gets a recorded message that the phone's been temporarily disconnected.

The tenant leaves the building very early, says good morning to the policeman guarding the front door, asks how the girl is. "I haven't heard." "Do you know if they caught the man who did it yet?" "I don't think so." She goes to church, kneels, prays for the girl's life and that the man is caught and that the whole city becomes more peaceful again, at least as peaceful as it was about twenty years ago, but if only one prayer's answered then that the girl lives. She sits, covers her eyes with her hands; just let things come into her. It's quiet in here, she thinks. For now, this is the only place.

The man who took her home the night before gets up around nine, has coffee, goes out for the *Times* and a quart of milk and two bagels, dumps half the newspaper sections into a trash can, reads the front page of the news section as he walks home, reads the sports and book sections while having a toasted bagel and coffee at home, looks at his watch, 9:42, still much too early, slips in a tape cassette, does warm-up exercises, goes out for a six-mile or one-hour run, whichever comes first, comes back, did good time—must have been all the alcohol last night that gave him so much sugar—showers, shaves, checks the time, 11:38, no, not yet; twelve, on Sunday, is really the earliest he can call someone he just met. If she worked as hard as she said she did this week—studying, painting, her waitress job every other weekday afternoon and all day Saturday—she'll need a good ten-hour sleep. Once she gets up she'll probably need an hour just to get started. One. Call her at one.

Gifts

I wrote a novel for Sarah and sent it to her. She wrote back "For me? How sweet. Nobody has ever done anything or presented me with anything near to what you've just given me. I'll treasure it always. I must confess I might not get around to reading it immediately, since I am tied up to my neck and beyond with things I'm forced to do first. But I can't describe my pleasure in receiving this and the overwhelming gratitude I'll always have in knowing it was written especially for me."

I painted a series of paintings and crated and shipped them to her and she wrote back "Are these really all for me? I only looked in one of them and it said '1st of a series of 15,' and I counted the other crates and came up with fourteen more and thought 'My God, I have the entire series.' You can't imagine how this gift moves me. I'll open the rest of the crates as soon as I find the time, as I have been unrelievedly busy these past few days and will be for weeks. The one I did open I'll hang above my fireplace if I can find the space among my other paintings and prints. Meanwhile, it's safely tucked away in a closet, so don't fear it will get hurt. Again, what can I say but my eternal thanks."

I wrote a sonata for her and called it "The Sarah Piece" and had it printed and sent her a copy and she wrote me "A musical composition in my name? And for the one instrument I can play if not competently then at least semipublicly okay? You've gone out of your way to honor and please me more than anyone has and a lot more than any person should expect another to for whatever the reasons, and as soon as I can sever myself from all the other things I'm doing and which I wish I had the time to tell you about, I'll sit down and try to learn this sonata or at least read it through. You can't believe the many good things that have happened to me lately and which I'm so involved in, but I'll definitely find the time to attend to my sonata in one of the ways I mentioned, on that you can bet. Once more my warmest thanks for your thoughtfulness and my respects for your creativeness, and my very best."

I carved sculptures for her, designed and built furniture for her, potted and baked earthenware for her, wrote poems, plays and essays for her and after I completed each of these projects I sent it to her and her replies were usually the same. Her thanks. I could never know how much it means to her. She is continually amazed by the diversity of my talents and skills. She will read, look at or use this newest thing as soon as she can. Then, after I sent her a coverlet I wove and thought good enough to use as a wall hanging and maybe the best thing I'd ever made, she wrote "You've sent me so many things that I don't know what to open or look at or hang or put in its rightful place or eat off of first. And not wanting to give any of your creative forms preference over the others, I'm going to set aside one of the dozen rooms here for your work and call that room the Arthur T. Reece Retreat in honor of you and put all your gifts in it so I know that whenever I want to go through any of these works or have found a place in one of the other rooms to put one of them or even when I want to think of you creating and making all these things for me, I can enter that room. The room, by the way, has no windows. It does have a washbasin and door but with no lock on it. It is a small room, once the maid's quarters of the previous owners, so most of the things you sent me will have to be piled on top of one another, though know that'll be done extra carefully. I am having the door taken off and the space it makes bricked up. I am cutting that room off from the rest of the house. I am going to set that separated room afire in honor of the great passion you've put into your work and your obvious deep feelings for me. I am honored, I am grateful, I am amazed and touched and of course ever thankful and moved, I have never known anyone more creative and generous than you. No, I am joking. I have given away all your gifts from the start and have told the post office and other delivery services to turn back any further envelope, package or crate coming from you. No, I am joking. I am disassociating myself from all the other men I know and whatever activities I'm now involved in and want you to come live with me immediately as loving soulmates and man, parents and wife. No, I am joking. I never received any of the things you claimed to friends you sent me and am beginning to doubt they all could have gotten lost along the way. No, I am joking. They all arrived but I quickly turned them into refuse. Aside from that, I am happily married, with child for the first time in my life, and wonder why you think you know me well enough to keep sending these things to me without my eventually getting disturbed and insulted by them and where you initially got my address and name. No, I am joking. I appreciate all you've done, have enjoyed the attention and sold whatever I could of these gifts for whatever I could get for them and with that money I am about to embark on a trip around the world with my newest lover who is also my best friend and one of our finest progressive artists. No, I am joking. It was nice of you to make all these things for me but I'm sorry to say, almost ashamed to after all I've said in my previous letters and just put you through, that I wasn't once, and this is the absolute truth now, impressed. When one has it one has it and you've proven over and over again that you never had it and so will never have it so why bother trying anything out again in any field or form or at least on me? You do and whatever it is you send me I shall throw up on before returning it to you cash on delivery in its envelope, box or crate."

I sent her a silver necklace someone else made but in my cover letter to her I said I fashioned it with my own homemade tools. She wrote back "For the first time, and I'm as serious now as I was at the end of my last letter, I love what you've made for me and think you've adopted a creative form that suits you perfectly and which you serve extraordinarily well. Good luck and success with it and much thanks." I sent her more of this person's jewelry and after the first few packages each one came back with a post office message stamped on it saying address unknown. I still send jewelry to her and other things I buy or sometimes find but say I made and they always come back. The few friends I know who know her say they also don't know where she's gone. The post office is right, they say. "Despite how much we all adored her and thought the feeling was mutual if not more so from her to some of us, she told no one she was going and left no forwarding address."

The

Student

━━◆

This begins more than four years ago. It was when I was driving a cab
in the day and going to college at night. I was a pre-dental student. I
lived in a single room. My folks were dead. I had no close relatives. I
was dating someone and had a number of friends. I had little time for
parties and movies though, what with my studying and job. My girlfriend, Louise, usually stayed with me weekends. We planned to get
married during my third year of dental school, when she'd be graduated and teaching second grade.

One Saturday, when Louise was studying her own college work in
my room, I was driving a man through the factory part of the city. I
suddenly felt this cold thing on the back of my neck. I swatted it from
behind. The thing came right back to the same spot. "It's a gun," the
man said. "Make another move it doesn't like and it'll bite off your
head."

"I'll do anything you say," I said.

"That's a smart hack."

"You want all my money, you can have it."

"Just stick to your driving."

"You want me to still drive to where you asked to go?"

"Drive around this block."

"And after that?"

"Just keep driving around this block."

He took the gun away from my neck. In the rearview mirror I saw him sitting in the middle of the backseat. He was nicely dressed in an overcoat, suit, tie and hat. His gloved hands held the gun between his knees and kept it pointing up at me.

I drove around the block several times.

"How many times you want me to drive around the block?" I said.

"Till I say for you to stop."

"And if I run out of gas?"

"No funny remarks."

"That wasn't intended to be funny. I'm low."

"You'll be lower if you make any more funny remarks."

"I mean I'm very low in gas. I was going to get a few dollars' worth right after I dropped you off."

"You'll be dropping off if you don't shut up fast."

I drove around the same block about two dozen times. The gun was still between his knees. Just the end of the barrel was visible now and still pointing at my head. Then the cab began making these bumping back and forth movements every few seconds.

"What's that?" he said.

"That's the gas tank going out of gas."

"I'm serious. What is it?"

"You must have never owned a car. Take a look at the gauge."

"Then get to a garage fast."

I told him I knew of one right around here. It was cold outside and all the windows were up but mine, which was opened just an inch. And there was no glass partition or steel cage separating the driver from the passenger section, as all the fleet cabs in the city are forced by law to have now. Not that a thick glass or cage would have stopped any caliber bullet from coming into me from behind, if I had wanted to yell for help through my window crack or signal with my hand or lights to a policeman if I saw one nearby.

"And no funny remarks or lowering the window an inch more or getting out of the cab," the man said, putting the gun in an overcoat side pocket, "or the trigger gets touched. It's a hair trigger too."

I wanted to ask him what exactly a hair trigger was, something I read of in newspapers and heard said about in movies and never looked up, but I knew he would think that a funny remark. Or maybe I wasn't as calm as all that and only imagined I wanted to ask him that question. Later on though, I told people I had asked him what a hair-pin trigger was and that he said "It's a trigger that releases the hammer that strikes the cartridge primer that sends the bullet up through the back of a cabby's head and out of his hair like a pin."

I drove the few blocks to the gas station and pulled up beside the gas pumps.

"Seven dollars of the cheaper grade," I told the attendant, "and a receipt."

"Why'd you ask for a receipt?" the man said when the attendant began putting in gas.

"I always get a receipt when I don't fill up at the taxi garage."

"No receipt," he said.

"But I need a receipt to get my seven dollars back. I've dealt with this guy. He knows that."

"I don't want you passing anything to him."

"What could I pass? He'll be the one passing me the receipt."

"No."

"That's seven dollars," the attendant said.

I gave him a ten.

"I'll get your change and receipt."

"No receipt," the man said to me.

"No receipt," I yelled to the attendant as he headed for the station office.

"It's no trouble," he said.

"No thanks."

"No three dollars either," the man said.

"I shouldn't wait for my three dollars?" I said.

"Get going."

"Forget the three dollars also," I yelled to the attendant as he left the office.

"But I got it right here."

"We're in a rush. Sorry."

"Sorry for what? Are you kidding?"

"Why'd you tell him we're in a rush?" the man said.

"I said what came into my head."

"Stupid."

"Really," the attendant said. "Three bucks tip is crazy," and he held the three dollars through the window space.

"Should I take it?" I said to the man in back.

"Why you asking me?"

"Is it yours?" the attendant said to him, his mouth at my window and waving the money through the space to the man. "Well really thanks, mister, but three dollars is a pretty large tip."

"Will you please take your change?" the man said. "Because I am in a rush."

"I'll take it," I said to the attendant.

"I shouldn't have said anything," he said. "Three dollars would have done me fine."

"Now please get moving," the man said, pointing to his watch.

"See you," I said to the attendant and drove out of the station. "Where you want to go now?"

"Around this block," the man said.

"This block?"

"You see another block?"

"There are lots of blocks around here. This, that and all the other blocks including the factory one we must have driven around a hundred times. It's a big neighborhood. An even bigger city."

"Shut your mouth and drive." He took the gun from his pocket and held it between his knees.

I drove around the block that had the gas station on the corner of it. The first time the attendant saw me he waved. He waved the second time also and then scratched his head when he saw me coming a third and fourth time. The fifth time he saw me he yelled "Hey, you're driving in circles." I shrugged. The man in the back said "Don't shrug. Don't make faces. Behave like your driving is perfectly normal." The next time the attendant saw me he yelled "You're getting me dizzy with your driving—you know that?" The time after that, he was pointing out my cab to a driver of another car in the gas station and yelling "What's your cab—locked to hidden street rails we don't know about?" Then he gave up on saying anything to me and only made the crazy sign with his finger screwing away at his temple, and the times after that he mostly wouldn't even look up.

We drove around the same block for about a half hour. Finally I said "You still want me to drive around this block?"

"Yes."

"That gas station guy's going to get suspicious."

"That's his trouble."

"He could call the police thinking something's wrong."

"Then that's their trouble."

"The police could try to stop us and you might use your gun on them and they might use their guns on you and I could get killed in the crossfire."

"What do you know?—Just keep driving."

"Why don't we drive around another block? One away from the gas station."

"This block."

"We drove around another block before."

"That was till you ran out of gas."

"I could run out of gas again. This stop-and-go driving drains the hell out of it."

"Then you'll get some more at the station."

"What could I ever say to that man the next time?"

"You'll say 'Fill her up, please, and no receipt.' And then exchange pleasantries about cars, auto parts and motor oils, or just read from one of the books on your seat."

"You must like that gas station very much."

"Save your remarks for the gas pumper."

"I will. I was just trying to be protective about myself then. I don't want to get hurt or cause any trouble in the least."

The gun was still pointing at me. I drove around the block another fifteen minutes. Every three times around or so the attendant looked at me and went right back to his work. Then I saw a policeman waving me down on the avenue around the block from the gas station.

"Keep driving around the block," the man said.

"But he wants me to stop."

"Pass him the next time you see him too."

"He'll have a car on our tail by then."

"Do as I say."

I drove past the policeman. Through the side mirror I saw him calling out for me to stop. Through the rearview mirror I saw the man putting the gun in his overcoat pocket. We passed the gas station. The attendant was wiping someone's dipstick. We went around the block. The policeman ran farther into the avenue this time and waved his nightstick for me to stop.

"The light's red," I said, passing the policeman.

"Go through it and around the block again and then stop where he says stop."

"Why not back up for him now? I could say I didn't see him the first time because I was keeping my eyes out for a certain address, and only saw him the second time when I was turning the corner and had mistakenly gone through the light."

He motioned me to continue around the block.

"You're the one asking for trouble now," I said.

"From you?"

"From the police. I could still back all the way up this block and around to where he is. It'll look better for us if I come around backward that way. More respectful, and as if I only passed him once and not twice."

"Shhh."

I drove around the block. The policeman was calling in from a police box on a lamppost. Seeing the cab, he dropped the receiver and blew his whistle at me. I stopped. He started over to us.

"Roll up your window," the man said.

I rolled it up. "What do I tell him when he gets here?"

"Cover your mouth when you talk to me now and don't turn around."

I put my hand over my mouth and said without turning around "Well, what do I?"

"Tell him you drove through the lights and didn't stop when he told you to because you wanted to help him lose some fat by his chasing after you."

I shook my head.

"Say what I said."

The policeman rapped my window with his stick. "Roll it down."

"Three inches," the man said.

I rolled it down three inches.

"Anything wrong in there?" the policeman asked the man.

"Nothing, thank you."

"Now let's hear you start explaining this," the policeman said to me.

"I'm very sorry, Officer."

"What about what you ordered me to say about him?" the man said.

"What he order you?" the policeman said.

"I think he should be the one to say it."

"That I only passed you because I wanted you to run a ways after me so you could lose a little weight."

"Get out," the policeman said.

"Do I?" I said into my hand without turning around.

"You're damn right you'll get out," the policeman said.

"I don't know what to do," I told him. I covered my mouth and said "What do I do?"

The policeman unsnapped his holster flap and tried opening the door. In the rearview the man made a turning motion with his hand for me to roll my window up.

"No need, Officer," I said, when he tried opening the rear door. "I'm coming out."

He stepped back, his hand on his holstered gun. I rolled up my window. He smashed my window with his stick.

The man slunk back into his seat screaming and then said "Get."

I drove off. Some glass had got in my cheek. The policeman shot once into the air. Then two more.

"Drive to the block with the movie theater on it," the man said, pointing to a movie theater a few blocks away.

"And the light?"

"No. This block here with the supermarket. Keep driving around it and don't stop for police or lights."

I drove through the red light and started around the block. We were on the avenue in front of the market completing our third trip around the block when I saw two police cars waiting for me in my lane.

"Make a U," he said.

I made a U-turn and then a left at the first sidestreet as he told me to do.

"Which block?" I said.

"Find another one around here. But a big one. If possible a block with the city's biggest avenues on opposite ends of it."

"There aren't any around here like that."

"Then drive across the park to the south side. I know of a beauty over there, right off Fourth."

I drove across town and was heading south through the park transverse when I saw that both lanes ahead were blocked with police cars.

"Around," he said, but through the side mirror I could see that the way back was blocked too.

"What now?" I said, slowing down.

"Get out and run."

I stopped the cab between the two police car blockades and said "If I run they might shoot me."

"And if you don't run I'll shoot you. And if you do run and suddenly stop I'll shoot you. And if you fall to the ground after you get out and suddenly stop I'll shoot you. I'll shoot you if you try climbing over the transverse wall or get out and yell to the police and me not to shoot you. Just get out and run either way down the road's dividing line to the police shouting threats that you're going to kill them, or I'll shoot you from behind. Now out," and he nudged the gun barrel against the back of my neck.

I got out, jumped to the ground and crawled underneath the cab. He began shooting through the floor. Two bullets hit my shoulder and arm, another ricocheted through my ear. The police drove up. They called out to me. They took the gun from the man and asked him why he had shot me. Shaking all over and between loud sobs and tears he said "This bum . . . this man . . . he forced me to drive with him as a hostage. I luckily disarmed him of that thing seconds before he was going to drive us straight into your cars and shoot every policeman he could see."

Even with two bullets and glass in me and blood coming out of my face and clothes, a policeman wrenched my head back by the hair and threw me against the cab and slammed my handcuffed hands on the hood and kicked my feet out behind me and told me to keep my legs spread apart and don't speak unless questioned or they'll knock me to the ground for good.

"But the man's lying. I was his hostage and was forced to drive around and taunt you guys."

I was punched in the back and head by two policemen till I rolled off the hood to the ground.

The man and I were driven in separate cars to the police station. An hour after I was arraigned and exhibited to the press for photographs, I was taken to the hospital, where my bullet and glass wounds were treated and also a gash in the back of my head that the policeman's ring had opened up.

I was brought to trial. My court-appointed lawyer advised me to stop repeating those ridiculous statements about the man forcing me to do all those things in my cab.

"He's a university professor," the lawyer said. "Has written several highly regarded textbooks on forensic psychiatry and medicine. And he and his wife have such an impeccable reputation and social standing in the city that he could never be thought to have done the bizarre things you claim. I don't believe you. The judge certainly won't believe you. The prosecuting attorney is too good for the jury to believe you. If you plead guilty to all charges and ask the court's mercy, I can get you off with only a few years. If you don't plead guilty, then the professor and that policeman and gas station attendant will testify against you and you can be sent away for thirty years."

I pleaded guilty and got six years. In prison I was taught mess hall cooking and worked in the kitchen there the last three years of my term. In the prison library I read as many books on psychology and psychiatry, including two of the professor's works, as any student could read in any university in the world.

Lots of times in prison I thought about getting revenge on that man once I got out. I thought I would wait for him outside his class, and only after I was sure he remembered me and the ride we took together, would I slam a two-by-four over his head, not caring if he got killed. But then I knew I could never do anything that fierce. So I thought I'd just walk up to him on the street and slap his face, and after I wrestled him to the ground, as he was a pretty small guy so probably easy to handle, I'd kick his legs and arms and maybe spit at him, and then just leave him there like that.

But I knew I wouldn't be capable of doing any of those things either. After reading those psychology and psychiatry books, I found I wasn't at all the type to go around kicking and slapping anyone for anything. I also learned from those books that the professor was the type who would always have a gun, or know where to get one, and that he would come after me and use it if I so much as accused him of the crimes I went to prison for and took a swing at his face. And he'd have all the right excuses too. He could say "That man tried to kill me for having told the truth about that day he kept me captive in his cab. For he swore to me in the cab that he'd get even with me if I ever talked. And he's phoned me a number of times since he left prison, with threats against my wife and me. So I got a gun. All right—I got it illegally"—if he couldn't get it legally and as the one he had in the cab must have been gotten—"but I was desperately afraid of him. And when he came for me I had to shoot him to save my life."

So I gave up on getting revenge. I was a model prisoner, got out in four years and returned to college, but this time to get a simple business degree in restaurant management. Louise, my old girlfriend, was too seriously involved with someone else to see me. Some of my old friends were still in the city. They all had fairly good jobs and a couple of them were married and had children. The few times I did meet some of them for beers, they asked me to tell the story about the professor and me. But I always told them it was best for my future career and personal well-being if I forgot that incident forever and if everybody else forgot about it too.

Most nights now I worked as a waiter. About once a week since I got the job a few months ago, that same man comes in the restaurant and sits at my station and orders drinks and a complete meal. Near the end of his dinner on the first night, he said "Aren't you the fellow who did that strange thing with the taxi and police that was such a popular news story a few years ago?"

I said "I'm the man, all right," and he said "I thought you looked familiar. You've clipped most of your hair and taken to wearing a mustache and eyeglasses, but I suppose those pictures of you on TV and in the papers left an indelible impression on me. I happen to have more than a morbid gossiper's concern in criminal cases and yours I have to admit was one of the more interesting ones." Then he excused himself for having brought up the subject, "since it must be embarrassing if not potentially damaging to you for anyone to repeat it in public," and didn't say another word to me for the rest of the meal except "Thank you" and "Goodbye."

Since then, after his first drink, he always asks if I'd mind speaking some more about that day he had talked about, and I always say I wouldn't.

"What I'm saying," he's said in a different way each time, "is I don't want you getting mad at me or anything. Because if you think I'm being nosy, even if it is with a professional interest in mind that could lead to a paper on the subject, please say so and I'll shut up and never ask you about it again."

He always asks just one question each dinner, though a different one each time. Such as "What prompted your doing it in the first place?" and "Didn't you think you could get killed in the act?" and "Where did you get the courage to face the police like that?" and "What was the significance of riding around the blocks so many times?" and "Why for a while did you settle on just one gas station in case you ran out of gas a second time?" and "Didn't you know that if caught you'd be jeopardizing your employment and social activities for life?" and "Did you really believe you were innocent as you first proclaimed to the press the day you were caught?" and "Didn't it occur to you that your passenger might have been killed by the police for being thought of as your accomplice or by a stray bullet aimed at you?"

I always make up an answer for him. Such as "At the time I intentionally wanted to get myself killed," and "I really can't say why I did anything that day because it was essentially another me who was responsible for the act," and "I went around and around those blocks to draw attention to myself, simple as that," and "I was too concerned with carrying out the crime itself and having a good time playing around with the police to pay any attention to the passenger in back."

My answer always seems to satisfy him for the time. He then apologizes for having brought up the subject again and changes the conversation by asking after my health or college work or if the dinner special looks good tonight, and throughout the rest of the meal acts somewhat frightened as if he thinks I'm about to pick up a chair and crash it down on him. Then he finishes his dinner and the bottle of wine he always orders with his meal, and leaves without ever giving me a tip.

All
Gone

He says goodbye, we kiss at the door, he rings for the elevator, I say "I'll call you when I find out about the tickets," he says "Anytime, as I'll be in all day working on that book jacket I'm behind on," waves to me as the elevator door opens and I shut the door.

I find out about the tickets and call him and he doesn't answer. Maybe he hasn't gotten home yet, though he usually does in half an hour. But it's Saturday and the subway's always much slower on weekends, and I call him half an hour later and he doesn't answer.

He could have got home and I missed him because he right away might have gone out to buy some necessary art supply or something, and I call him an hour later and he doesn't answer. I do warm-ups, go out and run my three miles along the river, come back and shower and call him and he doesn't answer. I dial him every half hour after that for the next three hours and then call Operator and she checks and says his phone's in working order.

I call his landlord and say "This is Maria Pierce, Eliot Schulter's good friend for about the last half-year—you know me. Anyway, could you do me a real big favor and knock on his door? I know it's an inconvenience but he's only one flight up and you see, he should be home and doesn't answer and I've been phoning and phoning him and am getting worried. I'll call you back in fifteen minutes. If he's in and for his own reasons didn't want to answer the phone or it actually is out of order, could you have him call me at home?"

I call the landlord back in fifteen minutes and he says "I did what you said and he didn't answer. That would've been enough for me. But you got me worried also, so I went downstairs for his duplicate keys and opened his door just a ways and yelled in for him and then walked in and he wasn't there, though his place looked okay."

"Excuse me, I just thought of something. Was his night-light on?"

"You mean the little small-watt-bulb lamp on his fireplace mantel?"

"That's the one. He always keeps it on at night to keep away burglars who like to jump in from his terrace."

"What burglars jumping in from where? He was never robbed that I know."

"The tenant before him said she was. Was it on?"

"That's different. Yes. I thought he'd forgotten about the light, so I shut it off. I was thinking about his electricity cost, but you think I did wrong?"

"No. It only means he never got home. Thanks."

I call every half hour after that till around six, when he usually comes to my apartment. But he never comes here without our first talking on the phone during the afternoon about all sorts of things: how our work's going, what the mail brought, what we might have for dinner that evening and do later and if there's anything he can pick up on the way here and so on. The concert's at eight and I still have to pick up the tickets from my friend who's giving them to me and can't go herself because her baby's sick and her husband won't go without her. I call her and say "I don't see how we can make the concert. Eliot's not here, hasn't called, doesn't answer his phone and from what his landlord said, I doubt he ever got home after he left me this morning."

"Does he have any relatives or close friends in the city for you to call?"

"No, he would have gone to his apartment directly—I know him. He had important work to finish, and the only close person other than myself to him is his mother in Seattle."

"Maybe he did get home but got a very sudden call to drop everything and fly out to her, so he didn't have the time to phone you, or when he did, your line was busy."

"No, we're close enough that he'd know it would worry me. He'd have called from the airport, someplace."

"Your line still could have been busy all the times you were trying to get him. But I'm sure everything's okay, and don't worry about the tickets. Expensive as they are, I'll put them down as a total loss.

Though if you are still so worried about him, phone the police in his neighborhood or even his mother in Seattle."

"Not his mother. There's no reason and I'd just worry her and Eliot would get angry at me. But the police is a good idea."

I call the police station in his precinct. The officer who answers says "We've nothing on a Mr. Schulter. But being that you say he left your apartment this morning, phone your precinct station," and she gives me the number. I call it and the officer on duty says "Something did come in today about someone of his name—let me think."

"Oh no."

"Hey, take it easy. It could be nothing. I'm only remembering that I saw an earlier bulletin, but what it was went right past me. What's your relationship to him before I start searching for it?"

"His closest friend. We're really very very close and his nearest relative is three thousand miles from here."

"Well, I don't see it in front of me. I'll locate it, though don't get excited when I'm away. It could be nothing. I might even be wrong. It was probably more like a Mr. Fullter or Schulton I read about, but not him. Want me to phone you back?"

"I'll wait, thanks."

"Let me take your number anyway, just in case I get lost."

He goes, comes back in a minute. "Now take it easy. It's very serious. He had no ID on him other than this artist society card with only his signature on it, which we were checking into, so we're grateful you called."

"Please, what is it?"

"According to this elderly witness, he was supposedly thrown on the subway tracks this morning and killed."

I scream, break down, hang up, pound the telephone table with my fists, the officer calls back and says "If you could please revive yourself, miss, we'd like you to come to the police station here and then, if you could by the end of the night sometime, to the morgue to identify your friend."

I say no, I could never go to the morgue, but then go with my best friend. She stays outside the body room when I go in, look and say "That's him." Later I call Eliot's mother and the next day her brother comes to the city and takes care of the arrangements to have Eliot flown to Seattle and his apartment closed down and most of his belongings sold or given away or put on the street. The uncle asks if I'd like to attend the funeral, but doesn't mention anything about providing airfare or where I would stay. Since I don't have much money saved and also think I'll be out of place there and maybe even looked down upon by his family I've never seen, I stay here and arrange on that same funeral day a small ceremony in the basement of a local church, where I and several of our friends and his employers speak about Eliot and read aloud excerpts of his letters to a couple of us and listen to parts of my opera records he most liked to play and for a minute bow our heads, hold hands and pray.

According to that elderly witness, Eliot was waiting for a train on the downtown platform of my stop when he saw a young man speaking abusively to a girl of about fifteen. When the girl continued to ignore him, he made several obscene gestures and said he was going to throw her to the platform and force her to do all sorts of sordid things to him and if he couldn't get her to do them there because people were watching, then in the men's room upstairs. The girl was frightened and started to walk away. The young man grabbed her wrist, started to twist it, stopped and said he would rip her arm off if she gave him a hard time, but didn't let go. There were a few people on the platform. Nobody said anything or tried to help her and in fact all of them except Eliot and this elderly man eventually moved to the other end of the platform or at least away from what was going on. Then Eliot went over to the young man, who was still holding the girl by her wrist, and very politely asked him to let her alone. Something like "Excuse me, I don't like to interfere in anyone's problems. But if this young lady doesn't want to be bothered by you, then I would really think you'd let her go."

"Listen, I know her, so mind your business," the young man said and she said to Eliot "No he don't." Then out of nowhere a friend of the young man ran down the subway stairs and said to him "What's this chump doing, horning in on your act?" The elderly man got up from a bench and started for the upstairs to get help. "You stay right here, grandpa," the first young man said, "or you'll get thrown on your back too." The elderly man stopped. Eliot said to the young men "Please, nobody should be getting thrown on their backs. And I hate to get myself any more involved in this, but for your own good you fellows ought to go now or just leave everybody here alone."

"And for your own good," one of the young men said, "you'd be wiser moving your ass out of here."

"I can only move it once I know this girl's out of danger with you two."

"She'll be plenty out of danger when you move your ass out of here, now move."

"Believe me, I'd like to, but how can I? Either you leave her completely alone now or I'll have to get the police."

That's when they jumped him, beat him to the ground and, when he continued to fight back with his feet, fists and butting his head, picked him up and threw him on the tracks. He landed on his head and cracked his skull and something like a blood clot suddenly shot through to the brain, a doctor later said. The girl had already run away. The young men ran the opposite way. The elderly man shouted at Eliot to get up, then at people to jump down to the tracks to help Eliot up, then ran in the direction the young men went to the token booth upstairs and told the attendant inside that an unconscious man was lying on the tracks and for her to do something quick to prevent a train from running over him. She phoned from the booth. He ran back to the platform and all the way to the other end of it yelling to the people around him "Stop the train. Man on the tracks, stop the local train." When the downtown local entered the station a minute later, he and most of the people along the platform screamed and waved the motorman to stop the train because someone was on the tracks. The train came to a complete stop ten feet from Eliot. A lot of the passengers were thrown to the floor and the next few days a number of them sued the city for the dizzy spells and sprained fingers and ripped clothes they said they got from the sudden train stop and also for the days and weeks they'd have to miss from their jobs because of their injuries. Anyway, according to that same doctor who examined Eliot at the hospital, he was dead a second or two after his head hit the train rail.

For a week after the funeral I go into my own special kind of mourning: seeing nobody, never leaving the apartment or answering phone calls, eating little and drinking too much, but mostly just sleeping or watching television while crying and lying in bed. Then I turn the television off, answer every phone call, run along the river for twice as many miles than I usually do, go out for a big restaurant dinner with a friend and return to my job.

The Saturday morning after the next Saturday after that I sit on the bench near the place on the subway platform where Eliot was thrown off. I stay there from eight to around one, on the lookout for the two young men. I figure they live in the neighborhood and maybe every Saturday have a job or something to go to downtown and after a few weeks they'll think everything's forgotten about them and their crime and they can go safely back to their old routines, like riding the subway to work at the station nearest their homes. The descriptions I have of them are the ones the elderly witness gave. He said he was a portrait painter or used to be and so he was absolutely exact about their height, age, looks, mannerisms and hair color and style and clothes. He also made detailed drawings of the men for the police, which I have copies of from the newspaper, and which so far haven't done the police any good in finding them.

What I'm really looking out for besides those descriptions are two young men who will try to pick up or seriously annoy or molest a teenage girl on the platform or do that to any reasonably young woman, including me. If I see them and I'm sure it's them I'll summon a transit policeman to arrest them and if there's none around then I'll follow the young men, though discreetly, till I see a policeman. And if they try and molest or terrorize me on the bench and no policeman's around, I'll scream at the top of my lungs till someone comes and steps in, and hopefully a policeman. But I just want those two young men caught, that's all, and am willing to risk myself a little for it, and though there's probably not much chance of it happening, I still want to give it a good try.

I do this every Saturday morning for months. I see occasional violence on the platform, like a man slapping his woman friend in the face or a mother hitting her infant real hard, but nothing like two or even one man of any description close to those young men terrorizing or molesting a woman or girl or even trying to pick one up. I do see men, both old and young, and a few who look no more than nine years old or ten, leer at women plenty as if they'd like to pick them up or molest them. Some men, after staring at a woman from a distance, then walk near to her when the train comes just to follow her through the same door into the car. But that's as far as it goes on the platform. Maybe when they both get in the car and especially when it's crowded, something worse happens. I know that a few times a year when I ride the subway, a pull or poke from a man has happened to me.

A few times a man has come over to the bench and once even a woman who looked manly and tried to talk to me, but I brushed them off with silence or a remark. Then one morning a man walks over when I'm alone on the bench and nobody else is around. I'm not worried, since he has a nice face and is decently dressed and I've seen him before here waiting for the train and all it seems he wants now is to sit down. He's a big man, so I move over a few inches to the far end of the bench to give him more room.

"No," he says, "I don't want to sit—I'm just curious. I've seen you in this exact place almost every Saturday for the last couple of months and never once saw you get on the train. Would it be too rude—"

"Yes."

"All right. I won't ask it. I'm sorry."

"No, go on, ask it. What is it you want to know? Why I sit here? Well, I've been here every Saturday for more than three months straight, if you're so curious to know, and why you don't see me get on the car is none of your business, okay?"

"Sure," he says, not really offended or embarrassed. "I asked for and got it and should be satisfied. Excuse me," and he walks away and stands near the edge of the platform, never turning around to me. When the local comes, he gets on it.

Maybe I shouldn't have been that sharp with him, but I don't like to be spoken to by men I don't know, especially in subways.

Next Saturday around the same time he comes downstairs again and stops by my bench.

"Hello," he says.

I don't say anything and look the other way.

"Still none of my business why you sit here every Saturday like this?"

I continue to look the other way.

"I should take a hint, right?"

"Do you think that's funny?"

"No."

"Then what do you want me to do, call a policeman?"

"Of course not. I'm sorry and I'm being stupid."

"Look, I wouldn't call a policeman. You seem okay. You want to be friendly or so it seems. You're curious besides, which is good. But to me it is solely my business and not yours why I sit here and don't want to talk to you and so forth and I don't know why you'd want to persist in it."

"I understand," and he walks away, stays with his back to me and gets on the train when it comes.

Next Saturday he walks down the stairs and stays near the platform edge about ten feet away reading a book. Then he turns to me and seems just about to say something and I don't know what I'm going to say in return, if anything, because he does seem polite and nice and intelligent and I actually looked forward a little to seeing and speaking civilly to him, when the train comes. He waves to me and gets on it. I lift my hand to wave back but quickly put it down. Why start?

Next Saturday he runs down the stairs to catch the train that's pulling in. He doesn't even look at me this time, so in a rush is he to get on the car. He gets past the doors just before they close and has his back to me when the train leaves. He must be late for someplace.

The next Saturday he comes down the stairs and walks over to me with two containers of coffee or tea while the train's pulling in. He keeps walking to me while the train doors open, close, and the train goes. I look at the advertisement clock. He's about fifteen minutes earlier than usual.

"How do you like your coffee if I can ask, black or regular? Or maybe you don't want any from me, if you do drink coffee, which would of course be all right too."

"Regular, but I don't want any, thanks."

"Come on, take it, it's not toxic and I can drink my coffee any old way. And it'll perk you up, not that you need perking up and certainly not from me," and he gives me a container. "Sugar?" and I say "Really, this is—" and he says "Come on: sugar?" and I nod and he pulls out of his jacket pocket a couple of sugar packets and a stirring stick. "I just took these on the way out of the shop without waiting for a bag, don't ask me why. The stick's probably a bit dirty, do you mind?" and I shake my head and wipe the stick though there's nothing on it. "Mind if I sit and have my coffee also?" and I say "Go ahead. It's not my bench and all that and I'd be afraid to think what you'd pull out of your pocket if I said no—probably your own bench and cocktail table," and he says "Don't be silly," and sits.

He starts talking about the bench, how the same oak one has been here for at least thirty years because that's how long he's lived in the neighborhood, then about the coffee, that it's good though always from the shop upstairs a little bitter, then why he happens to see me every Saturday: that he's recently divorced and has a child by that marriage who he goes to in Brooklyn once a week to spend the whole day with. He seems even nicer and more intelligent than I thought and comfortable to be with and for the first time I think he's maybe even good-looking when before I thought his ears stuck out too far and he had too thin a mouth and small a nose. He dresses well, anyway, and has a nice profile and his hair's stylish and neat and his face shaven clean which I like and no excessive jewelry or neck chain which I don't and in his other jacket pocket are a paperback and small ribbon-wrapped package, the last I guess a present for his little girl.

His train comes and when the doors open I say "Shouldn't you get on it?" and he says "I'll take the next one if you don't mind," and I say "I don't think it's up to me to decide," and he hunches his shoulders and gives me that expression "Well, I don't know what to say," and the train goes and when it's quiet again he continues the conversation, now about what I think of something that happened in Africa yesterday which he read in the paper today. I tell him I didn't read it and that maybe when I do read my paper it won't be the same as his and so might not have that news story and he says "What paper you read?" and I tell him and he says "Same one—front page, left-hand column," and I say "Anyway, on Saturdays I don't, and for my own reasons, have time for the newspaper till I get home later and really also don't have the time to just sit here and talk," and he says "Of course, of course," but seriously, as if he believes me, and we're silent for a while, drinking our coffees and looking at the tracks.

We hear another train coming and I say "I think you better get on this one," and he says "Okay. It's been great and I hope I haven't been too much of a nuisance," and I say "You really haven't at all," and he says "Mind if I ask your name?" and I say "Your train," and he yells to the people going into the subway car "Hold the door," and gets up and says to me "Mine's Vaughn," and shakes my hand and says "Next week," and runs to the train with his container and he's not past the door a second when the man who kept it open for him lets it close.

I picture him on his way to Brooklyn, reading his book, later in Prospect Park with his daughter as he said they would do if the good weather holds up and in an indoor ice-skating rink if it doesn't, and then go back to my lookout. People spit and throw trash on the tracks, a drunk or crazy man urinates on the platform, a boy defaces the tile wall with a marker pen and tells me to go shoot myself when I very politely suggest he stop, there's almost a fight between a man try-ing to get off the train and the one blocking his way who's trying to get on, which I doubt would have happened if both sides of the dou-ble door had opened, but again no sign of my two young men.

Vaughn's not there the next Saturday and the Saturday after that and the third Saturday he's not there I begin thinking that I'm think-ing more about him than I do of anybody or thing and spending more time looking at the staircase and around the platform for him than I do for those young men. I've gradually lost interest in finding them and over the last four months my chances have gotten worse and worse that I'll even recognize them if they ever do come down here and as far as their repeating that harassing-the-girl incident at this par-ticular station, well forget it, and I leave the station at noon instead of around my usual one and decide that was my last Saturday there.

A month later I meet Vaughn coming out of a supermarket when I'm going in. He's pulling a shopping cart filled with clean laundry at the bottom and two big grocery bags on top. It's Saturday, we're both dressed in T-shirts and shorts for the warm weather now, and I stop him by saying "Vaughn, how are you?" He looks at me as if he doesn't remember me. "Maybe because you can't place me anywhere else but on a subway bench. Maria Pierce. From the subway station over there."

"That's right. Suddenly your face was familiar, but you never gave me your name. What's been happening?" and I say "Nothing much I guess," and he says "You don't wait in subway stations anymore for whatever you were waiting for those days?" and I say "How would you know? You stopped coming yourself there and to tell you the truth I was sort of looking forward to a continuation of that nice chat we last had."

"Oh, let me tell you what went wrong. My ex-wife, giving me a day's notice, changed jobs and locations and took my daughter to Boston with her. I could have fought it, but don't like arguments. I only get to see her when I get up there, which hasn't happened yet, and maybe for August if I want."

"That's too bad. I remember how devoted you were."

"I don't know it's so bad. I'm beginning to enjoy my freedom every Saturday, as much as I miss my kid. But I got to go. Ice cream in the bag will soon be melting," and he says goodbye and goes.

If I knew his last name I might look him up in the phone book and call him and say something like "Since we live in the same neighborhood, would you care to meet for coffee one of these days? I owe you one and I'll even, if you're still curious, let you in on my big secret why I every Saturday for months waited at our favorite subway station." Then I think no, even if I did have his phone number, I gave him on the street a couple of openings to make overtures about seeing me again and he didn't take them because he didn't want to or whatever his reasons but certainly not because of his melting ice cream.

Several weeks later I read in the newspaper that those two young men got caught. They were in the Eighth Street subway station and tried to molest a policewoman dressed like an artist with even a sketchbook and drawing pen, and two plainclothesmen were waiting nearby. The police connected them up with Eliot's death. The two men later admitted to being on my subway platform that day but said they only started a fight with him because he tried to stop one of them from making a date with a girl the young man once knew. They said they told Eliot to mind his business, he refused, so they wrestled him to the ground and then said he could get up if he didn't make any more trouble. Eliot said okay, got up and immediately swung at them, missed, lost his footing and before either of them could grab him away, fell to the tracks. They got scared and ran to the street. They don't know the girl's last name or where she lives except that it's somewhere in the Bronx.

I buy all the newspapers that day and the next. One of them has a photo of the young men sticking their middle fingers up to the news photographers. They don't look anything like the young men I was on the lookout for, so either the witness's description of them or the printing of the photograph was bad, because I don't see how they could have physically changed so much in just a few months.

I continue to read the papers for weeks after that, hoping to find something about the young men going to trial, but don't. Then a month later a co-worker of mine who knew about Eliot and me says she saw on the television last night that the young men were allowed to plead guilty to a lesser charge of negligent manslaughter or something and got off with a jail term of from one to three years. "It seems the elderly man, that main witness to Eliot's murder, died of a fatal disease a while ago and the young woman witness could never be found. As for molesting the policewoman, that charge was dropped, though the news reporter never said why."

The

Batterer

—◀

My wife beats me up. Occasionally. I'm a relatively small man so she can beat me up without being afraid I'm going to beat her up back. Oh, I hit her back. Hard as I can sometimes. I got to protect myself. I'm a peaceful man and peace-loving, all that, but sometimes she gets so mad, and often over what seems the smallest thing, that she's got to take it out on something, and after she takes it out on something—a glass against the floor, tearing a piece of cloth apart—she takes it out on me. That's when I got to defend myself. I try all ways. First verbally. That sometimes works, but not usually. Then when she starts challenging me more, I walk away but she usually follows me wherever I go. When she starts swinging I try holding up my arms and deflecting her blows, but can't deflect all of them and even the ones I do deflect hurt my hands and arms.

That's when I got to stop being so peaceful and start defending myself. I hit back. I try for the blow that will incapacitate her without harming her, like in the arm where it'll hurt so much she can't swing it, but that one rarely works as my aim is never that good. When she really gets violent and uncontrollable I have to hit back hard and even aim for her belly or head. But she's much bigger than me and the harder I hit back the harder she hits me and because she hits harder than me and I'm smaller and can never get as ferocious as her, her hitting hurts me much more than mine does her.

I've gone to court about her beating me up. First time they wouldn't even hear me. Second time I made sure to come with X-rays and my doctor's report and the judge said "You're pressing assault charges against your wife? Where is the woman?"

My wife stood up.

"Do you beat this man as he says?" Several people in the court-room laughed and he banged his gavel for them to shut up.

"No," she said.

"That's a filthy lie," I said.

"Steady there, sir," the judge said, "or I'll get you for contempt."

"All I'm saying, Your Honor, is that she overpowers me and at times has nearly knocked me out. I never start the fights. I do everything I can to avoid and then stop them. This wound here—the one above my eye? She gave me that one two days ago."

"What about the one over my eye?" my wife shouted.

"That was in self-defense."

"Hell it was. You started it. You hit me. You tried to kill me so I swung back."

"If you don't like the treatment you get from your husband," the judge said, "why don't you move out?"

"Because I love him and all the other times he treats me very well."

"And if you don't like the treatment you say you get from her, why don't you move out?"

"I have," I said. "But for one reason or another I always go back. Probably this time I can't, or as long as she's still there or at least till something can be done about her. Because why should I move out for good and give away everything we own to her? And I like my apartment. It's cheap and cozy and where I live. If anyone's to move out, it should be her. She's the one beating me up, not the reverse."

"What are you asking of this court?"

"This is the Family Court, right? So if it wants us to stay a family then I want you to issue what I heard's called an order of protection prohibiting her from hitting me. That way I can move back with her. But if I come in here again from a beating then I want another order of protection issued forcing her to leave our apartment and never to try and see me again. If she still does after that and strikes me, then I want the court to next time get me victim's compensation from her or stick her in jail, since maybe those are the only things that will stop her from attacking me if the orders of protection don't."

"I'm sorry but your petition's denied. For one reason, you've no witness to the alleged beating and it seems that she could have just as easily pressed assault charges or asked for an order of protection against you. Secondly, this court doesn't like to interfere in domestic disputes except of the most serious kind and then mostly when it's the child or wife who gets battered by a parent or spouse. Even if your assault charge is true, I wouldn't think you'd come to this court to resolve the problem but would deal with it as a man in the privacy of your home, or just move out if you're unable to remedy things."

I tried to explain. "She's bigger than me," etcetera. "I'll end up getting killed by her if I hit her any harder than I already do to protect myself," but the judge started to laugh a little along with most of the courtroom.

I always take a hotel room after a bad beating and have always moved back. She sends me flowers and love letters and poems. I've heard of men batterers doing some of those things to get their wives back and there have been TV programs on it also—fictional and documentary and in the news—so maybe that's where she got the idea of those love gifts and romantic apologetic phone calls, though I'm almost sure she was sincere about them each of those last times.

But after a few weeks of this she always convinces me she'll never hit me again and, if anything, just a little love tap but nothing much harder than that. And when I go back, out of loneliness also, we usually have a normal life together for a few months. Kindness and sympathy and affection and even deep feelings and passion for one another, before something would happen. She'd ask me, as she did the last time, if I saw the thing she was searching for in the apartment, and if I said something just a little bit contentious like "Why should I?" or "You're always losing things around the house," as I might be very tired or just not feeling too good that day myself, she'd come right back with something like "Listen, I don't want to get into an argument about it. All I asked was if you saw it and if you didn't, don't give me any of that cynical crap back."

"I'm sorry."

"You're always sorry. Just don't do it again."

"I'm not always sorry and it's possible I might do it again. I'm just sorry this time for having said it and maybe making you even angrier. Because I can see you're in a foul mood."

"I'll really be in a foul mood if you keep that cynical chattering up."

"I'm not cynically chattering. Maybe the first thing I said was snappy, which I apologize for, but I'm now speaking reasonably to you. Anyway, when you're in a bad mood like this almost nothing will get you out of it, so mind if we drop the subject?"

"Yes I mind—a lot. I want to get this thing out into the open once and for all."

"Get what? You're just baiting me, can't you see? I haven't got enough scars on my face to let you know why I don't want to start up with you again?"

"You have to bring that up? My hitting you when you always started those fights, that's what argument you're going to use?"

"Forget it, this is ridiculous," and I go into the bedroom. She follows me.

"You're not going to stop I see," I say.

"No I'm not. I want to know why you had to bring up the fights when that wasn't what I had in mind."

"I know it's not in your mind. But it's what always happens when you get excited like this. You get into some wild emotional or mental state or both that winds up with you physically lashing out at me uncontrollably."

"Oh and you're in such perfect control. You're so perfectly normal. So damn sensitive and controlled."

"Those used to be qualities you liked in me. Just a few weeks ago you said it too."

"I was lying."

"Then don't say it next time."

"Don't tell me what to say or not say. But saying anything to you is a mistake. You're my life's curse, you know that? I never should've hooked up with you."

"Then unhook me, okay? I won't protest. But what I'll never be able to understand is why you get into moods like this that are almost over nothing and then insist on harping on the same theme or any theme just to get me to verbally fight with you when it's obvious I don't want to. Now stop, will you?"

"I'll verbally you. I'll stop you. I'll smack your damn ugly head off with my fist, that's how I'll verbally stop you."

"Now none of that. I don't want to go to court again. The judge'll believe me next time."

"He'll call you a faggot next time. A prissy little whimpery faggot and then laugh even harder in your face, that's what he'll do."

"The hell with reasoning with you then," and I get down on my knees to pull a valise out from under the bed.

"What're you doing?"

"Getting away, that you can bet. I'm not hanging around here waiting for you to drive a wedge into my head."

"Why, you too much the whimpery coward to stand up and talk back to me like a man?"

"Yes."

"You are, I was right, you faggot, so why didn't you say what your hang-ups were when you first met me and saved me the trouble of hooking up with you?"

"The truth is that talking to you doesn't work when you get like this and that's the last time I'm going to tell you that, the last."

"You saying something's wrong with my personality?"

"What are you, kidding me? Yes, goddamnit, I am."

"You bastard, you coward, you make me so mad I could bash your face in, I really could, you bastard, coward, faggot," and she swings at me and I duck and jump to my feet to protect myself but she connects with the next. Right to the mouth. I fly across the bed and a couple of my teeth I think fly someplace else. She weighs maybe fifty pounds more than me and has three inches on me too. She drags me off the bed by my feet and I land on my rear and she kicks me in the ribs. That really hurts and I'm spitting blood besides but I get up and she swings and I block her blow and hit her in the chest and that's all I had to do because now she's all over me with punches, screaming, swinging wildly, connecting every third or fourth time and before I know it she lands one to my jaw that knocks me to the floor. I feel sick. She's on top of me punching my face and hitting every time. All good shots. Nothing wild now. I can't protect myself. My whole face feels paralyzed and I want to throw up. I begin retching. She gets off me and says "That ought to teach you, you whimpering so-forth, you baby," and leaves the room and I hear the front door slam.

I'm really out of it this time. She never did a better job on me. I have to turn over and spit out a mouthful of blood to stop from gagging. I rest awhile and then crawl to the bathroom to see how bad it is and get a towel to stop the bleeding on my face. My face is a mess. Some of the welts have gashes on them, probably from her rings. I stop the bleeding in my mouth by sticking a rolled-up ball of wet toilet paper between my front teeth and upper lip. I wash myself, smear several streaks of iodine across my face and on my ears and when I feel steady enough I call my best friend.

"Herb, could you come over? Melanie really did a number on me this time. I might have to go to the hospital I think."

"I'll phone for an ambulance and run right over. Rest till I get there. Door unlocked?"

"I think so. Wow, my mouth hurts. I don't see her suddenly being so considerate to think of locking the door so burglars can't come in. If not, landlord's got the keys. I doubt I can get to the door myself."

I rest in bed. Herb comes with his wife in minutes. They wash my face and head and Debra says "Anything broken you think?"

"Maybe something in my chest. She kicked me. I think I blanked out but do remember a certain thumping going on down there when I was on the floor, but can't tell for sure. It now feels numb."

"We told you not to go back to her."

"I wasn't thinking. Believe me, never again."

"You do, you lose us as friends."

"I know. Thanks."

"If only she'd done it once when we were with you," Herb says, "you'd have had that witch in a sling by now and could have skipped all this."

"No chance. She's too careful that way. But maybe I got her this time only because of the extent of the beating and condition of my face."

Ambulance comes and takes me away. I'm examined. I have two broken ribs and a broken nose and cheekbone and concussion and have lost all my hearing in one ear and several missing teeth. I'm kept in the hospital for weeks. I ask to see the police and learn they also want to see me. She's pressed charges that I got drunk that night and tried to kill her. I tell them that's bull and press countercharges against her. My lawyer tells me "The best you can get from this is that if you drop charges against her, she'll drop hers against you. She's got too strong a case." And he reads me what she told the police: "He's an erratic drunk. Not a regular drinker as our friends will tell you, but once every other month at home he drinks too much and falls all over the place banging his head and face, which is how he cut his ears and such and lost the teeth. I even picked up the teeth this time to show him what he was doing to himself, but threw them out the window when he rushed at me like a mad dog. For when he gets drunk like that he also occasionally goes berserk and throws things and slaps out at anything in his way. Since I live with him, who else you think gets the brunt? And let's not be silly—you think I'd hit that man first? He might be a little smaller than me but he's wiry and quick and powerful and once or twice in the past he hit me so good that I wouldn't ever think of tangling with him except if I couldn't get out of the house and it was fight him or lose my life. That's what happened this time. The other times he battered me, though I never told our friends or even the ones who are just his friends and maybe believe him, because I was too ashamed and let's face it, the man supports me, and never reported him to you because I knew he'd really give me a licking after that. And then every time after that he moves away out of remorse and in a few weeks pleads with me to take him back. I always did as I'm a sucker for such slob talk and do depend on him for a lot of things and I'm not so young and pretty where I can get another guy that quick and also when he isn't so violently drunk like that he can be very sweet, but from now on I won't."

My lawyer says "The court will believe her rather than you which they always do in cases like this when the evidence isn't entirely in your favor. Besides, even if they've doubts you weren't lying, to most people the man's supposed to fight back. Please, whatever you do from now on, stay clear of her."

I drop charges, she drops hers, I'm ordered by the court to send her a certain sum of money every week if I'm going to live apart, and I move into a hotel, start looking for an apartment and, because of the notoriety our situation got, my boss asks me to look for another job. Month later Melanie calls and says "Thanks for this week's check."

"You're welcome."

"It's nice speaking to you again."

"It isn't for me."

"I want us to get back together, what do you say?"

"That last time was the last time of all the times and I never want to see or speak to you again," and hang up.

She calls back. "I promise the past won't be repeated. I got it all out of my system. I love you, need you, want you—please. Don't you even still like me a little bit and think of me or my body some? Don't you ever want to hold me again or want me to wrap myself around you at night like I used to and cuddle you to sleep?"

"Sometimes I think of you. I'll be honest. And not just think of you negatively. There were good times, yes, but when you got the adrenaline going till you turned into some horrible beast—well what do you think I am, permanently insane? Next time you'll kill or maim me to where I'll never again be able to stand. No. Definitely not."

"What can I do to make you change your mind and see how much I changed?"

"Nothing."

"Please. I can hear it in your voice. What? Tell me. For you I'll do anything."

"Two things for sure, though even then I can't promise I'll come back. One, tell the district attorney's office you did assault me those last few times and that I didn't strike you first. That way they won't think I'm making up stories and my boss and clients won't think I'm a little crazy. Then, if you beat me again, the city can also send you away or fine you or whatever they do to repeat offenders."

"No. They'll get me for perjury for swearing out untrue charges against you and maybe throw me in jail."

"Two, you have to start therapy right away. Group and individual both. And also go to a religious adviser every week to declare that you beat me repeatedly and nearly killed me last time and to keep going till they tell me you worked it out."

"I can't. People will think the worst things of me. It's crazy for a woman to be called a husband batterer. Society won't tolerate it. They'll say I'm wicked or insane and give me drugs or put me away. They'll also think I married a queer. A whimpering milquetoast. I don't want them to think that. I don't want them to think I married a man who can't stand up to anyone."

"You have my two stipulations."

"I can't meet them."

"Then that's it then, goodbye."

"But I swear I won't hit you again. Sweetheart, please, I love you, come home right now. I'll make it nice. I'll bathe you, make your favorite foods, take care of you in every way, do everything you want me to, take gladly all your commands."

"I don't want to command. I just wanted our relationship to be natural as possible, no fakeries or postures, can't you see? Beating isn't natural. Getting things out of your system is, but not like you do. Yours is vicious. Sadistic. You don't even stop when I'm down. No, first work out your problems or at least show me you've begun to by telling the district attorney's office and going to that therapy thing for a month. Only then I'll come back."

"If you don't come back now I'm really going to get mad."

"What, break my neck?"

"Yes."

"There, see? Oh, I wish I had a recording of this call. Forget it," and I hang up.

Hour later she knocks on my hotel room door. I say through the peephole "Go away or I'll call the desk."

"What'll you say: 'My wife wants to get into my room'?"

"Yes, I'll say that. Also that you want to murder me, that you tried it before and nearly succeeded and that I want protection from you."

"You don't need protection. I only want to speak gently to you."

"No."

She kicks the door. I say "Save your energy, I'm not opening up." She bangs her shoulder against the door. I say "I'm calling them so you better leave."

She's still banging. A paint seam runs down the entire middle of the door and the wood seems to be buckling. I call downstairs.

"Manager? Then assistant then, listen. There's a woman at my door who's my wife, all right, but we're legally separated and she's trying to get in my room to kill me, I'm not kidding. She won't go away. She's busting down the door now. Get up here. Six-G. She's a very big woman and I just recently got out of the hospital from a serious beating from her and I'm not allowed to get excited and certainly not to fight back."

They come upstairs. She yells "Let me go. He has someone in there—a prostitute, that's why I'm here."

"That true, Mr. Ridge?" a man says through the door.

"Absolutely not."

"I myself saw him accost her on the street before and ride the elevator up with her. I'm reporting this hotel for allowing whores in it."

"She's lying. I've no one. She's just trying to get in the room to attack me. Call the police, Fifth Precinct, Sergeant Abneg if he's in or any of his associates and ask them if they don't have a file on us about this beating thing."

"Could you open the door so we can see for ourselves? If you do have a woman in there, for one thing it's a single room and she's not a paying guest, and for another, if she is a prostitute then we'll have to ask you and the woman in there to leave. We don't allow that in this hotel."

"I told you. My wife just wants to get in here."

"Then we'll have to open the door ourselves. Sergio, the passkey."

They get the key in a minute and open the door. I'm at the other end of the room with a chair raised over my head ready to bring it down on her if she makes a move toward me. She screams "You whoremonger," and rushes at me. I bring the chair down. It hits her shoulder and she falls and gets up, drops again and while the two men are keeping me from hitting her again with the chair, she gets up and grabs an ashtray off a table and smashes it against my head. I go down.

"Ma'am," one of the men says.

She kicks me in the jaw. I hear the snap and know it's broken. She kicks it again and again and I go out. Next thing I know I'm in an ambulance driving through the city, a doctor leaning over me holding open one of my eyes.

I press charges against my wife from the hospital bed. The policewoman I speak to says "Your wife claims you had a prostitute in your room."

I can't speak but write on a pad: "She lies. I didn't."

"You might've that evening, as your wife said she distinctly saw you solicit a woman on the street and take her into your hotel and that's what got her so mad to knock on your room door."

I write: "Lies, lies, lies."

"The court will tend to believe her. If not for the prostitute, who you could've gotten rid of before your wife got upstairs, then that she broke your jaw in self-defense. She's witnesses to that."

I write: "Hit her with chair for frightened death of her that's why. She phoned hour before, said she'd kill me when she got to hotel."

"You'll never be believed. It's not my job to suggest this, but drop the charges."

I don't. Case is thrown out of court. I later file for divorce, charging physical cruelty. My wife fights the divorce and wins. At the courtroom she's so soft-spoken and sweet. Tells the judge I drink and beat her up every few months, etcetera. "But I still love him, don't ask me why after all he's put me through, and want him back."

I get a legal separation and file for divorce the long way and even then it might not be granted if she doesn't stop challenging it. "If you do get it despite her fighting it," my lawyer says, "you'll have to give her everything you own and more alimony a year than you now earn and which you'll have to continue giving even if she remarries."

I get my own apartment and go back to work. Melanie calls three to four times a week. She pleads with me to come back. I always hang up. Sometimes she follows me on the street, waits outside my office building and apartment house for me. I always get in a cab or duck into a subway and escape. She writes me ardent letters saying how she misses me, cries every night for me, wants me to make love to her, wants me to give her a child, letters like that. I rip them all up and eventually don't even open them.

I try and think of a way to get her to take one last unprovoked swing at me in front of witnesses. Then I could charge her with assault and maybe win this time and also get a quick divorce because of her physical cruelty and a legal writ preventing her from seeing and speaking to me again. But why bother, because the judge would probably say her hitting me again was caused by all the past times I'd provoked her. I'm also afraid that the next time she hits me she might batter my brains or eyes so much that I'd become blind or knocked into insensibility for good.

About six months after our courtroom battle and a few weeks after she stopped calling and sending letters, I get a phone call.

"It's me, don't hang up," she says. "I want to give you a quick uncontested divorce."

"What's the trick now?"

"No trick, darling, it's love. I met a beautiful man and we want to get married."

"I hope he's a foot taller and a hundred pounds heavier than you."

"He happens to be even thinner and shorter than you, but don't be mean."

"I can see why you want to marry him. So you can beat him up even worse than you did me."

"Not true."

"Don't tell me."

"And don't argue with me either. You want the divorce or not? Don't grant me it and you'll never see the end of me for a lifetime."

"I want it."

We agree to file for divorce on the grounds of mutual mental cruelty. We get the divorce in a month, and a week later she marries. I saw the man at the divorce court. He's a little guy all right, older and weaker-looking than me too. I wanted to warn him about her but then told myself to stay out of it. It's his business. And if I say anything he might not marry her and then she'll be on my back for life. Besides, if she does beat him up and he presses charges, the court and most of my old friends will know I wasn't crazy after all. Two men pressing assault charges against the same woman—that's no coincidence.

A year later she and her husband are in the newspaper. He's in a very bad coma. His sister, the article says, got a call from her brother saying Melanie was trying to break down their bedroom door to attack him. When the sister got to the apartment she found her brother on the floor and Melanie kicking him repeatedly in the head. The sister tore into her, knocked her out with a pan and then called the hospital and police.

Melanie's arrested. Her husband's still in a coma. A newsman calls me and says "Mrs. Delray's your ex-wife. So what do you think of the charges against her now—husband battering, attempted murder? Where it might end up a homicide, as he's got no more than a fifty-fifty chance to survive. Even if he does she'll still be in serious trouble, as he hasn't got any chance of being anything but totally brain-damaged for the rest of his life."

"If you don't mind I'll save what I have to say for the jury trial. Because I might be prejudicing the case if I told you all that happened to me and then because of some legal technicality she got away free," and I hang up.

Magna

as a Child

She gets on a train. A man makes a pass at her. "Hiya doing, darling?" She gets off the train. She waits on the platform. Another man comes over and says "Pardon me, young lady, but which way is uptown?"

"*This* the downtown side, that what you mean?"

"This is the downtown? That's the one I want. This the local side of the platform?"

"That's the local side there. This is the express."

"That's the one I want. The express. I have to get downtown in a hurry. Terrific business deal—you can't believe it. You're too young to understand that though."

"I suppose so."

She looks away from him, stands there, holds a book bag. She knows the man's a character. It happens so often. Men want to touch her on the subway, talk to her. They follow her on the street sometimes, and certainly give her looks wherever she goes. One took her hand the other week, held it gently enough, and said "Why don't you come home with me. It's a nice home. A really big apartment—anything you want in it could be yours. Antiques: they're yours. Not all, of course, but some, and the more valuable the better, far as I'm concerned. Lamps, chairs, dishes—anything of these is yours. Which one of those would you like?" "Do you mind?" she said, taking her hand from his. "No, really, I'm telling the truth. Whatever you want you can have. Lamps and chairs. Dishes too. All of them. Curtains. Brocaded curtains. Lazy Susans. Silent butlers. Know what those are? I got two, both sterling silver, engraved, but you can't tell what the initials are they're engraved so fancily. Whatever you want. You're that beautiful. Beautiful as a princess. You are a princess. What country you a princess of, beautiful young lady?" She had to walk across the street to get rid of him.

This one stands beside her. She knows he doesn't have to go uptown or down. He just wants to be with her. If not her, then another attractive girl. She knows he wants to be on the same train with her. She has an idea he's going to sit beside her on the train, talk to her and then get off with her at her stop and follow her on the street or walk beside her. She has this problem. Not a problem really, but because of her looks she attracts strange men like this, old and young, and they cause her problems. She happens to be very pretty. That's not being egotistical to admit it. People have told her it, and some have said, when she's said she's not that pretty, "Come on. You're gorgeous, don't deny it." But she's so young. Not even fourteen. Developed like a girl of eighteen maybe, and maybe older. Anyway, developed. And tall for her age. She might have already reached her full height. And men like her for her build and face. Young face, with very smooth clear skin, and her long blond hair. They like her hair. They often tell her about her hair, just as they comment to one another or tell her about her breasts, behind and legs. Here comes the train.

"Our train," the man says.

"Maybe just yours. I just realized I should take the local. It's a local stop I'm going to." She goes to the other side of the platform. The express comes. He doesn't get on it. All the people who got off it go up the stairs or wait on her side of the platform for the local. He comes over to her.

"The local, that's right," he says. "I have to take the local—I forgot. What stop you taking it to?"

"Excuse me," and she walks to the end of the platform. If there's a policeman around she'll stand by him. If the man comes over to her then, she'll report him. If the local comes and he doesn't get on it, she'll get on. If he gets on, she won't.

But there's no policeman. The man's coming toward her. That's it, she's had enough. Who should she report him to? Nobody really looks that safe or nice to talk to. She'll report him to that elderly man there, but when she gets closer to him she thinks he might be a derelict. That woman over there then.

"Excuse me, ma'am, but I'm having some trouble with that man there. He's been bothering me."

"What can I do for you, honey? Go upstairs. Tell the change clerk."

"If I can just stand with you I don't think he'll bother me anymore."

"Then I'm the one he might bother. Listen, honey, do what I say. Go upstairs, speak to the clerk in the booth. You want me to do it for you? I think I can in the time the next train comes."

"I don't want to be left down here with him. Can we go up together?"

"Better that you do it alone, honey. Maybe he won't follow. If he does I'll say something, but I don't want to miss my train."

She starts upstairs. The man starts up the stairs after her. She turns to him. The woman has her back to them, is looking down the tracks for the train. "Will you leave me alone, you crazy?"

He sticks his hand into his fly and pulls out his penis. He waves it at her. "Big, huh, and it's not even hard. Take a lick, kid. All you want. Free on the house and nobody here will mind. Go on, take a lick of it. It tastes real good."

She runs upstairs. He goes downstairs.

"That's awful," she hears the woman say, "just awful. What are you doing that for to that poor girl?"

Maybe he says or does something. By this time she's upstairs and she runs out of the station.

———

She comes home from her art lesson. Her mother says "Hello, sweetheart, have a nice day?" and kisses her cheek. She says she had a rotten day, maybe her worst except for when she was very sick. Her mother says "Here, let's sit down and talk."

"I don't have to sit down. I can't. I'm jumpy again just thinking about it. The art class wasn't bad—that's not it. Or not *that* bad. We had a live female model for once. Me, the big-shot, had been asking for one since they had the male model—"

"I didn't know you had male models. In the nude?"

"Sure, except for a strap down there, but when we finally got a female I almost died when I saw her body—a woman for the first time like that. It honestly scared me."

"Was she wearing drawers or something?"

"No—only he did, the male, though his behind cheeks showed.

And when he bent over to make the towel under him right, one testi- cle showed too, someone said—though I wasn't looking at the time because I had a feeling it'd happen. But the women don't. And when she undressed in the booth she didn't even pull the curtain, nor when she got dressed again. I think she should have. There were lots of boys my age too."

"I think she should have also. Complain to the teacher. You don't want to, I will, but I think you're old enough to complain when you think something's wrong. You do enough home. But tell me, sweet- heart, what was it that scared you about her so?"

"I didn't know women could get so big down there and different from me too."

"You know what you look like?"

"I've held a mirror to it. A teacher—in Hygiene—suggested us to."

"The model probably had babies. Don't let it scare you. You have plenty of time yet, and maybe she was also a little messy."

"And, well, I know what you're going to say, but I almost got molested on the subway going to Art. A man showed his penis."

"He exposed himself? Maybe you shouldn't take those classes anymore."

"No, I got away okay, I swear it, and since it was the first time ever, I don't think it'll happen again."

"I don't like it. Let me talk it over with Papa. But it was quite a day for genitalia for you. If you were old enough I'd advise your hav- ing a real drink. What about some cocoa or milk? I'll warm some for you."

"No, I'll be okay. You need help with dinner?"

"You're not just trying to bury it? You do feel better now that you got it out by telling me it?"

"Yes, Mom, yes. I won't let the experience with the man warp my future sexual and married life."

"That's a smart girl. Because he's destroyed, don't let you be."

Magna makes the salad, sets the table, does her homework, has supper, is told by her father to stay off the subways from now on unless she's traveling with someone, reads a novel she got out of the library last week with eleven other novels. She wants to read three novels a week for the next month. She thinks her mind needs it. She finished two this week and is almost done with this one—*Barchester Towers,* the longest and most boring of the three, or just the one whose language, style and consanguinity, as her teacher would say— she thinks that's the right word—but anyway, she got this far with it and if she doesn't finish it she'll be behind schedule. Then a friend calls.

"Magna," Sarah says, "I'm in love."

"Do tell me about it."

"Act more excited. It's big big news."

"Oh, do tell me about it."

"A boy in my school."

"Oh, a boy?"

"Don't be funny. A very tall masculine boy. He proposed to me today. Actually got on his knee. I said 'Get up, jerko, unless you want to be there for the next five years.' For in five years I should know, shouldn't I?"

"Am I believing this? Okay, I'm believing this. He just wants to get in your pants, Sarah. What's his name?"

"Not true and his name's Toby."

"Sounds like a clown. Drop him. No clowns allowed. Only serious names and serious professions. Charles, Henry, Ernest. Statesmen, physicians, writers, composers, choreographers, painters. Especially painters and all those in the plastic arts."

"Magna, you're too staid. You also should have a boyfriend."

"I almost did on the subway today. Listen to this. A man wanted to take me home. Said he'd give me anything. For starters, he showed me his penis."

"No."

"Actually, that was another one last week. Nothing exposed. This one today—and he was my second potential boyfriend in three minutes. The first on the subway went goo-goo with his eyes till I thought they'd pop out—but this one, well, he brought his thing out and said—Wait, are my folks around? No. He said 'Lick.' I could have killed him. He was insane. If I had a gun I would have shot it off—truly."

"You wouldn't."

"Maybe not, but I've been thinking, isn't there something they can do for men like that? Women too if they jump all over boys our age the same way? Oh, boys wouldn't mind. They're dumb enough to think it's great and they're so attractive if any woman suddenly pulled out her breast to them and said 'Suck, eat, crunch, squeeze.' But men. Maybe they could show them pictures of rats eating garbage same time they show them pictures of little and big girls."

"Good idea. We can show these films in movie theaters. We can charge admission and makes lots of money."

"I'm speaking of photographs, not movies, and you're missing my point besides."

"I'm not. Magna, you're getting too serious for me. But what did it look like this rope he had?"

"If you mean by rope, big, or if you're just using it as another word for any sized penis—"

"Was it ugly, I mean? Sounds as if it would be. With bumps and scales on it and disease leaking out."

"All of that. What do you think, I took time to stare? I felt sorry for him at first and also that he was very depraved, but most of all I was scared."

"So you admit that?"

"Sarah, why wouldn't I?"

"I don't know. I had nothing else to say. But you want to hear about Harry? That's my new flame."

"What happened to Toby?"

"Toby is what I wish his name was. I know you don't like it, but I do."

"Okay, okay, so long as your story doesn't have genitals in it. I'm tired of that today."

"Harry wouldn't do that. He might want to one day—with me, in a nice way, no creep flashing his raincoat on the street, I mean—but that's some day, not today. I met him in the lunchroom. In a half hour I knew he was it. He waited for me after school. Already sound too good to be true? He escorted me—that's the word he used—if he could; you know—to my ballet class."

"I like the word escort. He's sounding good. He have a friend?"

"He says he has a few and they're all almost as nice as he is. Harry's not modest. He also plays the cello."

"My favorite instrument."

"If that's so I won't let you near him. I told him the cello was the most beautiful instrument in the world, but I don't like any string sound but the guitar. And the mandolinski."

"Why the ski?"

"To give it a, well, a little Russian flavor. Because I love Russian everything—Russian dancing and Russian dancers especially. I've changed my name to ski, you know. Sarah Nortonski."

"Okayski, Miss Nortonski, any other newski?"

"Yes. You can sleep over this Friday. Mom says it's all right. And you know my dad didn't mind, since he has a crush on you."

"Sure he does."

"He does. He says 'How's your friend Magna? How come we see so little of her these days? Let me tell you,' he tells me, 'if I was a young woman of fourteen and wanted a good friend for life, Magna's the one I'd choose.' Other times he's called you beautiful, witty, charming, precocious—I love that. And brilliant, he once said—talented and brilliant and, my dear, what extraordinary poise. That's how he put it. He's in love with you, you cookie."

"Then think I want to sleep over your house?"

"Oh, he's in love with my mother also, but he's got a Russian crusher on you. You deserve it too. You're really everything he says."

"Why thank you, Ski. Sure I can come Friday. But I have to clear it with my folks. Hold on."

Magna goes into the living room. Her father says "I don't see why not," and her mother says "Let me speak to Mrs. Norton." The two women talk. The girls are both dears and a pleasure to have over, the mothers agree, and Friday will be fine.

"Great," Sarah says to Magna. "I can't wait. I'm going with Harry to a movie on Saturday or I would've asked you for that night too."

"Is he staying over Saturday?"

"Magna, how could you? This is an extension. And of course he's not. You know that."

"I'm sorry, that was dumb of me. Okay, got to run, unless you have other important news."

"How about you? I always talk, you never do."

"What I told you about Mr. Subway wasn't talking? And I saw a woman completely nude for the first time in my life today in art class. I suffered and I know why too. I'm going to end up looking like her, with my breasts and hips already large as they are. I don't think I'll have as much hair down there as she had, or I hope not, and never mounds of it under my arms and so dark, nor will I look so down and out, and so sad. But the body has to end up sagging like that, doesn't it?"

"Not with us dancers, my dear. Keeps the breasts and tushies tight—not just the legs. Ever see some of the old ones? Sixty, seventy years old. I've seen them in the showers and dressing rooms at ballet school and their bodies still look half great."

"Maybe I should give up painting for dancing then, but aren't we talking silly? Always the body, never the mind."

"Not you, just me. I can't stand to think deep or read. All I ever want to do with my life is eat like an Amazon and exercise and dance. Oh: see ballets and good ballet rehearsals too. But you're getting much too serious for me, and I got to scoot too. See you Friday, Brainstein, and come straight from school."

In bed that night she thinks about the model. The teacher told the class to go up and take a good look at her. "It's allowed. I checked beforehand with Astor and she said for the sake of art and higher learning, look anywhere you like and close as you want too, though keep a five-feet distance from her if you have a bad cold."

Magna stayed on her stool, drawing the model and the few students who went up to look at her. The teacher came up behind her and said "What're you concocting there, a basket of fruit? Take advantage—go up and give her a real inspection, unless it's against your principles or whatever, of course."

"It's not. It's just that, you know, I'm a little concerned she might think I'm just staring, no matter what you said she said. And I thought I had a pretty good drawing going till you came by, but if you still—" He was nodding his head, so she put the drawing down and went up to the model.

The model was on the floor on her back, legs spread apart, looking up at the wall clock. Magna stared at several parts of her body—hand, feet, shoulders—before she looked between her legs. It's so shiny and big. They're really not the prettiest things in the world, that's for sure, though penises, from what she's seen of them on statues and in photographs, aren't the nicest-looking things either and look stupid besides. But go back and draw it. Let Mr. Finkel think "Oh boy, this kid really got something from my lesson—maybe more, if she shows it to her folks, than I bargained for."

She made a large drawing of just the model's legs spread apart and her vagina and pubic area. Mr. Finkel came over, made believe he was handing her something and said "Here, kid, you get today's cigar. It's your best effort yet, not just for what you put in but what you left out also." She said "I think I know what you mean, but can you explain it further?" He said "Just think about it—you'll get it," and walked away. She still didn't know what he meant and doubted he did either. Just pretending to be profound, like most of her teachers, but anyway. . . .

She's been rubbing herself down there for the last few minutes. Door's closed and lights out and she's under the covers. She's tried to masturbate a few times but has either fallen asleep doing it or stopped because she thought one of her parents might walk in and turn the light on at the same time and catch her at it, and once when the light was on she thought there might be a tiny hole in the ceiling or walls someplace and one of her parents or the building's tenants might be looking through it. She knows where and how to rub and what she's supposed to do to complete it. She's read a couple of library books about it and what the end's supposed to be like, but she's never come near to feeling anything but a little titillation down there while she was doing it. She also read in one of those books that every woman, including married ones, should practice masturbation for all sorts of reasons—spiritual, political, like that—and sooner a younger woman learns how, better it'll be for her and all freedom-loving women in general, so she's never really felt much guilt over it but hasn't yet talked about it with anyone. She doesn't like the idea she's doing it so soon after she saw that man on the subway, but is sure that incident had nothing to do with it. In fact, more she thinks of him, less interested she is in continuing to rub herself, so she closes and opens her eyes a few times to get him out of her head, and also changes hands because the right one's become tired. The model today probably had more to do with it than anything else. Thinking of that woman's vagina probably made her think of her own, though without really knowing it, since right after she thought of her she found her hand rubbing down there. Sarah and her new boyfriend and the heavy petting she bets they'll start doing in a month if they stay together? No, she never thought of that till now, though again that's not to say somewhere deep inside she hadn't been thinking of it. But she still doesn't think so, nor anything related to Sarah's father being infatuated with her, something she already knew by his actions and looks and wishes he'd stop, more for her friendship with Sarah and Sarah's mother's sake than her own. Anyway, whatever it was that started her doing it, it's not working. She's been rubbing for around fifteen minutes, both hands are tired, she's beginning to ache down there from it, and she's no further along in getting excited as those books said she'd get than she was a few seconds after she started. Maybe she's doing it wrong or is just too young yet or the books left out something or some other reason. No big deal. It was more out of curiosity that she wanted to complete it than any other thing. She turns on the light, listens from her bed if anyone's behind the door, reads a little and falls asleep.

In one of her dreams there was a big bull with a long unicorn's horn on its head. She knows what those mean and knew in the dream. In the dream she said to the bull, when he stepped out from behind a bush and got into a charging position, "Come on, I know what you and that horn mean. You want to try and fool me with symbols and stuff, get more complicated, but don't come around like some old-time figure in art." She's become something of an expert on her dreams. Her youngest aunt's a psychotherapist and they've talked about their dreams a lot. The bull chased her after she lectured him on dreams and art. That was when she stopped interpreting within the dream, or even thought of it as one, and it became more like a normal dream. She was dressed only in white, even her socks and shoes. White's such an obvious symbol for her, though she didn't think of it then, but it can also stand for death, can't it?—in the Orient her aunt's said and she's read. Anyway, she was chased, fell back against a wall that had a few pillows on it, that suddenly became one huge pillow. A bed, what else? or something close to it. No? Yes. The bull charged from about ten feet away, head down, horn out, straight at her. She thought she'd be pierced by the horn and she screamed, so loud that she thinks she must have screamed outside of the dream too. The horn was a few inches from her stomach when she woke.

She's thirsty. She gets up and goes to the kitchen for some ice water or seltzer. Her mother's reading in the living room. "Everything all right, sweetheart? It's past two."

"I had a bad dream. Did you hear me scream?"

"No. It was that bad? Anything you want to talk about?"

"I don't know if it was that bad, just very revealing, I think."

"Tell me."

"I dreamt about a man about to penetrate me with an erection. In the stomach. But it's the same thing, isn't it—myself down there and my stomach? Only the man was a bull with a unicorn's horn, and the horn, well it has to be what I think it is to think it was an erection, right?"

"Sounds right. You haven't had any of those experiences—even close to it—have you?"

"Me? Not a chance. How would I? Where?"

"I'm not accusing you, I'm just naturally worried. So it was your whole day of bad experiences today. But anything else bothering you related to sex?"

"I don't know about bothering me, but another man got suggestive with me on the subway, right before the one who exposed himself. I just walked away."

"Maybe from now on let's take the bus."

"And Sarah's father. I didn't want to say anything for I don't want to hurt my friendship with her, but if she's telling the truth, he has a crush on me. Actually I know he has. I've seen the way he looks."

"You think you're old enough to tell?"

"I am. And not that he's evil or would do anything or anything, but he doesn't do a good job of hiding it."

"Then maybe you shouldn't sleep over there this Friday after all."

"Maybe for a while it's not a good idea. I can go over for afternoons and she can sleep here."

"Don't tell her the reasons though. It'd only hurt her. So, sweetheart, back to sleep?"

"I also tried to masturbate tonight and not for the first time too. That's all right also, considering everything, isn't it? I didn't want to tell you, but we were talking and I guess I really wanted to get it out, and now it is."

"What can I say? That I like hearing it? Not so much. The act itself is normal for young women as well as some older ones, I suppose—I'm not going to say at what specific age you do and you don't—but let's not talk about it anymore. It's not that nonsense that I don't like learning you're growing up, but maybe it's something you can try to save for your friends. But if anything is troubling you and you want to talk about it, no matter what it is, come to your father or me or both. Now off to bed."

"I want to get something cold to drink first."

"Not too cold or you'll have trouble sleeping."

Magna pours herself a glass of seltzer. Her mother goes back to her reading. Later her mother comes into Magna's room, thinks she's sleeping, pulls the covers up an inch or two to Magna's neck.

Only
the Cat
Escapes

Magna comes into the room. "Oh, Will, you're reading in bed. That's what I had decided to do. Would you mind if I joined you?"

"Come ahead."

She lies beside me on the bed and opens her book. I return to my book. She says after about a minute "Suppose I told you I don't want to read right now?"

"Let's say you just told me."

"That's what I meant. Suppose I did. What would you say?"

"I'd say 'What do you mean you don't want to read right now?'"

"And suppose I answered that I don't want to read right now because I have something else in mind?"

"Then I'd ask what that is."

"Let's say you have asked."

"Let's say I have."

"And let's say I then said I'd like to sleep with you right now."

"So?"

"Well, what's your reply?"

"My reply?" I put my book down and think. "My reply?" She puts her book on top of my book between us. Her cat jumps on the bed and lies on my feet. I say "Do you think your cat should be on the bed at a time like this?"

"What time is that?"

"A time when I'm about to say that I think it's a pretty good idea if we do sleep together right now."

"If you did say that then I'd say it probably isn't a good time for my cat to be on the bed."

"All right, let's say I said it."

"Then I suppose I should tell the cat to get off the bed."

"Why don't you?"

"I will."

Just then the cat jumps off the bed and runs underneath it.

"It seems," she says, "I didn't have to tell the cat to get off the bed."

"Seems so. But what next?"

"What next what? That I should do something about getting it out from under the bed and maybe even out of the room?"

"No, let it stay there, what's the harm? I mean about our sleeping together."

"About that I'd say I think we should start."

"And to that I'd say that I think we already did start when we began talking about it and put our books down."

"But we put our books down between us. That might end up being a little too uncomfortable for us if we actually do start sleeping with each other right now."

" 'Sleeping' as whatever figure of speech it is for 'making love,' I suppose. I mean, that is what you had in mind when you said 'sleeping,' isn't it?"

"First making love, then maybe sleeping together on this bed if we like."

"That's what I thought." I take the books in one hand and drop them on the floor. The cat runs out from under the bed and down the stairs.

"I didn't intend, I·want you to know, to scare the cat away by dropping the books."

"If you say so, then you didn't," she says.

"Didn't intend to."

"Right."

"But you did think I might have intended to scare it, isn't that so?"

"I thought you might have intended to, but I didn't worry about it much."

"You worried about it a little, though, no?"

"What happened was this. When you dropped the books and that cat ran out I thought for a second or two you might have intentionally scared my cat by dropping the books you were getting rid of for us and that that act could indicate something about your personality or nature or whatever it's called that I might not like about you. But it turned out not to be so. You didn't try to scare it. Or did you?"

"I didn't. I even forgot the cat was under the bed."

"Which I think is really, if I had had more time to think about it then, what I would have ended up thinking had happened. But where did we leave off after we stopped talking about figures of speech and sleeping together as meaning making love?"

"We left with that, I think. But are you saying you think we should try and carry on from that point?"

"Not try but do, if you still want to."

"Do you?"

"I'm sorry, but didn't I just say I did?"

"I do," I say.

"So do I."

"But if I had said I didn't, what would you have said?"

"I would have wondered why you didn't want to anymore."

"You would have wondered but would you have said it?"

"I might have. But because I do want to sleep with you or make love or both, I would have said it in a way which wouldn't have done anything to discourage you from wanting to sleep with me or make love or both, or I at least would have tried to say it in that way."

"What way would that be?"

"Gently. Sincerely. Lovingly, I suppose. Surely softly, if that isn't the same thing as saying it gently. But you know. I might have taken your hand." She takes my hand. "Like this. My hand around yours. And then got up on my side, like this, and said very gently and lovingly or not 'very' but just gently and lovingly and the rest of those ways . . . what was it I would have said? I forget."

"You mean before in response to my saying what would you have said if I had said I didn't want to sleep or make love with you or both anymore?"

"That's right. I would have said softly and sincerely, as I'm doing, lovingly and gently, as I'm still doing, and with my torso up on its side, as I've done and it still is, and my hands where they are now, 'Why don't you want to sleep with me or make love with me or do both with me now? Is it something I said?'"

"You would have said 'Is it something I said?'"

"I would have, yes," she says. "And if I had said all that in the way I said it and with my torso and hands the way they still are, what would you have said and done to me?"

"I would have got up on my side, facing you, as I'm now going to do, but carefully, so your hand wouldn't slip off my neck—"

"It's okay. If it slips I can put it back."

"And with my other hand still in your hand, as it still is, and also lovingly and sincerely and gently and softly, though maybe not as gently and softly as you said it, since I don't seem to be able to get my voice as gentle and soft as yours, possibly because of our respective sexes and because of that, our different vocal quality and tone. And maybe also because of our different personalities and sensibilities and backgrounds or something, though I don't know the physical and characteristical reasons why that should be so. But I would have said 'No, it wasn't anything you said. I simply don't want to make love or sleep with you right now, that's all.'"

She takes her hand off mine and other hand off my neck and says "You would have said that?"

"I wouldn't have."

"Then why'd you say it?"

"I didn't say it as if I meant it but just to see what your reaction would be like."

"And what would it be like?"

"Not 'would' but 'was.' You took both hands away from me but kept your torso on its side facing mine, and in a voice not as gentle and soft and loving as before but as sincere, you said 'You would have said that?'"

"Would you like to know why I reacted that way?"

"I can guess."

"Go ahead and guess then," she says.

"Because you probably believed that I didn't want to make love or sleep with you right now. Is that it?"

"I'm not saying."

"Can I ask how come?"

"You can ask."

"How come?"

"I'm not saying."

"Can I ask how come?"

"You already asked how come and I already said I'm not saying."

"That was to something else," I say. "But can I make a guess why you're not saying anything to any of my questions?"

"Make a guess. But I won't tell you if your guess is accurate or not."

"Can I ask how come?"

"Again, you can ask, but I'm not saying, I won't say, and that's that."

"You're not saying what?"

"I'm not saying, period."

"Why not? You answered all my other questions till now, if not directly then indirectly, but you gave me answers at least, just as I did to you in either of those two ways."

"I thought by me saying 'I'm not saying,' I was giving an indirect answer. You didn't get it?"

"No. But now that I know it was an indirect answer, maybe it'll be easier to get. Give me time to think."

She takes my hand.

"I think I'm getting it," I say.

She puts her other hand on the back of my neck.

"Now I get it. Or I'm almost sure I got it."

"From now on I'll only say 'what?'" she says.

"You don't want to talk anymore?"

"What?"

"You just want to make love or sleep or some other figure of speech with me, but you think talking about it too much sort of kills it?"

"What? What?" She brings her lips close to mine.

"You want to kiss and take off my clothes or have me take them off and also your clothes off or you want to take off your clothes by yourself? You want us to do all that or some of those or more?"

"What? What? What?"

"You want me to turn off the light or make it less bright by turning off one or two of the lamp's three bulbs, and you also want us to get closer, not just our lips, and do other things with our bodies and more? Am I right?"

"What? What? What? What?"

"Just say I'm right."

"What? What? What?"

"I'm sure I'm almost right."

"What? What?"

"I'm going to have to turn around to turn off the light or to turn it down, all right?"

"What?"

I turn around to the lamp on the night table on my side of the bed. Her hand slides off my neck onto my hip. Her other hand stays around mine but she's squeezing it now when she wasn't before. Her face is no longer near mine but it probably will be again once I turn the light off or down and turn back around. I turn off all three bulbs. It's still daylight out but gray because of the clouds and rain, and the room's dark, mostly because of the tall trees that surround the house. I turn around and face her. I can't see her face but can her form. She puts her hand back on my neck and her mouth close to mine. "I want—" I start to say, but she takes her hand off my neck and puts one finger across my lips to stop me from saying whatever I was going to say, which was "I want to tell you that I love you very very much," and takes her finger away and kisses my lips.

Frog's
Nanny

―

This is how he remembers it. He shits in his pants. Actually, it starts with him coming up to her—his memory of it always starts with him coming up to her and pointing between his legs. She says something like "Did you make doody in your pants?" He nods. Remembers nodding, not speaking. "Doody in your pants again?" Nods. Next thing he remembers she's pulling him into the bathroom, then that he's in the bathroom, long pants are off his legs, she slips his underpants off with the shit inside them, and holding the clean part of the underpants pushes the shit into his face. Then she picks him up by his underarms, holds him in front of the medicine chest mirror and tells him to look at himself. He doesn't want to. He's crying. "Look, I'm telling you to look!" He looks. Shit all over his face. Looked like hard mud. Just then he hears his father's voice. "Hello, anyone around?" He starts squirming in her arms to be let down. He wants to run to his father to show him what she did. He knows what she did was wrong. She lets him down. He runs out of the bathroom, through what they called the breakfast room into the kitchen where his father is. He points to his face. His father starts laughing very hard. That's all he remembers. Scene always goes blank then.

"Frieda's coming today," his mother said on the phone. "She particularly asked me to see if you could be here. I'd love for you to be here too." "I don't know if I can make it," he said. "Please do though. She'll be here at noon. She's always very punctual, to the point most of the time of getting here ten to fifteen minutes early. I'm taking her out to lunch. Would you like to join us?" "Now that I know I can't do." "Dobson's—for fish. She was thrilled with it the last time. Raved and raved. Even had a glass of wine." "No, thanks, Ma. If I come I can only spare an hour. Getting there and back will take another hour, which is really all I can spare. Two. Total."

He tells his wife that his mother called before. "Frieda's visiting her for the day. Both want me to be there. For lunch too, but that I'm definitely not doing."

"Your old nanny? What was the story you told about her—what she did to you?"

"What? Every morning rolling down my socks in a way where I could just hop out of bed and roll them up over my feet? Actually, she did that the night before. Left them at the end of my bed along with my—"

"Not the socks. The feces in your face. How'd that go again? I remember your father was in on it too. In the story."

"He laughed when he saw me."

"What do you think that was all about?"

"More I think of it, maybe he really did think it was funny. Here's this kid of his running up to him with shit all over his face. He had a great sense of humor. —No, he did. And for all he knew I might have tripped and fallen into it and maybe that's what he thought was so funny. His kid tripped headfirst into shit."

"But later he knew. You told him, didn't you? You were pointing, crying. And you told your mother later—you must have, or he did—but they still kept her on."

"Frieda was a gem, they thought. She ran the house. Kept the kids disciplined, quiet when necessary and out of the way. Three boys too, so no easy task. She gave them the time to do what they liked. Work, play, go off for two-week or weekend vacations whenever they wanted. Cruises, and once all summer in Europe. And she wasn't well paid either. None of the nannies then were."

"But she did lots of cruel things like that feces scene. She beat you, hit your face. Smacked your hands with a spatula that you said stung for hours later."

"That was Jadwiga, the Polish woman who replaced Frieda when Frieda married."

"Sent you to bed without your dinner several times."

"Both of them."

"Twisted your wrists till they burned. Right? Frieda?" He nods. "Face it, she was a sadist, but your parents permitted it."

"Look, you have to understand where she came from and the period. As for my parents, who knows if they didn't think that discipline—her kind—and it probably wasn't an uncommon notion then—attitude, belief, whatever—was what we needed. The kids. And okay, since they didn't want to discipline us like that themselves—didn't have the heart to, or the discipline for it or the time—she got anointed. *Appointed.* That wasn't intentional. I'm not that smart. Or just was tacitly allowed to. Anyway, Frieda came from Hanover. 1930 or so. A little hamlet outside. My father hired her right off the boat. Literally, almost. She was here for two or three days when he got her from an employment agency. And that had to be the way she was brought up herself. Germany, relatively poor and little educated, and very rigid, tough, hard, disciplined years."

"What did your father do after he stopped laughing? Did he clean your face?"

"I don't remember, but I'm sure he didn't. He would never touch it. The shit? That was Frieda's job. On her day off, my mother's."

"Can you remember though?"

"Let me see." Closes his eyes. "She put me down. I'd asked her to. You know all that. I ran into the kitchen. I see him coming, and then he's there. He's got on a business suit, white shirt and a tie. His office was in front of the building, you know."

"Yes."

"So it could have been around lunchtime. He came back to the apartment for lunch every workday. Did it through a door connecting the office and apartment."

"The door's not there now, is it?"

"On my mother's side it is—in the foyer—but she had that huge breakfront put up in front of it. On the other side it was sealed up when he gave up the office. I don't know why they didn't have the door sealed up on their side. Would have been safer from break-ins and more aesthetic. Maybe he thought he'd start up his practice again when he got well enough to. But after he gave up the office it was rented by another dentist. A woman. He sold her most of his equipment. And he wouldn't have been in a business suit then. White shirt and tie, yes. He wore them under his dental smock on even the hottest days. So now it makes me wonder. It was definitely a business suit I saw. A dark one. He must have come into the apartment through the front door, not the office door. It was probably a Sunday. Frieda got her day off during the week and a half day off on Sunday right after lunch. So I don't know. Maybe it was one of the Jewish holidays. He could have just come back from *shul.* But where were my brothers? They could have gone with him and were now playing outside. And my mother? She would have been in the kitchen cooking if it was a Jewish holiday. That was the time—the only time, just about, except for Thanksgiving and I don't know what—my father's birthday? Her father visiting? Which he did every other week till he died when I was six, though I don't ever remember seeing him, there or any other place—when she really went at it in the kitchen. The other times it was fairly quick and simple preparations and, occasionally, deli or chow mein brought in. Maybe we were going to my father's sister's—Ida and Jack's—in Brooklyn for dinner that night. We did that sometimes. She cooked kosher, if that's the right expression, and my father, raised on it, still fancied it, especially on Jewish holidays. Anyway, he approached. I was around three or four at the time. So if it was a nursery school day and not a serious Jewish holiday and I wasn't home from school because I was sick—but she never would have put shit in my face if I were sick—then it was the afternoon. My nursery school for the two years was always in the morning. But what about my father's business suit? Let's just say he closed the office for the day and had a suit on because he'd just come back from a dental convention downtown. He's there though. I see him coming through the living room into the kitchen. I run through the breakfast room—where we never had breakfast, except Sunday morning, just dinner—to the kitchen. The kitchen was where we had breakfast and lunch. Frieda's behind me. I don't remember seeing her, just always sensed she was. I hold out my arms to him. I'm also crying. I don't remember that there, but how could I not be? I think a little of the shit was getting into my mouth. I don't remember smelling it but do tasting it a little. All this might sound like extrapolation, exaggeration—what I didn't smell but did taste. But I swear it's not. Anyway, to it. Arms are out. Mine. I've a pleading look. I know it. I had never felt so humiliated, soiled, so sad, distressed—you name it. Dramatic, right? I'm telling you," opening his eyes, "I felt absolutely miserable and this had to be evident to him. So maybe when he saw me he took that kind of defense—laughter—rather than deal with it, try to comprehend it. But maybe not. Maybe he did think I tripped into it. So even though I was so distressed his first reaction might have been 'Oh my God, Howard's tripped into shit.' Maybe he thought it was our dog Joe's. Or dirt. That I'd been playing in one of the backyard planters, or that it was paint on my face. Clay. But no play clay's that color. Maybe it does get that way when you mix all the colors up. Anyway, my arms are out. Let me try to get beyond what I've so far can't remember about it. Past the blank." Shuts his eyes. "Arms. He's

there. Kitchen. I run to him. Frieda's behind me. Sense that. I'm crying. Have to. Pleading look. He laughs. Blank. Blank." Opens his
eyes. "No, didn't work. Most of my real old memories end like that.
Like a sword coming down. Whop! Maybe hypnosis would get me
past, but I tend to doubt those aids. Or can't see myself sitting there,
just submitting."

"But your mother. Didn't she say it never happened?"

"To me, yes. She says it happened to Alex. He says it did happen
to him but nothing about a kitchen or pair of pants, which she seems
to remember hearing he did it in, or my dad. That he was in a bathtub
by himself—one of the first times. Till then he had always bathed toe-
to-toe with Jerry, but Frieda thought they were too grown-up for that
so had it stopped—when he suddenly shit. Two big—"

"Come on, spare me."

"So he called out that he'd just made kaka in it. Frieda came,
grabbed some of it out of the water and put it in his face. He said he
never kakaed again in the tub or anywhere but in the potty, or at least
that he doesn't remember being anything but toiletized after that."

"How about you?"

"I don't know if what Frieda did to me stopped me from having
kaka accidents or even was the last time she put it in my face. I do
think it happened to me. For sure. Memory of it's too vivid for it not
to have happened, but I guess that doesn't have to be the case."

"So, are you going to see her?"

"Yes, I think so, you mind? I had Olivia two hours today, so I've
at least done part of my daily share. When I come back I'll take her to
the park or something and you can get back to work."

He goes to his mother's. Has the keys, lets himself in. "Hi, hi, it's
me," he says, walking through the living room. They're having coffee
and cookies in the kitchen. Frieda sees his mother look up at him and
smile and turns around. "Oh my, look who's here," she says. "What a
nice thing to do," and holds out her arms. He bends down and kisses
her cheek while she hugs him around the waist. Still that strong scent
of that German numbered cologne she always wore. He wondered on
the subway if he should bring the shit incident up. If it did happen to
him or has he been imagining it all this time? If he has been imagining
it, that'd say something about something he didn't know about himself before. But he'd never bring it up. It would embarrass her,
his mother, ultimately him. Or immediately him, seconds after he
asked it.

"You didn't bring the little one," Frieda says. "Or your wife. I
never met them and was hoping."

"I'm sorry, I didn't even think of it. Maybe no time to. When my mother called you were coming, I just ran right down."

His mother asks if he wants coffee. "Black, I remember, right?" Frieda says.

"Always black," his mother says.

Frieda talks about her life. He asked. "As I told Mrs. T., we're still living in the same small house in Ridgewood and we'll probably die there. That's Ridgewood Brooklyn, you know, not Queens. There, just over the line, it's always been very different. But our area's been much improved. Young people are living in. Excuse me, moving. Many good whites, blacks, Spanish—hard-working people, with families, and honest. You'd like this: some artists, even. For years we couldn't go out on the streets after six. Even during the days it was dangerous sometimes. We needed escorts—you had to pay for them; they simply didn't volunteer—just to go shopping." The same high reedy voice, trace of a German accent. Must be a more accurate way—a better way—to describe the distinctiveness of it, but will do for now. "Martin is as well as can be expected for someone his age." He asked. "He still does all the baking at home. Breads, rolls, pies, cakes—he does one from the first two and one from the second two every other day. I don't understand how we stay so thin, and he still only uses real butter, a hundred percent. The baking company gave him a good pension, and with the Social Security we both get—Dr. T. helped set it up for me. I really wasn't eligible to be paying for it at the time, but oh my God, could he finagle. For good reasons mostly, I'm saying, for he knew we'd need it later. So, we live all right and have no complaints other than those every old person has. But Mrs. T. looks wonderful, thank God," and she knocks twice on the table. "Such a tough life, but she never changes, never ages. She'll always be a beautiful bathing beauty and a showgirl, which she only stopped being, you know, a few years before I came to work for her. She's amazing," and squeezes his mother's hand. "The parties you gave then—I still see them in my head."

"That's what I just told you about yourself," his mother says. "Look at her. Everything's the same. She doesn't age."

"No no no no." She closes her eyes modestly. Those stove hoods for eyelids. Not stove hoods but something like them. Roll tops of rolltop desks. Her sister is very sick. He asked. "She lives with us now. She has since Fritz died. I don't want to say this, but it's possible she won't live out the year. Age is awful, awful, when it gets like that."

"Awful," his mother says. "No matter how good you feel one day; at our age, the next you could snap, go."

Her nephew married and moved to Atlanta and bought a house. He asked. "They want to have children. Buy a house after you have a child, Martin and I told them, but they wanted one first. He's an air controller, went to a special school for it. Six to six for months. We loaned him five thousand dollars of our savings for the house. After all, he's our only nephew and we love him, and his wife is like our only niece. So he's like our only son in many ways. You were like one of my children when I worked here. I can still see you pulling your wagon down the street. Red, do you remember?"

"I do if he doesn't. It said Fire Chief on the sides."

"I don't remember that," Frieda says, "but it probably did, since it was that color red. A very fine wagon—very sturdily made—and with a long metal handle he pulled. You were so small you couldn't even carry it up to the sidewalk."

"It was even almost too heavy for me," his mother says. "We got it from our friends the Kashas. It was their son Carl's."

"They were so old then they must be both dead now."

"He did about fifteen years ago. Bea—Mrs. Kasha—moved to Arizona and I never heard from her again."

"Too bad. Nice people. But I'd do most of the carrying up the steps for his wagon. The neighborhood was very safe then so we'd— your mother and I—let you go by yourself to the stores you could get to without crossing the street. Think of anyone letting their child do that today. He wasn't even four."

"He was so beautiful that today he'd be kidnapped the first time."

"You'd have a note in your hand. It would say this, when he went to Grossinger's, which is where he wanted to go most: 'Three sugar doughnuts, three jelly doughnuts,' and perhaps some Vienna or their special onion rolls and a challah or seeded rye. You had a charge there, didn't you?"

"At all the stores on Columbus. Gristede Brothers, Hazelkorn's kosher butcher. Al and Phil's greengrocers. Sam's hardware and so on. But sometimes we gave him money to buy. Shopkeepers were honest to a fault then, and when he did carry money I think the note always said to take the bills out of his pocket and put the change back in."

"It would have had to. So you'd go around the corner with your wagon and park it outside the store. Then you'd go inside and give the note to the saleslady, who was usually Mrs. Grossinger—"

"She passed away I think it was two years ago. She had a bad heart for years but never stopped going in every day."

"Oh, that's too bad; a very nice lady. I hope the store was kept up. There aren't any good home bakeries where we are."

"Her son runs it and even opened a branch store farther up Columbus."

"Good for him. So Mrs. Grossinger or the saleslady would give you whatever was on the note and you'd put the bags in your wagon one by one and start home. But sometimes I got so worried for you, or your mother did where she'd send me after you, that I'd follow you all the way there and back—maybe he was around five when he did this, what do you say?"

"I'd think at least five," his mother says.

"But this was how I was able to see all this. Not worried you'd be kidnapped. Just that you might cross the street. You never did. He was a very obedient boy, Howard. But once I found you sitting on the curb—you must have done this a few times because more than a few times a doughnut or roll was missing from a bag—eating one. Then he'd come home. I used to watch you from the street. You know, sneak up from behind car to car so you wouldn't see me following you. If someone saw me doing this with a boy today they'd think I was trying to kidnap him and I'd be arrested, no questions asked. But everyone around then knew I was your nanny. Then you'd leave your wagon out front and go into the building and apartment—the doors were always unlocked during the day—and ask me or one of your brothers or your mother to help you bring the wagon downstairs."

"What a memory you have."

"I don't remember most of that," he says. "Going into Grossinger's for sugar and jelly doughnuts I do, but no note or wagon. Sitting on the curb eating a roll or doughnut I've no mental picture of, I think, other than for what other people's accounts of it have put into my head."

"Believe me," Frieda says. "If you did it once, shopping with your wagon, you did it a dozen times. And when you got home, first thing you always asked for was one of those doughnuts or rolls or the end slice of the rye bread if it was rye. With no butter on it—no spread. Just the bread plain."

"I remember liking the end slice then. The tiny piece—no bigger than my thumb—but which was usually left in the bakery's bread slicer. In fact, I still have to fight my wife for it. At least for the heel of the bread, since it seems all the bread we get comes unsliced."

"How is Denise?"

"Fine."

"She's wonderful," his mother says. "As dear to me as any of my children, that's the way I look at her, terrible as that might be to say."

"It isn't. I'm sure Howard loves to hear it. And your daughter?" she says to him. "Olivia? You really should have brought her."

"Next time, I swear."

His mother asks Frieda about her trip to Germany this summer, her first time back there in about forty-five years. Then she starts talking about the European trip she took with his father more than twenty years ago and especially the overnight boat ride their tour took down the Rhine. It was in this room. His father walked in from there, he ran up to him from there, arms out. From where he's sitting—different table and chairs but same place, the small kitchen alcove—he sees it happening in front of him as if onstage. Two actors, playing father and son. "Frieda" must still be offstage or never gets on. He's in the first row, looking up at them, but very close. Or sitting level with them, three to four feet away, for it's theater-in-the-round. The two actors come from opposite directions—the father from stage left it that's the direction for Howard's left, the son from stage right. They stop, the father first, about two feet from each other. He points, with his arms still out, to his face. The young actor playing him does. He's asking for help, with his pointing and expression. He wants to be picked up or grabbed. The shit doesn't smell because it's makeup. The young actor gives the impression he just tasted a little of it. But he's not going to throw up. Howard didn't then, far as he can remember, and that's not what the young actor's face says, though he does look as if he's just gagged. The father bursts out laughing. He's wearing the same clothes his father wore that day. Dark suit, white shirt, tie. Howard doesn't recognize the son's clothes. The father continues to laugh but now seems somewhat repelled by him. Scene goes blank. Curtain comes down. He's left looking at the curtain. Or if it is theater-in-the-round, which it resembles more: blackout, and when the houselights come on thirty seconds later, the actors have left the stage. "Frieda," he says.

"Excuse me," she says to his mother. "Yes?"

"I'm sorry, I didn't mean to break in like that, but there's something I've often wanted to ask you about from the time when I was around five."

"You wanted to ask me it since you were five?"

"No, I mean, what I want to ask you about happened, or I think it did, when I was around five."

"Howard," his mother says, as if saying, since they had talked about it a few times, not to ask it.

"What is it?" Frieda says. To his mother: "What's the big mystery?"

"No mystery," Howard says. "Just that your memory's so good—phenomenal, really—that I wondered if you could remember it for me from that time."

"Why don't we keep it for lunch," his mother says. "I want you to join us. Frieda already told me she wants you to come too. Have anything you want."

"Let me just finish this, Mom. I don't think, if I'm gauging her right, she wants me to ask this, Frieda. Thinks it might offend you. Believe me, that's not my purpose. Whatever happened so long ago is over and past, period. We all—anyway, if it did happen, you were probably doing something—I know you were—that you thought right or necessary. Or just required for what you were hired for, or something. I'm not getting this out right—and I meant by that nothing disparaging about you, Mom—but just know I'm not asking this with any harm in mind whatsoever. None."

"What could it be? The mystery gets bigger and bigger. That I slapped you a few times? I'm sorry for that. I never wanted to. But sometimes, sweet and darling as you were, and beautiful—he was such a beautiful child, everyone thought so—you got out of control, like all children can. Out of my control."

"That's true. They could be something."

"I had three very wild boys to take care of sometimes, so sometimes I had to act like that. Rough. Mean. Slap one or the other. I always tried for the hands or backside first—to get control or they'd run over me. I had a lot of responsibility taking care of you all. Your mother understood that."

"I did. I wouldn't have accepted outright slaughter, but certainly corporal punishment is needed sometimes. You must do it with Olivia from time to time, spank her," she says to him. "Later, against your better judgment, you might even slap her face a couple of times. You'll see. Children can get to you."

"I don't know. If I did, I'd have Denise to deal with."

"She too. Calm as she is, and reasonable, she'd—"

"No, never. Not her, take it from me."

"But with Howard," Frieda says, "I just hope you'll have forgiven me by now. But if it had to be done sometimes, it had to be done."

"Of course. I'm not saying. But I was talking of once when you—at least my second-rate memory tells me this—when you pulled my hair and a big chunk came out. Did it? Where I walked around with a big bald spot for about a month?"

"I don't remember that."

"Neither do I," his mother says.

"To be honest, I do remember once putting filth in Alex's face. He was in the bath. He made in it. Number two. I felt I had to teach him somehow not to. I don't like it now. But that was about the worst I ever did, I think. In ways I don't like most of it now, but then I was so much younger, a new foreigner here—well, you know. Also, since your parents didn't object, and I always told them later what I did, I felt I had their approval. Am I wrong, Mrs. T.?"

"You had it. I'm not going to deny it now. Not for putting filth in their faces—this is the first I can remember hearing of that—but as Howard said, it's past, finished. But no matter what happened, all my boys couldn't have turned out better."

"Did anything like that ever happen in my face?" he asks Frieda. "In the bathtub? Anyplace?"

"No, you? You were toilet-trained earlier than the others, so it never got necessary. A year earlier than either of them. By the age of eighteen months, if I'm not wrong. Two years at the most, and that's for both things. You probably had the advantage of seeing them go to the potty on their own, and maybe even scolded or punished for doing it in their pants. So you followed them, did what they did or were supposed to—going to the toilet."

"That's the way it usually is," his mother says.

"He was ahead of the other two in many ways like that. Reading. Writing. Manners at the table. It could be just the reverse with the youngest, but wasn't with him. Dressing himself. Almost everything. Remember how you let him eat at the adult table, rather than here in the kitchen with me, two years before you let the other two?"

"Maybe because he was the last, and to give you a break from it finally, we let him join our table."

"No, I remember. Because he ate. Because he didn't drop things on the floor or talk loudly and interrupt at the table. He was a dream child. Active and a bit of a rascal at times, yes, but that's not so bad if it's not too often. But sweet, good-natured, helpful most times—a real young gentleman with a much older head than his age. If I had had children, boys or girls, I would have wanted them to be the way you were more than like your brothers. They were good, but you were almost perfect to bring up. You listened and watched. And what I did to Alex in the tub was the only time I think I ever did anything like that. I can't really remember it happening another time, before or after."

"I don't remember being toilet-trained so early. Well, of course I wouldn't, but it's interesting to know."

"He *was* a dream child," his mother says. "You never said it before, but I always knew you had a special place for Howard over the others."

"I did, but not by much, you understand. They were all wonderful. I felt very lucky with the family I ended up in. But maybe Howard was just a little more wonderful. A little." She smiles at him, reaches out to touch his cheek and then kisses it. He hugs her.

On the subway ride home he tries to remember the incident again. First of all, it happened. He knows it did or is almost a hundred percent sure. He runs to his father. First he walks bowlegged to Frieda, points to his crotch. She knows what it is, takes his hand and pulls him into the bathroom. She takes down his pants. His shoes—she takes them off, socks with them. Then she takes off the underpants carefully so the shit stays in them. She says "This will teach you never to do it in your pants again." That's new, but he thinks he just imagined she said it. Her face is angry. It was probably a thick shit, not messy. She puts it into his face. He cries—screams—and she picks him up and holds him in front of the mirror. He sees his face with the shit on most of it. Just then he hears his father. "Hello, anyone around?" Something like that. He squirms to get down, is let down, runs to him. She says "Go on, show him, and don't forget to tell him what you did." That's also new, but he really seems to remember it. His father's coming into the kitchen from the living room. Is in the kitchen, he is too. His arms are out. His father looks at him and bursts out laughing. He continues to look at him and laugh very hard.

Frog
Dances

—

He's passing a building in his neighborhood, looks into an apartment window on the second floor and sees a man around his age with a baby in his arms moving around the living room as if dancing to very beautiful music—a slow tragic movement from a Mahler symphony, for instance. The man seems so enraptured that Howard walks on, afraid if the man sees him looking at him his mood will be broken. He might feel self-conscious, embarrassed, leave the room or go over to the window with the baby to lower the shade or maybe even to stare back at Howard. Howard knows it can't always be like this between the man and his baby. That at times the man must slap the wall or curse out loud or something because the baby's screaming is keeping him from sleep or some work he has to do or wants to get done—but *still*. The man looked as happy as any man doing anything with anyone or alone. He wants to see it again. He goes back, looks around to see that nobody's watching him, and looks into the window. The man's dancing, eyes closed now, cheeks against the baby's head, arms wrapped around the baby. He kisses the baby's eyes and head as he sort of slides across the room. Howard thinks, I must have a child. I've got to get married. At my age—even if I have the baby in a year—some people will still think I'm its grandfather. But I want to go through what this man's experiencing, dance with my baby like that. Kiss its head, smell its hair and skin—everything.

And when the baby's asleep, dance with my wife or just hold her and kiss her something like that too. Someone to get up close to in bed every night for just about the rest of my life and to talk about the baby, and when it and perhaps its brother or sister are older, when they were babies, and every other thing. So: settled. He'll start on it tomorrow or the day after. He looks up at the window. Man's gone. "T'ank you, sir, t'ank you," and walks to the laundromat he was going to, to pick up his dried wash.

Next day he calls the three friends he thinks he can call about this. "Listen, maybe I've made a request something like this before, but this time I not only want to meet a woman and fall in love but I want to get married to her and have a child or two. So, do you know—and if you don't, please keep your ears and eyes open—someone you think very suitable for me and of course me for her too? I mean it. I had an experience last night—seeing a man holding what seemed like a one- to three-month-old baby very close and dancing around with it as if he were in dreamland—and I felt I've been missing out, and in a few years will have completely missed out, on something very important, necessary—you name it—in my life."

A friend calls back a few days later with the name of a woman she knows at work who's also looking to find a mate, fall in love and marry. "She's not about to jump into anything, you know. She's too sensible for that and already did it once with disastrous results, but fortunately no children. Her situation is similar to yours. She's thirty-four and she doesn't want to wait much longer to start a family, which she wants very much. She's extremely bright, attractive, has a good job, makes a lot of money but is willing to give it up or just go free-lance for a few years while she has her children. Besides that, she's a wonderful dear person. I think you two can hit it off. I told her about you and she'd like to meet you for coffee. Here's her office and home numbers."

He calls her and she says "Howard *who*?" "Howard Tetch. Freddy Gunn was supposed to have told you about me." "No, she didn't mention you that I can remember. Wait a second. Are you the fellow who saw a man dancing on the street with his baby and decided that you wanted to be that man?" "I didn't think she'd tell you that part, but yes, I am. It was through an apartment window I saw him. I was just walking. Anyway, I'm not much—I'm sure you're not also—for meeting someone blind like this, but Freddy seemed to think we've a lot in common and could have a good conversation. Would you care to meet for coffee one afternoon or night?" "Let's see, Howard. This week I'm tied up both at work and, in the few available nonwork hours, in my social life. It just happens to be one of those rare weeks—I'm not putting you on. Or putting you off, is more like it. Would you mind calling me again next week—in the middle, let's say?" "No, sure, I'll call."

He calls the next week and she says "Howard Tetch?" "Yes, I called you last week. Freddy Gunn's friend. You said—" "Oh, right, Howard. It's awful of me—please, I apologize. I don't know how I could have forgotten your name a second time. Believe me, it's the work. Sixty hours, seventy. How are you?" "Fine," he says, "and I was wondering if there was some time this week, or even on the weekend, we could—" "I really couldn't this week or the weekend. What I was doing last week extended into this one, and maybe even worse. Not the socializing, but those sixty-seventy-hours-a-week work. I'm not stringing you along, honestly. But I do have this profession that's very demanding sometimes—" "What is it you do?" "Whatever I do—and I wish I had the time to tell you, but I haven't. We'll talk it over when we meet. So you'll call me? I can easily understand why you wouldn't." "No, sure, next week then. I'll call."

He doesn't call back. A week later another friend calls and says he's giving a dinner party Saturday and "two very lovely and intelligent young women, both single, will be coming and I want you to meet them. Who can say? You might get interested in them both. Then you'll have a problem you wish never started by phoning around for possible brides and mothers for your future kids, right?" "Oh, I don't know," Howard says, "but sounds pretty good so far."

He goes to the party. One of these two women is physically beautiful, all right, but unattractive. Something about the way she's dressed—she's overdressed—and her perfume, makeup, self-important air or something, and she talks too much and too loudly. She also smokes—a lot—and every so often blows smoke on the person she's talking to, and both times she left her extinguished cigarette smoldering. He just knows—so he doesn't even approach her—he could never start seeing or not for too long a woman who smokes so much and so carelessly. The other woman—seems to be her friend—is pretty, has a nice figure, more simply dressed, no makeup or none he can make out, doesn't smoke or isn't smoking here, talks intelligently and has a pleasant voice. He introduces himself, they talk about different things, she tells him she recently got divorced and he says "I'm sorry, that can be very rough." "Just the opposite. We settled it quickly and friendly and since the day I left him I've never felt so free in my life. I love going out, or staying in when I want to, and partying late, meeting lots of people, but being unattached." She has a six-year-old son who lives with his father. "One child, that's all I ever wanted, and now I think even one was too many for me, much as I love him. Since his father wanted to take him, I thought why not? I see him every other weekend, or every weekend if that's what he wants, but he so far hasn't, and get him for a month in the summer. Lots of people disapprove, but they're not me. Many of them are hypocrites, for they're the same ones who feel so strongly that the husband—so why not the ex-husband who's the father of your child?—should take a much larger if not an equal role in the partnership. Well, it's still a partnership where our son's concerned, or at least till he's eighteen or twenty-one, isn't it? Do you disapprove too?" He says "No, if it works for you all and it's what you want and no one's hurt. Sure. Of course, there's got to be some sadness or remorse in a divorce where there's a child involved," and she says "Wrong again, with us. Having two parents was just too confusing for Riner. He thinks it's great having only one at a time to answer to, and another to fall back on just in case."

He takes her phone number, calls, they have dinner, he sees her to her apartment house after, shakes her hand in the lobby and says he'll call again if she doesn't mind, "for it was a nice evening: lively conversation, some laughs, many of them, in fact, and we seem to have several similar interests," and she says "So come on up. Even stay if you want; you don't seem like a masher." They go to bed and in the morning over coffee she says "I want to tell you something. I like you but don't want you getting any ideas about my being your one-and-only from now on. You should know from the start that I'm seeing several men, sleeping with three of them—they're all clean and straight, so don't worry. And you can be number four if you want, but I'm not for a long time getting seriously connected to anyone. You don't like the arrangement—no problem: here's my cheek to kiss and there's the door." He says he doesn't mind the arrangement for now, kisses her lips just before he leaves, but doesn't call again.

He sees a woman on a movie line waiting to go in. He's alone and she seems to be too. She's reading quite quickly a novel he liked a lot and never looks up from it at the people in front and behind her, at least while he's looking at her. Attractive, intelligent looking, he likes the casual way she's dressed, way her hair is, everything. He intentionally finds a seat two rows behind hers, watches her a lot and she never speaks to the person on either side of her. On the way out he does something he hasn't done in about twenty years. He gets alongside her and says "Pardon me, miss, but did you like the movie?" She smiles and says "It was a big disappointment, and you?" "Didn't care for it much either. Listen, this is difficult to do—introducing myself to a woman I've never met—like this, I mean, and something I haven't done in God knows how many years. But would you—my name is Howard Tetch—like to have a cup of coffee someplace or a beer and talk about the movie? That book too—I read it and saw you reading. If you don't, then please, I'm sorry for stopping you—I already think you're going to say no, and why shouldn't you?" "No, let's have coffee, but for me, tea." "Tea, yes, much healthier for you—that's what I'll have too."

They have tea, talk—the book, movie, difficulties of introducing yourself to strangers you want to meet, something she's wanted to do with a number of men—"I can admit it"—but never had the courage for it. He sees her to a taxi, next day calls her at work, they meet for tea, meet again for lunch, another time for a movie, go to bed, soon he's at her place more than his own. She's thirty-three and also wants to get married and have a child, probably two. "With the right person, of course. That'll take, once I meet him, about six months to find out. Then once it's decided, I'd like to get married no more than a month after that, or at least begin trying to conceive." The more time he spends at her place, the bossier and pettier she gets with him. She doesn't like him hanging the underpants he washes on the shower curtain rod. He says "What about if I hang them on a hanger over the tub?" but she doesn't like that either. "It looks shabby, like something in a squalid boardinghouse. Put them in the dryer with the rest of our clothes." "The elastic waistband stretches. So does the crotch part to where after a few dryer dryings you can see my balls. That's why I hand-wash them and hang them up like that." Problem's never resolved. He wrings his underpants out and hangs them on a hanger, with a few newspaper sheets underneath, in the foot of closet space she's set aside for his clothes. A couple of times when he does this she says the drops from the hanging underpants might go through the paper and ruin the closet floor. He puts more newspapers down and that seems to assuage her. She thinks he should shave before he gets into bed, not when he rises. He says "But I've always shaved, maybe since I started shaving my entire face, in the morning. That's what I do." "Well try changing your habits a little. You're scratchy. It hurts our lovemaking. My skin's fair, much smoother than yours, and your face against it at night is an irritant." "An irritant?" "It irritates my face, all right?" "Then we'll make love in the morning after I shave." "We can do that too," she says, "but like most couples, most of our lovemaking is at night. Also, while I'm on the subject, I wish you wouldn't get back into bed after you exercise in the morning. Your armpits smell. You sweat up the bed. If you don't want to shower after, wash your arms down with a wet washrag. Your back and chest too." "I only exercise those early times in the morning when I can't sleep anymore, or am having trouble sleeping. So I feel, long as I'm up, I should either read or do something I'm going to do later in the day anyway, like exercising. But from now on I'll do as you say with the washrag whenever I do exercise very early and then, maybe because the exercising's relaxed or tired me, get back into bed." She also thinks he hogs too much of the covers; he should try keeping his legs straight in front of him in bed rather than lying them diagonally across her side; he could perhaps shampoo more often—"Your hair gets to the sticky level sometimes." And is that old thin belt really right for when he dresses up? "If anything, maybe you can redye it." And does he have to wear jeans with a hole in the knee, even if it is only to go to the corner store? "What about you?" he finally says. "You read the *Times* in bed before we make love at night or just go to sleep, and then don't wash the newsprint off your hands. That gets on me. Probably also gets on the sheets and pillowcases, but of course only on your side of the bed, and your sheets and pillowcases, so why should I be griping, right? And your blouses. I'm not the only one who sweats. And after you have into one of yours—okay, you had a tough day at work and probably on the crowded subway to and from work and your body's reacted to it—that's natural. But you hang these blouses back up in the closet. On your side, that's fine with me, and I'm not saying the smell gets on my clothes. But it isn't exactly a great experience to get hit with it when I go into the closet for something. Anyway, I'm just saying." They complain like this some more, begin to quarrel, have a couple of fights where they don't speak to each other for an hour, a day, and soon agree they're not right for each other anymore and should break up. When he's packing his things to take back to his apartment, she says "I'm obviously not ready to be with only one man as much as I thought. I'm certainly not ready for marriage yet. As to having a child—to perhaps have *two*? I should really get my head looked over to have thought of that." "Well, I'm still ready," he says, "though maybe all this time I've been mistaken there too."

He meets a woman at an opening at an art gallery. They both were invited by the artist. She says she's heard about him from the artist. "Nothing much. Just that you're not a madman, drunk, drug addict or letch like most of the men he knows." He says "Gary, for some odd reason I don't know why, never mentioned you. Maybe because he's seeing you. Is he?" "What are you talking about? He's gay." "Oh.

He's only my colleague at school, so I don't know him that well. I know he's divorced and has three kids, but that's about it. May I be stupidly frank or just stupid and say I hope you're not that way too? Wouldn't mean I'd want to stop talking to you." "I can appreciate why you're asking that now. No, as mates, men are what I like exclusively. I didn't come here to meet one, but I've been in a receptive frame of mind for the last few months if something happens along." They separate at the drink table, eye each other a lot the next fifteen minutes, she waves for him to come over. "I have to go," she says. "The friend I came with has had her fill of this, and she's staying with me tonight. If you want to talk some more, I can call you tomorrow. You in the book?" "Hell, here's my number and best times to reach me," and he writes all this out and gives it to her.

She calls, they meet for a walk, have dinner the next night, she takes his hand as they leave the restaurant, kisses him outside, initiates a much deeper kiss along the street, he says "Lookit, why don't we go to my apartment—it's only a few blocks from here?" She says "Let's give it more time. I've had a lot of rushing from men lately. I'm not boasting, and I started some of it myself. It's simply that I know going too fast, from either of us, is no good, so what do you say?" They see each other about three times a week for two weeks. At the end of that time he says he wants to stay at her place that night or have her to his, "but you know, for bed." She says "I still think it'd be rushing. Let's give the main number some more time?" Two weeks later he says "Listen, I've got to sleep with you. All this heavy petting is killing me. I've got to see you completely naked, be inside you—the works. We've given it plenty of time. We like each other very much. But I need to sleep with you to really be in love with you. That's how I am." She says "I don't know what's wrong. I like you in every way. I'm almost as frustrated as you are over it. But something in me says that having sex with you now still wouldn't be sensible. That we're not ready for it yet. That what we have, in the long run, would be much better—could even end up in whatever we want from it. Living together. More, if that's what we ultimately want—if we hold out on this a while longer. It's partly an experiment on my part, coming after all my past involvement failures, but also partly what I most deeply feel will work, and so feel you have to respect that. So let's give it a little more time then, please?" He says "No. Call me if you not only want to see me again but want us to have sex together. From now on it has to be both. Not all the time, of course. But at least the next time if there's nothing—you know—physically, like a bad cold, wrong with one of us. I hate making conditions—it can't help the relationship—

but feel I have to. If I saw you in one of our apartments alone again I think I'd tear your clothes off and jump on you no matter how hard and convincingly you said no. It's awful, but there it is." She says "Let me think about it. Either way, I'll call."

She calls the next week and says "I think we better stop seeing each other. Even if I don't believe you would, what you said about tearing off my clothes scared me." "That's not it," he says. "I don't know what it is, but that's not it. Okay. Goodbye."

He misses her, wants to call her, resume things on her terms, dials her number two nights in a row but both times hangs up after the first ring.

He's invited to give a lecture at a university out of town. His other duty that day is to read the manuscripts of ten students and see them in an office for fifteen minutes each to discuss their work. The man who invited him is a friend from years ago. He says "What'd you think of the papers I sent you? All pretty good, but one exceptional. Flora's, right? She thinks and writes like someone who picked up a couple of postdoctorates in three years and then went on to five years of serious journalism. Easy style, terrific insights, nothing left un-turned, everything right and tight, sees things her teachers don't and registers these ideas better than most of them. She intimidates half the department, I'm telling you. They'd rather not have her in their classes, except to look at her. That's because she's brilliant. I can actu-ally say that about two of my students in fourteen years and the other's now dean of a classy law school. But hear me, Howard. Keep your mitts off her. That doesn't mean mine are on her or want to be. Oh, she's a honey, all right, and I've fantasized about her for sure. But I don't want anyone I'm inviting for good money messing with her and possibly messing up her head and the teaching career I've planned for her. Let some pimpleface do the messing; she'll get over it sooner. I want her to get out of here with top grades and great GREs and without being screwed over and made crestfallen for the rest of the semester by some visiting horn. Any of the other girls you'll be conferencing you can have and all at once if they so desire." "Listen, they all have to be way too young for me and aren't what I've been interested in for a long time, so stop fretting."

He sees two students. Flora's next on the list. He opens the office door and says to some students sitting on the floor against the corri-dor wall "One of you Ms. Selenika?" She raises her hand, stands, was writing in a pad furiously, has glasses, gold ear studs, medium-length blond hair, quite frizzy, little backpack, clear frames, tall, rustically dressed, pens in both breast pockets, what seem like dancer's legs, posture, neck. "Come in." They shake hands, sit, he says "I guess we should get right to your paper. Of course, what else is there? I mean, I'm always interested in where students come from. Their native areas, countries, previous education, what they plan to do after graduation. You know, backgrounds and stuff; even what their parents do. That can be very interesting. One student's father was police commissioner of New York. Probably the best one we had there in years. Another's mother was Mildred Kraigman. A comedian, now she's a character actress. Won an Academy Award? Well, she was once well known and you still see her name around, often for good causes. But those are my students where I teach. When I've time to digress, which I haven't with every student here. You all probably don't mind the fifteen minutes with me, but that's all we've got. So, your paper. I don't know why I went into all of that, do you?" She shakes her head, holds back a giggle. "Funny, right? But you can see how it's possible for me to run on with my students. As for your paper, I've nothing but admiration for it. I'm not usually that reserved or so totally complimentary, but here, well—no corrections. Not even grammatical or punctuational ones. Even the dashes are typed right and everything's before or after the quote marks where it belongs. Honestly, nothing to nitpick, even. I just wish I had had your astuteness—facility—you know, to create such clear succinct premises and then to get right into it and with such writing and literary know-how and ease; had had your skills, intelligence and instincts when I was your age, I mean. Would have saved a lot of catching up later on. Sure, we could go on for an hour about what you proposed in this and how you supported what you claimed, and so on. Let me just say that when I come across a student like you I just say 'Hands off; you're doing great without me so continue doing what you are on your own. If I see mistakes or anything I can add or direct you to, to possibly improve your work, I'll let you know.' And with someone like you I also say, which isn't so typical for me, 'If you see something you want to suggest about my work, or correct: be my guest.' In other words, I can only give you encouragement and treat you as my thinking equal and say 'More, more.' But your paper's perfect for what it is, which is a lot, and enlightened me on the subject enormously. But a subject which, if I didn't know anything about it before, I'd be very grateful to you after I read it for opening me up to it. You made it interesting and intriguing. What better way, right? Enough, I've said too much, not that I think compliments would turn you."

He looks away. She says something but he doesn't catch it. Something like "I'm no different than anyone else." He actually feels his heart pounding, mouth's parched, fingers feel funny. Looks at her. She's looking at him so seriously, fist holding up her chin, trying to make him out? Thinks he's being too obvious? "I'm sorry, you said something just now?" he says. "Oh nothing. Silly. Commonplace. I also tend to mumble." "But what?" "That I can be turned too, that's all." Smiles, big beautiful bright teeth, cute nose. Button pinned to her jacket, children in flames, caption in Chinese or Japanese. Or Korean or Vietnamese. What does he know? And turned how? That an oblique invitation? He once read a novel where the literature teacher took his student on the office floor. She willingly participated. In fact, she might have come to his office to make love. It was their first time. The teacher was married. He always thought that scene exaggerated—the author usually exaggerated or got sloppy when he wrote about sex—but the feeling the narrator had is the same he has now. Her brains, looks, body, little knapsack. He'd love right now to hold her, kiss her, undress her right here—hell with his friend. Hell with the rest of the students. They'd do it quickly. She'd understand. Even if it was their first time. He doubts it'd take him two minutes. Another minute for them both to undress. He bets she likes that kind of spontaneity. "I have got to make love to you," he could whisper. "Let's do it right now." He'd lock the door if it has a lock from the inside—he looks. Hasn't and he doesn't have the key. Now this would be something: opening the door to push the lock-button with all those students in the hall waiting for him. Instead he could put a chair up against the doorknob. They'd be quiet; to save time, just take their pants and shoes off and make love on the floor. Carpet seems clean. He could put his coat down. He wonders what such a young strong body like that looks and feels like. He looks at her, tries to imagine her naked. She says "Thanks for reading my paper and everything, but now I must be wasting your time. It's a rigorous day for you: all those conferences and papers to read and your lecture later on." "You're not wasting it." She opens the door. "Oh, maybe you won't go for this, but another student and I—my housemate—would like to invite you to a student reading after dinner." "Listen, maybe I can even take you both to dinner before the reading." "You're eating at the club with Dr. Wiggens, aren't you?" "Right; that's a must. Sure, tell me where to be and when. I haven't been to a good student reading in years." "This might not be good." "Even more fun. I like to see what goes on at different campuses. And after it, you'll be my guests for food and beer." "If he wants to and we're up to it, fine."

She sits at the back of his room during the lecture, laughs at all the right lines, claps hard but doesn't come up after.

"So how'd everything go today?" Wiggens asks at dinner. "Great bunch of kids," Howard says. "Incredibly keen and bright. Wish I had some like them in my own classes." "None of the girls made a pass at you?" his wife says. "Nah, I let them know I don't come easy." Wiggens says "That's the best approach. Why get all messy in a day and possibly go home a father-to-be with a social disease?" "What nonsense," she says. "One-night stands with students is the safest sport in town." They drop him off at his hotel, he goes inside the lobby, waits till their car leaves the driveway and runs to the building of the reading. He's already pretty tight. He sleeps through most of the stories and poems and the three of them go to a pizza place later. The housemate downs a beer, puts on his coat and says to Flora "Maybe I'll see you home." "Why'd he think you might not be home?" Howard says. "He meant for himself. He has a lover who occasionally kicks him out before midnight." They finish off the pitcher, have two brandies each, he says "This is not what I'm sup-posed to be doing here according to Wiggens, so don't let on to him, but may I invite you back to my room?" She says "I'm really too high to drive myself home and you're too high to drive me, so I guess I'll stay the night if you don't mind. You have twin beds?" "Sure, for twins. —No, okay," when she shakes her head that his humor's bad, "anything you want." When she takes off her clothes in his room he says "My goodness, your breasts. I had no idea they were so large. Why'd I think that?" "It's the way I dress. I'm extremely self-conscious about them. They've been a nuisance in every possible way." "I love large breasts." "Please, no more about them or I'm going to bed in my clothes." They shut off the lights. He's almost too drunk to do anything. In the morning he doesn't know if they even did anything. He says he wants to stay another night. "At my expense, in this same or a different hotel if you can't or don't want to put me up in your house. Take you to lunch and dinner and even a movie and where we'll start all over and do the whole thing right. The heck with Wiggens and his proscriptions." She says "My vagina hurts from last night. You were too rough. I couldn't do it again for a day." "So we did something? I was afraid I just passed out." "To be honest," she says, "it was horrendous. Never again when I and the guy I'm with are that stoned." "It'll be better. I can actually stay for two more nights, get some work done in your school library simply to keep busy and out of your hair all day, and we'll both stay relatively sober throughout." "No, it isn't a good idea. Where's it going to land us?" "Why, that you're way out here and I'm in New York? I'll fly out once a month for a few days." "Once a month." "Twice a month then.

Every other week. And the entire spring break. Or you can fly to New York. I'll pay your fare each time. And in the summer, a long vacation together. Rent a house on some coast. A trip to Europe if that's what you want. I don't make that much, but I can come up with it." "Let's talk about it again after you get to New York, but you go this afternoon as scheduled."

He calls from New York and she says "No, everything's too split apart. Not only where we live but the age and cultural differences. You're as nice as they come—sweet, smart and silly—but what you want for us is unattainable." "Think about it some more." He calls again and she says he got her at a bad moment. He writes twice and she doesn't answer. He calls again and her housemate, after checking with her, says she doesn't want to come to the phone. Howard says "So that's it then. Tell her."

He's invited to a picnic in Riverside Park for about twelve people. He doesn't want to go but the friend who's arranged it says "Come on, get out of the house already, you're becoming a hopeless old recluse." He meets a woman at the picnic. They both brought potato salad. "It wasn't supposed to happen like this," he says. "I was told to bring the coleslaw. But I didn't want to make the trip to the store just to buy cabbage, had a whole bag of potatoes around, so I made this salad. Anyway, yours is much better. You can see by what people have done to our respective bowls." "They're virtually identical," Denise says. "Eggs, celery, sweet pickles, fresh dill, store-bought mayonnaise, maybe mustard in both of them, and our potatoes cooked to the same softness, but I used salt." She gives him her phone number and says she hopes he'll call. He says "I wouldn't have asked for it if I didn't intend to. Truly."

He was attracted to her at the picnic but after it he thinks she was too eager for him to call. Well, that could be good—that she wants him to call, is available—but there were some things about her looks he didn't especially like. More he thinks of them, less he likes them. Nice face, wasn't that. But she seemed wider in the hips, larger in the nose, than he likes. Were her teeth good? Something, but nothing he can remember seeing, tells him they weren't. She was friendly, intelligent, no airs, good sense of humor. But if she's wide in the hips now, she's going to get wider older she gets. And noses, he's heard, and can tell from his own, grow longer with age. Everything else though . . .

He doesn't call her that week. On the weekend he bumps into a friend on the street who's walking with a very pretty woman. She can't be his girlfriend. The friend's married, much in love with his wife. And he has two young sons he dotes on and he'd never do anything that could lead to his being separated from them, but then you never know. Howard and the woman are introduced, she has a nice voice, unusually beautiful skin, and the three of them talk for a while. Her smile to him when they shake hands goodbye seems to suggest she wouldn't mind him contacting her. He calls his friend the next day and says "This woman you were with—Francine. If she's not married or anything like that, what do you think of my calling her?" "Fine, if you like. She's a great person, stunning looking as you saw, cultured, unattached—what else? One hell of a capable lawyer." "Why didn't you tell me about her before?" "You mean you're still searching for that ideal lifemate? I thought you gave that up." "No, I'm still looking, though maybe not as hard as I did. Went out with several women—a couple you even met. Nearly moved in with one, but nothing materialized beyond that with any of them, which has sort of discouraged me a little. But if I haven't found someone marriageable after a year, that's okay too, right? I've still plenty of time." "Then call Francine. She's been divorced for two years, no children, and from what she's let on in certain unguarded moments, I think she's seriously shopping around for a new lifemate herself." "What do you mean 'unguarded'? Is she very secretive, uncommunicative, cool or distant—like that?" "Hardly. Just that some things about herself she keeps inside."

Howard calls her. They make a date to go out for beers. He feels she's not right for him the moment she opens her apartment door. Something overdone in the way she's dressed for just beers at a local place. Also her apartment, which is practically garish. The books on the shelves say she isn't much of a serious reader, and same with the music on the radio, records on the shelf, prints on the walls. During their walk to the bar and then in the bar he find she's interested in a lot of things he isn't: money matters, big-time professional advancement, exercise classes, gossip about famous people, the trendy new restaurants, art exhibitions, movies, shows. They walk back to her building. She asks if he'd like to come up for a drink or tea. "No thanks, I've still plenty of work to do for tomorrow, but thank you." "If you'd like to phone me again, please do." "No, really, I don't think it would work out, but thanks for suggesting it. It's been a nice evening." "Actually, I doubt it has been for you, nor in many ways for me either. We're a bit different, that's easy to see, but I thought after a few times together we'd find much in common. Something told me that. What do you think?" "I don't think so, honestly. It's all right to say that, isn't it?" "I suppose, but it's probably not something we should go too deeply into," and she goes inside. He's walking uptown to his apartment when he sees a pay phone. Call Denise, he thinks. It's been two weeks since he said he would. He'll give a good excuse if he feels from what she says that he ought to. That he's been so steeped in his work that he didn't want to call till now just to say he'd be calling again to go out with her once he's done with this work. Or that he simply lost track of time with all the work he's been doing and also some personal things that are now over. He puts the coin in, thinks no, don't start anything, she isn't right for him. Her looks. The teeth. Something. Plump. Not plump but wider in the hips and he thinks heavier in the thighs than he likes, and her nose. And so sweet. Almost too damn too—even meek. He doesn't like meek and overly sweet women either who let the man do most of the speaking and decision making and so on. That's not what he wants. He wants something else. So he won't call her. He continues walking, passes another pay phone. Why not call her? Because he's a little afraid to. Already his stomach's getting butterflies. What would he say? Well, he'd say "Hello, it's Howard Tetch, and I know it's a bit presumptuous thinking you'd agree to this at the spur of something or another, but . . ." "But" what? Have a drink first. He goes into a bar, has a martini. After he drinks it he feels relaxed. One more. Then he should go home and, if he still wants to, call her tomorrow. He has another. Two, he tells himself, is his limit. Three and he's had it, not good for anything but sleep. But he doesn't want to be on the street with three. When he gets off the stool he feels high. He feels sexy when he gets to the street. He wants to have sex with someone tonight. He hasn't had sex with anyone since Flora and that was around three months ago and what does he remember of it? Her large breasts, that's all, which was before they had sex. He thinks of the man in the window holding the baby. The baby must be a month or two past a year old. It was April, right after his mother's birthday, so it was almost twelve months ago. Today or some day this or last week might be the baby's first birthday. The man might still be dancing with it at night, but by now the baby's probably saying words. "Hi. Bye." The man might have slept with his wife 350 times since that night, made love with her about 150 times. That would be about the number of times Howard thinks he'd make love to his wife in that time. But there is that period, maybe a month or two after the birth, maybe longer for some women if it was a particularly difficult delivery—a cesarean, for instance—when you don't have sex, or not where the man penetrates her. So, 100, 125. The woman he ends up with will have to be receptive to sex. As much as he, in her own way, or almost. If more so, fine. And sometimes do it when he wants to and she doesn't especially. That isn't so bad. It isn't that difficult for a woman to sort of loan her body like that, turn over on her side with her back to him and let him do it without even any movement on her part, and he'll do as much for her if it comes to it. And if the baby was a month or two old when he saw it in the window, then the man and his wife might have just around that time started to make love again, and even, for the first time in months, that night. For all he knows, that might account for the loving way the man danced with his child. No. But call her. He goes through his wallet, thought the slip with her number on it was inside, can't find it, dials Information, dials the number he gets and she says hello. "Hello, it's Howard Tetch, from that picnic in the park, how are you?" and she says "I'm all right, and you?" "Fine, just fine. Thank you. Listen, I called—well, I wanted to long before this but something always came up—to suggest we get together tonight. But I now realize it's much too late to. I'm sorry. This is an awful way to call after two weeks, but tomorrow?" "Tomorrow?" "Yes, would it be possible for us to meet sometime tomorrow or any day soon as we can? Evening? Late afternoon for a cup of something?" "Excuse me, Howard. This certainly isn't what I wanted to speak about first thing after enjoying your company at the picnic, but am I wrong in assuming you've had a bit to drink tonight which is influencing your speech and perhaps what you have to say?" "No, you're right, I have, and right in saying it to me. I shouldn't have called like this. But I was somewhat anxious about calling you, and just in calling any woman for the first time I'm not that . . . I get nervous, that's all. It's always awkward for me, no matter how anxious I was in wanting to call you. So I thought I needed a drink to brace me, you can say, and had two, at a bar just now, but martinis. I'm calling from the street, by the way." "I can hear." "What I meant by that is I have a home phone but was on the street, saw a phone, wanted to call, so called. Anyway, two martinis never hit me like this before. Never drink three martinis and think you'll have your head also, I always say. What am I saying I always say it? I'm saying it now, but probably have thought of it before. But I also had a drink at my apartment before I went out, so it was accumulative. Wine, gin. I'm not a problem drinker though." "I didn't say or think you were." "Little here, there, but only rarely in intoxicating quantities. Just that I didn't want that to be the reason you might not want us to meet." "All right. Call tomorrow if you still want to. Around six. We'll take it from there, okay?" "Yes." "Good. Goodnight."

He calls, they meet, have coffee, take a long walk after, the conversation never lulls, lots of things in common, no forced talk, good give and take, mutual interests, laughs, they touch upon serious subjects. Her teeth are fine. Her whole body. Everything's fine. Profile, full face. Some bumps, bulges, but what was he going on so about her hips and nose and so on? Scaring himself away maybe. They're right, all part of her, fit in just fine. She's also very intelligent, not meek, weak, just very peaceful, thoughtful, subdued, seemingly content with her life for the most part. They take the same bus home, he gets off first and says he'll call her soon, she says "That'll be nice," waves to him from the bus as it passes. He doesn't call her the next week. First he thinks give it a day or two before you call; see what you think. Then: this could get serious and something tells him she's still not exactly right for him. She's a serious person and would never have anything to do with him in any other way and maybe playing around is what he really wants right now. She may even be too intelligent for him, needing someone with larger ideas, deeper thoughts, better or differently read, a cleverer quicker way about him, smooth-spoken; she'd tire of him quickly.

He calls a woman he used to go out with but was never serious about more than a year ago and she says "Hello, Howard, what is it?" "Oops, doesn't sound good. Maybe I called at a wrong time." "Simply that you called is a surprise. How is everything?" "Thank you. Everything's fine. I thought you might want to get together. Been a while. What are you doing now, for instance?" "You're horny." "No I'm not." "You only used to call when you were horny. Call me when you're feeling like a normal human being. When you want to have dinner out, talk over whatever there's to talk over, but not to go to bed. I'm seeing someone. Even if I weren't. I could never again be around for you only when you have your hot pants on." "Of course. I didn't know you thought I was doing that. But I understand, will do as you say." The phone talk makes him horny. He goes out to buy a magazine with photos of nude women in it. He buys the raunchiest magazine he can find just from the cover photo and what the cover says is inside, sticks it under his arm inside his jacket, dumps it in a trash can a block away. He really doesn't like those magazines. Also something about having them in his apartment, and why not do something different with the rutty feeling he's got. A whorehouse. He buys a weekly at another newsstand that has articles on sex, graphic photos of couples, and in the back a couple of pages where they rate whorehouses, singles bars, porno flicks, peepshows and sex shops in the city. He goes home to read it. There's one on East Fifty-fourth that sounds all right. "Knockout gals, free drink, private showers, classy & tip-top." He goes outside and waits at a bus stop for a bus to take him to West Fifty-seventh, where he'll catch the crosstown. He has enough cash on him even if they charge a little more than the fifty dollars the weekly said they did, plus another ten for a tip. He wants to do it that much. He gets off at Sixty-fifth—butterflies again—will walk the rest of the way while he thinks if what he's doing is so smart. The woman could have a disease. One can always get rid of it with drugs. But some last longer than that. You have to experiment with several drugs before one works. And suppose there's one that can't be cured with drugs or not for years? No, those places—the expensive ones—are clean. They have to be or they'd lose their clients. He keeps walking to the house. Stops at a bar for a martini just to get back the sex feeling he had, has two, heads for the house again feeling good. No, this is ridiculous. His whoring days are over. They have been for about ten years. He'd feel embarrassed walking in and out of one; just saying what he's there for to the person at the front desk, if that's what they have, and then making small talk or not talk with the women inside, if they just sit around waiting for the men to choose them—even looking at the other men in the room would be embarrassing—and then with the woman he chooses. "What do you like, Howard?" or whatever name he gives. Howard. Why not? No last one. "You want me to do this or that or both or maybe you want to try something different?" It just isn't right besides. He still wants very much to have sex tonight—with a stranger, even—but not to pay for it. A singles bar? What are the chances? For him, nil, or near to it. He doesn't feel he has it in him anymore to approach women there or really anywhere. To even walk into one and find a free place at the bar would be difficult for him. Maybe Denise would see him this late. Try. If she doesn't want him up, she'll say so quickly enough. Or just say to her "You think it's too late to meet for a beer?" If she says something like "It's too late for me to go outside, why don't you come here," then he'll know she wants to have sex with him. She wouldn't have him up this late for any other reason. And if he comes up at this hour, she'll know what he's coming up for. If she can meet at a bar, then fine, he'll start his approach from there. Suppose she gets angry at him for calling so late and being so obvious in what he wants of her, especially after he said a week ago he'd call her soon? Then that's it with her then, since he doesn't feel there'll be anything very deep between them, so what he's really after is just sex. But don't call from a pay phone on the street. She may think he always walks the streets at night and get turned off by that.

He goes into a bar, buys a beer, tells himself to speak slowly and conscientiously and watch out for slurs and repeats, dials her number from a pay phone there. She says "Hello," doesn't seem tired, he says "It's Howard, how are you, I hope I'm not calling too late." "It's not that it's too late for me to receive a call, Howard, just that of the three to four calls from you so far, most have come this late. Makes me think . . . what? That your calls are mostly last-minute thoughts, emanating from some form of desperation perhaps. It doesn't make me feel good." "But they're not. And I'm sorry. I get impulsive sometimes. Not this time. You were on my mind—have been for days—and I thought about calling you tonight, then thought if it was getting too late to call you, but probably thought about it too long. Then, a little while before, thought 'Hell, call her, and I'll explain.' So some impulsiveness there after all." "All right. We have that down. So?" "So?" "So, you know, what is the reason you called?" "I wanted to know if you might like to meet at the Breakers for a drink, or maybe it's too late tonight for that too." "It probably is. Let me check the time. I don't have to. I know already. Way too late. If you want, why not come here." "That's what I'd like much better, really. You mean now, don't you?" "Not two hours from now, if you can help it." "Right. Is there anything I can pick up for you before I get there?" "Like what?" "Wine, beer? Anything you need? Milk?" "Just come, but without stopping for a drink along the way." "I already have. But so you won't get the wrong idea, it was because my phone wasn't working at home. Just tonight, which was a big surprise when I finally picked up the receiver to call you. So I went out to call from a public phone. But I didn't want to call from the street. Too noisy, and I also didn't want to give you the wrong idea that I'm always calling from the street. So I went into this bar I'm in to call but felt I should buy a beer from them first, even if I didn't drink it—though I did—part of it—rather than coming in only to use their phone. That's the way I am. I put all kinds of things in front of me." "Does seem so. Anyway, here's my address," and gives it and what street to get off if he takes the bus. "If you take the Broadway subway, get off at a Hundred-sixteenth and ride the front of the train, but not the first car, so you'll be right by the stairs. The subways, or at least that station at this hour, can be dangerous, so maybe to be safer you should take the bus or a cab." "A cab. That's what I'll do." "Good. See you."

He subways to her station, runs to her building. If she asks, he'll say he took a cab. They say hello, he takes off his jacket, she holds out her hand for it, probably to put it in what must be the coat closet right there. He hands it to her and says "I took the subway, by the way. Should have taken a cab, but I guess I'm still a little tight with money, I'm saying, from when I wasn't making much for years. I don't know why I mentioned that. It was a fast ride though—good connections—and I'm still panting somewhat from running down the hill to your building," has moved closer to her, she says "I didn't notice—you ran down the hill here?" he bends his head down, she raises hers and they kiss. They kiss again and when they separate she says "Your jacket—excuse me. It's on the floor." "Don't bother with it." "Don't be silly—it's a jacket," and picks it up, brushes it off and hangs it in the closet. He comes behind her while she's separating some of the coats, jackets and garment bags hanging in the closet, turns her around by her shoulders and they kiss. She says "Like a nightcap of some sort—seltzer?" "Really, nothing, thank you." "Then I don't know, I'm enjoying this but we should at least get out of this cramped utilitarian area. The next room. Or maybe, if we want, we should just go to bed." "Sure, if it's all right with you." "I'll have to wash up first." "Same here." "And I wouldn't mind, so long as you'd come with me, walking my dog." "You've a dog?" "It'll be quick, and I won't have to do it early in the morning."

They walk the dog, make love. They see each other almost every day for the next few weeks. Museums, movies, an opera, eat out or she cooks for them in her apartment or he cooks for them in his, a party given by friends of hers. They're walking around the food table there putting food on their plates when he says "I love you, you know that, right?" and she says "Me too, to you." "You do? Great." That night he dreams he's being carried high up in the sky by several party balloons, says "Good Christ, before this was fun, but now they better hold," wakes up, feels for her, holds her thigh and says to himself "This is it, I don't want to lose her, she's the best yet, or ever. Incredible that it really happened. Well, it could still go bust." He takes her to meet his mother, has dinner at her parents' apartment. He sublets his apartment, moves in with her. He can't get used to the dog. Walking it, cleaning up after it, its smells, hair on the couch and his clothes, the sudden loud barks which startle him, the dog licking his own erection, and tells her that as much as he knows she loves the dog, the city's really no place for it. She says "Bobby came with me and with me he stays. Sweetheart, think of it as a package deal and that Bobby's already pretty old." When his lease expires he gives up his apartment to the couple he sublet it to. He begins insisting to Denise that Bobby's long hair makes him sneeze and gives him shortness of breath, which is keeping him up lots of nights, and that the apartment's much too crowded with him. "If we ever have the baby we've talked about maybe having, it would mean getting an apartment with another bedroom at twice the rent we pay now, which we couldn't afford, or disposing of the dog somehow and staying with the baby here." She gives Bobby to a friend in the country. "If one day we do get a larger apartment," she says, "and Bobby's still alive, then I don't care how sick and feeble he might be then, he returns. Agreed?" "Agreed."

They marry a few months after that and a few months later she's pregnant. They planned it that way and it worked. They wanted to conceive the baby in February so they could spend most of the summer in Maine and have the baby in October, a mild month and where he'd be settled into the fall semester. He goes into the delivery room with her, does a lot of things he learned in the birth classes they took over the summer, to help her get through the more painful labor contractions. When their daughter's about a month old he starts dancing with her at night just as that man did three years ago. He has two Mahler symphonies on record, buys three more and dances to the slow movements and to the last half of the second side of a recording of Sibelius's Fifth Symphony. Denise loves to see him dancing like this. Twice she's said "May I cut in?" and they held the baby and each other and danced around the living room. Dancing with the baby against his chest, he soon found out, also helps get rid of her gas and puts her to sleep. He usually keeps a light on while he dances so he won't bump into things and possibly trip. Sometimes he closes his eyes—in the middle of the room—and dances almost in place while he kisses the baby's neck, hair, even where there's cradle cap, back, ears, face. Their apartment's on the third floor and looks out on other apartments in a building across the backyard. He doesn't think it would stop him dancing if he saw someone looking at him through one of those windows. He doesn't even think he'd lower the blinds. Those apartments are too far away—a hundred feet or more—to make him self-conscious about his dancing. If his apartment were on the first or second floor and fronted on the sidewalk, he'd lower the living room blinds at night. He'd do it even if he didn't have a baby or wasn't dancing with it. He just doesn't like people looking in at night from the street.

Frog

Made

Free

—◆

He suddenly seems to have lost all his marbles. Doesn't know where he is. Dark, feels movement, sounds of movement, so feels he's going someplace. A car, but no seat, just a rough wood floor he's on, so it isn't. Bed of a truck, totally enclosed, shaking back and forth, moving slowly, but not the sounds of one, outside or underneath. A train, bouncing like one. Sounding like it. How could it be? Not a real train. Sure, one with something pulling it and on tracks, but what's he, some bum tramping it in a boxcar? Smells like it, old hay, animal dung. He's sitting on a floor, still a rough wood floor, thick liquid on it where one of his hands touches, back up against someone's back, feet squashed against something like a crate or wall. Where's his family? He's no bum. Has a home, car, job, all small but as much as most, wife and kids he lives with, mother in a nearby city whom he helps support. They were with him just before, had to give away the dog, hours, a day, before he woke up. That's it: was asleep. "Denise? Denise?"

"Shh, go back to your snoring," man whose back he's against says. "It wasn't as loud."

"What's going on? What is it with this train?"

"And I'm going to tell you? Don't worry, it'll all turn out bad. Ha-ha, that's a good one. Sorry, go to sleep. Don't be afraid to, the ride's for a couple more days at least. Believe me, we're all here who were here, even the ones who aren't dead yet. Sorry again. I can't help

myself. I don't know what I'm saying. I don't even know if I said anything. Did I?"

"Shh, you too," someone says. "You're making more noise than
him now."

"Denise?" Howard yells.

"What's with this guy?" someone else says. "Hey, pipe down."

"We're over here," she says. "Directly across the car from you.
The girls are all right, sleeping now. People were kind enough to let
us move near the pail so the girls could relieve themselves right into
it. You were sleeping. You wouldn't budge. Rest, dear. Take care of
yourself. In the morning, come over."

He gets up. "Excuse me," he says, feeling bodies with his hands
and feet. Stepping on someone. "Get off me," a woman says.

"I'm sorry, really. But I want to get to my wife and children."

"You'll see them in the morning like she says."

"Stay where you are. . . . Go back to where you were. . . . You're
upsetting everything," other people say.

"No, now, please, I have to. This might be my last chance before
the train pulls in."

"Last chance nothing. Your foot's on my hand." He lifts his foot
and puts it down on someone else's or this same man's hand. "Just go
back to your spot, will you? Ah, it's likely already filled by three others. Come on, someone light a candle. Let this man get to his family."

Car stays dark. "Come on," the man says, "someone break down
and light a candle. This is Grisha Bischoff talking. If it's because you
don't want to spare a match, I'll loan you."

A candle's lit about twenty feet away. Little he can see, car's
packed full with bundles and people sleeping. Some look at him, one
eye, then blink shut. "Over here," Denise says, waving at him. "Excuse me, excuse me," he says. "My wife."

"Better to crawl over rather than step," a woman below him says.

"Right, I just wanted to be quick." Gets down, crawls over people. It takes a long time. "I'm sorry," he says. "I'm very sorry." Someone punches his back as he passes. "Imbecile," a man says. "Let him
be," someone else says. "He got permission. Maybe his kids need him
like he says." "They need him, I need him—when you're split up
you're sunk and that's final, but you have to make it hell for everybody else? Okay, okay, I'll get out of his way."

He gets to Denise. "I'm here, thank you, you can put out the candle, whoever it was." Candle goes out.

"There's only room for one adult here," Denise says, on her knees.

"Olivia's in a space for someone half her size. Eva's been on my chest. I'll make room somehow."

"Excuse me," he says, feeling for the person next to them and nudging his shoulder. "Could you just give us one or two inches?"

"There's no room to," the man says. "I don't have enough for my family or myself. Go back to your place. It was bad enough when she and your kids came here."

"I can't. I'll never get back. Thanks all the same." He feels for Olivia, picks her up, takes her spot, makes himself small, lays her facedown on him, feels for Denise's head, "It's me," he says, kisses her lips, for a while his lips stay on hers without moving, says "I didn't believe this just before. That we were here. I didn't know where I was, is more like it. Suddenly I was a kid, it seemed—a lost one. Parents gone; no brothers. In the dark, literally and the rest of it. I felt crazy. All I wanted was for you to be—"

"Go to sleep, my darling. Try to."

"I wish I could. We sleep most of the day; how could anyone sleep now? And the infection in my finger's killing me. When I crawled over I bumped it a dozen times and it now feels twice the size it was. It's a small inconvenience, and so what about the pain compared to all the other things, but if I can't soak and treat it it'll—"

"We'll try to do something in the morning. Maybe we can get some hot water, for your finger and to wash the girls. Sleep, though. We have a few hours to."

He kisses her, closes his eyes, head on her shoulder, one arm holding Olivia close, other on Eva's back. Very cold. Smell of shit and piss is worse here than where they were. The fucking slop pail. She had to move here? But the girls won't soil their clothes or less so than if they were over there. "If there was only something I could do for us."

"Like what?"

"Like everything."

"Right now there's nothing. Just stay close. No heroics unless it's a sure thing for us. Stay with us till the end. Wake up when I ask you. Help me keep the girls in a good mood. But now, sleep; not another word."

He doesn't sleep. Snoring of a woman close by keeps him up. Smells and cold. Weight of Olivia. Wailing every so often from people. Weeping, coughing, babies crying. Someone shouting, someone talking in his sleep. But Denise and the girls seem to sleep.

They go on like this for days. People die. No food except a little for the children. Some people share it. Olivia and Eva are always hungry and thirsty and complain and cry a lot about it. A bucket of water for the whole car is given them once a day. Bischoff distributes it in spoon-fuls. Howard's finger gets so swollen that he jabs it into a nail in the wall and keeps sucking it and it starts healing. There's a slit in the door and someone during the day is usually telling the car what the weather and scenery are like. Now it's hilly, now it's flat. Lots of big clouds in the sky, but nothing threatening. More people die. Corpses are piled on top of one another in a corner and what little hay can be found is strewn over them. The bottom ones begin to smell. Now it's clear out, now it's sleeting and looks as if it'll turn into snow. Some people seem to pray all day and night now. Train stops, goes, pulls into stations, drags along mostly, stays still for hours sometimes, one time for an entire night. They pass a pretty village, an oil refinery that goes on for miles, farmers working in fields. "Potatoes, they're trying to dig out that they might've missed," the slit-watcher says. "Turnips, cabbages, even a carrot or two. Sounds good, right? Look, a farmer's waving his pick at us. Hello, you lucky stiff. Look, a dog's running to the train. Do you kids hear him bark?" Nobody answers. Sunny, rainy. Denise and the girls sleep most of the time now. Olivia always seems to run a low fever and he's afraid it'll suddenly go out of control at night and she'll die. The slop pail's filled and starts running over. Some people talk of killing themselves. Bischoff gives an order. "Nobody kills himself. If you got pills or stuff that can do it, give them to me to use on someone who's really suffering or about to die. But we should be at the place soon we're going to and then let's hope it'll all be much better for us and most of us are even able to stay together as a group. Does anyone have some good stories to tell? Dreams, but interesting ones we can all appreciate? Then anything you want to make up for us or poems you remember from books or school? Does anyone have any food for the children?" Nobody answers. They haven't had a bucket of water for two days. During one stop someone asks a guard through the slit if they can get some water and also empty the slop pail. "Get rid of it through your hole there," the guard says. "You got little spoons. It can be done." "It'll probably make more of a mess than help us," Bischoff tells the car, "but what do we got to lose?" The pail's moved to the door. Denise wants to follow it, but Howard says "We got a good place together and now not such a filthy one, so let's stay." Someone's always spooning out slop through the slit, except at night. Some cardboard's turned into a funnel and they get rid of the slop faster. The pail keeps running over though, but not as much as before.

The train stops at a station. "I think this is it," the slit-watcher says. "Lots of lights, barbed wire and fences. Dogs, soldiers, march-ing prisoners in stripes who look like they're on their last leg. I hear lively band music from someplace, but it doesn't look good." "Don't worry, don't worry," Bischoff says. "They might be political prisoners you're seeing; we're not." They stay in the station till morning. Most of the groaning and crying's stopped. More people have died but nobody's piling them up. "It's snowing," the slit-watcher says. "Big flakes, but melting soon as they hit the ground. Plenty of activity outside, everyone being lined up, called to attention, even the dogs. Something's about to happen. A tall man in a greatcoat and officer's cap is pointing to the train."

The door suddenly opens and several men and women outside start shouting orders. One tells them to hurry out of the car and leave all their luggage on the platform, a second says to go to this or that truck. "What's going to happen to us?" Denise says in the car.

"I don't know," Howard says. "There's air though. Feel it coming in? Olivia, Eva—do you feel it? Already it smells better. Soon toilets, water for drinking and baths."

"Have we really got everything planned fully?" Denise whispers to him. "If they tell you to go one place, me another and the girls a third, or just split us up any other way but where we lose you or both of us lose the kids, what should we do?"

"What can we?"

"We could say no, stay with our children—that we have to, in other words. They're small, sick, need us. We don't want to lose them, we can say, lose them in both ways, and it's always taken the two of us to handle them."

"And be beaten down and the girls dragged away? I don't see it. I think we have to do what they want us to."

"We could ask graciously, civilly. Quick, we have to come to some final agreement. We can plead with them if that doesn't work—get on our knees even; anything."

"We can do that. I certainly will if it comes to that. But we'll see when our turn comes."

"It's coming; it's about to be here. I'm going to beg them first to keep us all together, and if that doesn't work, then for you to go with the girls. You'll last longer than I if it's as bad where they take us as it was in the car."

"One of us then will stay with the girls. If they don't go for it, then each of us with a child. Okay, that's what we'll say and then insist on until they start getting a little tough."

There's room to move around now. Half the people have left the car. He gets down on his knees and kisses the girls, stands them up between Denise and him and he hugs her and their legs touch the

children. "Should I start to worry now, Mother?" Olivia says and
Denise says "No, absolutely not, sweetheart—Daddy and I will take
care of you both."

"May it all be okay," he whispers in Denise's ear. "May it."

"Come on out of there," a man shouts. "All of you, out, out—
yours isn't the only car on the train."

"Goodbye all you lovely people," Bischoff says. "We did our best.
Now God be with you and everything else that's good and I hope to
see each of you in a warm clean room with tables of food."

Howard hands Eva to Denise, picks up Olivia and their ruck-
sacks. "This is how we'll split the kids if it has to come to it, okay? By
weight," and she nods and they walk out.

"All right, you," an officer says to Howard, "bags on the platform
and go to that truck, and you, lady, go to that truck with the children." "No," she says, "let us stay together. Please, the older girl—"
"I said do what I say," and he grabs Olivia to take her from Howard.
Howard pulls her back. "Do that—stop me, and I'll shoot you right
here in the head. Just one shot. That's all it'll take." Howard lets him
have Olivia. The officer puts her down beside Denise. "What will
happen to them?" Howard says.

"Next, come on—out with you and down the ramp, bags over
there. Richard, get them out faster. You go that way," to a man coming toward him and points past Howard, "and you two, the same
truck," to two young women. "Go, you both, what are you doing?—
with your children and to your trucks," he says to Denise and
Howard. "No more stalling." She stares at Howard as she drags
Olivia along. A soldier tugs at his sleeve and he goes to the other
truck. She's helped up into hers with the girls. Some more men and
young women climb into his truck. He can't see her or the girls in her
truck anymore. It's almost filled and then it's filled and it drives off.
"Denise," he screams. Many men are screaming women's names and
the names and pet names of children, and the people in that truck,
older people, mothers, children, are screaming to the people in his
truck, and a few people on the platform are screaming to one or the
other truck. Denise's truck disappears behind some buildings. He can
hear it and then he can't. Then his truck's filled and a soldier raps the
back of it with a stick and it pulls out. They'll never get our belongings to us, he thinks. What will the girls change into? It makes no difference to him what he has. They'll give him a uniform or he'll make
do. But Denise, the children. Denise, the children. "Oh no," and he
starts sobbing. Someone pats his back. "Fortunately, I had no one,"
the man says.

Frog

Takes

a Swim

Olivia doesn't want to play on the beach anymore, wants to go into the water but not to swim. "Just a little more till I finish this paragraph," "No," "All right," and puts down his book, walks her into a part of the lake where the sun is, lifts her under the arms and swings her above the water. "More, more, this is fun," and he does it some more, then says he can't, too tiring, let's rest, stands her up. "Too cold," she says. Holds her arms out. "Again." "Give me a few seconds." Looks out to the lake. Sailboat way off, or something with a sail. People jumping off the ledge into the water, but so far away that even from their shrieking he can't tell if they're kids or adults and which are male and which are female. Lily pads, closer, with flowers all over. Picks her up, swings her in a circle, her feet skimming the water, then her legs cutting through it. "Whee, this is great, better than swimming. Know what it reminds me of, Daddy?" and he indicates he doesn't and she says "Twirling around and getting dizzy dancing," and he does this till his arms ache, says "No more for now, I'm all hot from it, let me take a swim," stands in place holding her till he doesn't feel he'll fall if he walks, walks to shore and sets her down. "How can we do this—for me to swim? I can't just leave you." "Yes you can. I'll stay and play here." "No, someone has to watch you," while he's drying her. "We'll ask someone here to—would you mind that?" "Do I have to stay with that person?" "No. Just that if that person says come away from the edge of the water, for some reason—

a leech, maybe, or motorboat being put in—well, you do that, but that person won't have time to say much. I'll only go out for thirty strokes, kick my feet a few times while I'm on my back out there and maybe dive down once, and then swim in, a little slower than when I swam out as I'll probably do the breaststroke coming back, if that's it—you know, where the arms sort of push the water underwater. Like this—how could I be unsure what it's called?" and brings his arms to his chest, spreads them wide, brings them to his chest. "That's a stroke, like the crawl's a stroke," and demonstrates that one, even the breathing. "I think you said the first one's a breaststroke because it's your breast you're hitting." "Right. So, which person looks good to look after you?" "Her. She asked me what I was building with my mud before, and she was nice." Sitting by the beach, around twenty-five, noticed her when they walked down here and several times when he looked up from his book to see her reading hers, slim and nicely built from what he can see in the seated position she's been in since they got here, doesn't look like a local, magazine, travel and week-in-review sections of last Sunday's *Times* held down by a hairbrush and sandals. "Okay, let's ask her."

They go over. "Excuse me, but I'd like to—my name's Howard Tetch and this—" "Oh sure—Olivia. We chatted before. She's so pretty and well behaved, and sharp?—oh boy." "She is, which'll make what I want to say easier. I'd like to take a quick dip—" "Go ahead, I'll watch her." "But a very quick one. Thirty strokes out, thirty back or so, maybe a little whale movement on my back out there, but that's all. And she knows—" "Really, don't worry. Even if she can't swim or hold her breath underwater, she can go in up to her waist. I'll be right here, and I'm a WSI." "I'm sorry, don't know . . ." "Water safety instructor. I've two lifesaving badges, giving me the authority to save two adults of up to three hundred pounds total at one time." "Well, couldn't be better. Okay, kid. Up-to-your-knees, we'll say, but no higher and not for long. I don't want you catching a chill—getting one." "Anyhow, I don't want to go in again. I want to play here." "Fine. —By the way, your name's what?—just in case I get a cramp out there and have to shout for help. Only kidding—but what?" "Lita Reinekin." "Thanks, then, Mrs., Ms., Reinekin." "Lita," holding out her hand. "Lita," shaking it. "Okay, sweetie, Daddy's going in. Be good. Do what—" "I will," and she goes to her pail and things on the beach.

He throws the towel to their place on the grass, says to the woman "Think she needs her shirt?—nah, she's okay," walks into the water, turns around. Olivia's sitting in the muddy sand, her legs wrong, putting her two rubber adult figures into the pail. Woman's a few feet from her, book closed on a finger holding the page, he presumes, looking at Olivia. He splashes water behind his knees and on the back of his neck. Why's he doing that? He already adjusted to it when he was swinging her around. "Put your feet out, Olivia," and without looking at him, she does. He walks out some more, dives in, swims. Counts ten strokes, turns around. She's still playing on the beach. Should have told her to stay in the sun part of the beach, but he won't be out long. Swims fifteen strokes, turns around. Can't see her so well now. "Olivia . . . hi," he yells. "Hi, Olivia." She doesn't respond. He waves—maybe she's looking at him on the sly, which she does. The woman waves at him. Very nice, he thinks, she's very nice. And good-looking, and that long and what's probably a strong body. But WSI? Two people and three hundred pounds? How would she know what any two people weighed when they were drowning? People she didn't know, in other words. If they weighed more than that and one or both of them drowned, would she be penalized in some way for hav-ing tried to save them? Maybe he's missing the point. Ten more strokes, then thinks: give yourself ten more. Likes being this far out when nobody else is here. Ten more, looks around. People on the ledge seem to have left, sailboat's not around anymore, no motorboats today either. Hates those things. If one came close and didn't see him, what then? Yell, scream, wave frantically, then dive deep if it kept coming. When would he start diving? Depend how fast the boat was going, but something would tell him *now*. What an awful thought though, motorboat running smack into someone and maybe slicing off an arm or leg, and he shakes his head to get rid of it. Looks to shore. Can scarcely make out anything. The woman, he thinks, where she was sitting, and possibly that speck's Olivia, but he's kidding him-self. Some other movement on the grassy slope above them, really just blurs, and what looks like a light-colored blanket by a tree, but can't tell if anyone's on it. So quiet out here. Nothing as peaceful anywhere. Maybe the top of a secluded mountain where one sees nothing but trees and other mountains, and on the same kind of day: mild temper-ature, light breeze, mostly clear sky. Should get back. But she'll be okay. Gets on his back and looks at a bird, probably a hawk, circling way up in the sky. But time to get back. If she were calling him, would he even hear? And he's much farther out than he usually goes. There's always the chance of a sudden leg or stomach cramp, though he knows how to uncramp them. A motorboat could suddenly ap-proach, even that sailboat, and his sense of timing in diving might not be as good as he thinks.

Starts back, using the crawl for about fifteen strokes, then the breaststroke for about ten. Can see the beach fairly well now. Woman sitting where she was. Light blanket, if there was one, seems to be gone. Doesn't see Olivia or anybody else there. Some might have left, others gone into the woods, Olivia with them for some reason, picking berries, looking for exotic mushrooms or birds; to piss, even. Or she could be behind a tree or bush, playing hide-and-seek. Stares, doesn't see her. Ten more crawl strokes, stops. Woman reading. Their towels and shirts. Olivia's toys on the beach. If they're playing hide-and-seek, why's the woman reading? Pretending not to see her perhaps. "Hello . . . hello," he yells, treading water. She looks up. "Where's Olivia?" Stares at him; he can't make out her expression. He swims hard the rest of the way, stands when he's able to and yells while walking fast as he can through the water "Where'd Olivia go?" "What?" she says, cupping her ear. "Olivia—my daughter—where is she?" "Who?" "The girl I left with you. Is she in the woods? Or you let her go back to the car alone?" "I'm sorry, sir," standing when he gets right up to her, "but I don't know what you're talking about. You didn't leave anybody or anything with me. You were here by yourself before—" "By myself?" "Over there, and you went in the water—" "I went in only after you agreed to look after my girl. You said you were a WSI." "A WSI?" "Look, what is this, a joke on me? You two— together—and she's hiding somewhere?" "No, nothing." "Then you want me to panic, I'm panicking. You're nuts, fine, be nuts. But—oh, fuck you. —Olivia," he yells, listens. "Olivia, it's Daddy. Come out from wherever you are, and now." Listens, looks around, runs to the woods and yells "Olivia, do you hear me?" "If there was a girl—" the woman says. "There fucking was. And be quiet. I want to hear if she yells back." Listens. "Olivia," he yells. "If you're hiding, come out. Daddy's serious. Game's over if you're playing one. If the woman I left you with told you to play a game, she doesn't want you to play it anymore either. Now come out this second." Listens.

"Stay here," he says. "If you see her, tell her to wait till I come out." Runs to their spot, slips his sneakers on, runs into the woods shouting "Olivia, Olivia." Comes on a path and runs along it shouting "Olivia, it's me, Daddy, where are you?" Path ends and he runs back along it and out into the grass and says "You see her?" and she says "No, who?" and he says "Jesus, I'd like to bop you. What the hell's wrong with you—don't you understand anything?" She says "You've threatened me enough—I have to go," and he says "Please, I'm sorry, stay while I look," and runs into the woods at a clearing closer to the beach, trips, gets up, knee's bleeding, says "Screw it, fuck it, oh shit,

shit, shit," runs to the end of the clearing, shouts "Olivia, Olivia, it's Daddy, yell if you hear me; please, darling, yell," listens, squeezes his hands hard as he can, digs all his nails into his face till he's out of breath, runs into the woods a few feet, too thick, she'd never get through it and wouldn't even try, runs through the clearing to the grass, woman's putting her things in a canvas bag, he says "Don't go, whatever you do—I need someone to stay while I look up the hill for her, all right?" and she says "Really, this is crazy," and he says "Please, no more accusations from me, just give me a couple more minutes," and she nods and mouths Okay, he runs up the path to the parking area, stops several times to yell for Olivia and stare into the woods on both sides, gets to his car, nothing seems changed: windows down, things where he thinks they were, shouts "Olivia, you around here? Daddy's very worried about you, so yell if you hear me," listens, runs to the other car there which must be the woman's if she didn't walk here from wherever she's staying or park and take the woods' path from the ledge parking area, windows up, driver's door locked, pillow in back, New England road map and several spruce cones and a sand dollar on the dashboard, microbiology textbook and Magic Marker on the passenger seat, memorizes the Massachusetts license plate and car color and make, is about to run back when he thinks "Why not?" and puts his ear to the car trunk, knocks on it and says "Olivia, Olivia?" runs back, woman's in shirt and shorts and is fitting her feet into sandals, place where she was sitting's cleared, he yells from about twenty feet away "One more minute; just want to check the path to the ledge; I'll run, so I'll be right back," she slumps her shoulders and an expression that says "Enough's enough already, I have to go," runs on the ledge path about a quarter-mile shouting for Olivia and look-ing into the woods, nobody's at the ledge, towel draped over a tree branch but it's dry and could have been there for days, runs to the parking area, no cars or people, shouts her name and runs back along the path.

"Please, I know I said no more accusations, but this is unbeliev-ably crucial. I left my daughter with you—left her in your charge. I went for a swim." "Yes, I saw you. You went quite a ways out. I was even concerned for you somewhat." "Now listen, stop that bullshit. Those are our towels over there—Olivia's and mine. Two towels. I threw the second one over there right in front of you," and runs to the towels and holds them up. "Towels, goddamnit, towels. And beach toys—hers," and runs to the beach and holds up the pail and two shovels, pulls the two figures out of the pail and waves them in the air. "These are my daughter's. Pail, toys, everything. Who else's?

Nobody else is here." "Another child could have left—" "She was playing with them when I went in to swim. You were watching her, right from this spot here. She was still playing here when I last saw her from the water about forty strokes out. You had said she could even go into the water. That you were a—did she? Is that what happened? She's in there, under there, and you don't want to admit it? God no," and he runs in, stops because he doesn't want to churn up the water, walks around looking for her in it and then walks out a few feet, dives down, swims around underwater, when he comes up he looks back to see if the woman's still there. "One-seven, forty-two, PL, baby blue, Opel," he says to himself in case she goes. If she did anything why wouldn't she go? Because she's trying to pull something off. Because he has her name. Lita something. What the hell is it? Not important now. Goes down, again and again, looking for Olivia. If he sees her he'll dive for her and swim to shore with her and pump and pump and pump till he gets the water out and breathe air into her till she's alive or ask the woman, if she really is a water safety instructor, to do it or help. Sees something in the distance underwater and dives. It's a rock with a few long pieces of waving seaweed on it. She's nowhere around. She couldn't have gone out farther. She could have drifted out there before she sank. She would have screamed. He would have heard her. She could have screamed when he was on his back and water got in his ears. Still would have heard. Maybe she's in the weeds. Comes up and shouts "Did she go down in the weeds?" and points to the area of them sticking out of the water. She throws up her hands. Treads water and shouts "Save me the trouble looking. If she drowned then say so and maybe I can still save her. People can be underwater for twenty minutes and somehow still be revived. Where'd she go down if she went down, and if she didn't, then just say where she is or what happened to her?" and she shakes her head she didn't hear or doesn't understand. He swims to the weeds and dives to the part closest to shore, but the weeds stop him. Too thick. Treads through them a few feet, puts his face underwater to look. Can't see anything past the top. He's looking in the wrong place. He doesn't know where to look. Shore would be better, if only to threaten her some way unless she tells.

Swims to shore. Woman walks to him while he walks through the water to the beach and she says "Listen, I want to explain—" "Fine, quick, that's what I want." "I mean I want to be direct with you, though God knows what good it'll do me, so I'm saying I'm leaving. I don't know what you're searching for, but it has nothing to do with me and you have to start believing that, or just thinking about it, all right?" and she turns to leave and he says "But you saw me before. If I wasn't with my girl, who was I with?" "As I said—" "But the toys. The little kid's towel with the cartoon animals on it, and her clothes in my bag up there—shirt, pants, these little Japanese beach sandals— oh, why the hell my telling you? I have to get the police. And tell my wife. Maybe you're crazy or have some instant memory-loss affliction. Maybe Olivia went through the woods and came out some other place. Or got lost somehow, but I've got to get help in searching for her before it gets dark. Look, I don't know why you're saying this, denying it—you're obviously responsible for whatever—" "If I was—" "If you were, why would you have stayed? Because I have your name. I probably have your license plate. The Opel. One-seven PL, etcetera. Because people who were on the grass when we were all here saw me leave the girl with you. My daughter. If they noticed. So you know you're caught. So come on, will you, tell me already," and grabs her by the shoulders. "I mean it. Where the fuck is she? Tell me or I'll shake your fucking head off," and starts shaking her. "Get your hands off," and pulls his hands away. "Not till you tell me where she is." He swings her around and puts his arm around her neck and twists her arm behind her back and pushes it up till he knows it's hurting. She says "Stop that, stop," and tries to wrench free and he says "Tell me where she is or I'll break your arm off and strangle you right here. I'll do it. Now where is she?" "I don't know." "You know, you know." "I don't—please. You came alone. You have two towels but I never noticed them till you mentioned them. I was reading my book so I didn't see. I don't know anything about the beach toys and your bag of clothes. There was never a girl while I was here." "Liar, liar, liar," and pushes her arm up farther and she shouts in pain and he says "Last chance before I break it off," and waits but she's just shouting in pain and he wants to push it up more but can't. He doesn't want to break it. Wants to give her just so much pain before she tells him but he seems to have gone beyond that point and she's still not telling. "Damn your lying ass," and lets her arm go and from behind squeezes her neck with his forearm. She coughs, says "I'm having trouble breathing," and he says "That's the point. I'll cut the air in your windpipe. I'll even break your windpipe if I have to." "I don't know . . . imagining it . . . I wasn't, there isn't . . . my book . . . can't breathe," and then she's just choking and he wants to go on, he knows that at some point she has to tell him where Olivia is, but he seems to have gone too far, she's not getting any air in. He lets her go and she drops to the ground and gasps and spits and he looks at her to see if she'll say anything, then in the woods for Olivia, the lake to see if her body came up from where it sank, sees the same or different sailboat way off, a pile of stones by the beach, thinks "That's an idea." Woman's still on the ground. He runs to the pile, all too big, looks around, picks up a rock on the grass, one he can hold in one hand, runs back and gets down, she's stroking her throat, bends over her, face a few inches from hers and says "I'm going to smash this rock against your head but with such force that I'll split it open with the first crack. If you don't tell me where she is. Now tell me. You can see I mean business," and holds the rock over her face so she can see it. She says "I swear, don't know. Please, no more. I'd tell you by now if I knew. Swear." "Stay here. I'm not kidding. Don't move from this area. You can at least do that for me. If you see her, tell her to what? To wait. I'll be back or my wife will or the police. We're at Seven Bear Road in case you have to start moving with her for some reason. That she's very sick, or you are, and we're not back. Bear as in animal. Seven. We're summer renters. Tetch, Howard and Denise. Just Howard. The Brook Isle post office knows us and we have a phone for the summer in my name. You have it?" Nods. "I mean, everything I said about what to do and our name and address?" "Yes." "Or just immediately call, or if someone comes down here get him to call, the police." "I will."

Runs to the path to the car. Maybe Olivia was in the woods, lost, and found a path and it led to the car and she's now in it. Gets to it. Everything's the same. Car's pulling in. All just in swimsuits, man with his shirt off, woman, two kids. Says to the woman as she parks the car "You see a girl around four, about this height," holding out his hand, "long blond hair in a ponytail, very pretty, walking down that way to the main road or on the road?" She's shaking no. "In a bathing suit. Yellow. Red it was. Red-striped, one piece." "No, I'm sorry." Man beside her says "What is it, she lost?" "Lost. Or something. Too strange. I went for a swim." "You should never leave a child like that alone on a beach," the woman says. Kids have let themselves out of the car, father saying "You wait there by the door till we're finished with this man." "I didn't," Howard says. "I left her with a woman on the beach. She's still there, the woman. I almost killed her just now. She said she didn't know anything about it. It's ridiculous—she's lying—I left my daughter in her charge while I swam. I'm obviously going insane over it. With worry. Listen, I don't trust that woman. She's probably gone some other way out of the beach by now, though I'm sure that's her car. But if she's there, please, I told her to wait for my daughter. Olivia. Olivia Tetch. I'm Howard, at Seven Bear Road, for the summer. Remember that, if you see the girl. Or if the woman

612 The Stories of Stephen Dixon

tells you where my daughter is or what happened to her, which she
wouldn't to me. We've a listed phone. T-e-t-c-h. Because I need someone to stay here in case Olivia comes out of the woods—got lost, or
had been hiding—though why this woman would lie I don't know.
Maybe Olivia ran away from her, but something has to be wrong. But
please stay there till I come back or my wife or the police. Stay with
Olivia or bring her to our cottage on Bear Road. You know where
that is? Very near here." Man says no. "We know Bear Road," the
woman says. "Second one off 176 after the war monument." "Sure,
that's right, now I see it," the man says. "Our mailbox is right across
from our driveway with a big T on it in electrical tape. The Brook Isle
post office knows us. I'm going for the police now to get some
searchers in case she's still in the woods. But you, every now and then,
even if the woman's down there, yell out her name. Olivia. Yell it out
loud and for her to come to your voice—that her father told you to
yell for her—or for her to shout and you'll come to hers. Please, I
know I'm ruining everything for you today, but this is too important,
so you'll do it?" and the woman looks at the man and he thinks it
over quickly and says "Sure," and Howard runs to his car.

   Drives to the cottage. Denise is feeding the baby. She looks up
with a smile when he comes in, face drops when she sees his, and he
says "It's very bad, couldn't be worse. Olivia's disappeared," and
breaks down and she takes the baby off her breast and says "Tell me,"
and he quickly tells her. Phones the county police. Man there says
they'll get right on it: searching party for the woods, boats to drag the
lake, notify all the hospitals and trooper and police stations, someone
to speak to the woman and if she's not at the lake, to find her. Lita
what? He doesn't know, but her last name will come to him, he says.
"One of you stay home so we can always reach you." "My wife will.
I'll go back to the lake but first I'll drive around the area looking for
her, in addition to your troopers and the fire department people looking. I could recognize her from a distance and, up closer, immediately.
She might be in someone's car. She might be with someone who's giving her an ice cream treat at Lu-Ann's Drive-in or some such place.
She might be wandering along the road looking for home or a way
back to the lake and nobody's stopped her yet because they think
she's a local, no sneakers or sandals and in only a swimsuit and all."
"Probably little chance of that, it sounds like, but go ahead. The
trooper who goes to your house will get photos of her for us to copy
and pass around. You have them?" "Plenty." "Do you have that Lita's
last name yet?" "No. Lita something. If I keep saying her name it
could come to me, but that'll just be wasting time. Patchok comes to

mind, but that's not it. Don't even know why I thought of it. If the Opel's hers, you'll be able to trace her through it, won't you?" "That or we'll try to locate her by her first name. It's unusual enough, even for around here, if she gave you the right one, that is, and if she still isn't at the lake. Nothing we can do but try."

Howard makes calls to everyone he knows in the area whose number he remembers. Help look for Olivia. Go to the lake. Search with the troopers and firemen in the woods. Tell as many people as you can to help. Don't give up till it's declared hopeless. Tells Denise to look up the numbers of other people they know in the area and say the same things. "Also ask if they know a Lita. I forgot about that. And call the police every so often just to make sure they haven't been trying to get through to us and to keep after them. But make all your calls quick so the lines aren't tied up. Of course, you know that," and runs out of the house, drives around the area, asks everyone he speaks to at the various drive-ins and shops, after he's told them about Olivia and given her description, if they know or ever heard of a young woman named Lita. Nobody has. Goes to the post office, tells his story to the postmistress and asks if she knows of a woman named Lita. She doesn't but she calls several post offices in surrounding towns and none of the other postmasters have received mail for her. "Maybe that's her nickname," she says.

Goes to the lake. Lots of cars and people, couple of fire trucks. He speaks to the police chief he spoke to on the phone. "No trace of her so far. We ordered some hounds and a helicopter in. When it gets dark we'll try best as we can with searchlights and bullhorns, but I think by nine or ten we'll have covered every foot of these woods. That woman Lita was still here. She's in her car. It's not the Opel. Hers was parked along the main road and she said she walked in, so we let her go out and bring it to the lot. Your Opel wasn't here when we got here, so it could have been anyone's—another visitor, but in his own private lake spot—and not seeing any commotion yet, just drove away. We put a call out on it with the plate number you gave. That Miss Reinekin—" "That's it, that's the name." "Well, she said you attacked her real bad, and showed the bruises to prove it, and that she had nothing to do either with the girl or provoking you to threatening her life. That it's all in your head, she said, which is why she stayed—to tell us. Or that you did something previously to the girl and are trying to put the blame on her. Because you came to the lake alone, swam alone and when you came out of the water you went straight up to her and asked where's your daughter. She's from near Hartford, only here for a long weekend. Friends she's staying with are with her now. They're very respectable summer people, been coming up for years and before then the parents and grandparents of the man, and they say the woman's as truthful and right-minded as anyone they know. That she comes from a good family, well brought up and educated, never hurt anyone, and is a teacher engaged to a governor's assistant; the woman friend's known her since childhood. Just hearing all this and talking to Miss Reinekin, she doesn't seem like a child molester or kidnapper, but that's not for me to judge." "Let me speak to her." "If you don't mind someone taking down what you two say; and also no rough stuff from you, words or force." "Take down anything, and don't worry."

They go to the woman's car. She's in the backseat sitting between a man and woman, has a sweater on now, pants, glasses. "This is the man—" "She didn't wear glasses before," Howard says. "She only uses them for distance," the man says. "Let her speak. Can't she speak? Why isn't she speaking?" "She can speak but I chose then to speak for her. She's emotionally shaken. That rock over her head didn't help any." "I didn't hit her with it." "Held it over. Three inches away, if not two." "And strangling her," his wife says. "Strangling her, and nearly breaking her arm. She doesn't have to answer any more of your asinine charges or be talked threateningly to. She can even be demanding you be locked up and then suing you if she wants." "Gentlemen, let me continue," the chief says. "For the record, Miss Reinekin, this is the man you said accused you of doing something terrible to his daughter and then—" "If I hurt her, who wouldn't for his daughter? She's lucky I didn't do worse." "Anyway, I had nothing to do with it," she says. "But if this girl truly is missing—" "She's missing," the chief says. "We spoke to his wife. There's an older daughter, same description and age he gave, who's not home or anywhere to be seen. The whole county's out looking for her by now." "Then I'm sorry. It has to be the worst possible thing for the mother. But I've told everything I know of it. And Mr. Kaden here—he's not a lawyer but he knows something about it—has advised me not to talk about it further except in front of a lawyer. But a girl's missing, we all pray she's safe—" "Oh shit, just listen to her," Howard says. "—and I'll answer any more questions you have if it'll help find her. First, yes, he is the man who did all the things I said he did. I still don't know why. We hadn't said a word or even looked at the same time to one another till he came out of the water, though I did notice him go in and then swimming. Mostly the crawl but occasionally the breaststroke and once the butterfly stroke—" "I did no such stroke. I don't know how." "Well, it looked like the butterfly stroke by someone not that good at it, all that splashing and arm-flopping. But after he came out—" "He accused you and grabbed your arm and so on?" the chief says. Nods. "Nothing new to add?" Shakes her head. "Then you ought to go home, rest—we have your statement and now your identification of Mr. Tetch—and we'll go on with our search as though the girl were lost in the woods and no doubt contact you later." "You going to let her go just like that?" "It's been more than 'just that,' Mr. Tetch." "And I didn't say Olivia was lost in the woods. I said it's one of the main possibilities. I don't know where she is. She can be in that freaking water. She can be under a rock or down a well. This one knows though." "You said I may go, Officer? It's been, as you can see, too much of an afternoon for me and I don't want to say now what I really think about him." "Do you have any evidence for what you don't want to say?" the chief says. "I definitely suggest you don't say anything, Lita," Kaden says. "If there's an inquest or trial or anything like that—" "You fucking liars, with your inquests and trials," Howard says. "You fucking murderer and kidnapper," he says to her. "Or you're all murderers or kidnappers. Now where is she already? Where the goddamn fuck is she?" and tries opening the door, Kaden pulls it shut and locks it while his wife rolls up the window and Lita screams and covers her eyes. Howard bangs on the window, is led away by the chief and made to sit on the grass.

Lita drives off with Mrs. Kaden, Kaden drives behind them in Lita's car. Mazda, NXH #107, dark red, Connecticut. Search goes on for hours. He calls Denise every half hour from a police car. Last call she says friends have come and gone and been very kind but she needs to be with him. He's given his and Olivia's beach things and goes home. She puts some dinner on the table for him, weeps, checks the baby, weeps, says she has to control herself so she can think straight while there's still a chance Olivia can be found, says she doesn't understand any of it. "Now go over it, once more, maybe there's something we missed." He goes over it thoroughly. She says, "How can anything like this happen to her? Nothing has—I'm sure she's alive and we'll find her—but how can anyone do anything like that to her? How come they don't press that woman more? How can her friends protect her like that when they must know she's lying? The police should give her a lie detector test. They should have done it immediately. Or get a hypnotist to work on her—drugs, even, to draw out the truth—if she's crazy or has a mental or physical disorder where she can't remember things and one of those means would get her to say where Olivia is or what she did with her. What about where she's staying? Maybe the Kadens are involved. Some kind of satanic cult or just selling beautiful children or a ring for whatever kind of devious or money-making purpose—but in a basement there or someplace. Am I thinking straight or is all this part of my own growing craziness?" He says no, it's valid, "We have to try everything that's reasonable or possible," calls the police station, hoping it would relay the call to the chief's car, is told to call him at home. "The search has been called off," the chief says. "We'll resume it early tomorrow if you want." "I want." "Not even the dogs could turn up anything. They smelled blood but nothing human. They started digging up the ruins of an old cabin. That cabin must be three hundred years old. Nobody even knew an earlier settlement had been there—" "I'm not interested. Listen, my wife and I think you should give Miss Reinekin a lie detector test, and immediately. Or just get a hypnotist to hypnotize the truth out of her, or some serums or drugs to do it." "No can do. She's got to be suspected of a crime first and then agree to the test or drugs or hypnotism, and she's not." "Then what do you say to going to the Kadens' house where she's at? Anybody think of that? Olivia could be there. A satanic cult, let's say. Maybe they sell babies or slightly older children or are into all sorts of ugly things. The respectability and old-family stuff and all that lawyer-knowledge and holier-than-thou protest shit could be some kind of cover—some ruse." "Again, it wouldn't be a bad idea if anyone in the state or county police departments believed that, but we don't. The Kadens would have to be suspects too and they're anything but that. We put out queries on them and Miss Reinekin and they're as clean as they come. Try to listen to me now, Mr. Tetch—don't make trouble. We know how you both feel and our hearts go out to you as if she were our own child, but you don't want to be jailed at a time when your wife and other girl need you so much. A state's attorney and detectives will be out to see you tomorrow morning. Please be there. Then if you want to come where we'll be searching, you'll be more than welcome." "I've complete confidence in all your and your people's abilities, so of course I'll do what you say."

He looks up the Kaden address, tells Denise to take a couple of aspirins and maybe some port and try to get some sleep. "I know what I'm doing, honestly," when she says what he's doing probably isn't such a good idea, and drives to the road the Kadens' driveway leads to, parks, walks in a few hundred feet, ample moonlight, looks around, no outbuildings about, down to the beach, boathouse with a kayak and canoe, sailboat anchored in the water, different colored sail than the one he saw in the lake, wades out to it and looks inside, back up the path, looks through all the first-floor windows, sees them sitting beside a fireplace in the only lighted room in the house, Kaden reading a magazine and drinking wine or something pale in a wineglass, two women talking, fireplace going. Knocks on the door. Kaden comes to it. "You." "Listen, you've got to believe me, I'm not nuts. I had my daughter. I went for a swim. I left her with your friend. She's lying about everything. My wife and I are desperate. Right now she's going crazy from it. I'm about to too. You know what it means to lose a child like this? It's the worst feeling in the world. There is no other. Maybe if she got hit and killed by a car right in front of me. That's what it's like. Or the doctor's just told me she has cancer and only a month to live. If you have kids—" "Excuse me, but if you don't leave our property—and I mean right up to the public road—this minute, I'm phoning the police." "Hell with the police. Olivia might be here. There might even be a chance you don't know about it. Now you have to—" but he can see by his face he won't, so he pushes past him and goes inside. Kaden grabs his arm. He throws him against a wall, puts his fist under Kaden's nose and says "I'm only going to look around for my daughter. Don't stop me or I'll bust you, I'll even break you in two," and shoves him out the door, kicks but misses him, slams and latches the door, runs through the first floor turning on lights and opening doors looking for the basement, finds it, from another room the women are screaming for him to go. "Scream your bloody heads off; I'm looking, I'm looking." Goes downstairs, yells "Olivia, are you down here? Are you anywhere around here, Olivia?" Turns over boxes, looks behind a huge wine rack and stacks of newspapers and magazines, only door is to a toilet, nothing else to hide someone in or behind, nothing he can see to show anything strange going on. Runs upstairs; nobody's around. Runs through the first floor opening cupboards and a bathroom and closet doors. Runs upstairs to the guest bedroom, hallway bathroom, master bedroom, unused bedroom, kids' bedroom where when he turns the lights on two boys in double-decker bunks and the women start screaming. Checks every room and closet for an attic entrance. Guest bedroom a third time. Dresser and night table drawers for anything that might lead to something, woman's valise and handbag and under the bed and once more the shower stall. Goes downstairs. "Yes, this moment, walking right past me," Kaden says on the hallway phone. "Maybe he's now going to make good on his threat to bust me in two. Well, let him, since I'm not about to fight back. That's not what I do, and you're my aural witness on that, Chief Pollard . . . Now he's leaving the house. Good riddance I want to say to him . . . No, the children and women all seem to be okay. —Sure you're all right, boys? Doris?"

he yells upstairs. "We're fine, Daddy," a boy says. "Is he gone?" his wife says.

He starts up the driveway. "You should wait for them here," Kaden says from the porch. "Or they'll meet you at your place, Pollard told me to tell you. But they're on their way. You've got a number of serious complaints against you, sir. You'd better get yourself a good lawyer—one who'll be able to get you off with only a few years, for you can be certain I'll see that you're charged with everything that can be thrown at you. For slander, trespassing, verbal intimidation, assaulting Miss Reinekin, barging into a private home and tossing the occupants around like an ape. Whatever you've gone through and are going through, you can't do these things to people because of it. You have—it gives you—no moral license to, do you understand that, sir? No, you wouldn't."

Drives home, Pollard's waiting for him there, is arrested, taken to the police station, jailed overnight, state's attorney and detectives question him the next day, released on his own recognizance, search continues, he drinks himself to sleep every night, Denise is on medication for a while, search is ended, woman's exonerated, he's indicted for the disappearance of Olivia, Kaden never presses charges, Miss Reinekin drops hers, he asks for a lie detector test and passes it unqualifiedly, he asks to be hypnotized by a court-appointed hypnotist and is told his story didn't change one iota from the one he told before being hypnotized, state drops its case against him: no body or witnesses or evidence of any wrongdoing beyond parental neglect no matter how hard they looked, though the state's attorney feels sure, he tells reporters, that Howard's guilty of some heinous crime against his daughter which they'll find out about in time and charge him with and send him to prison or even execute him for. Denise doesn't know what to think through all this. She doesn't believe the woman was involved in Olivia's disappearance, but how couldn't she be if Howard says she was? That's not saying she thinks he had anything to do with it, she says, other than being irresponsible in leaving Olivia with a stranger, but how couldn't he have anything to do with it if the woman didn't? Did he lose Olivia someplace, she says once— "Quick, answer me now, no time to think of one, no or yes?" "No, absolutely not." Maybe, she says, both he and the woman are responsible in a way she hasn't figured out yet. "Are you lovers, and an accident happened with Olivia and you're covering up for each other in some way where you both assumed you'd get off?" "What am I supposed to answer to that?" "Of course; that was ridiculous of me, but I simply don't know what to think. I'm not afraid of you for Eva, but

I'm also not entirely comfortable with you for her and myself. I'm just confused." Goes on like that. She won't make love with him anymore, the few times he's felt like it since Olivia disappeared, and then she won't sleep in the same bed and then the same room with him. Then she brings Olivia's bed into Eva's room and sleeps there. She puts it all down as just part of her continuing grief and confusion.

Fall's come, it's cold, cottage isn't insulated, everyone they know has left, she wants to return to their apartment in the city, he wants her to stay with him here but in a heated house. "Maybe Olivia will turn up somehow. At the very least, if we're here and badgering the police, they'll continue looking for her more than they would if we weren't here, or at least not give up looking for her completely or investigating what might have happened that day. Maybe, while Miss Reinekin wasn't looking, someone came and snatched Olivia away—possibly one of the persons or a group of them sunbathing on the grass that day; or even the sailor of the sailboat I saw when I swam in the lake—and will want to turn himself in for whatever reason and also give up Olivia. Or Olivia could escape from her kidnapper—a door left unlocked a first time and she just walks out or something. I've read about such things—sometimes happening weeks later, sometimes years. That wouldn't explain why Miss Reinekin insists I was never at the lake with Olivia. Maybe she was threatened by this person or group not to say anything about the kidnapping or they'll kill her and maybe kill Olivia also, and that's why she's been lying all this time. Maybe Olivia was taken away at gunpoint. Lots of maybes, maybe one of them on target, or one future one. But I can't leave feeling Olivia might still be around here or in an area near here and that I might, by just sticking and looking around, think of or do something to get her back."

Denise leaves with Eva, he rents a room in town. He looks for Olivia or does something to help find her every day. Asks everyone he can about her in this county and the surrounding ones. Goes to houses and logging camps in the woods and other remote areas with photos of her. Places ads in newspapers with a photo of Olivia and him, asking if anyone was or knows anyone who was at the lake that day and saw him with Olivia or just saw anyone with her that day or any day since. Puts up her missing-child poster everywhere he can. Tries to generate news interest in her disappearance, by calling and sending letters to news editors, and when that doesn't work, in the story of the father obsessed with the search, so her picture will appear again in the papers and on local TV. Goes to the Kaden house sometimes. It's boarded up for the winter. Explores the beach and woods around the house, thinking he might have missed something the previous times; studies the house from all sides, trying to determine by the windows and dormers and roof shape and size of the walls whether he missed a room or two when he went through it. Would like to break inside, but he might get caught and jailed or ordered out of the county or even the state for a while. Many people in the area think he had something to do with Olivia's disappearing and that by staying on and looking for her so hard he's just trying to establish his innocence and get their sympathy. That's what the anonymous notes say that frequently come through the mail or are slipped into the letter box of his building and a couple of times under his door.

He searches through different parts of the lake woods almost every day. Goes into them in high boots because of the snow, calls out for her, nails her poster to trees, thinks he'll one time find a sign of her, something hanging from a tree branch or message or article of clothing left someplace, though maybe not till the spring thaw. Maybe there's a habitable cave in the woods no one knows about or a hut, same thing, but completely camouflaged. Pollard said the searching teams covered every part of the woods, but there had to be areas too thick for anyone to go into, or at least not without the cutting tools he always takes with him. He imagines coming on one of these huts— he's come on two already not shown on the town's survey maps he has, but with no doors or roofs—and looking inside the window, seeing Olivia and a man talking, eating. He smashes down the door with his foot and charges inside and knocks the man down and beats him, continues beating him with his fists or one of the tools till the man doesn't move. Till he's dead—the hell with him. Two or more men, he'd charge in the same way and use his tools on them, cutting through them, aiming for their faces and necks and groins, and then scoop up Olivia, dress her for the cold, or not dress her—just run with her to his car and drive to the one doctor in town.

He goes to the lake a lot, mostly to look around it but sometimes to think. Gone out on the ice several times to see what he could make out on the shore from there. Crisscrossed it, walked into every cove, stood in various spots on it to see if any smoke was coming from places where no houses were supposed to be. Once he thought he saw a girl around Olivia's height on the beach not far from where he lost her. Walked back without taking his eyes off her, yelled while he walked "Don't move, don't go away, stay there for godsakes, it's Daddy," then imagined her on shore when he got there and putting his coat and scarf around her and picking her up and kissing her head and hands all over and carrying her back to the road where he left the car—running with her, shouting "I've found her, my little baby; everybody, I've found her, found her."

Sits in the snow in the same place he last sat with her. Tries to bring her back. Talks to where she sat. Says "Olivia, please be here. Materialize from wherever you are. Just by some miracle or something, be with me now. Or walk through those woods there, say you've been kidnapped and you just broke free or they let you go. Please, my dearest child, come back. Daddy's heartbroken. He can't live without you. He's sad all the time knowing what might have happened and might still be happening to you. If it can only be a miracle that brings you back, you never have to tell me where you were or how you got back to me or anything about it. Never, I swear."

Later he calls the police chief as he usually does once a week and says "Please bear with me again, I know I've become a terrible nuisance to you, but is there anything new regarding my daughter here or in this country or the world?" "Nothing," Pollard says; "I wish there was." "But you're still doing your best to find her, right?" "Whatever there is to be done, and there isn't anything anymore without new information or leads on her, we're doing it, sir, you can count on it. If anyone calls the special phone number we set up for her, the news would reach me in minutes. And believe me, if I couldn't get hold of you by phone right away, I'd come, or send another officer, to wherever I thought you were. As I've said I don't know how many times, I fully understand how you feel, so you call me anytime you like."

Frog's
Mom

He's in his mother's neighborhood and decides to drop in. Though he
has the keys to her apartment, he'll ring the vestibule bell. If she
doesn't answer, he won't let himself in. She could be napping, resting,
taking a bath, just wanting her privacy. She's walking up the steps of
her building's areaway when he's coming down the block. "Mom?"
he yells from across the street. She doesn't look his way. "Mom,
Mom?" he yells, crossing the street. She reaches the sidewalk, holding
on to the wall and then the short iron fence on top of it to get there,
stops, takes a deep breath, and starts down to Columbus Avenue.
Probably has her hearing aid turned off or else not in. He starts to
run after her, then thinks follow her, see what she does for a while,
he's always been interested and has never done it before, maybe
because this is the first chance he's had. So he follows from about fifty
feet behind. If she sees him he'll say he just rang her apartment bell,
she didn't answer, he didn't want to disturb her by letting himself in if
she was home, and was heading now to Broadway to catch the subway or bus. She walks slowly. Every three buildings she stops to rest.
She looks at the sky or the tops of buildings while she's standing still,
to the sides, a couple of times behind. He doesn't wave and she
doesn't seem to notice him or not as her son. One time he pretends to
tie his shoe when she looks at him, another time when she turns his
way he actually has to tie that same shoe. She's carrying a small canvas
shopping bag and she probably has her handbag in it. She has on the

black sneakers he convinced her to buy a few years ago to make walking easier, or they could be a second pair. Black slacks, shirt and jacket and with her hair handsomely combed and pinned back, so she could be dressed for going to just about anywhere: a movie, stores, a stroll. Near the end of the block she stops and looks at the second-story window of the building she's in front of. She smiles and waves to it. The window opens, a woman's head sticks out. "How are you, Kathleen?" his mother says. "Fine, thanks; nice day for getting out, I'd say. How is everything?" "All right, considering. I thought I'd do a little shopping." "What I should do with the weather this nice. And the family?" "You know—you hear from them and you don't. And yours?" "As well as can be expected." "The same thing?" his mother says. "But worse." They chat for a few more minutes. He sits on a stoop, takes a book from his jacket pocket and pretends to read while listening to them. His mother tells her to try to come for lunch tomorrow or the next day. "Nothing elaborate; we'll talk." "The next day I can make it." "Then I'll see you there at noon if I don't see you on the street before then, dear." She waves, Kathleen waves, and she goes to the corner. She looks left and right, then across the avenue as if she's only now deciding which way to go. Left, crosses the street, stops at the third store along Columbus, goes inside, comes out with an ice cream cone, strawberry it seems, sits on the bench in front of the store and eats it. He looks in the window of a children's toy and clothing store next to the ice cream shop. If she sees him and calls out his name he'll say "Mom, oh hi, I was in the neighborhood, stopped to look at all the nice things in that store for Olivia and Eva, not that I'd ever buy anything—way too expensive—but I was on my way to see you. In fact I was going to call you at the corner phone there in about ten seconds. I guess I would have got nobody home." A young woman and her daughter sit beside her, filling up the bench, the girl right next to her. "Hello," she says to the girl. "You know, I once had a little girl—you're around what, seven, eight?" "Six." "Six? My, how much more grown up you look. And what am I talking about? I've a granddaughter your age and had two your age before they grew up and became big. But my daughter when she was six had long dark hair like yours and was slim and pretty like you too and she also loved ice cream cones. What's your favorite flavor? I bet I can guess." "Flavor?" "What ice cream cone do you like best?" her mother says to her. "Vanilla." "Say it to the lady, and in a loud clear voice; don't be shy or intimidated." "Vanilla!" "I've told her a hundred times: If there's anything I can do to prepare her for the adult world, it's that. I won't have her—you know, mealy." "My granddaughter too. But that was my favorite flavor when I was six," his mother says to the girl. "Till I switched to strawberry—I don't know why I did—and it was my daughter's favorite flavor all her life. Vanilla was." The two women talk while the girl eats her ice cream and looks at the traffic and people passing. The talk quickly gets into large families—the woman came from one, so did his mother—"The Jews years ago and the Irish forever," his mother says, "nothing insulting intended"— and then their voices gradually get lower and he hears the words "breasts . . . breast-feeding . . . warm compresses on them to draw the milk up, and also drinking dark beer and stout." His mother's giving advice— "I nursed all mine for more than a year and nobody thought I had the equipment for more than two months"—but it must be for someone the woman knows, for her breasts don't seem like a nursing mother's and her stomach's flat, and where's the baby if she has one? Maybe at home with a nanny or someone, and he could be all wrong about her breasts. A woman he knew who he thought was almost flat-chested, and when she took off her blouse the first time, "Oh my goodness, gosh, I had no idea, not that it should mean that much or I'd feel any different to you if they weren't so large, but still . . ." and went up to her from behind and put his hands around her on them. She still had her bra on and when she unhooked it and slid off the shoulder straps and twisted her head around to kiss him, breasts and bra fell into his hands. Palo Alto, back of a house by the train tracks, twenty-three years ago. The woman and daughter stand up; the two women shake hands. His mother finishes the ice cream in the cone, bites off a piece of the cone, looks around before spitting it into the paper napkin he didn't know she was holding, drops the napkin and cone into a trash can beside the bench and continues down Columbus. She still stops every forty feet or so, sometimes a deep breath. A young woman passing her looks at her standing still, stops a few feet away to look back at her, goes back and says "Is everything okay?" "Yes, thank you. Just resting, but I can make it fine to where I'm going, dear." "You're sure you're okay?" "Positively. You're a sweetheart for asking." Sidewalk's now crowded because of a row of vendors near the curb and the enclosed restaurant patios jutting out from the buildings. Her eyesight's not good and she refuses to wear her glasses outdoors, so there's even less chance she'll recognize him now. She does, he'll say "Mom, why hi, I was just over your place, rang the outside bell, no response, so I let myself in—I hope you don't mind—and when I saw you weren't home, thought you might be on Columbus or in one of the stores here and came to look for you. If you weren't, or I couldn't find you, I was even going to walk to

Broadway to D'Agostino's and Fairway, the two other places I thought you might be. Like to stop in for a coffee or snack someplace, on me?" She crosses the next street and goes into the supermarket at the corner. He follows her, picks up a basket by the door, puts a few beers in it from the cases stacked at the front of the store, too good a buy, loses her, looks up the nearest aisle, goes to the entrance and looks up the first aisle and sees her at a meat counter looking at what's there. She takes out a chicken—whole, parts, he can't tell—puts it in her cart, some beef—cubes for stew, looks like—at the dairy section gets cottage cheese, yogurt, two or three different foreign cheeses, goes down an aisle and gets scouring powder, big box of laundry detergent—how's she going to carry it all? Probably will have it delivered—Brillo, silver polish, floor wax, then several cans of tuna, seltzer, marmalade, English muffins, lettuce, carrots, radishes, scallions, bananas, kiwi, a cantaloupe. "You think this is ready?" she says to the woman who weighs the produce. The woman taps and smells the cantaloupe and presses its ends, says "Think I know what I'm doing? I see the regular man doing it, I do it. But he's off today, so don't go by me." "Let's say if you were thinking of buying it—would you?" "You're asking me that, customer to customer, I would, 'cause it's a great buy, and I'd keep it in a warm spot for a few days, but not the stove, you know? Now the bananas," weighing them—his mother puts the cantaloupe back— "yours are good, you could eat them while you're walking home. But the ones over there—too green, so I wouldn't touch them." "I think those are Spanish bananas—plantanos, I think they're called—and are supposed to be green. You cook them." "Do you? They look like green bananas to me that'll take weeks to ripen." "That reminds me," and she squeezes a number of avocados, puts two of them in her cart. "Nice talking to you, dear," she says. "Same here. Have a good one." Package each of figs and dates, jar of applesauce, several jars of baby food pear sauce, two six-packs of Dutch beer from the cases in front, and goes to the checkout counter, writes out two delivery forms, pays by check, says "I wrote on it to leave the packages by the door," gives a dollar tip for the delivery boy and leaves. He quickly pays for his beers on the express line, goes outside and sees her crossing the avenue at the corner. She buys a used book at a vendor's table on the sidewalk, goes into a card and party goods store at the corner and through the window he sees her smiling and another time laughing as she reads some cards. She takes one to the counter up front, he goes to the open door to listen. She sees him he'll say "Mom, hi, I happened to be in the neighborhood for something (he'll think of what), passed this store and saw you in it, but for some reason I could never stand these kinds of shops. Too what? Schlocky, meretricious, if I've got the word right for what I mean, and that cloying incense smell from the candles or something—soap, I don't know—though maybe that's all unfair of me and I don't really catch their value and worth—the stores', not of course the candles'. Anyway, I decided to wait out here till you came out or saw me from inside." But the beers. "Mom, hi, I was looking for you on Columbus, saw a good buy for Dutch beer advertised on Pioneer's window, so went in and bought a few and coming out of the store saw you crossing the avenue.... You were in Pioneer at the same time? Amazing, but I just shot in and out. Anyway, saw you were having such a good time browsing through the cards—they can be very funny, I know—that I thought I wouldn't spoil your fun so would just wait outside. What do you say? Like to have a bite or drink someplace?" She tells the salesman behind the counter how different cards are from what she remembers them ten, fifteen years ago. "I'm almost sure I told you this before, but I can't believe how risqué some of them are. I'm no prude, but do they really permit it? Can someone be arrested for sending one of the dirtier cards through the mail? I'm not joking. Monkeys doing it with people in one. Grotesque statues having orgies with figures in paintings. I'm sure it isn't only that my attitude can be a little out of date." "Oh no, we get complaints about them from every age. But plenty of people, and I'm not justifying the cards, find them funny and cute, and they cost more than the others, so the owner's happy. But you got a good traditional one—one of my favorites, both universal and clever. Whoever's getting it will get a big lift." He wonders who that is. Nobody's birthday or wedding anniversary's coming up that he knows, and from what the man said he doubts it's for a religious holiday. Friend of hers he doesn't know of? Better yet. He turns to the window as she leaves, looks at the party material while watching her reflection cross the avenue. How would he have explained his window-looking? "I was thinking of the kids—their birthdays—I know that's three and four months from now, but you have to plan ahead.... But what crap. And the prices!" She sits at a table in front of a Mexican restaurant. He sits at an outside table of the adjoining restaurant—Indian; he didn't even look—and when the waiter comes up, "No food, please; just a European or Japanese beer, or Indian if you got." She orders nachos and cheese and a draft beer. Draft he should have asked for. She leafs through the book she bought while she eats and drinks. She sees him he'll say "Mom, I don't believe it, patio-to-patio restaurants—what a fantastic surprise. I called you just ten minutes ago—

was in the neighborhood so thought 'Why not?' But wanting to know if you'd like to go out for exactly what you're having now, a snack and beer. I didn't know you liked those nacho things. I can't— the cholesterol; my doctor would have a heart attack—but you're incredible, arteries like a child's, and if I had known I would have suggested taking you to a Mexican restaurant long ago. There must be some things there I could eat. But think my patio will mind if I move my beer to yours? I'll just drink up and pay up and get a beer at your table." She reads several pages in the middle, the last page, closes the book and has a look as if she doesn't know by what she's read if she wants to read the whole book, looks at the people passing, lights one of those he supposes he could call them cheroots. A young man at a table on one side of her asks if he could bum one from her. "Of course—take two; less I smoke of these, the better." He takes one, asks what book she's reading, she lights his cheroot with her lighter. Asks if she reads a lot. Was she a teacher at one time? Has she always loved good literature? He wishes he read more. He wanted to read that very same book for years, but in college was too busy with studies, in graduate school too busy with his thesis and teaching, and now at his job too busy working. "Carry it with you," she says. "On the subway or whatever you take. Long elevator waits. That's what my son says he does and he gets an extra ten-fifteen pages a day in that way. Here; it only cost me a measly two dollars and I know after a few minutes with it I'll never finish it. At my age—well, anyway." He wants to give her the two dollars; she won't think of it. "Then let me treat you to another beer." "No, one's my limit in the afternoon." Thanks her and says he's going to do as she says: "Read between the cracks." She doesn't understand. "It's an expression: whenever I find a few minutes free." "That's it," smiles, pulls a newspaper out of her bag and reads. He sits back and opens the book and looks at her. "Excuse me, I don't mean to bother you again, but I just noticed you read without glasses. You've never worn them and you've read so much? What's your secret?" "I wear a pair for distance sometimes but don't really need them. Neither of my parents needed glasses either, though my father wore them because he thought they made him look more like Emperor Franz Josef." "Which emperor was he?" "Of Austria and Hungary before the First World War. He idolized him; emulated many of his mannerisms and dress; so much so there was a framed photograph of him—this big—over my parents' bed. Strange now when I mention it." The man thinks about it: one eye-brow up, couple of forehead furls. She reads the front page for a few minutes, pays, wishes the man a good day—he's startled away from the book, waves it at her and says "So far, great; thanks"—and heads back up Columbus. On the next block someone shouts "Mrs. Tetch? Pauline?" and runs over to her. Woman he knew from the neighborhood when he moved back to it fifteen years ago and introduced his mother to. They kiss, woman asks how she is, his mother says "All right, I suppose, for an old dust bag like me." If either sees him—he's looking at one of the sidewalk tables: unisex jewelry: rings, earrings, nose rings, clips and things for the hair—he'll say he was on the subway uptown, got off to see his mother—"But how are you, how are you, a great double surprise," and kiss them. The woman's talking about diet, health, alternative medicine, good food, lots of organically grown fruit juices and greens and grains, a mail-order house in Pennsylvania where you can get health foods sent to you—she'll bring her the catalog; "A lot more expensive than store-bought health food—you can even get fresh apples and carrots and bread and nondairy cheese—but it comes right to your door, so why not try it? It can give you a few extra years." "I'm too old to start into that," his mother says. "Where were you thirty years ago?" They talk for around ten minutes in the middle of the sidewalk. People have to walk around them; one man passing him says to his companion "What's with those two? Don't they know they're holding up traffic? People can be so unaware." He wants to say to him "Come on, give them a break; she's an old lady." He crosses the sidewalk to a store window; men's clothes, too fancy and expensive for him; but what would they say if they saw him? "You, the original cheap jeans and T-shirt guy, thinking of buying those clothes?" "Oh my God—hi. I was just on my way to see my mother. Truth is, I saw you two there but was curious, long as I was in the neighborhood and you were still busy talking, as to what these stores think men wear these days? Obviously plenty of men do wear what's in there, since half of them on the street have on a lot of the same stuff in the window along with some of the self-mutilating jewelry there on the sidewalk. But what a surprise. How are you both? I don't know which of you I should kiss first." The women are kissing goodbye. His mother holds and pats the woman's hand and says "You know I always had a special place in my heart for you the moment I first met you and was devastated for you when Barry died." "I know; thanks, Pauline; no one could have been kinder after." He forgot about Barry, doesn't think he's thought of him for years, even though he has two of his huge paintings hanging in his home, which the woman had given him, and had wheeled him in the park every day for an hour or so for a few weeks before he died. His mother continues up Columbus, stops, rests, looks in store windows—women's shoes, women's handbags and gloves—goes into a gourmet shop and has some things weighed; about a quarter-pound of sliced turkey breast, he sees through the window; salads scooped into half-pint and pint containers; a pickle and two onion rolls. She makes onion rolls better than he's bought anywhere, even when they're a couple of days old, but they're usually to give away; she hardly eats what she bakes. She puts the grocery bag into her shopping bag, stops in front of the ice cream store—she's not going to get another cone, is she?—sits on the bench. She tells the young man eating ice cream beside her that her heart suddenly started palpitating rapidly; she felt faint, that's why she's sitting without buying an ice cream. "Though I bought one from here just before." Should he go to her, say he overheard, is she all right, does she want him to hail a cab to get her home or to a doctor or hospital? The man says "Do you want me to do anything?" "Excuse me, what? My hearing aid is going on and off again." "I said do you want me to do anything for you—your heart?" "No, thank you, it's just about passed. It always does after I sit or lie down for a few minutes. It wasn't serious, so don't worry. And my hearing aid's working again." What would he say if she had died right in front of him? He wouldn't say anything. He'd get down on his knees, hold her to his face till the police or ambulance came, cry and cry, and only if somebody thought he was crazy and wanted to get him away from her, say "I'm her son." She asks where the man's bicycle is. He's in bicycling gear—backwards cap, shirt, special pants and shoes, fingerless gloves. He points to a bike fastened to a parking sign pole. "When you were buying your ice cream, weren't you afraid it would get stolen?" "Even the best bike thief couldn't break that lock in less than two minutes. It's made of the highest-tension steel—you'd need the kind of clippers that not even police cars carry—and I never keep my eyes off it for more than a minute." He's looking in the window of the children's toy and clothing store of before, would give the same excuse to her he thought up then. "From what I've read," she says, "these city thieves are always one step ahead of the police in the latest gadgets in everything—guns, bulletproof vests, picks for locks, even knockout darts. And maybe they'll just want to take the wheels and leave the lock and frame part behind. You always have to be more careful than you think." "If they're that desperate," but he can't hear the rest of what the man says because of a truck with a defective muffler and bouncing-around cargo driving past. She pretends to have heard, nodding while he talked, or maybe she's become adept at reading lips. She says she's completely better now, thanks him for his concern and walks to the corner and goes up her street. A landlord on the block stops her to talk. He turns around, opens his book and takes out a pen and uncaps it and holds it over a page. If either of them sees him he'll say he saw them just now but suddenly got an idea about this book, which he'll be teaching next term, and wanted to write it down before he forgot it. "Hi, how are you though? Nice to see you both. Funny, but I was just on my way to see you, Mom." The landlord says "You can't walk along Columbus—but every nice day, not only weekends— without getting bumped into or pushed into the street or asked or even threatened for money by beggars, though most of them look as if they live better than you or me. The clothes they got. And why aren't they working at a real job when they're so strong-looking and young? I'm not talking about the skinny women with the children, who are pitiful." "No one panhandled me this time," his mother says, "but I know what you mean. Maybe they're just—the healthier looking ones—not in their right minds." "Oh they're in their right minds, all right. To work like that for your money? Your hand out—sometimes two hands out for two people at once—and a few of the same words each time: 'Money for food?' 'Money to get back to Trenton?' One actually told me that, and next day he told me the same thing. 'Money for my babies?'—but you don't see the babies; it's just a line. And no physical effort in it either, and I hear some of the better ones pull in four to five hundred a week tax free and probably with Monday-Tuesday off. I'd take the job if it was offered me." "There must be more to it than that for most of them. Like I said: troubled heads; drugs. But I can never refuse anybody begging. It doesn't happen that often, and what's a dime?" "A dime? You give them a dime and they'll throw it back if not poke you. It's a dollar for coffee. It's two dollars for subway fare for him and his friend. It's five dollars to help get him a hotel suite so he doesn't die homeless in the street." "No they wouldn't. Still, I like Columbus better now. It's prettier, more exciting. You have a greater choice of places to eat." "But to shop? For the essentials?" "There are still some stores for that, or you go to Seventy-second or Amsterdam. But because of all the people walking and hanging around on it, the neighborhood's safer than it ever was." "This one's getting robbed, that one's being raped, and you say it's safer. Not the sidestreets. And the worst elements are coming here for a day, while before because they lived here you at least knew their face." "So it's the same. Or worse in ways. I forgot. I'd have to ask the police what they have to say." She then asks about a new form the city sent landlords regarding property taxes. "I don't understand it," the woman says. "As usual it's too complicated for the average nonlegal mind." "That's why I brought it up. Neither did I or Mr. Benjamin up the block, but I thought maybe you or your husband might." "No, but we're seeing our accountant early next week about lots of things and he's very good at those. If we find how to fill it out, want me or Lloyd to drop by and help you?" "Please or else I'll have to travel downtown to the city rent office for it. And of course you'll take home some fresh cookies I'm baking this weekend and a couple of frozen zucchini breads." She continues up the block, stops, deep breath, steps off the curb carefully, crosses the street and carefully steps onto the sidewalk in front of her building. She takes out her handbag, reaches into it, probably for keys, though he's told her to have her keys ready for use in her pocket before she even starts up the street, and if outside her pocket, then concealed in her hand. She takes out the card she bought, slips it most of the way out of the envelope and looks at it and smiles. Puts the card back into her bag and pulls out her keys. She looks around. He's told her to do this before she goes downstairs to her building, in case anyone's around who looks as if he might follow her into the vestibule. Anyone is, she's to walk to Columbus, where there are always more people than on her street, and if the person follows her, to go to a store marked Safe Haven on the window or door and tell someone there to call the police. She turns around, still looking for suspicious strangers, he supposes, and sees him across the street waving at her. She waves back and he crosses the street and says "Mom, how are you? I was in the neighborhood," and kisses her on the cheek.

Man,

Woman

and Boy

➤

They're sitting. "It's wrong," she says. He says "I know." She stands, he does right after her. "It's all wrong," she says. "I know," he says, "but what are we going to do about it?" She goes into the kitchen, he follows her. "It almost couldn't be worse," she says. "Between us—how could it be? I don't see how." "I agree," he says, "and I'd like to change it from bad to better but I don't know what to do." She pours them coffee. She puts on water for coffee. She fills the kettle with water. She gets the kettle off the stove, shakes it, looks inside and sees there's only a little water in it, turns on the faucet and fills the kettle halfway and then. And then? "Do you want milk, sugar?" she says. This after the water's dripped through the grounds in the coffee-maker, long after she said "I'm making myself coffee, you want some too?" He nodded. Now he says "You don't know how I like it by now?" "Black," she says. "Black as soot, black as ice. Black as the ace of spades, as the sky, a pearl, black as diamonds." "Whatever," he says, "whatever are you talking about?" "Just repeating something you once said. How you like your coffee." "I said that? Those, I mean—I said any of them? Never. You know me. I don't say stupid or foolish things, I try not to talk in clichés, I particularly dislike similes in my speech, and if I'm going to make a joke, I know beforehand it's going to get a laugh. But to get back to the problem." "The problem is this," she says. "We're two people, in one house, with only one child, and I'm not pregnant with a second. We have a master bed-

room and one other bedroom, so one for us and one for the child. We
have no room for guests. We have no guest room. The sofa's not comfortable enough to sleep on and doesn't pull out into a bed. We have
no sleeping bag for one of us to sleep on the floor. I don't want our
boy to sleep in the master bed with one of us while the other sleeps in
his bed. One of us has to go, is what I'm saying." "I understand you,"
he says. "The problem's probably what you said. It is, let's face it.
One of us has to go because both of us can't stay, and traditionally it's
been the man. But I don't want to go, I'd hate it. Not so much to
leave you but him. Not at all to leave you. I'm being honest. Don't
strike out against me for it, since it's not something I'm saying just to
hurt you." "I wouldn't," she says. "I like honesty. And the feeling's
mutual, which I'm also not saying just to get back at you for what you
said. But I'm not leaving the boy and traditionally the man is, in situations like this, supposed to, or simply has. We've seen it. Our friends,
and friends of friends we've heard of, who have split up. The child
traditionally stays with the woman. And it's easier, isn't it, for the one
without the child to leave than the one who stays with it, and also
ends up being a lot easier on the child. So I hope that's the way it'll
turn out. I think we both agree on that or have at least agreed on it in
our conversation just now." "Our conversation, which is continuing,"
he says. "Our conversation, which should conclude. It wouldn't take
you too long to pack, would it?" "You know me," he says, "I never
acquired much. Couple of dress shirts, two T-shirts, three pairs of
socks, not counting the pair I'm wearing, three or four handkerchiefs,
a tie. Two undershorts, including the one on me, pair of work pants in
addition to the good pants I've on. Sport jacket to match the good
pants, work jacket and coat, hat, muffler, boots, sneakers, the shoes
I'm wearing, and that should be it. Belt, of course. Bathing suit and
running shorts. Anything I leave behind—some books except the one
I'm reading and will take—I can pick up some other time. The tie, in
fact, I can probably leave here; I never use it." "You might," she says.
"Anyway, it's small enough to take and not use. Take everything so
you'll be done with it. So you're off then? Need any help packing?"
"For that amount of stuff? Nah. But one last time?" "What, one last
time?" she says. "A kiss, a smooch, a feel, a hug, a little bit of pressing
the old family flesh together, okay?" "You want to make me laugh?
I'll laugh. Cry? I'll do that too. Which do you want me to do?"
"Okey-doke, I got the message and was only kidding." "Oh yes, for
sure, only kidding, you." "What's that supposed to mean?" he says.
"Oh you don't know, for sure, oh yes, you bet." "If you're referring to
that smooch talk, what I meant was I'd like to be with my child for a

few minutes before I go. To hug, squeeze, kiss and explain that I'm not leaving him but you. That I'll see him periodically, or really as much as I can—every other day if you'll let me. You will let me, right?" "For the sake of him, of course, periodically. More coffee?" "No thanks," he says. "Then may I go to my room while you have this final get-together with him? Not final; while you say goodbye for now?" "Go on. I won't steal him."

They move backward, she to the couch, he to the chair. They never drank coffee, never made it; never had that conversation. They're both reading, or she is and he has the book on his lap. Their son's on the floor putting a picture puzzle together. It's a nice domestic scene, he thinks, quiet, the kind he likes best of all. Fire going in the fireplace—he made it. A good one too, though fires she makes are just as good. It doesn't give off much heat, fault of the fireplace's construction, but looks as if it does and is beautiful. Thermostat up to sixty-eight so, with the fire, high enough to keep the house warm, cozy. He has tea beside him on the side table. On the side table beside him. Beside his chair. A Japanese green tea, and he's shaved fresh ginger into it. Tea's now lukewarm. Tastes it; it is. He's been thinking these past few minutes and forgot about the tea. She has a cup of hot water with lemon in it. Not hot now—she might even have finished it—but was when he gave it to her. About ten minutes ago she said "Strange as this must sound"—he'd said he was making himself tea, would she like some or anything with boiling water?—"it's all I want. I wonder if it means I'm coming down with something." He said "You feel warm?" "No." "Anything ache—limbs, throat, extremities?" "Nope. I guess I'm not," and resumed reading. "What could you be coming down with, Mommy?" the boy said. "Your mommy means with a cold," he said. "Oh," the boy said and went back to his puzzle. I wonder, the man thinks, what that long parting scene I imagined means. It's not like that with us at all. We're a happy couple, a relatively happy one. Hell, happier than most it seems, more compatible and content and untroubled than most too. I still love her. Do I? Be honest. I still do. Very much so. Very much? Oh, well, most days not as passionately or crazily as I loved her when I first met her or the first six months or so of our being together before we got married or even the first six months or so of our marriage, but close enough to that. She still excites me. Very much so. Physically, intellectually. We make love a lot. About as much as when we first met, or after the first month we met. She often initiates it. Not because I don't. Lots of times she does when I'm thinking of initiating it but she starts it first. She doesn't seem dissatisfied. I'm not too. What's there to be dissatisfied about? A dozen or so years since we met and we still go at it like kids, or almost like kids—like adults, anyone—what I'm saying is, almost as if sometimes it's the first. I have fantasies about other women but what do they mean? Meaning, they don't mean much: I had them a week after I met her, they're fleeting and they probably exist just to make it even better with her, but probably not. They exist. That's the way I am. As long as I don't act on them, which I'd never do, for why would I? Which is what I'm saying. And she tells me she loves me almost every day. Tells me almost every day. And almost every night one of the last things she says to me, in the dark or just before or after she turns off the light, is "I love you, dearest." And I usually say "I love you too," which is true, very much so: I do, and then we'd briefly kiss and maybe later, maybe not, after I put down my reading, make love. So why'd I think of that scene? Just trying it out? Wondering how I'd feel? How would I? Awful, obviously. I couldn't live without her. Or I could but it'd be difficult, very, extremely trying, probably impossible or close. And without the boy? Never. As I said in the scene, I want to see him every day. He's such a good kid. I want to make him breakfast every morning till he's old enough to make his own, help him with his homework when he wants me to and go places with him—museums, the park, play ball with him, take walks with him—with him and her. Summer vacations, two to three weeks here or there, diving off rafts, long swims with him alongside me. Things like that. Libraries. He loves libraries and children's bookstores. Really odd that I thought of that scene then. Just trying it out as I said, that's all, or I suppose.

He gets up and gets on the floor and says "Need any help?" "No, Dad, thanks. If I do I'll tell you." "Sure now?" "Positive. I like to figure things out myself. That's the object of the puzzle, isn't it?" "Well, sometimes it's nice to do it with other people—it can be fun. But do what you want. And you're pretty good at this." "So far I am. I want to get up to one with a thousand pieces. This is only five hundred. But that's still two hundred more than the last one I did, which was two hundred fifty." "Two hundred fifty more than the last one," he says. "Two hundred fifty times two hundred fifty—no, I mean times two; or two hundred fifty plus another two hundred fifty equals—" "Five hundred. I know. Two hundred fifty times two hundred fifty is probably fifty thousand, or a hundred." "That's good. You're so smart." He touches the boy's cheek. "Okay, but if you need any help, whistle." "What for?" "I mean—it's just an expression, like what you said before: if you want me to help you'll tell me."

He goes over to his wife. She's reading and correcting manuscripts from her class. He puts his hand on top of her head. First he stood there thinking "Should I stay here till she notices me and looks up or should I put my hand on her head? On her head. Just standing here might seem peculiar to her. I'm sure if I was able to stand back and see myself standing here like this, it would seem peculiar." Now with his hand on her head he thinks "Actually, standing here with my hand on top of her head must also seem peculiar to her." Just as he's about to take his hand off, she looks up and grabs his hand with the one holding the pen. "Hello," she says. "Hello." "What's up?" she says. "Just admiring you." "You're a dear," she says. "You're the dear, a big one. I love you." "And I love you, my dearest." "And I love you very much," he says. "Very very." "Same with me, my dearest," she says. "Is that all? I mean, it's a lot and I like your hand here and holding it," and she squeezes it, "but may I return to my schoolwork unless you have anything further to say?" "Return, return," he says, and she pulls her hand away and holds the other side of the manuscripts with it. "Oh, Daddy and Mommy said they love each other," the boy says. "That's right, we did," he says. "We said it and we do." "Are you just saying that to me?" the boy says. "Ask your mother." "Well, Mom?" "Well, what?" she says, looking up from her manuscripts. "Do you really love Daddy or are you—" "Yes, of course, such a question, what do you think? Now may I return to my work? Eight more essays to grade in a little bit under an hour. That's when I think I'll be too sleepy for anything but sleep." "Oh yes?" he says. "Leave your mother then to her readings." "Not before you both kiss on the lips." "You ask for so much," he says. "All right with you, ma'am?" he says to her. "Come ahither and adither," she says and moves her head up, he bends over and puts his lips on hers. He sticks the tip of his tongue in in a way that he's sure the boy won't be able to see. Their tongues touch, eyes close. His does he knows—the eyes. He opens his and sees hers are closed. Closes his and opens them quickly: still closed. "Okay, you proved it," the boy says. "You can stop now."

They move into the dining room. About an hour earlier, two. The three of them. They're seated, eating. He avoids looking at her, she him. He doesn't want to talk. When he wants something near her he nudges his son and points to it and his son gives it to him or he just reaches over, sometimes even has to stand up, and gets it himself. When she wants something near him she asks their son, though he always puts the thing he took back in the spot it was on. He's angry at her and doesn't want to just talk to his son and ignore her. Something she said. That he doesn't do enough of the housework. "Hell I don't," he said. "I do at least half or most of the work most of the time." That wasn't it. He and she didn't say that. What then? Said to her "You know, I hate saying this, but the house could be neater. You going to take umbrage, take." Said this to her about an hour before dinner. Soon after he came home from work. She'd got home from work a couple of hours earlier. The boy was in his room doing homework. Or that's what she said he was supposed to be there for. "You know I like order. That the chaos you prefer, or simply don't mind living with, gets to me viscerally sometimes. Forget the 'viscerally.' I can't stand chaos, it makes me nervous, temperamental, like cigarette smoke does. Forget the cigarette smoke. I just can't stand it." "Then tidy up the place," she said. "It's not just tidying up that's needed; it's also the dirt and dust." "Then clean up the place too." "I don't clean up enough? I do most of the cleaning, it seems, plus most of the clothes washing and shopping and making the beds and fixing up the boy's room and cleaning the bird's cage and feeding it every night and our cooking and dishwashing and all that crap, and I just think it's your turn. The food I see you've done, though I made the salad before I left. But the rest." "Okay, I'll clean up," she said. "I've been busy, I am busy, I did the dinner except the salad, set the table, it's been a rough day at school, I've helped our son with his long division for an hour and still have a mess of essays to grade, but if you think the distribution of housework's been unequal, I'll do what you say. I wanted to say 'what the boss said,' but you might take umbrage. Umbrage; what a word." She cleaned up the living room and dining room. When she started to he said "I didn't mean now." Tidied up, swept the floors and rugs, dusted and polished the furniture, straightened the many books on the shelves, rubbed some stains on the wooden floor with a solution till she got them out. It looks and smells a lot better, he thought, place isn't a complete jumble, but she's making me feel guilty and she knows it. Why doesn't she do it periodically, as I do, and then it wouldn't come to this? "Do" meaning the cleaning; "this" being the disorder, dirty house, argument. The food was cooking, dinner was. He didn't want to eat with the two of them feeling about each other like this, but what could he say: "I don't want to eat right now, you go ahead without me," after she'd cooked it and just cleaned part of the house, and he'd, so to speak, started the argument? He'd come home mad because of something that happened at the office—more pettiness there, nothing that should have upset him. He took it out on her—might have taken it out on the boy if he'd been around—which isn't to say the place wasn't a visual assault when he got there, but it certainly wasn't enough of one to start an argument over, especially when he knew she'd taught most of the day and he could see she'd done some work at home: dinner, scrap paper scattered about showing she'd helped the boy with his long division. Besides, it just wasn't something that warranted arguing over anytime. He'd gone to work mad because this morning in bed—it all could have stemmed from this—he'd wanted to make love. One of those mornings: dreamt of lovemaking, woke up thinking of lovemaking, wanted very much to do it. She mumbled "Too tired, sweetie," and moved her neck away from his lips. He persisted. "I said I'm tired, too much so, don't want to, please let me sleep, I need it." Usually she gave in, even when she didn't feel like it. She knew it'd only take him a few minutes when he was like this and she could take the easiest and least-involved position and wouldn't even have to move to it since she was in it now—on her side with her back to him—and that he'd want to get out of bed right after to wash up, exercise, have coffee and read the paper, and prepare the breakfast table for their son and her. He pressed into her, put a hand on her breast through the nightgown, other hand between her legs. She had panties on. He hadn't known. He started to pull them down. "What, huh?" she said, as if startled awake. "Don't, dammit. I said I didn't want to and I certainly feel less like it now. Do it to your-self if you're so horny, but with me it'd be like with a corpse." "A corpse isn't warm." "Please?" "And I'm not horny; I just want you." "Sure," she said. "Oh yeah, you bet, oh boy," and moved a few inches away from him. "Bloody Christ," he said and got out of bed. "Bitch," he said softly but he thought loud enough for her to hear. She didn't respond, eyes were closed, she looked asleep. Faking it maybe, but who cares? They didn't talk at breakfast, which he ate standing up at the stove, she at the table he'd set. And he didn't look at her when he left for work. Put on his coat, got his briefcase, kissed his son, left. The pre-vious day during dinner they'd had an argument. Her mother had said to him on the phone "Are you treating my daughter nicely? Remember, she's our only child, one in a zillion, and I always want her treated well because nobody in the world deserves it better." "Have you asked either of us if she's been treating me nicely?" he said. "What a ques-tion," she said. Then "Let me talk to her if she's there—it's why I called." His wife later asked him what he'd said that made her mother so mad, and it started. "She's too nosy sometimes and she expects sen-sible gentle answers to these impossible, often hostile questions, and then she dismisses me as if I'm her houseboy-idiot." "You don't know how to talk to her and you never liked her and you don't know how to act civilly to anyone you don't like." "Is that right," he said, and so on. That morning he'd wanted to make love and they did. After, she said "Nothing really gets started with me when we make it lately, and I end up so frustrated. You—do you mind my saying this?—for the most part do it too quickly. You have to warm me up more and concentrate on the right spots, especially if you suddenly come on me unprepared, like when I'm asleep." "Listen, we're all responsible for our own orgasms," he said. "The hell we are." "I didn't mean it the way it might have come out, but we are to a certain degree, don't you think?" "You meant it and you show it," she said. "Just get yours, buster, and let whoever it is burn." "What 'whoever it is'?" he said. "It's only you." "Don't bullshit you don't know what I mean," she said, and so on. The previous day they fought about something, he forgets what: that she's been letting the gas gauge go almost to empty, that she took his stapler the other day and now he can't find it, that her personal trash in the bathroom waste-basket is starting to stink and it's her responsibility to dump it in the can outside or at least tie it up and stick it in the kitchen garbage bag. "So I forgot." "So from now on remember." "Don't fight," their son said, "please don't shout, please don't yell." They stopped but didn't talk to each other for a few hours. The previous night, when he was reading and at the same time falling asleep, she got into bed naked and said "You don't have to if you don't want to—no obligation," and he said "No, no, I can probably do it," and they made love and went to sleep holding each other, she kissing his hand, he the back of her head. Further back. The boy's born, and he drops to his knees in the birthing room he's so excited. Further. They're getting married and they both break down during the ceremony and cry. Further. They meet. Sees her at a cocktail party, introduces himself: "You probably have better things to do than talk to me," and she says "What a line—no, why?" His first wife, girlfriends, first he was smitten with in grade school. He's a boy, and his parents are arguing bitterly at the dinner table. He puts his hands over his ears and yells "Stop, can't you ever stop screaming at yourselves?" "Don't do that," his father says, pulling his hands off his ears. "What are you, crazy?" And he says "Yes," or "You made me," or "Why shouldn't I be?" and runs out of the room. "Go after the maniac," and his brother goes after him and says "It's no good for me either when they're like that, so come on back." Hears further back. From his mother's stomach. "Filthy rotten bitch." "And you. Stupid, cheap, pigheaded, a pill. Get lost. I hate your guts." "Not as much as I hate yours. Here." "And what's that?" "What you wanted so much. Your allowance. Take it and stick it up your ass," and so on. "Why'd I marry you?" and so on. "You don't think I ask that question too? With all I had and never any lip from anyone, what'd I need it for?" and so on.

He's in his chair, the man, wishing he'd made himself coffee or tea. Something hot to drink. He can think better with it. Son plays, wife reads. They'll probably make love tonight, he thinks. He's been nice all day, no arguments, she's smiled lovingly at him several times the last few hours. Kissed her when he got home, and she said "Ooh, that's some kiss; I love it." He can't wait. He's sure she'll come to bed ready. If she doesn't—well, how will he know? He can go to the bathroom and shake the case. Sometimes he can smell it on her too. The cream. Anyway, he can say—he's usually first in bed, usually reading—"I hope you're ready, I know I am." "Sure," she'll say if she isn't ready and go back to the bathroom. He loves her. They have their fights and disputes and sometimes he tells himself he hates her and doesn't want to live another second with her, but he really loves her. He should remember that. So beautiful. Still a very beautiful face. Her body still excites him. She's so smart, so good. He's lucky, particularly when he's so often a sonofabitch and fool. He should remember all that. He should call his mother now. Doesn't want to budge. Just wants to sit here remembering, digesting—something— the thoughts he just had about her. That he loves her. That no matter what, he loves her. "Time for bed," she says to their son. "Oh, I don't want to go yet," the boy says. "Do what your mother tells you," he says. "Okay," the boy says, "okay, but you don't have to talk rough." "I wasn't. And please clean up your puzzle. Nah, just forget it, it's late and you're going to bed; I'll do it." He looks at her. She's standing, her manuscripts are on the couch. Smiles at her. She smiles at him, he smiles back. The boy gets up and heads for the stairs. "Look," he says to her, "he's really going to bed without a fuss. What a kid." "I'll run his bath," she says, "you'll tell him a story after?" "I don't need anyone for that," the boy says. "I can fill my own tub—I know how much to—and I want to read by myself before I go to sleep." "You read?" the man says. "He reads?" to her. "Since when? I don't want him to. Soon I won't be able to do anything for him. He'll be brushing his own hair, combing his own teeth." "Daddy, you got those wrong. And I've been doing them a long time." "That's what I'm saying," he says. "Next you'll be cooking your own shoelaces, tying your own food. Go, go, don't let me stop you, big man," and blows a kiss at him. He didn't mean those first two to be switched around, but it turned out to be a good joke.

The boy runs upstairs. He gets on the floor, puts the—what do you call them? isolated, or incomplete, or unassembled or just-not-put-in-the-puzzle-yet—pieces in their box, doesn't know what to do with the partly completed puzzle, carefully slides it against the wall. Hears water running in the tub, lots of padding back and forth on the ceiling. "He's growing up so much," he says. "You haven't noticed before?" she says. "Of course, but the way he phrases things, and just now—no remonstrating." He sits beside her. "Mind?" "Go on." Puts his arm around her shoulder, pulls her to him. She looks at him. "Yes?" "This is the life," he says, "everything but the kid asleep." "Yes, it's very nice," and kisses his lips and goes back to reading. He continues looking at her. Wants to say "You're beautiful, you know; beautiful." Takes his arm away, for he feels it might be bothering her. She wants to concentrate. Good, she should. He leans his head back on the couch, looks at the ceiling. I go upstairs, he thinks. My son's in bed reading. He smells washed, his room's neat, he tidied it up without anyone asking. "All done for now?" I say. He puts the book on the floor and says "Forty-six; please remember the page for me?" "Will do. Goodnight, my sweet wonderful child," I say and kiss his lips, make sure the covers are over his shoulders. "Pillows all comfortable?" and he says "You could get them right, I don't mind." I fix the pillows, rest his head on them, turn the light off and go downstairs. "Like a beer or glass of wine?" I say. "If you'll share a bottle of beer with me," she says. We do. "I'm tired," I say. "Let's go to bed then," she says. We do. I'm in bed, naked, clothes piled beside me on the floor, glasses and book on my night table. She's still in—she's sitting on the other side of the bed, taking her clothes off. She was just in the bathroom a few minutes. "Dear," I say. "Not to worry," she says, "it's all taken care of. What's on your mind's on mine." All her clothes are off. I breathe deeply to see if I can smell her. I can: a little fresh cologne, cream she put in, something from her underarms. Or mine. I smell one when she's looking away. Nothing. "Can I shut off the light?" I say. "Please, I'm finished." I shut it off. She gets under the covers with me. We hug, kiss, rub each other very hard. She grabs me and I grab her. Something tells me it's going to be one of the best for me.

"Like a glass of wine, some beer?" he asks. "I don't want to get too sleepy," she says. "Maybe I can read a couple of more papers than I thought I could, so I won't have to do too many tomorrow." "Dad?" his son shouts from upstairs. "We're all out of toilet paper up here." "You checked the bathroom closet, the cabinet under the sink?" "Everyplace." "To the rescue." And he gets a roll out of the downstairs bathroom, runs upstairs, puts the roll in. He goes into his son's room. The boy's drawing at his desk, and he says "Don't you have to use the toilet?" "I did, but I was thinking of you and Mom." "That's very thoughtful, very. Come on now, though, you have to go to bed." The boy gets into bed. "Teeth all combed?" "Everything," the boy says. "You don't want the night-light on?" "I don't need it anymore." "Good, that's fine, but if you change your mind, okay too. Goodnight, my sweet wonderful kid," and he bends down and kisses him on the lips, turns the light off.

He undresses, brushes his teeth, flosses, washes his face, washes his penis and behind with a washrag, washes the washrag with soap and hangs it on the shower rod, walks a few steps downstairs and says softly "Sweetheart, I'm going to bed now, to read—you coming up soon?" "No. And don't wait up for me. I'm thinking now I'll just do the whole bunch of them, no matter how long it takes. Goodnight." "Goodnight." He gets into bed, opens a book, reads, feels sleepy, puts the book down, looks at her side of the bed and thinks "Remember what you promised to think about before? What was it? Bet you forgot." Thinks. "Ah," he says when he remembers what it was. "It's true," he thinks, "I really love her." "You hear that, dear," he says low, "do you hear that? I can't wait till you get into bed so I can hold ya." He puts the book and glasses on the night table, shuts off the light, lies on his back to see if anything else comes into his head, shuts his eyes, turns over on his side, falls asleep.

The stories have appeared in the following books: *Making a Break* (Latitudes Press, 1975); *No Relief* (Street Fiction Press, 1976); *Quite Contrary* (Harper & Row, 1979); *14 Stories* (Johns Hopkins University Press, 1980); *Movies* (North Point Press, 1983); *Time to Go* (Johns Hopkins University Press, 1984); *The Play & Other Stories* (Coffee House Press, 1989); *Love and Will* (British American Publishing, 1989); *All Gone* (Johns Hopkins University Press, 1990); *Friends* (Asylum Arts, 1990); *Frog* (British American Publishing, 1991); *Long Made Short* (Johns Hopkins University Press, 1993). "The Chess House" was published in *The Paris Review,* 1963.